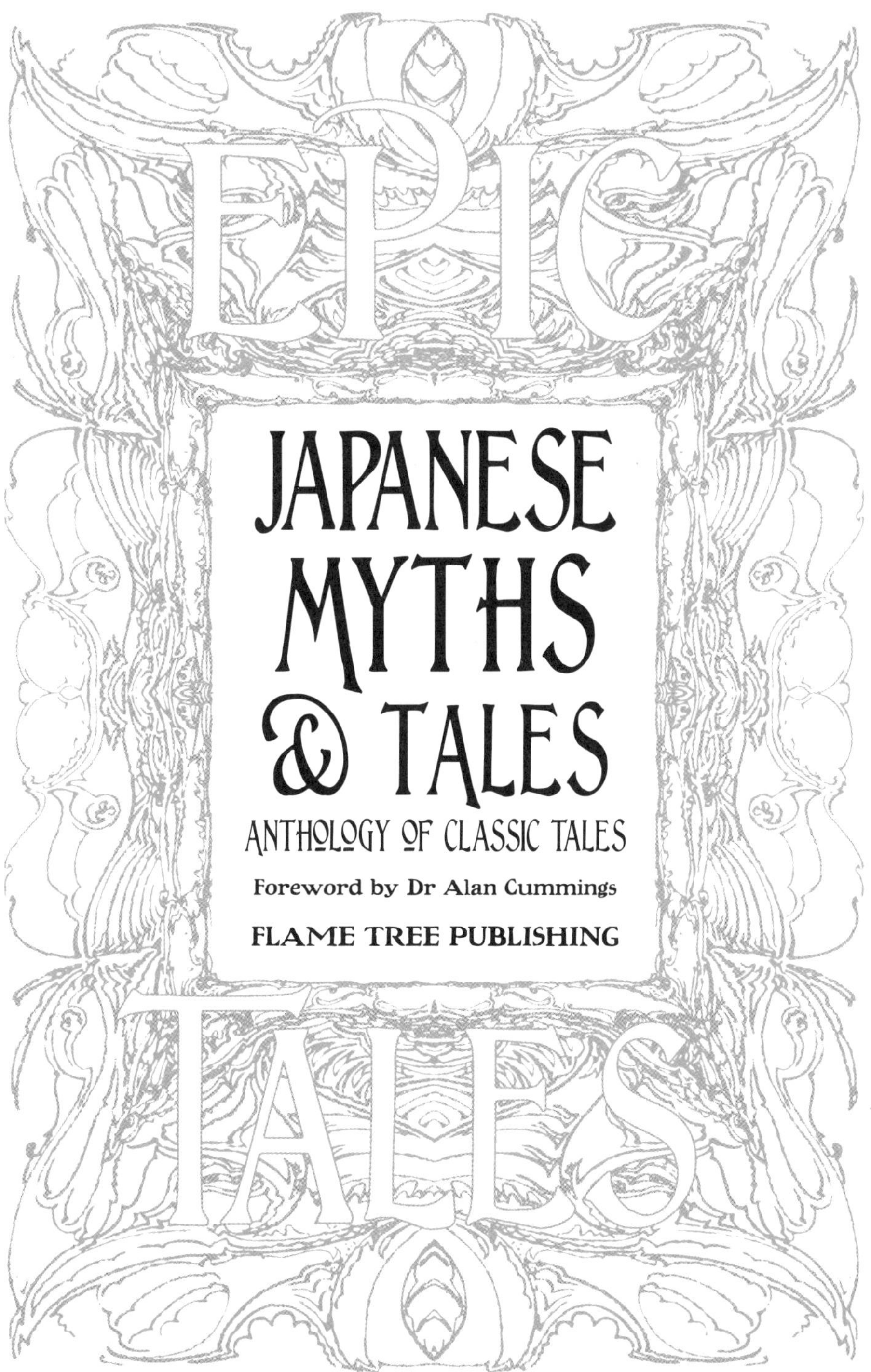

JAPANESE MYTHS & TALES

ANTHOLOGY OF CLASSIC TALES

Foreword by Dr Alan Cummings

FLAME TREE PUBLISHING

This is a FLAME TREE Book

Publisher & Creative Director: Nick Wells
Project Editor: Catherine Taylor

FLAME TREE PUBLISHING
6 Melbray Mews, Fulham,
London SW6 3NS, United Kingdom
www.flametreepublishing.com

First published 2019

19 21 23 22 20
1 3 5 7 9 10 8 6 4 2

ISBN: 978-1-78755-683-6

The cover image is created by Flame Tree Studio based on artwork by Vecster.

Incidental images by Shutterstock.com: Refluo, ADELART.
Full-page images based on woodblock prints by Katsukawa Shunshō (1726–93), Suzuki Harunobu (*c.* 1725–70), Isoda Koryūsai (1735–90), Hosoda (Chōbunsai) Eishi (1756–1829), Katsushika Hokusai (1760–1849), Utagawa Hiroshige (1797–1858) and Utagawa Toyokuni (1769–1825).

A copy of the CIP data for this book is available from the British Library.

Printed and bound in China

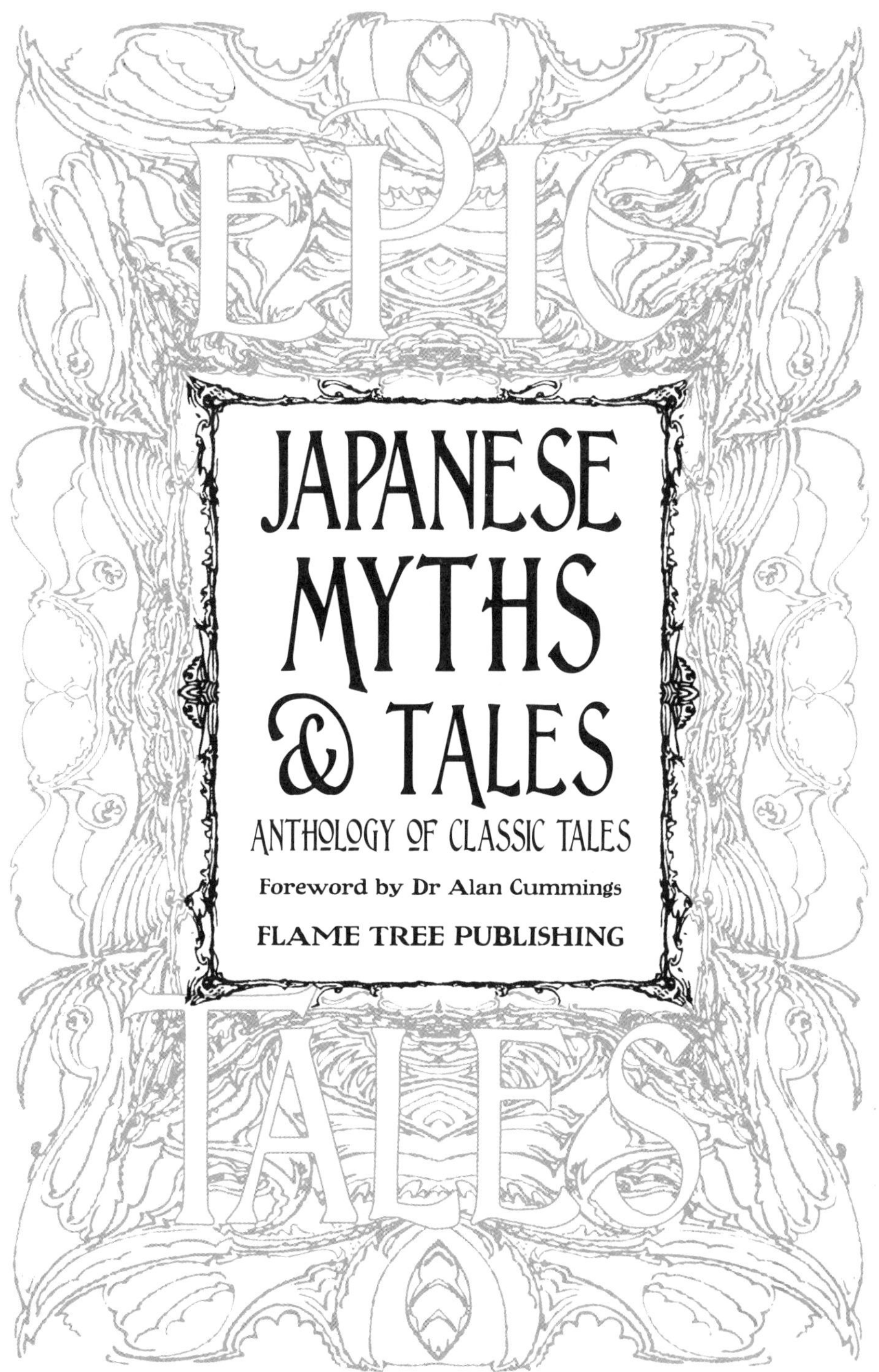

JAPANESE MYTHS & TALES

ANTHOLOGY OF CLASSIC TALES

Foreword by Dr Alan Cummings

FLAME TREE PUBLISHING

Contents

Leading Ladies & Affairs of the Heart

Ghost Stories & Supernatural Creatures

Legends of the Sea

Legends of Buddha & Buddhism

Fox & Animal Legends

Flowers & Trees

Legends of Mount Fuji

Bells, Mirrors, Fans & Tea

Foreword

THE MYTHS AND TALES anthologized in this volume are brought together from a long span of Japanese history and a wide range of geographical locations. Some, like the deeply strange story of the creation of the Japanese islands and their gods by the brother and sister deities Izanagi and Izanami, or the famous tale of Japan's prototype for martial heroism, Yamato Takeru, are taken from two myth-histories, the *Kojiki* and the *Nihon Shoki*, compiled and edited by the imperial court in the capital at the start of the eighth century. Others, like the tales of the shape-shifting, trickster fox spirits, or the chilling story of Yuki-Onna (the snow bride) are drawn from the culture of rural villages on the distant peripheries of the country. Japan's pioneering folklorist, Yanagita Kunio (1875–1962) was still able to find hamlets in rural north-eastern Japan and the islands of Okinawa where these stories were being passed down orally in the first decades of the twentieth century. Many of these stories continue to resonate in Japanese culture, through transformation into literature, theatre, children's stories, and more recently manga, anime and computer games.

The stories draw upon aspects of Japanese religious beliefs connected to the indigenous, animistic Shinto or to Buddhism, which was a later arrival to the archipelago. Shinto practice in particular is focused on shrines, which are believed to be the locations where *kami* (spirits, deities) reside. In Japanese belief, *kami* are wild and dangerous supernatural forces that are capable of causing destruction and calamity, but who can be appeased through the human intercession of worship and ritual. Once mollified, the *kami* can protect communities by ensuring that crops grow and the seasons turn, and they can also be petitioned for individual desires around marriage, childbirth, protection from illness and so on. Shinto shrines, like many of the stories in this volume, are thus situated at a liminal boundary between the civilized human world and the violent, teeming chaos of the natural world. They are both places where we are invited to come into contact with the unknown, the numinous, the supernatural.

The power of storytelling and language itself to act as an intervention between the human and supernatural worlds is another important theme seen in these stories. My personal favourite is the tale of Hōichi the Earless. Hōichi is a biwa hōshi, a blind man whose trade is the recitation of stories about the dead. He is renowned for his performances of The Tale of the Heike, a long, epic tale about the twelfth-century war between the Heike and the Genji warrior clans. The war ended in a climactic naval battle where the child emperor Antoku and most of the Heike were drowned. Japanese medieval belief held that the ghosts of powerful men who died in unhappy circumstances could wreak havoc on the human world, causing earthquakes, pestilence and other tragedies. But such is Hōichi's skill as a storyteller that the ghosts of Antoku and his drowned court summon him night after night to hear him recite the story of their deaths. By remembering them and performing their stories, Hōichi mediates between the human world and the world of the dead, his blindness creating a bridge between the realms. His singing of their story serves two audiences simultaneously: celebrating the Genji victors of the civil war, and pacifying the ghosts by reassuring them that they are remembered and valued. These stories still possess a unique power to bring us into contact with mysteries and truths that lie beyond our quotidian lives.

Dr Alan Cummings
SOAS, University of London

Publisher's Note

The Japanese language uses a logographic (as opposed to a phonetic) script, and thus it must of course be Romanized when translated into languages such as English, in order for names and places to be rendered legible to Western readers. There have been several systems for Romanizing Japanese throughout history, the three main ones being Hepburn, Kunrei-shiki and Nihon-shiki. Although Kunrei-shiki is the officially recognized system in Japan, Hepburn still tends to be favoured worldwide, but has itself experienced revisions over time. Owing to the mixture of sources used in compiling this collection, there may therefore be some inconsistency in spellings, depending on what Romanization system was preferred by the original author. However, some standardisation has been attempted where appropriate.

On a related note, these Romanization systems often use diacritical (accent) marks, such as the macron (¯), which indicates long vowel sounds, and the acute (´), above certain letters to clarify pronunciation, pitch and stress. However, the correct pronunciation of words can be hard to achieve even with some written explanation, as this needs to go hand in hand with proper appreciation of the mutual modifications of tone and rhythm, and so can only be properly acquired through oral instruction. Thus, due to this and the innate variation and inconsistency between the various sources used to compile this book, and the fact that some texts are direct translations from Japanese sources while others are inspired by traditional tales and written more simply, we have removed many of the accents in order for the reader to have an uncluttered and more accessible reading experience. (However, we have kept the macrons on most non-proper nouns since their absence can alter the meaning of a word.)

We also ask the reader to remember that while the myths and tales are timeless, much of the factual information, opinions regarding the nature of Japan and the Japanese, as well as the style of writing in this anthology, are of the era during which they were written.

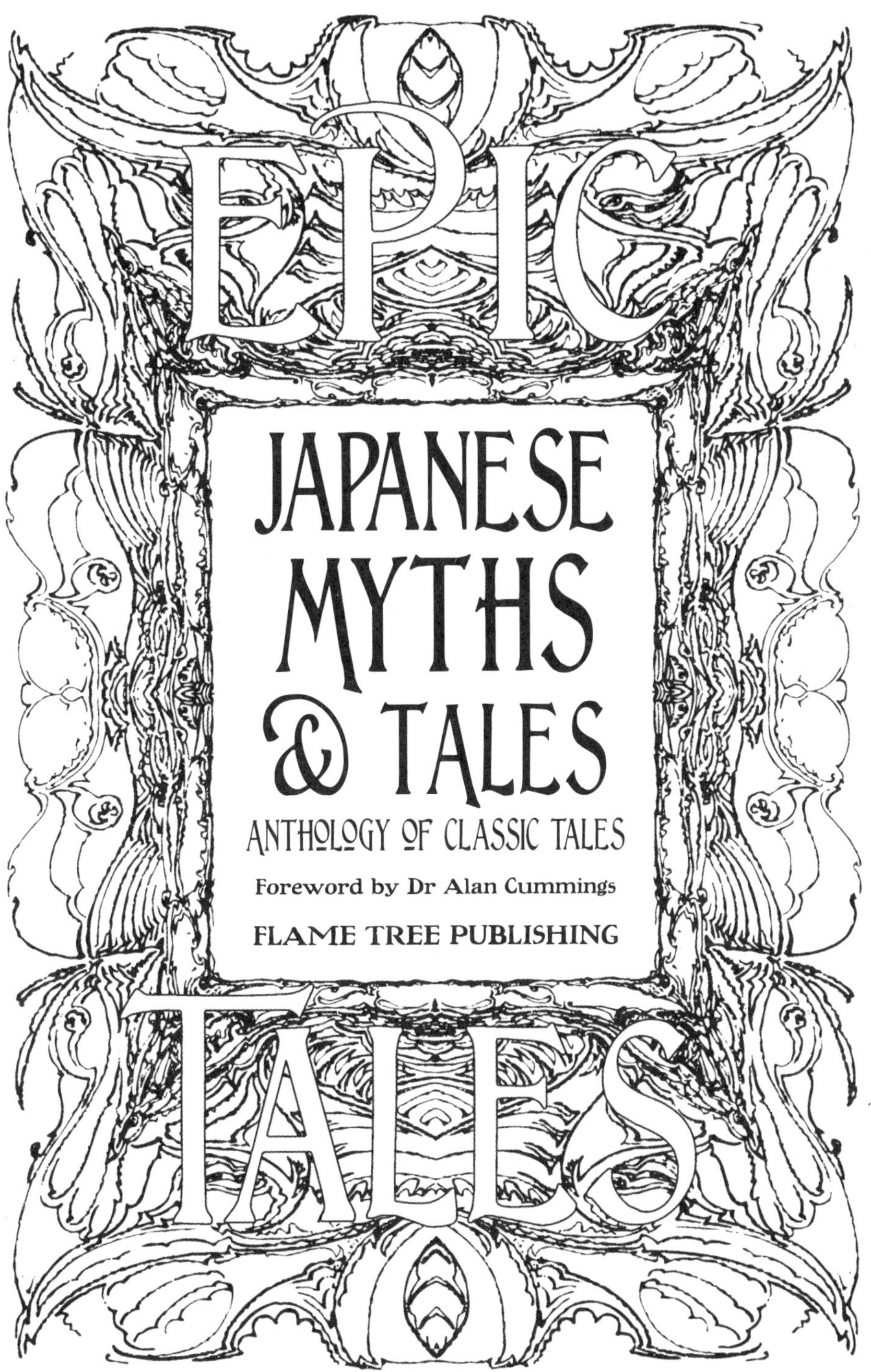
EPIC
JAPANESE MYTHS & TALES
ANTHOLOGY OF CLASSIC TALES
Foreword by Dr Alan Cummings
FLAME TREE PUBLISHING
TALES

Japanese Mythology

Introduction

JAPAN MAY HAVE ABSORBED the religion, art, and social life of China, but she set her own national seal upon what she borrowed from the Celestial Kingdom and created a world view and a mythology truly her own. The *Kojiki* and the *Nihon Shoki* are the sources from which we learn the early myths and legends of Japan. In their pages we are introduced to Izanagi and Izanami, Amaterasu, Susanoo, and numerous other divinities, and these august beings provide us with stories that are quaint, beautiful, quasi-humorous, and sometimes a little horrible. In studying Japanese legend one is particularly struck by its universality and also by its very sharp contrasts. The Japanese have described the red blossoms of azaleas as the fires of the Gods, and the white snow of Fuji as the garments of Divine Beings. Their legend, on the one hand at any rate, is essentially poetical, and those who worshipped Mount Fuji also had ghostly tales to tell about the smallest insect. Too much stress cannot be laid upon Japan's love of Nature. However, there is plenty of crude realism in Japanese legend. We are repelled by the Thunder God's favourite repast, amazed by the magical power of foxes and cats; and the story of 'Hōichi-the-Earless' and of the corpse-eating priest afford striking examples of the combination of the weird and the horrible. But first let us take a look at the origins and background of the people and their mythology.

Japanese Origins

Modern Japan exhibits a high degree of cultural homogeneity which derives from the centralization of power throughout most of the past 1500 years. However, the picture that has emerged over the years through archaeological and genetic research tells a different story. It seems that Japanese society in prehistoric times was characterized by a surprising diversity that has contributed silently to the later culture.

Although Japanese history has only been documented since the sixth century AD, with the introduction of a writing system from China, the hundreds of islands that make up Japan have been inhabited for thousands of years. Traces of the earliest population date back at least 50,000 years; these migrants must have made their way there overland, as Japan was linked to mainland Sakhalin in the north and to Korea in the south until about 12,000 years ago.

The Prehistoric Origins of Japanese Society

Around 12,000 years ago, a very long-lived, late-Palaeolithic and Neolithic culture emerged in Japan, known as the Jomon ('cord-marked') Culture, after its characteristic pottery. To the Jomon people goes the credit of having made the oldest pottery known to archaeologists; later samples of their work dating from 6000 BC have been discovered as far afield as Fiji. Though formerly dismissed as primitive hunter-gatherers, it is now known from archaeological sites such as Sannai Maruyama that the Jomon people developed a highly sophisticated society with large sedentary populations supported by marine products and some agriculture. The Jomon also engaged in long-distance trade both within Japan and overseas. Especially noteworthy are the high-quality ceramic figurines, known as *haniwa*, that provide valuable data concerning the appearance, dress and accoutrements of the Jomon people.

The Yayoi

The vibrant Jomon culture was transformed rapidly with the arrival of newcomers from the Asian mainland around 300 BC; they established the so-called Yayoi Culture by introducing innovations, such as iron-working, advanced rice cultivation and a more complex social organization. Although their numbers were probably small initially, it was these people who were to form the basis of much of the present-day Japanese population. At first they occupied the southern area of Japan, encroaching from the island of Kyushu and making their way northwards over the ensuing centuries until the emergence of the first large unified state of Yamato, which governed all of southern and central Japan (AD 300–710). This ancestry was corroborated in the 1990s by DNA studies of the Japanese population which indicate the presence of two main racial groups in Japan: the predominant one which has links to the Koreans and, surprisingly, the Tibetans, and which radiates out from south and central Japan; and the other, more ancient group, whose traces are strongest among the inhabitants of northern Japan and other outlying regions, including various small islands dotted all around the coast of the Japanese main islands, both to the north and to the south (including Okinawa).

Whether the Jomon people themselves had discovered rice cultivation independently, as now seems likely, it was the Yayoi people who introduced other new techniques and materials – such as the use of bronze and iron – which revolutionized life in Japan.

It was during the Yayoi period that a gradual consolidation of tribes took place, leading to the establishment of ever-larger political units that culminated in the Yamato state, which is believed to have been centred on central western Honshu. The power of its rulers, who claimed descent from the sun goddess Amaterasu, is demonstrated by the series of great *kofun* or tumuli that were constructed as graves for their dead, such as the enormous keyhole-shaped tomb on the Osaka plain dating from the early fifth century AD. Large portions of surviving Japanese mythology are intimately connected with the Yamato state, as the state derived its legitimacy from a belief that its rulers descended from the dominant gods and goddesses of mythology.

Focus on: Sannai Maruyama

Though little known outside of Japan, the extraordinary archaeological find of a large Neolithic Jomon coastal settlement at Sannai Maruyama in northern Japan in 1992 revolutionized our understanding of Jomon culture. Covering over 35 hectares, the site contains the remains of over 500 wooden buildings that functioned as dwellings, storage facilities and religious structures, forming a complex, planned settlement that was inhabited continuously between 3500 BC and 2000 BC. Based on the evidence of these buildings, it is believed that the average population of the settlement was in the region of 600; their culture represents a sedentary transitional phase between a purely hunter-gatherer society and an agrarian one. In addition, an enormous amount of pottery, ceramic figurines, stoneware, bone tools and wooden artefacts bear witness to the unexpectedly high level of sophistication of life here. Other materials found on the site, such as obsidian, asphalt and jade, suggest that the Sannai Maruyama inhabitants engaged in long-distance trade over hundreds of kilometres. Though largely marine-based, there is also clear evidence that the villagers' diet included the products of early agriculture, such as walnuts; and there is unprecedented evidence for rice cultivation, as well as indirect traces of alcohol production from fermented elderberries.

The Creation

Overall, Japanese mythology is rather monolithic in nature, lacking the richness of Mediterranean mythology, since it largely represents the ideology of the early centralized state of Yamato, although traces of rival or earlier beliefs may still be discerned. Therefore, the account of the creation of Japan and the events that immediately ensued seem to be unconnected with later sun goddess beliefs.

The Japanese creation myth as recounted in the *Kojiki* and *Nihon Shoki* does not tell of a creation *ex nihilo* but speaks of an unbounded, amorphous, chaotic mass. This existed for many aeons until an area of light and transparency arose within it – Takama-gahara, the High Plains of Heaven. Three primordial gods materialized there, followed by a further two lesser gods who in turn engendered five generations of gods culminating in the primal couple, Izanagi and Izanami. Little is related about the divine beings who existed before Izanagi and Izanami beyond their names; these may just be remembered remnants of earlier, lost mythologies.

Izanagi and Izanami

Izanagi and Izanami were charged by the other divinities with bringing creation to completion and to this end they stood on the Floating Bridge of Heaven and together stirred the oily brine below with a jewelled spear. Drops falling from this spear fell to produce the first island where they took up residence. There they were joined together as the first couple, but their offspring was the deformed Hiruko (Leach Child), whom they abandoned in a reed boat. In consultation with the other gods, it was found that this child had been deformed since, during their courtship ritual, the goddess Izanami had spoken first to Izanagi. When they re-enacted their marriage in the correct manner with precedence being given to the god Izanagi, Izanami was able to give birth successfully to a large number of offspring. This episode, it is believed by scholars, was included through Chinese patriarchal influences.

Among Izanami's children were the other islands that make up the Japanese archipelago, as well as the gods of the mountains, the plains, wind, trees and so on. While giving birth to her last child, Kagutsuchi, the god of fire, Izanami was so badly burnt that she died. As she lay dying, she gave birth to more divine beings, such as the god and goddess of metals and of earth, and finally Mizuhame-no-mikoto, the goddess of death. However, like the Greek Orpheus, Izanagi decided to seek out Izanami in the underworld of Yomi, the abode of darkness, and bring her back with him. Izanami said she would discuss this with the gods of the underworld, but as she disappeared into the gloom, she warned him not to look at her. Wanting to see her again, Izanagi broke off a tooth from his hair-comb and lit it as a torch. He was horrified to see that Izanami was now a maggot-infested, rotting corpse and tried to flee from her. Angered by his act, Izanami sent a horde of demon hags and warriors to pursue him. When he reached the entrance back into the realm of the living, Izanagi found three peaches which he threw at his pursuers and managed to turn them back. At this point, Izanami, now transformed into a demon, gave chase herself. Before she could reach him, Izanagi barred her way with a great boulder with which he sealed the entrance to the underworld. Here they confronted each other a final time and dissolved their marriage vows.

Focus on: Early Literary Sources

The first historical mention of Japan is found in AD 57 in the annals of the Chinese Han Dynasty in which Japan is described as a land divided into about a hundred tribal communities, lacking any central government. Later Chinese sources indicate that there was a degree of consolidation into larger political units in the following centuries, but the details are sparse. The Japanese themselves did not begin to keep accounts of their society until around AD 600 when a writing system was introduced, along with many other cultural innovations from China. The two main sources for Japanese mythology and early history are the *Kojiki* and the *Nihon Shoki*. The *Kojiki* or *Record of Ancient Matters* was compiled in Chinese in AD 712, but was based on earlier oral traditions. It relates various myths, legends and historical events concerning the imperial court from the age of the gods down to the time of the Empress Suiko (AD 593–628). The slightly later but longer *Nihon Shoki* or *Chronicles of Japan,* written in AD 720 betrays a greater influence of Chinese cultural attitudes, but covers broadly similar ground to the *Kojiki* although it relates events until AD 697. The theology of Shinto developed mainly through an interpretation of the mythology recorded in both the *Kojiki* and the *Nihon Shoki*.

Amaterasu, Sun Goddess

The sun goddess Amaterasu is of central significance to Japanese mythology, since the imperial family claimed descent from her until Japan's defeat in the Second World War. She is also unusual as a paramount female deity in a land where male pre-eminence has always been the norm, although there are stories connected with her that hint at male dissatisfaction with this state of affairs.

After his return from the underworld, Yomi (*see* page 18), Izanagi bathed to purify himself ritually from the pollution (*imi*) of contact with the dead. He then gave birth to a further sequence of gods and goddesses, culminating in the sun goddess Amaterasu, the moon god Tsuki-yomi and the storm god Susanoo. Before withdrawing from the world, Izanagi entrusted Amaterasu with rulership of the High Plains of Heaven, Tsuki-yomi with the realm of the night and Susanoo with the ocean. Susanoo was dissatisfied with his assignment and jealous of the ascendancy of his sister Amaterasu and so was banished by Izanagi.

Divine Conflict

Before he was due to leave, Susanoo arranged to meet with Amaterasu to say farewell but suspecting that he was plotting to overthrow her, Amaterasu armed herself and confronted her brother. He then challenged her to a contest which would prove who was really the mightiest – whoever could give birth to male gods would be the winner. Amaterasu took Susanoo's sword and broke it into three pieces from which she produced three goddesses, while Susanoo took her sacred *magatama* beads and produced five male gods. Amaterasu claimed she had won since his gods had come from *her* beads but Susanoo refused to accept defeat.

Susanoo then embarked on a series of foul outrages against Amaterasu, such as destroying the heavenly rice fields, defecating in the ritual hall of offerings and casting a skinned pony through the roof of the sacred weaving hall. This last act resulted in the death of one of Amaterasu's maidens after a shuttle pierced her genitals (according to some accounts it was Amaterasu herself who was injured). Either way, she was so terrified that she hid and sealed herself inside a cave. The entire human world and the heavens were cast into darkness and misery ensued. In vain the gods tried to entice her out with various stratagems but they all failed. Then the beautiful goddess of the dawn, Ama-no-uzume, who was the archetypal *miko* or shamaness, stood on an upturned rice barrel and began a sacred erotic dance baring her body. Hearing the excitement of the gods and their praises for Ama-no-uzume, Amaterasu peeped out of a crack and asked what was happening. She was told that the gods were rejoicing at the sight of a goddess more beautiful than herself. In disbelief, she opened the crack wider and as she gazed out, one of the gods held up a sacred mirror and Amaterasu saw her own reflection in it. While Amaterasu was entranced with her own reflection, one of the other gods seized her by the hand and pulled her out of the cave while others barred the cave with a magic rope. Upon this Amaterasu returned to the heavens where all the deities agreed to punish Susanoo with banishment from the heavens, fined him and cut off his beard and nails.

This account of divine rivalry may preserve distant memories of ancient power struggles in Japanese society between rival patriarchal and matriarchal systems of rule, although the outcome is uncharacteristic in world mythology inasmuch as it was the female, the goddess Amaterasu, who eventually emerged the winner rather than the male.

Focus on: Matriarchy in Japan

Various aspects of Japanese mythology and legendary records hint at a matriarchal system in early Japanese society. From the first to the third centuries AD, the Chinese noted that a number of the tribal groups were ruled by women. Whether this was a feature of Yayoi society or a vestige of the Jomon culture is uncertain, but it seems that women during this period sometimes combined leadership with religious duties of a shamanic nature. Queen Himiko is the first named ruler in Japan, of a state called Yamatai, known from Chinese historical records; she lived probably in the third century AD. Her name has intriguing implications for the myth of Amaterasu as it means 'sun daughter'. She is said to have been unmarried and some legends say she had a younger brother who brutally murdered her by thrusting a loom shuttle thrust into her vagina. Traces of the ancient shamanic role of women in Japan still persist in the shape of the *miko* priestess attendants found attached to Shinto shrines and the *itako* women who act as mediums between the living and the dead at various cultic centres, such as that at Mount Osorezan in northeastern Japan.

Susanoo, Storm God and The Izumo Cycle

A small but important group of myths known as the Izumo Cycle, concerning the activities of Susanoo and of his descendants, seems to preserve traditions from another tribal group unconnected with those who transmitted the main Amaterasu myths. In contrast to the Amaterasu cult associated with eastern central Japan, the Izumo Cycle is intimately linked with the coastal regions of western central Japan.

Izumo was the place where the god Susanoo lived after he was exiled from heaven. After he had killed an eight-headed monster, Susanoo married the princess Kusanada-hime and settled in Izumo. Myths tell of his expanding the territory and developing the region for human habitation.

Susanoo and Okuninushi

One of Susanoo's descendants, possibly his grandson, the god Okuninushi, also features in many of these myths as a bringer of civilization and culture. Okuninushi had numerous older brothers who wanted to marry Ya-gami-hime of neighbouring Inaba. Going to visit her, they meet a furless rabbit which they torment. Okuninushi kindly helps the rabbit regain its fur and in return is told that he will be the successful suitor of the princess while his brothers will become his retainers. This all comes true but his brothers soon become dissatisfied and quarrelsome. Though they manage to kill him twice, each time he comes back to life and he eventually decides to visit Yomi, the underworld, for advice about ridding himself of his troublesome brothers.

Suseri-hime

In the underworld, Okuninushi meets Suseri-hime, the daughter of Susanoo, and marries her without Susanoo's consent. Angered by this, Susanoo tries to kill Okuninushi three times but on each occasion Okuninushi is saved by a magic scarf given to him by Suseri-hime. Eventually the pair decide to escape to the land of the living while stealing a bow, sword and *koto* that belongs to Susanoo. Although Susanoo eventually catches up with him, he forgives Okuninushi out of admiration for his cunning and bravery. It is at this point that Okuninushi – Great Ruler of the Land – is given his name, foretelling his conquest of the whole country.

After his return from Yomi, the underworld, Okuninushi followed Susanoo's advice and hunted down his older brothers, eventually killing them all and becoming sole ruler of Izumo. Abandoning Ya-gami-hime, his earlier wife, he then went to live with Suseri-hime in a palace he built at Uga-no-yama in Izumo. After his return to Izumo, Okuninushi takes on many of the characteristics of a cultural hero, which perhaps reflects the early colonization and cultivation of that area. Much of the country was still wild and unformed at that time, and there was nothing but dense forests, swamps, ferocious animals and evil spirits. Mindful of Susanoo's prediction, Okuninushi began to clear the regions near Izumo with a magical weapon called Yachihoko, 'Eight Thousand Spears'. With it he walked tirelessly around the land and killed many demons, making places safe for people to live in.

A number of lesser myths are associated with Okuninushi, such as his encounter with the tiny, lame god Ku-e-hiko. Okuninushi adopts Ku-e-hiko as his brother and they become inseparable companions, continuing the work of clearing the land of evil and opening it up for habitation. Together they introduced silk worms and weaving, new crops and many medicinal herbs.

Focus on: Cultic Centres

The divine forces of nature or *kami* are thought to reside in rivers, rocks, mountains and trees, meaning that almost any feature in the Japanese landscape may act as a cultic centre. These may be marked by a small shrine for offerings or else just a *torii*, a stylized gateway demarking the boundary between the profane and the sacred. Other places in Japan are home to much larger shrines which act as national cultic centres though their importance has waned since the political demotion of Shinto in the wake of the Second World War. Most notable are the ancient great shrines at Ise and Izumo, both of which have their origins in prehistoric times. Ise in central Japan is connected with the sun goddess, Amaterasu, and Toyouke-no-okami, the god of rice and harvests. Until the fifteenth century the Ise shrine was considered to be so sacred that only members of the imperial family were allowed to visit it. The shrine at Izumo in western Japan is associated with Amaterasu's rival brother, Susanoo and his grandson, Okuninushi. A characteristic feature of all Shinto shrines is the complete absence of any form of iconographic depiction of the divinities enshrined in them. Instead, certain sacred objects are displayed on a simple altar such as a mirror, a sword or the comma-shaped *magatama* beads.

The Foundation of the Yamato State

Until very recently, the imperial family of Japan claimed an unbroken line of succession dating back to the mythical age when gods and goddesses roamed the earth. The myths relating the transition between the age of gods and humans hint at prehistoric events involving various rival tribes.

After Okuninushi and his descendants had made the land prosperous, their rule grew lax and evil gods once again made life unpleasant for the people. Amaterasu, who had wanted to extend her rule to that region for her descendants, decided to take advantage of the situation. After several failed attempts, she sent two trusted and brave gods, Futsunushi-no-mikoto and Takemikazuchi-no-mikoto, to tell Okuninushi to surrender the land to her. They sat on the tips of their upturned swords embedded in the crest of a wave in the sea off Inasa in Izumo and then delivered their ultimatum to him. Okuninushi was most impressed by this and after consulting with his son, he eventually conceded – on condition that a place should be reserved for him among the gods worshipped in Izumo.

The Origins of the Japanese State

After this, Okuninushi's clan was supplanted by Amaterasu's descendants. Her grandson Ninigi-no-mikoto came to earth carrying the three symbols of sovereignty: the mirror, the *magatama* beads and a sword. He had two sons – Hoderi (Fireshine) and Hoori (Fireshade).

Hoderi, the eldest, fished using a hook, while Hoori was a hunter. Hoori was dissatisfied and suggested changing their occupations, which they did but Hoori was unsuccessful, even losing the fishing hook. When Hoderi asked him to return it, he offered several substitutes but Hoderi insisted on having the original. Hoori drifted far out to sea in shame and eventually reached the palace of the sea god, Watatsumi-no-kami, who not only retrieved the fish hook but also gave Hoori his daughter in marriage. When the time came for Hoori to return home, Watatsumi-no-kami gave him two jewels, one to make the sea rise and one to make it fall. When Hoori got home, he returned the hook to Hoderi who, nevertheless, continued to complain, so Hoori then threw one jewel in the sea causing a flood. In terror, Hoderi begged for forgiveness so Hoori threw the other jewel into the sea and it receded. In gratitude, Hoderi swore that he would serve his younger brother in perpetuity.

The grandson of Hoori was Jimmu, the legendary first emperor of Japan. Jimmu seems to have set out from the island of Kyushu in the south in search of new lands to rule. When he and his followers reached the Kumano area, near present-day Osaka, a local deity put them in a deep sleep. However, Amaterasu appeared in a dream to one of Jimmu's retainers and revealed to him the existence of a magical sword. Awakening, the retainer found the sword and roused Jimmu. They then continued their march of conquest led by a giant crow. When Jimmu finally reached east central Japan, he married a local princess and founded the Yamato state. This state formed the precursor of the historic ruling hegemony.

Focus on: Shinto

Shinto is the indigenous religion which flourished in Japan before the introduction of Buddhism in the sixth century AD and has remained a vital force in all aspects of Japanese culture up to the present day. Shinto means 'the way of the gods' and as its name suggests, its central concern is the *kami*, a term that includes both the gods of myth and also the numinous powers inherent in all natural things. Though lacking a sophisticated metaphysical theology or philosophy, the aim of Shinto is to regulate human activities within the natural world in a harmonious manner. Unlike in Buddhism, the concept of ritual pollution (*imi*) – anything that disturbed the intrinsic harmony of nature – played an important role in Shinto in the past, and various methods of ritual cleansing were prescribed. Though early Shinto sacred places are natural features such as waterfalls, tall trees or imposing rocks, shrines were also built and maintained by families of ritual specialists who emerged by the sixth century AD; to a certain extent these places are still recognized as being sacred today. Although every town and village has its own Shinto shrine, those at Ise and Izumo are of national importance. Also associated with these shrines are colourful annual festivals (*matsuri*) in which the resident *kami* is paraded in a portable shrine.

Jizo, the God of Children

Jizo, the God of little children and the God who makes calm the troubled sea, is certainly the most lovable of the Buddhist divinities, though Kwannon, the Goddess of Mercy, has somewhat similar attributes. The most popular Gods, be they of the East or West, are those Gods with the most human qualities. Jizo, though of Buddhist origin, is essentially Japanese, and we may best describe him as being the creation of innumerable Japanese women who have longed to project into the Infinite, into the shrouded Beyond, a deity who should be a divine Father and Mother to the souls of their little ones. And this is just what Jizo is, a God essentially of the feminine heart, and not a being to be tossed about in the hair-splitting debates of hoary theologians. A study of the nature and characteristics of Jizo will reveal all that is best in the Japanese woman, for he assuredly reveals her love, her sense of the beautiful, and her infinite compassion. Jizo has all the wisdom of the Lord Buddha himself, with this important difference, namely, that Jizo has waived aside Nirvana, and does not sit upon the Golden Lotus, but has become, through an exquisitely beautiful self-sacrifice, the divine playmate and protector of Japanese children. He is the God of smiles and long sleeves, the enemy of evil spirits, and the one being who can heal the wound of a mother who has lost her child in death. We have a saying that all rivers find their way to the sea. To the Japanese woman who has laid her little one in the cemetery all rivers wind their silver courses into the place where the ever-waiting and ever-gentle Jizo is. That is why mothers who have lost their children in death write prayers on little slips of paper, and watch them float down the rivers on their way to the great spiritual Father and Mother who will answer all their petitions with a loving smile.

'The Dry Bed of the River of Souls'

Under the earth there is the Sai-no-Kawara, or 'the Dry Bed of the River of Souls'. This is the place where all children go after death, children and those who have never married. Here the little ones play with the smiling Jizo, and here it is that they build small towers of stones, for there are many in this river-bed. The mothers of these children, in the world above them, also pile up stones around the images of Jizo, for these little towers represent prayers; they are charms against the *oni* or wicked spirits. Sometimes in the Dry Bed of the River of Souls the *oni* for a moment gain a temporary victory, and knock down the little towers which the ghosts of children have built with so much laughter. When such a misfortune takes place the laughter ceases, and the little ones fly to Jizo for protection. He hides them in his long sleeves, and with his sacred staff drives away the red-eyed *oni*.

The place where the souls of children dwell is a shadowy and grey world of dim hills and vales through which the Sai-no-Kawara winds its way. All the children are clad in short white garments, and if occasionally the evil spirits frighten them there is always Jizo to dry their tears, always one who sends them back to their ghostly games again.

The following hymn of Jizo, known as 'The Legend of the Humming of the Sai-no-Kawara," gives us a beautiful and vivid conception of Jizo and this ghostly land where children play:

This abode of the souls of children is certainly not an ideal land. It is Jizo, and not his country, who has sprung from the hearts of Japanese women. The stern Buddhist teaching of cause and effect, of birth and re-birth, applies to even gentle infants. But if the great Wheel of Existence revolves with unerring force, and only fails to move when the desire for not-being is finally attained in Nirvana, Jizo lovingly stands at the foot of Destiny and makes easy the way where the feet of little children so softly patter.

The Cave of the Children's Ghosts

There is a cave in Japan known as Kyu-Kukedo-San, or Ancient Cavern, and far within its recess there is to be found an image of Jizo, with his mystic jewel and sacred staff. Before Jizo there is a little *torii* and a pair of *gohei*, both symbols of the Shinto faith; but, as Lafcadio Hearn observes, "this gentle divinity has no enemies; at the feet of the lover of children's ghosts both creeds unite in tender homage." Here it is that the ghosts of little children meet, softly whispering together as they stoop hither and thither in order to build their towers of stones. At night they creep over the sea from their Dry Bed of the River of Souls, and cover the sand in the cavern with their ghostly footsteps, building, ever building those prayers of stone, while Jizo smiles down upon their loving labour. They depart before the rising of the sun, for it is said that the dead fear to gaze upon the Sun Goddess, and most especially are these infants afraid of her bright gold eyes.

The Fountain of Jizo

Another beautiful sea-cave contains the Fountain of Jizo. It is a fountain of flowing milk, at which the souls of children quench their thirst. Mothers suffering from want of milk come to this fountain and pray to Jizo, and mothers having more milk than their infants require pray to the same God that he may take some of their milk and give it to the souls of children in his great shadowy kingdom. And Jizo is said to answer their prayers.

Kwannon, Goddess of Mercy

Kwannon, the Goddess of Mercy, resembles in many ways the no less merciful and gentle Jizo, for both renounced the joy of Nirvana that they might bring peace and happiness to others. Kwannon, however, is a much more complex divinity than Jizo, and though she is most frequently portrayed as a very beautiful and saintly Japanese woman, she nevertheless assumes a multitude of forms. We are familiar with certain Indian gods and goddesses with innumerable hands, and Kwannon is sometimes depicted as Senjiu-Kwannon, or Kwannon-of-the-Thousand-Hands. Each hand holds an object of some kind, as if to suggest that here indeed was a goddess ready in her love to give and to answer prayer to the uttermost.

Then there is Jiu-ichi-men-Kwannon, the Kwannon-of-the-Eleven-Faces. The face of Kwannon is here represented as "smiling with eternal youth and infinite tenderness," and in her glowing presence the ideal of the divine feminine is presented with infinite beauty of conception. In the tiara of Jiu-ichi-men-Kwannon are exquisite faces, a radiation, as it were, of miniature Kwannons. Sometimes the tiara of Kwannon takes another form, as in Bato-Kwannon, or Kwannon-with-the-Horse's-Head. The title is a little misleading, for such a graceful creature is very far from possessing a horse's head in any of her manifestations. Images of this particular Kwannon depict a horse cut out in the tiara. Bato-Kwannon is the Goddess to whom peasants pray for the safety and preservation of their horses and cattle, and Bato-Kwannon is not only said to protect dumb animals, particularly those who labour for mankind, but she extends her power to protecting their spirits and bringing them ease and a happier life than they experienced while on earth. In sharp contrast with the Kwannons we have already described is Hito-koto-Kwannon, the Kwannon who will only answer one prayer. The Gods of Love and Wisdom are frequently represented in conjunction with this Goddess, and the 'Twenty-eight Followers' are personifications of certain constellations. But in all the variations of Kwannon she preserves the same virgin beauty, and this Goddess of Mercy has not inappropriately been called the Japanese Madonna.

Kwannon in Chinese Myth

In China Kwannon is known as Kwanjin, and is the spiritual son of Amitâbha, but this divinity always appears as a goddess, as her images in both China and Japan testify. The Chinese claim that Kwanjin is of native origin, and was originally the daughter of the King of the Chow dynasty. She was sentenced to death by her father because she refused to marry, but the executioner's sword broke without inflicting a wound. We are told that later on her spirit went to Hell. There was something so radiantly beautiful about the spirit of Kwanjin that her very presence turned Hell into Paradise. The King of the Infernal Regions, in order to maintain the gloomy aspect of his realm, sent Kwanjin back to earth again, and he caused her to be miraculously transported on a lotus flower to the Island of Pootoo.

An Incarnation of Kwannon

Chujo Hime, a Buddhist nun, is generally regarded as the greatest early Japanese artist of embroidery, and, according to legend, she was an incarnation of Kwannon. Chujo Hime met with much cruel treatment from her stepmother, until she finally retired to the temple of Toema-dera, and there worked upon the wonderful lotus thread embroidery depicting the Buddhist Paradise. The design is so exquisite that we can easily understand the Japanese belief that the Gods helped this great artist in her work.

Kwannon the Mother

There is another remarkable embroidery, by Kano Hogai, depicting Kwannon as the Divine Mother, pouring forth from a crystal phial the water of creation. As this holy water falls in a series of bubbles, each bubble may be seen to contain a little babe with reverently folded hands. It is altogether a wonderful piece of work, and, turning from its pictorial beauty to study a description of its technicalities, we find that it took three years to execute, and that 12,100 different shades of silk, and twelve of gold thread, were used.

The 'Thirty-three Places' Sacred to Kwannon

There are thirty-three shrines sacred to Kwannon. All are carefully numbered, and are to be found in the provinces near Kyoto. The legend on page 45 may possibly account for the reverence bestowed upon the *Saikoku Sanjū-san Sho* (the 'Thirty-three Places'). The following is a complete list of the 'Thirty-three Places' sacred to Kwannon:

1. Fudaraku-ji, at Nachi, in Kishu.
2. Kimii-dera, near Wakayama, in Kishu.
3. Kokawa-dera, in Kishu.
4. Sefuku-ji, in Izumi.
5. Fujii-dera, in Kawachi.
6. Tsubosaka-dera, in Yamato.
7. Oka-dera, in Yamato.
8. Hase-dera, in Yamato.
9. Nan-eno, at Nara, in Yamato.
10. Mimuroto-dera, at Uji, in Yamashiro.
11. Kami Daigo-dera, at Uji, in Yamashiro.
12. Iwama-dera, in Omi.
13. Ishiyama-dera, near Otsu, in Omi.
14. Miidera, near Otsu, in Omi.
15. Ima-Gumano, at Kyoto, in Yamashiro.
16. Kiyomizu-dera, at Kyoto.

17. Rokuhara-dera, at Kyoto.
18. Rokkaku-do, at Kyoto.
19. Kodo, at Kyoto.
20. Yoshimine-dera, at Kyoto.
21. Anoji, in Tamba.
22. Sojiji, in Settsu.
23. Katsuo-dera, in Settsu.
24. Nakayama-dera, near Kobe, in Settsu.
25. Shin Kiyomizu-dera, in Harima.
26. Hokkeji, in Harima.
27. Shosha-san, in Harima.
28. Nareai-ji, in Tango.
29. Matsunoo-dera, in Wakasa.
30. Chikubu-shima, island in Lake Biwa, in Omi.
31. Chomeiji, in Omi.
32. Kwannonji, in Omi.
33. Tanigumi-dera, near Tarui, in Mino.

Benten, Goddess of the Sea

Benten, the Goddess of the Sea, is also one of the Seven Divinities of Luck; and she is romantically referred to as the Goddess of Love, Beauty, and Eloquence. She is represented in Japanese art as riding on a dragon or serpent, which may account for the fact that in certain localities snakes are regarded as being sacred. Images of Benten depict her as having eight arms. Six hands are extended above her head and hold a bow, arrow, wheel, sword, key, and sacred jewel, while her two remaining hands are reverently crossed in prayer. She resembles Kwannon in many ways, and images of the two goddesses are frequently seen together, but the shrines of Benten are usually to be found on islands.

The Gods of Luck

Daikoku, the God of Wealth, Ebisu, his son, the God of Labour, and Hotei, the God of Laughter and Contentment, belong to that cycle of deities known as the Gods of Luck.

Daikoku

Daikoku is represented with a Magic Mallet, which bears the sign of the Jewel, embodying the male and female spirit, and signifies a creative deity. A stroke of his Mallet confers wealth, and his second attribute is the Rat. Daikoku is, as we should suppose, an extremely popular deity, and he is frequently portrayed as a prosperous Chinese gentleman, richly apparelled, and is usually shown standing on bales of rice, with a bag of precious things on his shoulder. This genial and beneficent God is also depicted as seated on bales of rice, or showing his treasures to some eager and expectant child, or holding the Red Sun against his breast with one hand and grasping the Magic Mallet with the other.

Daikoku's attribute, a Rat, has an emblematic and moral meaning in connection with the wealth hidden in the God's bag. The Rat is frequently portrayed either in the bale of rice with its head peeping out, or in it, or playing with the Mallet, and sometimes a large number of rats are shown.

The Six Daikoku

1. Makura Daikoku, ordinary form with Mallet on lotus leaf.
2. Ojikara Daikoku, with sword and *vajra*.
3. Bika Daikoku, a priest, with Mallet in right hand, *vajra*-hilted sword in left.
4. Yasha Daikoku, with Wheel of the Law in his right hand.
5. Shinda Daikoku, a boy seated with a crystal in his left hand.
6. Mahakara Daikoku, seated female, with small bale of rice on her head.

Ebisu

Ebisu and his father Daikoku are usually pictured together: the God of Wealth seated upon bales of rice, pressing the Red Sun against his breast with one hand, and with the other holding the wealth-giving Mallet, while Ebisu is depicted with a fishing-rod and a great *tai* fish under his arm.

Hotei

Hotei, the God of Laughter and Contentment, is one of the most whimsical of the Japanese Gods. He is represented as extremely fat, carrying on his back a linen bag (*ho-tei*), from which he derives his name. In this bag he stows the Precious Things, but when in a particularly playful mood he uses it as a receptacle for merry and inquisitive children. Sometimes Hotei is represented in a broken-down and extremely shabby carriage drawn by boys, and is then known as the Waggon Priest. Again he is portrayed as carrying in one hand a Chinese fan and in the other his bag, or balancing at either end of a pole the bag of Precious Things and a boy.

Thunder Beings

There are many quaint legends in regard to thunder, and in Bakin's *Kumono Tayema Ama Yo No Tsuki* ('The Moon, shining through a Cloud-rift, on a Rainy Night') the famous Japanese novelist, who was an ardent believer in many of the superstitions of his country, had much to say in regard to Raiden, the God of Thunder, and the supernatural beings associated with him.

Raiden

Raiden is usually depicted as having red skin, the face of a demon, with two claws on each foot, and carrying on his back a great wheel or arc of drums. He is often found in company with Fugin, or with his son, Raitaro. When the Mongols attempted to invade Japan they were prevented from doing so by a great storm, and, according to legend, only three men escaped to tell the tale. Raiden's assistance in favour of Japan is often portrayed in Japanese art. He is depicted sitting on the clouds emitting lightnings and sending forth a shower of arrows upon the invaders. In China the Thunder God is regarded as a being ever on the look-out for wicked people. When he finds them, the Goddess of Lightning flashes a mirror upon those whom the God wishes to strike.

The Thunder Animal

Raiju, or Thunder Animal, appears to be more closely associated with lightning than with thunder. He is seen in forms resembling a weasel, badger, or monkey. In the *Shin-rai-ki* ('Thunder Record') we read the following: "On the twenty-second day of the sixth month of the second year of Meiwa [July 1766] a Thunder Animal fell at Oyama [Great Mountain], in the province of Sagami. It was captured by a farmer, who brought it to Edo, and exhibited it for money on the Riyo-goku Bridge. The creature was a little larger than a cat, and resembled a weasel: it had black hair, and five claws on each paw. During fine weather it was very tame and gentle; but, before and during a storm, exceedingly savage and unmanageable." In China the Thunder Animal is described as having "the head of a monkey, with crimson lips, eyes like mirrors, and two sharp claws on each paw." During a storm the Thunder Animal of Japan springs from tree to tree, and if any of the trees are found to have been struck by lightning it is believed to be the savage work of, the Thunder Animal's claws. This being, in common with the Thunder God himself, is said to have a weakness for human navels, so that for this reason many superstitious people endeavour, if possible, to lie flat on their stomachs during a thunderstorm. Bark torn by the Thunder Animal is carefully preserved, and is supposed to be an excellent remedy for toothache.

The Thunder Bird and Thunder Woman

Raicho, Thunder Bird, resembles a rook, but it has spurs of flesh, which, when struck together, produce a horrible sound. This is the bird to which the Emperor of Goto-bain referred in the following poem:

"In the shadow of the pine-tree of Shiro-yama
Thunder-birds rest, and spend the night."

These birds feed upon the tree-frog named *rai* (thunder), and are always seen flying about in the sky during a thunderstorm.

Little is known concerning Kaminari (Thunder Woman), except that on one occasion she is said to have appeared in the guise of a Chinese Empress.

Supernatural Beings

The Kappa

The *Kappa* is a river goblin, a hairy creature with the body of a tortoise and scaly limbs. His head somewhat resembles that of an ape, in the top of which there is a cavity containing a mysterious fluid, said to be the source of the creature's power. The chief delight of the *Kappa* is to challenge human beings to single combat, and the unfortunate man who receives an invitation of this kind cannot refuse. Though the *Kappa* is fierce and quarrelsome, he is, nevertheless, extremely polite. The wayfarer who receives his peremptory summons gives the goblin a profound bow. The courteous *Kappa* acknowledges the obeisance, and in inclining his head the strength-giving liquid runs out from the hollow in his cranium, and becoming feeble, his warlike characteristics immediately disappear. To defeat the *Kappa*, however, is just as unfortunate as to receive a beating at his hands, for the momentary glory of the conquest is rapidly followed by a wasting away of the unfortunate wayfarer. The *Kappa* possesses the propensities of a vampire, for he strikes people in the water, as they bathe in lake or river, and sucks their blood. In a certain part of Japan the *Kappa* is said to claim two victims every year. When they emerge from the water their skin becomes blanched, and they gradually pine away as the result of a terrible disease.

The Tengu

We will refer to the *Tengu* in the story of Yoshitsune and Benkei. In that legend, Yoshitsune, one of the greatest warriors of Old Japan, learnt the art of swordsmanship from the King of the *Tengu*. Professor B.H. Chamberlain (1850–1935), a leading Japanologist of his time, described the *Tengu* as "a class of goblins or gnomes that haunt the mountains and woodlands, and play many pranks. They have an affinity to birds; for they are winged and beaked, sometimes clawed. But often the beak becomes a large and enormously long human nose, and the whole creature is conceived as human, nothing bird-like remaining but the fan of feathers with which it fans itself. It is often dressed in leaves, and wears on its head a tiny cap." In brief, the *Tengu* are minor divinities, and are supreme in the art of fencing, and, indeed, in the use of weapons generally. The ideographs with which the name is written signify "heavenly dog," which is misleading, for the creature bears no resemblance to a dog, and is, as we have already described, partly human and partly bird-like in appearance. There are other confusing traditions in regard to the word *Tengu*, for it is said that the Emperor Jomei gave the name to a certain meteor "which whirled from east to west with a loud detonation." Then, again, a still more ancient belief informs us that the *Tengu* were emanations from Susanoo, the Impetuous Male, and again, that they were female demons with heads of beasts and great ears and noses of such enormous length that they could carry men on them and fly with their suspended burden for thousands of miles without fatigue, and in addition their teeth were so strong and so sharp that these female demons could bite through swords and spears. The *Tengu* is still believed to inhabit certain forests and the recesses of high mountains. Generally speaking, the *Tengu* is not a malevolent being, for he possesses a keen sense of humour, and is fond of a practical joke. Sometimes, however, the *Tengu* mysteriously hides human beings, and when finally they return to their homes they do so in a demented condition. This strange occurrence is known as *Tengu-kakushi*, or hidden by a *Tengu*, and features in a story later in this collection: 'The Adventures of Kiuchi Heizayemon'.

The Mountain Woman and the Mountain Man

The Mountain Woman's body is covered with long white hair. She is looked upon as an ogre (*kijo*), and, as such, figures in Japanese romance. She has cannibalistic tendencies, and is able to fly about like a moth and traverse pathless mountains with ease.

The Mountain Man is said to resemble a great darkhaired monkey. He is extremely strong, and thinks nothing of stealing food from the villages. He is, however, always ready to assist woodcutters, and will gladly carry their timber for them in exchange for a ball of rice. It is useless to capture or kill him, for an attack of any kind upon the Mountain Man brings misfortune, and sometimes death, upon the assailants.

Sennin

The *Sennin* are mountain recluses, and many are the legends told in connection with them. Though they have human form, they are, at the same time, immortal, and adepts in the magical arts. The first great Japanese *sennin* was Yosho, who was born at Noto AD 870. Just before his birth his mother dreamt that she had swallowed the sun, a dream that foretold the miraculous power of her child. Yosho was studious and devout, and spent most of his time in studying the 'Lotus of the Law'. He lived very simply indeed, and at length reduced his diet to a single grain of millet a day. He departed from the earth AD 901, having attained much supernatural power. He left his mantle hanging on the branch of a tree, together with a scroll bearing these words: "I bequeath my mantle to Emmei of Dogen-ji." In due time Emmei became a *sennin*, and, like his master, was able to perform many marvels. Shortly after Yosho's disappearance his father became seriously ill, and he prayed most ardently that he might see his well-loved son again. In reply to his prayers, Yosho's voice was heard overhead reciting the 'Lotus of the Law'. When he had concluded his recitations, he said to his stricken father: "If flowers are offered and incense burned on the 18th of every month, my spirit will descend and greet you, drawn by the perfume of the flowers and the blue smoke of incense."

Sennin are frequently depicted in Japanese art: Chokoro releasing his magic horse from a gigantic gourd; Gama with his wizard toad; Tekkai blowing his soul into space; Roko balancing himself on a flying tortoise; and Kume, who fell from his chariot of cloud because, contrary to his holy calling, he loved the image of a fair girl reflected in a stream.

Fire: Miraculous Lights

There are many varieties of fire apparitions in Japan. There is the ghost-fire, demon-light, fox-flame, flash-pillar, badger-blaze, dragon-torch, and lamp of Buddha. In addition supernatural fire is said to emanate from certain birds, such as the blue heron, through the skin, mouth, and eyes. There are also fire-wheels, or messengers from Hades, sea-fires, besides the flames that spring from the cemetery.

Baku

In Japan, among superstitious people, evil dreams are believed to be the result of evil spirits, and the supernatural creature called *Baku* is known as Eater of Dreams. The *Baku* like so many mythological beings, is a curious mingling of various animals. It has the face of a lion, the body of a horse, the tail of a cow, the forelock of a rhinoceros, and the feet of a tiger. Several evil dreams are mentioned in an old Japanese book, such as two snakes twined together, a fox with the voice of a man, blood-stained garments, a talking rice-pot, and so on. When a Japanese peasant awakens from an evil nightmare, he cries: "Devour, O *Baku*! devour my evil dream." At one time pictures of the *Baku* were hung up in Japanese houses and its name written upon pillows. It was believed that if the *Baku* could be induced to eat a horrible dream, the creature had the power to change it into good fortune.

The Dragon

The Dragon is undoubtedly the most famous of mythical beasts, but, though Chinese in origin, it has become intimately associated with Japanese mythology. The creature lives for the most part in the ocean, river, or lake, but it has the power of flight and rules over clouds and tempests. The Dragon of China and Japan resemble each other, with the exception that the Japanese variety has three claws, while that of the Celestial Kingdom has five. The Chinese Emperor Yao was said to be the son of a dragon, and many rulers of that country were metaphorically referred to as 'dragon-faced'. The Dragon has the head of a camel, horns of a deer, eyes of a hare, scales of a carp, paws of a tiger, and claws resembling those of an eagle. In addition it has whiskers, a bright jewel under its chin, and a measure on the top of its head which enables it to ascend to Heaven at will. This is merely a general description and does not apply to all dragons, some of which have heads of so extraordinary a kind that they cannot be compared with anything in the animal kingdom. The breath of the Dragon changes into clouds from which come either rain or fire. It is able to expand or contract its body, and in addition it has the power of transformation and invisibility. In both Chinese and Japanese mythology the watery principle is associated with the Dragon.

The Dragon (*Tatsu*) is one of the signs of the zodiac, and the four seas, which in the old Chinese conception limited the habitable earth, were ruled over by four Dragon Kings. The Celestial Dragon ruled over the Mansions of the Gods, the Spiritual Dragon presided over rain, the Earth Dragon marked the courses of rivers, and the Dragon or Hidden Treasure guarded precious metals and stones.

A white Dragon, which lived in a pond at Yamashiro, transformed itself every fifty years into a bird called *O-Goncho*, with a voice resembling the howling of a wolf. Whenever this bird appeared it brought with it a great famine. On one occasion, while Fuk Hi was standing by the Yellow River, the Yellow Dragon presented him with a scroll inscribed with mystic characters. This tradition is said to be the legendary origin of the Chinese system of writing.

Animals in Japanese Folklore

Inari, the Fox God

The fox takes an important place in Japanese legend, and the subject is of a far-reaching and complex kind. Inari was originally the God of Rice, but in the eleventh century he became associated with the Fox God, with attributes for good and evil, mostly for evil, so profuse and so manifold in their application that they cause no little confusion to the Western reader. All foxes possess supernatural powers to an almost limitless degree. They have the power of infinite vision; they can hear everything and understand the secret thoughts of mankind generally, and in addition they possess the power of transformation and of transmutation. The chief attribute of the bad fox is the power to delude human beings, and for this purpose it will take the form of a beautiful woman, and many are the legends told in this connection. If the shadow of a fox-woman chance to fall upon water, only the fox, and not the fair woman, is revealed. It is said that if a dog sees a fox-woman the feminine form vanishes immediately, and the fox alone remains.

Though the legends connected with the fox in Japan are usually associated with evil, Inari sometimes poses as a beneficent being, a being who can cure coughs and colds, bring wealth to the needy, and answer a woman's prayer for a child.

The Hare

The hare is supposed to attain, like the fox, tortoise, crane, and tiger, a fabulous age, extending to no less than a thousand years. In Taoist legends the hare is said to live in the moon, and is occupied in pounding, with pestle and mortar, the drugs that compose the Elixir of Life, while in other legends, as we have seen elsewhere, this animal is represented as pounding rice. Shaka Muni (the Lord Buddha), according to legend, is said to have sacrificed himself as a hare in order that he might appease the hunger of Indra, who drew the animal upon the moon by way of showing his admiration. The fur of the hare becomes white when it has lived for five hundred years, and we give below the famous legend from the *Kojiki* known as 'The White Hare of Inaba'.

The Badger

The badger in legend has much in common with the fox. It can adopt human form and assume the shape of the moon; but in many legends it is described as a humorous creature, an animal intensely fond of a practical joke. The badger is frequently depicted in legend and art as playing a tattoo on its protuberant and drum-like stomach, and it is for this reason that Japanese jesters are sometimes called badgers.

The Cat

The Japanese cat, with or without a tail, is very far from being popular, for this animal and the venomous serpent were the only two creatures that did not weep when the Lord Buddha died. Nipponese cats seem to be under a curse, and for the most part they are left to their own resources, resources frequently associated with supernatural powers. Like foxes and badgers, they are able to bewitch human beings. Professor B.H. Chamberlain wrote in *Things Japanese*: "Among Europeans an irreverent person may sometimes be heard to describe an ugly, cross old woman as a cat. In Japan, the land of topsy-turvydom, that nickname is colloquially applied to the youngest and most attractive – the singing-girls."

The Japanese cat, however, is regarded with favour among sailors, and the *mike-neko*, or cat of three colours, is most highly prized. Sailors the world over are said to be superstitious, and those of Japan do their utmost to secure a ship's cat, in the belief that this animal will keep off the spirits of the deep. Many sailors believe that those who are drowned at sea never find spiritual repose; they believe that they everlastingly lurk in the waves and shout and wail as junks pass by. To such men the breakers beating on the seashore are the white, grasping hands of innumerable spirits, and they believe that the sea is crowded with *O-bake*, honourable ghosts. The Japanese cat is said to have control over the dead.

The Dog

Generally speaking the dog in Japan is looked upon as a friendly animal, and in most legends he acquits himself well; but in the Oki Islands many of the inhabitants believe that all dogs have supernatural power, attributed to the fox elsewhere. Professor B.H. Chamberlain wrote: "The human beings in league with them are termed *inu-gami-mochi* – that is, 'dog-god owners.' When the spirit of such a magic dog goes forth on an errand of mischief its body remains behind, growing gradually weaker, and sometimes dying and falling to decay. When this happens the spirit on its return takes up its abode in the body of a wizard, who thereupon becomes more powerful than ever."

Birds

Various birds are mentioned in Japanese legend, such as the pheasant in the story of Momotaro, the *Ho-Ho* Bird, the Bridge of Magpies in the account of Tanabata, the mysterious light said to shine from the blue heron, and the Thunder Bird. The *sekirei*, or wagtails, are sacred to Izanagi and Izanami, for it was through these birds that these divinities first learnt the art of love, and not even the God of Scarecrows can frighten them. When the great hero Yamato-take died he was supposed to have been transformed into a white bird, and we read in the *Ho-jo-ki* that Chomei fancied he heard in the note of a copper pheasant the cry of his mother. Mythical creatures such as the *Tengu* possess certain bird-like qualities, but they cannot be classed under the heading of birds, and for this reason they are dealt with elsewhere.

Crickets and Cicadas

Much has been written about the Japanese *semi*, or tree-crickets, and it seems strange to us that these little creatures should be bought and placed in minute cages, where they sing with extraordinary sweetness. Lafcadio Hearn in *Kottō* gives us a pathetic story concerning one of these insects. He tells us that his servant forgot to feed it, and that gradually it ceased to sing, being forced at last to eat its own minute limbs.

The *minminzemi's* singing resembles the chanting of a Buddhist priest, while the green *semi*, or *higurashi*, makes a sound like the trilling of a tiny bell. The carrying of a dried beetle is said to increase one's wardrobe. It must be remembered in the legends that follow that according to Buddhist teaching all life is sacred, and, moreover, that on account of some sin the Buddhists believe that the soul of a man or woman can enter even the minute form of an insect.

Dragonflies

The dragonfly is frequently mentioned in Japanese poetry, but nowhere more pathetically than in the following lines written by Chiyo after the death of her little son:

"How far, I wonder, did he stray,
Chasing the burnished dragonfly today?"

Chiyo, in this exquisite fragment, suggests a very great deal, for in her mother-love there is no dismal conception of Death. She regards the future life of her little one as the happiest hour of playtime. Once more in these lines there is the Japanese idea of the soul coming back again.

Sanemori and Shiwan

Sanemori, who was a great warrior, was on one occasion, while riding on a horse, engaged in fighting an enemy. During the conflict his horse slipped and rolled into a rice-field. As the result of this mishap his antagonist was able to slay him, and from that hour Sanemori became a rice-devouring insect, known by the peasantry of Izumo as Sanemori-San. During certain summer nights the peasants light fires in their rice-fields in order to attract the insect, play upon flutes and beat gongs, crying: "O Sanemori, augustly deign to come hither!" A religious rite is then performed, and a straw representation of a rider upon a horse is either burnt or thrown into water. It is believed that this ceremony will successfully free the fields from the rice-devouring insect.

The *shiwan*, a small yellow insect that feeds upon cucumbers, is said to have once been a physician. This physician, guilty of some intrigue, was forced to leave his home, but in attempting to make his escape his foot caught in the sinuous coils of a cucumber vine, and he was killed by his pursuers. His angry ghost became a *shiwan*, and from that day to this the insect feeds upon cucumbers.

Fireflies

"For this willow-tree the season of budding would seem to have returned in the dark – look at the fireflies."

In ancient days firefly-hunting was one of the amusements of great nobles, but today it is the pastime of children only. These hunting parties, however, have lost none of their picturesqueness, and the flashing insect has been the theme of many an exquisite poem, such as: "Ah, the cunning fireflies! being chased, they hide themselves in the moonlight!"

Grown-up people, however, go out to see the fireflies with the same ardour with which they indulge in flower-viewing. To the minds of these great Nature-lovers the fireflies resemble dazzling petals of some strange fireflower or a host of wondering stars that has left the sky to wander upon the earth. During the summer thousands of people visit Uji in order to see the *Hotaru-Kassen*, or Firefly Battle. From the river-bank dart myriads of these flashing insects, and in a moment they form a great silver-shining cloud. The cloud breaks and the flowing river, once dark as black velvet, becomes a winding stretch of gleaming jewels. No wonder the Japanese poet cries: "Do I see only fireflies drifting with the current? Or is the Night itself drifting, with its swarming of stars?"

There is a legend connected with this fascinating spectacle. It is believed that the Minamoto-Firefly and the Taira-Firefly are the ghosts of the old warriors of the Minamoto and Taira clans. On the night of the twentieth day of the fourth month they fight a great battle on the Uji River. On that night all caged fireflies are set free in order that they may fight again the old clan battles of the twelfth century. The ghostly significance of fireflies is further strengthened by the fact that these insects are fond of swarming round willow-trees – the most eerie trees in Japan. Fireflies in ancient days were supposed to possess medicinal properties. Firefly ointment was said to render all poisons harmless, and, moreover, it had the power to drive away evil spirits and to preserve a house from the attacks of robbers.

Butterflies

It is in China rather than in Japan that the butterfly is connected with legend and folk-lore. The Chinese scholar Rosan is said to have received visits from two spirit maidens who regaled him with ghostly stories about these bright-winged insects.

It is more than probable that the legends concerning butterflies in Japan have been borrowed from China. Japanese poets and artists were fond of choosing for their professional appellation such names as 'Butterfly-Dream', 'Solitary Butterfly', 'Butterfly-Help' and so on. Though probably of Chinese origin, such ideas naturally appealed to the aesthetic taste of the Japanese people, and no doubt they played in early days the romantic game of butterflies.

The Emperor Genso used to make butterflies choose his loves for him. At a wine-party in his garden fair ladies would set caged butterflies free. These bright-coloured insects would fly and settle upon the fairest damsels, and those maidens immediately received royal favours.

In Japan the butterfly was at one time considered to be the soul of a living man or woman. If it entered a guest-room and pitched behind the bamboo screen it was a sure sign that the person whom it represented would shortly appear in the house. The presence of a butterfly in the house was regarded as a good omen, though of course everything depended on the individual typified by the butterfly.

The butterfly was not always the harbinger of good. When Taira-no-Masakado was secretly preparing for a revolt Kyoto was the scene of a swarm of butterflies, and the people who saw them were much frightened. Lafcadio Hearn suggests that these butterflies may have been the spirits of those fated to fall in battle, the spirits of the living who were stirred by a premonition of the near approach of death. Butterflies may also be the souls of the dead, and they often appear in this form in order to announce their final leave-taking from the body.

Tales of the Gods & Creation

Introduction

WE ARE TOLD THAT in the very beginning "Heaven and Earth were not yet separated, and the *In* and *Yo* not yet divided." The *In* and *Yo*, corresponding to the Chinese *Yang* and *Yin*, were the male and female principles. It was more convenient for the old Japanese writers to imagine the coming into being of creation in terms not very remote from their own manner of birth. We are told in the *Nihon Shoki* that these male and female principles "formed a chaotic mass like an egg which was of obscurely defined limits and contained germs." Eventually this egg was quickened into life, and the purer and clearer part was drawn out and formed Heaven, while the heavier element settled down and became Earth, which was "compared to the floating of a fish sporting on the surface of the water." A mysterious form resembling a reed-shoot suddenly appeared between Heaven and Earth, and as suddenly became transformed into a God called Kunitokotachi, ('Land-eternal-stand-of-august-thing'). We may pass over the other divine births until we come to the important deities known as Izanagi and Izanami ('Male-who-invites' and 'Female-who-invites'). About these beings has been woven an entrancing myth, the first in this section. We also present some tales and exploits of other gods, including Amaterasu, Susanoo, Ninigi, Uzume, Ko-no-Hana, the Sea God, Kwannon, Benten and the Thunder God.

Izanagi and Izanami

IZANAGI AND IZANAMI stood on the Floating Bridge of Heaven and looked down into the abyss. They inquired of each other if there were a country far, far below the great Floating Bridge. They were determined to find out. In order to do so they thrust down a jewel-spear, and found the ocean. Raising the spear a little, water dripped from it, coagulated, and became the island of Onogoro-jima ('Spontaneously-congeal-island').

Upon this island the two deities descended. Shortly afterwards they desired to become husband and wife, though as a matter of fact they were brother and sister; but such a relationship in the East has never precluded marriage. These deities accordingly set up a pillar on the island. Izanagi walked round one way, and Izanami the other. When they met, Izanami said: "How delightful! I have met with a lovely youth." One would have thought that this naive remark would have pleased Izanagi; but it made him, extremely angry, and he retorted: "I am a man, and by that right should have spoken first. How is it that on the contrary thou, a woman, shouldst have been the first to speak? This is unlucky. Let us go round again." So it happened that the two deities started afresh. Once again they met, and this time Izanagi remarked: "How delightful! I have met a lovely maiden." Shortly after this very ingenuous proposal Izanagi and Izanami were married.

When Izanami had given birth to islands, seas, rivers, herbs, and trees, she and her lord consulted together, saying: "We have now produced the Great-Eight-Island country, with the mountains, rivers, herbs, and trees. Why should we not produce someone who shall be the Lord of the Universe?"

The wish of these deities was fulfilled, for in due season Amaterasu, the Sun Goddess, was born. She was known as 'Heaven-Illumine-of-Great-Deity', and was so extremely beautiful that her parents determined to send her up the Ladder of Heaven, and in the high sky above to cast for ever her glorious sunshine upon the earth.

Their next child was the Moon God, Tsuki-yumi. His silver radiance was not so fair as the golden effulgence of his sister, the Sun Goddess, but he was, nevertheless, deemed worthy to be her consort. So up the Ladder of Heaven climbed the Moon God. They soon quarrelled, and Amaterasu said: "Thou art a wicked deity. I must not see thee face to face." They were therefore separated by a day and night, and dwelt apart.

The next child of Izanagi and Izanami was Susanoo ('The Impetuous Male'). We shall return to Susanoo and his doings later on, and content ourselves for the present with confining our attention to his parents.

Izanami gave birth to the Fire God, Kagutsuchi. The birth of this child made her extremely ill. Izanagi knelt on the ground, bitterly weeping and lamenting. But his sorrow availed nothing, and Izanami crept away into the Land of Yomi (Hades).

Her lord, however, could not live without her, and he too went into the Land of Yomi. When he discovered her, she said regretfully: "My lord and husband, why is thy coming so late? I have already eaten of the cooking-furnace of Yomi. Nevertheless, I am about to lie down to rest. I pray thee do not look at me."

Izanagi, moved by curiosity, refused to fulfil her wish. It was dark in the Land of Yomi, so he secretly took out his many-toothed comb, broke off a piece, and lighted it. The sight that greeted him was ghastly and horrible in the extreme. His once beautiful wife had now become a swollen and festering creature. Eight varieties of Thunder Gods rested upon her. The Thunder of the Fire, Earth, and Mountain were all there leering upon him, and roaring with their great voices.

Izanagi grew frightened and disgusted, saying: "I have come unawares to a hideous and polluted land." His wife retorted: "Why didst thou not observe that which I charged thee? Now am I put to shame."

Izanami was so angry with her lord for ignoring her wish and breaking in upon her privacy that she sent the Eight Ugly Females of Yomi to pursue him. Izanagi drew his sword and fled down the dark regions of the Underworld. As he ran he took off his headdress, and flung it to the ground. It immediately became a bunch of grapes. When the Ugly Females saw it, they bent down and ate the luscious fruit. Izanami saw them pause, and deemed it wise to pursue her lord herself.

By this time Izanagi had reached the Even Pass of Yomi. Here he placed a huge rock, and eventually came face to face with Izanami. One would scarcely have thought that amid such exciting adventures Izanagi would have solemnly declared a divorce. But this is just what he did do. To this proposal his wife replied: "My dear lord and husband, if thou sayest so, I will strangle to death the people in one day." This plaintive and threatening speech in no way influenced Izanagi, who readily replied that he would cause to be born in one day no less than fifteen hundred.

The above remark must have proved conclusive, for when we next hear of Izanagi he had escaped from the Land of Yomi, from an angry wife, and from the Eight Ugly Females. After his escape he was engaged in copious ablutions, by way of purification, from which numerous deities were born. We read in the *Nihon Shoki*: "After this, Izanagi, his divine task having been accomplished, and his spirit-career about to suffer a change, built himself an abode of gloom in the island of Ahaji, where he dwelt for ever in silence and concealment."

Amaterasu and Susanoo

SUSANOO, OR 'THE IMPETUOUS MALE', was the brother of Amaterasu, the Sun Goddess. Now Susanoo was a very undesirable deity indeed, and he figured in the Realm of the Japanese Gods as a decidedly disturbing element. His character has been clearly drawn in the *Nihon Shoki*, more clearly perhaps than that of any other deity mentioned in these ancient records. Susanoo had a very bad temper, which often resulted in many cruel and ungenerous acts. Moreover, in spite of his long beard, he had a habit of continually weeping and wailing. Where a child in a tantrum would crush a toy to pieces, the Impetuous Male, when in a towering rage, and without a moment's warning, would wither the once fair greenery of mountains, and in addition bring many people to an untimely end.

His parents, Izanagi and Izanami, were much troubled by his doings, and, after consulting together, they decided to banish their unruly son to the Land of Yomi. Susa, however, had a word to say in the matter. He made the following petition, saying: "I will now obey thy instructions and proceed to the Nether-Land (Yomi). Therefore I wish for a short time to go to the Plain of High Heaven and meet with my elder sister (Amaterasu), after which I will go away for ever." This apparently harmless request was granted, and Susanoo ascended to Heaven. His departure occasioned a great commotion of the sea, and the hills and mountains groaned aloud.

Now Amaterasu heard these noises, and perceiving that they denoted the near approach of her wicked brother Susanoo, she said to herself: "Is my younger brother coming with good intentions? I think it must be his purpose to rob me of my kingdom. By the charge which our parents gave to their children, each of us has his own allotted limits. Why, therefore, does he reject the kingdom to which he should proceed, and make bold to come spying here?"

Amaterasu then prepared for warfare. She tied her hair into knots and hung jewels upon it, and round her wrists "an august string of five hundred Yasaka jewels." She presented a very formidable appearance when in addition she slung over her back "a thousand-arrow quiver and a five-hundred-arrow quiver," and protected her arms with pads to deaden the recoil of the bowstring. Having arrayed herself for deadly combat, she brandished her bow, grasped her sword-hilt, and stamped on the ground till she had made a hole sufficiently large to serve as a fortification.

All this elaborate and ingenious preparation was in vain. The Impetuous Male adopted the manner of a penitent. "From the beginning," he said, "my heart has not been black. But as, in obedience to the stern behest of our parents, I am about to depart for ever to the Nether-Land, how could I bear to depart without having seen face to face thee my elder sister? It is for this reason that I have traversed on foot the clouds and mists and have come hither from afar. I am surprised that my elder sister should, on the contrary, put on so stern a countenance."

Amaterasu regarded these remarks with a certain amount of suspicion. Susanoo's filial piety and Susanoo's cruelty were not easily to be reconciled. She thereupon resolved to test his sincerity by a remarkable proceeding we need not describe. Suffice it to say that for the time being the test proved the Impetuous Male's purity of heart and general sincerity towards his sister.

But Susanoo's good behaviour was a very short-lived affair indeed. It happened that Amaterasu had made a number of excellent rice-fields in Heaven. Some were narrow and some were long, and Amaterasu was justly proud of these rice-fields. No sooner had she sown the seed in the spring than Susanoo broke down the divisions between the plots, and in the autumn let loose a number of piebald colts.

One day when he saw his sister in the sacred Weaving Hall, weaving the garments of the Gods, he made a hole through the roof and flung down a flayed horse. Amaterasu was so frightened that she accidentally wounded herself with the shuttle. Extremely angry, she determined to leave her abode; so, gathering her shining robes about her, she crept down the blue sky, entered a cave, fastened it securely, and there dwelt in seclusion.

Now the world was in darkness, and the alternation of night and day was unknown. When this dreadful catastrophe had taken place the Eighty Myriads of Gods assembled together on the bank of the River of Heaven and discussed how they might best persuade Amaterasu to grace Heaven once more with her shining glory. No less a God than 'Thought-combining', after much profound reasoning, gathered together a number of singing-birds from the Eternal Land. After sundry divinations with a deer's leg-bone, over a fire of cherry-bark, the Gods made a number of tools, bellows, and forges. Stars were welded together to form a mirror, and jewellery and musical instruments were eventually fashioned.

When all these things had been duly accomplished the Eighty Myriads of Gods came down to the rock-cavern where the Sun Goddess lay concealed, and gave an elaborate entertainment. On the upper branches of the True Sakaki Tree they hung the precious jewels, and on the middle branches the mirror. From every side there was a great singing of birds, which was only the prelude to what followed. Now Uzume ('Heavenly-alarming-female') took in her hand a spear wreathed with Eulalia grass, and made a headdress of the True Sakaki Tree. Then she placed a tub upside down, and proceeded to dance in a very immodest manner, till the Eighty Myriad Gods began to roar with laughter.

Such extraordinary proceedings naturally awakened the curiosity of Amaterasu, and she peeped forth. Once more the world became golden with her presence. Once more she dwelt in the Plain of High Heaven, and Susanoo was duly chastised and banished to the Yomi Land.

Susanoo and the Serpent

SUSANOO, HAVING DESCENDED from Heaven, arrived at the river Hi, in the province of Idzumo. Here he was disturbed by a sound of weeping. It was so unusual to hear any other than himself weep that he went in search of the cause of the sorrow. He discovered an old man and an old woman. Between them was a young girl, whom they fondly caressed and gazed at with pitiful eyes, as if they were reluctantly bidding her a last farewell. When Susanoo asked the old couple who they were and why they lamented, the old man replied: "I am an Earthly Deity, and my name is Ashinadzuchi ('Foot-stroke-elder'). My wife's name is Tenadzuchi ('Hand-stroke-elder'). This girl is our daughter, and her name is Kushinadahime ('Wondrous-Inada-Princess'). The reason of our weeping is that formerly we had eight children, daughters; but they have been devoured year by year by an eight-forked serpent, and now the time approaches for this girl to be devoured. There is no means of escape for her, and therefore do we grieve exceedingly."

The Impetuous Male listened to this painful recital with profound attention, and, perceiving that the maiden was extremely beautiful, he offered to slay the eight-forked serpent if her parents would give her to him in marriage as a fitting reward for his services. This request was readily granted.

Susanoo now changed Kushinadahime into a many-toothed comb and stuck it in his hair. Then he bade the old couple brew a quantity of *sake*. When the *sake* was ready, he poured it into eight tubs, and awaited the coming of the dreadful monster.

Eventually the serpent came. It had eight heads, and the eyes were red, "like winter-cherry." Moreover it had eight tails, and firs and cypress-trees grew on its back. It was in length the space of eight hills and eight valleys. Its lumbering progress was necessarily slow, but finding the *sake*, each head eagerly drank the tempting beverage till the serpent became extremely drunk, and fell asleep. Then Susanoo, having little to fear, drew his ten-span sword and chopped the great monster into little pieces. When he struck one of the tails his weapon became notched, and bending down he discovered a sword called the Murakumo-no-Tsurugi. Perceiving it to be a divine sword, he gave it to the Gods of Heaven.

Having successfully accomplished his task, Susanoo converted the many-toothed comb into Kushinadahime again, and at length came to Suga, in the province of Idzumo, in order that he might celebrate his marriage. Here he composed the following verse:

"Many clouds arise,
On all sides a manifold fence,
To receive within it the spouses,
They form a manifold fence:
Ah! that manifold fence!"

The Divine Messengers

NOW AT THAT TIME the Gods assembled in the High Plain of Heaven were aware of continual disturbances in the Central Land of Reed-Plains (Idzumo). We are told that "Plains, the rocks, tree-stems, and herbage have still the power of speech. At night they make a clamour like that of flames of fire; in the day-time they swarm up like flies in the fifth month." In addition certain deities made themselves objectionable. The Gods determined to put an end to these disturbances, and after a consultation Takamimusubi decided to send his grandchild Ninigi to govern the Central Land of Reed-Plains, to wipe out insurrection, and to bring peace and prosperity to the country. It was deemed necessary to send messengers to prepare the way in advance. The first envoy was Ama-no-ho; but as he spent three years in the country without reporting to the Gods, his son was sent in his place. He adopted the same course as his father, and defied the orders of the Heavenly Ones. The third messenger was Ame-waka ('Heaven-young-Prince'). He, too, was disloyal, in spite of his noble weapons, and instead of going about his duties he fell in love and took to wife Shita-teru-hime ('Lower-shine-Princess').

Now the assembled Gods grew angry at the long delay, and sent a pheasant down to ascertain what was going on in Idzumo. The pheasant perched on the top of a cassia-tree before Ame-waka's gate. When Ame-waka saw the bird he immediately shot it. The arrow went through the bird, rose into the Place of Gods, and was hurled back again, so that it killed the disloyal and idle Ame-waka.

The weeping of Lower-shine-Princess reached Heaven, for she loved her lord and failed to recognise in his sudden death the just vengeance of the Gods. She wept so loud and so pitifully that the Heavenly Ones heard her. A swift wind descended, and the body of Ame-waka floated up into the High Plain of Heaven. A mortuary house was made, in which the deceased was laid. Mr Frank Rinder writes: "For eight days and eight nights there was wailing and lamentation. The wild goose of the river, the heron, the kingfisher, the sparrow, and the pheasant mourned with a great mourning."

Now it happened that a friend of Ame-waka, Aji-shi-ki by name, heard the sad dirges proceeding from Heaven. He therefore offered his condolence. He so resembled the deceased that when Ame-waka's parents, relations, wife, and children saw him, they exclaimed: "Our lord is still alive!" This greatly angered Aji-shi-ki, and he drew his sword and cut down the mortuary house, so that it fell to the Earth and became the mountain of Moyama.

We are told that the glory of Aji-shi-ki was so effulgent that it illuminated the space of two hills and two valleys. Those assembled for the mourning celebrations uttered the following song:

"Like the string of jewels
Worn on the neck
Of the Weaving-maiden,
That dwells in Heaven:
Oh! the lustre of the jewels
Flung across two valleys
From Aji-suki-taka-hiko-ne!

"To the side-pool:
The side-pool
Of the rocky stream
Whose narrows are crossed
By the country wenches
Afar from Heaven,
Come hither, come hither!
(The women are fair)
And spread across thy net
In the side-pool
Of the rocky stream."

Two more Gods were sent to the Central Land of Reed-Plains, and these Gods were successful in their mission. They returned to Heaven with a favourable report, saying that all was now ready for the coming of the August Grandchild.

The Coming of the August Grandchild

Amaterasu presented her grandson Ninigi, or Prince Rice-Ear-Ruddy-Plenty, with many gifts. She gave him precious stones from the mountain-steps of Heaven, white crystal balls, and, most valuable gift of all, the divine sword that Susanoo had discovered in the serpent. She also gave him the star-mirror into which she had gazed when peeping out of her cave. Several deities accompanied Ninigi, including that lively maiden of mirth and dance Uzume, whose dancing, it will be remembered, so amused the Gods.

Ninigi and his companions had hardly broken through the clouds and arrived at the eight-forked road of Heaven, when they discovered, much to their alarm, a gigantic creature with large and brightly shining eyes. So formidable was his aspect that Ninigi and all his companions, except the merry and bewitching Uzume, started to turn back with intent to abandon their mission. But Uzume went up to the giant and demanded who it was that dared to impede their progress. The giant replied: "I am the Deity of the Field-paths. I come to pay my homage to Ninigi, and beg to have the honour to be his guide. Return to your master, O fair Uzume, and give him this message."

So Uzume returned and gave her message to the Gods, who had so ignominiously retreated. When they heard the good news they greatly rejoiced, burst once more through the clouds, rested on the Floating Bridge of Heaven, and finally reached the summit of Takachihi.

The August Grandchild, with the Deity of the Field-paths for guide, travelled from end to end of the kingdom over which he was to rule. When he had reached a particularly charming spot, he built a palace.

Ninigi was so pleased with the service the Deity of the Field-paths had rendered him that he gave that giant the merry Uzume to wife.

Ninigi, after having romantically rewarded his faithful guide, began to feel the stirring of love himself, when one day, while walking along the shore, he saw an extremely lovely maiden. "Who are you, most beautiful lady?" inquired Ninigi. She replied: "I am the daughter of the Great-Mountain-Possessor. My name is Ko-no-Hana, the Princess who makes the Flowers of the Trees Blossom."

Ninigi fell in love with Ko-no-Hana. He went with all haste to her father, Oho-yama, and begged that he would favour him with his daughter's hand.

Oho-yama had an elder daughter, Iha-naga, Princess Long-as-the-Rocks. As her name implies, she was not at all beautiful; but her father desired that Ninigi's children should have life as eternal as the life of rocks. He therefore presented both his daughters to Ninigi, expressing the hope that the suitor's choice would fall upon Iha-naga. Just as Cinderella, and not her ugly sisters, is dear to children of our own country, so did Ninigi remain true to his choice, and would not even look upon Iha-naga. This neglect made Princess Long-as-the-Rocks extremely angry. She cried out, with more vehemence than modesty: "Had you chosen me, you and your children would have lived long in the land. Now that you have chosen my sister, you and yours will perish as quickly as the blossom of trees, as quickly as the bloom on my sister's cheek."

However, Ninigi and Ko-no-Hana lived happily together for some time; but one day jealousy came to Ninigi and robbed him of his peace of mind. He had no cause to be jealous, and Ko-no-Hana much resented his treatment. She retired to a little wooden hut, and set it on fire. From the flames came three baby boys. We need only concern ourselves with two of them – Hoderi ('Fire-shine') and Hoori ('Fire-fade'). Hoori, as we shall see later on, was the grandfather of the first Mikado of Japan.

In the Palace of the Sea God

HODERI WAS A GREAT FISHERMAN, while his younger brother, Hoori, was an accomplished hunter. One day they exclaimed: "Let us for a trial exchange gifts." This they did, but the elder brother, who could catch fish to some purpose, came home without any spoil when he went a-hunting. He therefore returned the bow and arrows, and asked his younger brother for the fish-hook. Now it so happened that Hoori had lost his brother's fish-hook. The generous offer of a new hook to take the place of the old one was scornfully refused. He also refused to accept a heaped-up tray of fish-hooks. To this offer the elder brother replied: "These are not my old fish-hook: though they are many, I will not take them."

Now Hoori was sore troubled by his brother's harshness, so he went down to the sea-shore and there gave way to his grief. A kind old man by the name of Shiko-tsutsu no Oji

('Salt-sea-elder') said: "Why dost thou grieve here?" When the sad tale was told, the old man replied: "Grieve no more. I will arrange this matter for thee."

True to his word, the old man made a basket, set Hoori in it, and then sank it in the sea. After descending deep down in the water Hoori came to a pleasant strand rich with all manner of fantastic seaweed. Here he abandoned the basket and eventually arrived at the Palace of the Sea God.

Now this palace was extremely imposing. It had battlements and turrets and stately towers. A well stood at the gate, and over the well there was a cassia-tree. Here Hoori loitered in the pleasant shade. He had not stood there long before a beautiful woman appeared. As she was about to draw water, she raised her eyes, saw the stranger, and immediately returned, with much alarm, to tell her mother and father what she had seen.

The God of the Sea, when he had heard the news, "prepared an eightfold cushion" and led the stranger in, asking his visitor why he had been honoured by his presence. When Hoori explained the sad loss of his brother's fish-hook the Sea God assembled all the fishes of his kingdom, "broad of fin and narrow of fin." And when the thousands upon thousands of fishes were assembled, the Sea God asked them if they knew anything about the missing fish-hook. "We know not," answered the fishes. "Only the Red-woman (the *tai*) has had a sore mouth for some time past, and has not come." She was accordingly summoned, and on her mouth being opened the lost fish-hook was discovered.

Hoori then took to wife the Sea God's daughter, Toyotama ('Rich-jewel'), and they dwelt together in the palace under the sea. For three years all went well, but after a time Hoori hungered for a sight of his own country, and possibly he may have remembered that he had yet to restore the fish-hook to his elder brother. These not unnatural feelings troubled the heart of the loving Toyotama, and she went to her father and told him of her sorrow. But the Sea God, who was always urbane and courteous, in no way resented his son-in-law's behaviour. On the contrary he gave him the fish-hook, saying: "When thou givest this fish-hook to thy elder brother, before giving it to him, call to it secretly, and say, 'A poor hook!'" He also presented Hoori with the Jewel of the Flowing Tide and the Jewel of the Ebbing Tide, saying: "If thou dost dip the Tide-flowing Jewel, the tide will suddenly flow, and therewithal thou shalt drown thine elder brother. But in case thy elder brother should repent and beg forgiveness, if, on the contrary, thou dip the Tide-ebbing Jewel, the tide will spontaneously ebb, and therewithal thou shalt save him. If thou harass him in this way thy elder brother will of his own accord render submission."

Just before Hoori was about to depart his wife came to him and told him that she was soon to give him a child. Said she: "On a day when the winds and waves are raging I will surely come forth to the seashore. Build for me a house, and await me there."

Hoderi and Hoori Reconciled

When Hoori reached his own home he found his elder brother, who admitted his offence and begged for forgiveness, which was readily granted.

Toyotama and her younger sister bravely confronted the winds and waves, and came to the sea-shore. There Hoori had built a hut roofed with cormorant feathers, and there in due season she gave birth to a son. When Toyotama had blessed her lord with offspring, she turned into a dragon and slipped back into the sea. Hoori's son married his aunt, and was the father of four children, one of whom was Kamu-Yamato-Iware-Biko, who is said to have been the first human Emperor of Japan, and is now known as Jimmu Tenno.

The Thirty-three Places Sacred to Kwannon

WHEN THE GREAT BUDDHIST ABBOT of the eighth century, Tokudo Shonin, died, he was conducted into the presence of Emma-O, the Lord of the Dead. The castle in which Emma-O lived was resplendent with silver and gold, rosy pearls, and all manner of sparkling jewels. A light emanated from Emma-O too, and that dread God had a smile upon his face. He received the distinguished abbot with extreme courtesy, and thus addressed him:

"Tokudo Shonin, there are thirty-three places where Kwannon reveals her special favour, for behold she has, in her boundless love, divided herself into many bodies, so that he who cries for aid shall not cry in vain. Alas! men continue to go their evil ways, for they know not of these sacred shrines. They live their sordid lives and pass into Hell, a vast and countless number. Oh, how blind they are, how wayward, and how full of folly! If they were to make but a single pilgrimage to these thirty-three shrines sacred to our Lady of Mercy, a pure and wonderful light would shine from their feet, feet made spiritually strong to crush down all evil, to scatter the hundred and thirty-six hells into fragments. If, in spite of this pilgrimage, one should chance to fall into Hell, I will take his place and receive into myself all his suffering, for if this happened my tale of peace would be false, and I should indeed deserve to suffer. Here is a list of the thirty-and-three sacred shrines of Kwannon. Take it into the troubled world of men and women, and make known the everlasting mercy of Kwannon."

Tokudo, having carefully listened to all Emma-O had told him, replied: "You have honoured me with such a mission, but mortals are full of doubts and fears, and they would ask for some sign that what I tell them is indeed true."

Emma-O at once presented the abbot with his jewelled seal, and, bidding him farewell, sent him on his way accompanied by two attendants.

While these strange happenings were taking place in the Underworld the disciples of Tokudo perceived that though their master's body had lain for three days and nights the flesh had not grown cold. The devoted followers did not bury the body, believing that their master was not dead. And such was indeed the case, for eventually Tokudo awakened from his trance, and in his right hand he held the jewelled seal of Emma-O.

Tokudo lost no time in narrating his strange adventures, and when he had concluded his story he and his disciples set off on a pilgrimage to the thirty-three holy places over which the Goddess of Mercy presides.

Kwannon and the Deer

AN OLD HERMIT named Saion Zenji took up his abode on Mount Nariai in order that he might be able to gaze upon the beauty of Ama-no-Hashidate, a narrow fir-clad promontory dividing Lake Iwataki and Miyazu Bay. Ama-no-Hashidate is still regarded as one of the *Sankei*, or 'Three Great Sights', of Japan, and still Mount Nariai is considered the best spot from which to view this charming scene.

On Mount Nariai this gentle and holy recluse erected a little shrine to Kwannon not far from a solitary pine-tree. He spent his happy days in looking upon Ama-no-Hashidate and in chanting the Buddhist Scriptures, and his charming disposition and holy ways were much appreciated by the people who came to pray at the little shrine he had so lovingly erected for his own joy and for the joy of others.

The hermit's abode, delightful enough in mild and sunny weather, was dreary in the winter-time, for when it snowed the good old man was cut off from human intercourse. On one occasion the snow fell so heavily that it was piled up in some places to a height of twenty feet.

Day after day the severe weather continued, and at last the poor old hermit found that he had no food of any kind. Chancing to look out one morning, he saw that a deer was lying dead in the snow. As he gazed upon the poor creature, which had been frozen to death, he remembered that it was unlawful in the sight of Kwannon to eat the flesh of animals; but on thinking over the matter more carefully it seemed to him that he could do more good to his fellow creatures by partaking of this deer than by observing the strict letter of the law and allowing himself to starve in sight of plenty.

When Saion Zenji had come to this wise decision he went out and cut off a piece of venison, cooked it, and ate half, with many prayers of thanksgiving for his deliverance. The rest of the venison he left in his cooking-pot.

Eventually the snow melted, and several folk hastily wended their way from the neighbouring village, and ascended Mount Nariai, expecting to see that their good and much-loved hermit had forever passed away from this world. As they approached the shrine, however, they were rejoiced to hear the old man chanting, in a clear and ringing voice, the sacred Buddhist Scriptures.

The folk from the village gathered about the hermit while he narrated the story of his deliverance. When, out of curiosity, they chanced to peep into his cooking-pot, they saw, to their utter amazement, that it contained no venison, but a piece of wood covered with gold foil. Still wondering what it all meant, they looked upon the image of Kwannon in the little shrine, and found that a piece had been cut from her loins, and when they inserted the piece of wood the wound was healed. Then it was that the old hermit and the folk gathered about him realised that the deer had been none other than Kwannon, who, in her boundless love and tender mercy, had made a sacrifice of her own divine flesh.

Benten and the Dragon

IN A CERTAIN CAVE there lived a formidable dragon, which devoured the children of the village of Koshigoe. In the sixth century Benten was determined to put a stop to this monster's unseemly behaviour, and having caused a great earthquake she hovered in the clouds over the cave where the dread dragon had taken up his abode. Benten then descended from the clouds, entered the cavern, married the dragon, and was thus able, through her good influence, to put an end to the slaughter of little children. With the coming of Benten there arose from the sea the famous Island of Enoshima, which has remained to this day sacred to the Goddess of the Sea.

Benten-of-the-Birth-Water

HANAGAKI BAISHU, a young poet and scholar, attended a great festival to celebrate the rebuilding of the Amadera temple. He wandered about the beautiful grounds, and eventually reached the place of a spring from which he had often quenched his thirst. He found that what had originally been a spring was now a pond, and, moreover, that at one corner of the pond there was a tablet bearing the words *Tanjō-Sui* ('Birth-Water'), and also a small but attractive temple dedicated to Benten. While Baishu was noting the changes in the temple grounds the wind blew to his feet a charmingly written love-poem. He picked it up, and discovered that it had been inscribed by a female hand, that the characters were exquisitely formed, and that the ink was fresh.

Baishu went home and read and re-read the poem. It was not long before he fell in love with the writer, and finally he resolved to make her his wife. At length he went to the temple of Benten-of-the-Birth-Water, and cried: "Oh, Goddess, come to my aid, and help me to find the woman who wrote these wind-blown verses!" Having thus prayed, he promised to perform a seven days' religious service, and to devote the seventh night in ceaseless worship before the sacred shrine of Benten, in the grounds of the Amadera.

On the seventh night of the vigil Baishu heard a voice calling for admittance at the main gateway of the temple grounds. The gate was opened, and an old man, clad in ceremonial robes and with a black cap upon his head, advanced and silently knelt before the temple of Benten. Then the outer door of the temple mysteriously opened, and a bamboo curtain was partially raised, revealing a handsome boy, who thus addressed the old man: "We have taken pity on a young man who desires a certain love-union, and have called you to inquire into the matter, and to see if you can bring the young people together."

The old man bowed, and then drew from his sleeve a cord which he wound round Baishu's body, igniting one end in a temple-lantern, and waving his hand the while, as if beckoning some spirit to appear out of the dark night. In a moment a young girl entered the temple grounds, and, with her fan half concealing her pretty face, she knelt beside Baishu.

Then the beautiful boy thus addressed Baishu: "We have heard your prayer, and we have known that recently you have suffered much. The woman you love is now beside you." And having uttered these words the divine youth departed, and the old man left the temple grounds.

When Baishu had given thanks to Benten-of-the-Birth-Water he proceeded homeward. On reaching the street outside the temple grounds he saw a young girl, and at once recognised her as the woman he loved. Baishu spoke to her, and when she replied the gentleness and sweetness of her voice filled the youth with joy. Together they walked through the silent streets until at last they came to the house where Baishu lived. There was a moment's pause, and then the maiden said: "Benten has made me your wife," and the lovers entered the house together.

The marriage was an extremely fortunate one, and the happy Baishu discovered that his wife, apart from her excellent domestic qualities, was accomplished in the art of arranging flowers and in the art of embroidery, and that her delicate writing was not less pleasing than her charming pictures. Baishu knew nothing about her family, but as she had been presented to him by the Goddess Benten he considered that it was unnecessary to question her in the matter. There was only one thing that puzzled the loving Baishu, and that was that the neighbours seemed to be totally unaware of his wife's presence.

One day, while Baishu was walking in a remote quarter of Kyoto, he saw a servant beckoning to him from the gateway of a private house. The man came forward, bowed respectfully, and said: "Will you deign to enter this house? My master is anxious to have the honour of speaking to you." Baishu, who knew nothing of the servant or his master, was not a little surprised by this strange greeting, but he allowed himself to be conducted to the guest-room, and thus his host addressed him:

"I most humbly apologise for the very informal manner of my invitation, but I believe that I have acted in compliance with a message I received from the Goddess Benten. I have a daughter, and, as I am anxious to find a good husband for her, I sent her written poems to all the temples of Benten in Kyoto. In a dream the Goddess came to me, and told me that she had secured an excellent husband for my daughter, and that he would visit me during the coming winter. I was not inclined to attach very much importance to this dream; but last night Benten again revealed herself to me in a vision, and said that tomorrow the husband she had chosen for my daughter would call upon me, and that I could then arrange the marriage. The Goddess described the appearance of the young man so minutely that I am assured that you are my daughter's future husband."

These strange words filled Baishu with sorrow, and when his courteous host proposed to present him to the lady he was unable to summon up sufficient courage to tell his would-be father-in-law that he already had a wife. Baishu followed his host into another apartment, and to his amazement and joy he discovered that the daughter of the house was none other than his own wife! And yet there was a subtle difference, for the woman who now smiled upon him was the body of his wife, and she who had appeared before the temple of Benten-of-the-Birth-Water was her soul. We are told that Benten performed this miracle for the sake of her worshippers, and thus it came to pass that Baishu had a strange dual marriage with the woman he loved.

Daikoku's Rat

ACCORDING TO A CERTAIN OLD LEGEND, the Buddhist Gods grew jealous of Daikoku. They consulted together, and finally decided that they would get rid of the too popular Daikoku, to whom the Japanese offered prayers and incense. Emma-O, the Lord of the Dead, promised to send his most cunning and clever *oni*, Shiro, who, he said, would have no difficulty in conquering the God of Wealth. Shiro, guided by a sparrow, went to Daikoku's castle, but though he hunted high and low he could not find its owner. Finally Shiro discovered a large storehouse, in which he saw the God of Wealth seated. Daikoku called his Rat and bade him find out who it was who dared to disturb him. When the Rat saw Shiro he ran into the garden and brought back a branch of holly, with which he drove the *oni* away, and Daikoku remains to this day one of the most popular of the Japanese Gods. This incident is said to be the origin of the New Year's Eve charm, consisting of a holly leaf and a skewer, or a sprig of holly fixed in the lintel of the door of a house to prevent the return of the *oni*.

The Child of the Thunder God

NEAR MOUNT HAKUZAN there once lived a very poor farmer named Bimbo. His plot of land was extremely small, and though he worked upon it from dawn till sunset he had great difficulty in growing sufficient rice for himself and his wife.

One day, after a protracted drought, Bimbo dismally surveyed his dried-up rice sprouts. As he thus stood fearing starvation in the near future, rain suddenly descended, accompanied by loud claps of thunder. Just as Bimbo was about to take shelter from the storm he was nearly blinded by a vivid flash of lightning, and he prayed fervently to Buddha for protection. When he had done so he looked about him, and to his amazement saw a little baby boy laughing and crooning as he lay in the grass.

Bimbo took the infant in his arms, and gently carried him to his humble dwelling, where his wife greeted him with surprise and pleasure. The child was called Raitaro, the Child of Thunder, and lived with his foster-parents a happy and dutiful boy. He never played with other children, for he loved to roam in the fields, to watch the stream and the swift flight of clouds overhead.

With the coming of Raitaro there came prosperity to Bimbo, for Raitaro could beckon to clouds and bid them throw down their rain-drops only on his foster-father's field.

When Raitaro had grown into a handsome youth of eighteen he once again thanked Bimbo and his wife for all they had done for him, and told them that he must now bid farewell to his benefactors.

Almost before the youth had finished speaking, he suddenly turned into a small white dragon, lingered a moment, and then flew away.

The old couple ran to the door. As the white dragon ascended into the sky it grew bigger and bigger, till it was hidden behind a great cloud.

When Bimbo and his wife died a white dragon was carved upon their tomb in memory of Raitaro, the Child of Thunder.

Shokuro and the Thunder God

SHOKURO, in order to stand well with Tom, the magistrate of his district, promised him that he would catch the Thunder God. "If," said Shokuro, "I were to tie a human navel to the end of a kite, and fly it during a stormy day, I should be sure to catch Raiden, for the Thunder God would not be able to resist such a repast. The most difficult part of the whole business is to secure the meal."

With this scheme in view Shokuro set out upon a journey in quest of food for the Thunder God. On reaching a wood he chanced to see a beautiful woman named Chiyo. The ambitious Shokuro, without the least compunction, killed the maid, and, having secured his object, flung her corpse into a deep ditch. He then proceeded on his way with a light heart.

Raiden, while sitting on a cloud, happened to notice the woman's body lying in a ditch. He descended quickly, and, being fascinated by the beauty of Chiyo, he took from his mouth a navel, restored her to life, and together they flew away into the sky.

Some days later Shokuro was out hunting for the Thunder God, his kite, with its gruesome relic, soaring high over the trees as it flew hither and thither in a strong wind. Chiyo saw the kite, and descended nearer and nearer to the earth. At last she held it in her hands and saw what was attached. Filled with indignation, she looked down in order to see who was flying the kite, and was much astonished to recognise her murderer. At this juncture Raiden descended in a rage, only to receive severe chastisement at the hands of Shokuro, who then made his peace with Chiyo, and afterwards became a famous man in the village. Truly an astonishing story!

Heroes, Warriors & Adventure

Introduction

EARLY HEROES AND WARRIORS are always regarded as minor divinities, and the very nature of Shinto, associated with ancestor worship, has enriched those of Japan with many a fascinating legend. For strength, skill, endurance, and a happy knack of overcoming all manner of difficulties by a subtle form of quick-witted enterprise, the Japanese hero must necessarily take a high position among the famous warriors of other countries. There is something eminently chivalrous about the heroes of Japan. The most valiant men are those who champion the cause of the weak or redress evil and tyranny of every kind, and we trace in the Japanese hero, who is very far from being a crude swashbuckler, these most excellent qualities. He is not always above criticism, and sometimes we find in him a touch of cunning, but such a characteristic is extremely rare, and very far from being a national trait. An innate love of poetry and the beautiful has had its refining influence upon the Japanese hero, with the result that his strength is combined with gentleness.

Benkei is one of the most lovable of Japanese heroes. He possessed the strength of many men, his tact amounted to genius, his sense of humour was strongly developed, and the most loving of Japanese mothers could not have shown more gentleness when his master's wife gave birth to a child. We follow the two great warriors Yoshitsune and Benkei across the sea, over mountains, outwitting again and again their numerous enemies.

The Land of the Rising Sun has given us many more warriors worthy to rank with the Knights of King Arthur: Minamoto no Yorimasa, Minamoto no Yorimitsu (Raiko), Watanabe no Tsuna (or Isuna), Kintaro, Momotaro and Yamato Take(ru) to name but a few. More than one legend deals with the destruction of devils and goblins, and of the rescue of maidens who had the misfortune to be their captives. One hero slays a great monster that crouched upon the roof of the Emperor's palace, another despatches the Goblin of Oeyama, another thrusts his sword through a gigantic spider, and another slays a serpent.

Yorimasa

A LONG TIME AGO a certain Emperor became seriously ill. He was unable to sleep at night owing to a most horrible and unaccountable noise he heard proceeding from the roof of the palace, called the Purple Hall of the North Star. A number of his courtiers decided to lie in wait for this strange nocturnal visitor. As soon as the sun set they noticed that a dark cloud crept from the eastern horizon, and alighted on the roof of the august palace. Those who waited in the imperial bed-chamber heard extraordinary scratching sounds, as if what had at first appeared to be a cloud had suddenly changed into a beast with gigantic and powerful claws.

Night after night this terrible visitant came, and night after night the Emperor grew worse. He at last became so ill that it was obvious to all those in attendance upon him that unless something could be done to destroy this monster the Emperor would certainly die.

At last it was decided that Yorimasa was the one knight in the kingdom valiant enough to relieve his Majesty of these terrible hauntings. Yorimasa accordingly made elaborate preparations for the fray. He took his best bow and steel-headed arrows, donned his armour, over which he wore a hunting-dress, and a ceremonial cap instead of his usual helmet.

At sunset he lay in concealment outside the palace. While he thus waited thunder crashed overhead, lightning blazed in the sky, and the wind shrieked like a pack of wild demons. But Yorimasa was a brave man, and the fury of the elements in no way daunted him. When midnight came he saw a black cloud rush through the sky and rest upon the roof of the palace. At the north-east corner it stopped. Once more the lightning flashed in the sky, and this time he saw the gleaming eyes of a large animal. Noting the exact position of this strange monster, he pulled at his bow till it became as round as the full moon. In another moment his steel-headed arrow hit its mark. There was an awful roar of anger, and then a heavy thud as the huge monster rolled from the palace roof to the ground.

Yorimasa and his retainer ran forward and despatched the fearful creature they saw before them. This evil monster of the night was as large as a horse. It had the head of an ape, and the body and claws were like those of a tiger, with a serpent's tail, wings of a bird, and the scales of a dragon.

It was no wonder that the Emperor gave orders that the skin of this monster should be kept for all time as a curiosity in the Imperial treasure-house. From the very moment the creature died the Emperor's health rapidly improved, and Yorimasa was rewarded for his services by being presented with a sword called Shishi-wo, which means "the King of Lions." He was also promoted at Court, and finally married the Lady Ayame, the most beautiful of ladies-in-waiting at the Imperial Court.

Yoshitsune and Benkei

YOSHITSUNE'S FATHER, YOSHITOMO, had been killed in a great battle with the Taira. At that time the Taira clan was all-powerful, and its cruel leader, Kiyomori, did all he could to destroy Yoshitomo's children. But the mother of these children, Tokiwa, fled into hiding, taking her little ones with her. With characteristic Japanese fortitude, she finally consented to become the wife of the hated Kiyomori. She did so because it was the only way to save the lives of her children. She was allowed to keep Yoshitsune with her, and she daily whispered to him: "Remember thy father, Minamoto Yoshitomo! Grow strong and avenge his death, for he died at the hands of the Taira!"

When Yoshitsune was seven years of age he was sent to a monastery to be brought up as a monk. Though diligent in his studies, the young boy ever treasured in his heart the dauntless words of his brave, self-sacrificing mother. They stirred and quickened him to action. He used to go to a certain valley, where he would flourish his little wooden sword, and, singing fragments of war-songs, hit out at rocks and stones, desiring that he might one day become a great warrior, and right the wrongs so heavily heaped upon his family by the Taira clan.

One night, while thus engaged, he was startled by a great thunderstorm, and saw before him a mighty giant with a long red nose and enormous glaring eyes, bird-like claws, and feathered wings. Bravely standing his ground, Yoshitsune inquired who this giant might be, and was informed that he was King of the Tengu – that is, King of the elves of the mountains, sprightly little beings who were frequently engaged in all manner of fantastic tricks.

The King of the Tengu was very kindly disposed towards Yoshitsune. He explained that he admired his perseverance, and told him that he had appeared upon the scene with the meritorious intention of teaching him all that was to be learnt in the art of swordsmanship. The lessons progressed in a most satisfactory manner, and it was not long before Yoshitsune could vanquish as many as twenty small *tengu*, and this extreme agility stood Yoshitsune in very good stead, as we shall see later on in the story.

Now when Yoshitsune was fifteen years old he heard that there lived on Mount Hiei a very wild *bonze* (priest) by the name of Benkei. Benkei had for some time waylaid knights who happened to cross the Gojo Bridge of Kyoto. His idea was to obtain a thousand swords, and he was so brave, although such a rascal, that he had won from knights no less than nine hundred and ninety-nine swords by his lawless behaviour. When the news of these doings reached the ears of Yoshitsune he determined to put the teaching of the King of the Tengu to good use and slay this Benkei, and so put an end to one who had become a terror in the land.

One evening Yoshitsune started out, and, in order to establish the manner and bearing of absolute indifference, he played upon his flute till he came to the Gojo Bridge. Presently he saw coming towards him a gigantic man clad in black armour, who was none other than Benkei. When Benkei saw the youth he considered it to be beneath his dignity to attack what appeared to him to be a mere weakling, a dreamer who could play excellently, and no doubt write a pretty poem about the moon, which was then shining in the sky, but one who was in no way a warrior. This affront naturally angered Yoshitsune, and he suddenly kicked Benkei's halberd out of his hand.

Yoshitsune and Benkei Fight

Benkei gave a growl of rage, and cut about indiscriminately with his weapon. But the sprightliness of the *tengu* teaching favoured Yoshitsune. He jumped from side to side, from the front to the rear, and from the rear to the front again, mocking the giant with many a jest and many a peal of ringing laughter. Round and round went Benkei's weapon, always striking either the air or the ground, and ever missing its adversary.

At last Benkei grew weary, and once again Yoshitsune knocked the halberd out of the giant's hand. In trying to regain his weapon Yoshitsune tripped him up, so that he stumbled upon his hands and knees, and the hero, with a cry of triumph, mounted upon the now four-legged Benkei. The giant was utterly amazed at his defeat, and when he was told that the victor was none other than the son of Lord Yoshitomo he not only took his defeat in a manly fashion, but begged that he might henceforth become a retainer of the young conqueror.

From this time we find the names of Yoshitsune and Benkei linked together, and in all the stories of warriors, whether in Japan or elsewhere, never was there a more valiant and harmonious union of strength and friendship. We hear of them winning numerous victories over the Taira, finally driving them to the sea, where they perished at Dan-no-ura.

We get one more glimpse of Dan-no-ura from a legendary point of view. Yoshitsune and his faithful henchman arranged to cross in a ship from the province of Settsu to Saikoku. When they reached Dan-no-ura a great storm arose. Mysterious noises came from the towering waves, a far-away echo of the din of battle, of the rushing of ships and the whirling of arrows, of the footfall of a thousand men. Louder and louder the noise grew, and from the lashing crests of the waves there arose a ghostly company of the Taira clan. Their armour was torn and blood-stained, and they thrust out their vaporous arms and tried to stop the boat in which Yoshitsune and Benkei sailed. It was a ghostly reminiscence of the battle of Dan-no-ura, when the Taira had suffered a terrible and permanent defeat. Yoshitsune, when he saw this great phantom host, cried out for revenge even upon the ghosts of the Taira dead; but Benkei, always shrewd and circumspect, bade his master lay aside the sword, and took out a rosary and recited a number of Buddhist prayers. Peace came to the great company of ghosts, the wailing ceased, and gradually they faded into the sea which now became calm.

Legend tells us that fishermen still see from time to time ghostly armies come out of the sea and wail and shake their long arms. They explain that the crabs with dorsal markings are the wraiths of the Taira warriors. Later on we shall introduce another legend relating to these unfortunate ghosts, who seem never to tire of haunting the scene of their defeat.

The Goblin of Oeyama

IN THE REIGN OF THE EMPEROR ICHIJO many dreadful stories were current in Kyoto in regard to a demon that lived on Mount Oye. This demon could assume many forms. Sometimes appearing as a human being, he would steal into Kyoto, and leave many a home destitute of well-loved sons and daughters. These young men and women he took back to his mountain stronghold, and, sad to narrate, after making sport of them, he and his goblin companions made a great feast and devoured these poor young people. Even the sacred Court was not exempt from these awful happenings, and one day Kimitaka lost his beautiful daughter. She had been snatched away by the Goblin King, Shutendoji.

When this sad news reached the ears of the Emperor he called his council together and consulted how they might slay this dreadful creature. His ministers informed his Majesty that Raiko was a doughty knight, and advised that he should be sent with certain companions on this perilous but worthy adventure.

Raiko accordingly chose five companions and told them what had been ordained, and how they were to set out upon an adventurous journey, and finally to slay the King of the Goblins. He explained that subtlety of action was most essential if they wished for success in their enterprise, and that it would be well to go disguised as mountain priests, and to carry their armour and weapons on their backs, carefully concealed in unsuspicious-looking knapsacks. Before starting upon their journey two of the knights went to pray at the temple of Hachiman, the God of War, two at the shrine of Kwannon, the Goddess of Mercy, and two at the temple of Gongen.

When these knights had prayed for a blessing upon their undertaking they set out upon their journey, and in due time reached the province of Tamba, and saw immediately in front of them Mount Oye. The Goblin had certainly chosen the most formidable of mountains. Mighty rocks and great dark forests obstructed their path in every direction, while almost bottomless chasms appeared when least expected.

Just when these brave knights were beginning to feel just a little disheartened, three old men suddenly appeared before them. At first these newcomers were regarded with suspicion, but later on with the utmost friendliness and thankfulness. These old men were none other than the deities to whom the knights had prayed before setting out upon their journey. The old men presented Raiko with a jar of magical *sake* called Shimben-Kidoku-Shu ('a cordial for men, but poison for goblins'), advising him that he should by strategy get Shutendoji to drink it, whereupon he would immediately become paralysed and prove an easy victim for the final despatch. No sooner had these old men given the magical *sake* and proffered their valuable advice than a miraculous light shone round them, and they vanished into the clouds.

Once again Raiko and his knights, much cheered by what had happened, continued to ascend the mountain. Coming to a stream, they noticed a beautiful woman washing a blood-stained garment in the running water. She was weeping bitterly, and wiped away her tears with the long sleeve of her *kimono*. Upon Raiko asking who she was, she informed him that she was a princess, and one of the miserable captives of the Goblin King. When she was told that it was none other than the great Raiko who stood before her, and that he and his knights had come to kill the vile creature of that mountain, she was overcome with joy, and finally led the little band to a great palace of black iron, satisfying the sentinels by telling them that her followers were poor mountain priests who sought temporary shelter.

After passing through long corridors Raiko and his knights found themselves in a mighty hall. At one end sat the awful Goblin King. He was of gigantic stature, with bright red skin and a mass of white hair. When Raiko meekly informed him who they were, the Goblin King, concealing his mirth, bade them be seated and join the feast that was about to be set before them. Thereupon he clapped his red hands together, and immediately many beautiful damsels came running in with an abundance of food and drink, and as Raiko watched these women he knew that they had once lived in happy homes in Kyoto.

When the feast was in full progress Raiko took out the jar of magic *sake*, and politely begged the Goblin King to try it. The monster, without demur or suspicion, drank some of the *sake*, and found it so good that he asked for a second cup. All the goblins partook of the magic wine, and while they were drinking Raiko and his companions danced.

The power of this magical drink soon began to work. The Goblin King became drowsy, till finally he and his fellow goblins fell fast asleep. Then Raiko sprang to his feet, and he and his knights rapidly donned their armour and prepared for war. Once more the three deities appeared before them, and said to Raiko: "We have tied the hands and feet of the Demon fast, so you have nothing to fear. While your knights cut off his limbs do you cut off his head: then kill the rest of the *oni* (evil spirits) and your work will be done." Then these divine beings suddenly disappeared.

Raiko Slays the Goblin

Raiko and his knights, with their swords drawn, cautiously approached the sleeping Goblin King. With a mighty sweep Raiko's weapon came crashing down on the Goblin's neck. No sooner was the head severed than it shot up into the air, and smoke and fire poured out from the nostrils, scorching the valiant Raiko. Once more he struck out with his sword, and this time the horrible head fell to the floor, and never moved again. It was not long before these brave knights despatched the Demon's followers also.

There was a joyful exit from the great iron palace. Raiko's five knights carried the monster head of the Goblin King, and this grim spectacle was followed by a company of happy maidens released at last from their horrible confinement, and eager to walk once again in the streets of Kyoto.

The Goblin Spider

SOME TIME AFTER THE INCIDENT mentioned in the previous legend had taken place the brave Raiko became seriously ill, and was obliged to keep to his room. At about midnight a little boy always brought him some medicine. This boy was unknown to Raiko, but as he kept so many servants it did not at first awaken suspicion. Raiko grew worse instead of better, and always worse immediately after he had taken the medicine, so he began to think that some supernatural force was the cause of his illness.

At last Raiko asked his head servant if he knew anything about the boy who came to him at midnight. Neither the head servant nor anyone else seemed to know anything about him. By this time Raiko's suspicions were fully awakened, and he determined to go carefully into the matter.

When the small boy came again at midnight, instead of taking the medicine, Raiko threw the cup at his head, and drawing his sword attempted to kill him. A sharp cry of pain rang through the room, but as the boy was flying from the apartment he threw something at Raiko. It spread outward into a huge white sticky web, which clung so tightly to Raiko that he could hardly move. No sooner had he cut the web through with his sword than another enveloped him. Raiko then called for assistance, and his chief retainer met the miscreant in one of the corridors and stopped his further progress with extended sword. The Goblin threw a web over him too.

When he at last managed to extricate himself and was able to run into his master's room, he saw that Raiko had also been the victim of the Goblin Spider.

The Goblin Spider was eventually discovered in a cave writhing with pain, blood flowing from a sword-cut on the head. He was instantly killed, and with his death there passed away the evil influence that had caused Raiko's serious illness. From that hour the hero regained his health and strength, and a sumptuous banquet was prepared in honour of the happy event.

Another Version

There is another version of this legend, written by Kenko Hoshi, which differs so widely in many of its details from the one we have already given that it almost amounts to a new story altogether. To dispense with this version would be to rob the legend of its most sinister aspect, which has not hitherto been accessible to the general reader.

On one occasion Raiko left Kyoto with Tsuna, the most worthy of his retainers. As they were crossing the plain of Rendai they saw a skull rise in the air, and fly before them as if driven by the wind, until it finally disappeared at a place called Kagura ga Oka.

Raiko and his retainer had no sooner noticed the disappearance of the skull than they perceived before them a mansion in ruins. Raiko entered this dilapidated building, and saw an old woman of strange aspect. She was dressed in white, and had white hair; she opened her eyes with a small stick, and the upper eyelids fell back over her head like a hat; then she used the rod to open her mouth, and let her breast fall forward upon her knees. Thus she addressed the astonished Raiko:

"I am two hundred and ninety years old. I serve nine masters, and the house in which you stand is haunted by demons."

Having listened to these words, Raiko walked into the kitchen, and, catching a glimpse of the sky, he perceived that a great storm was brewing. As he stood watching the dark clouds gather he heard a sound of ghostly footsteps, and there crowded into the room a great company of goblins. Nor were these the only supernatural creatures which Raiko encountered, for presently he saw a being dressed like a nun. Her very small body was naked to the waist, her face was two feet in length, and her arms were white as snow and thin as threads. For a moment this dreadful creature laughed, and then vanished like a mist.

Raiko heard the welcome sound of a cock crowing, and imagined that the ghostly visitors would trouble him no more; but once again he heard footsteps, and this time he saw no hideous hag, but a lovely woman, more graceful than the willow branches as they wave in the breeze. As he gazed upon this lovely maiden his eyes became blinded for a moment on account of her radiant beauty. Before he could recover his sight he found himself enveloped in countless cobwebs. He struck at her with his sword, when she disappeared, and he found that he had but cut through the planks of the floor, and broken the foundation-stone beneath.

At this moment Tsuna joined his master, and they perceived that the sword was covered with *white* blood, and that the point had been broken in the conflict.

After much search Raiko and his retainer discovered a den in which they saw a monster with many legs and a head of enormous size covered with downy hair. Its mighty eyes shone like the sun and moon, as it groaned aloud: "I am sick and in pain!"

As Raiko and Tsuna drew near they recognised the broken sword-point projecting from the monster. The heroes then dragged the creature out of its den and cut off its head. Out of the deep wound in the creature's stomach gushed nineteen hundred and ninety skulls, and in addition many spiders as large as children. Raiko and his follower realised that the monster before them was none other than the Mountain Spider. When they cut open the great carcass they discovered, within the entrails, the ghostly remains of many human corpses.

The Ogre of Rashomon, or Watanabe Defeats the Ibaraki-doji

LONG, LONG AGO IN KYOTO, the people of the city were terrified by accounts of a dreadful ogre, who, it was said, haunted the Gate of Rashomon at twilight and seized whoever passed by. The missing victims were never seen again, so it was whispered that the ogre was a horrible cannibal, who not only killed the unhappy victims but ate them also. Now everybody in the town and neighbourhood was in great fear, and no one durst venture out after sunset near the Gate of Rashomon.

Now at this time there lived in Kyoto a general named Raiko, who had made himself famous for his brave deeds. Some time before this he made the country ring with his name, for he had attacked Oeyama, where a band of ogres lived with their chief, who instead of wine drank the blood of human beings. He had routed them all and cut off the head of the chief monster.

This brave warrior was always followed by a band of faithful knights. In this band there were five knights of great valour. One evening as the five knights sat at a feast quaffing *sake* in their rice bowls and eating all kinds of fish, raw, and stewed, and broiled, and toasting each other's healths and exploits, the first knight, Hojo, said to the others:

"Have you all heard the rumour that every evening after sunset there comes an ogre to the Gate of Rashomon, and that he seizes all who pass by?"

The second knight, Watanabe, answered him, saying:

"Do not talk such nonsense! All the ogres were killed by our chief Raiko at Oeyama! It cannot be true, because even if any ogres did escape from that great killing they would not dare to show themselves in this city, for they know that our brave master would at once attack them if he knew that any of them were still alive!"

"Then do you disbelieve what I say, and think that I am telling you a falsehood?"

"No, I do not think that you are telling a lie," said Watanabe; "but you have heard some old woman's story which is not worth believing."

"Then the best plan is to prove what I say, by going there yourself and finding out yourself whether it is true or not," said Hojo.

Watanabe, the second knight, could not bear the thought that his companion should believe he was afraid, so he answered quickly:

"Of course, I will go at once and find out for myself!"

So Watanabe at once got ready to go – he buckled on his long sword and put on a coat of armor, and tied on his large helmet. When he was ready to start he said to the others:

"Give me something so that I can prove I have been there!"

Then one of the men got a roll of writing paper and his box of Indian ink and brushes, and the four comrades wrote their names on a piece of paper.

"I will take this," said Watanabe, "and put it on the Gate of Rashomon, so tomorrow morning will you all go and look at it? I may be able to catch an ogre or two by then!" and he mounted his horse and rode off gallantly.

It was a very dark night, and there was neither moon nor star to light Watanabe on his way. To make the darkness worse a storm came on, the rain fell heavily and the wind howled like wolves in the mountains. Any ordinary man would have trembled at the thought of going out of doors, but Watanabe was a brave warrior and dauntless, and his honour and word were at stake, so he sped on into the night, while his companions listened to the sound of his horse's hoofs dying away in the distance, then shut the sliding shutters close and gathered round the charcoal fire and wondered what would happen – and whether their comrade would encounter one of those horrible Oni.

At last Watanabe reached the Gate of Rashomon, but peer as he might through the darkness he could see no sign of an ogre.

"It is just as I thought," said Watanabe to himself; "there are certainly no ogres here; it is only an old woman's story. I will stick this paper on the gate so that the others can see I have been here when they come tomorrow, and then I will take my way home and laugh at them all."

He fastened the piece of paper, signed by all his four companions, on the gate, and then turned his horse's head towards home.

As he did so he became aware that someone was behind him, and at the same time a voice called out to him to wait. Then his helmet was seized from the back. "Who are you?" said Watanabe fearlessly. He then put out his hand and groped around to find out who or what it was that held him by the helmet. As he did so he touched something that felt like an arm – it was covered with hair and as big round as the trunk of a tree!

Watanabe knew at once that this was the arm of an ogre, so he drew his sword and cut at it fiercely.

There was a loud yell of pain, and then the ogre dashed in front of the warrior.

Watanabe's eyes grew large with wonder, for he saw that the ogre was taller than the great gate, his eyes were flashing like mirrors in the sunlight, and his huge mouth was wide open, and as the monster breathed, flames of fire shot out of his mouth.

The ogre thought to terrify his foe, but Watanabe never flinched. He attacked the ogre with all his strength, and thus they fought face to face for a long time. At last the ogre, finding that he could neither frighten nor beat Watanabe and that he might himself be beaten, took to flight. But Watanabe, determined not to let the monster escape, put spurs to his horse and gave chase.

But though the knight rode very fast the ogre ran faster, and to his disappointment he found himself unable to overtake the monster, who was gradually lost to sight.

Watanabe returned to the gate where the fierce fight had taken place, and got down from his horse. As he did so he stumbled upon something lying on the ground.

Stooping to pick it up he found that it was one of the ogre's huge arms which he must have slashed off in the fight. His joy was great at having secured such a prize, for this was the best of all proofs of his adventure with the ogre. So he took it up carefully and carried it home as a trophy of his victory.

When he got back, he showed the arm to his comrades, who one and all called him the hero of their band and gave him a great feast. His wonderful deed was soon noised abroad in Kyoto, and people from far and near came to see the ogre's arm.

Watanabe now began to grow uneasy as to how he should keep the arm in safety, for he knew that the ogre to whom it belonged was still alive. He felt sure that one day or other, as soon as the ogre got over his scare, he would come to try to get his arm back again. Watanabe therefore had a box made of the strongest wood and banded with iron. In this he placed the arm, and then he sealed down the heavy lid, refusing to open it for anyone. He kept the box in his own room and took charge of it himself, never allowing it out of his sight.

Now one night he heard someone knocking at the porch, asking for admittance.

When the servant went to the door to see who it was, there was only an old woman, very respectable in appearance. On being asked who she was and what was her business, the old woman replied with a smile that she had been nurse to the master of the house when he was a little baby. If the lord of the house were at home she begged to be allowed to see him.

The servant left the old woman at the door and went to tell his master that his old nurse had come to see him. Watanabe thought it strange that she should come at that time of night, but at the thought of his old nurse, who had been like a foster-mother to him and whom he had not seen for a long time, a very tender feeling sprang up for her in his heart. He ordered the servant to show her in.

The old woman was ushered into the room, and after the customary bows and greetings were over, she said:

"Master, the report of your brave fight with the ogre at the Gate of Rashomon is so widely known that even your poor old nurse has heard of it. Is it really true, what everyone says, that you cut off one of the ogre's arms? If you did, your deed is highly to be praised!"

"I was very disappointed," said Watanabe, "that I was not able take the monster captive, which was what I wished to do, instead of only cutting off an arm!"

"I am very proud to think," answered the old woman, "that my master was so brave as to dare to cut off an ogre's arm. There is nothing that can be compared to your courage. Before I die it is the great wish of my life to see this arm," she added pleadingly.

"No," said Watanabe, "I am sorry, but I cannot grant your request."

"But why?" asked the old woman.

"Because," replied Watanabe, "ogres are very revengeful creatures, and if I open the box there is no telling but that the ogre may suddenly appear and carry off his arm. I have had a box made on purpose with a very strong lid, and in this box I keep the ogre's arm secure; and I never show it to anyone, whatever happens."

"Your precaution is very reasonable," said the old woman. "But I am your old nurse, so surely you will not refuse to show *me* the arm. I have only just heard of your brave act, and not being able to wait till the morning I came at once to ask you to show it to me."

Watanabe was very troubled at the old woman's pleading, but he still persisted in refusing. Then the old woman said:

"Do you suspect me of being a spy sent by the ogre?"

"No, of course I do not suspect you of being the ogre's spy, for you are my old nurse," answered Watanabe.

"Then you cannot surely refuse to show me the arm any longer." entreated the old woman; "for it is the great wish of my heart to see for once in my life the arm of an ogre!"

Watanabe could not hold out in his refusal any longer, so he gave in at last, saying:

"Then I will show you the ogre's arm, since you so earnestly wish to see it. Come, follow me!" and he led the way to his own room, the old woman following.

When they were both in the room Watanabe shut the door carefully, and then going towards a big box which stood in a corner of the room, he took off the heavy lid. He then called to the old woman to come near and look in, for he never took the arm out of the box.

"What is it like? Let me have a good look at it," said the old nurse, with a joyful face.

She came nearer and nearer, as if she were afraid, till she stood right against the box. Suddenly she plunged her hand into the box and seized the arm, crying with a fearful voice which made the room shake:

"Oh, joy! I have got my arm back again!"

And from an old woman she was suddenly transformed into the towering figure of the frightful ogre!

Watanabe sprang back and was unable to move for a moment, so great was his astonishment; but recognizing the ogre who had attacked him at the Gate of Rashomon, he determined with his usual courage to put an end to him this time. He seized his sword, drew it out of its sheath in a flash, and tried to cut the ogre down.

So quick was Watanabe that the creature had a narrow escape. But the ogre sprang up to the ceiling, and bursting through the roof, disappeared in the mist and clouds.

In this way the ogre escaped with his arm. The knight gnashed his teeth with disappointment, but that was all he could do. He waited in patience for another opportunity to dispatch the ogre. But the latter was afraid of Watanabe's great strength and daring, and never troubled Kyoto again. So once more the people of the city were able to go out without fear even at night time, and the brave deeds of Watanabe have never been forgotten!

The Adventures of Prince Yamato Take

KING KEIKO BADE HIS YOUNGEST SON, Prince Yamato, go forth and slay a number of brigands. Before his departure the Prince prayed at the shrines of Ise, and begged that Amaterasu, the Sun Goddess, would bless his enterprise. Prince Yamato's aunt was high-priestess of one of the Ise temples, and he told her about the task his father had entrusted to him. This good lady was much pleased to hear the news, and presented her nephew with a rich silk robe, saying that it would bring him luck, and perhaps be of service to him later on.

When Prince Yamato had returned to the palace and taken leave of his father, he left the court accompanied by his wife, the Princess Ototachibana, and a number of staunch followers, and proceeded to the Southern Island of Kiushiu, which was infested by brigands. The country was so rough and impassable that Prince Yamato saw at once that he must devise some cunning scheme by which he might take the enemy unawares.

Having come to this conclusion, he bade the Princess Ototachibana bring him the rich silk robe his aunt had given him. This he put on under the direction, no doubt, of his wife. He let down his hair, stuck a comb in it, and adorned himself with jewels. When he looked into a mirror he saw that the disguise was perfect, and that he made quite a handsome woman.

Thus gorgeously apparelled, he entered the enemy's tent, where Kumaso and Takeru were sitting. It happened that they were discussing the King's son and his efforts to exterminate their band. When they chanced to look up they saw a fair woman coming towards them.

Kumaso was so delighted that he beckoned to the disguised Prince and bade him serve wine as quickly as possible. Yamato was only too delighted to do so. He affected feminine shyness. He walked with very minute steps, and glanced out of the corner of his eyes with all the timidity of a bashful maiden.

Kumaso drank far more wine than was good for him. He still went on drinking just to have the pleasure of seeing this lovely creature pouring it out for him.

When Kumaso became drunk Prince Yamato flung down the wine-jar, whipped out his dagger, and stabbed him to death.

Takeru, when he saw what had happened to his brother, attempted to escape, but Prince Yamato leapt upon him. Once more his dagger gleamed in the air, and Takeru fell to the earth.

"Stay your hand a moment," gasped the dying brigand. "I would fain know who you are and whence you have come. Hitherto I thought that my brother and I were the strongest men in the kingdom. I am indeed mistaken."

"I am Yamato," said the Prince, "and son of the King who bade me kill such rebels as you!"

"Permit me to give you a new name," said the brigand politely. "From henceforth you shall be called Yamato Take, because you are the bravest man in the land."

Having thus spoken Takeru fell back dead.

The Wooden Sword

When the Prince was on his way to the capital he encountered another outlaw named Idzumo Takeru. Again resorting to strategy, he professed to be extremely friendly with this fellow. He cut a sword of wood and rammed it tightly into the sheath of his own steel weapon. He wore this whenever he expected to meet Takeru.

On one occasion Prince Yamato invited Takeru to swim with him in the river Hinokawa. While the brigand was swimming down-stream the Prince secretly landed, and, going to Takeru's clothes, lying on the bank, he managed to change swords, putting his wooden one in place of the keen steel sword of Takeru.

When Takeru came out of the water and put on his clothes the Prince asked him to show his skill with the sword. "We will prove," said he, "which is the better swordsman of the two."

Nothing loath, Takeru tried to unsheath his sword. It stuck fast, and as it happened to be of wood it was, of course, useless in any case. While the brigand was thus struggling Yamato cut off his head. Once again cunning had served him, and when he had returned to the palace he was feasted, and received many costly gifts from the King his father.

The 'Grass-Cleaving-Sword'

Prince Yamato did not long remain idle in the palace, for his father commanded him to go forth and quell an Ainu rising in the eastern provinces.

When the Prince was ready to depart the King gave him a spear made from a holly-tree called the 'Eight-Arms-Length-Spear'. With this precious gift Prince Yamato visited the temples of Ise. His aunt, the high-priestess, again greeted him. She listened with interest to all her nephew told her, and was especially delighted to know how well the robe she had given him had served in his adventures.

When she had listened to his story she went into the temple and brought forth a sword and a bag containing flints. These she gave to Yamato as a parting gift.

The sword was the sword of Murakumo, belonging to the insignia of the Imperial House of Japan. The Prince could not have received a more auspicious gift. This sword, it will be remembered, once belonged to the Gods, and was discovered by Susanoo.

After a long march Prince Yamato and his men found themselves in the province of Suruga. The governor hospitably received him, and by way of entertainment organised a deer-hunt. Our hero for once in a way was utterly deceived, and joined the hunt without the least misgiving.

The Prince was taken to a great and wild plain covered with high grass. While he was engaged in hunting down the deer he suddenly became aware of fire. In another moment he saw flames and clouds of smoke shooting up in every direction. He was surrounded by fire, from which there was, apparently, no escape. Too late the guileless warrior realised that he had fallen into a trap, and a very warm trap too!

Our hero opened the bag his aunt had given him, set fire to the grass near him, and with the sword of Murakumo he cut down the tall green blades on either side as quickly as possible. No sooner had he done so than the wind suddenly changed and blew the flames away from him, so that eventually the Prince made good his escape without the slightest burn of any kind. And thus it was that the sword of Murakumo came to be known as the 'Grass-Cleaving-Sword'.

The Sacrifice of Ototachibana

In all these adventures the Prince had been followed by his faithful wife, the Princess Ototachibana. Sad to say, our hero, so praiseworthy in battle, was not nearly so estimable in his love. He looked down on his wife and treated her with indifference. She, poor loyal soul, had lost her beauty in serving her lord. Her skin was burnt with the sun, and her garments were soiled and torn. Yet she never complained, and though her face became sad she made a brave effort to maintain her usual sweetness of manner.

Now Prince Yamato happened to meet the fascinating Princess Miyadzu. Her robes were charming, her skin delicate as cherry-blossom. It was not long before he fell desperately in love with her. When the time came for him to depart he swore that he would return again and make the beautiful Princess Miyadzu his wife. He had scarcely made this promise when he looked up and saw Ototachibana, and on her face was a look of intense sadness. But Prince Yamato hardened his heart, and rode away, secretly determined to keep his promise.

When Prince Yamato, his wife and men, reached the sea-shore of Idzu, his followers desired to secure a number of boats in order that they might cross the Straits of Kadzusa.

The Prince cried haughtily: "Bah! this is only a brook! Why so many boats? I could jump across it!"

When they had all embarked and started on their journey a great storm arose. The waves turned into water-mountains, the wind shrieked, the lightning blazed in the dark clouds, and the thunder roared. It seemed that the boat that carried the Prince and his wife must needs sink, for this storm was the work of Rin-Jin, King of the Sea, who was angry with the proud and foolish words of Prince Yamato.

When the crew had taken down the sails in the hope of steadying the vessel the storm grew worse instead of better. At last Ototachibana arose, and, forgiving all the sorrow her lord had caused her, she resolved to sacrifice her life in order to save her much-loved husband.

Thus spoke the loyal Ototachibana: "Oh, Rin-Jin, the Prince, my husband, has angered you with his boasting. I, Ototachibana, give you my poor life in the place of Yamato Take. I now cast myself into your great surging kingdom, and do you in return bring my lord safely to the shore."

Having uttered these words, Ototachibana leapt into the seething waves, and in a moment they dragged that brave woman out of sight. No sooner had this sacrifice been made than the storm abated and the sun shone forth in a cloudless sky.

Yamato Take safely reached his destination, and succeeded in quelling the Ainu rising.

Our hero had certainly erred in his treatment of his faithful wife. Too late he learnt to appreciate her goodness; but let it be said to his credit that she remained a loving memory till his death, while the Princess Miyadzu was entirely forgotten.

The Slaying of the Serpent

Now that Yamato Take had carried out his father's instructions, he passed through the province of Owari until he came to the province of Omi.

The province of Omi was afflicted with a great trouble. Many were in mourning, and many wept and cried aloud in their sorrow. The Prince, on making inquiries, was informed that a great serpent every day came down from the mountains and entered the villages, making a meal of many of the unfortunate inhabitants.

Prince Yamato at once started to climb up Mount Ibaki, where the great serpent was said to live. About half-way up he encountered the awful creature. The Prince was so strong that he killed the serpent by twisting his bare arms about it. He had no sooner done so than sudden darkness came over the land, and rain fell heavily. However, eventually the weather improved, and our hero was able to climb down the mountain.

When he reached home he found that his feet burned with a strange pain, and, moreover, that he felt very ill. He realised that the serpent had stung him, and, as he was too ill to move, he was carried to a famous mineral spring. Here he finally regained his accustomed health and strength, and for these blessings gave thanks to Amaterasu, the Sun Goddess.

The Adventures of Momotaro

ONE DAY, while an old woman stood by a stream washing her clothes, she chanced to see an enormous peach floating on the water. It was quite the largest she had ever seen, and as this old woman and her husband were extremely poor she immediately thought what an excellent meal this extraordinary peach would make. As she could find no stick with which to draw the fruit to the bank, she suddenly remembered the following verse:

"Distant water is bitter,
The near water is sweet;
Pass by the distant water
And come into the sweet."

This little song had the desired effect. The peach came nearer and nearer till it stopped at the old woman's feet. She stooped down and picked it up. So delighted was she with her discovery that she could not stay to do any more washing, but hurried home as quickly as possible.

When her husband arrived in the evening, with a bundle of grass upon his back, the old woman excitedly took the peach out of a cupboard and showed it to him.

The old man, who was tired and hungry, was equally delighted at the thought of so delicious a meal. He speedily brought a knife and was about to cut the fruit open, when it suddenly opened of its own accord, and the prettiest child imaginable tumbled out with a merry laugh.

"Don't be afraid," said the little fellow. "The Gods have heard how much you desired a child, and have sent me to be a solace and a comfort in your old age."

The old couple were so overcome with joy that they scarcely knew what to do with themselves. Each in turn nursed the child, caressed him, and murmured many sweet and affectionate words. They called him Momotaro, or 'Son of a Peach'.

When Momotaro was fifteen years old he was a lad far taller and stronger than boys of his own age. The making of a great hero stirred in his veins, and it was a knightly heroism that desired to right the wrong.

One day Momotaro came to his foster-father and asked him if he would allow him to take a long journey to a certain island in the North-Eastern Sea where dwelt a number of devils, who had captured a great company of innocent people, many of whom they ate. Their wickedness was beyond description, and Momotaro desired to kill them, rescue the unfortunate captives, and bring back the plunder of the island that he might share it with his foster-parents.

The old man was not a little surprised to hear this daring scheme. He knew that Momotaro was no common child. He had been sent from heaven, and he believed that all the devils in the world could not harm him. So at length the old man gave his consent, saying: "Go, Momotaro, slay the devils and bring peace to the land."

When the old woman had given Momotaro a number of rice-cakes the youth bade his foster-parents farewell, and started out upon his journey.

The Triumph of Momotaro

While Momotaro was resting under a hedge eating one of the rice-cakes, a great dog came up to him, growled, and showed his teeth. The dog, moreover, could speak, and threateningly begged that Momotaro would give him a cake. "Either you give me a cake," said he, "or I will kill you!"

When, however, the dog heard that the famous Momotaro stood before him, his tail dropped between his legs and he bowed with his head to the ground, requesting that he might follow 'Son of a Peach', and render to him all the service that lay in his power.

Momotaro readily accepted the offer, and after throwing the dog half a cake they proceeded on their way.

They had not gone far when they encountered a monkey, who also begged to be admitted to Momotaro's service. This was granted, but it was some time before the dog and the monkey ceased snapping at each other and became good friends.

Proceeding upon their journey, they came across a pheasant. Now the innate jealousy of the dog was again awakened, and he ran forward and tried to kill the bright-plumed creature. Momotaro separated the combatants, and in the end the pheasant was also admitted to the little band, walking decorously in the rear.

At length Momotaro and his followers reached the shore of the North-Eastern Sea. Here our hero discovered a boat, and after a good deal of timidity on the part of the dog, monkey, and pheasant, they all got aboard, and soon the little vessel was spinning away over the blue sea.

After many days upon the ocean they sighted an island. Momotaro bade the bird fly off, a winged herald to announce his coming, and bid the devils surrender.

The pheasant flew over the sea and alighted on the roof of a great castle and shouted his stirring message, adding that the devils, as a sign of submission, should break their horns.

The devils only laughed and shook their horns and shaggy red hair. Then they brought forth iron bars and hurled them furiously at the bird. The pheasant cleverly evaded the missiles, and flew at the heads of many devils.

In the meantime Momotaro had landed with his two companions. He had no sooner done so than he saw two beautiful damsels weeping by a stream, as they wrung out blood-soaked garments.

"Oh!" said they pitifully, "we are daughters of *daimyōs*, and are now the captives of the Demon King of this dreadful island. Soon he will kill us, and alas! there is no one to come to our aid." Having made these remarks the women wept anew.

"Ladies," said Momotaro, "I have come for the purpose of slaying your wicked enemies. Show me a way into yonder castle."

So Momotaro, the dog, and the monkey entered through a small door in the castle. Once inside this fortification they fought tenaciously. Many of the devils were so frightened that they fell off the parapets and were dashed to pieces, while others were speedily killed by Momotaro and his companions. All were destroyed except the Demon King himself, and he wisely resolved to surrender, and begged that his life might be spared.

"No," said Momotaro fiercely. "I will not spare your wicked life. You have tortured many innocent people and robbed the country for many years."

Having said these words he gave the Demon King into the monkey's keeping, and then proceeded through all the rooms of the castle, and set free the numerous prisoners he found there. He also gathered together much treasure.

The return journey was a very joyous affair indeed. The dog and the pheasant carried the treasure between them, while Momotaro led the Demon King.

Momotaro restored the two daughters or *daimyōs* to their homes, and many others who had been made captives in the island. The whole country rejoiced in his victory, but no one more than Momotaro's foster-parents, who ended their days in peace and plenty, thanks to the great treasure of the devils which Momotaro bestowed upon them.

My Lord Bag of Rice

ONE DAY THE GREAT HIDESATO came to a bridge that spanned the beautiful Lake Biwa. He was about to cross it when he noticed a great serpent-dragon fast asleep obstructing his progress. Hidesato, without a moment's hesitation, climbed over the monster and proceeded on his way.

He had not gone far when he heard someone calling to him. He looked back and saw that in the place of the dragon a man stood bowing to him with much ceremony. He was a strange-looking fellow with a dragon-shaped crown resting upon his red hair.

"I am the Dragon King of Lake Biwa," explained the red-haired man. "A moment ago I took the form of a horrible monster in the hope of finding a mortal who would not be afraid of me.

You, my lord, showed no fear, and I rejoice exceedingly. A great centipede comes down from yonder mountain, enters my palace, and destroys my children and grandchildren. One by one they have become food for this dread creature, and I fear soon that unless something can be done to slay this centipede I myself shall become a victim. I have waited long for a brave mortal. All men who have hitherto seen me in my dragon-shape have run away. You are a brave man, and I beg that you will kill my bitter enemy."

Hidesato, who always welcomed an adventure, the more so when it was a perilous one, readily consented to see what he could do for the Dragon King.

When Hidesato reached the Dragon King's palace he found it to be a very magnificent building indeed, scarcely less beautiful than the Sea King's palace itself. He was feasted with crystallised lotus leaves and flowers, and ate the delicacies spread before him with choice ebony chopsticks. While he feasted ten little goldfish danced, and just behind the goldfish ten carp made sweet music on the *koto* and *samisen*. Hidesato was just thinking how excellently he had been entertained, and how particularly good was the wine, when they all heard an awful noise like a dozen thunderclaps roaring together.

Hidesato and the Dragon King hastily rose and ran to the balcony. They saw that Mount Mikami was scarcely recognisable, for it was covered from top to bottom with the great coils of the centipede. In its head glowed two balls of fire, and its hundred feet were like a long winding chain of lanterns.

Hidesato fitted an arrow to his bowstring and pulled it back with all his might. The arrow sped forth into the night and struck the centipede in the middle of the head, but glanced off immediately without inflicting any wound. Again Hidesato sent an arrow whirling into the air, and again it struck the monster and fell harmlessly to the ground. Hidesato had only one arrow left. Suddenly remembering the magical effect of human saliva, he put the remaining arrow-head into his mouth for a moment, and then hastily adjusted it to his bow and took careful aim.

The last arrow struck its mark and pierced the centipede's brain. The creature stopped moving; the light in its eyes and legs darkened and then went out, and Lake Biwa, with its palace beneath, was shrouded in awful darkness. Thunder rolled, lightning flashed, and it seemed for the moment that the Dragon King's palace would topple to the ground.

The next day, however, all sign of storm had vanished. The sky was clear. The sun shone brightly. In the sparkling blue lake lay the body of the great centipede.

The Dragon King and those about him were overjoyed when they knew that their dread enemy had been destroyed. Hidesato was again feasted, even more royally than before. When he finally departed he did so with a retinue of fishes suddenly converted into men. The Dragon King bestowed upon our hero five precious gifts – two bells, a bag of rice, a roll of silk, and a cooking-pot.

The Dragon King accompanied Hidesato as far as the bridge, and then he reluctantly allowed the hero and the procession of servants carrying the presents to proceed on their way.

When Hidesato reached his home the Dragon King's servants put down the presents and suddenly disappeared.

The presents were no ordinary gifts. The rice-bag was inexhaustible, there was no end to the roll of silk, and the cooking-pot would cook without fire of any kind. Only the bells were without magical properties, and these were presented to a temple in the vicinity. Hidesato grew rich, and his fame spread far and wide. People now no longer called him Hidesato, but Tawara Toda, or 'My Lord Bag of Rice'.

The Transformation of Issunboshi

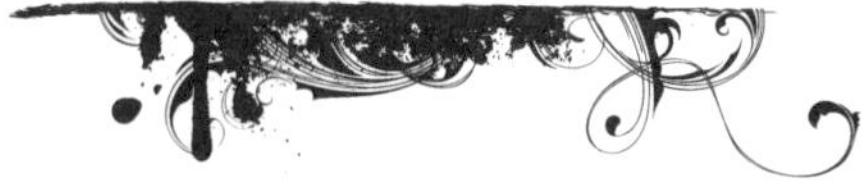

AN OLD MARRIED COUPLE went to the shrine of the deified Empress Jingo, and prayed that they might be blessed with a child, even if it were no bigger than one of their fingers. A voice was heard from behind the bamboo curtain of the shrine, and the old people were informed that their wish would be granted.

In due time the old woman gave birth to a child, and when she and her husband discovered that this miniature piece of humanity was no bigger than a little finger, they became extremely angry, and thought that the Empress Jingo had treated them very meanly indeed, though, as a matter of fact, she had fulfilled their prayer to the letter.

'One-Inch Priest'

The little fellow was called Issunboshi ('One-Inch Priest'), and every day his parents expected to see him suddenly grow up as other boys; but at thirteen years of age he still remained the same size as when he was born. Gradually his parents became exasperated, for it wounded their vanity to hear the neighbours describe their son as Little Finger, or Grain-of-Corn. They were so much annoyed that at last they determined to send Issunboshi away.

The little fellow did not complain. He requested his mother to give him a needle, a small soup-bowl, and a chop-stick, and with these things he set off on his adventures.

Issunboshi becomes a Page

His soup-bowl served as a boat, which he propelled along the river with his chop-stick. In this fashion he finally reached Kyoto. Issunboshi wandered about this city until he saw a large roofed gate. Without the least hesitation he walked in, and having reached the porch of a house, he cried out in a very minute voice: "I beg an honourable inquiry!"

Prince Sanjo himself heard the little voice, and it was some time before he could discover where it came from. When he did so he was delighted with his discovery, and on the little fellow begging that he might live in the Prince's house, his request was readily granted. The boy became a great favourite, and was at once made the Princess Sanjo's page. In this capacity he accompanied his mistress everywhere, and though so very small, he fully appreciated the honour and dignity of his position.

An Encounter with Oni

One day the Princess Sanjo and her page went to the Temple of Kwannon, the Goddess of Mercy, "under whose feet are dragons of the elements and the lotuses of Purity." As they were leaving the temple two *oni* (evil spirits) sprang upon them. Issunboshi took out his needle-sword from its hollow straw, and loudly denouncing the *oni*, he flourished his small weapon in their evil-looking faces.

One of the creatures laughed. "Why," said he scornfully, "I could swallow you, as a cormorant swallows a trout, and what is more, my funny little bean-seed, I will do so!"

The *oni* opened his mouth, and Issunboshi found himself slipping down a huge throat until he finally stood in the creature's great dark stomach. Issunboshi, nothing daunted, began boring away with his needle-sword. This made the evil spirit cry out and give a great cough, which sent the little fellow into the sunny world again.

The second *oni*, who had witnessed his companion's distress, was extremely angry, and tried to swallow the remarkable little page, but was not successful. This time Issunboshi climbed up the creature's nostril, and when he had reached the end of what seemed to him to be a very long and gloomy tunnel, he began piercing the *oni's* eyes. The creature, savage with pain, ran off as fast as he could, followed by his yelling companion.

Needless to say, the Princess was delighted with her page's bravery, and told him that she was sure her father would reward him when he was told about the terrible encounter.

The Magic Mallet

On their way home the Princess happened to pick up a small wooden mallet. "Oh!" said she, "this must have been dropped by the wicked *oni*, and it is none other than a lucky mallet. You have only to wish and then tap it upon the ground, and your wish, no matter what, is always granted. My brave Issunboshi, tell me what you would most desire, and I will tap the mallet on the ground."

After a pause the little fellow said: "Honourable Princess, I should like to be as big as other people."

The Princess tapped the mallet on the ground, calling aloud the wish of her page. In a moment Issunboshi was transformed from a bijou creature to a lad just like other youths of his age.

These wonderful happenings excited the curiosity of the Emperor, and Issunboshi was summoned to his presence. The Emperor was so delighted with the youth that he gave him many gifts and made him a high official. Finally, Issunboshi became a great lord and married Prince Sanjo's youngest daughter.

Kintaro, the Golden Boy

SAKATA KURANDO was an officer of the Emperor's bodyguard, and though he was a brave man, well versed in the art of war, he had a gentle disposition, and during his military career chanced to love a beautiful lady named Yaegiri. Kurando eventually fell into disgrace, and was forced to leave the Court and to become a travelling tobacco merchant. Yaegiri, who was much distressed by her lover's flight, succeeded in escaping from her home, and wandered up and down the country in the hope of meeting Kurando. At length she found him, but the unfortunate man, who, no doubt, felt deeply his disgrace and his humble mode of living, put an end to his humiliation by taking his miserable life.

Animal Companions

When Yaegiri had buried her lover she went to the Ashigara Mountain, where she gave birth to a child, called Kintaro, or the Golden Boy. Now Kintaro was remarkable for his extreme strength. When only a few years old his mother gave him an axe, with which he felled trees as quickly and easily as an experienced woodcutter. Ashigara Mountain was a lonely and desolate spot, and as there were no children with whom Kintaro could play, he made companions of the bear, deer, hare, and monkey, and in a very short time was able to speak their strange language.

One day, when Kintaro was sitting on the mountain, with his favourites about him, he sought to amuse himself by getting his companions to join in a friendly wrestling match. A kindly old bear was delighted with the proposal, and at once set to work to dig up the earth and arrange it in the form of a small dais. When this had been made a hare and a monkey wrestled together, while a deer stood by to give encouragement and to see that the sport was conducted fairly. Both animals proved themselves to be equally strong, and Kintaro tactfully rewarded them with tempting rice-cakes.

After spending a pleasant afternoon in this way, Kintaro proceeded to return home, followed by his devoted friends. At length they came to a river, and the animals were wondering how they should cross such a wide stretch of water, when Kintaro put his strong arms round a tree which was growing on the bank, and pulled it across the river so that it formed a bridge. Now it happened that the famous hero, Yorimitsu, and his retainers witnessed this extraordinary feat of strength, and said to Watanabe Tsuna: "This child is truly remarkable. Go and find out where he lives and all about him."

A Famous Warrior

So Watanabe Tsuna followed Kintaro and entered the house where he lived with his mother. "My master," said he, "Lord Yorimitsu, bids me find out who your wonderful son is." When Yaegiri had narrated the story of her life and informed her visitor that her little one was the son of Sakata Kurando, the retainer departed and told Yorimitsu all he had heard.

Yorimitsu was so pleased with what Watanabe Tsuna told him that he went himself to Yaegiri, and said: "If you will give me your child I will make him my retainer." The woman gladly consented, and the Golden Boy went away with the great hero, who named him Sakata Kintoki. He eventually became a famous warrior, and the stories of his wonderful deeds are recited to this day. Children regard him as their favourite hero, and little boys, who would fain emulate the strength and bravery of Sakata Kintoki, carry his portrait in their bosoms.

A Japanese Gulliver

SHIKAIYA WASOBIOYE was a man of Nagasaki, and possessed considerable learning, but disliked visitors. On the eighth day of the eighth month, in order to escape the admirers of the full moon, he set off in his boat, and had proceeded some distance, when the sky looked threatening, and he attempted to return, but the wind tore his sail and broke his mast. The poor man was tossed for three months on the waves, until at last he came to the Sea of Mud, where he nearly died of hunger, for there were no fishes to be caught.

At length he reached a mountainous island, where the air was sweet with the fragrance of many flowers, and in this island he found a spring, the waters of which revived him. At length Wasobioye met Jofuku, who led him through the streets of the main city, where all the inhabitants were spending their time in pursuit of pleasure. There was no death or disease on this island; but the fact that here life was eternal was regarded by many as a burden, which they tried to shake off by studying the magic art of death and the power of poisonous food, such as globe-fish sprinkled with soot and the flesh of mermaids.

When twenty years had passed by Wasobioye grew weary of the island, and as he had failed in his attempts to take his life, he started upon a journey to the Three Thousand Worlds mentioned in Buddhist Scriptures. He then visited the Land of Endless Plenty, the Land of Shams, the Land of the Followers of the Antique, the Land of Paradoxes, and, finally, the Land of Giants.

After Wasobioye had spent five months riding on the back of a stork through total darkness, he at length reached a country where the sun shone again, where trees were hundreds of feet in girth, where weeds were as large as bamboos, and men sixty feet in height. In this strange land a giant picked up Wasobioye, took him to his house, and fed him from a single grain of monster rice, with chopsticks the size of a small tree. For a few weeks Wasobioye attempted to catechise his host in regard to the doctrines of the old world whence he came, but the giant laughed at him and told him that such a small man could not be expected to understand the ways of big people, for their intelligences were in like proportion to their size.

Kazuma's Revenge

ABOUT TWO HUNDRED AND FIFTY YEARS AGO Ikeda Kunaishoyu was Lord of the Province of Inaba. Among his retainers were two gentlemen, named Watanabe Yukiye and Kawai Matazayemon, who were bound together by strong ties of friendship, and were in the habit of frequently visiting at one another's houses. One day Yukiye was sitting conversing with Matazayemon in the house of the latter, when, on a sudden, a sword that was lying in the raised part of the room caught his eye. As he saw it, he started and said:

"Pray tell me, how came you by that sword?"

"Well, as you know, when my Lord Ikeda followed my Lord Tokugawa Iyeyasu to fight at Nagakude, my father went in his train; and it was at the battle of Nagakude that he picked up this sword."

"My father went too, and was killed in the fight, and this sword, which was an heirloom in our family for many generations, was lost at that time. As it is of great value in my eyes, I do wish that, if you set no special store by it, you would have the great kindness to return it to me."

"That is a very easy matter, and no more than what one friend should do by another. Pray take it."

Upon this Yukiye gratefully took the sword, and having carried it home put it carefully away.

At the beginning of the ensuing year Matazayemon fell sick and died, and Yukiye, mourning bitterly for the loss of his good friend, and anxious to requite the favour which he had received in the matter of his father's sword, did many acts of kindness to the dead man's son – a young man twenty-two years of age, named Matagoro.

Now this Matagoro was a base-hearted cur, who had begrudged the sword that his father had given to Yukiye, and complained publicly and often that Yukiye had never made any present in return; and in this way Yukiye got a bad name in my Lord's palace as a stingy and illiberal man.

But Yukiye had a son, called Kazuma, a youth sixteen years of age, who served as one of the Prince's pages of honour. One evening, as he and one of his brother pages were talking together, the latter said:

"Matagoro is telling everybody that your father accepted a handsome sword from him and never made him any present in return, and people are beginning to gossip about it."

"Indeed," replied the other, "my father received that sword from Matagoro's father as a mark of friendship and good-will, and, considering that it would be an insult to send a present of money in return, thought to return the favour by acts of kindness towards Matagoro. I suppose it is money he wants."

When Kazuma's service was over, he returned home, and went to his father's room to tell him the report that was being spread in the palace, and begged him to send an ample present of money to Matagoro. Yukrye reflected for a while, and said:

"You are too young to understand the right line of conduct in such matters. Matagoro's father and myself were very close friends; so, seeing that he had ungrudgingly given me back the sword of my ancestors, I, thinking to requite his kindness at his death, rendered important services to Matagoro. It would be easy to finish the matter by sending a present of money; but I had rather take the sword and return it than be under an obligation to this mean churl, who knows not the laws which regulate the intercourse and dealings of men of gentle blood."

So Yukiye, in his anger, took the sword to Matagoro's house, and said to him:

"I have come to your house this night for no other purpose than to restore to you the sword which your father gave me;" and with this he placed the sword before Matagoro.

"Indeed," replied the other, "I trust that you will not pain me by returning a present which my father made you."

"Amongst men of gentle birth," said Yukiye, laughing scornfully, "it is the custom to requite presents, in the first place by kindness, and afterwards by a suitable gift offered with a free heart. But it is no use talking to such as you, who are ignorant of the first principles of good breeding; so I have the honour to give you back the sword."

As Yukiye went on bitterly to reprove Matagoro, the latter waxed very wroth, and, being a ruffian, would have killed Yukiye on the spot; but he, old man as he was, was a skilful swordsman, so Matagoro, craven-like, determined to wait until he could attack him unawares. Little suspecting any treachery, Yukiye started to return home, and Matagoro, under the pretence of attending him to the door, came behind him with his sword drawn and cut him in the shoulder. The older man, turning round, drew and defended himself; but having received a severe wound in the first instance, he fainted away from loss of blood, and Matagoro slew him.

The mother of Matagoro, startled by the noise, came out; and when she saw what had been done, she was afraid, and said – "Passionate man! what have you done? You are a murderer; and now your life will be forfeit. What terrible deed is this!"

"I have killed him now, and there's nothing to be done. Come, mother, before the matter becomes known, let us fly together from this house."

"I will follow you; do you go and seek out my Lord Abe Shirogoro, a chief among the Hatamotos, who was my foster-child. You had better fly to him for protection, and remain in hiding."

So the old woman persuaded her son to make his escape, and sent him to the palace of Shirogoro.

Now it happened that at this time the Hatamotos had formed themselves into a league against the powerful Daimyos; and Abe Shirogoro, with two other noblemen, named Kondo Noborinosuke and Midzuno Jiurozayemon, was at the head of the league. It followed, as a matter of course, that his forces were frequently recruited by vicious men, who had no means of gaining their living, and whom he received and entreated kindly without asking any questions as to their antecedents; how much the more then, on being applied to for an asylum by the son of his own foster-mother, did he willingly extend his patronage to him, and guarantee him against all danger. So he called a meeting of the principal Hatamotos, and introduced Matagoro to them, saying – "This man is a retainer of Ikeda Kunaishoyu, who, having cause of hatred against a man named Watanabe Yukiye, has slain him, and has fled to me for protection; this man's mother suckled me when I was an infant, and, right or wrong, I will befriend him. If, therefore, Ikeda Kunaishoyu should send to require me to deliver him up, I trust that you will one and all put forth your strength and help me to defend him."

"Ay! that will we, with pleasure!" replied Kondo Noborinosuke. "We have for some time had cause to complain of the scorn with which the Daimyos have treated us. Let Ikeda Kunaishoyu send to claim this man, and we will show him the power of the Hatamotos."

All the other Hatamotos, with one accord, applauded this determination, and made ready their force for an armed resistance, should my Lord Kunaishoyu send to demand the surrender of Matugoro. But the latter remained as a welcome guest in the house of Abe Shirogoro.

Now when Watanabe Kazuma saw that, as the night advanced, his father Yukiye did not return home, he became anxious, and went to the house of Matagoro to seek for him, and finding to his horror that he was murdered, fell upon the corpse and, embraced it, weeping. On a sudden, it flashed across him that this must assuredly be the handiwork of Matagoro; so he rushed furiously into the house, determined to kill his father's murderer upon the spot. But Matagoro had already fled, and he found only the mother, who was making her preparations for following her son to the house of Abe Shirogoro: so he bound the old woman, and searched all over the house for her son; but, seeing that his search was fruitless, he carried off the mother, and handed her over to one of the elders of the clan, at the same time laying information against Matagoro as his father's murderer. When the affair was reported to the Prince, he was very angry, and ordered that the old woman should remain bound and be cast into prison until the whereabouts of her son should be discovered. Then Kazuma buried his father's corpse with great pomp, and the widow and the orphan mourned over their loss.

It soon became known amongst the people of Abe Shirogoro that the mother of Matagoro had been imprisoned for her son's crime, and they immediately set about planning her rescue; so they sent to the palace of my Lord Kunaishoyu a messenger, who, when he was introduced to the councillor of the Prince, said:

"We have heard that, in consequence of the murder of Yukiye, my lord has been pleased to imprison the mother of Matagoro. Our master Shirogoro has arrested the criminal, and will deliver him up to you. But the mother has committed no crime, so we pray that she may be released from a cruel imprisonment: she was the foster-mother of our master, and he would fain intercede to save her life. Should you consent to this, we, on our side, will give up the murderer, and hand him over to you in front of our master's gate tomorrow."

The councillor repeated this message to the Prince, who, in his pleasure at being able to give Kazuma his revenge on the morrow, immediately agreed to the proposal, and the messenger returned triumphant at the success of the scheme. On the following day, the Prince ordered the mother of Matagoro to be placed in a litter and carried to the Hatamoto's dwelling, in charge of a retainer named Sasawo Danyemon, who, when he arrived at the door of Abe Shirogoro's house, said:

"I am charged to hand over to you the mother of Matagoro, and, in exchange, I am authorized to receive her son at your hands."

"We will immediately give him up to you; but, as the mother and son are now about to bid an eternal farewell to one another, we beg you to be so kind as to tarry a little."

With this the retainers of Shirogoro led the old woman inside their master's house, and Sasawo Danyemon remained waiting outside, until at last he grew impatient, and ventured to hurry on the people within.

"We return you many thanks," replied they, "for your kindness in bringing us the mother; but, as the son cannot go with you at present, you had better return home as quickly as possible. We are afraid we have put you to much trouble." And so they mocked him.

When Danyemon saw that he had not only been cheated into giving up the old woman, but was being made a laughing-stock of into the bargain, he flew into a great rage, and thought to break into the house and seize Matagoro and his mother by force; but, peeping into the courtyard, he saw that it was filled with Hatamotos, carrying guns and naked swords. Not caring then to die fighting a hopeless battle, and at the same time feeling that, after having been so cheated, he would be put to shame before his lord, Sasawo Danyemon went to the burial-place of his ancestors, and disembowelled himself in front of their graves.

When the Prince heard how his messenger had been treated, he was indignant, and summoning his councillors resolved, although he was suffering from sickness, to collect his retainers and attack Abe Shirogoro; and the other chief Daimyos, when the matter became publicly known, took up the cause, and determined that the Hatamotos must be chastised for their insolence. On their side, the Hatamotos put forth all their efforts to resist the Daimyos. So Edo became disturbed, and the riotous state of the city caused great anxiety to the Government, who took counsel together how they might restore peace. As the Hatamotos were directly under the orders of the Shogun, it was no difficult matter to put them down: the hard question to solve was how to put a restraint upon the great Daimyos. However, one of the Gorojin, named Matsudaira Idzu no Kami, a man of great intelligence, hit upon a plan by which he might secure this end.

There was at this time in the service of the Shogun a physician, named Nakarai Tsusen, who was in the habit of frequenting the palace of my Lord Kunaishoyu, and who for some time past had been treating him for the disease from which he was suffering. Idzu no Kami sent secretly for this physician, and, summoning him to his private room, engaged him in conversation, in the midst of which he suddenly dropped his voice and said to him in a whisper:

"Listen, Tsusen. You have received great favours at the hands of the Shogun. The Government is now sorely straitened: are you willing to carry your loyalty so far as to lay down your life on its behalf?"

"Ay, my lord; for generations my forefathers have held their property by the grace of the Shogun. I am willing this night to lay down my life for my Prince, as a faithful vassal should."

"Well, then, I will tell you. The great Daimyos and the Hatamotos have fallen out about this affair of Matagoro, and lately it has seemed as if they meant to come to blows. The country will be agitated, and the farmers and townsfolk suffer great misery, if we cannot quell the tumult. The Hatamotos will be easily kept under, but it will be no light task to pacify the great Daimyos. If you are willing to lay down your life in carrying out a stratagem of mine, peace will be restored to the country; but your loyalty will be your death."

"I am ready to sacrifice my life in this service."

"This is my plan. You have been attending my Lord Kunaishoyu in his sickness; tomorrow you must go to see him, and put poison in his physic. If we can kill him, the agitation will cease. This is the service which I ask of you."

Tsusen agreed to undertake the deed; and on the following day, when he went to see Kunaishoyu, he carried with him poisoned drugs. Half the draught he drank himself, and thus put the Prince off his guard, so that he swallowed the remainder fearlessly. Tsusen, seeing this, hurried away, and as he was carried home in his litter the death-agony seized him, and he died, vomiting blood.

My Lord Kunaishoyu died in the same way in great torture, and in the confusion attending upon his death and funeral ceremonies the struggle which was impending with the Hatamotos was delayed.

In the meanwhile the Gorojiu Idzu no Kami summoned the three leaders of the Hatamotos and addressed them as follows:

"The secret plottings and treasonable, turbulent conduct of you three men, so unbecoming your position as Hatamotos, have enraged my lord the Shogun to such a degree, that he has been pleased to order that you be imprisoned in a temple, and that your patrimony be given over to your next heirs."

Accordingly the three Hatamotos, after having been severely admonished, were confined in a temple called Kanyeiji; and the remaining Hatamotos, scared by this example, dispersed in peace. As for the great Daimyos, inasmuch as after the death of my Lord Kunaishoyu the Hatamotos were all dispersed, there was no enemy left for them to fight with; so the tumult was quelled, and peace was restored.

Thus it happened that Matagoro lost his patron; so, taking his mother with him, he went and placed himself under the protection of an old man named Sakurai Jiuzayemon. This old man was a famous teacher of lance exercise, and enjoyed both wealth and honour; so he took in Matagoro, and having engaged as a guard thirty Ronins, all resolute fellows and well skilled in the arts of war, they all fled together to a distant place called Sagara.

All this time Watanabe Kazuma had been brooding over his father's death, and thinking how he should be revenged upon the murderer; so when my Lord Kunaishoyu suddenly died, he went to the young Prince who succeeded him and obtained leave of absence to go and seek out his father's enemy. Now Kazuma's elder sister was married to a man named Araki Matayemon, who at that time was famous as the first swordsman in Japan. As Kazuma was but sixteen years of age, this Matayemon, taking into consideration his near relationship as son-in-law to the murdered man, determined to go forth with the lad, as his guardian, and help him to seek out Matagoro; and two of Matayemon's retainers, named Ishidome Busuke and Ikezoye Magohachi, made up their minds, at all hazards, to follow their master. The latter, when he heard their intention, thanked them, but refused the offer, saying that as he was now about to engage in a vendetta in which his life would be continually in jeopardy, and as it would be a lasting grief to him should either of them receive a wound in such a service, he must beg them to renounce their intention; but they answered:

"Master, this is a cruel speech of yours. All these years have we received nought but kindness and favours at your hands; and now that you are engaged in the pursuit of this murderer, we desire to follow you, and, if needs must, to lay down our lives in your service. Furthermore, we have heard that the friends of this Matagoro are no fewer than thirty-six men; so, however bravely you may fight, you will be in peril from the superior numbers of your enemy. However, if you are pleased to persist in your refusal to take us, we have made up our minds that there is no resource for us but to disembowel ourselves on the spot."

When Matayemon and Kazuma heard these words, they wondered at these faithful and brave men, and were moved to tears. Then Matayemon said:

"The kindness of you two brave fellows is without precedent. Well, then, I will accept your services gratefully."

Then the two men, having obtained their wish, cheerfully followed their master; and the four set out together upon their journey to seek out Matagoro, of whose whereabouts they were completely ignorant.

Matagoro in the meanwhile had made his way, with the old man Sakurai Jiuzayemon and his thirty Ronins, to Osaka. But, strong as they were in numbers, they travelled in great secrecy. The reason for this was that the old man's younger brother, Sakurai Jinsuke, a fencing-master by profession, had once had a fencing-match with Matayemon, Kazuma's brother-in-law, and had been shamefully beaten; so that the party were greatly afraid of Matayemon, and felt that, since he was taking up Kazuma's cause and acting as his guardian, they might be worsted in spite of their numbers: so they went on their way with great caution, and, having reached Osaka, put up at an inn in a quarter called Ikutama, and hid from Kazuma and Matayemon.

The latter also in good time reached Osaka, and spared no pains to seek out Matagoro. One evening towards dusk, as Matayemon was walking in the quarter where the enemy were staying, he saw a man, dressed as a gentleman's servant, enter a cook-shop and order some buckwheat porridge for thirty-six men, and looking attentively at the man, he recognized him as the servant of Sakurai Jiuzayemon; so he hid himself in a dark place and watched, and heard the fellow say:

"My master, Sakurai Jiuzayemon, is about to start for Sagara tomorrow morning, to return thanks to the gods for his recovery from a sickness from which he has been suffering; so I am in a great hurry."

With these words the servant hastened away; and Matayemon, entering the shop, called for some porridge, and as he ate it, made some inquiries as to the man who had just given so large an order for buckwheat porridge. The master of the shop answered that he was the attendant of a party of thirty-six gentlemen who were staying at such and such an inn. Then Matayemon, having found out all that he wanted to know, went home and told Kazuma, who was delighted at the prospect of carrying his revenge into execution on the morrow. That same evening Matayemon sent one of his two faithful retainers as a spy to the inn, to find out at what hour Matagoro was to set out on the following morning; and he ascertained from the servants of the inn, that the party was to start at daybreak for Sagara, stopping at Ise to worship at the shrine of Tersho Daijin.

Matayemon made his preparations accordingly, and, with Kazuma and his two retainers, started before dawn. Beyond Uyeno, in the province of Iga, the castle-town of the Daimyo Todo Idzumi no Kami, there is a wide and lonely moor; and this was the place upon which they fixed for the attack upon the enemy. When they had arrived at the spot, Matayemon went into a tea-house by the roadside, and wrote a petition to the governor of the Daimyo's castle-town for permission to carry out the vendetta within its precincts; then he addressed Kazuma, and said:

"When we fall in with Matagoro and begin the fight, do you engage and slay your father's murderer; attack him and him only, and I will keep off his guard of Ronins;" then turning to his two retainers, "As for you, keep close to Kazuma; and should the Ronins attempt to rescue Matagoro, it will be your duty to prevent them, and succour Kazuma." And having further laid down each man's duties with great minuteness, they lay in wait for the arrival of the enemy. Whilst they were resting in the tea-house, the governor of the castle-town arrived, and, asking for Matayemou, said:

"I have the honour to be the governor of the castle-town of Todo Idzumi no Kami. My lord, having learnt your intention of slaying your enemy within the precincts of his citadel, gives his consent; and as a proof of his admiration of your fidelity and valour, he has further sent you a detachment of infantry, one hundred strong, to guard the place; so that should any of the thirty-six men attempt to escape, you may set your mind at ease, for flight will be impossible."

When Matayemon and Kazurna had expressed their thanks for his lordship's gracious kindness, the governor took his leave and returned home. At last the enemy's train was seen in the distance. First came Sakurai Jiuzayemon and his younger brother Jinsuke; and next to them followed Kawai Matagoro and Takenouchi Gentan. These four men, who were the bravest and the foremost of the band of Ronins, were riding on pack-horses, and the remainder were marching on foot, keeping close together.

As they drew near, Kazuma, who was impatient to avenge his father, stepped boldly forward and shouted in a loud voice:

"Here stand I, Kazuma, the son of Yukiye, whom you, Matagoro, treacherously slew, determined to avenge my father's death. Come forth, then, and do battle with me, and let us see which of us twain is the better man."

And before the Ronins had recovered from their astonishment, Matayemon said:

"I, Arake Matayemon, the son-in-law of Yukiye, have come to second Kazuma in his deed of vengeance. Win or lose, you must give us battle."

When the thirty-six men heard the name of Matayemon, they were greatly afraid; but Sakurai Jiuzayemon urged them to be upon their guard, and leaped from his horse; and Matayemon, springing forward with his drawn sword, cleft him from the shoulder to the nipple of his breast, so that he fell dead. Sakurai Jinsuke, seeing his brother killed before his eyes, grew furious, and shot an arrow at Matayemon, who deftly cut the shaft in two with his dirk as it flew; and Jinsuke, amazed at this feat, threw away his bow and attacked Matayemon, who, with his sword in his right hand and his dirk in his left, fought with desperation. The other Ronins attempted to rescue Jinsuke, and, in the struggle, Kazuma, who had engaged Matagoro, became separated from Matayemon, whose two retainers, Busuke and Magohachi, bearing in mind their master's orders, killed five Ronins who had attacked Kazuma, but were themselves badly wounded. In the meantime, Matayemon, who had killed seven of the Ronins, and who the harder he was pressed the more bravely he fought, soon cut down three more, and the remainder dared not approach him. At this moment there came up one Kano Tozayemon, a retainer of the lord of the castle-town, and an old friend of Matayemon, who, when he heard that Matayemon was this day about to avenge his father-in-law, had seized his spear and set out, for the sake of the good-will between them, to help him, and act as his second, and said:

"Sir Matayemon, hearing of the perilous adventure in which you have engaged, I have come out to offer myself as your second."

Matayemon, hearing this, was rejoiced, and fought with renewed vigour. Then one of the Ronins, named Takenouchi Gentan, a very brave man, leaving his companions to do battle with

Matayemon, came to the rescue of Matagoro, who was being hotly pressed by Kazuma, and, in attempting to prevent this, Busuke fell covered with wounds. His companion Magohachi, seeing him fall, was in great anxiety; for should any harm happen to Kazuma, what excuse could he make to Matayemon? So, wounded as he was, he too engaged Takenouchi Gentan, and, being crippled by the gashes he had received, was in deadly peril. Then the man who had come up from the castle-town to act as Matayemon's second cried out:

"See there, Sir Matayemon, your follower who is fighting with Gentan is in great danger. Do you go to his rescue, and second Sir Kazuma: I will give an account of the others!"

"Great thanks to you, sir. I will go and second Kazuma."

So Matayemon went to help Kazuma, whilst his second and the infantry soldiers kept back the surviving Ronins, who, already wearied by their fight with Matayemon, were unfit for any further exertion. Kazuma meanwhile was still fighting with Matagoro, and the issue of the conflict was doubtful; and Takenouchi Gentan, in his attempt to rescue Matagoro, was being kept at bay by Magohachi, who, weakened by his wounds, and blinded by the blood which was streaming into his eyes from a cut in the forehead, had given himself up for lost when Matayemon came and cried:

"Be of good cheer, Magohachi; it is I, Matayemon, who have come to the rescue. You are badly hurt; get out of harm's way, and rest yourself."

Then Magohachi, who until then had been kept up by his anxiety for Kazuma's safety, gave in, and fell fainting from loss of blood; and Matayemon worsted and slew Gentan; and even then, although be had received two wounds, he was not exhausted, but drew near to Kazuma and said:

"Courage, Kazuma! The Ronins are all killed, and there now remains only Matagoro, your father's murderer. Fight and win!"

The youth, thus encouraged, redoubled his efforts; but Matagoro, losing heart, quailed and fell. So Kazuma's vengeance was fulfilled, and the desire of his heart was accomplished.

The two faithful retainers, who had died in their loyalty, were buried with great ceremony, and Kazuma carried the head of Matagoro and piously laid it upon his father's tomb.

So ends the tale of Kazuma's revenge.

A Story of The Otokodate of Edo

CHOBEI OF BANDZUIN was the chief of the Otokodate of Edo. He was originally called Itaro, and was the son of a certain Ronin who lived in the country. One day, when he was only ten years of age, he went out with a playfellow to bathe in the river; and as the two were playing they quarrelled over their game, and Itaro, seizing the other boy, threw him into the river and drowned him.

Then he went home, and said to his father:

"I went to play by the river today, with a friend; and as he was rude to me, I threw him into the water and killed him."

When his father heard him speak thus, quite calmly, as if nothing had happened, he was thunderstruck, and said:

"This is indeed a fearful thing. Child as you are, you will have to pay the penalty of your deed; so tonight you must fly to Edo in secret, and take service with some noble Samurai, and perhaps in time you may become a soldier yourself."

With these words he gave him twenty ounces of silver and a fine sword, made by the famous swordsmith Rai Kunitoshi, and sent him out of the province with all dispatch. The following morning the parents of the murdered child came to claim that Itaro should be given up to their vengeance; but it was too late, and all they could do was to bury their child and mourn for his loss.

Itaro made his way to Edo in hot haste, and there found employment as a shop-boy; but soon tiring of that sort of life, and burning to become a soldier, he found means at last to enter the service of a certain Hatamoto called Sakurai Shozayemon, and changed his name to Tsunehei. Now this Sakurai Shozayemon had a son, called Shonosuke, a young man in his seventeenth year, who grew so fond of Tsunehei that he took him with him wherever he went, and treated him in all ways as an equal.

When Shonosuke went to the fencing-school Tsunehei would accompany him, and thus, as he was by nature strong and active, soon became a good swordsman.

One day, when Shozayemon had gone out, his son Shonosuke said to Tsunehei:

"You know how fond my father is of playing at football: it must be great sport. As he has gone out today, suppose you and I have a game?"

"That will be rare sport," answered Tsunehei. "Let us make haste and play, before my lord comes home."

So the two boys went out into the garden, and began trying to kick the football; but, lacking skill, do what they would, they could not lift it from the ground. At last Shonosuke, with a vigorous kick, raised the football; but, having missed his aim, it went tumbling over the wall into the next garden, which belonged to one Hikosaka Zempachi, a teacher of lance exercise, who was known to be a surly, ill-tempered fellow.

"Oh, dear! what shall we do?" said Shonosuke. "We have lost my father's football in his absence; and if we go and ask for it back from that churlish neighbour of ours, we shall only be scolded and sworn at for our pains."

"Oh, never mind," answered Tsunehei; "I will go and apologize for our carelessness, and get the football back."

"Well, but then you will be chidden, and I don't want that."

"Never mind me. Little care I for his cross words." So Tsunehei went to the next-door house to reclaim the ball.

Now it so happened that Zempachi, the surly neighbour, had been walking in his garden whilst the two youths were playing; and as he was admiring the beauty of his favourite chrysanthemums, the football came flying over the wall and struck him full in the face. Zempachi, not used to anything but flattery and coaxing, flew into a violent rage at this; and while he was thinking how he would revenge himself upon anyone who might be sent to ask for the lost ball, Tsunehei came in, and said to one of Zempachi's servants:

"I am sorry to say that in my lord's absence I took his football, and, in trying to play with it, clumsily kicked it over your wall. I beg you to excuse my carelessness, and to be so good as to give me back the ball."

The servant went in and repeated this to Zempachi, who worked himself up into a great rage, and ordered Tsunehei to be brought before him, and said:

"Here, fellow, is your name Tsunehei?"

"Yes, sir, at your service. I am almost afraid to ask pardon for my carelessness; but please forgive me, and let me have the ball."

"I thought your master, Shozayemon, was to blame for this; but it seems that it was you who kicked the football."

"Yes, sir. I am sure I am very sorry for what I have done. Please, may I ask for the ball?" said Tsunehei, bowing humbly.

For a while Zempachi made no answer, but at length he said:

"Do you know, villain, that your dirty football struck me in the face? I ought, by rights, to kill you on the spot for this; but I will spare your life this time, so take your football and be off." And with that he went up to Tsunehei and beat him, and kicked him in the head, and spat in his face.

Then Tsunehei, who up to that time had demeaned himself very humbly, in his eagerness to get back the football, jumped up in a fury, and said:

"I made ample apologies to you for my carelessness, and now you have insulted and struck me. Ill-mannered ruffian! take back the ball, – I'll none of it;" and he drew his dirk, and cutting the football in two, threw it at Zempachi, and returned home.

But Zempachi, growing more and more angry, called one of his servants, and said to him:

"That fellow, Tsunehei, has been most insolent: go next door and find out Shozayemon, and tell him that I have ordered you to bring back Tsunehei, that I may kill him."

So the servant went to deliver the message.

In the meantime Tsunehei went back to his master's house; and when Shonosuke saw him, he said:

"Well, of course you have been ill treated; but did you get back the football?"

"When I went in, I made many apologies; but I was beaten, and kicked in the head, and treated with the greatest indignity. I would have killed that wretch, Zempachi, at once, but that I knew that, if I did so while I was yet a member of your household, I should bring trouble upon your family. For your sake I bore this ill-treatment patiently; but now I pray you let me take leave of you and become a Ronin, that I may be revenged upon this man."

"Think well what you are doing," answered Shonosuke. "After all, we have only lost a football; and my father will not care, nor upbraid us."

But Tsimehei would not listen to him, and was bent upon wiping out the affront that he had received. As they were talking, the messenger arrived from Zempachi, demanding the surrender of Tsunehei, on the ground that he had insulted him: to this Shonosuke replied that his father was away from home, and that in his absence he could do nothing.

At last Shozayemon came home; and when he heard what had happened he was much grieved, and at a loss what to do, when a second messenger arrived from Zempachi, demanding that Tsunehei should be given up without delay. Then Shozayemon, seeing that the matter was serious, called the youth to him, and said:

"This Zempachi is heartless and cruel, and if you go to his house will assuredly kill you; take, therefore, these fifty riyos, and fly to Osaka or Kyoto, where you may safely set up in business."

"Sir," answered Tsunehei, with tears of gratitude for his lord's kindness, "from my heart I thank you for your great goodness; but I have been insulted and trampled upon, and, if I lay down my life in the attempt, I will repay Zempachi for what he has this day done."

"Well, then, since you needs must be revenged, go and fight, and may success attend you! Still, as much depends upon the blade you carry, and I fear yours is likely to be but a sorry weapon, I will give you a sword;" and with this he offered Tsunehei his own.

"Nay, my lord," replied Tsunehei; "I have a famous sword, by Rai Kunitoshi, which my father gave me. I have never shown it to your lordship, but I have it safely stowed away in my room."

When Shozayemon saw and examined the sword, he admired it greatly, and said, "This is indeed a beautiful blade, and one on which you may rely. Take it, then, and bear yourself nobly in the fight; only remember that Zempachi is a cunning spearsman, and be sure to be very cautious."

So Tsunehei, after thanking his lord for his manifold kindnesses, took an affectionate leave, and went to Zempachi's house, and said to the servant:

"It seems that your master wants to speak to me. Be so good as to take me to see him."

So the servant led him into the garden, where Zempachi, spear in hand, was waiting to kill him. When Zempachi saw him, he cried out:

"Ha! so you have come back; and now for your insolence, this day I mean to kill you with my own hand."

"Insolent yourself!" replied Tsunehei. "Beast, and no Samurai! Come, let us see which of us is the better man."

Furiously incensed, Zempachi thrust with his spear at Tsunehei; but he, trusting to his good sword, attacked Zempachi, who, cunning warrior as he was, could gain no advantage. At last Zempachi, losing his temper, began fighting less carefully, so that Tsunehei found an opportunity of cutting the shaft of his spear. Zempachi then drew his sword, and two of his retainers came up to assist him; but Tsunehei killed one of them, and wounded Zempachi in the forehead. The second retainer fled affrighted at the youth's valour, and Zempachi was blinded by the blood which flowed from the wound on his forehead. Then Tsunehei said:

"To kill one who is as a blind man were unworthy a soldier. Wipe the blood from your eyes, Sir Zempachi, and let us fight it out fairly."

So Zempachi, wiping away his blood, bound a kerchief round his head, and fought again desperately. But at last the pain of his wound and the loss of blood overcame him, and Tsunehei cut him down with a wound in the shoulder and easily dispatched him.

Then Tsunehei went and reported the whole matter to the Governor of Edo, and was put in prison until an inquiry could be made. But the Chief Priest of Bandzuin, who had heard of the affair, went and told the governor all the bad deeds of Zempachi, and having procured Tsunehei's pardon, took him home and employed him as porter in the temple. So Tsunehei changed his name to Chobei, and earned much respect in the neighbourhood, both for his talents and for his many good works. If any man were in distress, he would help him, heedless of his own advantage or danger, until men came to look up to him as to a father, and many youths joined him and became his apprentices. So he built a house at Hanakawado, in Asakusa, and lived there with his apprentices, whom he farmed out as spearsmen and footmen to the Daimyos and Hatamotos, taking for himself the tithe of their earnings. But if any of them were sick or in trouble, Chobei would nurse and support them, and provide physicians and medicine. And the fame of his goodness went abroad until his apprentices were more than two thousand men, and were employed in every part of the city. But as for Chobei, the more he prospered, the more he gave in charity, and all men praised his good and generous heart.

This was the time when the Hatamotos had formed themselves into bands of Otokodate, of which Midzuno Jiurozayemon, Kondo Noborinosuke, and Abe Shirogoro were the chiefs. And the leagues of the nobles despised the leagues of the wardsmen, and treated them with scorn, and tried to put to shame Chobei and his brave men; but the nobles' weapons recoiled upon themselves, and, whenever they tried to bring contempt upon Chobei, they themselves were brought to ridicule. So there was great hatred on both sides.

One day, that Chobei went to divert himself in a tea-house in the Yoshiwara, he saw a felt carpet spread in an upper room, which had been adorned as for some special occasion; and he asked the master of the house what guest of distinction was expected. The landlord replied that my Lord Jiurozayemon, the chief of the Otokodate of the Hatamotos, was due there that afternoon. On hearing this, Chobei replied that as he much wished to meet my Lord Jiurozayemon, he would lie down and await his coming. The landlord was put out at this, and knew not what to say; but yet he dare not thwart Chobei, the powerful chief of the Otokodate. So Chobei took off his clothes and laid himself down upon the carpet. After a while my Lord Jiurozayemon arrived, and going upstairs found a man of large stature lying naked upon the carpet which had been spread for him.

"What low ruffian is this?" shouted he angrily to the landlord.

"My lord, it is Chobei, the chief of the Otokodate," answered the man, trembling.

Jiurozayemon at once suspected that Chobei was doing this to insult him; so he sat down by the side of the sleeping man, and lighting his pipe began to smoke. When he had finished his pipe, he emptied the burning ashes into Chobei's navel; but Chobei, patiently bearing the pain, still feigned sleep. Ten times did Jiurozayemon fill his pipe, and ten times he shook out the burning ashes on to Chobei's navel; but he neither stirred nor spoke. Then Jiurozayemon, astonished at his fortitude, shook him, and roused him, saying:

"Chobei! Chobei! wake up, man."

"What is the matter?" said Chobei, rubbing his eyes as though he were awaking from a deep sleep; then seeing Jiurozayemon, he pretended to be startled, and said, "Oh, my lord, I know not who you are; but I have been very rude to your lordship. I was overcome with wine, and fell asleep: I pray your lordship to forgive me."

"Is your name Chobei?"

"Yes, my lord, at your service. A poor wardsman, and ignorant of good manners, I have been very rude; but I pray your lordship to excuse my ill-breeding."

"Nay, nay; we have all heard the fame of Chobei, of Bandzuin, and I hold myself lucky to have met you this day. Let us be friends."

"It is a great honour for a humble wardsman to meet a nobleman face to face."

As they were speaking, the waitresses brought in fish and wine, and Jiurozayemon pressed Chobei to feast with him; and thinking to annoy Chobei, offered him a large wine-cup, which, however, he drank without shrinking, and then returned to his entertainer, who was by no means so well able to bear the fumes of the wine. Then Jiurozayemon hit upon another device for annoying Chobei, and, hoping to frighten him, said:

"Here, Chobei, let me offer you some fish;" and with those words he drew his sword, and, picking up a cake of baked fish upon the point of it, thrust it towards the wardsman's mouth. Any ordinary man would have been afraid to accept the morsel so roughly offered; but Chobei simply opened his mouth, and taking the cake off the sword's point ate it without wincing. Whilst Jiurozayemon was wondering in his heart what manner of man this was, that nothing could daunt, Chobei said to him:

"This meeting with your lordship has been an auspicious occasion to me, and I would fain ask leave to offer some humble gift to your lordship in memory of it. Is there anything which your lordship would specially fancy?"

"I am very fond of cold macaroni."

"Then I shall have the honour of ordering some for your lordship;" and with this Chobei went downstairs, and calling one of his apprentices, named Token Gombei, who was waiting for him, gave him a hundred riyos, and bade him collect all the cold macaroni to be found in the neighbouring cook-shops and pile it up in front of the tea-house. So Gombei went home, and, collecting Chobei's apprentices, sent them out in all directions to buy the macaroni. Jiurozayemon all this while was thinking of the pleasure he would have in laughing at Chobei for offering him a mean and paltry present; but when, by degrees, the macaroni began to be piled mountain-high around the tea-house, he saw that he could not make a fool of Chobei, and went home discomfited.

At this time there lived in the province of Yamato a certain Daimyo, called Honda Dainaiki, who one day, when surrounded by several of his retainers, produced a sword, and bade them look at it and say from what smith's workshop the blade had come.

"I think this must be a Masamune blade," said one Fuwa Banzayemon.

"No," said Nagoya Sanza, after examining the weapon attentively, "this certainly is a Muramasa."

A third Samurai, named Takagi Umanojo, pronounced it to be the work of Shidzu Kanenji; and as they could not agree, but each maintained his opinion, their lord sent for a famous connoisseur to decide the point; and the sword proved, as Sanza had said, to be a genuine Muramasa. Sanza was delighted at the verdict; but the other two went home rather crestfallen. Umanojo, although he had been worsted in the argument, bore no malice nor ill-will in his heart; but Banzayemon, who was a vainglorious personage, puffed up with the idea of his own importance, conceived a spite against Sanza, and watched for an opportunity to put him to shame. At last, one day Banzayemon, eager to be revenged upon Sanza, went to the Prince, and said, "Your lordship ought to see Sanza fence; his swordsmanship is beyond all praise. I know that I am no match for him; still, if it will please your lordship, I will try a bout with him;" and the Prince, who was a mere stripling, and thought it would be rare sport, immediately sent for Sanza and desired he would fence with Banzayemon. So the two went out into the garden, and stood up facing each other, armed with wooden swords. Now Banzayemon was proud of his skill, and thought he had no equal in fencing; so he expected to gain an easy victory over Sanza, and promised himself the luxury of giving his adversary a beating that should fully make up for the mortification which he had felt in the matter of the dispute about the sword. It happened, however, that he had undervalued the skill of Sanza, who, when he saw that his adversary was attacking him savagely and in good earnest, by a rapid blow struck Banzayemon so sharply on the wrist that he dropped the sword, and, before he could pick it up again, delivered a second cut on the shoulder, which sent him rolling over in the dust. All the officers present, seeing this, praised Sanza's skill, and Banzayemon, utterly stricken with shame, ran away home and hid himself.

After this affair Sanza rose high in the favour of his lord; and Banzayemon, who was more than ever jealous of him, feigned sickness, and stayed at home devising schemes for Sanza's ruin.

Now it happened that the Prince, wishing to have the Muramasa blade mounted, sent for Sanza and entrusted it to his care, ordering him to employ the most cunning workmen in the manufacture of the scabbard-hilt and ornaments; and Sanza, having received the blade, took it home, and put it carefully away. When Banzayemon heard of this, he was overjoyed; for he saw that his opportunity for revenge had come. He determined, if possible, to kill Sanza, but at any rate to steal the sword which had been committed to his care by the Prince, knowing full well that if Sanza lost the sword he and his family would be ruined. Being a single man, without wife or child, he sold his furniture, and, turning all his available property into money, made ready to fly the country. When his preparations were concluded, he went in the middle of the night to Sanza's house and tried to get in by stealth; but the doors and shutters were all carefully bolted from the inside, and there was no hole by which he could effect an entrance. All was still, however, and the people of the house were evidently fast asleep; so he climbed up to the second storey, and, having contrived to unfasten a window, made his way in. With soft, cat-like footsteps he crept downstairs, and, looking into one of the rooms, saw Sanza and his wife sleeping on the mats, with their little son Kosanza, a boy of thirteen, curled up in his quilt between them. The light in the night-lamp was at its last flicker, but, peering through the gloom, he could just see the Prince's famous Muramasa sword lying on a sword-rack in the raised part of the room: so he crawled stealthily along until he could reach it, and stuck it in his girdle. Then, drawing near to Sanza, he bestrode his sleeping body, and, brandishing the sword made a thrust at his throat; but in his excitement his hand shook, so that he missed his aim, and only scratched Sanza, who, waking with a start and trying to jump up, felt himself held down by a man standing over him. Stretching out his hands, he would have wrestled with his enemy; when Banzayemon, leaping back, kicked over the night-lamp, and throwing open the shutters, dashed into the garden. Snatching up his sword, Sanza rushed out after him; and his wife, having lit a lantern and armed herself with a halberd, went out, with her son Kosanza, who carried a drawn dirk, to help her husband. Then Banzayemon, who was hiding in the shadow of a large pine-tree, seeing the lantern and dreading detection, seized a stone and hurled it at the light, and, chancing to strike it, put it out, and then scrambling over the fence unseen, fled into the darkness. When Sanza had searched all over the garden in vain, he returned to his room and examined his wound, which proving very slight, he began to look about to see whether the thief had carried off anything; but when his eye fell upon the place where the Muramasa sword had lain, he saw that it was gone. He hunted everywhere, but it was not to be found. The precious blade with which his Prince had entrusted him had been stolen, and the blame would fall heavily upon him. Filled with grief and shame at the loss, Sanza and his wife and child remained in great anxiety until the morning broke, when he reported the matter to one of the Prince's councillors, and waited in seclusion until he should receive his lord's commands.

It soon became known that Banzayemon, who had fled the province, was the thief; and the councillors made their report accordingly to the Prince, who, although he expressed his detestation of the mean action of Banzayemon, could not absolve Sanza from blame, in that he had not taken better precautions to insure the safety of the sword that had been committed to his trust. It was decided, therefore, that Sanza should be dismissed from his service, and that his goods should be confiscated; with the proviso that should he be able to find Banzayemon, and recover the lost Muramasa blade, he should be restored to his former position. Sanza, who from the first had made up his mind that his punishment would be severe, accepted the decree without a murmur; and, having committed his wife and son to the care of his relations, prepared to leave the country as a Ronin and search for Banzayemon.

Before starting, however, he thought that he would go to his brother-officer, Takagi Umanojo, and consult with him as to what course he should pursue to gain his end. But this Umanojo, who was by nature a churlish fellow, answered him unkindly, and said:

"It is true that Banzayemon is a mean thief; but still it was through your carelessness that the sword was lost. It is of no avail your coming to me for help: you must get it back as best you may."

"Ah!" replied Sanza, "I see that you too bear me a grudge because I defeated you in the matter of the judgment of the sword. You are no better than Banzayemon yourself."

And his heart was bitter against his fellow men, and he left the house determined to kill Umanojo first and afterwards to track out Banzayemon; so, pretending to start on his journey, he hid in an inn, and waited for an opportunity to attack Umanojo.

One day Umanojo, who was very fond of fishing, had taken his son Umanosuke, a lad of sixteen, down to the sea-shore with him; and as the two were enjoying themselves, all of a sudden they perceived a Samurai running towards them, and when he drew near they saw that it was Sanza. Umanojo, thinking that Sanza had come back in order to talk over some important matter, left his angling and went to meet him. Then Sanza cried out:

"Now, Sir Umanojo, draw and defend yourself. What! were you in league with Banzayemon to vent your spite upon me? Draw, sir, draw! You have spirited away your accomplice; but, at any rate, you are here yourself, and shall answer for your deed. It is no use playing the innocent; your astonished face shall not save you. Defend yourself, coward and traitor!" and with these words Sanza flourished his naked sword.

"Nay, Sir Sanza," replied the other, anxious by a soft answer to turn away his wrath; "I am innocent of this deed. Waste not your valour on so poor a cause."

"Lying knave!" said Sanza; "think not that you can impose upon me. I know your treacherous heart;" and, rushing upon Umanojo, he cut him on the forehead so that he fell in agony upon the sand.

Umanosuke in the meanwhile, who had been fishing at some distance from his father, rushed up when he saw him in this perilous situation and threw a stone at Sanza, hoping to distract his attention; but, before he could reach the spot, Sanza had delivered the death-blow, and Umanojo lay a corpse upon the beach.

"Stop, Sir Sanza – murderer of my father!" cried Umanosuke, drawing his sword, "stop and do battle with me, that I may avenge his death."

"That you should wish to slay your father's enemy," replied Sanza, "is but right and proper; and although I had just cause of quarrel with your father, and killed him, as a Samurai should, yet would I gladly forfeit my life to you here; but my life is precious to me for one purpose – that I may punish Banzayemon and get back the stolen sword. When I shall have restored that sword to my lord, then will I give you your revenge, and you may kill me. A soldier's word is truth; but, as a pledge that I will fulfil my promise, I will give to you, as hostages, my wife and boy. Stay your avenging hand, I pray you, until my desire shall have been attained."

Umanosuke, who was a brave and honest youth, as famous in the clan for the goodness of his heart as for his skill in the use of arms, when he heard Sanza's humble petition, relented, and said:

"I agree to wait, and will take your wife and boy as hostages for your return."

"I humbly thank you," said Sanza. "When I shall have chastised Banzayemon, I will return, and you shall claim your revenge."

So Sanza went his way to Edo to seek for Banzayemon, and Umanosuke mourned over his father's grave.

Now Banzayemon, when he arrived in Edo, found himself friendless and without the means of earning his living, when by accident he heard of the fame of Chobei of Bandzuin, the chief of the Otokodate, to whom he applied for assistance; and having entered the fraternity, supported himself by giving fencing-lessons. He had been plying his trade for some time, and had earned some little reputation, when Sanza reached the city and began his search for him. But the days and months passed away, and, after a year's fruitless seeking, Sanza, who had spent all his money without obtaining a clue to the whereabouts of his enemy, was sorely perplexed, and was driven to live by his wits as a fortune-teller. Work as he would, it was a hard matter for him to gain the price of his daily food, and, in spite of all his pains, his revenge seemed as far off as ever, when he bethought him that the Yoshiwara was one of the most bustling places in the city, and that if he kept watch there, sooner or later he would be sure to fall in with Banzayemon. So be bought a hat of plaited bamboo, that completely covered his face, and lay in wait at the Yoshiwara.

One day Banzayemon and two of Chobei's apprentices Token Gombei and Shirobei, who, from his wild and indocile nature, was surnamed 'the Colt', were amusing themselves and drinking in an upper storey of a tea-house in the Yoshiwara, when Token Gombei, happening to look down upon the street below, saw a Samurai pass by, poorly clad in worn-out old clothes, but whose poverty-stricken appearance contrasted with his proud and haughty bearing.

"Look there!" said Gombei, calling the attention of the others; "look at that Samurai. Dirty and ragged as his coat is, how easy it is to see that he is of noble birth! Let us wardsmen dress ourselves up in never so fine clothes, we could not look as he does."

"Ay," said Shirobei, "I wish we could make friends with him, and ask him up here to drink a cup of wine with us. However, it would not be seemly for us wardsmen to go and invite a person of his condition."

"We can easily get over that difficulty," said Banzayemon. "As I am a Samurai myself, there will be no impropriety in my going and saying a few civil words to him, and bringing him in."

The other two having joyfully accepted the offer, Banzayemon ran downstairs, and went up to the strange Samurai and saluted him, saying:

"I pray you to wait a moment, Sir Samurai. My name is Fuwa Banzayemon at your service. I am a Ronin, as I judge from your appearance that you are yourself. I hope you will not think me rude if I venture to ask you to honour me with your friendship, and to come into this tea-house to drink a cup of wine with me and two of my friends."

The strange Samurai, who was no other than Sanza, looking at the speaker through the interstices of his deep bamboo hat, and recognizing his enemy Banzayemon, gave a start of surprise, and, uncovering his head, said sternly:

"Have you forgotten my face, Banzayemon?"

For a moment Banzayemon was taken aback, but quickly recovering himself, he replied, "Ah! Sir Sanza, you may well be angry with me; but since I stole the Muramasa sword and fled to Edo I have known no peace: I have been haunted by remorse for my crime. I shall not resist your vengeance: do with me as it shall seem best to you; or rather take my life, and let there be an end of this quarrel."

"Nay," answered Sanza, "to kill a man who repents him of his sins is a base and ignoble action. When you stole from me the Muramasa blade which had been confided to my care by my lord, I became a disgraced and ruined man. Give me back that sword, that I may lay it before my lord, and I will spare your life. I seek to slay no man needlessly."

"Sir Sanza, I thank you for your mercy. At this moment I have not the sword by me, but if you will go into yonder tea-house and wait awhile, I will fetch it and deliver it into your hands."

Sanza having consented to this, the two men entered the tea-house, where Banzayemon's two companions were waiting for them. But Banzayemon, ashamed of his own evil deed, still pretended that Sanza was a stranger, and introduced him as such, saying:

"Come Sir Samurai, since we have the honour of your company, let me offer you a wine-cup."

Banzayemon and the two men pressed the wine-cup upon Sanza so often that the fumes gradually got into his head and he fell asleep; the two wardsmen, seeing this, went out for a walk, and Banzayemon, left alone with the sleeping man, began to revolve fresh plots against him in his mind. On a sudden, a thought struck him. Noiselessly seizing Sanza's sword, which he had laid aside on entering the room, he stole softly downstairs with it, and, carrying it into the back yard, pounded and blunted its edge with a stone, and having made it useless as a weapon, he replaced it in its scabbard, and running upstairs again laid it in its place without disturbing Sanza, who, little suspecting treachery, lay sleeping off the effects of the wine. At last, however, he awoke, and, ashamed at having been overcome by drink, he said to Banzayemon:

"Come, Banzayemon, we have dallied too long; give me the Muramasa sword, and let me go."

"Of course," replied the other, sneeringly, "I am longing to give it back to you; but unfortunately, in my poverty, I have been obliged to pawn it for fifty ounces of silver. If you have so much money about you, give it to me and I will return the sword to you."

"Wretch!" cried Sanza, seeing that Banzayemon was trying to fool him, "have I not had enough of your vile tricks? At any rate, if I cannot get back the sword, your head shall be laid before my lord in its place. Come," added he, stamping his foot impatiently, "defend yourself."

"With all my heart. But not here in this tea-house. Let us go to the Mound, and fight it out."

"Agreed! There is no need for us to bring trouble on the landlord. Come to the Mound of the Yoshiwara."

So they went to the Mound, and drawing their swords, began to fight furiously. As the news soon spread abroad through the Yoshiwara that a duel was being fought upon the Mound, the people flocked out to see the sight; and among them came Token Gombei and Shirobei, Banzayemon's companions, who, when they saw that the combatants were their own friend and the strange Samurai, tried to interfere and stop the fight, but, being hindered by the thickness of the crowd, remained as spectators. The two men fought desperately, each driven by fierce rage against the other; but Sanza, who was by far the better fencer of the two, once, twice, and again dealt blows which should have cut Banzayemon down, and yet no blood came forth. Sanza, astonished at this, put forth all his strength, and fought so skilfully, that all the bystanders applauded him, and Banzayemon, though he knew his adversary's sword to be blunted, was so terrified that he stumbled and fell. Sanza, brave soldier that he was, scorned to strike a fallen foe, and bade him rise and fight again. So they engaged again, and Sanza, who from the beginning had had the advantage, slipped and fell in his turn; Banzayemon, forgetting the mercy which had been shown to him, rushed up, with bloodthirsty joy glaring in his eyes, and stabbed Sanza in the side as he lay on the ground. Faint as he was, he could not lift his hand to save himself; and his craven foe was about to strike him again, when the bystanders all cried shame upon his baseness. Then Gombei and Shirobei lifted up their voices and said:

"Hold, coward! Have you forgotten how your own life was spared but a moment since? Beast of a Samurai, we have been your friends hitherto, but now behold in us the avengers of this brave man."

With these words the two men drew their dirks, and the spectators fell back as they rushed in upon Banzayemon, who, terror-stricken by their fierce looks and words, fled without having dealt the death-blow to Sanza. They tried to pursue him, but he made good his escape, so the two men returned to help the wounded man. When he came to himself by dint of their kind treatment, they spoke to him and comforted him, and asked him what province he came from, that they might write to his friends and tell them what had befallen him. Sanza, in a voice faint from pain and loss of blood, told them his name and the story of the stolen sword, and of his enmity against Banzayemon. "But," said he, "just now, when I was fighting, I struck Banzayemon more than once, and without effect. How could that have been?" Then they looked at his sword, which had fallen by his side, and saw that the edge was all broken away. More than ever they felt indignant at the baseness of Banzayemon's heart, and redoubled their kindness to Sanza; but, in. spite of all their efforts, he grew weaker and weaker, until at last his breathing ceased altogether. So they buried the corpse honourably in an adjoining temple, and wrote to Sanza's wife and son, describing to them the manner of his death.

Now when Sanza's wife, who had long been anxiously expecting her husband's return, opened the letter and learned the cruel circumstances of his death, she and her son Kosanza mourned bitterly over his loss. Then Kosanza, who was now fourteen years old, said to his mother:

"Take comfort, mother; for I will go to Edo and seek out this Banzayemon, my father's murderer, and I will surely avenge his death. Now, therefore, make ready all that I need for this journey."

And as they were consulting over the manner of their revenge, Umanosuke, the son of Umanojo, whom Sanza had slain, having heard of the death of his father's enemy, came to the house. But he came with no hostile intent. True, Sanza had killed his father, but the widow and the orphan were guiltless, and he bore them no ill-will; on the contrary, he felt that Banzayemon was their common enemy. It was he who by his evil deeds had been the cause of all the mischief that had arisen, and now again, by murdering Sanza, he had robbed Umanosuke of his revenge. In this spirit he said to Kosanza:

"Sir Kosanza, I hear that your father has been cruelly murdered by Banzayemon at Edo. I know that you will avenge the death of your father, as the son of a soldier should: if, therefore, you will accept my poor services, I will be your second, and will help you to the best of my ability. Banzayemon shall be my enemy, as he is yours."

"Nay, Sir Umanosuke, although I thank you from my heart, I cannot accept this favour at your hands. My father Sanza slew your noble father: that you should requite this misfortune thus is more than kind, but I cannot think of suffering you to risk your life on my behalf."

"Listen to me," replied Umanosuke, smiling, "and you will think it less strange that I should offer to help you. Last year, when my father lay a bleeding corpse on the sea-shore, your father made a covenant with me that he would return to give me my revenge, so soon as he should have regained the stolen sword. Banzayemon, by murdering him on the Mound of the Yoshiwara, has thwarted me in this; and now upon whom can I avenge my father's death but upon him whose baseness was indeed its cause? Now, therefore, I am determined to go with you to Edo, and not before the murders of our two fathers shall have been fully atoned for will we return to our own country."

When Kosanza heard this generous speech, he could not conceal his admiration; and the widow, prostrating herself at Umanosuke's feet, shed tears of gratitude.

The two youths, having agreed to stand by one another, made all ready for their journey, and obtained leave from their prince to go in search of the traitor Banzayemon. They reached Edo without meeting with any adventures, and, taking up their abode at a cheap inn, began to make their inquiries; but, although they sought far and wide, they could learn no tidings of their enemy. When three months had passed thus, Kosanza began to grow faint-hearted at their repeated failures; but Umanosuke supported and comforted him, urging him to fresh efforts. But soon a great misfortune befell them: Kosanza fell sick with ophthalmia, and neither the tender nursing of his friend, nor the drugs and doctors upon whom Umanosuke spent all their money, had any effect on the suffering boy, who soon became stone blind. Friendless and penniless, the one deprived of his eyesight and only a clog upon the other, the two youths were thrown upon their own resources. Then Umanosuke, reduced to the last extremity of distress, was forced to lead out Kosanza to Asakusa to beg sitting by the roadside, whilst he himself, wandering hither and thither, picked up what he could from the charity of those who saw his wretched plight. But all this while he never lost sight of his revenge, and almost thanked the chance which had made him a beggar, for the opportunity which it gave him of hunting out strange and hidden haunts of vagabond life into which in his more prosperous condition he could not have penetrated. So he walked to and fro through the city, leaning on a stout staff, in which he had hidden his sword, waiting patiently for fortune to bring him face to face with Banzayemon.

Now Banzayemon, after he had killed Sanza on the Mound of the Yoshiwara, did not dare to show his face again in the house of Chobei, the Father of the Otokodate; for he knew that the two men, Token Gombei and Shirobei "the loose Colt," would not only bear an evil report of him, but would even kill him if he fell into their hands, so great had been their indignation at his cowardly Conduct; so he entered a company of mountebanks, and earned his living by showing tricks of swordsmanship, and selling tooth-powder at the Okuyama, at Asakusa. One day, as he was going towards Asakusa to ply his trade, he caught sight of a blind beggar, in whom, in spite of his poverty-stricken and altered appearance, he recognized the son of his enemy. Rightly he judged that, in spite of the boy's apparently helpless condition, the discovery boded no weal for him; so mounting to the upper storey of a tea-house hard by, he watched to see who should come to Kosanza's assistance. Nor had he to wait long, for presently he saw a second beggar come up and speak words of encouragement and kindness to the blind youth; and looking attentively, he saw that the new-comer was Umanosuke. Having thus discovered who was on his track, he went home and sought means of killing the two beggars; so he lay in wait and traced them to the poor hut where they dwelt, and one night, when he knew Umanosuke to be absent, he crept in. Kosanza, being blind, thought that the footsteps were those of Umanosuke, and jumped up to welcome him; but he, in his heartless cruelty, which not even the boy's piteous state could move, slew Kosanza as he helplessly stretched out his hands to feel for his friend. The deed was yet unfinished when Umanosuke returned, and, hearing a scuffle inside the hut, drew the sword which was hidden in his staff and rushed in; but Banzayemon, profiting by the darkness, eluded him and fled from the hut. Umanosuke followed swiftly after him; but just as he was on the point of catching him, Banzayemon, making a sweep backwards with his drawn sword, wounded Umanosuke in the thigh, so that he stumbled and fell, and the murderer, swift of foot, made good his escape. The wounded youth tried to pursue him again, but being compelled by the pain of his wound to desist, returned home and found his blind companion lying dead, weltering in his own blood. Cursing his unhappy fate, he called in the beggars of the fraternity to which he belonged, and between them they buried Kosanza, and he himself being too poor to procure a surgeon's aid, or to buy healing medicaments for his wound, became a cripple.

It was at this time that Shirai Gompachi (see 'The Loves of Gompachi and Komurasaki' on page 123), who was living under the protection of Chobei, the Father of the Otokodate, was in love with Komurasaki, the beautiful courtesan who lived at the sign of the Three Sea-shores, in the Yoshiwara. He had long exhausted the scanty supplies which he possessed, and was now in the habit of feeding his purse by murder and robbery, that he might have means to pursue his wild and extravagant life. One night, when he was out on his cutthroat business, his fellows, who had long suspected that he was after no good, sent one of their number, named Seibei, to watch him. Gompachi, little dreaming that anyone was following him, swaggered along the street until he fell in with a wardsman, whom he cut down and robbed; but the booty proving small, he waited for a second chance, and, seeing a light moving in the distance, hid himself in the shadow of a large tub for catching rain-water till the bearer of the lantern should come up. When the man drew near, Gompachi saw that he was dressed as a traveller, and wore a long dirk; so he sprung out from his lurking-place and made to kill him; but the traveller nimbly jumped on one side, and proved no mean adversary, for he drew his dirk and fought stoutly for his life. However, he was no match for so skilful a swordsman as Gompachi, who, after a sharp struggle, dispatched him, and carried off his purse, which contained two hundred riyos. Overjoyed at having found so rich a prize, Gompachi was making off for the Yoshiwara, when Seibei, who, horror-stricken, had seen both murders, came up and began to upbraid him for his wickedness. But Gompachi was so smooth-spoken and so well liked by his comrades, that he easily persuaded Seibei to hush the matter up, and accompany him to the Yoshiwara for a little diversion. As they were talking by the way, Seibei said to Gompachi:

"I bought a new dirk the other day, but I have not had an opportunity to try it yet. You have had so much experience in swords that you ought to be a good judge. Pray look at this dirk, and tell me whether you think it good for anything."

"We'll soon see what sort of metal it is made of," answered Gompachi. "We'll just try it on the first beggar we come across."

At first Seibei was horrified by this cruel proposal, but by degrees he yielded to his companion's persuasions; and so they went on their way until Seibei spied out a crippled beggar lying asleep on the bank outside the Yoshiwara. The sound of their footsteps aroused the beggar, who seeing a Samurai and a wardsman pointing at him, and evidently speaking about him, thought that their consultation could bode him no good. So he pretended to be still asleep, watching them carefully all the while; and when Seibei went up to him, brandishing his dirk, the beggar, avoiding the blow, seized Seibei's arm, and twisting it round, flung him into the ditch below. Gompachi, seeing his companion's discomfiture, attacked the beggar, who, drawing a sword from his staff, made such lightning-swift passes that, crippled though he was, and unable to move his legs freely, Gompachi could not overpower him; and although Seibei crawled out of the ditch and came to his assistance, the beggar, nothing daunted, dealt his blows about him to such good purpose that he wounded Seibei in the temple and arm. Then Gompachi, reflecting that after all he had no quarrel with the beggar, and that he had better attend to Seibei's wounds than go on fighting to no purpose, drew Seibei away, leaving the beggar, who was too lame to follow them, in peace. When he examined Seibei's wounds, he found that they were so severe that they must give up their night's frolic and go home. So they went back to the house of Chobei, the Father of the Otokodate, and Seibei, afraid to show himself with his sword-cuts, feigned sickness, and went to bed. On the following morning Chobei, happening to need his apprentice Seibei's services, sent for him, and was told that he was sick; so he went to the room, where he lay abed, and, to his astonishment, saw the cut upon his temple. At first the wounded man refused to answer any questions as to how he had been hurt; but at last, on being pressed by Chobei, he told the whole story of what had taken place the night before. When Chobei heard the tale, be guessed that the valiant beggar must be some noble Samurai in disguise, who, having a wrong to avenge, was biding his time to meet with his enemy; and wishing to help so brave a man, he went in the evening, with his two faithful apprentices, Token Gombei and Shirobei "the loose Colt," to the bank outside the Yoshiwara to seek out the beggar. The latter, not one whit frightened by the adventure of the previous night, had taken his place as usual, and was lying on the bank, when Chobei came up to him, and said:

"Sir, I am Chobei, the chief of the Otokodate, at your service. I have learnt with deep regret that two of my men insulted and attacked you last night. However, happily, even Gompachi, famous swordsman though he be, was no match for you, and had to beat a retreat before you. I know, therefore, that you must be a noble Samurai, who by some ill chance have become a cripple and a beggar. Now, therefore, I pray you tell me all your story; for, humble wardsman as I am, I may be able to assist you, if you will condescend to allow me."

The cripple at first tried to shun Chobei's questions; but at last, touched by the honesty and kindness of his speech, he replied:

"Sir, my name is Takagi Umanosuke, and I am a native of Yamato;" and then he went on to narrate all the misfortunes which the wickedness of Banzayemon had brought about.

"This is indeed a strange story," said Chobei who had listened with indignation. "This Banzayemon, before I knew the blackness of his heart, was once under my protection. But after he murdered Sanza, hard by here, he was pursued by these two apprentices of mine, and since that day he has been no more to my house."

When he had introduced the two apprentices to Umanosuke, Chobei pulled forth a suit of silk clothes befitting a gentleman, and having made the crippled youth lay aside his beggar's raiment, led him to a bath, and had his hair dressed. Then he bade Token Gombei lodge him and take charge of him, and, having sent for a famous physician, caused Umanosuke to undergo careful treatment for the wound in his thigh. In the course of two months the pain had almost disappeared, so that he could stand easily; and when, after another month, he could walk about a little, Chobei removed him to his own house, pretending to his wife and apprentices that he was one of his own relations who had come on a visit to him.

After a while, when Umanosuke had become quite cured, he went one day to worship at a famous temple, and on his way home after dark he was overtaken by a shower of rain, and took shelter under the eaves of a house, in a part of the city called Yanagiwara, waiting for the sky to clear. Now it happened that this same night Gompachi had gone out on one of his bloody expeditions, to which his poverty and his love for Komurasaki drove him in spite of himself, and, seeing a Samurai standing in the gloom, he sprang upon him before he had recognized Umanosuke, whom he knew as a friend of his patron Chobei. Umanosuke drew and defended himself, and soon contrived to slash Gompachi on the forehead; so that the latter, seeing himself overmatched, fled under the cover of the night. Umanosuke, fearing to hurt his recently healed wound, did not give chase, and went quietly back to Chobei's house. When Gompachi returned home, he hatched a story to deceive Chobei as to the cause of the wound on his forehead. Chobei, however, having overheard Umanosuke reproving Gompachi for his wickedness, soon became aware of the truth; and not caring to keep a robber and murderer near him, gave Gompachi a present of money, and bade him return to his house no more.

And now Chobei, seeing that Umanosuke had recovered his strength, divided his apprentices into bands, to hunt out Banzayemon, in order that the vendetta might be accomplished. It soon was reported to him that Banzayemon was earning his living among the mountebanks of Asakusa; so Chobei communicated this intelligence to Umanosuke, who made his preparations accordingly; and on the following morning the two went to Asakusa, where Banzayemon was astonishing a crowd of country boors by exhibiting tricks with his sword.

Then Umanosuke, striding through the gaping rabble, shouted out:

"False, murderous coward, your day has come! I, Umanosuke, the son of Umanojo, have come to demand vengeance for the death of three innocent men who have perished by your treachery. If you are a man, defend yourself. This day shall your soul see hell!"

With these words he rushed furiously upon Banzayemon, who, seeing escape to be impossible, stood upon his guard. But his coward's heart quailed before the avenger, and he soon lay bleeding at his enemy's feet.

But who shall say how Umanosuke thanked Chobei for his assistance; or how, when he had returned to his own country, he treasured up his gratitude in his heart, looking upon Chobei as more than a second father?

Thus did Chobei use his power to punish the wicked, and to reward the good – giving of his abundance to the poor, and succouring the unfortunate, so that his name was honoured far and near. It remains only to record the tragical manner of his death.

We have already told how my lord Midzuno Jiurozayemon, the chief of the associated nobles, had been foiled in his attempts to bring shame upon Chobei, the Father of the Otokodate; and how, on the contrary, the latter, by his ready wit, never failed to make the proud noble's weapons recoil upon him. The failure of these attempts rankled in the breast of Jiurozayemon, who hated Chobei with an intense hatred, and sought to be revenged upon him. One day he sent a retainer to Chobei's house with a message to the effect that on the following day my lord Jiurozayemon would be glad to see Chobei at his house, and to offer him a cup of wine, in return for the cold macaroni with which his lordship had been feasted some time since. Chobei immediately suspected that in sending this friendly summons the cunning noble was hiding a dagger in a smile; however, he knew that if he stayed away out of fear he would be branded as a coward, and made a laughing-stock for fools to jeer at. Not caring that Jiurozayemon should succeed in his desire to put him to shame, he sent for his favourite apprentice, Token Gombei, and said to him:

"I have been invited to a drinking-bout by Midzuno Jiurozayemon. I know full well that this is but a stratagem to requite me for having fooled him, and maybe his hatred will go the length of killing me. However, I shall go and take my chance; and if I detect any sign of foul play, I'll try to serve the world by ridding it of a tyrant, who passes his life in oppressing the helpless farmers and wardsmen. Now as, even if I succeed in killing him in his own house, my life must pay forfeit for the deed, do you come tomorrow night with a burying-tub, and fetch my corpse from this Jiurozayemon's house."

Token Gombei, when he heard the "Father" speak thus, was horrified, and tried to dissuade him from obeying the invitation. But Chobei's mind was fixed, and, without heeding Gombei's remonstrances, he proceeded to give instructions as to the disposal of his property after his death, and to settle all his earthly affairs.

On the following day, towards noon, he made ready to go to Jiurozayemon's house, bidding one of his apprentices precede him with a complimentary present. Jiurozayemon, who was waiting with impatience for Chobei to come, so soon as he heard of his arrival ordered his retainers to usher him into his presence; and Chobei, having bade his apprentices without fail to come and fetch him that night, went into the house.

No sooner had he reached the room next to that in which Jiurozayemon was sitting than he saw that his suspicions of treachery were well founded; for two men with drawn swords rushed upon him, and tried to cut him down. Deftly avoiding their blows, however, he tripped up the one, and kicking the other in the ribs, sent him reeling and breathless against the wall; then, as calmly as if nothing had happened he presented himself before Jiurozayemon, who, peeping through a chink in the sliding-doors, had watched his retainers' failure.

"Welcome, welcome, Master Chobei," said he. "I always had heard that you were a man of mettle, and I wanted to see what stuff you were made of; so I bade my retainers put your courage to the test. That was a masterly throw of yours. Well, you must excuse this churlish reception: come and sit down by me."

"Pray do not mention it, my lord," said Chobei, smiling rather scornfully. "I know that my poor skill is not to be measured with that of a noble Samurai; and if these two good gentlemen had the worst of it just now, it was mere luck – that's all."

So, after the usual compliments had been exchanged, Chobei sat down by Jiurozayemon, and the attendants brought in wine and condiments. Before they began to drink, however, Jiurozayemon said:

"You must be tired and exhausted with your walk this hot day, Master Chobei. I thought that perhaps a bath might refresh you, so I ordered my men to get it ready for you. Would you not like to bathe and make yourself comfortable?"

Chobei suspected that this was a trick to strip him, and take him unawares when he should have laid aside his dirk. However, he answered cheerfully:

"Your lordship is very good. I shall be glad to avail myself of your kind offer. Pray excuse me for a few moments."

So he went to the bath-room, and, leaving his clothes outside, he got into the bath, with the full conviction that it would be the place of his death. Yet he never trembled nor quailed, determined that, if he needs must die, no man should say he had been a coward. Then Jiurozayemon, calling to his attendants, said:

"Quick! lock the door of the bath-room! We hold him fast now. If he gets out, more than one life will pay the price of his. He's a match for any six of you in fair fight. Lock the door, I say, and light up the fire under the bath; and we'll boil him to death, and be rid of him. Quick, men, quick!"

So they locked the door, and fed the fire until the water hissed and bubbled within; and Chobei, in his agony, tried to burst open the door, but Jiurozayemon ordered his men to thrust their spears through the partition wall and dispatch him. Two of the spears Chobei clutched and broke short off; but at last he was struck by a mortal blow under the ribs, and died a brave man by the hands of cowards.

That evening Token Gombei, who, to the astonishment of Chobei's wife, had bought a burying-tub, came, with seven other apprentices, to fetch the Father of the Otokodate from Jiurozayemon's house; and when the retainers saw them, they mocked at them, and said:

"What, have you come to fetch your drunken master home in a litter?"

"Nay," answered Gombei, "but we have brought a coffin for his dead body, as he bade us."

When the retainers heard this, they marvelled at the courage of Chobei, who had thus wittingly come to meet his fate. So Chobei's corpse was placed in the burying-tub, and handed over to his apprentices, who swore to avenge his death. Far and wide, the poor and friendless mourned for this good man. His son Chomatsu inherited his property; and his wife remained a faithful widow until her dying day, praying that she might sit with him in paradise upon the cup of the same lotus-flower.

Many a time did the apprentices of Chobei meet together to avenge him; but Jiurozayemon eluded all their efforts, until, having been imprisoned by the Government in the temple called Kanyeiji, at Uyeno, as is related in the story of "Kazuma's Revenge," he was placed beyond the reach of their hatred.

So lived and so died Chobei of Bandzuin, the Father of the Otokodate of Edo.

The Wonderful Adventures of Funakoshi Jiuyemon

IN THE OLDEN TIME, in the island of Shikoku there lived one Funakoshi Jiuyemon, a brave Samurai and accomplished man, who was in great favour with the prince, his master. One day, at a drinking-bout, a quarrel sprung up between him and a brother-officer, which resulted in a duel upon the spot, in which Jiuyemon killed his adversary. When Jiuyemon awoke to a sense of what he had done, he was struck with remorse, and he thought to disembowel himself; but, receiving a private summons from his lord, he went to the castle, and the prince said to him:

"So it seems that you have been getting drunk and quarrelling, and that you have killed one of your friends; and now I suppose you will have determined to perform *hara-kiri*. It is a great pity, and in the face of the laws I can do nothing for you openly. Still, if you will escape and fly from this part of the country for a while, in two years' time the affair will have blown over, and I will allow you to return."

And with these words the prince presented him with a fine sword, made by Sukesada, and a hundred ounces of silver, and, having bade him farewell, entered his private apartments; and Jiuyemon, prostrating himself, wept tears of gratitude; then, taking the sword and the money, he went home and prepared to fly from the province, and secretly took leave of his relations, each of whom made him some parting present. These gifts, together with his own money, and what he had received from the prince, made up a sum of two hundred and fifty ounces of silver, with which and his Sukesada sword he escaped under cover of darkness, and went to a sea-port called Marugame, in the province of Sanuki, where he proposed to wait for an opportunity of setting sail for Osaka. As ill luck would have it, the wind being contrary, he had to remain three days idle; but at last the wind changed; so he went down to the beach, thinking that he should certainly find a junk about to sail; and as he was looking about him, a sailor came up, and said:

"If your honour is minded to take a trip to Osaka, my ship is bound thither, and I should be glad to take you with me as passenger."

"That's exactly what I wanted. I will gladly take a passage," replied Jiuyemon, who was delighted at the chance.

"Well, then, we must set sail at once, so please come on board without delay."

So Jiuyemon went with him and embarked; and as they left the harbour and struck into the open sea, the moon was just rising above the eastern hills, illumining the dark night like a noonday sun; and Jiuyemon, taking his place in the bows of the ship, stood wrapt in contemplation of the beauty of the scene.

Now it happened that the captain of the ship, whose name was Akagoshi Kuroyemon, was a fierce pirate who, attracted by Jiuyemon's well-to-do appearance, had determined to decoy him on board, that he might murder and rob him; and while Jiuyemon was looking at the moon, the pirate and his companions were collected in the stern of the ship, taking counsel together in whispers as to how they might slay him. He, on the other hand, having for some time past fancied their conduct somewhat strange, bethought him that it was not prudent to lay aside his sword, so he went towards the place where he had been sitting, and had left his weapon lying, to fetch it, when he was stopped by three of the pirates, who blocked up the gangway, saying:

"Stop, Sir Samurai! Unluckily for you, this ship in which you have taken a passage belongs to the pirate Akagoshi Kuroyemon. Come, sir! whatever money you may chance to have about you is our prize."

When Jiuyemon heard this he was greatly startled at first, but soon recovered himself, and being an expert wrestler, kicked over two of the pirates, and made for his sword; but in the meanwhile Shichirohei, the younger brother of the pirate captain, had drawn the sword, and brought it towards him, saying:

"If you want your sword, here it is!" and with that he cut at him; but Jiuyemon avoided the blow, and closing with the ruffian, got back his sword. Ten of the pirates then attacked him with spear and sword; but he, putting his back against the bows of the ship, showed such good fight that he killed three of his assailants, and the others stood off, not daring to approach him. Then the pirate captain, Akagoshi Kuroyemon, who had been watching the fighting from the stern, seeing that his men stood no chance against Jiuyemon's dexterity, and that he was only losing them to no purpose, thought to shoot him with a matchlock. Even Jiuyemon, brave as he was, lost heart when he saw the captain's gun pointed at him, and tried to jump into the sea; but one of the pirates made a dash at him with a boat-hook, and caught him by the sleeve; then Jiuyemon, in despair, took the fine Sukesada sword which he had received from his prince, and throwing it at his captor, pierced him through the breast so that he fell dead, and himself plunging into the sea swam for his life. The pirate captain shot at him and missed him, and the rest of the crew made every endeavour to seize him with their boat-hooks, that they might avenge the death of their mates; but it was all in vain, and Jiuyemon, having shaken off his clothes that he might swim the better, made good his escape. So the pirates threw the bodies of their dead comrades into the sea, and the captain was partly consoled for their loss by the possession of the Sukesada sword with which one of them had been transfixed.

As soon as Jiuyemon jumped over the ship's side, being a good swimmer, he took a long dive, which carried him well out of danger, and struck out vigorously; and although he was tired and distressed by his exertions, he braced himself up to greater energy, and faced the waves boldly. At last, in the far distance, to his great joy, he spied a light, for which he made, and found that it was a ship carrying lanterns marked with the badge of the governor of Osaka; so he hailed her, saying:

"I have fallen into great trouble among pirates: pray rescue me."

"Who and what are you?" shouted an officer, some forty years of age.

"My name is Funakoshi Jiuyemon, and I have unwittingly fallen in with pirates this night. I have escaped so far: I pray you save me, lest I die."

"Hold on to this, and come up," replied the other, holding out the butt end of a spear to him, which he caught hold of and clambered up the ship's side. When the officer saw before him a handsome gentleman, naked all but his loincloth, and with his hair all in disorder, he called to his servants to bring some of his own clothes, and, having dressed him in them, said:

"What clan do you belong to, sir?"

"Sir, I am a Ronin, and was on my way to Osaka; but the sailors of the ship on which I had embarked were pirates;" and so he told the whole story of the fight and of his escape.

"Well done, sir!" replied the other, astonished at his prowess. "My name is Kajiki Tozayemon, at your service. I am an officer attached to the governor of Osaka. Pray, have you any friends in that city?"

"No, sir, I have no friends there; but as in two years I shall be able to return to my own country, and re-enter my lord's service, I thought during that time to engage in trade and live as a common wardsman."

"Indeed, that's a poor prospect! However, if you will allow me, I will do all that is in my power to assist you. Pray excuse the liberty I am taking in making such a proposal."

Jiuyemon warmly thanked Kajiki Tozayemon for his kindness; and so they reached Osaka without further adventures.

Jiuyemon, who had secreted in his girdle the two hundred and fifty ounces which he had brought with him from home, bought a small house, and started in trade as a vendor of perfumes, tooth-powder, combs, and other toilet articles; and Kajiki Tozayemon, who treated him with great kindness, and rendered him many services, prompted him, as he was a single man, to take to himself a wife. Acting upon this advice, he married a singing-girl, called O Hiyaku.

Now this O Hiyaku, although at first she seemed very affectionately disposed towards Jiuyemon, had been, during the time that she was a singer, a woman of bad and profligate character; and at this time there was in Osaka a certain wrestler, named Takasegawa Kurobei, a very handsome man, with whom O Hiyaku fell desperately in love; so that at last, being by nature a passionate woman, she became unfaithful to Jiuyemon. The latter, little suspecting that anything was amiss, was in the habit of spending his evenings at the house of his patron Kajiki Tozayemon, whose son, a youth of eighteen, named Tonoshin, conceived a great friendship for Jiuyemon, and used constantly to invite him to play a game at checkers; and it was on these occasions that O Hiyaku, profiting by her husband's absence, used to arrange her meetings with the wrestler Takasegawa.

One evening, when Jiuyemon, as was his wont, had gone out to play at checkers with Kajiki Tonoshin, O Hiyaku took advantage of the occasion to go and fetch the wrestler, and invite him to a little feast; and as they were enjoying themselves over their wine, O Hiyaku said to him:

"Ah! Master Takasegawa, how wonderfully chance favours us! and how pleasant these stolen interviews are! How much nicer still it would be if we could only be married. But, as long as Jiuyemon is in the way, it is impossible; and that is my one cause of distress."

"It's no use being in such a hurry. If you only have patience, we shall be able to marry, sure enough. What you have got to look out for now is, that Jiuyemon does not find out what we are about. I suppose there is no chance of his coming home tonight, is there?"

"Oh dear, no! You need not be afraid. He is gone to Kajiki's house to play checkers; so he is sure to spend the night there."

And so the guilty couple went on gossiping, with their minds at ease, until at last they dropped off asleep.

In the meanwhile Jiuyemon, in the middle of his game at checkers, was seized with a sudden pain in his stomach, and said to Kajiki Tonoshin, "Young sir, I feel an unaccountable pain in my stomach. I think I had better go home, before it gets worse."

"That is a bad job. Wait a little, and I will give you some physic; but, at any rate, you had better spend the night here."

"Many thanks for your kindness," replied Jiuyemon; "but I had rather go home."

So he took his leave, and went off to his own house, bearing the pain as best he might. When he arrived in front of his own door, he tried to open it; but the lock was fastened, and he could not get in, so he rapped violently at the shutters to try and awaken his wife. When O Hiyaku heard the noise, she woke with a start, and roused the wrestler, saying to him in a whisper:

"Get up! get up! Jiuyemon has come back. You must hide as fast as possible."

"Oh dear! oh dear!" said the wrestler, in a great fright; "here's a pretty mess! Where on earth shall I hide myself?" and he stumbled about in every direction looking for a hiding-place, but found none.

Jiuyemon, seeing that his wife did not come to open the door, got impatient at last, and forced it open by unfixing the sliding shutter and, entering the house, found himself face to face with his wife and her lover, who were both in such confusion that they did not know what to do. Jiuyemon, however, took no notice of them, but lit his pipe and sat smoking and watching them in silence. At last the wrestler, Takasegawa, broke the silence by saying:

"I thought, sir, that I should be sure to have the pleasure of finding you at home this evening, so I came out to call upon you. When I got here, the Lady O Hiyaku was so kind as to offer me some wine; and I drank a little more than was good for me, so that it got into my head, and I fell asleep. I must really apologize for having taken such a liberty in your absence; but, indeed, although appearances are against us, there has been nothing wrong."

"Certainly," said O Hiyaku, coming to her lover's support, "Master Takasegawa is not at all to blame. It was I who invited him to drink wine; so I hope you will excuse him."

Jiuyemon sat pondering the matter over in his mind for a moment, and then said to the wrestler, "You say that you are innocent; but, of course, that is a lie. It's no use trying to conceal your fault. However, next year I shall, in all probability, return to my own country, and then you may take O Hiyaku and do what you will with her: far be it from me to care what becomes of a woman with such a stinking heart."

When the wrestler and O Hiyaku heard Jiuyemon say this quite quietly, they could not speak, but held their peace for very shame.

"Here, you Takasegawa," pursued he; "you may stop here tonight, if you like it, and go home tomorrow."

"Thank you, sir," replied the wrestler, "I am much obliged to you; but the fact is, that I have some pressing business in another part of the town, so, with your permission, I will take my leave;" and so he went out, covered with confusion.

As for the faithless wife, O Hiyaku, she was in great agitation, expecting to be severely reprimanded at least; but Jiuyemon took no notice of her, and showed no anger; only from that day forth, although she remained in his house as his wife, he separated himself from her entirely.

Matters went on in this way for some time, until at last, one fine day, O Hiyaku, looking out of doors, saw the wrestler Takasegawa passing in the street, so she called out to him:

"Dear me, Master Takasegawa, can that be you! What a long time it is since we have met! Pray come in, and have a chat."

"Thank you, I am much obliged to you; but as I do not like the sort of scene we had the other day, I think I had rather not accept your invitation."

"Pray do not talk in such a cowardly manner. Next year, when Jiuyemon goes back to his own country, he is sure to give me this house, and then you and I can marry and live as happily as possible."

"I don't like being in too great a hurry to accept fair offers."

"Nonsense! There's no need for showing such delicacy about accepting what is given you."

And as she spoke, she caught the wrestler by the hand and led him into the house. After they had talked together for some time, she said:

"Listen to me, Master Takasegawa. I have been thinking over all this for some time, and I see no help for it but to kill Jiuyemon and make an end of him."

"What do you want to do that for?"

"As long as he is alive, we cannot be married. What I propose is that you should buy some poison, and I will put it secretly into his food. When he is dead, we can be happy to our hearts' content."

At first Takasegawa was startled and bewildered by the audacity of their scheme; but forgetting the gratitude which he owed to Jiuyemon for sparing his life on the previous occasion, he replied:

"Well, I think it can be managed. I have a friend who is a physician, so I will get him to compound some poison for me, and will send it to you. You must look out for a moment when your husband is not on his guard, and get him to take it."

Having agreed upon this, Takasegawa went away, and, having employed a physician to make up the poison, sent it to O Hiyaku in a letter, suggesting that the poison should be mixed up with a sort of macaroni, of which Jiuyemon was very fond. Having read the letter, she put it carefully away in a drawer of her cupboard, and waited until Jiuyemon should express a wish to eat some macaroni.

One day, towards the time of the New Year, when O Hiyaku had gone out to a party with a few of her friends, it happened that Jiuyemon, being alone in the house, was in want of some little thing, and, failing to find it anywhere, at last bethought himself to look for it in O Hiyaku's cupboard; and as he was searching amongst the odds and ends which it contained, he came upon the fatal letter. When he read the scheme for putting poison in his macaroni, he was taken aback, and said to himself, "When I caught those two beasts in their wickedness I spared them, because their blood would have defiled my sword; and now they are not even grateful for my mercy. Their crime is beyond all power of language to express, and I will kill them together."

So he put back the letter in its place, and waited for his wife to come home. So soon as she made her appearance he said:

"You have come home early, O Hiyaku. I feel very dull and lonely this evening; let us have a little wine."

And as he spoke without any semblance of anger, it never entered O Hiyaku's mind that he had seen the letter; so she went about her household duties with a quiet mind.

The following evening, as Jiuyemon was sitting in his shop casting up his accounts, with his counting-board in his hand, Takasegawa passed by, and Jiuyemon called out to him, saying:

"Well met, Takasegawa! I was just thinking of drinking a cup of wine tonight; but I have no one to keep me company, and it is dull work drinking alone. Pray come in, and drink a bout with me."

"Thank you, sir, I shall have much pleasure," replied the wrestler, who little expected what the other was aiming at; and so he went in, and they began to drink and feast.

"It's very cold tonight," said Jiuyemon, after a while; "suppose we warm up a little macaroni, and eat it nice and hot. Perhaps, however, you do not like it?"

"Indeed, I am very fond of it, on the contrary."

"That is well. O Hiyaku, please go and buy a little for us."

"Directly," replied his wife, who hurried off to buy the paste, delighted at the opportunity for carrying out her murderous design upon her husband. As soon she had prepared it, she poured it into bowls and set it before the two men; but into her husband's bowl only she put poison. Jiuyemon, who well knew what she had done, did not eat the mess at once, but remained talking about this, that, and the other; and the wrestler, out of politeness, was obliged to wait also. All of a sudden, Jiuyemon cried out:

"Dear me! whilst we have been gossiping, the macaroni has been getting cold. Let us put it all together and warm it up again. As no one has put his lips to his bowl yet, it will all be clean; so none need be wasted." And with these words he took the macaroni that was in the three bowls, and, pouring it altogether into an iron pot, boiled it up again. This time Jiuyemon served out the food himself, and, setting it before his wife and the wrestler, said:

"There! make haste and eat it up before it gets cold."

Jiuyemon, of course, did not eat any of the mess; and the would-be murderers, knowing that sufficient poison had been originally put into Jiuyemon's bowl to kill them all three, and that now the macaroni, having been well mixed up, would all be poisoned, were quite taken aback, and did not know what to do.

"Come! make haste, or it will be quite cold. You said you liked it, so I sent to buy it on purpose. O Hiyaku! come and make a hearty meal. I will eat some presently."

At this the pair looked very foolish, and knew not what to answer; at last the wrestler got up and said:

"I do not feel quite well. I must beg to take my leave; and, if you will allow me, I will come and accept your hospitality tomorrow instead."

"Dear me! I am sorry to hear you are not well. However, O Hiyaku, there will be all the more macaroni for you."

As for O Hiyaku, she put a bold face upon the matter, and replied that she had supped already, and had no appetite for any more.

Then Jiuyemon, looking at them both with a scornful smile, said:

"It seems that you, neither of you, care to eat this macaroni; however, as you, Takasegawa, are unwell, I will give you some excellent medicine;" and going to the cupboard, he drew out the letter, and laid it before the wrestler. When O Hiyaku and the wrestler saw that their wicked schemes had been brought to light, they were struck dumb with shame.

Takasegawa, seeing that denial was useless, drew his dirk and cut at Jiuyemon; but he, being nimble and quick, dived under the wrestler's arm, and seizing his right hand from behind, tightened his grasp upon it until it became numbed, and the dirk fell to the ground; for, powerful man as the wrestler was, he was no match for Jiuyemon, who held him in so fast a grip that he could not move. Then Jiuyemon took the dirk which had fallen to the ground, and said:

"Oh! I thought that you, being a wrestler, would at least be a strong man, and that there would be some pleasure in fighting you; but I see that you are but a poor feckless creature, after all. It would have defiled my sword to have killed such an ungrateful hound with it; but luckily here is your own dirk, and I will slay you with that."

Takasegawa struggled to escape, but in vain; and O Hiyaku, seizing a large kitchen knife, attacked Jiuyemon; but he, furious, kicked her in the loins so violently that she fell powerless, then brandishing the dirk, he cleft the wrestler from the shoulder down to the nipple of his breast, and the big man fell in his agony. O Hiyaku, seeing this, tried to fly; but Jiuyemon, seizing her by the hair of the head, stabbed her in the bosom, and, placing her by her lover's side, gave her the death-blow.

On the following day, he sent in a report of what he had done to the governor of Osaka, and buried the corpses; and from that time forth he remained a single man, and pursued his trade as a seller of perfumery and such-like wares; and his leisure hours he continued to spend as before, at the house of his patron, Kajiki Tozayemon.

One day, when Jiuyemon went to call upon Kajiki Tozayemon, he was told by the servant-maid, who met him at the door, that her master was out, but that her young master, Tonoshin, was at home; so, saying that he would go in and pay his respects to the young gentleman, he entered the house; and as he suddenly pushed open the sliding-door of the room in which Tonoshin was sitting, the latter gave a great start, and his face turned pale and ghastly.

"How now, young sir!" said Jiuyemon, laughing at him, "surely you are not such a coward as to be afraid because the sliding-doors are opened? That is not the way in which a brave Samurai should behave."

"Really I am quite ashamed of myself," replied the other, blushing at the reproof; "but the fact is that I had some reason for being startled. Listen to me, Sir Jiuyemon, and I will tell you all about it. Today, when I went to the academy to study, there were a great number of my fellow-students gathered together, and one of them said that a ruinous old shrine, about two miles and a half to the east of this place, was the nightly resort of all sorts of hobgoblins, who have been playing pranks and bewitching the people for some time past; and he proposed that we should all draw lots, and that the one upon whom the lot fell should go tonight and exorcise those evil beings; and further that, as a proof of his having gone, he should write his name upon a pillar in the shrine. All the rest agreed that this would be very good sport; so I, not liking to appear a coward, consented to take my chance with the rest; and, as ill luck would have it, the lot fell upon me. I was thinking over this as you came in, and so it was that when you suddenly opened the door, I could not help giving a start."

"If you only think for a moment," said Jiuyemon, "you will see that there is nothing to fear. How can beasts and hobgoblins exercise any power over men? However, do not let the matter trouble you. I will go in your place tonight, and see if I cannot get the better of these goblins, if any there be, having done which, I will write your name upon the pillar, so that everybody may think that you have been there."

"Oh! thank you: that will indeed be a service. You can dress yourself up in my clothes, and nobody will be the wiser. I shall be truly grateful to you."

So Jiuyemon having gladly undertaken the job, as soon as the night set in made his preparations, and went to the place indicated – an uncanny-looking, tumble-down, lonely old shrine, all overgrown with moss and rank vegetation. However, Jiuyemon, who was afraid of nothing, cared little for the appearance of the place, and having made himself as comfortable as he could in so dreary a spot, sat down on the floor, lit his pipe, and kept a sharp look-out for the goblins. He had not been waiting long before he saw a movement among the bushes; and presently he was surrounded by a host of elfish-looking creatures, of all shapes and kinds, who came and made hideous faces at him. Jiuyemon quietly knocked the ashes out of his pipe, and then, jumping up, kicked over first one and then another of the elves, until several of them lay sprawling in the grass; and the rest made off, greatly astonished at this unexpected reception. When Jiuyemon took his lantern and examined the fallen goblins attentively, he saw that they were all Tonoshin's fellow-students, who had painted their faces, and made themselves hideous, to frighten their companion, whom they knew to be a coward: all they got for their pains, however, was a good kicking from Jiuyemon, who left them groaning over their sore bones, and went home chuckling to himself at the result of the adventure.

The fame of this exploit soon became noised about Osaka, so that all men praised Jiuyemon's courage; and shortly after this he was elected chief of the Otokodate, or friendly society of the wardsmen, and busied himself no longer with his trade, but lived on the contributions of his numerous apprentices.

Now Kajiki Tonoshin was in love with a singing girl named Kashiku, upon whom he was in the habit of spending a great deal of money. She, however, cared nothing for him, for she had a sweetheart named Hichirobei, whom she used to contrive to meet secretly, although, in order to support her parents, she was forced to become the mistress of Tonoshin. One evening, when the latter was on guard at the office of his chief, the Governor of Osaka, Kashiku sent word privately to Hichirobei, summoning him to go to her house, as the coast would be clear.

While the two were making merry over a little feast, Tonoshin, who had persuaded a friend to take his duty for him on the plea of urgent business, knocked at the door, and Kashiku, in a great fright, hid her lover in a long clothes-box, and went to let in Tonoshin, who, on entering the room and seeing the litter of the supper lying about, looked more closely, and perceived a man's sandals, on which, by the light of a candle, he saw the figure seven. Tonoshin had heard some ugly reports of Kashiku's proceedings with this man Hichirobei, and when he saw this proof before his eyes he grew very angry; but he suppressed his feelings, and, pointing to the wine-cups and bowls, said:

"Whom have you been feasting with tonight?"

"Oh!" replied Kashiku, who, notwithstanding her distress, was obliged to invent an answer, "I felt so dull all alone here, that I asked an old woman from next door to come in and drink a cup of wine with me, and have a chat."

All this while Tonoshin was looking for the hidden lover; but, as he could not see him, he made up his mind that Kashiku must have let him out by the back door; so he secreted one of the sandals in his sleeve as evidence, and, without seeming to suspect anything, said:

"Well, I shall be very busy this evening, so I must go home."

"Oh! won't you stay a little while? It is very dull here, when I am all alone without you. Pray stop and keep me company."

But Tonoshin made no reply, and went home. Then Kashiku saw that one of the sandals was missing, and felt certain that he must have carried it off as proof; so she went in great trouble to open the lid of the box, and let out Hichirobei. When the two lovers talked over the matter, they agreed that, as they both were really in love, let Tonoshin kill them if he would, they would gladly die together: they would enjoy the present; let the future take care of itself.

The following morning Kashiku sent a messenger to Tonoshin to implore his pardon; and he, being infatuated by the girl's charms, forgave her, and sent a present of thirty ounces of silver to her lover, Hichirobei, on the condition that he was never to see her again; but, in spite of this, Kashiku and Hichirobei still continued their secret meetings.

It happened that Hichirobei, who was a gambler by profession, had an elder brother called Chobei, who kept a wine-shop in the Ajikawa Street, at Osaka; so Tonoshin thought that he could not do better than depute Jiuyemon to go and seek out this man Chobei, and urge him to persuade his younger brother to give up his relations with Kashiku; acting upon this resolution, he went to call upon Jiuyemon, and said to him:

"Sir Jiuyemon, I have a favour to ask of you in connection with that girl Kashiku, whom you know all about. You are aware that I paid thirty ounces of silver to her lover Hichirobei to induce him to give up going to her house; but, in spite of this, I cannot help suspecting that they still meet one another. It seems that this Hichirobei has an elder brother – one Chobei; now, if you would go to this man and tell him to reprove his brother for his conduct, you would be doing me a great service. You have so often stood my friend, that I venture to pray you to oblige me in this matter, although I feel that I am putting you to great inconvenience."

Jiuyemon, out of gratitude for the kindness which he had received at the hands of Kajiki Tozayemon, was always willing to serve Tonoshin; so he went at once to find out Chobei, and said to him:

"My name, sir, is Jiuyemon, at your service; and I have come to beg your assistance in a matter of some delicacy."

"What can I do to oblige you, sir?" replied Chobei, who felt bound to be more than usually civil, as his visitor was the chief of the Otokodate.

"It is a small matter, sir," said Jiuyemon. "Your younger brother Hichirobei is intimate with a woman named Kashiku, whom he meets in secret. Now, this Kashiku is the mistress of the son of a gentleman to whom I am under great obligation: he bought her of her parents for a large sum of money, and, besides this, he paid your brother thirty ounces of silver some time since, on condition of his separating himself from the girl; in spite of this, it appears that your brother continues to see her, and I have come to beg that you will remonstrate with your brother on his conduct, and make him give her up."

"That I certainly will. Pray do not be uneasy; I will soon find means to put a stop to my brother's bad behaviour."

And so they went on talking of one thing and another, until Jiuyemon, whose eyes had been wandering about the room, spied out a very long dirk lying on a cupboard, and all at once it occurred to him that this was the very sword which had been a parting gift to him from his lord: the hilt, the mountings, and the tip of the scabbard were all the same, only the blade had been shortened and made into a long dirk. Then he looked more attentively at Chobei's features, and saw that he was no other than Akagoshi Kuroyemon, the pirate chief. Two years had passed by, but he could not forget that face.

Jiuyemon would have liked to have arrested him at once; but thinking that it would be a pity to give so vile a robber a chance of escape, he constrained himself, and, taking his leave, went straightway and reported the matter to the Governor of Osaka. When the officers of justice heard of the prey that awaited them, they made their preparations forthwith. Three men of the secret police went to Chobei's wine-shop, and, having called for wine, pretended to get up a drunken brawl; and as Chobei went up to them and tried to pacify them, one of the policemen seized hold of him, and another tried to pinion him. It at once flashed across Chobei's mind that his old misdeeds had come to light at last, so with a desperate effort he shook off the two policemen and knocked them down, and, rushing into the inner room, seized the famous Sukesada sword and sprang upstairs. The three policemen, never thinking that he could escape, mounted the stairs close after him; but Chobei with a terrible cut cleft the front man's head in sunder, and the other two fell back appalled at their comrade's fate. Then Chobei climbed on to the roof, and, looking out, perceived that the house was surrounded on all sides by armed men. Seeing this, he made up his mind that his last moment was come, but, at any rate, he determined to sell his life dearly, and to die fighting; so he stood up bravely, when one of the officers, coming up from the roof of a neighbouring house, attacked him with a spear; and at the same time several other soldiers clambered up. Chobei, seeing that he was overmatched, jumped down, and before the soldiers below had recovered from their surprise he had dashed through their ranks, laying about him right and left, and cutting down three men. At top speed he fled, with his pursuers close behind him; and, seeing the broad river ahead of him, jumped into a small boat that lay moored there, of which the boatmen, frightened at the sight of his bloody sword, left him in undisputed possession. Chobei pushed off, and sculled vigorously into the middle of the river; and the officers – there being no other boat near – were for a moment baffled. One of them, however, rushing down the river bank, hid himself on a bridge, armed with. a spear, and lay in wait for Chobei to pass in his boat; but when the little boat came up, he missed his aim, and only scratched Chobei's elbow; and he, seizing the spear, dragged down his adversary into the river, and killed him as he was struggling in the water; then, sculling for his life, he gradually drew near to the sea. The other officers in the mean time had secured ten boats, and, having come up with Chobei, surrounded him; but he, having formerly been a pirate, was far better skilled in the management of a boat than his pursuers, and had no great difficulty in eluding them; so at last he pushed out to sea, to the great annoyance of the officers, who followed him closely.

Then Jiuyemon, who had come up, said to one of the officers on the shore:

"Have you caught him yet?"

"No; the fellow is so brave and so cunning that our men can do nothing with him."

"He's a determined ruffian, certainly. However, as the fellow has got my sword, I mean to get it back by fair means or foul: will you allow me to undertake the job of seizing him?"

"Well, you may try; and you will have officers to assist you, if you are in peril."

Jiuyemon, having received this permission, stripped off his clothes and jumped into the sea, carrying with him a policeman's mace, to the great astonishment of all the bystanders. When he got near Chobei's boat, he dived and came up alongside, without the pirate perceiving him until he had clambered into the boat. Chobei had the good Sukesada sword, and Jiuyemon was armed with nothing but a mace; but Chobei, on the other hand, was exhausted with his previous exertions, and was taken by surprise at a moment when he was thinking of nothing but how he should scull away from the pursuing boats; so it was not long before Jiuyemon mastered and secured him.

For this feat, besides recovering his Sukesada sword, Jiuyemon received many rewards and great praise from the Governor of Osaka. But the pirate Chobei was cast into prison.

Hichirobei, when he heard of his brother's capture, was away from home; but seeing that he too would be sought for, he determined to escape to Edo at once, and travelled along the Tokaido, the great highroad, as far as Kuana. But the secret police had got wind of his movements, and one of them was at his heels disguised as a beggar, and waiting for an opportunity to seize him.

Hichirobei in the meanwhile was congratulating himself on his escape; and, little suspecting that he would be in danger so far away from Osaka, he went to a house of pleasure, intending to divert himself at his ease. The policeman, seeing this, went to the master of the house and said:

"The guest who has just come in is a notorious thief, and I am on his track, waiting to arrest him. Do you watch for the moment when he falls asleep, and let me know. Should he escape, the blame will fall upon you."

The master of the house, who was greatly taken aback, consented of course; so he told the woman of the house to hide Hichirobei's dirk, and as soon as the latter, wearied with his journey, had fallen asleep, he reported it to the policeman, who went upstairs, and having bound Hichirobei as he lay wrapped up in his quilt, led him back to Osaka to be imprisoned with his brother.

When Kashiku became aware of her lover's arrest, she felt certain that it was the handiwork of Jiuyemon; so she determined to kill him, were it only that she might die with Hichirobei. So hiding a kitchen knife in the bosom of her dress, she went at midnight to Jiuyemon's house, and looked all round to see if there were no hole or cranny by which she might slip in unobserved; but every door was carefully closed, so she was obliged to knock at the door and feign an excuse.

"Let me in! let me in! I am a servant-maid in the house of Kajiki Tozayemon, and am charged with a letter on most pressing business to Sir Jiuyemon."

Hearing this, one of Jiuyemon's servants, thinking her tale was true, rose and opened the door; and Kashiku, stabbing him in the face, ran past him into the house. Inside she met another apprentice, who had got up, aroused by the noise; him too she stabbed in the belly, but as he fell he cried out to Jiuyemon, saying:

"Father, father! take care! Some murderous villain has broken into the house."

And Kashiku, desperate, stopped his further utterance by cutting his throat. Jiuyemon, hearing his apprentice cry out, jumped up, and, lighting his night-lamp, looked about him in the half-gloom, and saw Kashiku with the bloody knife, hunting for him that she might kill him. Springing upon her before she saw him, he clutched her right hand, and, having secured her, bound her with cords so that she could not move. As soon as he had recovered from his surprise, he looked about him, and searched the house, when, to his horror, he found one of his apprentices dead, and the other lying bleeding from a frightful gash across the face. With the first dawn of day, he reported the affair to the proper authorities, and gave Kashiku in custody. So, after due examination, the two pirate brothers and the girl Kashiku were executed, and their heads were exposed together.

Now the fame of all the valiant deeds of Jiuyemon having reached his own country, his lord ordered that he should be pardoned for his former offence, and return to his allegiance; so, after thanking Kajiki Tozayemon for the manifold favours which he had received at his hands, he went home, and became a Samurai as before.

Leading Ladies & Affairs of the Heart

Introduction

SELF-LESS HEROINES, doomed lovers and romance feature heavily in Japanese myth and folkore, often as a device to illustrate the importance of filial piety. 'The Bamboo Cutter and the Moon Maiden' is adapted from a tenth-century story called *Taketori Monogatari*, and is the earliest example of the Japanese romance. All the characters in this very charming legend are Japanese, but most of the incidents have been borrowed from China. Mr F.V. Dickins wrote concerning the *Taketori Monogatari*: "The art and grace of the story of the Lady Kaguya are native, its unstrained pathos, its natural sweetness, are its own, and in simple charm and purity of thought and language it has no rival in the fiction of either the Middle Kingdom or of the Dragonfly Land."

One of the most romantic of the old Japanese festivals is the Festival of Tanabata. The story that inspired it is the famous one of 'The Star Lovers', Tanabata (more often known as Orihime) and Hikoboshi, from the Chinese tale of 'The Cowherd and the Weaver Girl', in which the lovers are punished for their disrespect by being separated, only to be allowed to meet once a year.

Snow-time in Japan has a beauty peculiarly its own, and it is a favourite theme of Japanese poets and artists. Because it is so particularly beautiful it is surprising to find that Yuki-Onna, the Lady of the Snow, is very far from being a benevolent and attractive spirit. All the artistry and poetry of snow vanish in her malignant presence, for she represents Death, with attributes not unlike that of a vampire. But Japan is full of sharp and surprising contrasts, and the delicate and beautiful jostle with the ugly and horrible.

The Bamboo Cutter and the Moon Maiden

LONG AGO THERE LIVED an old bamboo-cutter by the name of Sanugi no Miyakko. One day, while he was busy with his hatchet in a grove of bamboos, he suddenly perceived a miraculous light, and on closer inspection discovered in the heart of a reed a very small creature of exquisite beauty. He gently picked up the tiny girl, only about four inches in height, and carried her home to his wife. So delicate was this little maiden that she had to be reared in a basket.

Now it happened that the Bamboo Cutter continued to set about his business, and night and day, as he cut down the reeds, he found gold, and, once poor, he now amassed a considerable fortune.

The child, after she had been but three months with these simple country folk, suddenly grew in stature to that of a full-grown maid; and in order that she should be in keeping with such a pleasing, if surprising, event, her hair, hitherto allowed to flow in long tresses about her shoulders, was now fastened in a knot on her head. In due season the Bamboo Cutter named the girl the Lady Kaguya, or 'Precious-Slender-Bamboo-of-the-Field-of-Autumn'. When she had been named a great feast was held, in which all the neighbours participated.

The Wooing of the 'Precious-Slender-Bamboo-of-the-Field-of-Autumn'

Now the Lady Kaguya was of all women the most beautiful, and immediately after the feast the fame of her beauty spread throughout the land. Would-be lovers gathered around the fence and lingered in the porch with the hope of at least getting a glimpse of this lovely maiden. Night and day these forlorn suitors waited, but in vain. Those who were of humble origin gradually began to recognise that their love-making was useless. But five wealthy suitors still persisted, and would not relax their efforts. They were Prince Ishizukuri and Prince Kuramochi, the Sadaijin Dainagon Abe no Miushi, the Chiunagon Otomo no Miyuki, and Morotada, the Lord of Iso. These ardent lovers bore "the ice and snow of winter and the thunderous heats of midsummer with equal fortitude." When these lords finally asked the Bamboo Cutter to bestow his daughter upon one of them, the old man politely explained that the maiden was not really his daughter, and as that was so she could not be compelled to obey his own wishes in the matter.

At last the lords returned to their mansions, but still continued to make their supplications more persistently than ever. Even the kindly Bamboo Cutter began to remonstrate with the Lady Kaguya, and to point out that it was becoming for so handsome a maid to marry, and that among the five noble suitors she could surely make a very good match. To this the wise Kaguya replied: "Not so fair am I that I may be certain of a man's faith, and were I to mate with one whose heart proved fickle what a miserable fate were mine! Noble lords, without doubt, are these of whom thou speakest, but I would not wed a man whose heart should be all untried and unknown."

It was finally arranged that Kaguya should marry the suitor who proved himself the most worthy. This news brought momentary hope to the five great lords, and when night came they assembled before the house where the maiden dwelt "with flute music and with singing, with chanting to accompaniments and piping, with cadenced tap and clap of fan." Only the Bamboo Cutter went out to thank the lords for their serenading. When he had come into the house again, Kaguya thus set forth her plan to test the suitors:

"In Tenjiku (Northern India) is a beggar's bowl of stone, which of old the Buddha himself bore, in quest whereof let Prince Ishizukuri depart and bring me the same. And on the mountain Horai, that towers over the Eastern ocean, grows a tree with roots of silver and trunk of gold and fruitage of pure white jade, and I bid Prince Kuramochi fare thither and break off and bring me a branch thereof. Again, in the land of Morokoshi men fashion fur-robes of the pelt of the Flame-proof Rat, and I pray the Dainagon to find me one such. Then of the Chiunagon I require the rainbow-hued jewel that hides its sparkle deep in the dragon's head; and from the hands of the Lord Iso would I fain receive the cowry-shell that the swallow brings hither over the broad sea-plain."

The Begging-bowl of the Lord Buddha

The Prince Ishizukuri, after pondering over the matter of going to distant Tenjiku in search of the Lord Buddha's begging-bowl, came to the conclusion that such a proceeding would be futile. He decided, therefore, to counterfeit the bowl in question. He laid his plans cunningly, and took good care that the Lady Kaguya was informed that he had actually undertaken the journey. As a matter of fact this artful suitor hid in Yamato for three years, and after that time discovered in a hill-monastery in Tochi a bowl of extreme age resting upon an altar of Binzuru (the Succourer in Sickness). This bowl he took away with him, and wrapped it in brocade, and attached to the gift an artificial branch of blossom.

When the Lady Kaguya looked upon the bowl she found inside a scroll containing the following:

"Over seas, over hills
hath thy servant fared, and weary
and wayworn he perisheth:
O what tears hath cost this
bowl of stone,
what floods of streaming tears!"

But when the Lady Kaguya perceived that no light shone from the vessel she at once knew that it had never belonged to the Lord Buddha. She accordingly sent back the bowl with the following verse:

"Of the hanging dewdrop
not even the passing sheen
dwells herein:
On the Hill of Darkness, the Hill

of Ogura,
what couldest thou hope to find?"

The Prince, having thrown away the bowl, sought to turn the above remonstrance into a compliment to the lady who wrote it.

"Nay, on the Hill of Brightness
what splendour
will not pale?
Would that away from the light
of thy beauty
the sheen of yonder Bowl might
prove me true!"

It was a prettily turned compliment by a suitor who was an utter humbug. This latest poetical sally availed nothing, and the Prince sadly departed.

The Jewel-bearing Branch of Mount Horai

Prince Kuramochi, like his predecessor, was equally wily, and made it generally known that he was setting out on a journey to the land of Tsukushi in quest of the Jewel-bearing Branch. What he actually did was to employ six men of the Uchimaro family, celebrated craftsmen, and secure for them a dwelling hidden from the haunts of men, where he himself abode, for the purpose of instructing the craftsmen as to how they were to make a Jewel-bearing Branch identical with the one described by the Lady Kaguya.

When the Jewel-bearing Branch was finished, he set out to wait upon the Lady Kaguya, who read the following verse attached to the gift:

"Though it were at the peril
of my very life,
without the Jewel-laden Branch
in my hands never again
would I have dared to return!"

The Lady Kaguya looked sadly upon this glittering branch, and listened without interest to the Prince's purely imaginative story of his adventures. The Prince dwelt upon the terrors of the sea, of strange monsters, of acute hunger, of disease, which were their trials upon the ocean. Then this incorrigible story-teller went on to describe how they came to a high mountain rising out of the sea, where they were greeted by a woman bearing a silver vessel which she filled with water. On the mountain were wonderful flowers and trees, and a stream "rainbow-hued, yellow as gold, white as silver, blue as precious *ruri* (lapis lazuli); and the stream was spanned by bridges built up of divers gems, and by it grew trees laden with dazzling jewels, and from one of these I broke off the branch which I venture now to offer to the Lady Kaguya."

No doubt the Lady Kaguya would have been forced to believe this ingenious tale had not at that very moment the six craftsmen appeared on the scene, and by loudly demanding payment for the ready-made Jewel-Branch, exposed the treachery of the Prince, who made a hasty retreat. The Lady Kaguya herself rewarded the craftsmen, happy, no doubt, to escape so easily.

The Flameproof Fur-Robe

The Sadaijin (Left Great Minister) Abe no Miushi commissioned a merchant, by the name of Wokei, to obtain for him a fur-robe made from the Flame-proof Rat, and when the merchant's ship had returned from the land of Morokoshi it bore a fur-robe, which the sanguine Sadaijin imagined to be the very object of his desire. The Fur-Robe rested in a casket, and the Sadaijin, believing in the honesty of the merchant, described it as being "of a sea-green colour, the hairs tipped with shining gold, a treasure indeed of incomparable loveliness, more to be admired for its pure excellence than even for its virtue in resisting the flame of fire."

The Sadaijin, assured of success in his wooing, gaily set out to present his gift to the Lady Kaguya, offering in addition the following verse:

"Endless are the fires of love
that consume me, yet unconsumed
is the Robe of Fur:
dry at last are my sleeves,
for shall I not see her face this day!"

At last the Sadaijin was able to present his gift to the Lady Kaguya. Thus she addressed the Bamboo Cutter, who always seems to have been conveniently on the scene at such times: "If this Robe be thrown amid the flames and be not burnt up, I shall know it is in very truth the Flame-proof Robe, and may no longer refuse this lord's suit." A fire was lighted, and the Robe thrown into the flames, where it perished immediately. "When the Sadaijin saw this his face grew green as grass, and he stood there astonished." But the Lady Kaguya discreetly rejoiced, and returned the casket with the following verse:

"Without a vestige even left
thus to burn utterly away,
had I dreamt it of this Robe of Fur.
Alas the pretty thing! far otherwise
would I have dealt with it."

The Jewel in the Dragon's Head

The Chiunagon Otomo no Miyuki assembled his household and informed his retainers that he desired them to bring him the Jewel in the Dragon's head.

After some demur they pretended to set off on this quest. In the meantime the Chiunagon was so sure of his servants' success that he had his house lavishly adorned throughout with exquisite lacquer-work, in gold and silver. Every room was hung with brocade, the panels rich with pictures, and over the roof were silken cloths.

Weary of waiting, the Chiunagon after a time journeyed to Naniwa and questioned the inhabitants if any of his servants had taken boat in quest of the Dragon. The Chiunagon learnt that none of his men had come to Naniwa, and, considerably displeased at the news, he himself embarked with a helmsman.

Now it happened that the Thunder God was angry and the sea ran high. After many days the storm grew so severe and the boat was so near sinking that the helmsman ventured to remark: "The howling of the wind and the raging of the waves and the mighty roar of the thunder are signs of the wrath of the God whom my lord offends, who would slay the Dragon of the deep, for through the Dragon is the storm raised, and well it were if my lord offered a prayer."

As the Chiunagon had been seized with a terrible sickness, it is not surprising to find that he readily took the helmsman's advice. He prayed no less than a thousand times, enlarging on his folly in attempting to slay the Dragon, and solemnly vowed that he would leave the Ruler of the deep in peace.

The thunder ceased and the clouds dispersed, but the wind was as fierce and strong as ever. The helmsman, however, told his master that it was a fair wind and blew towards their own land.

At last they reached the strand of Akashi, in Harima. But the Chiunagon, still ill and mightily frightened, vowed that they had been driven upon a savage shore, and lay full length in the boat, panting heavily, and refusing to rise when the governor of the district presented himself.

When the Chiunagon at last realised that they had not been blown upon some savage shore he consented to land. No wonder the governor smiled when he saw the wretched appearance of the discomfited lord, chilled to the very bone, with swollen belly and eyes lustreless as sloes.

At length the Chiunagon was carried in a litter to his own home. When he had arrived his cunning servants humbly told their master how they had failed in the quest. Thus the Chiunagon greeted them: "Ye have done well to return empty-handed. Yonder Dragon, assuredly, has kinship with the Thunder God, and whoever shall lay hands on him to take the jewel that gleams in his head shall find himself in peril. Myself am sore spent with toil and hardship, and no guerdon have I won. A thief of men's souls and a destroyer of their bodies is the Lady Kaguya, nor ever will I seek her abode again, nor ever bend ye your steps thitherward."

When the women of his household heard of their lord's adventure they laughed till their sides were sore, while the silken cloths he had caused to be drawn over the roof of his mansion were carried away, thread by thread, by the crows to line their nests with.

The Royal Hunt

Now the fame of the Lady Kaguya's beauty reached the court, and the Mikado, anxious to gaze upon her, sent one of his palace ladies, Fusago, to go and see the Bamboo Cutter's daughter, and to report to his Majesty of her excellences.

However, when Fusago reached the Bamboo Cutter's house the Lady Kaguya refused to see her. So the palace lady returned to court and reported the matter to the Mikado. His Majesty, not a little displeased, sent for the Bamboo Cutter, and made him bring the Lady Kaguya to court that he might see her, adding: "A hat of nobility, perchance, shall be her father's reward."

The old Bamboo Cutter was an admirable soul, and mildly discountenanced his daughter's extraordinary behaviour. Although he loved court favours and probably hankered after so distinguished a hat, it must be said of him that he was first of all true to his duty as a father.

When, on returning to his home, he discussed the matter with the Lady Kaguya, she informed the old man that if she were compelled to go to court it would certainly cause her death, adding: "The price of my father's hat of nobility will be the destruction of his child."

The Bamboo Cutter was deeply affected by these words, and once more set out on a journey to the court, where he humbly made known his daughter's decision.

The Mikado, not to be denied even by an extraordinarily beautiful woman, hit on the ingenious plan of ordering a Royal Hunt, so arranged that he might unexpectedly arrive at the Bamboo Cutter's dwelling, and perchance see the lady who could set at defiance the desires of an emperor.

On the day appointed for the Royal Hunt, therefore, the Mikado entered the Bamboo Cutter's house. He had no sooner done so than he was surprised to see in the room in which he stood a wonderful light, and in the light none other than the Lady Kaguya.

His Majesty advanced and touched the maiden's sleeve, whereupon she hid her face, but not before the Mikado had caught a glimpse of her beauty. Amazed by her extreme loveliness, and taking no notice of her protests, he ordered a palace litter to be brought; but on its arrival the Lady Kaguya suddenly vanished. The Emperor, perceiving that he was dealing with no mortal maid, exclaimed: "It shall be as thou desirest, maiden; but 'Tis prayed that thou resume thy form, that once more thy beauty may be seen."

So the Lady Kaguya resumed her fair form again. As his Majesty was about to be borne away he composed the following verse:

"Mournful the return
of the Royal Hunt,
and full of sorrow the
brooding heart;
for she resists and stays behind,
the Lady Kaguya!"

The Lady Kaguya thus made answer:

"Under the roof o'ergrown
with hopbine
long were the years
she passed.
How may she dare to look upon
The Palace of Precious Jade?"

The Celestial Robe of Feathers

In the third year after the Royal Hunt, and in the spring-time, the Lady Kaguya continually gazed at the moon. On the seventh month, when the moon was full, the Lady Kaguya's sorrow increased so that her weeping distressed the maidens who served her. At last they came to the Bamboo Cutter, and said: "Long has the Lady Kaguya watched the moon, waxing in melancholy with the waxing thereof, and her woe now passes all measure, and sorely she weeps and wails; wherefore we counsel thee to speak with her."

When the Bamboo Cutter communed with his daughter, he requested that she should tell him the cause of her sorrow, and was informed that the sight of the moon caused her to reflect upon the wretchedness of the world.

During the eighth month the Lady Kaguya explained to her maids that she was no ordinary mortal, but that her birthplace was the Capital of Moonland, and that the time was now at hand when she was destined to leave the world and return to her old home.

Not only was the Bamboo Cutter heart-broken at this sorrowful news, but the Mikado also was considerably troubled when he heard of the proposed departure of the Lady Kaguya. His Majesty was informed that at the next full moon a company would be sent down from that shining orb to take this beautiful lady away, whereupon he determined to put a check upon this celestial invasion. He ordered that a guard of soldiers should be stationed about the Bamboo Cutter's house, armed and prepared, if need be, to shoot their arrows upon those Moonfolk, who would fain take the beautiful Lady Kaguya away.

The old Bamboo Cutter naturally thought that with such a guard to protect his daughter the invasion from the moon would prove utterly futile. The Lady Kaguya attempted to correct the old man's ideas on the subject, saying: "Ye cannot prevail over the folk of yonder land, nor will your artillery harm them nor your defences avail against them, for every door will fly open at their approach, nor may your valour help, for be ye never so stout-hearted, when the Moonfolk come vain will be your struggle with them." These remarks made the Bamboo Cutter exceedingly angry. He asserted that his nails would turn into talons – in short, that he would completely annihilate such impudent visitors from the moon.

Now while the royal guard was stationed about the Bamboo Cutter's house, on the roof and in every direction, the night wore away. At the hour of the Rata great glory, exceeding the splendour of the moon and stars, shone around. While the light still continued a strange cloud approached, bearing upon it a company of Moonfolk. The cloud slowly descended until it came near to the ground, and the Moonfolk assembled themselves in order. When the royal guard perceived them every soldier grew afraid at the strange spectacle; but at length some of their number summoned up sufficient courage to bend their bows and send their arrows flying; but all their shafts went astray.

On the cloud there rested a canopied car, resplendent with curtains of finest woollen fabric, and from out the car a mighty voice sounded, saying: "Come thou forth, Miyakko Maro!"

The Bamboo Cutter tottered forth to obey the summons, and received for his pains an address from the chief of the Moonfolk commencing with, "Thou fool," and ending up with a command that the Lady Kaguya should be given up without further delay.

The car floated upward upon the cloud till it hovered over the roof. Once again the same mighty voice shouted: "Ho there, Kaguya! How long wouldst thou tarry in this sorry place?"

Immediately the outer door of the storehouse and the inner lattice-work were opened by the power of the Moonfolk, and revealed the Lady Kaguya and her women gathered about her.

The Lady Kaguya, before taking her departure, greeted the prostrate Bamboo Cutter and gave him a scroll bearing these words: "Had I been born in this land, never should I have quitted it until the time came for my father to suffer no sorrow for his child; but now, on the contrary, must I pass beyond the boundaries of this world, though sorely against my will. My silken mantle I leave behind me as a memorial, and when the moon lights up the night let my father gaze upon it. Now my eyes must take their last look and I must mount to yonder sky, whence I fain would fall, meteorwise, to earth."

Now the Moonfolk had brought with them, in a coffer, a Celestial Feather Robe and a few drops of the Elixir of Life. One of them said to the Lady Kaguya: "Taste, I pray you, of this Elixir, for soiled has your spirit become with the grossnesses of this filthy world."

The Lady Kaguya, after tasting the Elixir, was about to wrap up some in the mantle she was leaving behind for the benefit of the old Bamboo Cutter, who had loved her so well, when one of the Moonfolk prevented her, and attempted to throw over her shoulders the Celestial Robe, when the Lady Kaguya exclaimed: "Have patience yet awhile; who dons yonder robe changes his heart, and I have still somewhat to say ere I depart." Then she proceeded to write the following to the Mikado:

"Your Majesty deigned to send a host to protect your servant, but it was not to be, and now is the misery at hand of departing with those who have come to bear her away with them. Not permitted was it to her to serve your Majesty, and despite her will was it that she yielded not obedience to the Royal command, and wrung with grief is her heart thereat, and perchance your Majesty may have thought the Royal will was not understood, and was opposed by her, and so will she appear to your Majesty lacking in good manners, which she would not your Majesty deemed her to be, and therefore humbly she lays this writing at the Royal Feet. And now must she don the Feather Robe and mournfully bid her lord farewell."

Having delivered this scroll into the hands of the captain of the host, together with a bamboo joint containing the Elixir, the Feather Robe was thrown over her, and in a moment all memory of her earthly existence departed.

Then the Lady Kaguya entered the car, surrounded by the company of Moonfolk, and the cloud rapidly rose skyward till it was lost to sight.

The sorrow of the Bamboo Cutter and of the Mikado knew no bounds. The latter held a Grand Council, and inquired which was the highest mountain in the land. One of the councillors answered: "In Suruga stands a mountain, not remote from the capital, that towers highest towards heaven among all the mountains of the land." Whereupon his Majesty composed the following verse:

"Never more to see her!
Tears of grief overwhelm me,
and as for me,
with the Elixir of Life
what have I to do?"

Then the scroll, which the Lady Kaguya had written, together with the Elixir, was given to Tsuki no Iwakasa. These he was commanded to take to the summit of the highest mountain in Suruga, and, standing upon the highest peak, to burn the scroll and the Elixir of Life.

So Tsuki no Iwakasa heard humbly the Royal command, and took with him a company of warriors, and climbed the mountain and did as he was bidden. And it was from that time forth that the name of Fuji (*Fuji-yama*, 'Never Dying') was given to yonder mountain, and men say that the smoke of that burning still curls from its high peak to mingle with the clouds of heaven.

The Star Lovers

THE GOD OF THE FIRMAMENT had a lovely daughter, by name, and she spent her time in weaving for her august father. One day, while she sat at her loom, she chanced to see a handsome lad leading an ox, and she immediately fell in love with him. Tanabata's father, reading her secret thoughts, speedily consented to their marriage. Unfortunately, however, they loved not wisely, but too well, with the result that Tanabata neglected her weaving, and Hikoboshi's ox was allowed to wander at large over the High Plain of Heaven. The God of the Firmament became extremely angry, and commanded that these too ardent lovers should henceforth be separated by the Celestial River. On the seventh night of the seventh month, provided the weather was favourable, a great company of birds formed a bridge across the river, and by this means the lovers were able to meet. Their all too brief visit was not even a certainty, for if there were rain the Celestial River would become too wide for even a great bridge of magpies to span, and the lovers would be compelled to wait another weary year before there was even a chance of meeting each other again.

No wonder that on the Festival of the Weaving Maiden little children should sing, "*Tenki ni nari*" ("Oh, weather, be clear!"). When the weather is fine and the Star Lovers meet each other after a weary year's waiting it is said that the stars, possibly Lyra and Aquila, shine with five different colours – blue, green, red, yellow, and white – and that is why the poems are written on paper of these colours.

The Robe of Feathers

IT WAS SPRING-TIME, and along Mio's pine-clad shore there came a sound of birds. The blue sea danced and sparkled in the sunshine, and Hairukoo, a fisherman, sat down to enjoy the scene. As he did so he chanced to see, hanging on a pine-tree, a beautiful robe of pure white feathers.

As Hairukoo was about to take down the robe he saw coming toward him from the sea an extremely lovely maiden, who requested that the fisherman would restore the robe to her.

Hairukoo gazed upon the lady with considerable admiration. Said he: "I found this robe, and I mean to keep it, for it is a marvel to be placed among the treasures of Japan. No, I cannot possibly give it to you."

"Oh," cried the maiden pitifully, "I cannot go soaring into the sky without my robe of feathers, for if you persist in keeping it I can never more return to my celestial home. Oh, good fisherman, I beg of you to restore my robe!"

The fisherman, who must have been a hard-hearted fellow, refused to relent. "The more you plead," said he, "the more determined I am to keep what I have found."

Thus the maiden made answer:

"Speak not, dear fisherman! speak not that word!
Ah! know'st thou not that, like the hapless bird
Whose wings are broke, I seek, but seek in vain,
Reft of my wings, to soar to heav'n's blue plain?"

After further argument on the subject the fisherman's heart softened a little. "I will restore your robe of feathers," said he, "if you will at once dance before me."

Then the maiden replied: "I will dance it here – the dance that makes the Palace of the Moon turn round, so that even poor transitory man may learn its mysteries. But I cannot dance without my feathers."

"No," said the fisherman suspiciously. "If I give you this robe you will fly away without dancing before me."

This remark made the maiden extremely angry. "The pledge of mortals may be broken," said she, "but there is no falsehood among the Heavenly Beings."

These words put the fisherman to shame, and, without more ado, he gave the maiden her robe of feathers.

The Moon-Lady's Song

When the maiden had put on her pure white garment she struck a musical instrument and began to dance, and while she danced and played she sang of many strange and beautiful things concerning her far-away home in the Moon. She sang of the mighty Palace of the Moon, where thirty monarchs ruled, fifteen in robes of white when that shining orb was full, and fifteen robed in black when the Moon was waning. As she sang and played and danced she blessed Japan, "that earth may still her proper increase yield!"

The fisherman did not long enjoy this kindly exhibition of the Moon-Lady's skill, for very soon her dainty feet ceased to tap upon the sand. She rose into the air, the white feathers of her robe gleaming against the pine-trees or against the blue sky itself. Up, up she went, still playing and singing, past the summits of the mountains, higher and higher, until her song was hushed, until she reached the glorious Palace of the Moon.

Yuki-Onna, the Snow-Bride

MOSAKU AND HIS APPRENTICE MINOKICHI journeyed to a forest, some little distance from their village. It was a bitterly cold night when they neared their destination, and saw in front of them a cold sweep of water. They desired to cross this river, but the ferryman had gone away, leaving his boat on the other side of the water, and as the weather was too inclement to admit of swimming across the river they were glad to take shelter in the ferryman's little hut.

Mosaku fell asleep almost immediately he entered this humble but welcome shelter. Minokichi, however, lay awake for a long time listening to the cry of the wind and the hiss of the snow as it was blown against the door.

Minokichi at last fell asleep, to be soon awakened by a shower of snow falling across his face. He found that the door had been blown open, and that standing in the room was a fair woman in dazzlingly white garments. For a moment she stood thus; then she bent over Mosaku, her breath coming forth like white smoke. After bending thus over the old man for a minute or two she turned to Minokichi and hovered over him. He tried to cry out, for the breath of this woman was like a freezing blast of wind. She told him that she had intended to treat him as she had done the old man at his side, but forbore on account of his youth and beauty. Threatening Minokichi with instant death if he dared to mention to anyone what he had seen, she suddenly vanished.

Then Minokichi called out to his beloved master: "Mosaku, Mosaku, wake! Something very terrible has happened!" But there was no reply. He touched the hand of his master in the dark, and found it was like a piece of ice. Mosaku was dead!

During the next winter, while Minokichi was returning home, he chanced to meet a pretty girl by the name of Yuki. She informed him that she was going to Edo, where she desired to find a situation as a servant. Minokichi was charmed with this maiden, and he went so far as to ask if she were betrothed, and hearing that she was not, he took her to his own home, and in due time married her.

Yuki presented her husband with ten fine and handsome children, fairer of skin than the average. When Minokichi's mother died her last words were in praise of Yuki, and her eulogy was echoed by many of the country folk in the district.

One night, while Yuki was sewing, the light of a paper lamp shining upon her face, Minokichi recalled the extraordinary experience he had had in the ferryman's hut. "Yuki," said he, "you remind me so much of a beautiful white woman I saw when I was eighteen years old. She killed my master with her ice-cold breath. I am sure she was some strange spirit, and yet tonight she seems to resemble you!"

Yuki flung down her sewing. There was a horrible smile on her face as she bent close to her husband and shrieked: "It was I, Yuki-Onna, who came to you then, and silently killed your master! Oh, faithless wretch, you have broken your promise to keep the matter secret, and if it were not for our sleeping children I would kill you now! Remember, if they have aught to complain of at your hands I shall hear, I shall know, and on a night when the snow falls I *will* kill you!"

Then Yuki-Onna, the Lady of the Snow, changed into a white mist, and, shrieking and shuddering, passed through the smoke-hole, never to return again.

Kyuzaemon's Ghostly Visitor

KYUZAEMON, A POOR FARMER, had closed the shutters of his humble dwelling and retired to rest. Shortly before midnight he was awakened by loud tapping. Going to the door, he exclaimed: "Who are you? What do you want?"

The strange visitor made no attempt to answer these questions, but persistently begged for food and shelter. The cautious Kyuzaemon refused to allow the visitor to enter, and, having seen that his dwelling was secure, he was about to retire to bed again, when he saw standing beside him a woman in white flowing garments, her hair falling over her shoulders.

"Where did you leave your *geta*?" demanded the frightened farmer.

The white woman informed him that she was the visitor who had tapped upon his door. "I need no *geta*," she said, "for I have no feet! I fly over the snow-capped trees, and should have proceeded to the next village, but the wind was blowing strongly against me, and I desired to rest awhile."

The farmer expressed his fear of spirits, whereupon the woman inquired if her host had a *butsudan* (a family altar). Finding that he had, she bade him open the *butsudan* and light a lamp. When this was done the woman prayed before the ancestral tablets, not forgetting to add a prayer for the still much-agitated Kyuzaemon.

Having paid her respects at the *butsudan*, she informed the farmer that her name was Oyasu, and that she had lived with her parents and her husband, Isaburo. When she died her husband left her parents, and it was her intention to try to persuade him to go back again and support the old people.

Kyuzaemon began to understand as he murmured to himself: "Oyasu perished in the snow, and this is her spirit I see before me." However, in spite of this recollection he still felt much afraid. He sought the family altar with trembling footsteps, repeating over and over again: "Namu Amida Butsu!" ("Hail, Omnipotent Buddha!")

At last the farmer went to bed and fell asleep. Once he woke up to hear the white creature murmur farewell; but before he could make answer she had disappeared.

The following day Kyuzaemon went to the next village, and called upon Isaburo, whom he now found living with his father-in-law again. Isaburo informed him that he had received numerous visits from the spirit of his wife in the guise of Yuki-Onna. After carefully considering the matter Kyuzaemon found that this Lady of the Snow had appeared before Isaburo almost immediately after she had paid him such a mysterious visit. On that occasion Isaburo had promised to fulfil her wish, and neither he nor Kyuzaemon were again troubled with her who travels in the sky when the snow is falling fast.

The Maiden of Unai

THE MAIDEN UNAI dwelt with her parents in the village of Ashinoya. She was extremely beautiful, and it so happened that she had two most ardent and persistent lovers – Mubara, who was a native of the same countryside, and Chinu; who came from Izumi. These two lovers might very well have been twins, for they resembled each other in age, face, figure, and stature. Unfortunately, however, they both loved her with an equal passion, so that it was impossible to distinguish between them. Their gifts were the same, and there appeared to be no difference in their manner of courting. We get a good idea of the formidable aspect of these two lovers in the following, taken from Mushimaro's poem on the subject:

"With jealous love these champions twain
The beauteous girl did woo;
Each had his hand on the hilt of his sword,
And a full-charged quiver, too,

"Was slung o'er the back of each champion fierce,
And a bow of snow-white wood
Did rest in the sinewy hand of each;
And the twain defiant stood."

In the meantime, the Maiden of Unai grew sick at heart. She never accepted the gifts of either Mubara or Chinu, and yet it distressed her to see them standing at the gate month after month, never relaxing for a moment the ardent expression of their feeling toward her.

The Maiden of Unai's parents do not seem to have appreciated the complexity of the situation, for they said to her: "Sad it is for us to have to bear the burden of thine unseemly conduct in thus carelessly from month to month, and from year to year, causing others to sorrow. If thou wilt accept the one, after a little time the other's love will cease."

These well-meant words brought no consolation or assistance to the poor Maiden of Unai, so her parents sent for the lovers, explained the pitiful situation, and decided that he who should shoot a water-bird swimming in the river Ikuta, which flowed by the platform on which the house was built, should have their daughter in marriage. The lovers were delighted at this decision, and anxious to put an end to this cruel suspense. They pulled their bow-strings at the same instant, and together their arrows struck the bird, one in the head and the other in the tail, so that neither could claim to be the better marksman. When the Maiden of Unai saw how entirely hopeless the whole affair was, she exclaimed:

"Enough, enough! yon swiftly flowing wave
Shall free my soul from her long anxious strife:
Men call fair Settsu's stream the stream of life,
But in that stream shall be the maiden's grave!"

With these melodramatic words she flung herself from the platform into the surging water beneath.

The maid's parents, who witnessed the scene, shouted and raved on the platform, while the devoted lovers sprang into the river. One held the maiden's foot, and the other her hand, and in a moment the three sank and perished. In due time the maiden was buried with her lovers on either side, and to this day the spot is known as the 'Maiden's Grave'. In the grave of Mubara there was a hollow bamboo-cane, together with a bow, a quiver, and a long sword; but nothing had been placed in the grave of Chinu.

Some time afterwards a stranger happened to pass one night in the neighbourhood of the grave, and he was suddenly disturbed by hearing the sound of fighting. He sent his retainers to inquire into the matter, but they returned to him saying they could hear or see nothing of an unusual nature. While the stranger pondered over the love-story of the Maiden of Unai he fell asleep. He had no sooner done so than he saw before him, kneeling on the ground, a blood-stained man, who told him that he was much harassed by the persecutions of an enemy, and begged that the stranger would lend him his sword. This request was reluctantly granted. When the stranger awoke he was inclined to think the whole affair a dream; but it was no passing fantasy of the night, for not only was his sword missing, but he heard near at hand the sound of a great combat. Then the clash of weapons suddenly ceased, and once more the blood-stained man stood before him, saying: "By thine honourable assistance have I slain the foe that had oppressed me during these many years." So we may infer that in the spirit world Chinu fought and slew his rival, and after many years of bitter jealousy was finally able to call the Maiden of Unai his own.

The Maiden with the Wooden Bowl

IN ANCIENT DAYS there lived an old couple with their only child, a girl of remarkable charm and beauty. When the old man fell sick and died his widow became more and more concerned for her daughter's future welfare.

One day she called her child to her, and said: "Little one, your father lies in yonder cemetery, and I, being old and feeble, must needs follow him soon. The thought of leaving you alone in the world troubles me much, for you are beautiful, and beauty is a temptation and a snare to men. Not all the purity of a white flower can prevent it from being plucked and dragged down in the mire. My child, your face is all too fair. It must be hidden from the eager eyes of men, lest it cause you to fall from your good and simple life to one of shame."

Having said these words, she placed a lacquered bowl upon the maiden's head, so that it veiled her attractions. "Always wear it, little one," said the mother, "for it will protect you when I am gone."

Shortly after this loving deed had been performed the old woman died, and the maiden was forced to earn her living by working in the rice-fields. It was hard, weary work, but the girl kept a brave heart and toiled from dawn to sunset without a murmur. Over and over again her strange appearance created considerable comment, and she was known throughout the country as the "Maiden with the Bowl on her Head." Young men laughed at her and tried to peep under the vessel, and not a few endeavoured to pull off the wooden covering; but it could not be removed, and laughing and jesting, the young men had to be content with a glimpse of the lower part of the fair maiden's face. The poor girl bore this rude treatment with a patient but heavy heart, believing that out of her mother's love and wisdom would come some day a joy that would more than compensate for all her sorrow.

One day a rich farmer watched the maiden working in his rice-fields. He was struck by her diligence and the quick and excellent way she performed her tasks. He was pleased with that bent and busy little figure, and did not laugh at the wooden bowl on her head. After observing her for some time, he came to the maiden, and said: "You work well and do not chatter to your companions. I wish you to labour in my rice-fields until the end of the harvest."

When the rice harvest had been gathered and winter had come the wealthy farmer, still more favourably impressed with the maiden, and anxious to do her a service, bade her become an inmate of his house. "My wife is ill," he added, "and I should like you to nurse her for me."

The maiden gratefully accepted this welcome offer. She tended the sick woman with every care, for the same quiet diligence she displayed in the rice-fields was characteristic of her gentle labour in the sick-room. As the farmer and his wife had no daughter they took very kindly to this orphan and regarded her as a child of their own.

At length the farmer's eldest son returned to his old home. He was a wise young man who had studied much in gay Kyoto, and was weary of a merry life of feasting and frivolous pleasure. His father and mother expected that their son would soon grow tired of his father's house and its quiet surroundings, and every day they feared that he would come to them, bid farewell, and return once more to the city of the Mikado. But to the surprise of all the farmer's son expressed no desire to leave his old home.

One day the young man came to his father, and said: "Who is this maiden in our house, and why does she wear an ugly black bowl upon her head?"

When the farmer had told the sad story of the maiden his son was deeply moved; but, nevertheless, he could not refrain from laughing a little at the bowl. The young man's laughter, however, did not last long. Day by day the maiden became more fascinating to him. Now and again he peeped at the girl's half-hidden face, and became more and more impressed by her gentleness of manner and her nobility of nature. It was not long before his admiration turned into love, and he resolved that he would marry the Maiden with the Bowl on her Head. Most of his relations were opposed to the union. They said: "She is all very well in her way, but she is only a common servant. She wears that bowl in order to captivate the unwary, and we do not think it hides beauty, but rather ugliness. Seek a wife elsewhere, for we will not tolerate this ambitious and scheming maiden."

From that hour the maiden suffered much. Bitter and spiteful things were said to her, and even her mistress, once so good and kind, turned against her. But the farmer did not change his opinion. He still liked the girl, and was quite willing that she should become his son's wife, but, owing to the heated remarks of his wife and relations, he dared not reveal his wishes in the matter.

All the opposition, none too kindly expressed, only made the young man more desirous to achieve his purpose. At length his mother and relations, seeing that their wishes were useless, consented to the marriage, but with a very bad grace.

The young man, believing that all difficulties had been removed, joyfully went to the Maiden with the Bowl on her Head, and said: "All troublesome opposition is at an end, and now nothing prevents us from getting married."

"No," replied the poor maiden, weeping bitterly, "I cannot marry you. I am only a servant in your father's house, and therefore it would be unseemly for me to become your bride."

The young man spoke gently to her. He expressed his ardent love over and over again, he argued, he begged; but the maiden would not change her mind. Her attitude made the relations extremely angry. They said that the woman had made fools of them all, little knowing that she dearly loved the farmer's son, and believed, in her loyal heart, that marriage could only bring discord in the home that had sheltered her in her poverty.

That night the poor girl cried herself to sleep, and in a dream her mother came to her, and said: "My dear child, let your good heart be troubled no more. Marry the farmer's son and all will be well again." The maiden woke next morning full of joy, and when her lover came to her and asked once more if she would become his bride, she yielded with a gracious smile.

Great preparations were made for the wedding, and when the company assembled, it was deemed high time to remove the maiden's wooden bowl. She herself tried to take it off, but it remained firmly fixed to her head. When some of the relations, with not a few unkind remarks, came to her assistance, the bowl uttered strange cries and groans. At length the bridegroom approached the maiden, and said: "Do not let this treatment distress you. You are just as dear to me with or without the bowl," and having said these words, he commanded that the ceremony should proceed.

Then the wine-cups were brought into the crowded apartment and, according to custom, the bride and bridegroom were expected to drink together the 'Three times three' in token of their union. Just as the maiden put the wine-cup to her lips the bowl on her head broke with a great noise, and from it fell gold and silver and all manner of precious stones, so that the maiden who had once been a beggar now had her marriage portion. The guests were amazed as they looked upon the heap of shining jewels and gold and silver, but they were still more surprised when they chanced to look up and see that the bride was the most beautiful woman in all Japan.

The Loves of Gompachi and Komurasaki

ABOUT TWO HUNDRED AND THIRTY YEARS AGO there lived in the service of a daimyo of the province of Inaba a young man, called Shirai Gompachi, who, when he was but sixteen years of age, had already won a name for his personal beauty and valour, and for his skill in the use of arms. Now it happened that one day a dog belonging to him fought with another dog belonging to a fellow-clansman, and the two masters, being both passionate youths, disputing as to whose dog had had the best of the fight, quarrelled and came to blows, and Gompachi slew his adversary; and in consequence of this he was obliged to flee from his country, and make his escape to Edo.

And so Gompachi set out on his travels.

One night, weary and footsore, he entered what appeared to him to be a roadside inn, ordered some refreshment, and went to bed, little thinking of the danger that menaced him: for as luck would have it, this inn turned out to be the trysting-place of a gang of robbers, into whose clutches he had thus unwittingly fallen. To be sure, Gompachi's purse was but scantily furnished, but his sword and dirk were worth some three hundred ounces of silver, and upon these the robbers (of whom there were ten) had cast envious eyes, and had determined to kill the owner for their sake; but he, all unsuspicious, slept on in fancied security.

In the middle of the night he was startled from his deep slumbers by someone stealthily opening the sliding door which led into his room, and rousing himself with an effort, he beheld a beautiful young girl, fifteen years of age, who, making signs to him not to stir, came up to his bedside, and said to him in a whisper:

"Sir, the master of this house is the chief of a gang of robbers, who have been plotting to murder you this night for the sake of your clothes and your sword. As for me, I am the daughter of a rich merchant in Mikawa: last year the robbers came to our house, and carried off my father's treasure and myself. I pray you, sir, take me with you, and let us fly from this dreadful place."

She wept as she spoke, and Gompachi was at first too much startled to answer; but being a youth of high courage and a cunning fencer to boot, he soon recovered his presence of mind, and determined to kill the robbers, and to deliver the girl out of their hands. So he replied:

"Since you say so, I will kill these thieves, and rescue you this very night; only do you, when I begin the fight, run outside the house, that you may be out of harm's way, and remain in hiding until I join you."

Upon this understanding the maiden left him, and went her way. But he lay awake, holding his breath and watching; and when the thieves crept noiselessly into the room, where they supposed him to be fast asleep, he cut down the first man that entered, and stretched him dead at his feet. The other nine, seeing this, laid about them with their drawn swords, but Gompachi, fighting with desperation, mastered them at last, and slew them. After thus ridding himself of his enemies, he went outside the house and called to the girl, who came running to his side, and joyfully travelled on with him to Mikawa, where her father dwelt; and when they reached Mikawa, he took the maiden to the old man's house, and told him how, when he had fallen among thieves, his daughter had come to him in his hour of peril, and saved him out of her great pity; and how he, in return, rescuing her from her servitude, had brought her back to her home. When the old folks saw their daughter whom they had lost restored to them, they were beside themselves with joy, and shed tears for very happiness; and, in their gratitude, they pressed Gompachi to remain with them, and they prepared feasts for him, and entertained him hospitably: but their daughter, who had fallen in love with him for his beauty and knightly valour, spent her days in thinking of him, and of him alone. The young man, however, in spite of the kindness of the old merchant, who wished to adopt him as his son, and tried hard to persuade him to consent to this, was fretting to go to Edo and take service as an officer in the household of some noble lord; so he resisted the entreaties of the father and the soft speeches of the daughter, and made ready to start on his journey; and the old merchant, seeing that he would not be turned from his purpose, gave him a parting gift of two hundred ounces of silver, and sorrowfully bade him farewell.

But alas for the grief of the maiden, who sat sobbing her heart out and mourning over her lover's departure! He, all the while thinking more of ambition than of love, went to her and comforted her, and said: "Dry your eyes, sweetheart, and weep no more, for I shall soon come back to you. Do you, in the meanwhile, be faithful and true to me, and tend your parents with filial piety."

So she wiped away her tears and smiled again, when she heard him promise that he would soon return to her. And Gompachi went his way, and in due time came near to Edo.

But his dangers were not yet over; for late one night, arriving at a place called Suzugamori, in the neighbourhood of Edo, he fell in with six highwaymen, who attacked him, thinking to make short work of killing and robbing him. Nothing daunted, he drew his sword, and dispatched two out of the six; but, being weary and worn out with his long journey, he was sorely pressed, and the struggle was going hard with him, when a wardsman, who happened to pass that way riding in a chair, seeing the affray, jumped down from his chair and drawing his dirk came to the rescue, and between them they put the robbers to flight.

Now it turned out that this kind tradesman, who had so happily come to the assistance of Gompachi, was no other than Chobei of Bandzuin, the chief of the *Otokodate*, or Friendly Society of the wardsmen of Edo – a man famous in the annals of the city, whose life, exploits, and adventures are recited to this day, and form the subject of another tale.

When the highwaymen had disappeared, Gompachi, turning to his deliverer, said:

"I know not who you may be, sir, but I have to thank you for rescuing me from a great danger."

And as he proceeded to express his gratitude, Chobei replied:

"I am but a poor wardsman, a humble man in my way, sir; and if the robbers ran away, it was more by good luck than owing to any merit of mine. But I am filled with admiration at the way you fought; you displayed a courage and a skill that were beyond your years, sir."

"Indeed," said the young man, smiling with pleasure at hearing himself praised; "I am still young and inexperienced, and am quite ashamed of my bungling style of fencing."

"And now may I ask you, sir, whither you are bound?"

"That is almost more than I know myself, for I am a *ronin,* and have no fixed purpose in view."

"That is a bad job," said Chobei, who felt pity for the lad. "However, if you will excuse my boldness in making such an offer, being but a wardsman, until you shall have taken service I would fain place my poor house at your disposal."

Gompachi accepted the offer of his new but trusty friend with thanks; so Chobei led him to his house, where he lodged him and hospitably entertained him for some months. And now Gompachi, being idle and having nothing to care for, fell into bad ways, and began to lead a dissolute life, thinking of nothing but gratifying his whims and passions; he took to frequenting the Yoshiwara, the quarter of the town which is set aside for tea-houses and other haunts of wild young men, where his handsome face and figure attracted attention, and soon made him a great favourite with all the beauties of the neighbourhood.

About this time men began to speak loud in praise of the charms of Komurasaki, or 'Little Purple', a young girl who had recently come to the Yoshiwara, and who in beauty and accomplishments outshone all her rivals. Gompachi, like the rest of the world, heard so much of her fame that he determined to go to the house where she dwelt, at the sign of 'The Three Sea-coasts', and judge for himself whether she deserved all that men said of her. Accordingly he set out one day, and having arrived at 'The Three Sea-coasts', asked to see Komurasaki; and being shown into the room where she was sitting, advanced towards her; but when their eyes met, they both started back with a cry of astonishment, for this Komurasaki, the famous beauty of the Yoshiwara, proved to be the very girl whom several months before Gompachi had rescued from the robbers' den, and restored to her parents in Mikawa. He had left her in prosperity and affluence, the darling child of a rich father, when they had exchanged vows of love and fidelity; and now they met in a common stew in Edo. What a change! what a contrast! How had the riches turned to rust, the vows to lies!

"What is this?" cried Gompachi, when he had recovered from his surprise. "How is it that I find you here pursuing this vile calling, in the Yoshiwara? Pray explain this to me, for there is some mystery beneath all this which I do not understand."

But Komurasaki – who, having thus unexpectedly fallen in with her lover that she had yearned for, was divided between joy and shame – answered, weeping:

"Alas! my tale is a sad one, and would be long to tell. After you left us last year, calamity and reverses fell upon our house; and when my parents became poverty-stricken, I was at my wits' end to know how to support them: so I sold this wretched body of mine to the master of this house, and sent the money to my father and mother; but, in spite of this, troubles and misfortunes multiplied upon them, and now, at last, they have died of misery and grief. And, oh! lives there in this wide world so unhappy a wretch as I! But now that I have met you again – you who are so strong – help me who am weak. You saved me once – do not, I implore you, desert me now!!" and as she told her piteous tale the tears streamed from her eyes.

"This is, indeed, a sad story," replied Gompachi, much affected by the recital. "There must have been a wonderful run of bad luck to bring such misfortune upon your house, which but a little while ago I recollect so prosperous. However, mourn no more, for I will not forsake you. It is true that I am too poor to redeem you from your servitude, but at any rate I will contrive so that you shall be tormented no more. Love me, therefore, and put your trust in me." When she heard him speak so kindly she was comforted, and wept no more, but poured out her whole heart to him, and forgot her past sorrows in the great joy of meeting him again.

When it became time for them to separate, he embraced her tenderly and returned to Chobei's house; but he could not banish Komurasaki from his mind, and all day long he thought of her alone; and so it came about that he went daily to the Yoshiwara to see her, and if any accident detained him, she, missing the accustomed visit, would become anxious and write to him to inquire the cause of his absence. At last, pursuing this course of life, his stock of money ran short, and as, being a *ronin* and without any fixed employment, he had no means of renewing his supplies, he was ashamed of showing himself penniless at 'The Three Sea-coasts'. Then it was that a wicked spirit arose within him, and he went out and murdered a man, and having robbed him of his money carried it to the Yoshiwara.

From bad to worse is an easy step, and the tiger that has once tasted blood is dangerous. Blinded and infatuated by his excessive love, Gompachi kept on slaying and robbing, so that, while his outer man was fair to look upon, the heart within him was that of a hideous devil. At last his friend Chobei could no longer endure the sight of him, and turned him out of his house; and as, sooner or later, virtue and vice meet with their reward, it came to pass that Gompachi's crimes became notorious, and the Government having set spies upon his track, he was caught red-handed and arrested; and his evil deeds having been fully proved against him, he was carried off to the execution ground at Suzugamori, the 'Bell Grove', and beheaded as a common male-factor.

Now when Gompachi was dead, Chobei's old affection for the young man returned, and, being a kind and pious man, he went and claimed his body and head, and buried him at Meguro, in the grounds of the Temple called Boronji.

When Komurasaki heard the people at Yoshiwara gossiping about her lover's end, her grief knew no bounds, so she fled secretly from 'The Three Sea-coasts', and came to Meguro and threw herself upon the newly-made grave. Long she prayed and bitterly she wept over the tomb of him whom, with all his faults, she had loved so well, and then, drawing a dagger from her girdle, she plunged it in her breast and died. The priests of the temple, when they saw what had happened, wondered greatly and were astonished at the loving faithfulness of this beautiful girl, and taking compassion on her, they laid her side by side with Gompachi in one grave, and over the grave they placed a stone which remains to this day, bearing the inscription "The Tomb of the Shiyoku". And still the people of Edo visit the place, and still they praise the beauty of Gompachi and the filial piety and fidelity of Komurasaki.

The Outcast Maiden and the Hatamoto

ONCE UPON A TIME, some two hundred years ago, there lived at a place called Honjo, in Edo, a Hatamoto named Takoji Genzaburo; his age was about twenty-four or twenty-five, and he was of extraordinary personal beauty. His official duties made it incumbent on him to go to the Castle by way of the Adzuma Bridge, and here it was that a strange adventure befel him. There was a certain Outcast, who used to earn his living by going out every day to the Adzuma Bridge, and mending the sandals of the passers-by. Whenever Genzaburo crossed the bridge, the Outcast used always to bow to him. This struck him as rather strange; but one day when Genzaburo was out alone, without any retainers following him, and was passing the Adzuma Bridge, the thong of his sandal suddenly broke: this annoyed him very much; however, he recollected the Outcast cobbler who always used to bow to him so regularly, so he went to the place where he usually sat, and ordered him to mend his sandal, saying to him: "Tell me why it is that every time that I pass by this bridge, you salute me so respectfully."

When the Outcast heard this, he was put out of countenance, and for a while he remained silent; but at last taking courage, he said to Genzaburo, "Sir, having been honoured with your commands, I am quite put to shame. I was originally a gardener, and used to go to your honour's house and lend a hand in trimming up the garden. In those days your honour was very young, and I myself little better than a child; and so I used to play with your honour, and received many kindnesses at your hands. My name, sir, is Chokichi. Since those days I have fallen by degrees info dissolute habits, and little by little have sunk to be the vile thing that you now see me."

When Genzaburo heard this he was very much surprised, and, recollecting his old friendship for his playmate, was filled with pity, and said, "Surely, surely, you have fallen very low. Now all you have to do is to presevere and use your utmost endeavours to find a means of escape from the class into which you have fallen, and become a wardsman again. Take this sum: small as it is, let it be a foundation for more to you." And with these words he took ten riyos out of his pouch and handed them to Chokichi, who at first refused to accept the present, but, when it was pressed upon him, received it with thanks. Genzaburo was leaving him to go home, when two wandering singing-girls came up and spoke to Chokichi; so Genzaburo looked to see what the two women were like. One was a woman of some twenty years of age, and the other was a peerlessly beautiful girl of sixteen; she was neither too fat nor too thin, neither too tall nor too short; her face was oval, like a melon-seed, and her complexion fair and white; her eyes were narrow and bright, her teeth small and even; her nose was aquiline, and her mouth delicately formed, with lovely red lips; her eyebrows were long and fine; she had a profusion of long black hair; she spoke modestly, with a soft sweet voice; and when she smiled, two lovely dimples appeared in her cheeks; in all her movements she was gentle and refined. Genzaburo fell in love with her at first sight; and she, seeing what a handsome man he was, equally fell in love with him; so that the woman that was with her, perceiving that they were struck with one another, led her away as fast as possible.

Genzaburo remained as one stupefied, and, turning to Chokichi, said, "Are you acquainted with those two women who came up just now?"

"Sir," replied Chokichi, "those are two women of our people. The elder woman is called O Kuma, and the girl, who is only sixteen years old, is named O Koyo. She is the daughter of one Kihachi, a chief of the Outcasts. She is a very gentle girl, besides being so exceedingly pretty; and all our people are loud in her praise."

When he heard this, Genzaburo remained lost in thought for a while, and then said to Chokichi, "I want you to do something for me. Are you prepared to serve me in whatever respect I may require you?"

Chokichi answered that he was prepared to do anything in his power to oblige his honour. Upon this Genzaburo smiled and said, "Well, then, I am willing to employ you in a certain matter; but as there are a great number of passers-by here, I will go and wait for you in a tea-house at Hanakawado; and when you have finished your business here, you can join me, and I will speak to you." With these words Genzaburo left him, and went off to the tea-house.

When Chokichi had finished his work, he changed his clothes, and, hurrying to the tea-house, inquired for Genzaburo, who was waiting for him upstairs. Chokichi went up to him, and began to thank him for the money which he had bestowed upon him. Genzaburo smiled, and handed him a wine-cup, inviting him to drink, and said:

"I will tell you the service upon which I wish to employ you. I have set my heart upon that girl O Koyo, whom I met today upon the Adzuma Bridge, and you must arrange a meeting between us."

When Chokichi heard these words, he was amazed and frightened, and for a while he made no answer. At last he said:

"Sir, there is nothing that I would not do for you after the favours that I have received from you. If this girl were the daughter of any ordinary man, I would move heaven and earth to comply with your wishes; but for your honour, a handsome and noble Hatamoto, to take for his concubine the daughter of an Outcast is a great mistake. By giving a little money you can get the handsomest woman in the town. Pray, sir, abandon the idea."

Upon this Genzaburo was offended, and said:

"This is no matter for you to give advice in. I have told you to get me the girl, and you must obey."

Chokichi, seeing that all that he could say would be of no avail, thought over in his mind how to bring about a meeting between Genzaburo and O Koyo, and replied:

"Sir, I am afraid when I think of the liberty that I have taken. I will go to Kihachi's house, and will use my best endeavours with him that I may bring the girl to you. But for today, it is getting late, and night is coming on; so I will go and speak to her father tomorrow."

Genzaburo was delighted to find Chokichi willing to serve him.

"Well," said he, "the day after tomorrow I will await you at the tea-house at Oji, and you can bring O Koyo there. Take this present, small as it is, and do your best for me."

With this he pulled out three riyos from his pocket and handed them to Chokichi. who declined the money with thanks, saying that he had already received too much, and could accept no more; but Genzaburo pressed him, adding, that if the wish of his heart were accomplished he would do still more for him. So Chokichi, in great glee at the good luck which had befallen him, began to revolve all sorts of schemes in his mind; and the two parted.

But O Koyo, who had fallen in love at first sight with Genzaburo on the Adzuma Bridge, went home and could think of nothing but him. Sad and melancholy she sat, and her friend O Kuma tried to comfort her in various ways; but O Koyo yearned, with all her heart, for Genzaburo; and the more she thought over the matter, the better she perceived that she, as the daughter of an Outcast, was no match for a noble Hatamoto. And yet, in spite of this, she pined for him, and bewailed her own vile condition.

Now it happened that her friend O Kuma was in love with Chokichi, and only cared for thinking and speaking of him; one day, when Chokichi went to pay a visit at the house of Kihachi the Outcast chief, O Kuma, seeing him come, was highly delighted, and received him very politely; and Chokichi, interrupting her, said:

"O Kuma, I want you to answer me a question: where has O Koyo gone to amuse herself today?"

"Oh, you know the gentleman who was talking with you the other day, at the Adzuma Bridge? Well, O Koyo has fallen desperately in love with him, and she says that she is too low-spirited and out of sorts to get up yet."

Chokichi was greatly pleased to hear this, and said to O Kuma:

"How delightful! Why, O Koyo has fallen in love with the very gentleman who is burning with passion for her, and who has employed me to help him in the matter. However, as he is a noble

Hatamoto, and his whole family would be ruined if the affair became known to the world, we must endeavour to keep it as secret as possible."

"Dear me!" replied O Kuma; "when O Koyo hears this, how happy she will be, to be sure! I must go and tell her at once."

"Stop!" said Chokichi, detaining her; "if her father, Master Kihachi, is willing, we will tell O Koyo directly. You had better wait here a little until I have consulted him;" and with this he went into an inner chamber to see Kihachi; and, after talking over the news of the day, told him how Genzaburo had fallen passionately in love with O Koyo, and had employed him as a go-between. Then he described how he had received kindness at the hands of Genzaburo when he was in better circumstances, dwelt on the wonderful personal beauty of his lordship, and upon the lucky chance by which he and O Koyo had come to meet each other.

When Kihachi heard this story, he was greatly flattered, and said:

"I am sure I am very much obliged to you. For one of our daughters, whom even the common people despise and shun as a pollution, to be chosen as the concubine of a noble Hatamoto – what could be a greater matter for congratulation!"

So he prepared a feast for Chokichi, and went off at once to tell O Koyo the news. As for the maiden, who had fallen over head and ears in love, there was no difficulty in obtaining her consent to all that was asked of her.

Accordingly Chokichi, having arranged to bring the lovers together on the following day at Oji, was preparing to go and report the glad tidings to Genzaburo; but O Koyo, who knew that her friend O Kuma was in love with Chokichi, and thought that if she could throw them into one another's arms, they, on their side, would tell no tales about herself and Genzaburo, worked to such good purpose that she gained her point. At last Chokichi, tearing himself from the embraces of O Kuma, returned to Genzaburo, and told him how he had laid his plans so as, without fail, to bring O Koyo to him, the following day, at Oji, and Genzaburo, beside himself with impatience, waited for the morrow.

The next day Genzaburo, having made his preparations, and taking Chokichi with him, went to the tea-house at Oji, and sat drinking wine, waiting for his sweetheart to come.

As for O Koyo, who was half in ecstasies, and half shy at the idea of meeting on this day the man of her heart's desire, she put on her holiday clothes, and went with O Kuma to Oji; and as they went out together, her natural beauty being enhanced by her smart dress, all the people turned round to look at her, and praise her pretty face. And so after a while, they arrived at Oji, and went into the tea-house that had been agreed upon; and Chokichi, going out to meet them, exclaimed:

"Dear me, Miss O Koyo, his lordship has been all impatience waiting for you: pray make haste and come in."

But, in spite of what he said, O Koyo, on account of her virgin modesty, would not go in. O Kuma, however, who was not quite so particular, cried out:

"Why, what is the meaning of this? As you've come here, O Koyo, it's a little late for you to be making a fuss about being shy. Don't be a little fool, but come in with me at once." And with these words she caught fast hold of O Koyo's hand, and, pulling her by force into the room, made her sit down by Genzaburo.

When Genzaburo saw how modest she was, he reassured her, saying:

"Come, what is there to be so shy about? Come a little nearer to me, pray."

"Thank you, sir. How could I, who am such a vile thing, pollute your nobility by sitting by your side?" And, as she spoke, the blushes mantled over her face; and the more Genzaburo looked at her, the more beautiful she appeared in his eyes, and the more deeply he became enamoured of her charms. In the meanwhile he called for wine and fish, and all four together made a feast of it. When Chokichi and O Kuma saw how the land lay, they retired discreetly into another chamber, and Genzaburo and O Koyo were left alone together, looking at one another.

"Come," said Genzaburo, smiling, "hadn't you better sit a little closer to me?"

"Thank you, sir; really I'm afraid."

But Genzaburo, laughing at her for her idle fears, said:

"Don't behave as if you hated me."

"Oh, dear! I'm sure I don't hate you, sir. That would be very rude; and, indeed, it's not the case. I loved you when I first saw you at the Adzuma Bridge, and longed for you with all my heart; but I knew what a despised race I belonged to, and that I was no fitting match for you, and so I tried to be resigned. But I am very young and inexperienced, and so I could not help thinking of you, and you alone; and then Chokichi came, and when I heard what you had said about me, I thought, in the joy of my heart, that it must be a dream of happiness."

And as she spoke these words, blushing timidly, Genzaburo was dazzled with her beauty, and said:

"Well, you're a clever child. I'm sure, now, you must have some handsome young lover of your own, and that is why you don't care to come and drink wine and sit by me. Am I not right, eh?"

"Ah, sir, a nobleman like you is sure to have a beautiful wife at home; and then you are so handsome that, of course, all the pretty young ladies are in love with you."

"Nonsense! Why, how clever you are at flattering and paying compliments! A pretty little creature like you was just made to turn all the men's heads – a little witch."

"Ah! those are hard things to say of a poor girl! Who could think of falling in love with such a wretch as I am? Now, pray tell me all about your own sweetheart: I do so long to hear about her."

"Silly child! I'm not the sort of man to put thoughts into the heads of fair ladies. However, it is quite true that there is someone whom I want to marry."

At this O Koyo began to feel jealous.

"Ah!" said she, "how happy that someone must be! Do, pray, tell me the whole story." And a feeling of jealous spite came over her, and made her quite unhappy.

Genzaburo laughed as he answered:

"Well, that someone is yourself, and nobody else. There!" and as he spoke, he gently tapped the dimple on her cheek with his finger; and O Koyo's heart beat so, for very joy, that, for a little while, she remained speechless. At last she turned her face towards Genzaburo, and said:

"Alas! your lordship is only trifling with me, when you know that what you have just been pleased to propose is the darling wish of my heart. Would that I could only go into your house as a maid-servant, in any capacity, however mean, that I might daily feast my eyes on your handsome face!"

"Ah! I see that you think yourself very clever at hoaxing men, and so you must needs tease me a little;" and, as he spoke, he took her hand, and drew her close up to him, and she, blushing again, cried:

"Oh! pray wait a moment, while I shut the sliding-doors."

"Listen to me, O Koyo! I am not going to forget the promise which I made you just now; nor need you be afraid of my harming you; but take care that you do not deceive me."

"Indeed, sir, the fear is rather that you should set your heart on others; but, although I am no fashionable lady, take pity on me, and love me well and long."

"Of course! I shall never care for another woman but you."

"Pray, pray, never forget those words that you have just spoken."

"And now," replied Genzaburo, "the night is advancing, and, for today, we must part; but we will arrange matters, so as to meet again in this tea-house. But, as people would make remarks if we left the tea-house together, I will go out first."

And so, much against their will, they tore themselves from one another, Genzaburo returning to his house, and O Koyo going home, her heart filled with joy at having found the man for whom she had pined; and from that day forth they used constantly to meet in secret at the tea-house; and Genzaburo, in his infatuation, never thought that the matter must surely become notorious after a while, and that he himself would be banished, and his family ruined: he only took care for the pleasure of the moment.

Now Chokichi, who had brought about the meeting between Genzaburo and his love, used to go every day to the tea-house at Oji, taking with him O Koyo; and Genzaburo neglected all his duties for the pleasure of these secret meetings. Chokichi saw this with great regret, and thought to himself that if Genzaburo gave himself up entirely to pleasure, and laid aside his duties, the secret would certainly be made public, and Genzaburo would bring ruin on himself and his family; so he began to devise some plan by which he might separate them, and plotted as eagerly to estrange them as he had formerly done to introduce them to one another.

At last he hit upon a device which satisfied him. Accordingly one day he went to O Koyo's house, and, meeting her father Kihachi, said to him:

"I've got a sad piece of news to tell you. The family of my lord Genzaburo have been complaining bitterly of his conduct in carrying on his relationship with your daughter, and of the ruin which exposure would bring upon the whole house; so they have been using their influence to persuade him to hear reason, and give up the connection. Now his lordship feels deeply for the damsel, and yet he cannot sacrifice his family for her sake. For the first time, he has become alive to the folly of which he has been guilty, and, full of remorse, he has commissioned me to devise some stratagem to break off the affair. Of course, this has taken me by surprise; but as there is no gainsaying the right of the case, I have had no option but to promise obedience: this promise I have come to redeem; and now, pray, advise your daughter to think no more of his lordship."

When Kihachi heard this he was surprised and distressed, and told O Koyo immediately; and she, grieving over the sad news, took no thought either of eating or drinking, but remained gloomy and desolate.

In the meanwhile, Chokichi went off to Genzaburo's house, and told him that O Koyo had been taken suddenly ill, and could not go to meet him, and begged him to wait patiently until she should send to tell him of her recovery. Genzaburo, never suspecting the story to be false, waited for thirty days, and still Chokichi brought him no tidings of O Koyo. At last he met Chokichi, and besought him to arrange a meeting for him with O Koyo.

"Sir," replied Chokichi, "she is not yet recovered; so it would be difficult to bring her to see your honour. But I have been thinking much about this affair, sir. If it becomes public, your honour's family will be plunged in ruin. I pray you, sir, to forget all about O Koyo."

"It's all very well for you to give me advice," answered Genzaburo, surprised; "but, having once bound myself to O Koyo, it would be a pitiful thing to desert her; I therefore implore you once more to arrange that I may meet her."

However, he would not consent upon any account; so Genzaburo returned home, and, from that time forth, daily entreated Chokichi to bring O Koyo to him, and, receiving nothing but advice from him in return, was very sad and lonely.

One day Genzaburo, intent on ridding himself of the grief he felt at his separation from O Koyo, went to the Yoshiwara, and, going into a house of entertainment, ordered a feast to be prepared, but, in the midst of gaiety, his heart yearned all the while for his lost love, and his merriment was but mourning in disguise. At last the night wore on; and as he was retiring along the corridor, he saw a man of about forty years of age, with long hair, coming towards him, who, when he saw Genzaburo, cried out, "Dear me! why this must be my young lord Genzaburo who has come out to enjoy himself."

Genzaburo thought this rather strange; but, looking at the man attentively, recognized him as a retainer whom he had had in his employ the year before, and said:

"This is a curious meeting: pray, what have you been about since you left my service? At any rate, I may congratulate you on being well and strong. Where are you living now?"

"Well, sir, since I parted from you I have been earning a living as a fortune-teller at Kanda, and have changed my name to Kaji Sazen. I am living in a poor and humble house; but if your lordship, at your leisure, would honour me with a visit – "

"Well, it's a lucky chance that has brought us together, and I certainly will go and see you; besides, I want you to do something for me. Shall you be at home the day after tomorrow?"

"Certainly, sir, I shall make a point of being at home."

"Very well, then, the day after tomorrow I will go to your house."

"I shall be at your service, sir. And now, as it is getting late, I will take my leave for tonight."

"Good night, then. We shall meet the day after tomorrow." And so the two parted, and went their several ways to rest.

On the appointed day Genzaburo made his preparations, and went in disguise, without any retainers, to call upon Sazen, who met him at the porch of his house, and said, "This is a great honour! My lord Genzaburo is indeed welcome. My house is very mean, but let me invite your lordship to come into an inner chamber."

"Pray," replied Genzaburo, "don't make any ceremony for me. Don't put yourself to any trouble on my account."

And so he passed in, and Sazen called to his wife to prepare wine and condiments; and they began to feast. At last Genzaburo, looking Sazen in the face, said, "There is a service which I want you to render me – a very secret service; but as if you were to refuse me, I should be put to shame, before I tell you what that service is, I must know whether you are willing to assist me in anything that I may require of you."

"Yes; if it is anything that is within my power, I am at your disposal."

"Well, then," said Genzaburo, greatly pleased, and drawing ten riyos from his bosom, "this is but a small present to make to you on my first visit, but pray accept it."

"No, indeed! I don't know what your lordship wishes of me; but, at any rate, I cannot receive this money. I really must beg your lordship to take it back again."

But Genzaburo pressed it upon him by force, and at last he was obliged to accept the money. Then Genzaburo told him the whole story of his loves with O Koyo – how he had first met her and fallen in love with her at the Adzuma Bridge; how Chokichi had introduced her to him at the tea-house at Oji, and then when she fell ill, and he wanted to see her again, instead of bringing her to him, had only given him good advice; and so Genzaburo drew a lamentable picture of his state of despair.

Sazen listened patiently to his story, and, after reflecting for a while, replied, "Well, sir, it's not a difficult matter to set right: and yet it will require some little management.

However, if your lordship will do me the honour of coming to see me again the day after tomorrow, I will cast about me in the meanwhile, and will let you know then the result of my deliberations."

When Genzaburo heard this he felt greatly relieved, and, recommending Sazen to do his best in the matter, took his leave and returned home. That very night Sazen, after thinking over all that Genzaburo had told him, laid his plans accordingly, and went off to the house of Kihachi, the Outcast chief, and told him the commission with which he had been entrusted.

Kihachi was of course greatly astonished, and said, "Some time ago, sir, Chokichi came here and said that my lord Genzaburo, having been rebuked by his family for his profligate behaviour, had determined to break off his connection with my daughter. Of course I knew that the daughter of an Outcast was no fitting match for a nobleman; so when Chokichi came and told me the errand upon which he had been sent, I had no alternative but to announce to my daughter that she must give up all thought of his lordship. Since that time she has been fretting and pining and starving for love. But when I tell her what you have just said, how glad and happy she will be! Let me go and talk to her at once." And with these words, he went to O Koyo's room; and when he looked upon her thin wasted face, and saw how sad she was, he felt more and more pity for her, and said, "Well, O Koyo, are you in better spirits today? Would you like something to eat?"

"Thank you, I have no appetite."

"Well, at any rate, I have some news for you that will make you happy. A messenger has come from my lord Genzaburo, for whom your heart yearns."

At this O Koyo, who had been crouching down like a drooping flower, gave a great start, and cried out, "Is that really true? Pray tell me all about it as quickly as possible."

"The story which Chokichi came and told us, that his lordship wished to break off the connection, was all an invention. He has all along been wishing to meet you, and constantly urged Chokichi to bring you a message from him. It is Chokichi who has been throwing obstacles in the way. At last his lordship has secretly sent a man, called Kaji Sazen, a fortune-teller, to arrange an interview between you. So now, my child, you may cheer up, and go to meet your lover as soon as you please."

When O Koyo heard this, she was so happy that she thought it must all be a dream, and doubted her own senses.

Kihachi in the meanwhile rejoined Sazen in the other room, and, after telling him of the joy with which his daughter had heard the news, put before him wine and other delicacies. "I think," said Sazen, "that the best way would be for O Koyo to live secretly in my lord Genzaburo's house; but as it will never do for all the world to know of it, it must be managed very quietly; and further, when I get home, I must think out some plan to lull the suspicions of that fellow Chokichi, and let you know my idea by letter. Meanwhile O Koyo had better come home with me tonight: although she is so terribly out of spirits now, she shall meet Genzaburo the day after tomorrow."

Kihachi reported this to O Koyo; and as her pining for Genzaburo was the only cause of her sickness, she recovered her spirits at once, and, saying that she would go with Sazen immediately, joyfully made her preparations. Then Sazen, having once more warned Kihachi to keep the matter secret from Chokichi, and to act upon the letter which he should send him, returned home, taking with him O Koyo; and after O Koyo had bathed and dressed her hair, and painted herself and put on beautiful clothes, she came out looking so lovely that no princess in the land could vie with her; and Sazen, when he saw her, said to himself that it was no wonder that Genzaburo had fallen in love with her; then, as it was getting late, he advised her to go to rest, and, after showing her to her apartments, went to his own room and wrote his letter to Kihachi, containing the scheme which he had devised. When Kihachi received his instructions, he was filled with admiration at Sazen's ingenuity, and, putting on an appearance of great alarm and agitation, went off immediately to call on Chokichi, and said to him:

"Oh, Master Chokichi, such a terrible thing has happened! Pray, let me tell you all about it."

"Indeed! what can it be?"

"Oh! sir," answered Kihachi, pretending to wipe away his tears, "my daughter O Koyo, mourning over her separation from my lord Genzaburo, at first refused all sustenance, and remained nursing her sorrows until, last night, her woman's heart failing to bear up against her great grief, she drowned herself in the river, leaving behind her a paper on which she had written her intention."

When Chokichi heard this, he was thunderstruck, and exclaimed, "Can this really be true! And when I think that it was I who first introduced her to my lord, I am ashamed to look you in the face."

"Oh, say not so: misfortunes are the punishment due for our misdeeds in a former state of existence. I bear you no ill-will. This money which I hold in my hand was my daughter's; and in her last instructions she wrote to beg that it might be given, after her death, to you, through whose intervention she became allied with a nobleman: so please accept it as my daughter's legacy to you;" and as he spoke, he offered him three riyos.

"You amaze me!" replied the other. "How could I, above all men, who have so much to reproach myself with in my conduct towards you, accept this money?"

"Nay; it was my dead daughter's wish. But since you reproach yourself in the matter when you think of her, I will beg you to put up a prayer and to cause masses to be said for her."

At last, Chokichi, after much persuasion, and greatly to his own distress, was obliged to accept the money; and when Kihachi had carried out all Sazen's instructions, he returned home, laughing in his sleeve.

Chokichi was sorely grieved to hear of O Koyo's death, and remained thinking over the sad news; when all of a sudden looking about him, he saw something like a letter lying on the spot where Kihachi had been sitting, so he picked it up and read it; and, as luck would have it, it was the very letter which contained Sazen's instructions to Kihachi, and in which the whole story which had just affected him so much was made up. When he perceived the trick that had been played upon him, he was very angry, and exclaimed, "To think that I should have been so hoaxed by that hateful old dotard, and such a fellow as Sazen! And Genzaburo, too! – out of gratitude for the favours which I had received from him in old days, I faithfully gave him good advice, and all in vain. Well, they've gulled me once; but I'll be even with them yet, and hinder their game before it is played out!" And so he worked himself up into a fury, and went off secretly to prowl about Sazen's house to watch for O Koyo, determined to pay off Genzaburo and Sazen for their conduct to him.

In the meanwhile Sazen, who did not for a moment suspect what had happened, when the day which had been fixed upon by him and Genzaburo arrived, made O Koyo put on her best clothes, smartened up his house, and got ready a feast against Genzaburo's arrival. The latter came punctually to his time, and, going in at once, said to the fortune-teller, "Well, have you succeeded in the commission with which I entrusted you?"

At first Sazen pretended to be vexed at the question, and said, "Well, sir, I've done my best; but it's not a matter which can be settled in a hurry. However, there's a young lady of high birth and wonderful beauty upstairs, who has come here secretly to have her fortune told; and if your lordship would like to come with me and see her, you can do so."

But Genzaburo, when he heard that he was not to meet O Koyo, lost heart entirely, and made up his mind to go home again. Sazen, however, pressed him so eagerly, that at last he went upstairs to see this vaunted beauty; and Sazen, drawing aside a screen, showed him O Koyo, who was sitting there. Genzaburo gave a great start, and, turning to Sazen, said, "Well, you certainly are a first-rate hand at keeping up a hoax. However, I cannot sufficiently praise the way in which you have carried out my instructions."

"Pray, don't mention it, sir. But as it is a long time since you have met the young lady, you must have a great deal to say to one another; so I will go downstairs, and, if you want anything, pray call me." And so he went downstairs and left them.

Then Genzaburo, addressing O Koyo, said, "Ah! it is indeed a long time since we met. How happy it makes me to see you again! Why, your face has grown quite thin. Poor thing! have you been unhappy?" And O Koyo, with the tears starting from her eyes for joy, hid her face; and her heart was so full that she could not speak. But Genzaburo, passing his hand gently over her head and back, and comforting her, said, "Come, sweetheart, there is no need to sob so. Talk to me a little, and let me hear your voice."

At last O Koyo raised her head and said, "Ah! when I was separated from you by the tricks of Chokichi, and thought that I should never meet you again, how tenderly I thought of you! I thought I should have died, and waited for my hour to come, pining all the while for you. And when at last, as I lay between life and death, Sazen came with a message from you, I thought it was all a dream." And as she spoke, she bent her head and sobbed again; and in Genzaburo's eyes she seemed more beautiful than ever, with her pale, delicate face; and he loved her better than before. Then she said, "If I were to tell you all I have suffered until today, I should never stop."

"Yes," replied Genzaburo, "I too have suffered much;" and so they told one another their mutual griefs, and from that day forth they constantly met at Sazen's house.

One day, as they were feasting and enjoying themselves in an upper storey in Sazen's house, Chokichi came to the house and said, "I beg pardon; but does one Master Sazen live here?"

"Certainly, sir: I am Sazen, at your service. Pray where are you from?"

"Well, sir, I have a little business to transact with you. May I make so bold as to go in?" And with these words, he entered the house.

"But who and what are you?" said Sazen.

"Sir, I am an Outcast; and my name is Chokichi. I beg to bespeak your goodwill for myself: I hope we may be friends."

Sazen was not a little taken aback at this; however, he put on an innocent face, as though he had never heard of Chokichi before, and said, "I never heard of such a thing! Why, I thought you were some respectable person; and you have the impudence to tell me that your name is Chokichi, and that you're one of those accursed Outcasts. To think of such a shameless villain coming and asking to be friends with me, forsooth! Get you gone! – the quicker, the better: your presence pollutes the house."

Chokichi smiled contemptuously, as he answered, "So you deem the presence of an Outcast in your house a pollution – eh? Why, I thought you must be one of us."

"Insolent knave! Begone as fast as possible."

"Well, since you say that I defile your house, you had better get rid of O Koyo as well. I suppose she must equally be a pollution to it."

This put Sazen rather in a dilemma; however, he made up his mind not to show any hesitation, and said, "What are you talking about? There is no O Koyo here; and I never saw such a person in my life."

Chokichi quietly drew out of the bosom of his dress the letter from Sazen to Kihachi, which he had picked up a few days before, and, showing it to Sazen, replied, "If you wish to dispute the genuineness of this paper, I will report the whole matter to the Governor of Edo; and Genzaburo's family will be ruined, and the rest of you who are parties in this affair will come in for your share of trouble. Just wait a little."

And as he pretended to leave the house, Sazen, at his wits' end, cried out, "Stop! stop! I want to speak to you. Pray, stop and listen quietly. It is quite true, as you said, that O Koyo is in my house; and really your indignation is perfectly just. Come! let us talk over matters a little. Now you yourself were originally a respectable man; and although you have fallen in life, there is no reason why your disgrace should last for ever. All that you want in order to enable you to escape out of this fraternity of Outcasts is a little money. Why should you not get this from Genzaburo, who is very anxious to keep his intrigue with O Koyo secret?"

Chokichi laughed disdainfully. "I am ready to talk with you; but I don't want any money. All I want is to report the affair to the authorities, in order that I may be revenged for the fraud that was put upon me."

"Won't you accept twenty-five riyos?"

"Twenty-five riyos! No, indeed! I will not take a fraction less than a hundred; and if I cannot get them I will report the whole matter at once."

Sazen, after a moment's consideration, hit upon a scheme, and answered, smiling, "Well, Master Chokichi, you're a fine fellow, and I admire your spirit. You shall have the hundred riyos you ask for; but, as I have not so much money by me at present, I will go to Genzaburo's house and fetch it. It's getting dark now, but it's not very late; so I'll trouble you to come with me, and then I can give you the money tonight."

Chokichi consenting to this, the pair left the house together.

Now Sazen, who as a Ronin wore a long dirk in his girdle, kept looking out for a moment when Chokichi should be off his guard, in order to kill him; but Chokichi kept his eyes open, and did not give Sazen a chance. At last Chokichi, as ill-luck would have it, stumbled against a stone and fell; and Sazen, profiting by the chance, drew his dirk and stabbed him in the side; and as Chokichi, taken by surprise, tried to get up, he cut him severely over the head, until at last he fell dead. Sazen then looking around him, and seeing, to his great delight, that there was no one near, returned home. The following day, Chokichi's body was found by the police; and when they examined it, they found nothing upon it save a paper, which they read, and which proved to be the very letter which Sazen had sent to Kihachi, and which Chokichi had picked up. The matter was immediately reported to the governor, and, Sazen having been summoned, an investigation was held. Sazen, cunning and bold murderer as he was, lost his self-possession when he saw what a fool he had been not to get back from Chokichi the letter which he had written, and, when he was put to a rigid examination under torture, confessed that he had hidden O Koyo at Genzaburo's instigation, and then killed Chokichi, who had found out the secret. Upon this the governor, after consulting about Genzaburo's case, decided that, as he had disgraced his position as a Hatamoto by contracting an alliance with the daughter of an Outcast, his property should be confiscated, his family blotted out, and himself banished. As for Kihachi, the Outcast chief, and his daughter O Koyo, they were handed over for punishment to the chief of the Outcasts, and by him they too were banished; while Sazen, against whom the murder of Chokichi had been fully proved, was executed according to law.

The Story of Princess Hase

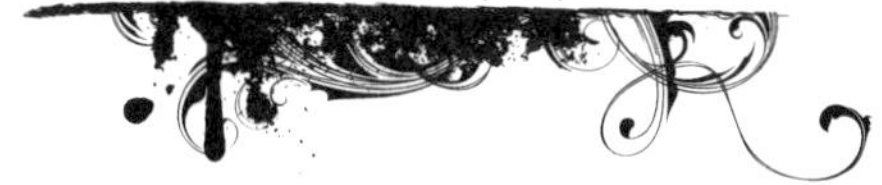

MANY, MANY YEARS AGO there lived in Nara, the ancient Capital of Japan, a wise State minister, by name Prince Toyonari Fujiwara. His wife was a noble, good, and beautiful woman called Princess Murasaki (Violet). They had been married by their respective families according to Japanese custom when very young, and had lived together happily ever since. They had, however, one cause for great sorrow, for as the years went by no child was born to them. This made them very unhappy, for they both longed to see a child of their own who would grow up to gladden their old age, carry on the family name, and keep up the ancestral rites when they were dead. The Prince and his lovely wife, after long consultation and much thought, determined to make a pilgrimage to the temple of Hase-no-Kwannon (Goddess of Mercy at Hase), for they believed, according to the beautiful tradition of their religion, that the Mother of Mercy, Kwannon, comes to answer the prayers of mortals in the form that they need the most. Surely after all these years of prayer she would come to them in the form of a beloved child in answer to their special pilgrimage, for that was the greatest need of their two lives. Everything else they had that this life could give them, but it was all as nothing because the cry of their hearts was unsatisfied.

So the Prince Toyonari and his wife went to the temple of Kwannon at Hase and stayed there for a long time, both daily offering incense and praying to Kwannon, the Heavenly Mother, to grant them the desire of their whole lives. And their prayer was answered.

A daughter was born at last to the Princess Murasaki, and great was the joy of her heart. On presenting the child to her husband, they both decided to call her Hase-Hime, or the Princess of Hase, because she was the gift of the Kwannon at that place. They both reared her with great care and tenderness, and the child grew in strength and beauty.

When the little girl was five years old her mother fell dangerously ill and all the doctors and their medicines could not save her. A little before she breathed her last she called her daughter to her, and gently stroking her head, said:

"Hase-Hime, do you know that your mother cannot live any longer? Though I die, you must grow up a good girl. Do your best not to give trouble to your nurse or any other of your family. Perhaps your father will marry again and someone will fill my place as your mother. If so do not grieve for me, but look upon your father's second wife as your true mother, and be obedient and filial to both her and your father. Remember when you are grown up to be submissive to those who are your superiors, and to be kind to all those who are under you. Don't forget this. I die with the hope that you will grow up a model woman."

Hase-Hime listened in an attitude of respect while her mother spoke, and promised to do all that she was told. There is a proverb which says "As the soul is at three so it is at one hundred," and so Hase-Hime grew up as her mother had wished, a good and obedient little Princess, though she was now too young to understand how great was the loss of her mother.

Not long after the death of his first wife, Prince Toyonari married again, a lady of noble birth named Princess Terute. Very different in character, alas! to the good and wise Princess Murasaki, this woman had a cruel, bad heart. She did not love her step-daughter at all, and was often very unkind to the little motherless girl, saying to herself:

"This is not my child! this is not my child!"

But Hase-Hime bore every unkindness with patience, and even waited upon her step-mother kindly and obeyed her in every way and never gave any trouble, just as she had been trained by her own good mother, so that the Lady Terute had no cause for complaint against her.

The little Princess was very diligent, and her favourite studies were music and poetry. She would spend several hours practicing every day, and her father had the most proficient of masters he could find to teach her the koto (Japanese harp), the art of writing letters and verse. When she was twelve years of age she could play so beautifully that she and her step-mother were summoned to the Palace to perform before the Emperor.

It was the Festival of the Cherry Flowers, and there were great festivities at the Court. The Emperor threw himself into the enjoyment of the season, and commanded that Princess Hase should perform before him on the koto, and that her mother Princess Terute should accompany her on the flute.

The Emperor sat on a raised dais, before which was hung a curtain of finely-sliced bamboo and purple tassels, so that His Majesty might see all and not be seen, for no ordinary subject was allowed to look upon his sacred face.

Hase-Hime was a skilled musician though so young, and often astonished her masters by her wonderful memory and talent. On this momentous occasion she played well. But Princess Terute, her step-mother, who was a lazy woman and never took the trouble to practice daily, broke down in her accompaniment and had to request one of the Court ladies to take her place. This was a great disgrace, and she was furiously jealous to think that she had failed where her step-daughter succeeded; and to make matters worse the Emperor sent many beautiful gifts to the little Princess to reward her for playing so well at the Palace.

There was also now another reason why Princess Terute hated her step-daughter, for she had had the good fortune to have a son born to her, and in her inmost heart she kept saying:

"If only Hase-Hime were not here, my son would have all the love of his father."

And never having learned to control herself, she allowed this wicked thought to grow into the awful desire of taking her step-daughter's life.

So one day she secretly ordered some poison and poisoned some sweet wine. This poisoned wine she put into a bottle. Into another similar bottle she poured some good wine. It was the occasion of the Boys' Festival on the fifth of May, and Hase-Hime was playing with her little brother. All his toys of warriors and heroes were spread out and she was telling him wonderful stories about each of them. They were both enjoying themselves and laughing merrily with their attendants when his mother entered with the two bottles of wine and some delicious cakes.

"You are both so good and happy." said the wicked Princess Terute with a smile, "that I have brought you some sweet wine as a reward – and here are some nice cakes for my good children."

And she filled two cups from the different bottles.

Hase-Hime, never dreaming of the dreadful part her step-mother was acting, took one of the cups of wine and gave to her little step brother the other that had been poured out for him.

The wicked woman had carefully marked the poisoned bottle, but on coming into the room she had grown nervous, and pouring out the wine hurriedly had unconsciously given the poisoned cup to her own child. All this time she was anxiously watching the little Princess, but to her amazement no change whatever took place in the young girl's face. Suddenly the little boy screamed and threw himself on the floor, doubled up with pain. His mother flew to him, taking the precaution to upset the two tiny jars of wine which she had brought into the room, and lifted him up. The attendants rushed for the doctor, but nothing could save the child – he died within the hour in his mother's arms. Doctors did not know much in those ancient times, and it was thought that the wine had disagreed with the boy, causing convulsions of which he died.

Thus was the wicked woman punished in losing her own child when she had tried to do away with her step-daughter; but instead of blaming herself she began to hate Hase-Hime more than ever in the bitterness and wretchedness of her own heart, and she eagerly watched for an opportunity to do her harm, which was, however, long in coming.

When Hase-Hime was thirteen years of age, she had already become mentioned as a poetess of some merit. This was an accomplishment very much cultivated by the women of old Japan and one held in high esteem.

It was the rainy season at Nara, and floods were reported every day as doing damage in the neighbourhood. The river Tatsuta, which flowed through the Imperial Palace grounds, was swollen to the top of its banks, and the roaring of the torrents of water rushing along a narrow bed so disturbed the Emperor's rest day and night, that a serious nervous disorder was the result. An Imperial Edict was sent forth to all the Buddhist temples commanding the priests to offer up continuous prayers to Heaven to stop the noise of the flood. But this was of no avail.

Then it was whispered in Court circles that the Princess Hase, the daughter of Prince Toyonari Fujiwara, second minister at Court, was the most gifted poetess of the day, though still so young, and her masters confirmed the report. Long ago, a beautiful and gifted maiden-poetess had moved Heaven by praying in verse, had brought down rain upon a land famished with drought – so said the ancient biographers of the poetess Ono-no-Komachi. If the Princess Hase were to write a poem and offer it in prayer, might it not stop the noise of the rushing river and remove the cause of the Imperial illness? What the Court said at last reached the ears of the Emperor himself, and he sent an order to the minister Prince Toyonari to this effect.

Great indeed was Hase-Hime's fear and astonishment when her father sent for her and told her what was required of her. Heavy, indeed, was the duty that was laid on her young shoulders – that of saving the Emperor's life by the merit of her verse.

At last the day came and her poem was finished. It was written on a leaflet of paper heavily flecked with gold-dust. With her father and attendants and some of the Court officials, she proceeded to the bank of the roaring torrent and raising up her heart to Heaven, she read the poem she had composed, aloud, lifting it heavenwards in her two hands.

Strange indeed it seemed to all those standing round. The waters ceased their roaring, and the river was quiet in direct answer to her prayer. After this the Emperor soon recovered his health.

His Majesty was highly pleased, and sent for her to the Palace and rewarded her with the rank of Chinjo – that of Lieutenant-General – to distinguish her. From that time she was called Chinjo-hime, or the Lieutenant-General Princess, and respected and loved by all.

There was only one person who was not pleased at Hase-Hime's success. That one was her stepmother. Forever brooding over the death of her own child whom she had killed when trying to poison her step-daughter, she had the mortification of seeing her rise to power and honour, marked by Imperial favour and the admiration of the whole Court. Her envy and jealousy burned in her heart like fire. Many were the lies she carried to her husband about Hase-Hime, but all to no purpose. He would listen to none of her tales, telling her sharply that she was quite mistaken.

At last the step-mother, seizing the opportunity of her husband's absence, ordered one of her old servants to take the innocent girl to the Hibari Mountains, the wildest part of the country, and to kill her there. She invented a dreadful story about the little Princess, saying that this was the only way to prevent disgrace falling upon the family – by killing her.

Katoda, her vassal, was bound to obey his mistress. Anyhow, he saw that it would be the wisest plan to pretend obedience in the absence of the girl's father, so he placed Hase-Hime in a palanquin and accompanied her to the most solitary place he could find in the wild district. The poor child knew there was no good in protesting to her unkind step-mother at being sent away in this strange manner, so she went as she was told.

But the old servant knew that the young Princess was quite innocent of all the things her step-mother had invented to him as reasons for her outrageous orders, and he determined to save her life. Unless he killed her, however, he could not return to his cruel task-mistress, so he decided to stay out in the wilderness. With the help of some peasants he soon built a little cottage, and having sent secretly for his wife to come, these two good old people did all in their power to take care of the now unfortunate Princess. She all the time trusted in her father, knowing that as soon as he returned home and found her absent, he would search for her.

Prince Toyonari, after some weeks, came home, and was told by his wife that his daughter Hime had done something wrong and had run away for fear of being punished. He was nearly ill with anxiety. Everyone in the house told the same story – that Hase-Hime had suddenly disappeared, none of them knew why or whither. For fear of scandal he kept the matter quiet and searched everywhere he could think of, but all to no purpose.

One day, trying to forget his terrible worry, he called all his men together and told them to make ready for a several days' hunt in the mountains. They were soon ready and mounted, waiting at the gate for their lord. He rode hard and fast to the district of the Hibari Mountains, a great company following him. He was soon far ahead of everyone, and at last found himself in a narrow picturesque valley.

Looking round and admiring the scenery, he noticed a tiny house on one of the hills quite near, and then he distinctly heard a beautiful clear voice reading aloud. Seized with curiosity as to who could be studying so diligently in such a lonely spot, he dismounted, and leaving his horse to his groom, he walked up the hillside and approached the cottage. As he drew nearer his surprise increased, for he could see that the reader was a beautiful girl. The cottage was wide open and she was sitting facing the view. Listening attentively, he heard her reading the Buddhist scriptures with great devotion. More and more curious, he hurried on to the tiny gate and entered the little garden, and looking up beheld his lost daughter Hase-Hime. She was so intent on what she was saying that she neither heard nor saw her father till he spoke.

"Hase-Hime!" he cried, "it is you, my Hase-Hime!"

Taken by surprise, she could hardly realize that it was her own dear father who was calling her, and for a moment she was utterly bereft of the power to speak or move.

"My father, my father! It is indeed you – oh, my father!" was all she could say, and running to him she caught hold of his thick sleeve, and burying her face burst into a passion of tears.

Her father stroked her dark hair, asking her gently to tell him all that had happened, but she only wept on, and he wondered if he were not really dreaming.

Then the faithful old servant Katoda came out, and bowing himself to the ground before his master, poured out the long tale of wrong, telling him all that had happened, and how it was that he found his daughter in such a wild and desolate spot with only two old servants to take care of her.

The Prince's astonishment and indignation knew no bounds. He gave up the hunt at once and hurried home with his daughter. One of the company galloped ahead to inform the household of the glad news, and the step-mother hearing what had happened, and fearful of meeting her husband now that her wickedness was discovered, fled from the house and returned in disgrace to her father's roof, and nothing more was heard of her.

The old servant Katoda was rewarded with the highest promotion in his master's service, and lived happily to the end of his days, devoted to the little Princess, who never forgot that she owed her life to this faithful retainer. She was no longer troubled by an unkind step-mother, and her days passed happily and quietly with her father.

As Prince Toyonari had no son, he adopted a younger son of one of the Court nobles to be his heir, and to marry his daughter Hase-Hime, and in a few years the marriage took place. Hase-Hime lived to a good old age, and all said that she was the wisest, most devout, and most beautiful mistress that had ever reigned in Prince Toyonari's ancient house. She had the joy of presenting her son, the future lord of the family, to her father just before he retired from active life.

To this day there is preserved a piece of needle-work in one of the Buddhist temples of Kyoto. It is a beautiful piece of tapestry, with the figure of Buddha embroidered in the silky threads drawn from the stem of the lotus. This is said to have been the work of the hands of the good Princess Hase.

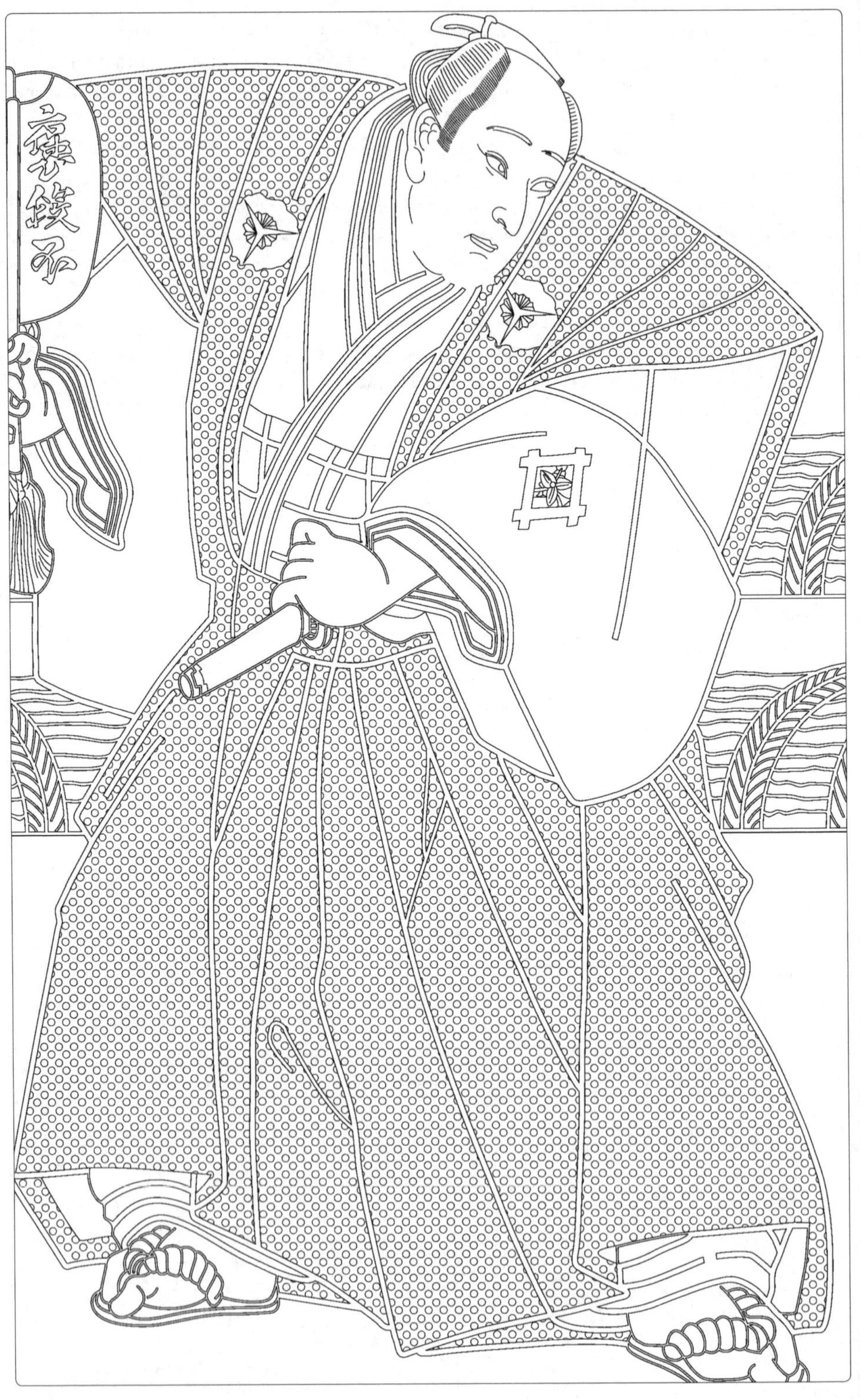

Ghost Stories & Supernatural Creatures

Introduction

SOME OF THE LEGENDS in this chapter were adapted by Frederick Hadland Davis from stories in Lafcadio Hearn's *Kwaidan* and *Glimpses of Unfamiliar Japan*. In its widest sense, the word *kaidan* can indicate any ghost or horror story, but these tales tend to originate from or evoke the folklore and world of Edo period Japan. Classic *kaidan* usually include some element of vengeance on the part of the spirit for mistreatment in their lifetime – the two long sagas at the end of this section (*The Yotsuya Kwaidan or O'Iwa Inari* and *The Bancho Sarayashiki or The Lady of The Plates*) are particularly famous *kaidan* – the poor maidservant who haunts a well in the second story will be familiar to fans of the horror film *Ring*.

Supernatural beings populate many a Japanese tale. In addition to the fearsome demons or ogres known as *oni*, whom we have already encountered in some of the heroes' exploits, in the following stories we meet the *tengu* and other species of (often man-eating) goblin, *kappas*, fire ghosts, sea monsters and all manner of spirits and demons.

A Kakemono Ghost

SAWARA WAS A PUPIL in the house of the artist Tenko, who was a kind and able master, while Sawara, even at the commencement of his art studies, showed considerable promise. Kimi, Tenko's niece, devoted her time to her uncle and in directing the affairs of the household generally. Kimi was beautiful, and it was not long before she fell desperately in love with Sawara. This young pupil regarded her as very charming, one to die for if need be, and in his heart he secretly loved her. His love, however, unlike Kimi's, was not demonstrative, for he had his work to attend to, and so, to be sure, had Kimi; but work with Sawara came before his love, and with Kimi it was only love that mattered.

One day, when Tenko was paying a visit, Kimi came to Sawara, and, unable to restrain her feelings any longer, told him of her love, and asked him if he would like to marry her. Having made her request, she set tea before her lover, and awaited his answer.

Sawara returned her affection, and said that he would be delighted to marry her, adding, however, that marriage was not possible until after two or three years, when he had established a position for himself and had become a famous artist.

Sawara, in order to add to his knowledge of art, decided to study under a celebrated painter named Myokei, and, everything having been arranged, he bade farewell to his old master and Kimi, promising that he would return as soon as he had made a name for himself and become a great artist.

Two years went by and Tenko and Kimi heard no news of Sawara. Many admirers of Kimi came to her uncle with offers of marriage, and Tenko was debating as to what he should do in the matter, when he received a letter from Myokei, saying that Sawara was doing good work, and that he desired that his excellent pupil should marry his daughter.

Tenko imagined, perhaps not without some reason, that Sawara had forgotten all about Kimi, and that the best thing he could do was to give her in marriage to Yorozuya, a wealthy merchant, and also to fulfil Miyokei's wish that Sawara should marry the great painter's daughter. With these intentions Tenko resolved to employ strategy, so he called Kimi to him, and said:

"Kimi, I have had a letter from Myokei, and I am afraid the sad news which it contains will distress you. Myokei wishes Sawara to marry his daughter, and I have told him that I fully approve of the union. I feel sure that Sawara has neglected you, and I therefore wish that you should marry Yorozuya, who will make, I am sure, a very good husband."

When Kimi heard these words she wept bitterly, and without a word went to her room.

In the morning Tenko entered Kimi's apartment, but his niece had gone, and the protracted search that followed failed to discover her whereabouts.

When Myokei had received Tenko's letter he told the promising young artist that he wished him to marry his daughter, and thus establish a family of painters; but Sawara was amazed to hear this extraordinary news, and explained that he could not accept the honour of becoming his son-in-law because he was already engaged to Tenko's niece.

Sawara, all too late, sent letters to Kimi, and, receiving no reply, he set out for his old home, shortly after the death of Myokei.

When he reached the little house where he had received his first lessons in the art of painting he learnt with anger that Kimi had left her old uncle, and in due time he married Kiku ('Chrysanthemum'), the daughter of a wealthy farmer.

Shortly after Sawara's marriage the Lord of Aki bade him paint the seven scenes of the Islands of Kabakari-jima, which were to be mounted on gold screens. He at once set out for these islands, and made a number of rough sketches. While thus employed he met along the shore a woman with a red cloth round her loins, her hair loose and falling about her shoulders. She carried shell-fish in her basket, and as soon as she saw Sawara she recognised him.

"You are Sawara and I am Kimi," said she, "to whom you are engaged. It was a false report about your marriage with Myokei's daughter, and my heart is full of joy, for now nothing prevents our union."

"Alas! poor, much-wronged Kimi, that cannot be!" replied Sawara. "I thought that you deserted Tenko, and that you had forgotten me, and believing these things to be true I have married Kiku, a farmer's daughter."

Kimi, without a word, sprang forward like a hunted animal, ran along the shore, and entered her little hut, Sawara running after her and calling her name over and over again. Before his very eyes he saw Kimi take a knife and thrust it into her throat, and in another moment she lay dead upon the ground. Sawara wept as he gazed upon her still form, noticed the wistful beauty of Death upon her cheek, and saw a new glory in her wind-blown hair. So fair and wonderful was her presence now that when he had controlled his weeping he made a sketch of the woman who had loved him so well, but so pitifully. Above the mark of the tide he buried her, and when he reached his own home he took out the rough sketch, painted a picture of Kimi, and hung the *kakemono* on the wall.

Kimi Finds Peace

That very night he awoke to find that the figure on the *kakemono* had come to life, that Kimi with the wound in her throat, the dishevelled hair, stood beside him. Night after night she came, a silent, pitiful figure, until at last Sawara, unable to bear these visitations any longer, presented the *kakemono* to the Korinji Temple and sent his wife back to her parents. The priests of the Korinji Temple prayed every day for the soul of Kimi, and by and by Kimi found peace and troubled Sawara no more.

The Peony Lantern

TSUYU ('MORNING DEW') was the only daughter of Iijima. When her father married again she found she could not live happily with her stepmother, and a separate house was built for her, where she lived with her servant-maid Yone.

One day Tsuyu received a visit from the family physician, Yamamoto Shijo accompanied by a handsome young *samurai* named Hagiwara Shinzaburo. These young people fell in love with each other, and at parting Tsuyu whispered to Shinzaburo: "*Remember! if you do not come to see me again I shall certainly die*!"

Shinzaburo had every intention of seeing the fair Tsuyu as frequently as possible. Etiquette, however, would not allow him to visit her alone, so that he was compelled to rely on the old doctor's promise to take him to the villa where his loved one lived. The old doctor, however, having seen more than the young people had supposed, purposely refrained from keeping his promise.

Tsuyu, believing that the handsome young *samurai* had proved unfaithful, slowly pined away and died. Her faithful servant Yone also died soon afterwards, being unable to live without her mistress, and they were buried side by side in the cemetery of Shin-Banzui-In.

Shortly after this sad event had taken place the old doctor called upon Shinzaburo and gave him full particulars of the death of Tsuyu and her maid.

Shinzaburo felt the blow keenly. Night and day the girl was in his thoughts. He inscribed her name upon a mortuary tablet, placed offerings before it, and repeated many prayers.

The Dead Return

When the first day of the Festival of the Dead arrived he set food on the Shelf of Souls and hung out lanterns to guide the spirits during their brief earthly sojourn. As the night was warm and the moon at her full, he sat in his verandah and waited. He felt that all these preparations would not be in vain, and in his heart he believed that the soul of Tsuyu would come to him.

Suddenly the stillness was broken by the sound of *kara-kon*, *kara-kon*, the soft patter of women's *geta*. There was something strange and haunting about the sound. Shinzaburo rose and peeped over the hedge. He saw two women. One was carrying a long-shaped lantern with silk peonies stuck in at the upper end; the other wore a lovely robe covered with designs of autumnal blossom. In another moment he recognised the sweet figure of Tsuyu and her maid Yone.

When Yone had explained that the wicked old doctor had told them that Shinzaburo was dead, and the young *samurai* had likewise informed his visitors that he, too, had learnt from the same source that his loved one and her maid had departed this life, the two women entered the house, and remained there that night, returning home a little before sunrise. Night after night they came in this mysterious manner, and always Yone carried the shining peony-lantern, always she and her mistress departed at the same hour.

A Spy

One night Tomozo, one of Shinzaburo's servants, who lived next door to his master, chanced to hear the sound of a woman's voice in his lord's apartment. He peeped through a crack in one of the sliding doors, and perceived by the night-lantern within the room that his master was talking with a strange woman under the mosquito-net. Their conversation was so extraordinary that Tomozo was determined to see the woman's face. When he succeeded in doing so his hair stood on end and he trembled violently, for he saw the face of a dead woman, a woman long dead. There was no flesh on her fingers, for what had once been fingers were now a bunch of jangling bones. Only the upper part of her body had substance; below her waist there was but a dim, moving shadow. While Tomozo gazed with horror upon such a revolting scene a second woman's figure sprang up from within the room. She made for the chink and for Tomozo's eye behind it. With a shriek of terror the spying Tomozo fled to the house of Hakuodo Yusai.

Yusai's Advice

Now Yusai was a man well versed in all manner of mysteries; but nevertheless Tomozo's story made considerable impression upon him, and he listened to every detail with the utmost amazement. When the servant had finished his account of the affair Yusai informed him that his master was a doomed man if the woman proved to be a ghost, that love between the living and the dead ended in the destruction of the living.

However, apart from critically examining this strange event, Yusai took practical steps to rescue this young *samurai* from so horrible a fate. The next morning he discussed the matter with Shinzaburo, and told him pretty clearly that he had been loving a ghost, and that the sooner he got rid of that ghost the better it would be for him. He ended his discourse by advising the youth to go to the district of Shitaya, in Yanaka-no-Sasaki, the place where these women had said they lived.

The Mystery is Revealed

Shinzaburo carried out Yusai's advice, but nowhere in the quarter of Yanaka-no-Sasaki could he find the dwelling-place of Tsuyu. On his return home he happened to pass through the temple Shin-Banzui-In. There he saw two tombs placed side by side, one of no distinction, and the other large and handsome, adorned with a peony-lantern swinging gently in the breeze. Shinzaburo remembered that this lantern and the one carried by Yone were identical, and an acolyte informed him that the tombs were those of Tsuyu and Yone. Then it was that he realised the strange meaning of Yone's words: "*We went away, and found a very small house in Yanaka-no-Sasaki. There we are now just barely able to live by doing a little private work.*" Their house, then, was a grave. The ghost of Yone carried the peony-lantern, and the ghost of Tsuyu wound her fleshless arms about the neck of the young *samurai*.

Holy Charms

Shinzaburo, now fully aware of the horror of the situation, hastily retraced his steps and sought counsel from the wise, far-seeing Yusai. This learned man confessed his inability to help him further in the matter, but advised him to go to the high-priest Ryoseki, of Shin-Banzui-In, and gave him a letter explaining what had taken place.

Ryoseki listened unmoved to Shinzaburo's story, for he had heard so many bearing on the same theme, the evil power of Karma. He gave the young man a small gold image of Buddha, which he instructed him to wear next his skin, telling him that it would protect the living from the dead. He also gave him a holy *sutra*, called "Treasure-Raining Sutra," which he was commended to recite in his house every night; and lastly he gave him a bundle of sacred texts. Each holy strip he was to paste over an opening in his house.

By nightfall everything was in order in Shinzaburo's house. All the apertures were covered with sacred texts, and the air resounded with the recitation of the 'Treasure-Raining Sutra', while the little gold Buddha swayed upon the *samurai's* breast. But somehow or other peace did not come to Shinzaburo that night. Sleep refused to close his weary eyes, and just as a temple bell ceased booming he heard the old *karan-koron, karan-koron* – the patter of ghostly *geta*! Then the sound ceased. Fear and joy battled within Shinzaburo's heart. He stopped reciting the holy *sutra* and looked forth into the night. Once more he saw Tsuyu and her maid with the peony-lantern. Never before had Tsuyu looked so beautiful or so alluring;

but a nameless terror held him back. He heard with bitter anguish the women speaking together. He heard Yone tell her mistress that his love had changed because his doors had been made fast against them, followed by the plaintive weeping of Tsuyu. At last the women wandered round to the back of the house. But back and front alike prevented their entry, so potent were the sacred words of the Lord Buddha.

The Betrayal

As all the efforts of Yone to enter Shinzaburo's house were of no avail, she went night after night to Tomozo and begged him to remove the sacred texts from his master's dwelling. Over and over again, out of intense fear, Tomozo promised to do so, but with the coming of daylight he grew brave and decided not to betray one to whom he owed so much. One night, however, Yone refused to be trifled with. She threatened Tomozo with awful hatred if he did not take away one of the sacred texts, and in addition she pulled such a terrible face that Tomozo nearly died of fright.

Tomozo's wife Mine happened to awake and hear the voice of a strange woman speaking to her husband. When the ghost-woman had vanished Mine gave her lord cunning counsel to the effect that he should consent to carry out Yone's request provided that she would reward him with a hundred *ryō*.

Two nights later, when this wicked servant had received his reward, he gave Yone the little gold image of Buddha, took down from his master's house one of the sacred texts, and buried in a field the *sutra* which his master used to recite. This enabled Yone and her mistress to enter the house of Shinzaburo once more, and with their entry began again this horrible love of the dead, presided over by the mysterious power of Karma.

When Tomozo came the next morning to call his master as usual, he obtained no response to his knocking. At last he entered the apartment, and there, under the mosquito-net, lay his master dead, and beside him were the white bones of a woman. The bones of 'Morning Dew' were twined round the neck of one who had loved her too well, of one who had loved her with a fierce passion that at the last had been his undoing.

Hōichi-the-Earless

IT IS SAID THAT for seven hundred years after this great battle the sea and coast in the vicinity have been haunted by the ghosts of the Taira clan. Mysterious fires shone on the waves, and the air was filled with the noise of warfare. In order to pacify the unfortunate spirits the temple of Amidaji was built at Akamagaseki, and a cemetery was made close by, in which were various monuments inscribed with the names of the drowned Emperor and his principal followers. This temple and cemetery pacified the ghostly visitants to a certain extent, but from time to time many strange things happened, as we shall gather from the following legend.

There once lived at the Amidaji temple a blind priest named Hōichi. He was famous for his recitation and for his marvellous skill in playing upon the *biwa* (a four-stringed lute), and he was particularly fond of reciting stories in connection with the protracted war between the Taira and Minamoto clans.

One night Hōichi was left alone in the temple, and as it was a very warm evening he sat out on the verandah, playing now and again upon his *biwa*. While thus occupied he heard someone approaching, someone stepping across the little back garden of the temple. Then a deep voice cried out from below the verandah: "Hōichi!" Yet again the voice sounded: "Hōichi!"

Hōichi, now very much alarmed, replied that he was blind, and would be glad to know who his visitor might be.

"My lord," began the stranger, "is now staying at Akamagaseki with many noble followers, and he has come for the purpose of viewing the scene of the battle of Dan-no-ura. He has heard how excellently you recite the story of the conflict, and has commanded me to escort you to him in order that you may show him your skill. Bring your *biwa* and follow me. My lord and his august assembly now await your honourable presence."

Hōichi, deeming that the stranger was some noble *samurai*, obeyed immediately. He donned his sandals and took his *biwa*. The stranger guided him with an iron hand, and they marched along very quickly. Hōichi heard the clank of armour at his side; but all fear left him, and he looked forward to the honour of showing his skill before a distinguished company.

Arriving at a gate, the stranger shouted: "*Kaimon*!" Immediately the gate was unbarred and opened, and the two men passed in. Then came the sound of many hurrying feet, and a rustling noise as of screens being opened. Hōichi was assisted in mounting a number of steps, and, arriving at the top, he was commanded to leave his sandals. A woman then led him forward by the hand till he found himself in a vast apartment, where he judged that a great company of people were assembled. He heard the subdued murmur of voices and the soft movement of silken garments. When Hōichi had seated himself on a cushion the woman who had led him bade him recite the story of the great battle of Dan-no-ura.

Hōichi began to chant to the accompaniment of his *biwa*. His skill was so great that the strings of his instrument seemed to imitate the sound of oars, the movement of ships, the shouting of men, the noise of surging waves, and the whirring of arrows. A low murmur of applause greeted Hōichi's wonderful performance. Thus encouraged, he continued to sing and play with even greater skill. When he came to chant of the perishing of the women and children, the plunge of Niidono into the sea with the infant Emperor in her arms, the company began to weep and wail.

When the performance was over the woman who had led Hōichi told him that her lord was well pleased with his skill, and that he desired him to play before him for the six following nights. "The retainer," added she, "who brought you tonight will visit your temple at the same hour tomorrow. You must keep these visits secret, and may now return to your abode."

Once more the woman led Hōichi through the apartment, and having reached the steps the same retainer led him back to the verandah at the back of the temple where he lived.

The next night Hōichi was again led forth to entertain the assembly, and he met with the same success. But this time his absence was detected, and upon his return his fellow priest questioned him in regard to the matter. Hōichi evaded his friend's question, and told him that he had merely been out to attend some private business.

His questioner was by no means satisfied. He regretted Hōichi's reticence and feared that there was something wrong, possibly that, the blind priest had been bewitched by evil spirits. He bade the men-servants keep a strict watch upon Hōichi, and to follow him if he should again leave the temple during the night.

Once more Hōichi left his abode. The men-servants hastily lit their lanterns and followed him with all speed; but though they walked quickly, looked everywhere, and made numerous inquiries, they failed to discover Hōichi, or learn anything concerning him. On their return, however, they were alarmed to hear the sound of a *biwa* in the cemetery of the temple, and on entering this gloomy place they discovered the blind priest. He sat at the tomb of Antoku Tenno, the infant Emperor, where he twanged his *biwa* loudly, and as loudly chanted the story of the battle of Dan-no-ura. About him on every side mysterious fires glowed, like a great gathering of lighted candles.

"Hōichi! Hōichi!" shouted the men. "Stop your playing at once! You are bewitched, Hōichi!" But the blind priest continued to play and sing, rapt, it seemed, in a strange and awful dream.

The men-servants now resorted to more extreme measures. They shook him, and shouted in his ear: "Hōichi, come back with us at once!"

The blind priest rebuked them, and said that such an interruption would not be tolerated by the noble assembly about him.

The men now dragged Hōichi away by force. When he reached the temple his wet clothes were taken off and food and drink set before him.

By this time Hōichi's fellow priest was extremely angry, and he not unjustly insisted upon a full explanation of his extraordinary behaviour. Hōichi, after much hesitation, told his friend all that had happened to him. When he had narrated his strange adventures, the priest said:

"My poor fellow! You ought to have told me this before. You have not been visiting a great house of a noble lord, but you have been sitting in yonder cemetery before the tomb of Antoku Tenno. Your great skill has called forth the ghosts of the Taira clan. Hōichi, you are in great danger, for by obeying these spirits you have assuredly put yourself in their power, and sooner or later they will kill you. Unfortunately I am called away tonight to perform a service, but before I go I will see that your body is covered with sacred texts."

Before night approached Hōichi was stripped, and upon his body an acolyte inscribed, with writing-brushes, the text of the *sutra* known as *Hannya-Shin-Kyō*. These texts were written upon Hōichi's breast, head, back, face, neck, legs, arms, and feet, even upon the soles thereof.

Then the priest said: "Hōichi, you will be called again tonight. Remain silent, sit very still, and continually meditate. If you do these things no harm will befall you."

That night Hōichi sat alone in the verandah, scarcely moving a muscle and breathing very softly.

Once more he heard the sound of footsteps. "Hōichi!" cried a deep voice. But the blind priest made no answer. He sat very still, full of a great fear.

His name was called over and over again, but to no effect. "This won't do," growled the stranger. "I must see where the fellow is." The stranger sprang into the verandah and stood beside Hōichi, who was now shaking all over with the horror of the situation.

"Ah!" said the stranger. "This is the *biwa*, but in place of the player I see – only two ears! Now I understand why he did not answer. He has no mouth, only his two ears! Those ears I will take to my lord!"

In another moment Hōichi's ears were torn off, but in spite of the fearful pain the blind priest remained mute. Then the stranger departed, and when his footsteps had died away the only sound Hōichi heard was the trickling of blood upon the verandah, and thus the priest found the unfortunate man upon his return.

"Poor Hōichi!" cried the priest. "It is all my fault. I trusted my acolyte to write sacred texts on every part of your body. He failed to do so on your ears. I ought to have seen that he carried out my instructions properly. However, you will never be troubled with those spirits in future." From that day the blind priest was known as *Mimi-nashi-Hōichi*, 'Hōichi-the-Earless'.

The Corpse-eater

MUSO KOKUSHI, A PRIEST, lost his way while travelling through the province of Mino. Despairing of finding a human abode, he was about to sleep out in the open, when he chanced to discover a little hermitage, called *anjitsu*. An aged priest greeted him, and Muso requested that he would give him shelter for the night. "No," replied the old priest angrily, "I never give shelter to anyone. In yonder valley you will find a certain hamlet; seek a night's repose there."

With these rather uncivil words, Muso took his departure, and reaching the hamlet indicated he was hospitably received at the headman's dwelling. On entering the principal apartment, the priest saw a number of people assembled together. He was shown into a separate room, and was about to fall asleep, when he heard the sound of lamentation, and shortly afterwards a young man appeared before him, holding a lantern in his hand.

"Good priest," said he, "I must tell you that my father has recently died. We did not like to explain the matter upon your arrival, because you were tired and much needed rest. The number of people you saw in the principal apartment had come to pay their respects to the dead. Now we must all go away, for that is the custom in our village when anyone dies, because strange and terrible things happen to corpses when they are left alone; but perhaps, being a priest, you will not be afraid to remain with my poor father's body."

Muso replied that he was in no way afraid, and told the young man that he would perform a service, and watch by the deceased during the company's absence. Then the young man, together with the other mourners, left the house, and Muso remained to perform his solitary night vigil.

After Muso had undertaken the funeral ceremonies, he sat meditating for several hours. When the night had far advanced, he was aware of the presence of a strange Shape, so terrible in aspect that the priest could neither move nor speak. The Shape advanced, raised the corpse, and quickly devoured it. Not content with this horrible meal, the mysterious form also ate the offerings, and then vanished.

The next morning the villagers returned, and they expressed no surprise, on hearing that the corpse had disappeared. After Muso had narrated his strange adventure he inquired if the priest on the hill did not sometimes perform the funeral service. "I visited him last night at his *anjitsu*, and though he refused me shelter, he told me where I might rest."

The villagers were amazed at these words, and informed Muso that there was certainly no priest and no *anjitsu* on yonder hill. They were positive in their assertion, and assured Muso that he had been deluded in the matter by some evil spirit. Muso did not reply, and shortly afterwards he took his departure, determined if possible to unravel the mystery.

Muso had no difficulty in finding the *anjitsu* again. The old priest came out to him, bowed, and exclaimed that he was sorry for his former rudeness. "I am ashamed," added he, "not only because I gave you no shelter, but because you have seen my real shape. You have seen me devour a corpse and the funeral offerings. Alas! good sir, I am a *jikininki* (man-eating goblin), and if you will bear with me I will explain my wretched condition.

"Many years ago I used to be a priest in this district, and I performed a great number of burial services; but I was not a good priest, for I was not influenced by true religion in performing my tasks, and thought only of the good and fine clothes I could get out of my calling. For that reason I was reborn a *jikininki*, and have ever since devoured the corpses of all those who died in this district. I beg that you will have pity on my miserable plight, and repeat certain prayers on my behalf, that I may speedily find peace and make an end of my great wickedness."

Immediately after these words had been spoken, the recluse and his hermitage suddenly vanished, and Muso found himself kneeling beside a moss-covered tomb, which was probably the tomb of the unfortunate priest.

The Ghost Mother

A PALE-FACED WOMAN crept down a street called Nakabaramachi, entered a certain shop, and purchased a small quantity of *midzu-ame*. Every night, at a late hour, she came, always haggard of countenance and always silent. The shopkeeper, who took a kindly interest in her, followed her one night, but seeing that she entered a cemetery, he turned back, puzzled and afraid.

Once again the mysterious woman came to the little shop, and this time she did not buy *midzu-ame*, but beckoned the shopkeeper to follow her. Down the street went the pale-faced woman, followed by the seller of amber syrup and some of his friends. When they reached the cemetery the woman disappeared into a tomb, and those without heard the weeping of a child. When the tomb was opened they saw the corpse of the woman they had followed, and by her side a living child, laughing at the lantern-light and stretching forth its little hands towards a cup of *midzu-ame*. The woman had been prematurely buried and her babe born in the tomb. Every night the silent mother went forth from the cemetery in order that she might bring back nourishment for her child.

The Futon of Tottori

IN TOTTORI THERE WAS a small and modest inn. It was a new inn, and as the landlord was poor he had been compelled to furnish it with goods purchased from a second-hand shop in the vicinity. His first guest was a merchant, who was treated with extreme courtesy and given much warm *sake*. When the merchant had drunk the refreshing rice wine he retired to rest and soon fell asleep. He had not slumbered long when he heard the sound of children's voices in his room, crying pitifully: "Elder Brother probably is cold?" "Nay, thou probably art cold?" Over and over again the children repeated these plaintive words. The merchant, thinking that children had strayed into his room by mistake, mildly rebuked them and prepared to go to sleep again. After a moment's silence the children again cried: "Elder Brother probably is cold?" "Nay, thou probably art cold?"

The guest arose, lit the *andon* (night-light), and proceeded to examine the room. But there was no one in the apartment; the cupboards were empty, and all the *shōji* (paper-screens) were closed. The merchant, lay down again, puzzled and amazed. Once more he heard the cry, close to his pillow: "Elder Brother probably is cold?" "Nay, thou probably art cold?" The cries were repeated, and the guest, cold with horror, found that the voices proceeded from his *futon*(quilt).

He hurriedly descended the stairs and told the innkeeper what had happened. The landlord was angry. "You have drunk too much warm *sake*," said he. "Warm *sake* has brought you evil dreams." But the guest paid his bill and sought lodging elsewhere.

On the following night another guest, slept in the haunted room, and he, too, heard the same mysterious voices, rated the innkeeper, and hastily took his departure. The landlord then entered the apartment himself. He heard the pitiful cries of children coming from one *futon*, and now was forced to believe the strange story his two guests had told him.

The next day the landlord went to the second-hand shop where he had purchased the *futon*, and made inquiries. After going from one shop to another, he finally heard the following story of the mysterious *futon*:

There once lived in Tottori a poor man and his wife, with two children, boys of six and eight years respectively. The parents died, and the poor children were forced to sell their few belongings, until one day they were left with only a thin and much-worn *futon* to cover them at night. At last they had no money to pay the rent, and not even the wherewithal to purchase food of any kind.

When the period of the greatest cold came, the snow gathered so thickly about the humble dwelling that the children could do nothing but wrap the *futon* about them, and murmur to each other in their sweet, pathetic way: "Elder Brother probably is cold?" "Nay, thou probably art cold?" And sobbing forth these words they clung together, afraid of the darkness and of the bitter, shrieking wind.

While their poor little bodies nestled together, striving to keep each other warm, the hard-hearted landlord entered, and finding that there was no one to pay the rent, he turned the children out of the house, each clad only in one thin *kimono*. They tried to reach a temple of Kwannon, but the snow was too heavy, and they hid behind their old home. A *futon* of snow covered them and they fell asleep on the merciful bosom of the Gods, and were finally buried in the cemetery of the Temple of Kwannon-of-the-Thousand-Arms.

When the innkeeper heard this sad story he gave the *futon* to the priests of the Kwannon temple, prayers were recited for the children's souls, and from that hour the *futon* ceased to murmur its plaintive cries.

The Return

IN THE VILLAGE OF MOCHIDA-NO-URA there lived a peasant. He was extremely poor, but, notwithstanding, his wife bore him six children. Directly a child was born, the cruel father flung it into a river and pretended that it had died at birth, so that his six children were murdered in this horrible way.

At length, as years went by, the peasant found himself in a more prosperous position, and when a seventh child was born, a boy, he was much gratified and loved him dearly.

One night the father took the child in his arms, and wandered out into the garden, murmuring ecstatically: "What a beautiful summer night!"

The babe, then only five months old, for a moment assumed the speech of a man, saying: "The moon looks just as it did when you last threw me in the river!"

When the infant had uttered these words he became like other children; but the peasant, now truly realising the enormity of his crime, from that day became a priest.

A Test of Love

THERE WAS ONCE a certain fair maiden who, contrary to Japanese custom, was permitted to choose her own husband. Many suitors sought her hand, and they brought her gifts and fair poems, and said many loving words to her. She spoke kindly to each suitor, saying: "I will marry the man who is brave enough to bear a certain test I shall impose upon him, and whatever that test of love may be, I expect him, on the sacred honour of a *samurai*, not to divulge it." The suitors readily complied with these conditions, but one by one they left her, with horror upon their faces, ceased their wooing, but breathed never a word concerning the mysterious and awful secret.

At length a poor *samurai*, whose sword was his only wealth, came to the maiden, and informed her that he was prepared to go through any test, however severe, in order that he might make her his wife.

When they had supped together the maiden left the apartment, and long after midnight returned clad in a white garment. They went out of the house together, through innumerable streets where dogs howled, and beyond the city, till they came to a great cemetery. Here the maiden led the way while the *samurai* followed, his hand upon his sword.

When the wooer was able to penetrate the darkness he saw that the maiden was digging the ground with a spade. She dug with extreme haste, and eventually tore off the lid of a coffin. In another moment she snatched up the corpse of a child, tore off an arm, broke it, and commenced to eat one piece, flinging the other to her wooer, crying: "If you love me, eat what I eat!"

Without a moment's hesitation the *samurai* sat down by the grave and began to eat one half of the arm. "Excellent!" he cried, "I pray you give me more!" At this point of the legend the horror happily disappears, for neither the *samurai* nor the maiden ate a corpse – the arm was made of delicious confectionery!

The maiden, with a cry of joy, sprang to her feet, and said: "At last I have found a brave man! I will marry you, for you are the husband I have ever longed for, and until this night have never found."

The Kappa's Promise

IN IZUMO the village people refer to the *Kappa* as *Kawako* ('The Child of the River'). Near Matsue there is a little hamlet called Kawachi-mura, and on the bank of the river Kawachi there is a small temple known as Kawako-no-miya, that is, the temple of the *Kawako* or *Kappa*, said to contain a document signed by this river goblin. Concerning this document the following legend is recorded.

In ancient days a *Kappa* dwelt in the river Kawachi, and he made a practice of seizing and destroying a number of villagers, and in addition many of their domestic animals. On one occasion a horse went into the river, and the *Kappa*, in trying to capture it, in some way twisted his neck, but in spite of considerable pain he refused to let his victim go. The frightened horse sprang up the river bank and ran into a neighbouring field with the Kappa still holding on to the terrified animal. The owner of the horse, together with many villagers, securely bound the Child of the River. "Let us kill this horrible creature," said the peasants, "for he has assuredly committed many horrible crimes, and we should do well to be rid of such a dreadful monster." "No," replied the owner of the horse, "we will not kill him. We will make him swear never to destroy any of the inhabitants or the domestic animals of this village." A document was accordingly prepared, and the *Kappa* was asked to peruse it, and when he had done so to sign his name. "I cannot write," replied the penitent *Kappa*, "but I will dip my hand in ink and press it upon the document." When the creature had made his inky mark, he was released and allowed to return to the river, and from that day to this the *Kappa* has remained true to his promise.

Tobikawa Imitates a Tengu

TOBIKAWA, AN EX-WRESTLER who lived in Matsue, spent his time in hunting and killing foxes. He did not believe in the various superstitions concerning this animal, and it was generally believed that his great strength made him immune from the witchcraft of foxes. However, there were some people of Matsue who prophesied that Tobikawa would come to an untimely end as the result of his daring deeds and disbelief in supernatural powers.

Tobikawa was extremely fond of practical jokes, and on one occasion he had the hardihood to imitate the general appearance of a *Tengu*, feathers, long nose, claws, and all. Having thus disguised himself he climbed up into a tree belonging to a sacred grove. Presently the peasants observed him, and deeming the creature they saw to be a *Tengu*, they began to worship him and to place many offerings about the tree. Alas! the dismal prophecy came true, for while the merry Tobikawa was trying to imitate the acrobatic antics of a *Tengu*, he slipped from a branch and was killed.

The Adventures of Kiuchi Heizayemon

ONE EVENING, Kiuchi Heizayemon, a retainer, mysteriously disappeared. Kiuchi's friends, when they heard of what had taken place, searched for him in every direction. Eventually they discovered the missing man's clogs, scabbard, and sword; but the sheath was bent like the curved handle of a tea-kettle. They had no sooner made this lamentable discovery than they also perceived Kiuchi's girdle, which had been cut into three pieces. At midnight, those who searched heard a strange cry, a voice calling for help. Suzuki Shichiro, one of the party, chanced to look up, and he saw a strange creature with wings standing upon the roof of a temple. When the rest of the band had joined their comrade, they all looked upon the weird figure, and one said: "I believe it is nothing but an umbrella flapping in the wind." "Let us make quite sure," replied Suzuki Shichiro, and with these words he lifted up his voice, and cried loudly: "Are you the lost Kiuchi?" "Yes," was the reply, "and I pray that you will take me down from this temple as speedily as possible."

When Kiuchi had been brought down from the temple roof, he fainted, and remained in a swoon for three days. At length, gaining consciousness, he gave the following account of his strange adventure:

"The evening when I disappeared I heard someone shouting my name over and over again, and going out I discovered a black-robed monk, bawling 'Heizayemon!' Beside the monk stood a man of great stature; his face was red, and his dishevelled hair fell upon the ground. 'Climb up on yonder roof,' he shouted fiercely. I refused to obey such an evil-faced villain, and drew my sword, but in a moment he bent the blade and broke my scabbard into fragments. Then my girdle was roughly torn off and cut into three pieces. When these things had been done, I was carried to a roof, and there severely chastised. But this was not the end of my trouble, for after I had been beaten, I was forced to seat myself on a round tray. In a moment I was whirled into the air, and the tray carried me with great speed to many regions. When it appeared to me that I had travelled through space for ten days, I prayed to the Lord Buddha, and found myself on what appeared to be the summit of a mountain, but in reality it was the roof of the temple whence you, my comrades, rescued me."

A Globe of Fire

FROM THE BEGINNING OF MARCH to the end of June there may be seen in the province of Settsu a globe of fire resting on the top of a tree, and within this globe there is a human face. In ancient days there once lived in Nikaido district of Settsu province a priest named

Nikobo, famous for his power to exorcise evil spirits and evil influences of every kind. When the local governor's wife fell sick, Nikobo was requested to attend and see what he could do to restore her to health again. Nikobo willingly complied, and spent many days by the bedside of the suffering lady. He diligently practised his art of exorcism, and in due time the governor's wife recovered.

But the gentle and kind-hearted Nikobo was not thanked for what he had done; on the contrary, the governor became jealous of him, accused him of a foul crime, and caused him to be put to death. The soul of Nikobo flashed forth in its anger and took the form of a miraculous globe of fire, which hovered over the murderer's house. The strange light, with the justly angry face peering from it, had its effect, for the governor was stricken with a fever that finally killed him. Every year, at the time already indicated, Nikobo's ghost pays a visit to the scene of its suffering and revenge.

The Ghostly Wrestlers

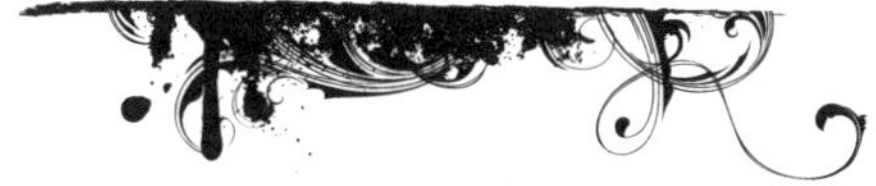

IN OMI PROVINCE, at the base of the Katada hills, there is a lake. During the cloudy nights of early autumn a ball of fire emerges from the margin of the lake, expanding and contracting as it floats toward the hills. When it rises to the height of a man it reveals two shining faces, to develop slowly into the torsos of two naked wrestlers, locked together and struggling furiously. The ball of fire, with its fierce combatants, floats slowly away to a recess in the Katada hills. It is harmless so long as no one interferes with it, but it resents any effort to retard its progress.

According to a legend concerning this phenomenon, we are informed that a certain wrestler, who had never suffered a defeat, waited at midnight for the coming of this ball of fire. When it reached him he attempted to drag it down by force, but the luminous globe proceeded on its way, and hurled the foolish wrestler to a considerable distance.

The Shōjō's White Sake

THE SHŌJŌ IS A SEA MONSTER with bright red hair, and is extremely fond of drinking large quantities of sacred white *sake*. The following legend will give some account of this creature and the nature of his favourite beverage.

We will refer later to the miraculous appearance of Mount Fuji. On the day following this alleged miracle a poor man named Yurine, who lived near this mountain, became extremely ill, and feeling that his days were numbered, he desired to drink a cup of *sake* before he died. But there was no rice wine in the little hut, and his boy, Koyuri, desiring if possible to fulfil his father's dying wish, wandered along the shore with a gourd in his hand. He had not gone far when he heard someone calling his name. On looking about him he discovered two strange-looking creatures with long red hair and skin the colour of pink cherry-blossom, wearing green seaweed girdles about their loins. Drawing nearer, he perceived that these beings were drinking white *sake* from large flat cups, which they continually replenished from a great stone jar.

"My father is dying," said the boy, "and he much desires to drink a cup of *sake* before he departs this life. But alas! we are poor, and I know not how to grant him his last request."

"I will fill your gourd with this white *sake*," replied one of the creatures, and when he had done so Koyuri ran with haste to his father.

The old man drank the white *sake* eagerly. "Bring me more," he cried, "for this is no common wine. It has given me strength, and already I feel new life flowing through my old veins."

So Koyuri returned to the seashore, and the red-haired creatures gladly gave him more of their wine; indeed, they supplied him with the beverage for five days, and by the end of that time Yurine was restored to health again.

Now Yurine's neighbour was a man called Mamikiko, and when he heard that Yurine had recently obtained a copious supply of *sake* he grew jealous, for above all things he loved a cup of rice wine. One day he called Koyuri and questioned him in regard to the matter, saying: "Let me taste the *sake*." He roughly snatched the gourd from the boy's hand and began to drink, making a wry face as he did so. "This is not *sake*!" he exclaimed fiercely; "it is filthy water," and having said these words, he began to beat the boy, crying: "Take me to those red people you have told me about. I will get from them fine *sake*, and let the beating I have given you warn you never again to play a trick upon me."

Koyuri and Mamikiko went along the shore together, and presently they came to where the red-haired creatures were drinking. When Koyuri saw them he began to weep.

"Why are you crying?" said one of the creatures. "Surely your good father has not drunk all the *sake* already?"

"No," replied the boy, "but I have met with misfortune. This man I bring with me, Mamikiko by name, drank some of the *sake*, spat it out immediately, and threw the rest away, saying that I had played a trick upon him and given him foul water to drink. Be so good as to let me have some more *sake* for my father."

The red-haired man filled the gourd, and chuckled over Mamikiko's unpleasant experience.

"I should also like a cup or *sake*" said Mamikiko. "Will you let me have some?"

Permission having been granted, the greedy Mamikiko filled the largest cup he could find, smiling over the delicious fragrance. But directly he tasted the *sake* he felt sick, and angrily remonstrated with the red-haired creature.

The red man thus made answer: "You are evidently not aware that I am a *Shōjō*, and that I live near the Sea Dragon's Palace. When I heard of the sudden appearance of Mount Fuji I came here to see it, assured that such an event was a good omen and foretold of the prosperity and perpetuity of Japan. While enjoying the beauty of this fair mountain I met Koyuri, and had the good fortune to save his honest father's life by giving him some of our sacred white *sake* that restores youth to human beings, together with an increase in years, while to *Shōjō* it vanquishes death. Koyuri's father is a good man, and the *sake* was thus able to exert its full and beneficent power upon him; but you are greedy and selfish, and to all such this *sake* is poison."

"*Poison*?" groaned the now contrite Mamikiko. "Good *Shōjō*, have mercy upon me and spare my life!"

The *Shōjō* gave him a powder, saying: "Swallow this in *sake* and repent of your wickedness."

Mamikiko did so, and this time he found that the white *sake* was delicious. He lost no time in making friends with Yurine, and some years later these men took up their abode on the southern side of Mount Fuji, brewed the *Shōjō's* white *sake*, and lived for three hundred years.

How an Old Man Lost His Wen

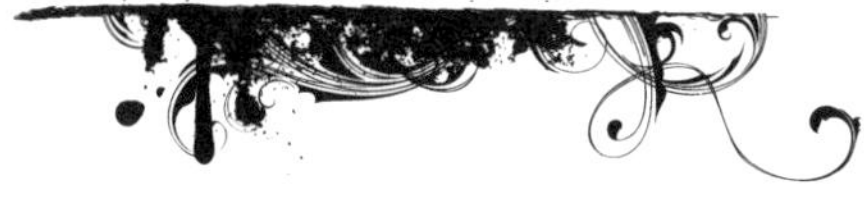

THERE WAS ONCE AN OLD MAN who had a wen on his right cheek. This disfigurement caused him a good deal of annoyance, and he had spent a considerable sum of money in trying to get rid of it. He took various medicines and applied many lotions, but instead of the wen disappearing or even diminishing, it increased in size.

One night, while the old man was returning home laden with firewood, he was overtaken by a terrible thunderstorm, and was forced to seek shelter in a hollow tree. When the storm had abated, and just as he was about to proceed on his journey, he was surprised to hear a sound of merriment close at hand. On peeping out from his place of retreat, he was amazed to see a number of demons dancing and singing and drinking. Their dancing was so strange that the old man, forgetting caution, began to laugh, and eventually left the tree in order that he might see the performance better. As he stood watching, he saw that a demon was dancing by himself, and, moreover, that the chief of the company was none too pleased with his very clumsy antics. At length the leader of the demons said: "Enough! Is there no one who can dance better than this fellow?"

When the old man heard these words, it seemed that his youth returned to him again, and having at one time been an expert dancer, he offered to show his skill. So the old man danced before that strange gathering of demons, who congratulated him on his performance, offered him a cup of *sake*, and begged that he would give them the pleasure of several other dances.

The old man was extremely gratified by the way he had been received, and when the chief of the demons asked him to dance before them on the following night, he readily complied. "That is well," said the chief, "but you must leave some pledge behind you. I see that you have a wen on your right cheek, and that will make an excellent pledge. Allow me to take it off for you." Without inflicting any pain, the chief removed the wen, and having accomplished this extraordinary feat, he and his companions suddenly vanished.

The old man, as he walked towards his home, kept on feeling his right cheek with his hand, and could scarcely realise that after many years of disfigurement he had at last the good fortune to lose his troublesome and unsightly wen. At length he entered his humble abode, and his old wife was none the less pleased with what had taken place.

A wicked and cantankerous old man lived next door to this good old couple. For many years he had been afflicted with a wen on his left cheek, which had failed to yield to all manner of medical treatment. When he heard of his neighbour's good fortune, he called upon him and listened to the strange adventures with the demons. The good old man told his neighbour where he might find the hollow tree, and advised him to hide in it just before sunset.

The wicked old man found the hollow tree and entered it. He had not remained concealed more than a few minutes when he rejoiced to see the demons. Presently one of the company said: "The old man is a long time coming. I made sure he would keep his promise."

At these words the old man crept out of his hiding-place, flourished his fan, and began to dance; but, unfortunately, he knew nothing about dancing, and his extraordinary antics caused the demons to express considerable dissatisfaction. "You dance extremely ill," said one of the company, "and the sooner you stop the better we shall be pleased; but before you depart we will return the pledge you left with us last night." Having uttered these words, the demon flung the wen at the right cheek of the old man, where it remained firmly fixed, and could not be removed. So the wicked old man, who had tried to deceive the demons, went away with a wen on either side of his face.

The Ghost of Sakura

IN THE PROVINCE OF SHIMOSA, and the district of Soma, Hotta Kaga no Kami was lord of the castle of Sakura, and chief of a family which had for generations produced famous warriors. When Kaga no Kami, who had served in the Gorojiu, the cabinet of the Shogun, died at the castle of Sakura, his eldest son Kotsuke no Suke Masanobu inherited his estates and honours, and was appointed to a seat in the Gorojiu; but he was a different man from the lords who had preceded him. He treated the farmers and peasants unjustly, imposing additional and grievous taxes, so that the tenants on his estates were driven to the last extremity of poverty; and although year after year, and month after month, they prayed for mercy, and remonstrated against this injustice, no heed was paid to them, and the people throughout the villages were reduced to the utmost distress. Accordingly, the chiefs of the one hundred and thirty-six villages, producing a total revenue of 40,000 kokus of rice, assembled together in council and determined unanimously to present a petition to the Government, sealed with their seals, stating that their repeated remonstrances had been taken no notice of by their local authorities. Then they assembled in numbers before the house of one of the councillors of their lord, named Ikeura Kazuye, in order to show the petition to him first, but even then no notice was taken of them; so they returned home, and resolved, after consulting together, to proceed to their lord's yashiki, or palace, at Edo, on the seventh day of the tenth month. It was determined, with one accord, that one hundred and forty-three village chiefs should go to Edo; and the chief of the village of Iwahashi, one Sogoro, a man forty-eight years of age, distinguished for his ability and judgment, ruling a district which produced a thousand kokus, stepped forward, and said:

"This is by no means an easy matter, my masters. It certainly is of great importance that we should forward our complaint to our lord's palace at Edo; but what are your plans? Have you any fixed intentions?"

"It is, indeed, a most important matter," rejoined the others; but they had nothing further to say. Then Sogoro went on to say:

"We have appealed to the public office of our province, but without avail; we have petitioned the Prince's councillors, also in vain. I know that all that remains for us is to lay our case before our lord's palace at Edo; and if we go there, it is equally certain that we shall not be listened to – on the contrary, we shall be cast into prison. If we are not attended to here, in our own province, how much less will the officials at Edo care for us. We might hand our petition into the litter of one of the Gorojiu, in the public streets; but, even in that case, as our lord is a member of the Gorojiu, none of his peers would care to examine into the rights and wrongs of our complaint, for fear of offending him, and the man who presented the petition in so desperate a manner would lose his life on a bootless errand. If you have made up your minds to this, and are determined, at all hazards, to start, then go to Edo by all means, and bid a long farewell to parents, children, wives, and relations. This is my opinion."

The others all agreeing with what Sogoro said, they determined that, come what might, they would go to Edo; and they settled to assemble at the village of Funabashi on the thirteenth day of the eleventh month.

On the appointed day all the village officers met at the place agreed upon, – Sogoro, the chief of the village of Iwahashi, alone being missing; and as on the following day Sogoro had not yet arrived, they deputed one of their number, named Rokurobei, to inquire the reason. Rokurobei arrived at Sogoro's house towards four in the afternoon, and found him warming himself quietly over his charcoal brazier, as if nothing were the matter. The messenger, seeing this, said rather testily:

"The chiefs of the villages are all assembled at Funabashi according to covenant, and as you, Master Sogoro, have not arrived, I have come to inquire whether it is sickness or some other cause that prevents you."

"Indeed," replied Sogoro, "I am sorry that you should have had so much trouble. My intention was to have set out yesterday; but I was taken with a cholic, with which I am often troubled, and, as you may see, I am taking care of myself; so for a day or two I shall not be able to start. Pray be so good as to let the others know this."

Rokurobei, seeing that there was no help for it, went back to the village of Funabashi and communicated to the others what had occurred. They were all indignant at what they looked upon as the cowardly defection of a man who had spoken so fairly, but resolved that the conduct of one man should not influence the rest, and talked themselves into the belief that the affair which they had in hand would be easily put through; so they agreed with one accord to start and present the petition, and, having arrived at Edo, put up in the street called Bakurocho. But although they tried to forward their complaint to the various officers of their lord, no one would listen to them; the doors were all shut in their faces, and they had to go back to their inn, crestfallen and without success.

On the following day, being the 18th of the month, they all met together at a tea-house in an avenue, in front of a shrine of Kwannon Sama; and having held a consultation, they determined that, as they could hit upon no good expedient, they would again send for Sogoro to see whether he could devise no plan. Accordingly, on the 19th, Rokurobei and one Jiuyemon started for the village of Iwahashi at noon, and arrived the same evening.

Now the village chief Sogoro, who had made up his mind that the presentation of this memorial was not a matter to be lightly treated, summoned his wife and children and his relations, and said to them:

"I am about to undertake a journey to Edo, for the following reasons: Our present lord of the soil has increased the land-tax, in rice and the other imposts, more than tenfold, so that pen and paper would fail to convey an idea of the poverty to which the people are reduced, and the peasants are undergoing the tortures of hell upon earth. Seeing this, the chiefs of the various villages have presented petitions, but with what result is doubtful. My earnest desire, therefore, is to devise some means of escape from this cruel persecution. If my ambitious scheme does not succeed, then shall I return home no more; and even should I gain my end, it is hard to say how I may be treated by those in power. Let us drink a cup of wine together, for it may be that you shall see my face no more. I give my life to allay the misery of the people of this estate. If I die, mourn not over my fate; weep not for me."

Having spoken thus, he addressed his wife and his four children, instructing them carefully as to what he desired to be done after his death, and minutely stating every wish of his heart. Then, having drunk a parting cup with them, he cheerfully took leave of all present, and went to a tea-house in the neighbouring village of Funabashi, where the two messengers, Rokurobei and Jiuyemon, were anxiously awaiting his arrival, in order that they might recount to him all that had taken place at Edo.

"In short," said they, "it appears to us that we have failed completely; and we have come to meet you in order to hear what you propose. If you have any plan to suggest, we would fain be made acquainted with it."

"We have tried the officers of the district," replied Sogoro, "and we have tried my lord's palace at Edo. However often we might assemble before my lord's gate, no heed would be given to us. There is nothing left for us but to appeal to the Shogun."

So they sat talking over their plans until the night was far advanced, and then they went to rest. The winter night was long; but when the cawing of the crows was about to announce the morning, the three friends started on their journey for the tea-house at Asakusa, at which, upon their arrival, they found the other village elders already assembled.

"Welcome, Master Sogoro," said they. "How is it that you have come so late? We have petitioned all the officers to no purpose, and we have broken our bones in vain. We are at our wits' end, and can think of no other scheme. If there is any plan which seems good to you, we pray you to act upon it."

"Sirs," replied Sogoro, speaking very quietly, "although we have met with no better success here than in our own place, there is no use in grieving. In a day or two the Gorojiu will be going to the castle; we must wait for this opportunity, and following one of the litters, thrust in our memorial. This is my opinion: what think you of it, my masters?"

One and all, the assembled elders were agreed as to the excellence of this advice; and having decided to act upon it, they returned to their inn.

Then Sogoro held a secret consultation with Jiuyemon, Hanzo, Rokurobei, Chinzo, and Kinshiro, five of the elders, and, with their assistance, drew up the memorial; and having heard that on the 26th of the month, when the Gorojiu should go to the castle, Kuze Yamato no Kami would proceed to a palace under the western enclosure of the castle, they kept watch in a place hard by. As soon as they saw the litter of the Gorojiu approach, they drew near to it, and, having humbly stated their grievances, handed in the petition; and as it was accepted, the six elders were greatly elated, and doubted not that their hearts' desire would be attained; so they went off to a tea-house at Riyogoku, and Jiuyemon said:

"We may congratulate ourselves on our success. We have handed in our petition to the Gorojiu, and now we may set our minds at rest; before many days have passed, we shall hear good news from the rulers. To Master Sogoro is due great praise for his exertions."

Sogoro, stepping forward, answered, "Although we have presented our memorial to the Gorojiu, the matter will not be so quickly decided; it is therefore useless that so many of us should remain here: let eleven men stay with me, and let the rest return home to their several villages. If we who remain are accused of conspiracy and beheaded, let the others agree to reclaim and bury our corpses. As for the expenses which we shall incur until our suit is concluded, let that be according to our original covenant. For the sake of the hundred and thirty-six villages we will lay down our lives, if needs must, and submit to the disgrace of having our heads exposed as those of common malefactors."

Then they had a parting feast together, and, after a sad leave-taking, the main body of the elders went home to their own country; while the others, wending their way to their quarters waited patiently to be summoned to the Supreme Court. On the 2nd day of the 12th month, Sogoro, having received a summons from the residence of the Gorojiu Kuze Yamato no Kami, proceeded to obey it, and was ushered to the porch of the house, where two councillors, named Aijima Gidaiyu and Yamaji Yori, met him, and said:

"Some days since you had the audacity to thrust a memorial into the litter of our lord Yamato no Kami. By an extraordinary exercise of clemency, he is willing to pardon this heinous offence; but should you ever again endeavour to force your petitions; upon him, you will be held guilty of riotous conduct;" and with this they gave back the memorial.

"I humbly admit the justice of his lordship's censure. But oh! my lords, this is no hasty nor ill-considered action. Year after year, affliction upon affliction has been heaped upon us, until at last the people are without even the necessaries of life; and we, seeing no end to the evil, have humbly presented this petition. I pray your lordships of your great mercy to consider our case" and deign to receive our memorial. Vouchsafe to take some measures that the people may live, and our gratitude for your great kindness will know no bounds."

"Your request is a just one," replied the two councillors after hearing what he said; "but your memorial cannot be received: so you must even take it back."

With this they gave back the document, and wrote down the names of Sogoro and six of the elders who had accompanied him. There was no help for it: they must take back their petition, and return to their inn. The seven men, dispirited and sorrowful, sat with folded arms considering what was best to be done, what plan should be devised, until at last, when they were at their wits' end, Sogoro said, in a whisper:

"So our petition, which we gave in after so much pains, has been returned after all! With what face can we return to our villages after such a disgrace? I, for one, do not propose to waste my labour for nothing; accordingly, I shall bide my time until some day, when the Shogun shall go forth from the castle, and, lying in wait by the roadside, I shall make known our grievances to him, who is lord over our lord. This is our last chance."

The others all applauded this speech, and, having with one accord hardened their hearts, waited for their opportunity.

Now it so happened that, on the 20th day of the 12th month, the then Shogun, Prince Iyemitsu, was pleased to worship at the tombs of his ancestors at Uyeno; and Sogoro and the other elders, hearing this, looked upon it as a special favour from the gods, and felt certain that this time they would not fail. So they drew up a fresh memorial, and at the appointed time Sogoro hid himself under the Sammaye Bridge, in front of the black gate at Uyeno. When Prince Iyemitsu passed in his litter, Sogoro clambered up from under the bridge, to the great surprise of the Shogun's attendants, who called out, "Push the fellow on one side;" but, profiting by the confusion, Sogoro, raising his voice and crying, "I wish to humbly present a petition to his Highness in person," thrust forward his memorial, which he had tied on to the end of a bamboo stick six feet long, and tried to put it into the litter; and although there were cries to arrest him, and he was buffeted by the escort, he crawled up to the side of the litter, and the Shogun accepted the document. But Sogoro was arrested by the escort, and thrown into prison. As for the memorial, his Highness ordered that it should be handed in to the Gorojiu Hotta Kotsuke no Suke, the lord of the petitioners.

When Hotta Kotsuke no Suke had returned home and read the memorial, he summoned his councillor, Kojima Shikibu, and said:

"The officials of my estate are mere bunglers. When the peasants assembled and presented a petition, they refused to receive it, and have thus brought this trouble upon me. Their folly has been beyond belief; however, it cannot be helped. We must remit all the new taxes, and you must inquire how much was paid to the former lord of the castle. As for this Sogoro, he is not the only one who is at the bottom of the conspiracy; however, as this heinous offence of his in going out to lie in wait for the Shogun's procession is unpardonable, we must manage to get him given up to us by the Government, and, as an example for the rest of my people, he shall be crucified – he and his wife and his children; and, after his death, all that he possesses shall be confiscated. The other six men shall be banished; and that will suffice."

"My lord," replied Shikibu, prostrating himself, "your lordship's intentions are just. Sogoro, indeed, deserves any punishment for his outrageous crime. But I humbly venture to submit that his wife and children cannot be said to be guilty in the same degree: I implore your lordship mercifully to be pleased to absolve them from so severe a punishment."

"Where the sin of the father is great, the wife and children cannot be spared," replied Kotsuke no Suke; and his councillor, seeing that his heart was hardened, was forced to obey his orders without further remonstrance.

So Kotsuke no Suke, having obtained that Sogoro should be given up to him by the Government, caused him to be brought to his estate of Sakura as a criminal, in a litter covered with nets, and confined him in prison. When his case had been inquired into, a decree was issued by the Lord Kotsuke no Suke that he should be punished for a heinous crime; and on the 9th day of the 2nd month of the second year of the period styled Shoho (AD 1644) he was condemned to be crucified. Accordingly Sogoro, his wife and children, and the elders of the hundred and thirty-six villages were brought before the Court-house of Sakura, in which were assembled forty-five chief officers. The elders were then told that, yielding to their petition, their lord was graciously pleased to order that the oppressive taxes should be remitted, and that the dues levied should not exceed those of the olden time. As for Sogoro and his wife, the following sentence was passed upon them:

"Whereas you have set yourself up as the head of the villagers; whereas, secondly, you have dared to make light of the Government by petitioning his Highness the Shogun directly, thereby offering an insult to your lord; and whereas, thirdly, you have presented a memorial to the Gorojiu; and, whereas, fourthly, you were privy to a conspiracy: for these four heinous crimes you are sentenced to death by crucifixion. Your wife is sentenced to die in like manner; and your children will be decapitated.

"This sentence is passed upon the following persons:

"Sogoro, chief of the village of Iwahashi, aged 48.

"His wife, Man, aged 38.

"His son, Gennosuke, aged 13.

"His son, Sohei, aged 10.

"His son, Kihachi, aged 7."

The eldest daughter of Sogoro, named Hatsu, nineteen years of age, was married to a man named Jiuyemon, in the village of Hakamura, in Shitachi, beyond the river, in the territory of Matsudaira Matsu no Kami (the Prince of Sendai). His second daughter, whose name was Saki, sixteen years of age, was married to one Tojiuro, chief of a village on the property of my lord Naito Geki. No punishment was decreed against these two women.

The six elders who had accompanied Sogoro were told that although by good rights they had merited death, yet by the special clemency of their lord their lives would be spared, but that they were condemned to banishment. Their wives and children would not be attainted, and their property would be spared. The six men were banished to Oshima, in the province of Idzu.

Sogoro heard his sentence with pure courage.

The six men were banished; but three of them lived to be pardoned on the occasion of the death of the Shogun, Prince Genyuin, and returned to their country.

According to the above decision, the taxes were remitted; and men and women, young and old, rejoiced over the advantage that had been gained for them by Sogoro and by the six elders, and there was not one that did not mourn for their fate.

When the officers of the several villages left the Court-house, one Zembei, the chief of the village of Sakato, told the others that he had some important subjects to speak to them upon, and begged them to meet him in the temple called Fukushoin. Every man having consented, and the hundred and thirty-six men having assembled at the temple, Zembei addressed them as follows:

"The success of our petition, in obtaining the reduction of our taxes to the same amount as was levied by our former lord, is owing to Master Sogoro, who has thus thrown away his life for us. He and his wife and children are now to suffer as criminals for the sake of the one hundred and thirty-six villages. That such a thing should take place before our very eyes seems to me not to be borne. What say you, my masters?"

"Ay! ay! what you say is just from top to bottom," replied the others. Then Hanzayemon, the elder of the village of Katsuta, stepped forward and said:

"As Master Zembei has just said, Sogoro is condemned to die for a matter in which all the village elders are concerned to a man. We cannot look on unconcerned. Full well I know that it is useless our pleading for Sogoro; but we may, at least, petition that the lives of his wife and children may be spared."

The assembled elders having all applauded this speech, they determined to draw up a memorial; and they resolved, should their petition not be accepted by the local authorities, to present it at their lord's palace in Edo, and, should that fail, to appeal to the Government. Accordingly, before noon on the following day, they all affixed their seals to the memorial, which four of them, including Zembei and Hanzayemon, composed, as follows:

"With deep fear we humbly venture to present the following petition, which the elders of the one hundred and thirty-six villages of this estate have sealed with their seals. In consequence of the humble petition which we lately offered up, the taxes have graciously been reduced to the rates levied by the former lord of the estate, and new laws have been vouchsafed to us. With reverence and joy the peasants, great and small, have gratefully acknowledged these favours. With regard to Sogoro, the elder of the village of Iwahashi, who ventured to petition his highness the Shogun in person, thus being guilty of a heinous crime, he has been sentenced to death in the castle-town. With fear and trembling we recognize the justice of his sentence. But in the matter of his wife and children, she is but a woman, and they are so young and innocent that they cannot distinguish the east from the west: we pray that in your great clemency you will remit their sin, and give them up to the representatives of the one hundred and thirty-six villages, for which we shall be ever grateful. We, the elders of the villages, know not to what extent we may be transgressing in presenting this memorial. We were all guilty of affixing our seals to the former petition; but Sogoro, who was chief of a large district, producing a thousand kokus of revenue, and was therefore a man of experience, acted for the others; and we grieve that he alone should suffer for all. Yet in his case we reverently admit that there can be no reprieve. For his wife and children, however, we humbly implore your gracious mercy and consideration.

"Signed by the elders of the villages of the estate, the 2nd year of Shoho, and the 2nd month."

Having drawn up this memorial, the hundred and thirty-six elders, with Zembei at their head, proceeded to the Court-house to present the petition, and found the various officers seated in solemn conclave. Then the clerk took the petition, and, having opened it, read it aloud; and the councillor, Ikeura Kazuye, said:

"The petition which you have addressed to us is worthy of all praise. But you must know that this is a matter which is no longer within our control. The affair has been reported to the Government; and although the priests of my lord's ancestral temple have interceded for Sogoro, my lord is so angry that he will not listen even to them, saying that, had he not been one of the Gorojiu, he would have been in danger of being ruined by this man: his high station alone saved him. My lord spoke so severely that the priests themselves dare not recur to the subject. You see, therefore, that it will be no use your attempting to take any steps in the matter, for most certainly your petition will not be received. You had better, then, think no more about it." And with these words he gave back the memorial.

Zembei and the elders, seeing, to their infinite sorrow, that their mission was fruitless, left the Court-house, and most sorrowfully took counsel together, grinding their teeth in their disappointment when they thought over what the councillor had said as to the futility of their attempt. Out of grief for this, Zembei, with Hanzayemon and Heijiuro, on the 11th day of the 2nd month (the day on which Sogoro and his wife and children suffered), left Ewaradai, the place of execution, and went to the temple Zenkoji, in the province of Shinshiu, and from thence they ascended Mount Koya in Kishiu, and, on the 1st day of the 8th month, shaved their heads and became priests; Zembei changed his name to Kakushin, and Hanzayemon changed his to Zensho: as for Heijiuro, he fell sick at the end of the 7th month, and on the 11th day of the 8th month died, being forty-seven years old that year. These three men, who had loved Sogoro as the fishes love water, were true to him to the last. Heijiuro was buried on Mount Koya. Kakushin wandered through the country as a priest, praying for the entry of Sogoro and his children into the perfection of paradise; and, after visiting all the shrines and temples, came back at last to his own province of Shimosa, and took up his abode at the temple Riukakuji, in the village of Kano, and in the district of Imban, praying and making offerings on behalf of the souls of Sogoro, his wife and children. Hanzayemon, now known as the priest Zensho, remained at Shinagawa, a suburb of Edo, and, by the charity of good people, collected enough money to erect six bronze Buddhas, which remain standing to this day. He fell sick and died, at the age of seventy, on the 10th day of the 2nd month of the 13th year of the period styled Kambun. Zembei, who, as a priest, had changed his name to Kakushin, died, at the age of seventy-six, on the 17th day of the 10th month of the 2nd year of the period styled Empo. Thus did those men, for the sake of Sogoro and his family, give themselves up to works of devotion; and the other villagers also brought food to soothe the spirits of the dead, and prayed for their entry into paradise; and as litanies were repeated without intermission, there can be no doubt that Sogoro attained salvation.

"In paradise, where the blessings of God are distributed without favour, the soul learns its faults by the measure of the rewards given. The lusts of the flesh are abandoned; and the soul, purified, attains to the glory of Buddha."

On the 11th day of the 2nd month of the 2nd year of Shoho, Sogoro having been convicted of a heinous crime, a scaffold was erected at Ewaradai, and the councillor who resided at Edo and the councillor who resided on the estate, with the other officers, proceeded to the place in all solemnity. Then the priests of Tokoji, in the village of Sakenaga, followed by coffin-bearers, took their places in front of the councillors, and said:

"We humbly beg leave to present a petition."

"What have your reverences to say?"

"We are men who have forsaken the world and entered the priesthood," answered the monks, respectfully; "and we would fain, if it be possible, receive the bodies of those who are to die, that we may bury them decently. It will be a great joy to us if our humble petition be graciously heard and granted."

"Your request shall be granted; but as the crime of Sogoro was great, his body must be exposed for three days and three nights, after which the corpse shall be given to you."

At the hour of the snake (10 am), the hour appointed for the execution, the people from the neighbouring villages and the castle-town, old and young, men and women, flocked to see the sight: numbers there were, too, who came to bid a last farewell to Sogoro, his wife and children, and to put up a prayer for them. When the hour had arrived, the condemned were dragged forth bound, and made to sit upon coarse mats. Sogoro and his wife closed their eyes, for the sight was more than they could bear; and the spectators, with heaving breasts and streaming eyes, cried "Cruel!" and "Pitiless!" and taking sweetmeats and cakes from the bosoms of their dresses threw them to the children. At noon precisely Sogoro and his wife were bound to the crosses, which were then set upright and fixed in the ground. When this had been done, their eldest son Gennosuke was led forward to the scaffold, in front of the two parents. Then Sogoro cried out:

"Oh! cruel, cruel! what crime has this poor child committed that he is treated thus? As for me, it matters not what becomes of me." And the tears trickled down his face.

The spectators prayed aloud, and shut their eyes; and the executioner himself, standing behind the boy, and saying that it was a pitiless thing that the child should suffer for the father's fault, prayed silently. Then Gennosuke, who had remained with his eyes closed, said to his parents:

"Oh! my father and mother, I am going before you to paradise, that happy country, to wait for you. My little brothers and I will be on the banks of the river Sandzu, and stretch out our hands and help you across. Farewell, all you who have come to see us die; and now please cut off my head at once."

With this he stretched out his neck, murmuring a last prayer; and not only Sogoro and his wife, but even the executioner and the spectators could not repress their tears; but the headsman, unnerved as he was, and touched to the very heart, was forced, on account of his office, to cut off the child's head, and a piteous wail arose from the parents and the spectators.

Then the younger child Sohei said to the headsman, "Sir, I have a sore on my right shoulder: please, cut my head off from the left shoulder, lest you should hurt me. Alas! I know not how to die, nor what I should do."

When the headsman and the officers present heard the child's artless speech, they wept again for very pity; but there was no help for it, and the head fell off more swiftly than water is drunk up by sand. Then little Kihachi, the third son, who, on account of his tender years, should have been spared, was butchered as he was in his simplicity eating the sweetmeats which had been thrown to him by the spectators.

When the execution of the children was over, the priests of Tokoji took their corpses, and, having placed them in their coffins, carried them away, amidst the lamentations of the bystanders, and buried them with great solemnity.

Then Shigayemon, one of the servants of Danzayemon, the chief of the Outcasts, who had been engaged for the purpose, was just about to thrust his spear, when O Man, Sogoro's wife, raising her voice, said:

"Remember, my husband, that from the first you had made up your mind to this fate. What though our bodies be disgracefully exposed on these crosses? – we have the promises of the gods before us; therefore, mourn not. Let us fix our minds upon death: we are drawing near to paradise, and shall soon be with the saints. Be calm, my husband. Let us cheerfully lay down our single lives for the good of many. Man lives but for one generation; his name, for many. A good name is more to be prized than life."

So she spoke; and Sogoro on the cross, laughing gaily, answered:

"Well said, wife! What though we are punished for the many? Our petition was successful, and there is nothing left to wish for. Now I am happy, for I have attained my heart's desire. The changes and chances of life are manifold. But if I had five hundred lives, and could five hundred times assume this shape of mine, I would die five hundred times to avenge this iniquity. For myself I care not; but that my wife and children should be punished also is too much. Pitiless and cruel! Let my lord fence himself in with iron walls, yet shall my spirit burst through them and crush his bones, as a return for this deed."

And as he spoke, his eyes became vermilion red, and flashed like the sun or the moon, and he looked like the demon Razetsu.

"Come," shouted he, "make haste and pierce me with the spear."

"Your wishes shall be obeyed," said the Outcast, Shigayemon, and thrust in a spear at his right side until it came out at his left shoulder, and the blood streamed out like a fountain. Then he pierced the wife from the left side; and she, opening her eyes, said in a dying voice:

"Farewell, all you who are present. May harm keep far from you. Farewell! farewell!" and as her voice waxed faint, the second spear was thrust in from her right side, and she breathed out her spirit. Sogoro, the colour of his face not even changing, showed no sign of fear, but opening his eyes wide, said:

"Listen, my masters! all you who have come to see this sight. Recollect that I shall pay my thanks to my lord Kotsuke no Suke for this day's work. You shall see it for yourselves, so that it shall be talked of for generations to come. As a sign, when I am dead, my head shall turn and face towards the castle. When you see this, doubt not that my words shall come true."

When he had spoken thus, the officer directing the execution gave a sign to the Outcast, Shigayemon, and ordered him to finish the execution, so that Sogoro should speak no more. So Shigayemon pierced him twelve or thirteen times, until he died. And when he was dead, his head turned and faced the castle. When the two councillors beheld this miracle, they came down from their raised platform, and knelt down before Sogoro's dead body and said:

"Although you were but a peasant on this estate, you conceived a noble plan to succour the other farmers in their distress. You bruised your bones, and crushed your heart, for their sakes. Still, in that you appealed to the Shogun in person, you committed a grievous crime, and made light of your superiors; and for this it was impossible not to punish you. Still we admit that to include your wife and children in your crime, and kill them before your eyes, was a cruel deed. What is done, is done, and regret is of no avail. However, honours shall be paid to your spirit: you shall be canonized as the Saint Daimiyo, and you shall be placed among the tutelar deities of my lord's family."

With these words the two councillors made repeated reverences before the corpse; and in this they showed their faithfulness to their lord. But he, when the matter was reported to him, only laughed scornfully at the idea that the hatred of a peasant could affect his feudal lord; and said that a vassal who had dared to hatch a plot which, had it not been for his high office, would have been sufficient to ruin him, had only met with his deserts. As for causing him to be canonized, let him be as he was. Seeing their lord's anger, his councillors could only obey. But it was not long before he had cause to know that, though Sogoro was dead, his vengeance was yet alive.

The relations of Sogoro and the elders of the villages having been summoned to the Court-house, the following document was issued:

"Although the property of Sogoro, the elder of the village of Iwahashi, is confiscated, his household furniture shall be made over to his two married daughters; and the village officials will look to it that these few poor things be not stolen by lawless and unprincipled men.

"His rice-fields and corn-fields, his mountain land and forest land, will be sold by auction. His house and grounds will be given over to the elder of the village. The price fetched by his property will be paid over to the lord of the estate.

"The above decree will be published, in full, to the peasants of the village; and it is strictly forbidden to find fault with this decision.

"The 12th day of the 2nd month, of the 2nd year of the period Shoho."

The peasants, having heard this degree with all humility, left the Court-house. Then the following punishments were awarded to the officers of the castle, who, by rejecting the petition of the peasants in the first instance, had brought trouble upon their lord:

"Dismissed from their office, the resident councillors at Edo and at the castle-town.

"Banished from the province, four district governors, and three bailiffs, and nineteen petty officers.

"Dismissed from office, three metsukes, or censors, and seven magistrates.

"Condemned to *hara-kiri*, one district governor and one Edo bailiff.

"The severity of this sentence is owing to the injustice of the officials in raising new and unprecedented taxes, and bringing affliction upon the people, and in refusing to receive the petitions of the peasants, without consulting their lord, thus driving them to appeal to the Shogun in person. In their avarice they looked not to the future, but laid too heavy a burden on the peasants, so that they made an appeal to a higher power, endangering the honour of their lord's house. For this bad government the various officials are to be punished as above."

In this wise was justice carried out at the palace at Edo and at the Court-house at home. But in the history of the world, from the dark ages down to the present time, there are few instances of one man laying down his life for the many, as Sogoro did: noble and peasant praise him alike.

As month after month passed away, towards the fourth year of the period Shoho, the wife of my lord Kotsuke no Suke, being with child, was seized with violent pains; and retainers were sent to all the different temples and shrines to pray by proxy, but all to no purpose: she continued to suffer as before. Towards the end of the seventh month of the year, there appeared, every night, a preternatural light above the lady's chamber; this was accompanied by hideous sounds as of many people laughing fiendishly, and sometimes by piteous wailings, as though myriads of persons were lamenting. The profound distress caused by this added to her sufferings; so her own privy councillor, an old man, took his place in the adjoining chamber, and kept watch. All of a sudden, he heard a noise as if a number of people were walking on the boards of the roof of my lady's room; then there was a sound of men and women weeping; and when, thunderstruck, the councillor was wondering what it could all be, there came a wild burst of laughter, and all was silent. Early the following morning, the old women who had charge of my lady's household presented themselves before my lord Kotsuke no Suke, and said:

"Since the middle of last month, the waiting-women have been complaining to us of the ghostly noises by which my lady is nightly disturbed, and they say that they cannot continue to serve her. We have tried to soothe them, by saying that the devils should be exorcised at once, and that there was nothing to be afraid of. Still we feel that their fears are not without reason, and that they really cannot do their work; so we beg that your lordship will take the matter into your consideration."

"This is a passing strange story of yours; however, I will go myself tonight to my lady's apartments and keep watch. You can come with me."

Accordingly, that night my lord Kotsuke no Suke sat up in person. At the hour of the rat (midnight) a fearful noise of voices was heard, and Sogoro and his wife, bound to the fatal crosses, suddenly appeared; and the ghosts, seizing the lady by the hand, said:

"We have come to meet you. The pains you are suffering are terrible, but they are nothing in comparison with those of the hell to which we are about to lead you."

At these words, Kotsuke no Suke, seizing his sword, tried to sweep the ghosts away with a terrific cut; but a loud peal of laughter was heard, and the visions faded away. Kotsuke no Suke, terrified, sent his retainers to the temples and shrines to pray that the demons might be cast out; but the noises were heard nightly, as before. When the eleventh month of the year came round, the apparitions of human forms in my lady's apartments became more and more frequent and terrible, all the spirits railing at her, and howling out that they had come to fetch her. The women would all scream and faint; and then the ghosts would disappear amid yells of laughter. Night after night this happened, and even in the daytime the visions would manifest themselves; and my lady's sickness grew worse daily, until in the last month of the year she died, of grief and terror. Then the ghost of Sogoro and his wife crucified would appear day and night in the chamber of Kotsuke no Suke, floating round the room, and glaring at him with red and flaming eyes. The hair of the attendants would stand on end with terror; and if they tried to cut at the spirits, their limbs would be cramped, and their feet and hands would not obey their bidding. Kotsuke no Suke would draw the sword that lay by his bedside; but, as often as he did so, the ghosts faded away, only to appear again in a more hideous shape than before, until at last, having exhausted his strength and spirits, even he became terror-stricken. The whole household was thrown into confusion, and day after day mystic rites and incantations were performed by the priests over braziers of charcoal, while prayers were recited without ceasing; but the visions only became more frequent, and there was no sign of their ceasing. After the 5th year of Shoho, the style of the years was changed to Keian; and during the 1st year of Keian the spirits continued to haunt the palace; and now they appeared in the chamber of Kotsuke no Suke's eldest son, surrounding themselves with even more terrors than before; and when Kotsuke no Suke was about to go to the Shogun's castle, they were seen howling out their cries of vengeance in the porch of the house. At last the relations of the family and the members of the household took counsel together, and told Kotsuke no Suke that without doubt no ordinary means would suffice to lay the ghosts; a shrine must be erected to Sogoro, and divine honours paid to him, after which the apparitions would assuredly cease. Kotsuke no Suke having carefully considered the matter and given his consent, Sogoro was canonized under the name of Sogo Daimiyo, and a shrine was erected in his honour. After divine honours had been paid to him, the awful visions were no more seen, and the ghost of Sogoro was laid for ever.

In the 2nd year of the period Keian, on the 11th day of the 10th month, on the occasion of the festival of first lighting the fire on the hearth, the various Daimyos and Hatamotos of distinction went to the castle of the Shogun, at Edo, to offer their congratulations on this occasion. During the ceremonies, my lord Hotta Kotsuke no Suke and Sakai Iwami no Kami, lord of the castle of Matsumoto, in the province of Shinshiu, had a quarrel, the origin of which was not made public; and Sakai Iwami no Kami, although he came of a brave and noble family, received so severe a wound that he died on the following day, at the age of forty-three; and in consequence of this, his family was ruined and disgraced. My lord Kotsuke no Suke, by great good fortune, contrived to escape from the castle, and took refuge in his own house, whence, mounting a famous horse called Hira-Abumi, he fled to his castle of Sakura, in Shimosa, accomplishing the distance, which is about sixty miles, in six hours. When he arrived in front of the castle, he called out in a loud voice to the guard within to open the gate, answering, in reply to their challenge, that he was Kotsuke no Suke, the lord of the castle. The guard, not believing their ears, sent word to the councillor in charge of the castle, who rushed out to see if the person demanding admittance were really their lord. When he saw Kotsuke no Suke, he caused the gates to be opened, and, thinking it more than strange, said:

"Is this indeed you, my lord? What strange chance brings your lordship hither thus late at night, on horseback and alone, without a single follower?"

With these words he ushered in Kotsuke no Suke, who, in reply to the anxious inquiries of his people as to the cause of his sudden appearance, said:

"You may well be astonished. I had a quarrel today in the castle at Edo, with Sakai Iwami no Kami, the lord of the castle of Matsumoto, and I cut him down. I shall soon be pursued; so we must strengthen the fortress, and prepare for an attack."

The household, hearing this, were greatly alarmed, and the whole castle was thrown into confusion. In the meanwhile the people of Kotsuke no Suke's palace at Edo, not knowing whether their lord had fled, were in the greatest anxiety, until a messenger came from Sakura, and reported his arrival there.

When the quarrel inside the castle of Edo and Kotsuke no Suke's flight had been taken cognizance of, he was attainted of treason, and soldiers were sent to seize him, dead or alive. Midzuno Setsu no Kami and Goto Yamato no Kami were charged with the execution of the order, and sallied forth, on the 13th day of the 10th month, to carry it out. When they arrived at the town of Sasai, they sent a herald with the following message:

"Whereas Kotsuke no Suke killed Sakai Iwami no Kami inside the castle of Edo, and has fled to his own castle without leave, he is attainted of treason; and we, being connected with him by ties of blood and of friendship, have been charged to seize him."

The herald delivered this message to the councillor of Kotsuke no Suke, who, pleading as an excuse that his lord was mad, begged the two nobles to intercede for him. Goto Yamato no Kami upon this called the councillor to him, and spoke privately to him, after which the latter took his leave and returned to the castle of Sakura.

In the meanwhile, after consultation at Edo, it was decided that, as Goto Yamato no Kami and Midzuno Setsu no Kami were related to Kotsuke no Suke, and might meet with difficulties for that very reason, two other nobles, Ogasawara Iki no Kami and Nagai Hida no Kami, should be sent to assist them, with orders that should any trouble arise they should send a report immediately to Edo. In consequence of this order, the two nobles, with five thousand men, were about to march for Sakura, on the 15th of the month, when a messenger arrived from that place bearing the following despatch for the Gorojiu, from the two nobles who had preceded them:

"In obedience to the orders of His Highness the Shogun, we proceeded, on the 13th day of this month, to the castle of Sakura, and conducted a thorough investigation of the affair. It is true that Kotsuke no Suke has been guilty of treason, but he is out of his mind; his retainers have called in physicians, and he is undergoing treatment by which his senses are being gradually restored, and his mind is being awakened from its sleep. At the time when he slew Sakai Iwami no Kami he was not accountable for his actions, and will be sincerely penitent when he is aware of his crime. We have taken him prisoner, and have the honour to await your instructions; in the meanwhile, we beg by these present to let you know what we have done.
"(Signed) Goto Yamato No Kami.
Midzuno Setsu No Kami.
To the Gorojiu, 2nd year of Keian, 2nd month, 14th day."

This despatch reached Edo on the 16th of the month, and was read by the Gorojiu after they had left the castle; and in consequence of the report of Kotsuke no Suke's madness, the second expedition was put a stop to, and the following instructions were sent to Goto Yamato no Kami and Midzuno Setsu no Kami:

"With reference to the affair of Hotta Kotsuke no Suke, lord of the castle of Sakura, in Shimosa, whose quarrel with Sakai Iwami no Kami within the castle of Edo ended in bloodshed. For this heinous crime and disregard of the sanctity of the castle, it is ordered that Kotsuke no Suke be brought as a prisoner to Edo, in a litter covered with nets, that his case may be judged.
"2nd year of Keian, 2nd month.
(Signed by the Gorojiu) Inaba Mino No Kami.
Inouye Kawachi No Kami.
Kato Ecchiu No Kami."

Upon the receipt of this despatch, Hotta Kotsuke no Suke was immediately placed in a litter covered with a net of green silk, and conveyed to Edo, strictly guarded by the retainers of the two nobles; and, having arrived at the capital, was handed over to the charge of Akimoto Tajima no Kami. All his retainers were quietly dispersed; and his empty castle was ordered to be thrown open, and given in charge to Midzuno Iki no Kami.

At last Kotsuke no Suke began to feel that the death of his wife and his own present misfortunes were a just retribution for the death of Sogoro and his wife and children, and he was as one awakened from a dream. Then night and morning, in his repentance, he offered up prayers to the sainted spirit of the dead farmer, and acknowledged and bewailed his crime, vowing that, if his family were spared from ruin and re-established, intercession should be made at the court of the Mikado, at Kiyoto, on behalf of the spirit of Sogoro, so that, being worshipped with even greater honours than before, his name should be handed down to all generations.

In consequence of this it happened that the spirit of Sogoro having relaxed in its vindictiveness, and having ceased to persecute the house of Hotta, in the 1st month of the 4th year of Keian, Kotsuke no Suke received a summons from the Shogun, and, having been forgiven, was made lord of the castle of Matsuyama, in the province of Dewa, with a revenue of twenty thousand kokus. In the same year, on the 20th day of the 4th month, the Shogun, Prince Iyemitsu, was pleased to depart this life, at the age of forty-eight; and whether by the forgiving spirit of the prince, or by the divine interposition of the sainted Sogoro, Kotsuke no Suke was promoted to the castle of Utsu no Miya, in the province of Shimotsuke, with a revenue of eighty thousand kokus; and his name was changed to Hotta Hida no Kami. He also received again his original castle of Sakura, with a revenue of twenty thousand kokus: so that there can be no doubt that the saint was befriending him. In return for these favours, the shrine of Sogoro was made as beautiful as a gem. It is needless to say how many of the peasants of the estate flocked to the shrine: any good luck that might befall the people was ascribed to it, and night and day the devout worshipped at it.

Zenroku's Ghost

ABOUT TEN YEARS AGO there lived a fishmonger, named Zenroku, in the Mikawa-street, at Kanda, in Edo. He was a poor man, living with his wife and one little boy. His wife fell sick and died, so he engaged an old woman to look after his boy while he himself went out to sell his fish. It happened, one day, that he and the other hucksters of his guild were gambling; and this coming to the ears of the authorities, they were all thrown into prison. Although their offence was in itself a light one, still they were kept for some time in durance while the matter was being investigated; and Zenroku, owing to the damp and foul air of the prison, fell sick with fever. His little child, in the meantime, had been handed over by the authorities to the charge of the petty officers of the ward to which his father belonged, and was being well cared for; for Zenroku was known to be an honest fellow, and his fate excited much compassion.

One night Zenroku, pale and emaciated, entered the house in which his boy was living; and all the people joyfully congratulated him on his escape from jail. "Why, we heard that you were sick in prison. This is, indeed, a joyful return." Then Zenroku thanked those who had taken care of the child, saying that he had returned secretly by the favour of his jailers that night; but that on the following day his offence would be remitted, and he should be able to take possession of his house again publicly. For that night, he must return to the prison. With this he begged those present to continue their good offices to his babe; and, with a sad and reluctant expression of countenance, he left the house.

On the following day, the officers of that ward were sent for by the prison authorities. They thought that they were summoned that Zenroku might be handed back to them a free man, as he himself had said to them; but to their surprise, they were told that he had died the night before in prison, and were ordered to carry away his dead body for burial. Then they knew that they had seen Zenroku's ghost; and that when he said that he should be returned to them on the morrow, he had alluded to his corpse. So they buried him decently, and brought up his son, who is alive to this day.

The Money-lender's Ghost

ABOUT THIRTY YEARS AGO there stood a house at Mitsume, in the Honjo of Edo, which was said to be nightly visited by ghosts, so that no man dared to live in it, and it remained untenanted on that account. However, a man called Miura Takeshi, a native of the province of Oshiu, who came to Edo to set up in business as a fencing-master, but was too poor to hire a house, hearing that there was a haunted house, for which no tenant could be found, and that the owner would let any man live in it rent free, said that he feared neither man nor devil, and obtained leave to occupy the house. So he hired a fencing-room, in which he gave his lessons by day, and after midnight returned to the haunted house.

One night, his wife, who took charge of the house in his absence, was frightened by a fearful noise proceeding from a pond in the garden, and, thinking that this certainly must be the ghost that she had heard so much about, she covered her head with the bed-clothes and remained breathless with terror. When her husband came home, she told him what had happened; and on the following night he returned earlier than usual, and waited for the ghostly noise. At the same time as before, a little after midnight, the same sound was heard – as though a gun had been fired inside the pond. Opening the shutters, he looked out, and saw something like a black cloud floating on the water, and in the cloud was the form of a bald man. Thinking that there must be some cause for this, he instituted careful inquiries, and learned that the former tenant, some ten years previously, had borrowed money from a blind shampooer, and, being unable to pay the debt, had murdered his creditor, who began to press him for his money, and had thrown his head into the pond.

The fencing-master accordingly collected his pupils and emptied the pond, and found a skull at the bottom of it; so he called in a priest, and buried the skull in a temple, causing prayers to be offered up for the repose of the murdered man's soul. Thus the ghost was laid, and appeared no more.

How Tajima Shume Was Tormented by a Devil of His Own Creation

ONCE UPON A TIME, a certain Ronin, Tajima Shume by name, an able and well-read man, being on his travels to see the world, went up to Kiyoto by the Tokaido. One day, in the neighbourhood of Nagoya, in the province of Owari, he fell in with a wandering priest, with whom he entered into conversation. Finding that they were bound for the same place, they agreed to travel together, beguiling their weary way by pleasant talk on divers matters; and so by degrees, as they became more intimate, they began to speak without restraint about their private affairs; and the priest, trusting thoroughly in the honour of his companion, told him the object of his journey.

"For some time past," said he, "I have nourished a wish that has engrossed all my thoughts; for I am bent on setting up a molten image in honour of Buddha; with this object I have wandered through various provinces collecting alms and (who knows by what weary toil?) we have succeeded in amassing two hundred ounces of silver – enough, I trust, to erect a handsome bronze figure."

What says the proverb? "He who bears a jewel in his bosom bears poison." Hardly had the Ronin heard these words of the priest than an evil heart arose within him, and he thought to himself, "Man's life, from the womb to the grave, is made up of good and of ill luck. Here am I, nearly forty years old, a wanderer, without a calling, or even a hope of advancement in the world. To be sure, it seems a shame; yet if I could steal the money this priest is boasting about, I could live at ease for the rest of my days;" and so he began casting about how best he might compass his purpose. But the priest, far from guessing the drift of his comrade's thoughts, journeyed cheerfully on, till they reached the town of Kuana. Here there is an arm of the sea, which is crossed in ferry-boats, that start as soon as some twenty or thirty passengers are gathered together; and in one of these boats the two travellers embarked. About half-way across, the priest was taken with a sudden necessity to go to the side of the boat; and the Ronin, following him, tripped him up whilst no one was looking, and flung him into the sea. When the boatmen and passengers heard the splash, and saw the priest struggling in the water, they were afraid, and made every effort to save him; but the wind was fair, and the boat running swiftly under the bellying sails, so they were soon a few hundred yards off from the drowning man, who sank before the boat could be turned to rescue him.

When he saw this, the Ronin feigned the utmost grief and dismay, and said to his fellow-passengers, "This priest, whom we have just lost, was my cousin: he was going to Kiyoto, to visit the shrine of his patron; and as I happened to have business there as well, we settled to travel together. Now, alas! by this misfortune, my cousin is dead, and I am left alone."

He spoke so feelingly, and wept so freely, that the passengers believed his story, and pitied and tried to comfort him. Then the Ronin said to the boatmen:

"We ought, by rights, to report this matter to the authorities; but as I am pressed for time, and the business might bring trouble on yourselves as well, perhaps we had better hush it up for the present; and I will at once go on to Kiyoto and tell my cousin's patron, besides writing home about it. What think you, gentlemen?" added he, turning to the other travellers.

They, of course, were only too glad to avoid any hindrance to their onward journey, and all with one voice agreed to what the Ronin had proposed; and so the matter was settled. When, at length, they reached the shore, they left the boat, and every man went his way; but the Ronin, overjoyed in his heart, took the wandering priest's luggage, and, putting it with his own, pursued his journey to Kiyoto.

On reaching the capital, the Ronin changed his name from Shume to Tokubei, and, giving up his position as a Samurai, turned merchant, and traded with the dead man's money. Fortune favouring his speculations, he began to amass great wealth, and lived at his ease, denying himself nothing; and in course of time he married a wife, who bore him a child.

Thus the days and months wore on, till one fine summer's night, some three years after the priest's death, Tokubei stepped out on to the verandah of his house to enjoy the cool air and the beauty of the moonlight. Feeling dull and lonely, he began musing over all kinds of things, when on a sudden the deed of murder and theft, done so long ago, vividly recurred to his memory, and he thought to himself, "Here am I, grown rich and fat on the money I wantonly stole. Since then, all has gone well with me; yet, had I not been poor, I had never turned assassin nor thief. Woe betide me! what a pity it was!" and as he was revolving the matter in his mind, a feeling of remorse came over him, in spite of all he could do. While his conscience thus smote him, he suddenly, to his utter amazement, beheld the faint outline of a man standing near a fir-tree in the garden: on looking more attentively, he perceived that the man's whole body was thin and worn and the eyes sunken and dim; and in the poor ghost that was before him he recognized the very priest whom he had thrown into the sea at Kuana. Chilled with horror, he looked again, and saw that the priest was smiling in scorn. He would have fled into the house, but the ghost stretched forth its withered arm, and, clutching the back of his neck, scowled at him with a vindictive glare, and a hideous ghastliness of mien, so unspeakably awful that any ordinary man would have swooned with fear. But Tokubei, tradesman though he was, had once been a soldier, and was not easily matched for daring; so he shook off the ghost, and, leaping into the room for his dirk, laid about him boldly enough; but, strike as he would, the spirit, fading into the air, eluded his blows, and suddenly reappeared only to vanish again: and from that time forth Tokubei knew no rest, and was haunted night and day.

At length, undone by such ceaseless vexation, Tokubei fell ill, and kept muttering, "Oh, misery! misery! – the wandering priest is coming to torture me!" Hearing his moans and the disturbance he made, the people in the house fancied he was mad, and called in a physician, who prescribed for him. But neither pill nor potion could cure Tokubei, whose strange frenzy soon became the talk of the whole neighbourhood.

Now it chanced that the story reached the ears of a certain wandering priest who lodged in the next street. When he heard the particulars, this priest gravely shook his head, as though he knew all about it, and sent a friend to Tokubei's house to say that a wandering priest, dwelling hard by, had heard of his illness, and, were it never so grievous, would undertake to heal it by means of his prayers; and Tokubei's wife, driven half wild by her husband's sickness, lost not a moment in sending for the priest, and taking him into the sick man's room.

But no sooner did Tokubei see the priest than he yelled out, "Help! help! Here is the wandering priest come to torment me again. Forgive! forgive!" and hiding his head under the coverlet, he lay quivering all over. Then the priest turned all present out of the room, put his mouth to the affrighted man's ear, and whispered:

"Three years ago, at the Kuana ferry, you flung me into the water; and well you remember it."

But Tokubei was speechless, and could only quake with fear.

"Happily," continued the priest, "I had learned to swim and to dive as a boy; so I reached the shore, and, after wandering through many provinces, succeeded in setting up a bronze figure to Buddha, thus fulfilling the wish of my heart. On my journey homewards, I took a lodging in the next street, and there heard of your marvellous ailment. Thinking I could divine its cause, I came to see you, and am glad to find I was not mistaken. You have done a hateful deed; but am I not a priest, and have I not forsaken the things of this world? and would it not ill become me to bear malice? Repent, therefore, and abandon your evil ways. To see you do so I should esteem the height of happiness. Be of good cheer, now, and look me in the face, and you will see that I am really a living man, and no vengeful goblin come to torment you."

Seeing he had no ghost to deal with, and overwhelmed by the priest's kindness, Tokubei burst into tears, and answered, "Indeed, indeed, I don't know what to say. In a fit of madness

I was tempted to kill and rob you. Fortune befriended me ever after; but the richer I grew, the more keenly I felt how wicked I had been, and the more I foresaw that my victim's vengeance would some day overtake me. Haunted by this thought, I lost my nerve, till one night I beheld your spirit, and from that time forth fell ill. But how you managed to escape, and are still alive, is more than I can understand."

"A guilty man," said the priest, with a smile, "shudders at the rustling of the wind or the chattering of a stork's beak: a murderer's conscience preys upon his mind till he sees what is not. Poverty drives a man to crimes which he repents of in his wealth. How true is the doctrine of Moshi, that the heart of man, pure by nature, is corrupted by circumstances."

Thus he held forth; and Tokubei, who had long since repented of his crime, implored forgiveness, and gave him a large sum of money, saying, "Half of this is the amount I stole from you three years since; the other half I entreat you to accept as interest, or as a gift."

The priest at first refused the money; but Tokubei insisted on his accepting it, and did all he could to detain him, but in vain; for the priest went his way, and bestowed the money on the poor and needy. As for Tokubei himself, he soon shook off his disorder, and thenceforward lived at peace with all men, revered both at home and abroad, and ever intent on good and charitable deeds.

Little Silver's Dream of the Shōjō

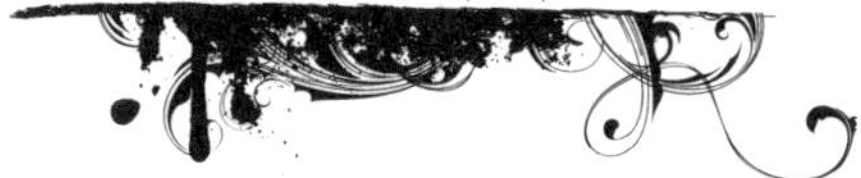

KO GIN SAN (MISS LITTLE SILVER) was a young maid who did not care for strange stories of animals, so much as for those of wonder-creatures in the form of human beings. Even of these, however, she did not like to dream, and when the foolish old nurse would tell her ghost stories at night, she was terribly afraid they would appear to her in her sleep.

To avoid this, the old nurse told her to draw pictures of a tapir, on the sheet of white paper, which, wrapped round the tiny pillow, makes the pillow-case of every young lady, who rests her head on two inches of a bolster in order to keep her well-dressed hair from being mussed or rumpled.

Old grannies and country folks believe that if you have a picture of a tapir under the bed or on the paper pillow-case, you will not have unpleasant dreams, as the tapir is said to eat them.

So strongly do some people believe this that they sleep under quilts figured with the device of this long-snouted beast. If in spite of this precaution one should have a bad dream, he must cry out on awaking, "tapir, come eat, tapir, come eat"; when the tapir will swallow the dream, and no evil results will happen to the dreamer.

Little Silver listened with both eyes and open mouth to this account of the tapir, and then making the picture and wrapping it around her pillow, she fell asleep. I suspect that the kowameshi (red rice) of which she had eaten so heartily at supper time, until her waist strings tightened, had something to do with her travels in dream-land.

She thought she had gone down to Osaka, and there got on a junk and sailed far away to the southwest, through the Inland sea. One night the water seemed full of white ghosts of men and women. Some of them were walking on, and in, the water. Some were running about. Here and there groups appeared to be talking together. Once in a while the junk would run against one of them; and when Little Silver looked to see if he were hurt or knocked over, she could see nothing until the junk passed by, when the ghost would appear standing in the same place, as though the ship had gone through empty air.

Occasionally a ghost would come up to the side of the ship, and in a squeaky voice ask for a dipper. While she would be wondering what a ghost wanted to do with a dipper, a sailor would quietly open a locker, take out a dipper having no bottom, and give one every time he was asked for them. Little Silver noticed a large bundle of these dippers ready. The ghosts would then begin to bail up water out of the sea to empty it in the boat. All night they followed the junk, holding on with one hand to the gunwale, while they vainly dipped up water with the other, trying to swamp the boat. If dippers with bottoms in them had been given them, the sailors said, the boat would have been sunk. When daylight appeared the shadowy host of people vanished.

In the morning they passed an island, the shores of which were high rocks of red coral. A great earthen jar stood on the beach, and around it lay long-handled ladles holding a half-gallon or more, and piles of very large shallow red lacquered wine cups, which seemed as big as the full moon. After the sun had been risen some time, there came down from over the hills a troop of the most curious looking people. Many were short, little wizen-faced folks, that looked very old; or rather, they seemed old before they ought to be. Some were very aged and crooked, with hickory-nut faces, and hair of a reddish gray tint. All the others had long scarlet locks hanging loose over their heads, and streaming down their backs. Their faces were flushed as if by hard drinking, and their pimpled noses resembled huge red barnacles. No sooner did they arrive at the great earthen jar than they ranged themselves round it. The old ones dipped out ladles full, and drank of the wine till they reeled. The younger ones poured the liquor into cups and drank. Even the little infants guzzled quantities of the yellow sake from the shallow cups of very thin red-lacquered wood.

Then began the dance, and wild and furious it was. The leather-faced old sots tossed their long reddish-grey locks in the air, and pirouetted round the big sake jar. The younger ones of all ages clapped their hands, knotted their handkerchiefs over their foreheads, waved their dippers or cups or fans, and practiced all kinds of antics, while their scarlet hair streamed in the wind or was blown in their eyes.

The dance over, they threw down their cups and dippers, rested a few minutes and then took another heavy drink all around.

"Now to work" shouted an old fellow whose face was redder than his half-bleached hair, and who having only two teeth like tusks left looked just like an *oni* (imp.) As for his wife, her teeth had long ago fallen out and the skin of her face seemed to have added a pucker for every year since a half century had rolled over her head.

Then Little Silver looked and saw them scatter. Some gathered shells and burned them to make lime. Others carried water and made mortar, which they thickened by a pulp made of paper, and a glue made by boiling fish skin. Some dived under the sea for red coral, which they hauled up by means of straw ropes, in great sprigs as thick as the branches of a tree. They quickly ran up a scaffold, and while some of the scarlet-headed plasterers smeared the walls, others below passed up the tempered mortar on long shell shovels, to the hand mortar-boards. Even at work they had casks and cups of sake at hand, while children played in the empty kegs and licked the gummy sugar left in some of them.

"What is that house for?" asked Little Silver of the sailors.

"Oh, that is the Kura (storehouse) in which the King of the Shōjō stores the treasures of life, and health, and happiness, and property, which men throw away, or exchange for the sake, which he gives them, by making funnels of themselves."

"Oh, Yes," said Little Silver to herself, as she remembered how her father had said of a certain neighbour who had lately been drinking hard, "he swills sake like a Shōjō."

She also understood why picnic or "chow-chow" boxes were often decorated with pictures of Shōjō, with their cups and dippers. For, at these picnics, many men get drunk; so much so indeed, that after a while the master of the feast orders very poor and cheap wine to be served to the guests. He also replaces the delicate wine cups of egg-shell porcelain, with big thick tea-cups or wooden bowls, for the guests when drunk, do not know the difference.

She also now understood why it was commonly said of a Mr Matsu, who had once been very rich but was now a poor sot, "His property has all gone to the Shōjō."

Just then the ship in which she was sailing struck a rock, and the sudden jerk woke up Little Silver, who cried out, "Tapir, come eat; tapir, come eat."

No tapir came, but if he had I fear Little Silver would have been more frightened than she was by her dream of the ghosts; for next morning she laughed to think how they had all their work a-dipping water for nothing, and at her old nurse for thinking a picture of a tapir could keep off dreams.

The Goblin of Adachigahara

Long, long ago there was a large plain called Adachigahara, in the province of Mutsu in Japan. This place was said to be haunted by a cannibal goblin who took the form of an old woman. From time to time many travelers disappeared and were never heard of more, and the old women round the charcoal braziers in the evenings, and the girls washing the household rice at the wells in the mornings, whispered dreadful stories of how the missing folk had been lured to the goblin's cottage and devoured, for the goblin lived only on human flesh. No one dared to venture near the haunted spot after sunset, and all those who could, avoided it in the daytime, and travelers were warned of the dreaded place.

One day as the sun was setting, a priest came to the plain. He was a belated traveler, and his robe showed that he was a Buddhist pilgrim walking from shrine to shrine to pray for some blessing or to crave for forgiveness of sins. He had apparently lost his way, and as it was late he met no one who could show him the road or warn him of the haunted spot.

He had walked the whole day and was now tired and hungry, and the evenings were chilly, for it was late autumn, and he began to be very anxious to find some house where he could obtain a night's lodging. He found himself lost in the midst of the large plain, and looked about in vain for some sign of human habitation.

At last, after wandering about for some hours, he saw a clump of trees in the distance, and through the trees he caught sight of the glimmer of a single ray of light. He exclaimed with joy:

"Oh. surely that is some cottage where I can get a night's lodging!"

Keeping the light before his eyes he dragged his weary, aching feet as quickly as he could towards the spot, and soon came to a miserable-looking little cottage. As he drew near he saw that it was in a tumble-down condition, the bamboo fence was broken and weeds and grass pushed their way through the gaps. The paper screens which serve as windows and doors in Japan were full of holes, and the posts of the house were bent with age and seemed scarcely able to support the old thatched roof. The hut was open, and by the light of an old lantern an old woman sat industriously spinning.

The pilgrim called to her across the bamboo fence and said:

"O Baa San (old woman), good evening! I am a traveler! Please excuse me, but I have lost my way and do not know what to do, for I have nowhere to rest tonight. I beg you to be good enough to let me spend the night under your roof."

The old woman as soon as she heard herself spoken to stopped spinning, rose from her seat and approached the intruder.

"I am very sorry for you. You must indeed be distressed to have lost your way in such a lonely spot so late at night. Unfortunately I cannot put you up, for I have no bed to offer you, and no accommodation whatsoever for a guest in this poor place!"

"Oh, that does not matter," said the priest; "all I want is a shelter under some roof for the night, and if you will be good enough just to let me lie on the kitchen floor I shall be grateful. I am too tired to walk further tonight, so I hope you will not refuse me, otherwise I shall have to sleep out on the cold plain." And in this way he pressed the old woman to let him stay.

She seemed very reluctant, but at last she said:

"Very well, I will let you stay here. I can offer you a very poor welcome only, but come in now and I will make a fire, for the night is cold."

The pilgrim was only too glad to do as he was told. He took off his sandals and entered the hut. The old woman then brought some sticks of wood and lit the fire, and bade her guest draw near and warm himself.

"You must be hungry after your long tramp," said the old woman. "I will go and cook some supper for you." She then went to the kitchen to cook some rice.

After the priest had finished his supper the old woman sat down by the fire-place, and they talked together for a long time. The pilgrim thought to himself that he had been very lucky to come across such a kind, hospitable old woman. At last the wood gave out, and as the fire died slowly down he began to shiver with cold just as he had done when he arrived.

"I see you are cold," said the old woman; "I will go out and gather some wood, for we have used it all. You must stay and take care of the house while I am gone."

"No, no," said the pilgrim, "let me go instead, for you are old, and I cannot think of letting you go out to get wood for me this cold night!"

The old woman shook her head and said:

"You must stay quietly here, for you are my guest." Then she left him and went out.

In a minute she came back and said:

"You must sit where you are and not move, and whatever happens don't go near or look into the inner room. Now mind what I tell you!"

"If you tell me not to go near the back room, of course I won't," said the priest, rather bewildered.

The old woman then went out again, and the priest was left alone. The fire had died out, and the only light in the hut was that of a dim lantern. For the first time that night he began to feel that he was in a weird place, and the old woman's words, "Whatever you do don't peep into the back room," aroused his curiosity and his fear.

What hidden thing could be in that room that she did not wish him to see? For some time the remembrance of his promise to the old woman kept him still, but at last he could no longer resist his curiosity to peep into the forbidden place.

He got up and began to move slowly towards the back room. Then the thought that the old woman would be very angry with him if he disobeyed her made him come back to his place by the fireside.

As the minutes went slowly by and the old woman did not return, he began to feel more and more frightened, and to wonder what dreadful secret was in the room behind him. He must find out.

"She will not know that I have looked unless I tell her. I will just have a peep before she comes back," said the man to himself.

With these words he got up on his feet (for he had been sitting all this time in Japanese fashion with his feet under him) and stealthily crept towards the forbidden spot. With trembling hands he pushed back the sliding door and looked in. What he saw froze the blood in his veins. The room was full of dead men's bones and the walls were splashed and the floor was covered with human blood. In one corner skull upon skull rose to the ceiling, in another was a heap of arm bones, in another a heap of leg bones. The sickening smell made him faint. He fell backwards with horror, and for some time lay in a heap with fright on the floor, a pitiful sight. He trembled all over and his teeth chattered, and he could hardly crawl away from the dreadful spot.

"How horrible!" he cried out. "What awful den have I come to in my travels? May Buddha help me or I am lost. Is it possible that that kind old woman is really the cannibal goblin? When she comes back she will show herself in her true character and eat me up at one mouthful!"

With these words his strength came back to him and, snatching up his hat and staff, he rushed out of the house as fast as his legs could carry him. Out into the night he ran, his one thought to get as far as he could from the goblin's haunt. He had not gone far when he heard steps behind him and a voice crying: "Stop! stop!"

He ran on, redoubling his speed, pretending not to hear. As he ran he heard the steps behind him come nearer and nearer, and at last he recognized the old woman's voice which grew louder and louder as she came nearer.

"Stop! stop, you wicked man, why did you look into the forbidden room?"

The priest quite forgot how tired he was and his feet flew over the ground faster than ever. Fear gave him strength, for he knew that if the goblin caught him he would soon be one of her victims. With all his heart he repeated the prayer to Buddha:

"Namu Amida Butsu, Namu Amida Butsu."

And after him rushed the dreadful old hag, her hair flying in the wind, and her face changing with rage into the demon that she was. In her hand she carried a large blood-stained knife, and she still shrieked after him, "Stop! stop!"

At last, when the priest felt he could run no more, the dawn broke, and with the darkness of night the goblin vanished and he was safe. The priest now knew that he had met the Goblin of Adachigahara, the story of whom he had often heard but never believed to be true. He felt that he owed his wonderful escape to the protection of Buddha to whom he had prayed for help, so he took out his rosary and bowing his head as the sun rose he said his prayers and made his thanksgiving earnestly. He then set forward for another part of the country, only too glad to leave the haunted plain behind him.

The Yotsuya Kwaidan or O'Iwa Inari

O'Mino and Densuke

YOTSUYA IS A SUBURB – at the extreme west of Edo-Tokyo. Its streets are narrow and winding, though hilly withal; especially on the southern edge toward the Aoyama district, still devoted to cemeteries and palaces, sepulchres whited without and within. Echizenbori would be at the other extremity of the great city. It fronts eastward on the bank of the Sumidagawa. The populous and now poverty stricken districts of Honjo and Fukagawa beyond the wide stream, with other qualities, deprive it of any claim of going to extremes. In fact Echizenbori is a very staid and solid section of Edo-Tokyo. Its streets are narrow; and many are the small shops to purvey for the daily needs of its inhabitants. But these rows of shops are sandwiched in between great clumps of stores, partly warehouses and partly residences of the owners thereof. These stores line the canals of Echizenbori, water courses crowded with junks carrying their ten tons, or their hundreds of tons, of freight – precious cargoes of rice to go into these stores in bulk, of *shoyu* (soy) by the hundred kegs, of sakarazumi (charcoal from Shimosa) by the thousand *tawara* (bale), of fish dried and fresh, of *takuan* or *daikon* (the huge white radish) pickled in salt and rice bran, of all the odds and ends of material in the gross which go to make up the necessities of living in a great city. If Echizenbori then can make its show of poverty, and very little *display* of wealth, it is not one of the poor quarters of this capital city of Nippon.

Crossing the Takabashi from Hachobori and plunging down the narrow street opposite; a short turn to the right, a plunge down another narrow street and a turn to the right; one comes to the high cement wall, in its modernness of type a most unusual attachment to shrine or temple. The gate is narrow and formal; almost like the entrance to a garden or smaller burying ground. Within all is changed from the busy outside world. The area inclosed is small – perhaps a square of a hundred and fifty feet – but marked in lines by a maze of lanterns of the cheap iron variety, set on cheap wooden posts. On the right is seen a minor shrine or two dedicated to the Inari goddess. On the left is a small building devoted to votive offerings, the crude and the more elaborate. The most striking is the offering of a little *geisha* lady, and portrays an heroic scene of early days. There are other portraitures, in which perhaps a wandering lover is seen as a hero, to the lady's eyes, of these later times. On the outside of the structure are posted up by the hundred pictures of once woebegone ladies, now rejoicing in the potent influence of the Tamiya shrine to restore to them the strayed affections of husband or lover. Next in line is an open, shed-like structure. It is a poor chance if here the casual visitor does not encounter one or two of the petitioners, patiently trotting round in a circle from front to back, and reciting their prayers in this accomplishment of 'the hundred turns'. Just opposite, and close by, is the shrine itself. This is in part a massive store-house set back in the domestic structure, with the shrine of the Inari facing the visitor. The floor space at the sides and before it often is piled high with tubs of *shoyu* and *sake*, with bundles of charcoal, such negotiable articles as the wealthier shopkeeper can offer to the mighty lady; and long tresses of hair of women too poor to offer anything else, or wise enough to know that a woman could make no greater sacrifice. And is not the object of their worship a woman? Numerous are these severed strands. Entering the shrine and passing the pleasant spoken warden at its entrance, peddling his charms and giving advice where often it is sadly needed – perhaps the more valuable of his two public duties – to the left within is the Oku-no-In, the inner shrine containing the *ihai* or memorial tablet of O'Iwa (Oiwa). That the shrine is popular and wealthy; that the lady is feared, venerated, and her dreadful powers much sought after; this is plain to the eye in the crowded elaborateness of this inner holy place of the larger sacred structure.

Now Echizenbori is not a particularly old quarter of the city. Long after Edo was established, the city, step by step, fought its way down to the river; filling in lagoons and swamps, and driving their waters into the canals which were to furnish very largely the means of communication for its traffic. Yotsuya on the contrary is old. Its poverty is of later date. In the Edo days it was a favourite site for the homes of *dōshin*, *yakunin*, and a whole herd of the minor officials who had the actual working of the great Tokugawa machine of government in their hands. In the maps of Ansei 4th year (1857) the shrine of the O'Iwa Inari figures in Samoncho, in its Teramachi; a small part of the great mass of red, indicating temples and shrines and their lands, which then covered a large part of Yotsuya. How then did it come to pass that the shrine was removed to this far off site in Echizenbori, with such incongruous surroundings? The explanation must be found in our story.

When the Tenwa year period (1681–83) opened, long resident at Yotsuya Samoncho had been Tamiya Matazaemon. By status he was a minor official or *dōshin* under the Tokugawa administration. These *dōshin* held highest rank of the permanent staff under the bureaucratic establishment; and on these men lay the main dependence for smoothness of working of the machinery of the Government. Matazaemon was the perfect type of the under-official of the day; smooth, civilly impertinent to his equals, harsh to his inferiors, and all unction and abjectness to his superiors. Indeed, he laid more stress on those immediately above him than on the more removed. To serve the greater lord he served his immediate officer, being careful to allow to the latter all the credit. No small part of his function was to see that ceremonial form and precedent were carried out to the letter. It was the accurate and ready knowledge of these which was of greatest import to his chief, indeed might save the latter from disaster. Matazaemon's readiness and conduct rendered him deservedly valued. Hence he enjoyed the double salary of thirty *tawara* of rice, largely supplemented by gifts coming to him as teacher in *hanaike* (the art of flower arrangement) and of the *cha-no-yu* (tea ceremony). He had a more than good house, for one of his class, facing on the wide Samoncho road, and with a garden on the famous Teramachi or long street lined with temples and which runs eastward from that thoroughfare. The garden of Tamiya almost faced the entrance to the Gwanshoji, which is one of the few relics of the time still extant. It was large enough to contain some fifteen or twenty fruit trees, mainly the *kaki* or persimmon, for Matazaemon was of practical mind. Several cherry trees, however, periodically displayed their bloom against the rich dark green foliage of the fruit trees; and in one corner, to set forth the mystic qualities of a small Inari shrine relic of a former owner, were five or six extremely ancient, gnarled, and propped up plum trees, sufficient in number to cast their delicate perfume through garden and house in the second month (March).

Such was the home of Matazaemon; later that of O'Iwa San. It was pretentious enough to make display with a large household. But the master of Tamiya was as close-fisted and hard and bitter as an unripe *biwa* (medlar). His wealth was the large and unprofitable stone which lay within; the acid pulp, a shallow layer, all he had to give to society in his narrow-minded adherence to official routine; the smooth, easily peeled skin the outward sign of his pretentions to social status and easily aroused acidity of temper. With most of his neighbours, and all his relatives, he had a standing quarrel. Secure in his lord's favour as an earnest officer, so little did he care for the dislike of the ward residents that he was ever at drawn swords with the head of his ward-association, Ito Kwaiba. As for the relatives, they were only too ready to come to closer intimacy; and Matazaemon knew it.

His household consisted of his wife O'Naka, his daughter O'Mino, and the man servant Densuke. The garden Matazaemon would allow no one to attend to but himself. The two women did all the work of the household which ordinarily would fall to woman-kind, with something more. Densuke performed the heavier tasks, accompanied his master on his outings, and represented his contribution to the service of the ward barrier, the Okido, on the great Koshu-Kaido and just beyond the Obangumi. The barrier cut off Yotsuya from the Naito-Shinjuku district, and, as an entrance into Edo, was of considerable importance. When the time of service came Densuke appeared in full uniform and with his pike. A handsome young fellow of nineteen years, the women, especially O'Mino, saw to it that his appearance should be a credit to the House. His progress up the wide Samoncho, up to his disappearance into the great highway, was watched by O'Mino – and by the neighbours, who had much sharper eyes and tongues than Matazaemon and his wife. They marvelled.

With ground for marvel. In the eyes of her parents O'Mino was the most beautiful creature ever created. Occasionally Matazaemon would venture on criticism. "Naka, something is to be said to Mino. Too much powder is used on the face. Unless the colour of the skin be very dark, the use of too much powder is not good. Mino is to be warned against excess." Thus spoke the official in his most official tone and manner. Wife and daughter heard and disobeyed; the wife because she was ruled by her daughter, and the daughter because she would emulate the fair skin of Densuke and be fairer in his eyes. O'Mino had suffered both from fate and fortune. She had been born ugly; with broad, flat face like unto the moon at full, or a dish. Her back was a little humped, her arms disproportionately long, losing in plumpness what they gained in extension. She seemed to have no breasts at all, the chest forming a concavity in correspondence to the convexity of the back, with a smoothness much like the inner surface of a bowl. This perhaps was no disadvantage – under the conditions. So much for fate. But fortune had been no kinder. 'Blooming' into girlhood, she had been attacked by smallpox. Matazaemon was busy, and knew nothing of sick nursing. O'Naka was equally ignorant, though she was well intentioned. Of course the then serving wench knew no more than her mistress. O'Mino was allowed to claw her countenance and body, as the itching of the sores drove her nearly frantic. In fact, O'Naka in her charity aided her. The result was that she was most hideously pock-marked. Furthermore, the disease cost her an eye, leaving a cavity, a gaping and unsightly wound, comparable to the dumplings called *kuzumanju*, white puffy masses of rice dough with a depression in the centre marked by a dab of the dark-brown bean paste. The neighbours used to say that O'Mino was *nin san bake shichi* – that is, three parts human and seven parts apparition. The more critical reduced her humanity to the factor one. The children had no name for her but "Oni" (fiend). They had reason for this. They would not play with her, and treated her most cruelly. O'Mino, who was of no mild temperament, soon learned to retaliate by use of an unusually robust frame, to which was united by nature and circumstances her father's acidity of character. When the odds were not too great all the tears were not on O'Mino's side; but she suffered greatly, and learned with years that the Tamiya garden was her safest playground.

O'Mino grew into a woman. Affection had to find some outlet. Not on the practical and very prosaic mother; not on the absorbed and crabbed father; but on Densuke, on the *samurai's* attendant or *chūgen*, it fell. All manner of little services were rendered to him; even such as would appropriately fall within his own performance. At first O'Mino sought out little missions for him to perform, out of the line of his usual duties, and well rewarded in coin. This was at his first appearance in the house. Then she grew bolder. Densuke found his clothing undergoing mysterious repairs and replacement. His washing, even down to the loin cloths, was undertaken by the Ojosan. Densuke did not dare to question or thwart her. Any trifling fault O'Mino took on herself, as due to her meddling. She became bolder and bolder, and sought his assistance in her own duties, until finally they were as man and maid employed in the same house. Matazaemon noted little increases in the house expenses. O'Mino took these as due to her own extravagance. The father grunted a little at these unusual expenditures. "What goes out at one end must be cut off at the other end. Densuke, oil is very expensive. At night a light is not needed. Be sure, therefore, on going to bed to extinguish the light." Densuke at once obeyed his master's order; and that very night, for the first time, O'Mino boldly sought his couch. Confused, frightened, overpowered by a passionate woman, Densuke sinned against his lord, with his master's daughter as accomplice.

Henceforth Densuke had what O'Mino was willing to give him. On Matazaemon's going forth to his duties, O'Mino, and O'Naka under her orders, did all his household work. The only return required was submission to the exigencies of the Ojosan. This was no slight obligation. Densuke at times thought of escape, to his home at Togane village in Kazusa, to his uncle Kyubei in the Kanda quarter of Edo. O'Mino seemed to divine his thoughts. She would overload him with favours; or openly express her purpose of following wherever he went in life. Kanda? Kyubei was a well-known hanger-on at the Tamiya. Matazaemon entered him up in his expense book at so much a year. Togane? He could not get there except through Kyubei. Matazaemon had farms there, and the *nanushi* or village bailiff was his servant. Besides, he would be a runaway. Matazaemon surely would come down on Kyubei as the security. So the months passed, and matters were allowed to drift. Perhaps it was some gossip of the quarter which reached the deaf ears of Matazaemon. As he was about to go forth one day he followed the figure of O'Mino sharply with his little eyes all screwed up. "Naka, there seems change in the figure of Mino. Surely the gossip of the neighbours as to Densuke is not true? Mino is said to harbour a child by him. In such case it would be necessary to kill them both. Warn Mino in time; a *chūgen* is not one to become the adopted son (*muko*) of the Tamiya. He is an excellent lad, and costs but little. His habits are not riotous. To dismiss him thus causelessly would not only be unjust, but to no profit. Mino giving heed to the warning, all will be well." With this the lord of the household stalked forth to the house entrance. Receiving his clogs from O'Mino, he stalked forth to his official attendance. The two women, prostrate in salutation at his exit, raised their heads to watch him stalk.

It was a frightened face that O'Naka turned to her daughter. In whispering voice – "The honoured father's words have been heard? If not, it is to be said that gossip of the neighbourhood has come to his ears as to relations with Densuke. He notices that an *obi* is not often worn; and when worn is soon discarded. However, a man's eye is not so apt in such matters. Even in this Naka cannot speak positively. Doubtless the report is not true." O'Mino, if ugly, was anything but obtuse. Her mother must know; and yet not know. "My honoured father does not consider the difference of age and status in Densuke. Densuke is but a boy. This Mino has passed her twenty-third year. Moreover, surely she deserves a better husband than a *chūgen*. Least of all would she give her father cause for regret or painful thoughts. Can a woman be pregnant otherwise than by a man?" O'Mino, respectfully prostrate, with this raised her head. The two women looked each other in the face. Finally O'Naka said – "With joy is the answer heard. But Matazaemon San is of hasty temper. In his suspicions even he is to be avoided. However, the business of the house is to be performed. This will take the time until late in the day. Tradesmen may come for payments of the month. In the closet ten *ryō* in silver will be found. Here are the keys to the chests. It would be well to take an inventory of the effects. The winter is at hand. It is time to make warmer provision for it. Be sure to observe circumspection." With these words, and a sad look at her erring daughter, O'Naka donned street garb, threw a *haori* (cloak) over her shoulders, climbed down into her clogs, and their patter soon disappeared down the street.

Her departure was almost coincident with the reappearance of Densuke. His attendance on the master to the offices of the palace stables accomplished, for the time being he had returned. Thus did Matazaemon effect an outward state and an household economy. None too willing was the presence of Densuke. He was faithful in his way to O'Mino, and much afraid of her. Even in the most private intercourse to him she was the Ojosan, the daughter of the House; but he had no other recourse than the Tamiya. Once assured of him, O'Mino had cut off all the previous flow of coin, and with it the means of his rare indiscretions at the Shinjuku pleasure quarter. Besides, their interviews took place in the darkness of night. In the daytime O'Naka usually was present, who, lacking other company, sought that of her daughter, and moreover was unwilling to be too complacent in the intrigue she saw going on. As soon as the sound of Densuke's steps was heard, O'Mino called him. There was a sharpness in her tone, a note of alarmed decision, that frightened and chilled him. Humbly he sought her presence. A glance showed the absence of O'Naka, yet as usual he prostrated himself in salutation. In that position he did not see her face. She said impatiently – "For salutation there is no time nor occasion. It is no longer the Ojosan who speaks; it is the wife. My father knows all concerning this Mino and Densuke. On his return he is sure to take the occasion of the presence of both to kill us. It is his right and our duty to submit to his punishment. But to do so consigns the infant in the womb from darkness to darkness. This is too dreadful to contemplate. Unfilial though it be, we must run away. Make up your mind to do so." Densuke looked up. She was bent in meditation over this flight. The corners of the mouth widened out, the eyelid drooping more conspicuously than ever and forming a heavy fold over the empty socket, the bald brow, the scanty hair at the sides in disordered whisps and strands, all these made her a hideous mask. He could not endure the sight. Timidly he said – "Terrible news indeed! How has it happened? Surely, honoured lady, you have been very rash; nay, somewhat clumsy withal. Cannot women take their pleasure with whom they please without such dire results? Ah! Such luxury, such pleasant surroundings! All must be abandoned. This Densuke will seek his native village in Kazusa. And the Ojosan whither will she go; what will she do?"

Was the question asked in innocence, or in deepest guile? O'Mino could not have answered, well as she thought she knew Densuke. He felt a hand on his shoulder. He sprang up in fright, hardly knowing whether it was a demon, or O'Mino turned demon, who confronted him. Her mouth half open, her large, white, shining, even teeth all displayed, her single eye darting malignant gleams, and the empty socket and its fold quivering and shaking, she was a frightful object. "To speak of pleasure without the consequences, such talk is that of a fool. Densuke was taken for the relationship of the two worlds. Now you would abandon me. Very well – do so. But this Mino does not perish by her father's sword. The well is at hand. Within three days I shall reappear and hunt you out. Torn to pieces the wretched man shall die a miserable death. Better would it be now to die with Mino. A last salutation...." Two vigorous arms seized his neck. Densuke gave a cry of anguish as the sharp teeth marked the ear. Letting him go, she sprang to the *rōka* (verandah). Frightened as he was, Densuke was too quick for her. He grasped her robe. "Nay! The Ojosan must not act so desperately. Densuke spoke as one clumsy, and at a loss what to do ... yes ... we must run away ... there is the uncle, Kawai, in Kanda. To him Densuke will go, and there learn the will of Tamiya Dono." O'Mino's tragic attitude lapsed. At once she was the practical woman of the house. She gave thanks for her mother's foresight. "The escape is not as of those unprovided. Here are ten *ryō* in silver. A bundle is to be made of the clothing and other effects. This is to be carried by Densuke. And the uncle: Mino presenting herself for the first time as wife, a present is to be brought. What should it be?" She talked away, already busy with piling clothes, quilts (*futon*), toilet articles onto a large *furoshiki* or square piece of cloth. Then she arrayed her person with greatest care, and in the soberest and richest fashion as the newly-wed wife. With time Densuke managed to get his breath amid this vortex of unexpected confusion into which he had been launched. "The uncle's teeth are bad. Soft *takuan* is just the thing. For long he has eaten little else. Four or five stalks are sufficient." He went to the kitchen to secure this valued gift. Then he collected his own possessions. With the huge bundle of the *furoshiki* on his shoulders; with straw raincoat, sun hat, clogs for wet and dry weather, piled on the top, and the stalks of the *takuan* dangling down; "it was just as if they were running away from a fire." As Densuke departed O'Mino closely observed him. He was too subdued, too scared to give her anxiety. Later she left the house to join him at the Hanzo-bashi, far enough removed from Yotsuya. It was then Tenwa, 2nd year, 11th month (December, 1682).

Kawai San Of Kandu Ku

This uncle of Densuke, Kawai Kyubei by name, was a rice dealer, with a shop in Matsudacho of the Kanda district. The distance to go was far. As with all ladies, O'Mino kept Densuke waiting long at the Hanzo-bashi. Indeed, there was much romance about this ugly, neglected, hard girl. She waited until the sound of O'Naka's clogs was heard. Then she halted at the corner of Teramachi until she could see her mother's figure in the dusk; see it disappear into the house. When she went down the street toward the Samegabashi she was crying. It was late therefore – after the hour of the pig (9 pm) – when the pair reached Kanda. The business of the day was long over in this business section of Edo. The houses were tightly closed. On reaching the entrance of Kyubei's house said Densuke – "Ojosan, condescend to wait here for a moment. The uncle is to be informed. Deign to have an eye to the *furoshiki*. Please don't let the dogs bite into or insult the *takuan*." He pounded on the door. Said a voice within – "Obasan (Auntie)! Obasan! Someone knocks. Please go and open for them." The more quavering and softer tones of an old woman made answer – "No, it is not my turn and time to go to the door. Get up; and first make inquiry before entrance is allowed. With little to lose, loss is much felt. Ah! Tamiya Dono in the Yotsuya has been sadly neglected." The scolding tones hummed on. Grumbling, the old man was lighting a rush. "'Tis agreed; 'Tis agreed. Tomorrow without fail this Kyubei visits Tamiya. Ah! It is no jest to go to that house. Not only is the distance great, but...." He had the door open, and his mouth too. "Densuke! Graceless fellow! But what are you doing here, and at this hour? No; the luck is good. There is a big bundle with you, a huge bundle." He spied the *takuan* and his face broadened into a smile. "Ah! If dismissed, it has been with honour. Doubtless the *takuan* is for this Kyubei. Thanks are felt. But is all this stuff Densuke's? He has not stolen it? Doubtless a woman is at the bottom of the affair. Never mind;

an opportunity presents itself to offer you as *muko* – at the Tatsuya in Yokomachi. Of late a boy has been hoped for, but another girl presented herself. A *muko* now will be welcome. The wife is getting past child-bearing, and there is little hope of a son. The Tatsuya girl is just the thing. In a few months she will be fit to be a wife. She...."

Densuke edged a word into this stream. "The honoured uncle is right. The cause of Densuke's appearance is a woman." The old man made a face. Said he – "Well, in such a case it is good to be out of it. This Kyubei has heard talk of Densuke – and of all things with the Ojosan! That would be terrible indeed. But how is the Oni (demon)? What a sight she is! Bald, one-eyed, hairless, with a face like a dish and no nose – Kyubei came suddenly on her at dusk in the Yotsuya. Iya! It was cold feet and chills for him for the space of seven days. It is that which keeps Kyubei from Yotsuya, although a little aid would go far. The last dealings in rice notes were not favourable. Besides, account is soon to be rendered to Tamiya Dono. But though wicked of temper and ugly, O'Mino San is rich. Even for the demon in time a good match will be found. She will be the wife of an honoured *kenin* (vassal), and the husband will buy *geisha* and *jorō* with the money. Such is the expectation of Tamiya Dono. Don't allow any trifling there. Remember that she is the daughter of a *go-kenin*. They talk of Densuke in the Yotsuya. Of course it is all talk. Don't allow it to happen." Densuke found an opening. The words meant one thing; the expression another. "It is not *going* to happen." Kyubei looked at him aghast as he took in the meaning. "What! With the demon? Densuke has committed the carnal sin with the demon? Oh, you filthy scoundrel! Rash, inconsiderate boy! Obasan! Obasan!... What did she pay you for the deed?... This low fellow Densuke, this foolish rascal of a nephew, has been caught in fornication with the demon.... What a fool! How is it that death has been escaped? And you have run away. Doubtless a pregnancy has followed. After putting his daughter to death Tamiya Dono will surely hunt out Densuke. Or perhaps keep O'Mino San until he catches the interloper. Sinning together, both will die together. Ah! To cross the Sanzu no Kawa, to climb the Shide no Yama, with the demon as company: terrific! It is terrific! And what has become of her? Why fall into such a trap, with a woman old and ugly? Her riches are not for you. Caught here, the *tatami* of Kyubei will be spoiled."

Densuke countered. He spoke in the old man's ear. "Refusing consent, she threatened to kill herself and haunt this Densuke as O'Bake (apparition). The Ojisan (uncle) has seen the Ojosan. Would he be haunted by her, be seized and killed with torture?... And then – here she stands, just at the door." The old man spluttered, and gasped, and went on his nose in abject salutation – "Oh, the fool!... the Ojosan is here in person ... he would trifle with the devil!... the low rascal would seduce the honoured daughter of Tamiya ... put ten hags in a row and pick out the worst ... will the Ojosan condescend to honour Kyubei's place.... Oh! She's a very O'Bake already. Pregnancy with a beautiful woman is bad enough. With this demon it makes her an apparition ... condescend to enter; deign to enter." O'Mino slowly came forward. That what had been said by the rash and unconscious Kyubei had escaped her ear was unlikely. The humility of demeanor hardly veiled the offended dignity of her approach. "Densuke has spoken truth. We come as husband and wife. Condescend to give shelter for the time being, and become the intercessor with Tamiya Dono. Such is the prayer of this Mino." As she spoke she bowed low on the *tatami* (mats). Kyubei caught the hint; for if she had heard the talk of Densuke, she had assuredly heard his still louder ejaculations and ill-timed wit. The Obasan was in a rage at him. Taking the conduct of affairs in her own hand – "Condescend to make this poor dwelling a home for as long as desired. Plainly the visitors have not come empty handed. Ma! Ma! 'Tis like an escape from a fire. Densuke is a strong lad to shoulder such a burden. But he always has been something of an ass. As for Matazaemon Dono, tomorrow the Ojisan shall attend to the affair, and see what is to be expected. Meanwhile, deign to be as in Samoncho itself." The kindly old woman pushed Kyubei and his clumsy apologies out of the way. She busied herself about O'Mino. The two women understood each other. The varied contents of the *furoshiki* were quickly stowed away. A little supper was prepared for the hungry fugitives. Kyubei sat by, his eyes dazzled by the wealth of goods displayed, and his nostrils shifting under the acrid perfume of the *takuan* and remembrance of his stupidity.

The next morning Kyubei was up betimes. Matazaemon was no dawdler. It was best to catch him satisfied with the morning meal, and perhaps beset by the night's regret over the loss of his daughter. In no way was it a pleasant mission. Kyubei's pace became a crawl as he approached the garden gate on Teramachi. He put in an appearance at the kitchen side. O'Naka was here established, engaged in her duties and surely awaiting him. At sight of him she burst into what was half laugh and half tears. "Ah! It is Kyubei San. Doubtless he comes on the part of Mino and Densuke. It is kind of Kyubei to befriend them. The Danna (master) is very angry indeed. An only daughter, and one on whom he depended for a *muko*, he is much upset. Please go in and talk with him. Show anger at the runaways. To agree with him may somewhat soothe his passion. Condescend so to act." Kyubei winked. And turn some of this anger on himself? Well, agreement might rouse the spirit of contradiction in Tamiya Dono. It was a characteristic of this hide-bound official. Matazaemon was drinking the last sips of tea from his rice bowl when the *shōji* were gently pushed apart, and the head of Kyubei inserted in the opening. At first he paid no attention. Then as one in haste – "Ah! Is it Kyubei? He comes early today – and hardly to apply for anything. The rice notes are not yet due for some weeks." His tone was grim; the usual indifferent benevolence of demeanor toward a townsman was conspicuously absent. Kyubei felt chilled. Densuke must not sacrifice his good uncle to his own folly.

Said Kyubei – "Yet it is to seek the honoured benevolence of Tamiya Dono that Kyubei comes." Matazaemon turned sharp around toward him. Frightened, the townsman continued – "Densuke has acted very wickedly. The low, lascivious rascal has dared to seduce the honoured daughter of the House. Both are now harboured at the house of this Kyubei, who now makes report. Their lives are in the hand of Tamiya Dono. But Kyubei would make earnest plea for delay. O'Mino San being pregnant, the child would be sent from darkness to darkness – a terrible fate. May it be condescended to show the honoured mercy and benevolence. Evil and unfilial though the action of the two has been, yet 'benevolence weighs the offence; justice possesses two qualities.' Such are the words of Koshi (Confucius)." The eyes of Matazaemon twinkled. He had heard that Kyubei was on the verge of shaving his head (turning priest). Truly the townsman was profitting by the exhortations of his teacher. After a time he said – "The memory of Kyubei is excellent. Don't let it fail him on the present occasion. For such a deed as has been committed the punishment is death, meted out by the hand of this Matazaemon. The fact ascertained, it was intended to kill them both. The flight of Mino and Densuke has altered the complexion of the affair. It is no longer necessary to inflict the extreme penalty. O'Mino is disowned for seven births. Neither she nor Densuke is to appear before this Matazaemon. If the talk of the ward be true, in exchange for a loyal service Densuke has secured a beautiful bride. There can be no regrets." Then, taking a sprightly and jeering air, "But this Kyubei has been the one to exercise benevolence. Matazaemon now learns that the two runaways have been received by him. Entertain them well; entertain them well. Thanks are due to Kyubei San – from them. Doubtless he is much occupied with his guests. Less will be seen of him in Yotsuya.... But official duties press. This Matazaemon must leave. Don't be in haste. Stay and take some tea.... Naka! Naka! Tea for Kyubei San;

the *baori* (cloak) of Matazaemon.... *Sayonara*.... Ah! The rice notes this Matazaemon took up for Kyubei San, they fall due with the passage of the weeks. But Kyubei is one who always meets his obligations. As to that there is no anxiety." With this last fling the prostrate Kyubei heard the sound of the clogs of Matazaemon on the flagged walk outside. A departing warning to O'Naka as to the tea, and steps were heard near-by. He raised his head, to confront the mistress of the house.

O'Naka spoke with tears in her eyes – a salve to the alarmed and wounded feelings of Kyubei. "Don't be frightened. After all Matazaemon is a *samurai*. To press Kyubei, or any tradesman, is beyond him. But this Naka cannot see her daughter! To add to his anger would bring disaster on her and the unborn child. Alas! Anyhow, give Mino this money; and these articles of value, properly her own. Her mirror has been forgotten in the hasty flight." O'Naka brought forth one of those elaborate polished silver surfaces, used by the ladies of Nippon in these later luxurious days of the Shogunate. It was only now that it became the property of O'Mino. It was part of the wedding outfit of O'Naka herself. With this little fiction the mother continued – "When the child is born allow the grandmother at least a distant sight of it. Perhaps it will resemble Tamiya; be like its mother, and soften a father's heart." Now she wept bitterly; and Kyubei wept with her – bitterly. "Like the mother! The Buddhas of Daienji would indeed weep at the appearance of such a monster." This was his thought; not expressed with the humble gratitude, prostration, and promises which he fully intended to keep. Kyubei reverentially accepted the mirror, the goods, the money. Taking his leave of Yotsuya – a long one he feared – with sighs he set out for Kanda. Here he made his report. Said the old townsman with severity – "The will of the parent is not to be disobeyed. It is the duty of this Kyubei to see to its performance." He had O'Naka more in mind than the master of Tamiya. O'Mino might yet be the goose to lay golden eggs. A goose of such plumage! Kyubei made a wry face in the darkness of the corridor.

Takahashi Daihachiro

Some means of support had to be found. Employed in a *kenin's* house, and leaving it under such conditions, kindred occupation was out of the question. There was a sort of black list among these officials to cover all grades of their service. Time and the host of servants of some great House would get the lad back into the only occupation he understood. Trusting to some such accident of fortune, Kyubei made Densuke his agent on commission. Densuke was no idler. Kyubei managed to meet the Tamiya security for his loans, largely through the efforts of the younger man. The married couple at this time set up their establishment in Gorobeicho of Kyobashi Ku. Coming and going, often with no definite task in hand, Densuke to all appearance was an out-and-out idler. For the first time released from the trammels of her class, O'Mino could attend the theatres and farce shows of the capital. She delighted in acting this part of a tradesman's wife. Moreover she was very sure of not meeting with Matazaemon, of whom she was in great fear. Bound to the *formulae* of his class, her father might feel bound to cut her down on sight.

One day Densuke was idling and hanging over the parapet of the Nihonbashi. Some fishermen were violently quarrelling in the fish market on the bank just below the bridge. As he looked on with interest a hand was laid on his shoulder. Turning, he saw a man, partly in the dress of a *chūgen*, partly in that of a menial attendant of one of the larger *yashiki* (nobleman's mansion). Scars of burns on his hands and arms, patches of rice flour and bran, showed that he was a cook. His eye was severe and his manner abrupt as he rebuked Densuke. "An idle fellow! This Tarobei never fails to come across Densuke as an idler, or on the way to Asakusa with the worthy wife. Is he fit for nothing?" Densuke was a mild man. To this man with a grievance his answer was soft. Besides he had no liking for the cook's knife stuck in the girdle, and handy to carve fish or flesh. He said – "Perchance the idleness is more in appearance than fact. Buying and selling on commission the task is an irregular one. It is true, however, that this Densuke has no settled labour. Alas! Former days in the service of a *samurai* are much to be regretted." – "Can you cook rice?" was the abrupt interruption. "This Densuke knows the 'Sanryaku' fairly well. Is more needed?" The man looked at him dumbfounded. "The 'Sanryaku' – what's that?" – "Knowledge of the 'Sanryaku' enables one to meet all the requirements of a *bushi* (knight). At the school in Kazusa Togane the priest who taught this Densuke, at one time a *samurai*, was far more taken with the 'Sanryaku' than with the *Sutra* (Scripture); the lessons taught applied more to Bushido (the knight's way) than to Butsudo (the way of the Buddha).... But to the point; this Densuke for three years cooked the rice at Tamiya in Yotsuya. First there is the *toro-toro* of bubbling water; then the *biri-biri*, as what little remains passes as steam through the rice grains. Then the sharp whistling cry of a baby from the pot on the slow fire (*murashite*). The task is done, and the vessel is removed from the stove." The man looked with respect on this learned cook. Said he – "Densuke is the man. Tarobei must leave the kitchen of Geishu Sama at once. The mother is ill in Aki province. A substitute is to be found. The salary – is next to nothing; but the perquisites are numerous, and the food ample to feed several Densuke and their wives. Deign to accept." Densuke did not hesitate – "The obligation lies with Densuke. But how secure the position? There is Tamiya...." The man laughed. "There are many Densuke in Edo; and no connection between the *yashiki* of Matsudaira Aki no Kami and the house of a *dōshin* in Yotsuya. There is small likelihood of meeting old acquaintances. Be sure to remember that it is Densuke of Kyobashi; not Densuke of Yotsuya. This pass will answer to the gate-man. Substitutes are common. Whether it be Densuke or Tarobei who cooks the rice makes no difference; provided the rice be well cooked. Tarobei's service lies elsewhere; to Densuke San deep his obligation." He held out the pass, and Densuke took it.

With mutual salutation and joy in heart they parted. Densuke betook himself to the *yashiki* of Matsudaira Aki no Kami at Kasumigaseki. No difficulties were encountered. Tarobei was not so superlative as a cook that the substitute could not be better than the original. At this place Densuke acted the part of the *komatsukibatta*. This is a narrow brown weevil, some three parts of an inch in length, and which stands on its head making the repeated movements of *o'jigi*, much as at a ceremonial encounter in Nippon. Densuke was not long in becoming well liked. He was ready to run errands for all, outside of the hours of his duties. From those higher up in the *yashiki* these errands brought him coin. Every month he could bring O'Mino twenty to thirty *mon* in "cash"; apart from the ample rations of rice and *daikon* bestowed on the kitchen staff. Nay: as cook at times fish could not be allowed to spoil, and fell to the perquisites of Densuke. Thus time passed; and with it the delivery of O'Mino, and the crisis in the affairs of Densuke approached. Now Geishu Sama was a fourth month *daimyō*. Hence with the iris blossoms he took his departure from Edo to the government of his fief in Aki province. The Sakuji Machibugyo, one Takahashi Daihachiro, plead illness on this occasion of the exodus. As unable to accompany his lord he remained in Edo. On plea of convenience he established himself in the abandoned quarters of the *ashigaru* or common soldiers, situated right over Densuke's cooking stoves. Entirely removed from the bustle of the household, except during Densuke's now rare attendance, he secured complete isolation and quiet. Densuke went on cooking for Takahashi Sama, just as if it had been for the whole military household. Daihachiro was a forbidding kind of man; and it was with no amiable look that he greeted Densuke when the latter appeared very late to prepare the meal. It being the 5th month 5th day (the *sekku*) of Tenwa 3rd year (30th May, 1683), perhaps he suspected Densuke of preparation for, and participation in, the great festival which was in progress. "Densuke is very late. This Daihachiro has made the trial; to find out that he is no cook. Indeed the right hand has been severely burnt. A cook should be on time – for the meal, not the *matsuri*." Densuke was all apology – "Nay, Danna Sama; it is not the festival which has detained Densuke. An infant was expected today by the wife. Hence Densuke's neglect. Deign to pardon him." – "A baby being born is no reason why Daihachiro should starve. Prepare the meal in haste. The rice is to be soft; and please see that the fish also is soft. Make the sauce not too sharp. It would give great trouble to make the bath in the quarters. In Owarimachi, or Kubomachi, good bath-houses are to be found." Densuke took the hint. At once he recommended one he thought befitting the great man's greatness. "Well: *Sayonara*. See that the meal is ready by the return." Off stalked Takahashi Daihachiro, towel dangling from his hand, and toothbrush and bran bag in his bosom.

Densuke gave a sigh of relief as he left the court. Daihachiro often employed him on missions, and was never particularly generous even when the transaction was decidedly shady. Densuke was dreadfully afraid of him. Somehow he felt as if Daihachiro was Fate – his fate. Turning to his stoves, the pots and the pans, the meal soon was in successful preparation. As Densuke lifted the cover to inspect the rice – splash! A great red spot spread in widening circle over the white mass. In fright Densuke clapped on the lid of the pot. He looked upward, to locate this unusual condiment to his provision. On his forehead he received in person a second consignment. Applying his finger to his head, and then to his nose – "Blood! Ah! O'Take's fierce cat has caught a rat and is chewing it in the room above. How vexatious! If the Danna should find out...." Hastily he tried to shove his equipment to one side. This would not do. The massive stone blocks forming the furnace were too heavy for Densuke to move unaided. Somewhat helpless he looked around. The rice was almost done; ready for the process of *murashite*, or simmering over the slow fire. The fish, carefully prepared, as yet was to be cooked. All was to be ready against the return of Daihachiro Sama. Ah! Again the dropping began. As finding some channel in the rough boarding of the ceiling it came fast. His kitchen began to look like the place where the Outcasts slaughter beasts. Densuke shuddered.

Circumstances, the results involved, make the timid brave. Grasping a pole Densuke started up the ladder leading to the loft and the quarters of the *ashigaru*. Arrived at the top his eyes took in the poor apartment. The rafters and beams of a low-cast roof; six wretched (Loo-choo) mats on the floor, for the men to sit, and sleep, and live upon; such its bare equipment. In the middle of the mats was a great red stain. Densuke was at once attracted to it. "A cat would eat a rat; but it would not wipe up the blood." His eyes were caught by the straw basket used to store away the raincoats. This was all stained red at the bottom. Going close up he found it was wet. Perhaps the cat was at work inside. Densuke raised the cover and looked in. In alarm he sprang back. On the trunk and limbs of a body was placed a freshly severed head. Without replacing the cover, with pole uplifted over his head in defence, Densuke backed toward the ladder. His one idea was to flee this *yashiki*. As he reached the top of the steps the voice of Daihachiro was heard below – "A pest on such filthy bath-houses; and filthier patrons.... What! No rice yet, Densuke? Ah! Where is the fellow?" Densuke looked down, to meet the altered countenance of Daihachiro looking up. He retreated as the latter sprang up the ladder. Daihachiro gave a rapid glance. He saw the raised cover of the basket.

The next moment the bosom of Densuke's dress was harshly grasped, and he himself was forced down on the floor. Gloomily Daihachiro regarded him – "Rash and curious fellow! Why not keep to your pots and pans? Densuke loses his life; and Daihachiro a fool for a cook." He had drawn his sword to strike. Densuke clung to his knees in petition – "Pardon, master! Pardon! This Densuke is no idle gossip. The dripping blood threatened to spoil the meal. Thinking the cat was eating a rat, fearing the anger of the Danna Sama if the meal had to be re-cooked, Densuke came up here to chase the animal away. Thus the crime was discovered...." – "Crime!" thundered Daihachiro. "Ah! This intermeddler must certainly die. By the word of a *samurai*...." In his terror Densuke almost put his hand over the irrevocable sentence. He spoke with life at stake. "Deign, master, to pardon Densuke. He has committed no offence; knows of no offence in others. Densuke has seen nothing. Life is a jewel, to be kept at any cost. Densuke is far too insignificant to deserve the anger of Takahashi Sama." He grovelled in the abject terror of his petition.

Takahashi Daihachiro hesitated. An idea seemed to occur to him, at sight of the man's fear-struck state. He smiled grimly. "Densuke saw the head?" – "'Tis so," admitted Densuke. "But to see a head means nothing." Daihachiro dragged him over to the raincoat basket. Holding him down, he grasped the head by the cue and lifted it out. "Look!" Densuke gave a cry of surprise at sight of the features of a once neighbour. "It is the head of Iseya Jusuke, the money lender of Hachobori; a hard man. Surely the Danna...." – "Just so," replied Daihachiro, carelessly throwing the mortuary relic back into the basket. "Borrowing five *ryō*, in six months with the interest the sum now due is twenty-five *ryō*. Pleading illness Daihachiro remained in Edo, to try and soften the usurer. He threatened a report to my lord; grew insolent beyond measure. The sword drawn, he was killed forthwith.... Here Densuke finds his use and saves his life. This body is an awkward impediment. Densuke must take and cast it away. Otherwise, a second head is added to this first. With one already to dispose of a second gives no difficulty. Decide: is it agreed? Moreover there will be payment." He took out a money belt (*dōmaki*), that of Jusuke. Densuke recognized it. Daihachiro had robbed Jusuke, after killing him. Lovingly he ran the golden *ryō* through his fingers. Seventy of them Densuke counted. Daihachiro picked out three *ryō*. "Here is payment. Life is spared, and it is agreed to cast away the body." Stammered Densuke – "On the rubbish heap?" Daihachiro looked at him – "You fool! Why not proclaim that Densuke murdered Jusuke? Once the gate is passed – and this Daihachiro goes in company so far – it is Densuke who is the murderer of Jusuke. Remain in this place until night. Then off with the body; pitch it into the ditch of Kuroda Ke, or that of Saio Dono. Daihachiro now takes his meal. There is nothing wrong with it?" He looked meaningly at Densuke. The latter, with eyes on the shining sword, at once denied all defilement. He now plumed himself on the care taken of the Danna's interests. Daihachiro descended; to feed at ease and keep watch over the unwilling Densuke.

In the 5th month (June) the days are long. Densuke was a coward; and for company had the corpse of the murdered Jusuke. To the poor cook the time passed was torture. He was continually going to the stair and calling down – "Danna Sama, has the time come?... Ah! The sky is light. The streets at night will be full of people with lanterns. Plainly O'Tento Sama (the Sun) has forgotten to decline in the West. Alas! This Densuke is most unlucky." At last the hour of the dog was passing (7–9 pm). Daihachiro appeared. "Now for the corpse! Wrap it up in this matting.... Coward! Is Densuke afraid of a dead man?" He took the body and cut the tendons of arms and legs. Then he placed the head on the belly. Doubling the limbs over the body so as to hold the head he wrapped the matting around the whole. The outside he covered with some red raincoats – "in case of accidental stains." Then he strongly roped the whole together. He stood back to inspect a truly admirable job. Densuke wondered how many usurers Daihachiro had thus disposed of. His speculations were interrupted. Everything was ready. "Now! the loan of Densuke's back." Groaned Densuke – "Danna Sama, a request." – "What?" asked Daihachiro. "Condescend to put a board between the body of Densuke and that of Jusuke. The head might seize and bite me with its teeth." Daihachiro snorted with laughter, contempt, and anger mixed. "What a cowardly rascal you are! Off with it as it is." Said Densuke respectfully and firmly – "The task is that of Densuke. Condescend so far to favour him." His obvious terror threatened collapse even of the influence of Daihachiro. An old remnant of the back of a corselet was at hand. Said Daihachiro – "This is still better. It is metal. In it goes. Now off with you." Stalking along in the rear of the unfortunate cook, Daihachiro kept within easy distance of a sword blow. At the gate he said – "Pray grant passage. Densuke takes washing of this Daihachiro – bed quilts and *futon* to be renovated." – "Respectfully heard and understood." The gate-man let fall the bar and stood aside. Densuke passed into the street. A little way off he looked around. Takahashi Daihachiro had disappeared. Now indeed it was an affair between Densuke and Jusuke.

The Appearance Of O'Iwa San

Shouldering his pack Densuke made off down the broad space lined by the white walls of the *yashiki*. In this quarter of the *bushi* the highway was not crowded with citizens and their lanterns. Densuke had high hopes of an early disposition of the incubus. He approached the ditch which protected the wall of the *yashiki* of Prince Kuroda. When about to put down the bundle a hail reached him from the *samurai* on guard at the Kuroda gate. "Heigh there, rascal! Wait!" But Densuke did not wait. In terror he gave the load a shift on his shoulder and started off almost at a run. On doing so there was a movement within. The cold sweat stood out on the unhappy man's forehead. A moment, and would the teeth of Jusuke be fastened in his shoulder? "Ah! Jusuke San! Good neighbour! This Densuke is but the wretched agent. 'Tis Daihachiro Sama who killed Jusuke. Deign to pursue and haunt Takahashi Sama. Jusuke San! Jusuke San!" Fright gave him strength and boldness. The Tora no Mon (Tiger gate) of the castle should be the place of disposal. Here the ditch was deep and dark. But to its very edge swarmed the people with their lanterns on this night of festival in early summer. The moor of Kubomachi was his next goal. At this period it really was open ground. With a sigh of relief Densuke let the bundle slip from his now weary shoulders. Alive he would have laughed at the idea of carrying the portly Jusuke. Yet here the usurer bestrode him, far heavier weight than on other unfortunate clients. "Let's have a look at him; address him face to face." His hand was on the knot, when a woman's voice spoke in his ear. Densuke did not wait to ascertain the nature of her solicitation. He sped away into the darkness, toward the distant city. Without goal, he found himself at Shiodome. Crossing the Shimbashi he entered on the crowded and lighted Owaricho. It was only the hour of the pig (9 pm), and the house lanterns as yet burned brightly. He hesitated, with the idea of turning toward Shiba, of trying his luck in this still rustic district; or on the seashore, not far off.

A man close by greeted him. "Iya! Densuke San at last is found. The honoured wife suffers great anxiety. Thinking that the festival might be the attraction this Goemon set out to find you. Deign to hasten at once to Gorobeicho." Densuke shifted his burden away from the man. Did it not already somewhat taint the air? His nostrils were wide open in alarmed inquiry. He made excuses. With his heavy pack he would follow after slowly. He was overwhelmed by his neighbour's kindness. Goemon offered to share the work. Densuke did more than refuse. Unable to shake off his companion in stolid desperation he took his way to his home in the tenement (*nagaya*). "Tadaima" (just now – present), he called from the doorway. Entering the shabby room he put down the *furoshiki* in a distant corner. Going to the Butsudan, or house altar, at once he lit the lamps. O'Mino eyed him with astonishment. "What's that?" she asked, pointing to the bundle – "Washing of Daihachiro Sama" – "But Mino is ill. So situated she cannot do washing. How negligent!" – "It makes no matter," replied Densuke recklessly. O'Mino did not like the tone of his voice. She eyed him sharply. Then more pressing matters urged. "Weary as you are it is to be regretted; but money must be in hand, for the midwife and other expenses. A few hours, and this Mino will be unable to leave her bed – for three turns (weeks). There is cooking and washing to be done. Please go to Kyubei San and ask the loan of a *ryō*. Perhaps he will give half." – "He will give nothing," was the surly reply of Densuke. "Of loans he has grown tired of late. As the uncle is the only stay in dire necessity care must be taken not to offend. Moreover, the loan is unnecessary. Here are three *ryō*." He brought out the shining oblong pieces. O'Mino's eyes were bright with terror. "Ah! Has Densuke turned thief? How was this money secured? What has happened? Why so late in returning?" But Densuke was made confident and ready of tongue by the physical helplessness of O'Mino. "Don't be alarmed. Densuke is neither thief nor murderer. He is no Shirai Gompachi. Perhaps there is a corpse within, not washing. Would the Ojosan see a head, arms, legs, freshly severed?" He laughed harshly as she turned her head from him to the bundle, then back again. "This money was given to Densuke by Takahashi Sama; in return for faithful service in an important matter. Don't be frightened. It has been honestly earned." Said O'Mino, almost to herself – "But Daihachiro Sama is not one to give such a sum as three *ryō*. He is always in debt. The wife of Jusuke San complains of his delays with her husband. However...." Confidence restored, she bade Densuke put the money in the drawer of the toilet stand. Then he was to prepare some food; for themselves, and for the neighbours ready to assist at the expected birth.

Densuke did so, his eyes shifting from O'Mino to the stove, from the stove to the deadly bundle. Finally he removed the *furoshiki* to their outer room, mumbling some excuse as to the foulness of a buck-basket. He returned to his cooking. Barely tasting some food O'Mino soon was sound asleep. Densuke observed her. "Ugly, rich, a very *O'Bake* in appearance is the Ojosan; and yet she takes as husband a spiritless creature, such as is this Densuke. Is it good or bad fortune? How grateful would be her advice." He went to bed himself in the outer room; to spend a hideous night of nightmare in company with the dead Jusuke, who now did taint the air with that indefinable pollution of even the freshest corpse. Wild visions floated through the brain of Densuke. The neighbours would assemble. The food was ready. Ah! Here comes the wife of Jusuke San. She demands her husband. A moment, and Densuke was stealing from the house entrance into the darkness. The river? Ah! That was it. The canal of Hachobori was close at hand to Jusuke's own home. It would float him to his very door. Densuke soon saw himself at the river bank. No one was at hand. Splash! In went the foul burden. There it was again. But now it was Jusuke in person. "Jusuke San! Jusuke San! Pardon! 'Twas not this Densuke who killed you. Seek vengeance of Daihachiro Sama. He is the murderer." In his terror he lost all fear of being heard. He shouted at the top of his lungs. But Jusuke laid a heavy hand on him. With one long drawn out groan Densuke – awoke.

O'Mino was leaning close over him, her face spectre-like with pain. Seeing that he was awake she took away her hand. "What is the matter with you? All night you have been shouting and mumbling in sleep. Just now it was 'Jusuke San! Jusuke San! Daihachiro Sama!'

It is indeed a matter of Jusuke San. The time of Mino is at hand; the pains begin. Go at once to the house of Jusuke, and ask his wife O'Yoshi to condescend her aid." Densuke sprang up. An idea flashed into his mind. He would go to Hachobori and make full confession. Which was the most important? O'Yoshi as confessor or as midwife? With his brain thus puzzled over an answer he started off. His last injunction to O'Mino was – "by no means meddle with the bundle of Daihachiro Sama." There could have been no more direct invitation to her to do so. For a short time O'Mino did nothing but eye the strange bundle. Then she was on her knees before it, examining it. "Rain coats as wrapping! And tied with rope: a queer kind of washing. What a strange odour! Pickled *daikon* (*nukamisozuke*)?" She shook it. Something inside went *gotsu-gotsu*. This was too much for her curiosity. Her old suspicion came back, that Densuke had turned robber. She poked a little hole in the straw wrapping. Some kind of cloth covering was within; a *kimono* without doubt. Through its tissue something shone white. The kitchen knife was close at hand on the brazier (*hibachi*). She reached out, and in a moment the rope was severed. "Oya! Oya!" Out rolled a head. An arm, two helpless flexible legs were extended before her. With a scream of horror O'Mino fell flat on her back. Lying stretched out she uttered one sharp cry after another. The neighbouring wives came hurrying in, a stream of humanity. "What is wrong? A young wife screams not without cause. Oya! Oya! O'Mino San has given birth to a baby and a head. Iya! Head, limbs, body – a monstrous parturition!" With the woman groaning in the pain of her delivery, the wives in confusion, children flying to summon the men folk, the whole district was in an uproar. In the midst of the confusion arrived Densuke and the wife of Jusuke. As yet he had not found courage to confess. He was still "deciding." A neighbour greeted him – "Densuke San! Strange things have happened to O'Mino San. She has given birth to a head and a baby at the same time. Hasten, Densuke San! Hasten!" Densuke did hasten; but it was to disappear down the nearest byway in headlong flight. Amazed and confounded the wife of Jusuke proceeded alone to the house; as the first thing to set eyes on the head of her husband, eyes still open and glaring in death. With a cry she precipitated herself upon it; took it in her arms. The midwife, summoned in haste, parted infant from mother. Thus did O'Iwa San come forth into the world.

The affair was grave. The *kenshi* (coroner) was soon on the scene. O'Mino with feeble voice told what she knew. "Deign to examine into the affair beyond the surface. My husband Densuke is not the man to commit this crime. Ask the neighbours, who know him. Last night he brought three *ryō*, given him by Takahashi Daihachiro Sama, the Sakuji Machibugyo of Geishu Ko. He said that it was for important service rendered. There is no doubt that Takahashi San is the murderer. Deign to examine well; show benevolence.... Ah! This Mino shall have vengeance. For seven lives Daihachiro shall be pursued...." Her eyes became injected with blood. Her breast heaved painfully in the attempt to get air. The women around her gave cries of alarm. O'Mino sank back in a pool of blood. She had died in the midst of her curse. Said one present – "This Tokichi would not be the honoured Sakuji Sama; nay, not for the full seven existences in human form." The others felt as he did. Even the *kenshi* drew up his shoulders a little at the frightful mask of the dead woman's face. He could learn but little. Kyubei, soon at hand, petitioned for the dead body of O'Mino and the custody of the infant. The neighbours corroborated the story of O'Mino; but Densuke had disappeared. Daihachiro never had confidence in his agent. His preparations for flight had been made before Densuke's discovery, and almost together with Densuke he had passed out the gate of Geishu Sama, with the seventy *ryō* provided by Jusuke. Report being made to the Machibugyo a "grass dividing" search was made, without result. No trace of either man was found. As for the child born under these auspicious conditions, Kyubei went at once to

Tamiya Matazaemon and made report. With bowed head the old man awaited the decision. Said Matazaemon – "The name giving is to take place on the seventh night. Kyubei will not fail to be present." He did not speak further. Thus the offence of the parents was pardoned in O'Iwa the infant; the grandchild of a man and woman passing the period of middle age.

The Affair of The Shiba Kiridoshi

It was Genroku 8th year (1695). O'Iwa, a girl of twelve years, could understand what came to her ears. In dealing with each other the Nipponese are very exact and exacting. The New Year must start with a clean balance sheet for the tradesman – all bills paid and collected. The last night of the dying year, and its last few hours; this time is the busiest and most anxious. Zensuke, the *banto* (clerk) of the Shimaya dry goods shop, accompanied by one Jugoro, was passing the Shiba Kiridoshi. It was the hour of the tiger (3 am). Of the two, Jugoro was the fighting man. Jurozaemon of the Shimaya had provided him with a short sword and sent him as guard to Zensuke, who would have more than three hundred *ryo* in gold. Said Jugoro – "Banto San, whither now? The hour is late." – "It is never late on the *omisoka* (31st of the 12th month)," replied Zensuke tersely. "However, there remains but one account to collect; at Nishikubo. We will hasten." – "Go on ahead," said Jugoro. "A moment here for a necessity." Thus the two men became separated by nearly a *cho* (100 yards). The district was one of *yashiki* and temples. The white walls of the former blended with the white carpet of snow on the ground. At any hour it was no busy place; now it was desolate. The high banks of the cutting crowned by woods and approached through the trees, made it an ideal place for a hold-up. Zensuke hesitated. He slowed his pace to allow his companion to join him. He thought he saw something move in the darkness close by. From behind a tree just before him came a *samurai*. Two others followed this man from the shadows. The heads of all three men were covered by *zukin* (hoods). They wore vizors. "Wait!" Zensuke stopped in fright. "What suspicious rascal is this, travelling the quarter at this hour? Probably some clerk making off with his master's funds. Come now! Give them into better keeping. Low fellow! You are fairly trapped." Zensuke began to retreat, but two of the men were now behind him. He began to shout for Jugoro. The latter came up at a run – "Honoured Sirs! This is the Banto San of the Shimaya of Honjo Itchome. He is collecting the house bills. Deign not to disturb him." – "Shut up!" was the reply of the leader. "Another fellow of the same kidney. Look to him." Roughly he thrust his hand into Zensuke's bosom and began to hustle and fumble the clerk. When Jugoro would interfere the two other men prevented him. With fright he saw the money belt of the *banto* dangling from the man's hand. The nature of the affair was plain. "Heigh! Jokes don't go, honoured sirs. We are not suspicious fellows. Condescend to pardon us." As he spoke he took advantage of the negligence of his opponents, their interest in the struggle of Zensuke and their leader, to wrench himself free. At once his sword was out. Jugoro was of no mean skill. None of his wardsmen could face him. One man received severe wounds in scalp and face. The other lost part of his hand. But Jugoro was no match for the odds of two trained soldiers. He was soon cut down. Meanwhile Zensuke was shouting lustily for aid. At this period there was a guard called the *tsujiban* (cross-roads watch). It was mostly composed of oldish men not fit for active service. Such regulations as there were they observed. These were very severe; but, as with the present day police, kept them to their post. They rarely troubled themselves to patrol their district. From these men there could be little hope of aid. Just then, however, the train of some lord came in sight. With one hand the leader held Zensuke by the bosom of his robe. The hand holding the money belt was already thrust in his own bosom. In a moment it would be free. Then Zensuke would go in company with Jugoro to the Yellow Fountain (in Hell). His captor gave a startled cry. "The train of Geishu Sama! Lose no time!"

As he wrenched himself away Zensuke sank his teeth deep into the man's hand. With a howl of pain the fellow made off, exchanging a little finger for the three hundred and twenty-five *ryo* in Zensuke's *domaki*.

The *bantō* crouched in conventional attitude by the roadside. His distress was plain; the prostrate body of a man evidence of some unusual condition. A *samurai* left the passing train and came up to investigate. "Ah! Robbery and murder: follow behind to the *tsujiban*. It is their affair." With moans and groans Zensuke made his report. He was indignant at the luxury of these watchmen, toasting at their fire. They noted it; looked at each other and out into the snowy night, and laughed with contempt. For a tradesman's money belt were they to disturb themselves? They questioned him harshly, in such way as to excuse any further effort on their part. Surely the thieves by this time were at the other end of Edo. Two of them, however, did accompany Zensuke to the scene of the hold-up. Casting an eye over Jugoro's mangled corpse, said one – "A good fight: the occasion has been missed. As perhaps the criminal this man is to be bound. Probably his intent was to run away with the master's funds." Roughly they seized him, hustled him back to the guardhouse. Trussed up Zensuke had to spend the hours in alarm and fear. Luckily the *kenshi* soon appeared. It was the *ōmisoka*. No official business would be performed during the three days following. Jugoro could hardly exercise patience and remain as he was for that space of time. So the examination was duly held. The Shimaya soon secured the body of Jugoro and the release of Zensuke. The latter's evidence was put on record; none too satisfactory, as the concealing *zukin* prevented any recognition or description of the features of the assailants. He only knew of the cries of impatience at wounds received, and knew that he had left his mark on his own opponent. How then were they to be run down? The *kenshi* showed some impatience. Said he to the captain of the *tsujiban* – "Why truss up this man, even though a tradesman? He has all his own fingers, and the corpse lacks none." He touched the severed finger with his baton. With this all were dismissed, and to all seeming the affair was forgotten.

The Tokugawa had their plain-clothes police. One of the most noted was Magome Yaemon of Hachobori. His great grandfather had captured Marubashi Chuya, of note in the rebellion of Yui Shosetsu at the time of the fourth Shogun Iyetsuna Ko. One day this Magome Dono, in company with a *yakunin* (constable) named Kuma, was rummaging the poorer districts of Shitaya Hirokoji. The two men were disguised as charcoal burners, and attracted little attention. All the legitimate profession in the way of medicine and pharmacy had been ransacked by the magistrate (*machibugyō*) of the south district. Yaemon felt sure that there were still some by-ways. "Who's that fellow?" he asked Kuma. The constable laughed. "He's a *sunekiri* (shin-cutter). The rascals can be told by their tough dark blue cotton socks, the coarse straw sandals, and the banded leggings. Deign to note the long staff he carries. They peddle plasters – shin plasters, guaranteed to cure any wound, to stop any flow of blood. A man's arm hangs but by a strip of skin; the blood flows in torrents. Apply the plaster and the flow ceases at once, the arm heals. They drive a roaring trade, even among the *bushi* (*samurai*); selling a shell here, two there. As for their real usefulness...." He laughed. They followed after the man and soon came to a guard house. Said Magome San – "Detain that man yonder. He is to be examined." The ward officer was a little surprised – "Respectfully heard and understood. It is old Yamabayashi Yogen." Soon the man entered the guard house. Said the official drily – "Magome Dono is here to talk with Yogen. What has he been up to?" But the old fellow was confident. "Thanks are felt." With the ease of the righteous and prosperous he passed into the presence of Yaemon. The latter greeted him with a non-official genial smile. "Ah! This is Yamabayashi Yogen, the head of the *Sunekiri*. And business?" – "Truly this Yogen is grateful. Man was born with teeth. Men and women still seek each other's company. So long as such endures Yogen finds profit." – "And plasters?" – "They are the affair of Tokichi. Would his worship deign to examine him ... condescend dismissal. At once he presents himself."

Thus in short order the straight haired, unshaven, low browed Tokichi stuck his head into the Sanbashi guard house. "Deign to pardon this Tokichi. The honoured benevolence...." The ward officer eyed him knowingly and quizzically. "Shut up! Magome Dono has questions to ask about clients. Wait until the questions deal with the doings of Tokichi. That will be well. Then it will be time enough to lie. Meanwhile, be sure and tell the truth." With this disinterested advice Tokichi was passed to the presence. Once more conscience spoke louder than caution. "The honoured benevolence, the honoured pity; condescend the honoured examination into the innocence of Tokichi." Yaemon laughed. "Fortunately it is not a matter of Tokichi, but of his plasters. Who bought these at this year's Shogwatsu (New Year)? Be careful in answer. The case is a bad one." Tokichi considered. "The first day of the New Year a man came. His purchase of salve was large. In the course of the past three months he has been many times to buy. His visits now are wider spaced, and he praises the goods – as he ought. No hand ever had a worse poisoned wound. He...." – "Age and appearance?" interrupted Yaemon, now all attention. He had struck a trail. "Perhaps fifty years; fair of complexion, tall, and stout. By his lordly manner he must at least be a *go-kenin*, or a charlatan." Who was this man? Yaemon felt sure that he was about to learn something of interest. Kuma was given his instructions. "Go daily to the shop of this man and receive his report. As to the *samurai* in question be circumspect. Evidently he is no ordinary person. A *samurai* is to be summoned, not disgraced by arrest – if he is a *samurai*." So Kuma with several aides established himself in the rear of Tokichi's shop. The man not having put in an appearance for several weeks, the wait, if uncertain, was soon rewarded. On the 25th day of the 3rd month (May) he presented himself. Kuma recognized him at once by the description; sooner than Tokichi, who was engaged in filling his little shells with the marvellous salve. The officer's decision was prompt. At a call Tokichi turned from his drugs. "Ah! the honoured Sir. And the arm, does it honourably progress?" – "Progress could not be better. This is probably the last visit." In replying the man eyed Tokichi with some astonishment. The latter made his bows, first to the newcomer, then to the indefinite rear of the establishment. "Indeed the drug is all that is claimed for it. The wound being poisoned, at one time it looked as if the hand, nay arm, must go. These House doctors are notoriously good for nothing. Just as nothing can surpass your product, good leech. Here is money for two shells of its virtues." He held out a silver *bu*. Busied with his preparations Tokichi looked in vain toward the rear apartment. After as long delay as he could contrive he passed the shells and a heap of copper change over to the customer. As soon as the latter had left the shop Tokichi bolted for the rear. Kuma was gone. His aides were calmly smoking their pipes and drinking the poor tea (*bancha*) of Tokichi.

Kuma had little trouble in following his man to Okachimachi in Shitaya. He found near by a shop for the sale of everything, from tobacco to *daikon* (radish), both odoriferous, yet lacking perfume. Said Kuma – "A question or so: this tall *samurai*, an oldish man, who lives close by; who is he?" The woman in charge hesitated. Then dislike overcame discretion. "Ah! With the hand wrapped in a bandage; his name is Sakurai Kichiro Tayu. Truly he is a bad man. That he should quarrel with his own class is no great matter. Maimed as he is, thrice report has been made to the guard house, but in each case he has escaped further process. He is a dreadful fellow; one who never pays a debt, yet to whom it is dangerous to refuse credit. Already nearly a *ryō* is due to this Echigoya. It has been the bad luck to support him and his family during the past six months." Said Kuma – "Thus maimed, to hold his own in quarrels he must be a notable fencer as well as brawler. Was the wound so received?" – "Iya! That is not known. Some quarrel at the New Year's festivities probably was the cause. Before that time he was sound enough." She laughed. "He has two friends; Kahei San and Miemon San. They are birds of a feather; and all partly plucked. Perhaps they quarrelled in company, but if so have made it up. Sakurai San is a match for the two others." She looked at Kuma, to see if he had more to say. Indifferent he picked out a strand of tobacco. "He shouldered this Gobei into the ditch close by here. Fortunate is it to have escaped worse injury." Satisfied with his inquiries he took his way in haste to his master. The eyes of Yaemon and his aid shone with enjoyment. Surely they had the men of the Shiba Kiridoshi.

Magome Yaemon at once sought out the *machibugyō's* office. His lordship heard the report. "Different disorders require different treatment. Of two of these men this Gemba knows something. The other man is hard to place, and evidently not so easy to deal with." Two *dōshin* and *yakunin* were sent at once to the addresses indicated. To capture Nakagawa Miemon and Imai Kahei was an easy task. The *dōshin* and *yakunin* sent to the house of Sakurai formed a band of twenty men. The house surrounded, without ceremony the officer and an aid entered. "On the lord's mission: Sakurai San is wanted at the office of Matsuda Dono. If resistance be made it will be necessary to use the rope. Pray accompany me." Sakurai Kichiro divined the object of the arrest. "The affair at the Kiridoshi has been scented out. The manner of that rascally drug seller was strange today." The officer had planted himself right before the sword rack. Sakurai could neither kill anybody, nor cut belly. He turned to his wife. "There is a matter on hand to be explained. Absence will probably be prolonged. Already the day is far advanced.... Ah! Is it Kichitaro?" A boy of seven years had rushed into the room. "Pretty fellow!... Honoured Sir, be patient. The separation is no short one. No resistance is made. We go the same road.... Taro; rude fellow! Salute the gentleman." The boy obeyed, with grave ceremony and a hostility which divined an unpleasant mission. "Your father leaves you. It is now the time to obey the mother in all she says. Remember well, or the end will be a bad one." Wife and child clung to him, frightened and now weeping. It was an arrest; their mainstay was being taken from them. In the last caresses he had time to bend down and whisper to O'Ren – "In the toilet box is a scroll sealed up. All is there explained. Read and destroy it. In later days at discretion let our son know." Roughly he pushed woman and boy aside. With rapid stride he reached the entrance. The *yakunin* confronted him. He laughed and waved a hand. "There is no resistance. We go the same road." The *dōshin* permitted the laxity of discipline. He had his orders.

Meanwhile the examination of the other two men was in progress at the office of the *machibugyō*. As the biggest fool of the two, Nakagawa Miemon was the first summoned to the presence of Matsuda Dono. Said the Judge – "Nakagawa Uji, there is a slight inquiry to make. How were those scars on the face come by? These are marks of wounds not long since received. Consider well and remember." The tone of menace staggered Miemon. He had anticipated some rebuke for slight infraction of the peace, not unusual with these men. "Naruhodo! Has the Shiba Kiridoshi matter cropped up?" He hesitated – "The story is a long one, and a foolish one. To weary the honoured ears...." Matsuda Gemba caught him up with impatient gesture. "Answer the question, and truly. Nakagawa Miemon is noted neither for judgment nor sobriety." The man caught up the last phrase as a cue. Eagerly he spoke, the doors of the jail opening wide for exit – "So it is indeed. Wine never benefited man; much less a *samurai*. Hence, with Kahei and Sakurai Uji, it was decided to forswear wine forever. It was determined to make a pilgrimage to Kompira San. There the vow of abstinence was to be taken; on its holy ground. All went well. We met at Nihonbashi. Alas! At the Kyobashi the perfume of a grog shop reached our noses. The vow had not yet been taken. The ground was not holy. Just one last drink before setting out. But the Buddha was unfavourable. Once begun, the drinking was adjourned to a cook shop. There the bout continued all day. Wine lent us the wings of *tengu*. We travelled the road to Kompira San in a dream. In the progress Kahei and this Miemon quarrelled. Swords were drawn, and we cut each other. These wounds on head and face were the portion of this Miemon. Kahei had his hand nearly severed. Sakurai San, who was asleep, aroused by the noise, sprang up to part us. He is a man to be feared; but in my rage I sank my teeth in his hand. The bite of man or beast is poison. His wound was worse than that of either of us."

Gemba Dono was in conversation with his chamberlain. He let Miemon talk away. He was not one to say too little. As barely having listened he asked – "When was this fight? The day of the vow and journey to Kompira? Truly the result has been the vengeance of offended deity." – "The twelfth month tenth day," naturally replied Miemon. Gemba forced him to repeat the answer. Several times he put the query in different forms. Miemon, fool that he was, stuck to the date. Then said the magistrate – "Miemon, you are a liar. Moreover, you are a murderer. On the 13th day, on going up to the castle, this Gemba had converse with your lord. At that time Nakagawa Miemon was summoned to carry out a mission. As a man of whom report had been made you were noted well. At that time you had no wound.... Tie him up, and take him away." The *yakunin* fell on him from all sides. In a trice he was trussed up and removed.

Then appeared Imai Kahei. Kahei was cunning, but also a coward. To the questions of the *machibugyō* he procrastinated in his answers, confused them all he could. What had Miemon said? "He spoke of the eloquence of Imai San; of Kahei Uji as the clever man, the one to tell the tale properly. Now let us have the true statement of the case." Such was Gemba's reply. It was flattering. Unable to help himself Kahei set sail on his sea of lies. "We all like wine...." – "Ah! After all you are agreed." Gemba smiled pleasantly. Kahei took courage – "But wine costs money. Together we went to Kuraya Jibei, a money-lender living at Kuramae no Saka, as is well known." Gemba nodded assent. "Of him two *ryō* were borrowed, on agreement to repay ten *ryō* as interest within a month. The nearest grog shop was sought, and it was the hour of the rat (11 pm) before the return was started. At the Teobashi a band of drunkards was encountered. Without cause these men forced a quarrel on us. Thus was the hand of Kahei nearly severed. This is the truth." – "And what was the date of this money bond?" Imai hesitated. He had caught a glimpse of the drug seller Tokichi on being brought into the place. Without doubt the Kiridoshi affair was in question. He must antedate his wound. "Kahei does not remember with certainty. Perhaps it was the seventeenth day; before the Kwannon festival of the eighteenth day." He mumbled, and was frightened. Said Gemba sharply – "Speak distinctly; the seventeenth day?" – "Hei! Hei! Some time in the last decade of the month; the nineteenth or twentieth day – not later; not later." Matsuda Gemba almost leaped at him. "Oh, you liar! On the last day of the year you came, in person, to this Gemba to anticipate the New Year's gift (*sebo*). At that time you had no wound. Yet the drug seller sees you next day with maimed hand. It was not at Teobashi, but at Shiba Kiridoshi, that the wound was received.... Tie him up, and away with him." The *yakunin* came forward. Imai made a spasmodic attempt to rise. They threw him down, and in a moment he was keeping company with Nakagawa Miemon.

Gemba Dono braced himself for the more serious task. So did his *yakunin*. A glance showed the magistrate that he had mistaken his man. Sakurai Kichiro came forward with calm and dignity. Making his ceremonial salutation to the judge he came at once to the point. "What lies Miemon and Kahei have told, this Kichiro knows not. The fact is that we three plotted together to rob the fatly supplied purses of the *bantō* making their rounds in settlement of accounts at the close of the year. Hence the *bantō* of the Shimaya, Zensuke, lost his money belt, and a man of the same stamp, one Jugoro, was killed. All three of us are guilty of the murder...." As he would proceed Gemba held up his hand. "Bring in the other two men. Continue, Kichiro." Said Sakurai – "Miemon was badly cut about the head and face. Kahei nearly lost his hand. This Kichiro would have killed the clerk, but the procession of Geishu Sama came in sight, and recognition was feared. Of the three hundred and twenty-five *ryō* secured...." The eyes of Nakagawa and Imai stood out. Aghast they had followed the confession of Sakurai Kichiro, with full intention to deny its truth. Now they were in a fury. "What! Three hundred and twenty-five *ryō*! And we had but ten *ryō* apiece. You jest, Sakurai Uji.... Oh! The low fellow! The villain! A very beast! A swine!"

Gemba Dono could ask for nothing more. With smiling face and courtesy he turned to Sakurai Kichiro. "Why did Kichiro take the three hundred *ryō*, giving to these fellows such a paltry sum?" Answered Kichiro – "As deserving no more. They are paltry fellows; little better than common soldiers (*ashigaru*). But there is more to tell, now the end is reached. The true name of Sakurai Kichiro is Takahashi Daihachiro, at one time a retainer of Matsudaira Aki no Kami. Pressed by the money lender Jusuke, I killed him and had the body disposed of by one Densuke, the cook at the soldiers' quarters of the *yashiki*. This was in Tenwa 3rd year 5th month (June 1683). Fleeing to avoid arrest the occupation of writing teacher was taken up at Yuki in Shimosa. Densuke, too, had fled, and hither he came as a wandering beggar. Fearing his tongue I killed him; and mutilating the corpse, threw it into the castle moat close by. A beggar found dead, no inquiry was made." – "When did this take place?" asked Gemba. "Just one year later – Jokyo 1st year 5th month." He made a little movement. Nakagawa and Imai broke out into protest at the completeness of this confession, but Sakurai turned fiercely on them. "Shut up! To undergo public trial would bring shame on all *kerai* throughout the land; would cause people to fear our caste. We three planned the deed and secured the money." He put his arms behind his back. The *yakunin*, stepping softly, roped him up almost with respect. A wave of Gemba's hand and the guilty men were removed. Unable to help themselves, Nakagawa and Imai made confession to avoid the torture in what was now a hopeless case. Later the sentences of condemnation were issued. Degraded from their status the three men were taken to the execution ground of Shinagawa, and there decapitated.

The wife of Takahashi Daihachiro did not wait these proceedings. The confession of her husband was in her hands before he himself told everything to Matsuda Gemba. Before night she had decamped with her son. At eight years of age Kichitaro was placed as disciple (*deshi*) at the Joshinji of Fukagawa. Receiving the name of Myoshin he became the favourite of the rector (*jūshoku*) of the temple. The mother now became reduced to the greatest penury. For a time she was bawd in the Honjo Warigesui district. Subsequently she was promoted to the position of favourite sultana (wife) of her master Toemon, local head of his profession. Her name now was O'Matsu. When Myoshin was thirteen years old in some way he was told that she was dead. Henceforth he had no stay in the world but the worthy priest, who became a second and better father to him. This treatment found its usual and virtuous reward. At eighteen years, now a priest and learned in priestly ways, he took to himself the contents of the temple strong box. Fifty *ryō* soon disappeared in the company of the harlots of Fukagawa Yagura-Shita. A prolonged absence of Myoshin aroused the inquiries of the other monks, and the eyes of the rector were soon opened as to his unworthy proselyte, the blighted issue of a miserable stock.

Negotiations: The Business of a Marriage Broker (Nakodo)

The presence of O'Iwa created an upheaval in the Samoncho household. The wet nurse required brought with her a train of servants. With the child's growth this was maintained, even increased. The young lady (Ojosan) found herself graduated into one with a *status* to maintain. All the niggardly habits of Matazaemon were thrown to the winds with the advent of this grandchild. The affection never shown outwardly to the mother, was lavished on her daughter. At seven years of age O'Iwa underwent the common enough infliction of smallpox. It showed itself on the anniversary day of O'Mino's death, and the child's sickness afforded but mutilated rites for the memorial service of the mother. Matazaemon would have abandoned all his duties, himself to nurse the child. O'Naka loved O'Iwa for self and daughter. She had sense enough to drive the old man into a corner of the room, then out of it; and further expostulations sent him to his duties. Who, in those iron days, would accept such excuse for absence? The child worried through, not unscathed. Her grandmother's qualifications as nurse have been mentioned. O'Iwa was a plain girl. She had the flat plate-like face of her mother. The eyes were small, disappearing behind the swollen eyelids, the hair was scanty, the disease added its black pock marks which stood thick and conspicuous on a fair skin. Otherwise she was spared by its ravages, except:

Whatever her looks O'Iwa compensated for all by her disposition. She had one of those balanced even temperaments, with clear judgment, added to a rare amiability. Moreover she possessed all the accomplishments and discipline of a lady. At eleven years Matazaemon unwillingly had sought and found a place for her in attendance on her ladyship of the great Hosokawa House. O'Iwa's absence made no difference in his household. The train of servants was maintained, to be disciplined for her return, to be ready on this return. Perhaps it was a pleasing fiction to the fond mind of the aging man that she would return, soon, tomorrow. O'Naka acquiesced in the useless expense and change in her habits. She always acquiesced; yet her own idea would have been to make a good housekeeper of O'Iwa – like herself, to sew, cook, wash, clean – a second O'Mino. She could not understand the new turn of Matazaemon's mind. As for O'Iwa, she grew to girlhood in the Hosokawa House, learned all the accomplishments of her own house and what the larger scale of her new position could teach her; everything in the way of etiquette and the polite arts, as well as the plainer tasks of housekeeping, she was likely ever to be called on to perform. The plain child grew into the plain woman; perhaps fortunately for her. The *okugata* (her ladyship) was a jealous woman. Her spouse was mad on women. Every nubile maid (*koshimoto*) in the *yashiki* was a candidate for concubinage. His wife countered by as hideous a collection of females as her own House and her lord's retainers could furnish. O'Iwa attracted from the first by her lack of all physical attraction. His lordship tried to get used to her with the passage of years – and failed. He could not stomach the necessary advances. But the girl's admirable temper and even judgment secured the esteem of all. These latter qualities captivated the whole household. It was O'Iwa who performed all duties for her ladyship, took them in charge as her substitute. For the first time in his life Oki no Kami found something in a woman apart from her sex. When the time came for O'Iwa to depart, the regret of lord and lady was substantially expressed in their gifts. But his lordship had to admit failure. Not a retainer could be found willing to take the daughter of Tamiya as wife. So far O'Iwa's mission at the *yashiki* had failed. O'Naka knew this. Matazaemon never gave it thought; so glad he was to get her back. He received the honoured words and presents with humble and delighted thanks. O'Iwa reentered her home, a recovered jewel. She was the Ojosan, the lady daughter.

A first step of hers was gradually to get rid of a good part of the superfluous train. O'Iwa was a very practical girl.

Matazaemon was now old and ill. He was nearing his seventieth year. The one idea in his head was the *muko*, the son to be adopted as husband of the heir of the House; the mate to be secured for O'Iwa, and the posterity to be secured for his House. As a little girl O'Iwa had been much courted – in fun. Watanabe Juzo, Natsume Kyuzo, Imaizumi Jinzaemon, many others the growing 'sparks' of Samoncho and roundabout, could not forbear this amusement with the little '*Bakemono*' (apparition). Of their ill intent O'Iwa knew nothing. Indeed a short experience with O'Iwa disarmed derision. Most of the unseemly lovers came genuinely to like the girl, unless inherent malice and ugliness of disposition, as with Natsume and Akiyama Chozaemon, made their sport more than mere pastime. But as grown men they could not face the results of the final step, and no parent was harsh enough to graft his unwilling stock on O'Iwa's persimmon trees. The girl was clever enough to know this. It was Hoei 6th year (1709) and she was now twenty-six years old. It was indirectly at her suggestion that Matazaemon sought the aid of Kondo Rokurobei. This man lived just behind the large inclosure of the Sainenji, on the hill slope which dips steeply down to the Samegabashi. The relationship was very distant at best; but with nearer relatives in general, and with Yoemon his brother in particular, the master of Tamiya had deadly feud. To them he would not turn to find a husband for O'Iwa.

Thus it happened that one day in the seventh month (August) Rokurobei was awaiting the appearance of Yamada Chobei. He really knew little about the man, but Chobei at one time had been resident in the ward. He had undergone vicissitudes, and now was a dealer in metals and a kind of broker in everything under the sign of Musashiya. He had a wide acquaintance over Edo in his different businesses, and was the easy and slip-shod means by which Rokurobei would avoid the more arduous part of the task laid on him by Matazaemon. Chobei was not long in putting in an appearance. All affairs were gifts of the gods to a man who lived on wind. Kazaguruma Chobei – Windmill Chobei – he was called. His flittings were so noiseless and erratic, just like the little paper windmills made for children, that the nickname applied exactly fitted him. The maid in announcing him showed no particular politeness. "Wait here a moment.... Danna Sama (master), Chobei San, the metal dealer, requests an interview." – "Ah! Pass him here at once.... Is it Chobei? Please sit down." Chobei had followed almost on the girl's footsteps. She drew aside to make room for him, then flirted out in haste. Poverty and dislike had no influence in Yotsuya in those days. She seemed to scent the man.

Chobei looked with envy at the comfortable Rokurobei. The day was hot. The thin *kimono* fallen about his loins, the latter's garb was a pair of drawers and a thin shirt. He sat looking out on the garden, with its shade of large trees, its shrubbery and rock work. Everything was dripping with the water industriously splashed to this side and to that by the serving man. The tea was brought and Kondo at last remembered that he had a guest. As he turned – "It is a long time since a visit has been paid. Deign to pardon the intrusion." Chobei sighed in making this remark. The irony was lost on his fat host. As Rokurobei seemed unwilling, or hardly to know how to impart the subject concerning which he had summoned him, Chobei continued – "And the honoured health, is it good? The honoured business, is it on some matter of moment that Chobei is summoned?" Rokurobei woke up under the direct question. He, too, sighed. Chobei was noted for a greed which inspired fear. For money he would do anything. 'Blindman Chobei' had been his nickname of old days in the ward. Kondo remembered this. He liked money, too. It brought in so much comfort. He hated to part with comfort. It was to be a question between himself and Chobei how much of his hard-earned commission was to be parted with. This last thought completely aroused him. "It is a matter of securing a *muko*. This Rokurobei is the one charged with the task. As a son-in-law outside the ward is desired, no one has wider circulation and better opportunities than Chobei San. Hence the desire for a consultation." Chobei whistled inwardly. Outside the ward! What was wrong with the case. Here was coin to be turned up by the circumspect. "Surely there are young fellows enough in Samoncho, fit to be *muko*. Of course with impediments...." – "It is the daughter of Tamiya; O'Iwa San. Matazaemon Dono has commissioned this Rokurobei to secure a *muko*." Chobei whistled outwardly. "For O'Iwa San!..." – "She is no beauty, as Chobei evidently knows. Wealth compensates for other deficiencies. At all events his aid is desired." – "For how much?" Chobei spoke bluntly. If Rokurobei had forgotten Chobei, Chobei had not forgotten Rokurobei. He went on – "To get a price for damaged goods is no sinecure. Fortunately she is only out of repair on the surface.... Say ten *ryō*?" Kondo laughed scornfully – "And they call Chobei 'the Blind-man'! Rather is it vision magnified. The entertainment should be the reward; with what Chobei collects from the happy bridegroom." Chobei replied gravely – "With such a wealthy connection the future of Kondo Dono is to be envied. Chobei has to realize his future at once. Not a *ryō* less can he afford." Plainly he was in earnest, as was the long conversation which followed. Finally Chobei emerged with partial success, and half the sum named as stipend for his labours.

He began them at once. The next day he was at the metal market in Kanda. In course of chaffering over wares he never bought – "You fellows always have some *rōnin* in train; a fine, handsome fellow for whom a wife is needed. Application is made. Jinzaemon, you have a candidate." – "Not for the kind of wife Chobei San provides." Those present laughed loudly at the sally. Chobei did not wink. He explained. "No bad provision is this one. Rich, with an income of thirty *tawara*, a fine property in reversion, and but twenty-five years old. The man therefore must be fit to pose as a *samurai*; able to read and write, to perform official duty, he must be neither a boy nor a man so old as to be incapable. Come now! Does no one come forward? *Rōnin* are to be had. A *ryō* for aid to this Chobei." – "Too cheap as an offer," was Jinzaemon's retort. "A *rōnin* is one to be handled with care. Those favoured with acquaintance of the honoured *bushi* often part with life and company at the same date. Those without lords are equally testy as those in quarters." He spoke with the bluntness of the true Edokko, the peculiar product of the capital; men who were neither farmers nor provincials, but true descendants of the men of the guild of Bandzuin Chobei. He jested, but the subject interested the crowd. Said one – "Does Chobei San get the *ryō* out of groom or bride? She is a bold wench, unmarried at that age; and none too chaste eh, Chobei San? She will provide the husband with wife and child to hand, or in the making. Or, are matters the other way? Has she been tried and found wanting? Is she impotent, or deformed; or is Chobei making fools of us?" Answered Chobei slowly – "No; she is a little ugly. The face round and flat, shining, with black pock marks, making it look like speckled pumice, rouses suspicion of leprosy. This, however, is not the case. At all events she is a woman." All were now roaring with laughter – "A very beauty indeed! Just the one for Chobei's trade! Too honied was his speech. He would market anything. But in this market it is a matter of hard cash; without credit. This is a bit of goods too wilted. Even Chobei cannot sell it." – "You lie!" said Chobei in a towering passion. "At the first hint of ill-fortune threatening wine supply or pleasure, there is not one of you who would not turn to Chobei to find the money needed. Sisters, daughters, wives, aunts ... mothers are for sale." He was choking with rage. "Sell her? Chobei can and will." Angered by the final item on his family list, a man nearby gave him a sharp poke in the back. Others voiced resentment, perhaps would have given it material form. The canal was spoken of. Chobei took the hint. He did not wait for a ducking. At a sharp pace he trotted off toward his tenement at Asakusa Hanagawado. For a while he would avoid the metal market. He regretted his display of temper. It was in the necessities of other trades that he found the material of his own, and flourished.

In plain terms Kazaguruma Chobei was a pimp for the Yoshiwara and kindred quarters. His other occupations were mere channels accessory to this main business. Hence his seasons of increase and decline. Just now he was in a period of decline. His eagerness in this Tamiya affair was sharpened. Pushing his way through the Kuramae of Asakusa suddenly a hopeful light came into his eye. Abruptly he made his way to the side of the roadway. Here boarding covered the ditch, removing the occupant of a booth erected thereon, and would-be clients, from the passing stream of humanity. There was a table in the booth, and on it were several books, a vessel containing water, brushes (*fude*), scrolls for writing, and a box containing divining sticks. It was the stand of a strolling fortune-teller. At the time the occupant was engaged in gathering together his professional apparatus, with the evident purpose to decamp. Chobei did not delay in accosting him. "Ah! The Sensei; Kazuma Uji finds the day too hot to pry into the future. Does the Sensei leave his clients to their fate, or have the clients abandoned the Sensei? Deign to come along with Chobei. Perhaps he, too, can tell fortunes. At all events the wife has been forewarned; the bath is ready. It will put life into both of us." The young man laughed and hastened his operations, nodding assent – "Thanks are felt, Chobei San. Indeed this Kazuma has but to continue the art of prophecy if he would foretell his own fate. No one will buy the future when money is so needed for the present. Besides this is a pleasure ground. Men have no hankering to learn of possible worse luck than being here. All the fools have died – except their prophet." He shouldered his scanty apparatus, and with rapid stride the two men pushed their way up the crowded street toward the great gate of the temple. In his haste Chobei yet had time to eye, from time to time, his companion, always gaining encouragement from the palpable seediness made more plain by a handsome person. The two were neighbours in a house-row (*nagaya*) of the Hanagawado, that poverty-stricken district along the river close to the great amusement ground, and furnishing those who perform its baser tasks. On arrival Chobei called out – "O'Taki! O'Taki! The bath, is it ready? The Sensei, Kazuma San, honours us with his company. Make all ready for his reception.... Sensei, condescend to enter; please come up."

Yanagibara Kazuma dropped his clogs in the vestibule. As he entered the room – "Pray pardon the intrusion. This Kazuma feels much in the way. He is continually putting his neighbours of the *nagaya* to inconvenience; too great the kindness of Chobei San and wife." O'Taki laughed deprecatingly. Truly this was a handsome young man. In this 6th year of Hoei (1709) Yanagibara Kazuma was twenty-one years of age. O'Taki was thirty odd. She appreciated masculine beauty all the more. Chobei grunted from heat and the merest trace of discomfiture. He had his limit, even in his business. Quickly he shook off his *kimono*, and fan in hand squatted in his loin cloth. "Ah! 'Tis hot beyond endurance. Business is bad – from Yoshiwara to Yotsuya." O'Taki looked up at the last word. He continued – "The Sensei takes precedence. Kazuma Uji, deign to enter the bath. All is ready?" His wife nodded assent. Kazuma followed the example of Chobei. In a trice he was naked as his mother bore him. Chobei burst out into phrases of admiration – "What a splendid fellow! Ah! Waste of material! If a woman Kazuma San would be a fortune to himself and to Chobei.... Taki, note the skin of the Sensei. It has the texture of the finest paper. How regrettable!" He drew back for the better inspection of the sum total of his subject's charms. O'Taki drew closer for the same purpose. Chobei sighed – "It is plain enough that Kazuma San is not a woman. An error of Nature! Somehow the age at which a woman becomes of use, is that at which a boy becomes a mere burden. He is fit for nothing but to be a story-teller.... And you, Taki, what are you about?" The lady of his affections was far advanced in the process of disrobing. She protested. "Does not the Sensei need aid in the bath? How cleanse the back, the shoulders. This Taki would aid him." – "Immodest wench!" bellowed Chobei. "The Sensei needs no such aid. Why! You ... Taki ... one would take you for a charcoal ball (*tadon*), so dark your skin. Nay! For two of them, for a cluster piled in a box, so round the buttocks and belly. The Sensei wants no aid from such an ugly jade. This Chobei can do what is needed; with as much skill and better purpose than a woman." Kazuma modestly interposed in this incipient quarrel between husband and wife. "Nay, the matter is of no importance. Kazuma is grateful for such kindness, but aid is not needed. His arm is long." He held it out, almost simian in proportion and slenderness, the one proportional defect of this handsome body. The quarrel of Chobei and O'Taki lapsed before his pleasant smile.

Seated over tea said Chobei – "This Chobei, too, has claimed to be a diviner. Don't deny it. The Sensei at one time has been a priest." Kazuma looked at him with surprise, even misgiving. Explained Chobei – "The manner in which the Sensei takes up the cup betrays him; in both hands, with a little waving of the vessel and shake of the head. The rust of the priest's garb clings close." Said Kazuma – "Chobei San is a clever fellow. It is true. At one time I was priest." – "Whereabouts?" asked Chobei. "At the Reigan of Fukagawa," replied the prophet – "Ah! Reiganji; and later would return to the life of a *samurai*. Such pose and manner possessed by the Sensei are only gained in good company. He would reassume the status. This Chobei was not always as he is. Wine, women, gambling, have brought him to pimping. The buying of *geisha* and *jorō* cost the more as they imply the other two vices. Wife, status, fortune; all are gone. Such has been Chobei's fate." – "Not the only case of the kind," grumbled his partner in concubinage. "And the wife, what has become of her?" – "None of Taki's affair, as she is no longer an issue. Would the jade be jealous?" He glowered at her. "But Kazuma San, this Chobei is not only diviner, to tell fortunes. He can make them." Kazuma laughed. "Don't joke. Chobei San's line of business has already cost this Kazuma fortune and position." – "To secure a better one. Kazuma San is a *rōnin* (without lord), a man of education, and of fine appearance. He is just the one to become a *muko*." – "In some tradesman's family?" The *samurai* spoke with disdain. Said Chobei eagerly – "No: Chobei prophesied the return of Kazuma Uji to his own caste." – "At what cost?" said Kazuma coolly. "The honour of a *samurai* cannot stand open taint. Kazuma has no desire to cut belly at too early a date, to save the situation for others. Has the woman erred, and is the father's sword dulled?" – "It is no such case," answered Chobei. "The parents, rather grandparents, are fools in pride. The girl is twenty-five years old, rich, and, one must admit, not too good looking. It is by a mere chance, a former connection, that the affair comes into Chobei's hands. As Kazuma Uji knows, it is not much in his line. Let us share the good luck together." – "Is she a monster; one of those long-necked, pop-eyed *rokurokubi*?" – "That can be determined at the meeting," said the cautious Chobei. "She is somewhat pock-marked, as with others. It is a matter of luck. Chobei's position forces him to fall back on Kazuma San as the only likely man to recommend. Deign not to refuse to come to his aid." – "Rich, and granddaughter of people old in years." He eyed Chobei quizzically. The latter nodded agreement. "No matter what her looks, this Kazuma accepts with thanks – unless this be a jest of Chobei San." Chobei slightly coughed – "There is a commission...." – "Ah! Then the foundation is rock. As to commission, assuredly; Kazuma is not rich, nor in funds." – "But will be. At ten *ryō* it is a cheap affair."

– "Agreed," replied the diviner carelessly. "The money will be paid." – "With the delivery of the goods." Chobei now was all gaiety – "Of the Rokurokubi, the monster with sextuple lengthed neck," laughed Kazuma Sensei as he took his leave. He was engaged to meet Chobei the next day at the house of Kondo Rokurobei in Yotsuya.

Iemon Appears

In his difficult mission Kondo Rokurobei had hopes of Chobei; but not much more. It was with no small pleasure that he heard the announcement of his visit the next morning. The maid was a shade more civil – "Please wait." Kondo was decidedly so. He greeted Chobei with an effusion which Chobei noted. The tea brought, the two men faced each other over the cups. To Kondo's inquiring look – "Honoured master the task is a difficult one." He retailed his experience at the Kanda market. Kondo was somewhat discomfited. He had put a different interpretation on the early visit of Chobei. Continued the latter – "A difficult task, but not hopeless. Surely five *ryō* is very small remuneration." Kondo's eye lit up. Chobei had his man. "It is all this Kondo is qualified to give. Chobei knows Tamiya Dono. After all it is he who pays, and Chobei can claim but his share. However, the matter is not urgent. A bad turn with Matazaemon, and O'Naka will be much easier to deal with ... unless it be Yoemon who interposes." He made a wry face; joined in by Chobei. Kondo went on – "It is matter of regret to have troubled you. The parents of Natsume Kyuzo show signs of breaking off present negotiations and coming round to us. This is a matter of yesterday, and on hearing that the affair of O'Iwa San was definitely in the hands of Rokurobei." Chobei was frightened. Was this the cause of Kondo's joy? Had he misinterpreted on his entrance? He put out a hand, as if to stop the talk of his host. "Deign to allow the money question to stand as agreed. Such step would put this Chobei in an awkward position. The man is found, and soon will be here. Probably even Kondo Dono will be satisfied." – "Who is he?" asked Kondo. – "One Yanagibara Kazuma. He has practised divination at Asakusa...." – "A charlatan! A quack doctor! Chobei, are you mad?" Rokurobei pushed back his cushion and his cue in horror. Not a word did he say of Natsume Kyuzo. Chobei smiled. He had been trapped; but he had detected Kondo. "Don't be alarmed. The man is a *rōnin*, his divination of small account and due to temporary stress. Kondo Dono will soon judge of the man by his appearance. Let the subject of Kazuma San be dropped – with that of Natsume San. Our bargain has been made firm." Kondo looked down. He felt a little injured. Continued Chobei – "For his man Chobei cannot answer if all be known. Pray follow my plan, and precede us to the house of Matazaemon. He must not see O'Iwa at this juncture. Tamiya Dono is ill and not visible. The Obasan is wise enough to do as she is told. Years have drilled that into her. O'Iwa has taken cold. Her hair is loose and she cannot think of appearing. Make this known when the time comes to serve the wine. Meanwhile send her off on some mission; to the house of Akiyama, or that of the newly-wed Imaizumi." – "But the man must see the girl," protested Kondo. Answered Chobei – "He must see the property. It is with that Chobei intends he shall become enamoured. He is not to see the girl until she is his wife. To keep the estate he will cleave to the woman. Trust Chobei for a knowledge of men's hearts ... at least that of Yanagibara Kazuma." Perhaps he spoke a little too plainly. Rokurobei had a last touch of conscience – "Chobei, what manner of man is this one you bring? What is his real nature? Tamiya is upright as the walls of the Honmaru (castle). And Yanagibara Kazuma...." Chobei's brow wrinkled. He was spared an answer. Said the maid – "Yanagibara Sama would see the master." – "Show him in at once," said Rokurobei.

He rose, as much in amazement as in courtesy. Kazuma was a striking figure as he entered the room. His dress of white Satsuma was of finest quality, and perfectly aligned. The *haori* (cloak) was of the corrugated Akashi crape. In his girdle he wore the narrow swords then coming into fashion, with finely lacquered scabbards. In person he was tall, fair, with high forehead and big nose. Slender and sinewy every movement was lithe as that of a cat. Kondo gasped as he made the accustomed salutations. "This man for O'Iwa! Bah! A fox has stolen a jewel." All his compunction and discretion vanished before this unusual presence. Kazuma gracefully apologized for his intrusion, thus uninvited. Kondo stammered protests and his delight at the opportunity of meeting Yanagibara Dono. Chobei smiled inward and outward delight at thus summarily removing any too pointed objections of Kondo. For absolute self-possession in this awkward situation the younger man easily carried the palm. Kazuma acted as would a man double his years. Chobei was not only delighted, but astonished. "Whence had the Sensei produced all this wondrous get-up? Was he in real fact a magician?" Kazuma knew, but he was not one to enlighten Chobei or anyone else. After talk on general matters the affair of the meeting was broached. Said Kondo Rokurobei – "Thus to trouble Yanagibara Dono requires apology, but the affair is not without advantage. The lady is the daughter of Tamiya, a *dōshin* and favoured by the Hosokawa House. This Kondo is honoured in presenting Kazuma Dono in Yotsuya." – "Nay, fear enters. The honour of this meeting with Kondo Dono is as great as the intrusion has been unseemly. Deign to pardon the precipitancy of this Kazuma." Kondo protested in his turn. Said Chobei – "The presentation made, doubtless the matter is as good as concluded. But Tamiya Dono is ill; this visit is unexpected. If Kondo Dono would deign to precede, and ascertain how matters are at Tamiya, it would be well." To this Kondo assented. Making his excuses he set out for Samoncho, bubbling over with excitement, and praying that the matter would have certain issue; and thus establish him for life on the shoulders of the wealthy Tamiya. Prayers? Indeed he did stop on the road, one lined with the ecclesiastical structures. Kondo had too much at stake, not to invoke all likely aid.

With his departure Chobei began to go into the externals of the House of Tamiya. As they walked along – "Congenial surroundings." This was with a grin and a wave of the hand toward the long line of temple buildings and graveyards they were passing. "Not much savour of present lodging in Hanagawado. Eh! Kazuma Uji, even Chobei notes the difference." He stopped opposite the Gwanshoji and looked across the way. The fruit was already formed on the trees of Matazaemon's garden. "Persimmons of a hundred momme (375 grammes) each; twenty cartloads for the profit of the house at the fall of the year." As they passed in the entrance on Samoncho he pointed to a store-house. "Stuffed with rice, from the farms of Tamiya in Kazusa. No husks to be found in it." – "Who said there were?" said Kazuma testily. His eyes were taking in the wide proportions of the garden, the spreading roof and eaves of a stately mansion. As they passed along the *rōka* to a sitting room Chobei called his attention to the fret work (*rama-shōji*) between the rooms, the panelled ceilings, the polished and rare woodwork of *tokonoma* (alcoves). A *kakemono* of the severe Kano school was hung in the sitting room alcove, a beautifully arranged vase of flowers stood beneath it. Matazaemon could not use his legs, but his hands were yet active. Of his visitors he knew nothing; least of all of Chobei. Kondo Rokurobei appeared. With him was an old lady. O'Naka bowed to the ground before the proposed son-in-law. She was in a flutter over the beautiful man destined for O'Iwa. The admirable courtesy of his manners, the tender softness of voice, robbed her of what little judgment she had. Her only fear was that the candidate for honours and the Tamiya would escape.

Said Chobei – "Asakusa is a long distance; the occasion exceptional. Cannot the Ojosan favour us by pouring the wine?" The old woman hummed and hawed. Kondo, too, seemed put out. "As a matter of fact O'Iwa is not presentable. She has taken cold, and just now is in bed. Perhaps the Obasan will urge her further, now that Yanagibara Uji is present." O'Naka at once rose, like to an automaton, the spring of which has been pressed. She disappeared, to return and repeat her lesson. "Wilful as a child! One would suppose her such. Illness she would disregard, but her hair is not made up. She cannot think of appearing before company. Truly she is vexing." – "Not so," defended Chobei. "She could not show higher regard than by refusing to appear before a future husband in careless attire. It is a guarantee of conduct when married. She is much to be commended for such respect. All women like to appear well. A man in the neighbourhood, and rice powder and rouge are at once applied. How neglect such an elaborate structure as the hair? Trust Chobei's judgment as to women."

O'Naka thought that he spoke well, but like most men with great conceit. Kazuma looked out towards the beautiful garden. He took the chance to smile, for he had soon ascertained that Kondo knew little about his agent; was in fact a precipitate, testy man. However, he was a little put out at not seeing the would-be bride. At an opportunity he stepped out, to see more of the house and its surroundings. Chobei came up to him as he stood on the *rōka*. His voice was coaxing and pleading. "Is it not a fine prospect – for Kazuma Dono?" His voice hung on the "Dono". "Nay, don't let escape this splendid piece of luck. Long has Chobei interested himself in his neighbour. Such a beautiful exterior should have a proper setting. Marry O'Iwa San and Kazuma Dono is master of Tamiya. Is it agreed?" Kazuma looked down in thought. At his age there are ideals of the other sex, hard to put aside. Said he – "Not to see the lady.... Is she so horrible?" Chobei protested. "Not so! The lady is a mere item, well fitted to go with this fine house, this beautiful garden, these store-houses filled with goods. Look: Tamiya Dono is a man of double rations. The property has *nagaya* for attendants. For long this has not been used. Tamiya will not rent it out. It will be so much revenue added to the stipend of the House, and will replace the old man's uncertain income from his accomplishments as master of *hanaike* and *cha-no-yu*." Kazuma looked around, following the pointing finger of Chobei. He was in sad straits. His only future was this position of a *muko*. No matter what the woman might be, there was compensation. To Chobei's direct question he made answer – "Yes."

The affair of the marriage suffered no delays. Chobei had struck home. Kazuma was so impressed with the surroundings, especially after a return to his own miserable quarters, that the matter of the interview took a minor place to the inspection of his future property. Within the week he had removed to the house of Kondo Rokurobei. The latter introduced him to his future associates in the ward by a succession of fish and wine dinners dear to the heart of the men of Nippon. These neighbours were astonished at the future son-in-law of the Tamiya. This man was to be the husband of the O'Bake? Was he mad, or drunk? Perhaps the latter, for neither themselves nor Kazuma had the opportunity to be particularly sober during this period of festivity. Of course there was an introduction to Matazaemon, the other principal involved. As Kondo carefully explained, no set date could be made for this interview. Tamiya Dono was ill, and to be seen at a favourable time. As ill luck would have it, on the very day the interview was permitted O'Iwa San received an urgent summons from the Okugata of the Hosokawa House. This could not be disregarded, and her absence on the second occasion was easily explained and condoned. Kondo certainly made no effort, and Kazuma no suggestion, for a meeting in the three days intervening before the formal marriage.

At evening the guests met in the reception rooms of Tamiya. In a private apartment were Kondo Rokurobei and his wife, O'Iwa, and Iemon. The latter name had been assumed by Kazuma on his formal registration in the Tamiya House. It was Chobei who had purchased the *wataboshi*, or wadded hood, of floss silk worn by the bride on this great occasion of her life. Iemon could see but little within its depths, except the shining light of her countenance. Joy perhaps? At least this curiosity was soon to be satisfied. Nine times – three times three – were the *sake* cups drained. Kondo Rokurobei joined the hands of the train, exhorting them to mutual forbearance, O'Iwa to unquestioning obedience to the husband. He pattered over the maxims of the Dojikun of Kaibara Yekken in this strange case, as he had done twenty times before with favourable results. Yekken's book was comparatively recent, only a few decades old, and the woman's guide. Truly the position of the *nakōdo* was no easy one, if it was to bring him at odds with either House involved. He felt complacent. This pair at least presented less complications in that line than usual. What there was of doubtful issue came now to the test. At this crisis he cast an eye to the *rōka* (verandah) to see that Chobei really was at hand as promised. Then the strings of the *wataboshi* were loosed. The hood concealing the face of O'Iwa was removed.

Iemon rose to his feet as if impelled by springs; then hurriedly he sat again with some mumbled excuse and trembling hands. He could not take his eyes from the shining white of the face before him, the glazed smooth surface left in many places between the black of the pock marks. The removal of the hood had somewhat disarrayed the hair, leaving the broad expanse of forehead more prominent, the puffed heavy eyelids in the face more conspicuous. In the depths shone two tiny points, the eyes. Indeed, as Chobei afterwards described it, eyelids and eyes had the appearance of *kuzumanju*, the dumplings of white rice paste with the black dots of dark brown bean paste sunk deep in the centre. Never had O'Iwa appeared to such disadvantage. She was now engaged in removing the white garment, to appear in her proper array as bride and wife. Iemon took advantage of this absence to step to the *rōka*. In leaving the room Kondo had given a wink to Chobei. Iemon almost ran into him. He seized him by the arm. The young man's voice was excited. He spoke in a whisper, as one who could barely find speech. With satisfaction Chobei noted that he was frightened, not angered. "What is that? Who is that creature?" were the first words of Iemon. Replied Chobei coldly – "That is the wife of Tamiya Iemon; O'Iwa San, daughter of Matazaemon Dono; your wife to eight thousand generations." Then roughly – "Deign, Iemon San, not to be a fool. In the purchase of cow or horse, what does the buyer know of the animal? Its real qualities remain to be ascertained. O'Iwa San is ugly. That much Chobei will admit. She is pock-marked, perhaps stoops a little. But if the daughter of the rich Tamiya, a man with this splendid property, had been a great beauty, this Iemon would not have become the *muko* of Tamiya, the future master of its wealth. What qualification had he for such a position – a diviner, a man whose pedigree perhaps would not stand too much search." He looked keenly at Iemon, and noted with satisfaction how the last thrust had gone home. Chobei must know more of Iemon, ex-Kazuma. He determined on that for the future.

He continued – "Withdrawal at this juncture would merely create scandal. Matazaemon is not so bereft of friends that such a step would not cause serious displeasure in high quarters. The insult would find an avenger. Then consider please: the old man is kept alive by the anxiety to see his granddaughter established in life, the line of the Tamiya assured. He will die within the month. If the old woman hangs on too long" – he halted speech for a moment, then coldly – "give her lizard to eat. A diviner, doubtless Iemon San knows Kondo Rokurobei by this time. He will never prejudice the man who holds in his hands the purse of the Tamiya.

Iemon San and O'Iwa San are left alone. Good luck to you, honoured Sir, in the encounter. In this Chobei a counsellor and friend always is to be found; and one by no means lacking experience of the world. As for the woman, she is your wife; one to take charge of the house and affairs of Iemon Dono is to hand. No other *rusu* could be found so earnest in duty and so cheap, as O'Iwa San. Take a concubine. This Chobei will purchase one for you; such a one as will be the object of envy and desire to the whole of young Edo. His opportunities in that line are exceptional. Come! To turn on the lights. On our part at least there is nothing to conceal." Iemon did not pay attention to the hint. The one thought harassing him must out – "lop-sided and – a leper!" He spoke with despair and conviction, eyes fastened on Chobei, and such a frightened look that even Chobei had pity. One foot in the room he turned back. "That is not so – absolutely." Iemon could not disbelieve the earnest testimony. Said Chobei – "The wounds of smallpox were no trivial ones. In healing the scars were such in places as form over burns. Hence the shining surface. Positively there is no leprous taint in Tamiya." He was gratified by the sigh which came from Iemon, sign of the immense weight lifted off the young man's mind. "Bah! leave things to the future, and – enjoy the present. O'Iwa cannot grow ugly with age. So much is gained. What difference will her looks make to Iemon thirty years hence? She is a woman. Make a child on her. Then you are free to turn elsewhere."

At once he began to place lights everywhere, as a sign to Kondo that all was well. This worthy came forward with other guests, to congratulate the Tamiya House on being once more in young and vigorous hands. It was Iemon himself who gave the signal to retire. How matters went alone with his bride has reference to one of those occasions over which the world draws the veil of decency. In the morning O'Iwa arose early to attend to the matutinal needs of her spouse. The ablutions performed, Iemon sat down to tea, as exquisite and exquisitely served as in any dream in literature of how such ceremony of the opening day should be performed. Then the morning meal was brought, under the same supervision of this woman, as expert in all the technique of her craft as she was ugly in feature; and that was saying much. Iemon watched her movements in the room with curiosity, mixed with a little pain and admiration. He was quick to note the skill with which she concealed the slight limp, due to the shrinking of the sinews of one leg and causing an unevenness of gait. It was a blemish in the little quick movements of a woman of surpassing grace; who by art had conquered disease and an ungainly figure.

O'Iwa had left the room for a moment to get flowers to place in the vases, offering to the *hotoke* (Spirits of the departed) in the Butsudan. On his return Iemon held the *ihai* (memorial tablets) in his hands. A priest, these had at once attracted his notice. "Kangetsu Shinshi; Kangetsu Shimmyo; O'Iwa San, these people have died on the same day of the month – and the year?" – "Is on the back of the *ihai*," replied O'Iwa. "No; it is not a case of suicide together." Then seeing his evident curiosity she motioned him to sit as she poured tea, ready for a long story. With its progress voice and manner grew more strained and earnest. She never took her eyes from the *tatami* (mats). "The tablets are those of the father and mother of this Iwa. My mother's name was Mino. Daughter of Tamiya she acted badly with my father Densuke, a mere servant in the house. This Densuke was a good man, but his status of *chūgen* made my grandfather very angry. He drove the twain from the house. Thus deprived of means to live, my father took a position as cook in the *yashiki* of a great noble. Here he was frightened into becoming the tool of a very wicked man. Having killed an usurer this man forced my father to dispose of the body under penalty of death if he refused. The body being placed in a cloth, my father had carried it to his house. During his short absence my mother's curiosity led her into untying the bundle. Her screams aroused the neighbourhood. As they entered she was seized with convulsions, and gave birth to this Iwa, thus brought into the world together with the exposure of the crime. My father, doubtless warned by the crowd, fled from Edo. My mother had but time to tell her story to the *kenshi*. Then she died. A year later to the day my father's dead body was found floating in the castle moat, near the town of Yuki in Shimosa. A beggar man, but little inquiry was made into the crime. For long the cause and the criminal were unknown. Then a *bantō* was robbed in the Shiba Kiridoshi; his companion was killed. The criminals were traced, and on confession were put to death. The leader and most wicked of them also confessed to the murder of the usurer Jusuke and to that of my father Densuke. My father had met him again in Yuki town, and had aroused in him fear of denunciation of past crimes. He spoke of 'this Densuke' as a superstitious, haunted fool; thus in his wickedness regarding my father's remorse and desire to clear up the strange affair. The execution of this man removed all chance of my avenging the deaths of father and mother on himself. But he has left behind a son. The one wish of this Iwa is to meet with Kichitaro; to avenge on him the wickedness of his father Takahashi Daihachiro." Iemon at first had followed in idle mood her story. With the development of the details he showed an attention which grew in intensity at every stage. With the mention of the name of Takahashi Daihachiro he gave a violent start. Yanagibara Kazuma, Iemon Tamiya – what were these but names to cover this Kichitaro, the one-time priest Myoshin of the Joshinji at Reigan Fukagawa, and son of Daihachiro.

Strange was this retributory fate which had brought these two into the most intimate relations of husband and wife. When Iemon could control his voice he said – "That O'Iwa San should have this feeling in reference to the wicked Daihachiro can be understood. But why such hatred toward this Kichitaro? Surely the boy is not to be held guilty of the father's offence!" – "That is a man's way of reasoning," answered O'Iwa. "A woman, ignorant and foolish, has but her feelings to consult. To seven births this Iwa will clutch and chew the wicked son of a wicked father. Against Kichitaro is the vow made." She raised her head. Iemon turned away shuddering. She had aged into a hag. The shining face, the marks like black spots in pumice standing out, the mere dots of eyes in their puffy bed, the spreading mouth with its large shining teeth – all turned the plain gentle girl into a very demon. The certainty, the intensity, of a malignant hate was driven into Iemon. He was so frightened that he even nodded assent to her last words. The gentle voice of O'Iwa added – "Iwa is ugly; perhaps annoys by the tale. Leave the affair to her and to the enemy. To Iemon she is bound for two existences. Deign to drop all formality; call her Iwa, and condescend to regard her with affection." And Iemon covenanted with himself so to do. The present should compensate for the past. But in the days which followed O'Iwa sat on him as a nightmare. He felt the impress of her teeth at his throat, and would wake up gasping. Time made the situation familiar. He carefully lulled her into a blind admiration and belief in her husband Iemon. There seemed no likelihood of O'Iwa learning the truth; or believing it, if she did.

If Old Acquaintance Be Forgot

Matazaemon's illness justified all the predictions of Chobei. In the course of the month it was plain that his last hold on life was rapidly weakening. In that time Iemon had won golden opinions from household and neighbours. His face was beautiful, and this they saw. His heart was rotten to the core, and this he kept carefully concealed. The incentive of his fear of O'Iwa kept up the outward signs of good-will. He found this easier with the passage of the days. Plain as she was in face and figure, no one could help being attracted by the goodness of O'Iwa's disposition. Iemon, in his peculiar situation, placed great hopes on this, even if discovery did take place. Day following day he began to discount this latter contingency. To a feeling of half liking, half repugnance, was added a tinge of contempt for one so wrapped in her immediate surroundings, whose attention was so wholly taken up with the matter in hand. She easily could be kept in ignorance, easily be beguiled.

One day Iemon was summoned to the old man's bedside. He was shocked at the change which had taken place in a few hours. Propped upon pillows Matazaemon would speak a few last words. With a shade of his old impertinent official smile and manner – "The Tamiya is to be congratulated on its great good fortune in the entrance of one so well qualified by appearance and manners to uphold its reputation. Deign, honoured Muko San, to accept the thanks of this Matazaemon. All else has been placed in the hands of Iemon – goods, reputation, granddaughter." Iemon bowed flat in acknowledgment and protest at the good-will expressed. Continued Matazaemon – "There is one matter close to the old man's heart. Concerning that he would make his last request to the admirable heart of Iemon. Iwa is a plain girl. The end of time for man, and the carping comment of neighbours come to his ears, have opened the eyes of Matazaemon to the truth. Great has been the favour in disregarding this plainness and taking her to wife. Everything is in the hands of Iemon San. Consider her happiness and deign to use her well. Abstain if possible from taking a concubine. At all events conceal the fact from Iwa, if it be deigned to keep such company. Plainness and jealousy go together. Faithful and upright, such a disposition as hers is not to be strained on that point. She would be very unhappy. Better the light women of Shinjuku Nakacho, than one who takes the place of the wife. Condescend to remember this last request of Tamiya Matazaemon." He clasped the hand of Iemon, and tears were in his eyes as he spoke. Iemon, too, was affected. It almost frightened him to be left alone with O'Iwa. "Deign not to consider such unlikely contingency. The amiability of O'Iwa is compensation for the greatest beauty. Who could think of injuring her in any way? Perhaps a child soon will be the issue. With this in mind condescend to put aside all gloomy thoughts. Concentrate the honoured will on life, and complete recovery to health will follow. Such, indeed, is the daily prayer of this Iemon at the Myogyoji."

Matazaemon smiled faintly – with gratification or grimness? Perhaps death unseals the vision. Often indeed did Iemon present himself at the family temple; he the substitute for the Master of Tamiya. But as often did his feet return by the diametrically opposite direction, running the gauntlet of the charms of the frail beauties of Nakacho. Iemon held on to the hand of Matazaemon, swearing and forswearing himself with the greatest earnestness and the best of intentions. Suddenly he raised his head. The emotion aroused by the interview had been too much for the old man's fluttering heart. His head had slipped down sideways on the pillow. A little stream of dark bitter refuse flowed from the mouth and choked him. He was dead.

Great was the grief of wife and grandchild; great was the importance of Iemon, now in very fact Master of Tamiya. Whether or not he followed the advice of Chobei, and gave the old woman *tokage* (lizard); whether her constant small journeys to the houses of neighbours, reciting a litany of praise of this wondrous son-in-law; whether the loss of the companion of so many years wore out the feeble frame; it is fact that O'Naka followed her lord before the maple leaf turned red. Again the Tamiya was the scene of the funereal chanting of the priest. The corpse removed with the provision for the guests and watchers at the wake, the seventh night of the death observed, with this removal of the deceased spirit from the scenes of its former activities Iemon could turn himself without impediment to the life of the future. Outward change there was none. He was the same kind and affectionate husband as of former days. Neighbours, anticipating some change of manner, were still louder in their praises. One day there appeared at Tamiya two intimates, Natsume Kyuzo and Imaizumi Jinzaemon. "Iemon Uji, a matter of importance presses. We are on our way to the ward head, Ito Kwaiba Dono. Deign to go in company. You are known to be an expert at *go*, a game at which the old man prides himself for skill. He chafes at the presence of this unknown rival, heard of but not yet tested. A dinner and wine are at stake. Without Iemon Uji we do not dare to present ourselves. Condescend to go in company. To know the great man of the ward, the wealthy Ito Kwaiba, is of advantage even to Tamiya." Iemon laughed and assented. He was soon dressed for the greater ceremony of a first visit. All three climbed down into their clogs, and set out for the house of the Kumi-gashira near Samegabashi.

If Iemon had been impressed by the wealth of Tamiya, he felt insignificant before that of the head of Yotsuya. Ito Kwaiba was a man of sixty-four years, retaining much of the vigour of his youth. For the past ten years he had added *go* to his twin passions for wine and women, neither of which seemed to have made any impression on a keenness of sight which could read the finest print by the scanty light of an *andon*, teeth which could chew the hard and tough dried *mochi* (rice paste) as if bean confection, and an activity of movement never to be suspected from his somewhat heavy frame. At the name of Tamiya he looked up with much curiosity, and Iemon thought his greeting rather brusque. He saluted with great respect – "Truly fear is inspired. For long no visit has been paid to the honoured head. Coming thus without invitation is very rude. Intrusion is feared." – "Nay! Nay!" replied Kwaiba, apparently attracted by the splendid externals of Iemon. "The failure to visit is reciprocal. In fact, Tamiya and this Kwaiba have been at odds these many years. Visits had altogether ceased. This, however, is no matter for the younger generation. But Iemon San is indeed a fine fellow. So Kwaiba had heard from all he met. Ah! A fellow to put all the girls in a flutter. He is the very image of this Kwaiba in younger years. The husbands were little troubled when he was around. The fair ones were attracted. Well, well: they all had their turn at Kwaiba; and Kwaiba has stood the pace. He is as good today as ever; in some ways.... And it is a man like Iemon San who has married the – lady of Tamiya." Iemon knew the term "O'Bake" had nearly slipped out. Knowing O'Iwa's attractiveness of temperament, feeling touched in his own conceit, this astonished and satirical reception he met with on every side nettled him more than a little. Perhaps Kwaiba noted it. With greatest unction he urged a cushion and at once changed the subject. "Iemon San is noted as a *go* player. This Kwaiba is a mere amateur. It is for him to ask odds in making request for a game.... Ho! Heigh! The *go* board and stones!"

Kwaiba and Iemon were the antagonists. Natsume and Imaizumi sat at the sides of the board. Kwaiba, confident in his powers, readily accepted the deprecatory answer of Iemon at its face value. The game was to be on even terms. Iemon really was an expert of the sixth grade; certainly of several grades superiority to Kwaiba. The latter's brows knit as his position rapidly became imperilled. Natsume was in a ferment. Fish or wine? If Iemon sought Kwaiba's favour by a preliminary sound thrashing at his favourite game, the prospects of either were small. He dropped his tobacco pipe. In picking it up he gave the buttocks of Iemon a direct and severe pinch. Iemon was too astonished to cry out. His ready mind sought a motive for this unexpected assault and pain. The face of Natsume was unmoved, that of Imaizumi anxious. A glance at Kwaiba's attitude enlightened him. Politeness and a dinner were at stake. Even Natsume and Imaizumi wondered and admired at what followed. The blunder of Iemon was a stroke of genius, the inspiration of an expert player. It was a slight blunder, not obvious to the crudeness of Kwaiba; but it opened up the whole of Iemon's position and put the game in his antagonist's hands. Kwaiba promptly seized the advantage. His triumphant glance shifted continually from Iemon to the onlookers, as the former struggled bravely with a desperate position. Kwaiba won this first game somewhat easily. A second he lost by a bare margin. In the third he scored success in a manner to make evident his superiority over a really expert player. Confident in his championship of the ward, he was all geniality as at the end he sorted and swept back the *go* stones into their polished boxes. "*Go-ishi* of Shingu; soft as a woman's hands. But never mind the sex. Now for fish and wine.... However, Hana can serve the liquor for us." To the servant – "Heigh! Some refreshments for the honoured guests; and convey the request of Kwaiba to O'Hana San, to be present."

With the wine appeared O'Hana San. She was a beautiful girl. Of not more than twenty years, on the graceful sloping shoulders was daintily set a head which attracted attention and admiration. The face was a pure oval – of the *uri* or melon, as the Nipponese class it – with high brow, and was framed in long hair gathered below the waist and reaching nearly to her ankles with its heavy luxuriant mass. She was dressed for the hot season of the year in a light coloured Akashi crape, set off by an *obi* or broad sash of peach colour in which were woven indistinct and delicate wavy designs. The sleeves, drawn a little back, showed the arms well up to the shoulder. Glimpses of a beautifully moulded neck and bosom appeared from time to time as she moved here and there in her preparation of the service of the wine utensils. The delicate tissue of the dress seemed to caress the somewhat narrow hips of a girlish figure. Every movement was studied and graceful. This O'Hana had belonged to the Fukadaya at Yagura no Shita of Fukagawa. She had been what is known as an *obitsuke* harlot, wearing the *obi* in the usual form, without the loose overrobe or *shikake* of the common women. "In the period of Tempo (1830-1843) all Fukagawa harlots were dressed in this manner." Attracted by her beauty old Kwaiba had ransomed her and made her his concubine. For nearly two years she had held this position in his house. In serving the wine she came to the front and knelt before Iemon as first to receive it. In handing him the tray with the cup she looked into his face. The start on the part of both was obvious. Some of the wine was spilled.

Said Kwaiba – "Then Iemon Uji, you know this woman?" His tone was hard and truculent. It conveyed the suspicion of the jealous old male. Iemon's former profession stood him in good stead. He had a glib tongue, and no intention to deny what had been made perfectly obvious – "It is fact, and nothing to be ashamed of on the part of Iemon; except as to attendant conditions beyond control. I was a diviner on the public highway." – "So 'twas heard," grumbled Kwaiba. "Without customers, and with no use for the diviner's lens but to charr the rafters of the garret in which you lived." Iemon did not care to notice the attack. He merely said – "Deign not to find amusement in what really is a serious matter to one who has to suffer poverty. While seated at the diviner's stand attention was drawn by a girl coming down the Kuramae. Slouching along close by her was a drunken *samurai*. From time to time he lurched entirely too close to her. Turning unexpectedly her sunshade caught in his *haori* (cloak), which thereby was slightly torn. At once he flew into a great rage. Laying hands on her he showed no disposition to accept her excuses. 'Careless wench! You have torn my dress. How very impudent of you. Unless you at once accompany me to the tea house close by, to serve the wine and please me, pardon, there is none; be sure of that.' The people had gathered like a black mountain. Nothing was to be seen but heads. O'Hana San was in the greatest embarrassment, unable to free herself from the insults and importunities of the drunken fellow. The *samurai* was hid under the diviner's garb. Stepping from the stand I interposed in the girl's behalf, making apology, and pointing out the rudeness of his behaviour to the drunkard. Instead of becoming calm he raised his fist and struck me in the face. His condition gave the advantage without use of arms. Locking a leg in his tottering supports I threw him down into the ditch. Then with a word to O'Hana San to flee at once, we disappeared in different directions. The *samurai* Iemon again became the diviner. That part of his role this Iemon regrets; but a weapon he could not draw in the quarrel. Later on meeting O'Hana San at the Kwannon temple of Asakusa thanks were received, for what was a very trivial service." – "And again renewed," said the beauty, raising her downcast face to look direct into that of Iemon. Said Kwaiba – "Ah! That's the tale, is it? A fortunate encounter, and a strange reunion; but the world is full of such. O'Hana, it comes in most befitting that opportunity is afforded to favour the rescuer with something of greater value than thanks. Pray serve him with wine." Then did Kwaiba take the matter as a man of the world. But he was no fool, "this old *tanuki* (badger) of a thousand autumns' experience on hill and in dale." He understood very well that between Iemon and O'Hana there had been a closer connection than that of mere accident.

Love Knots

Many were the visits paid by Iemon to contest at *go* with Ito Kwaiba. Rapid was the progress of the love affair between a young man and a young woman, both inspired with a consuming passion for each other. In former days – something more than two years before – when Iemon was priest in the Joshinji of the Reigan district of Fukagawa, and was spending the money of the *osho* so freely, he had met O'Hana at the Fukagawa of Yagura no Shita. Just entering on her career, she at once captivated him with a permanent passion. It was in her company that the funds of the temple had been cast to the four winds of heaven. His love had been fully reciprocated by O'Hana. The one purpose was to ransom the lady, and then to live together as husband and wife. Such was the engagement plighted between them. However, the ransom figure was large. Iemon – or Kazuma at that time, he dropped his priestly name when out of bounds – had already planned a larger raid than usual on the ecclesiastical treasury. Warned by O'Hana that his operations had been discovered, he had sought safety in flight; not without a last tearful parting with his mistress, and assurance that fate somehow would bring them again together. The engagement thus entered on was to flourish under the new conditions.

As to this pursuit of O'Hana, in which the maiden was coy and willing, the lover circumspect and eager, or at least thought he was, those around the pair were soon well informed; that is, with the exception of the most interested – O'Iwa and Kwaiba. The marked neglect which now ensued O'Iwa took in wifely fashion; and attributing it to some passing attraction of Shinjuku Nakacho, she did not take it to heart as she would have done if a concubine had been at issue. As for Kwaiba, the usually astute and prying old man was so immersed in his *go* as to be struck blind, deaf, and dumb. The matter coming to the ears of Kondo Rokurobei, the worthy gentleman was seriously alarmed. If true, the old man had indeed reached a parting of the ways, at which he had to satisfy Iemon, Master of Tamiya, O'Iwa, his ward, and Ito Kwaiba, the powerful influence in the daily life of all of them. That night there was a meeting at the house of Kwaiba, a competition in *gidayu* recitation, dancing, and poetry (*uta*) making. He presented himself in season at the door of the Tamiya. "Ah! O'Iwa San; and tonight does Iemon join the company at the house of the *Kumi-gashira*? Rokurobei comes from Kawagoe, and perhaps is not too late to find company on the road." – "Oya! Is it Kondo Sama? Iya! the Danna has but begun his preparations.... Iemon! The Danna of Yotsuyazaka has come; for company on the way to Ito Sama's house.... Deign to enter. In a short time Iemon will be ready." Kondo looked at her quizzically. There was no sign of distress or misgivings in this quarter. He felt encouraged. Probably the rumour was false or exaggerated; perhaps it was wholly due to the malice of Akiyama Chozaemon, from whom that day he had heard it.

He turned to greet Iemon, who emerged ready for the street. At the entrance they halted. Said Iemon – "It will be a long drawn-out affair. Deign to retire, and not await the return." Replied O'Iwa – "A small matter. The sound of the Danna's footstep will arouse Iwa to receive him." Iemon laughed. "How so? How distinguish my steps from those of Akiyama San or other constant callers?" Said O'Iwa gravely – "When the wife can no longer distinguish the husband's footstep, then affection has departed. O'Iwa will be ready to receive Iemon, no matter what the hour." – "And, indeed, a late one," put in Kondo. "The party consists mainly of young men. After it they will adjourn to Nakacho. Is it allowed to Iemon Dono to accompany them?" O'Iwa winced a little. "The Master is always master, within and without the house. He will do as he pleases." – "Gently said; like a true wife. Truly such a married pair are rarely to be encountered. They are the mandarin duck and drake of Morokoshi transplanted to Yotsuya. Rokurobei feels proud of his guardianship." As he and Iemon took their way along the Teramachi, he said – "Iemon is indeed a wonderful man. He is handsome and pursued by the women. O'Iwa undeniably is ugly; yet never is there failure to show her respect and consideration, in private as well as public. One's life here in Yotsuya is open to all the neighbours, and these speak well of Iemon." Said the younger man, in matter of fact tone – "Who could fail toward Iwa? She is amiability itself. Plain, perhaps, but gentleness is the compensating quality, a truer source of household wealth than beauty." – "Well spoken! Deign to keep it in heart, for the neighbours' tongues wag as to Iemon and O'Hana. Malice can cause as much unhappiness as downright wickedness. Besides, Kwaiba is no man to trifle with." Iemon was a little put out and alarmed at the directness of Kondo's reference. "Be sure there is nothing in such talk. A slight service, rendered in earlier days, makes O'Hana San more cordial to one otherwise a stranger. The excess shown is perhaps to be discouraged. But Ito Dono is good company and has good wine; and besides really is a good *go* player. It would be loss to shun his house."

Kondo noted a first symptom on their arrival. He spoke sharply to the maid – "Middle age in company with youth plainly finds a poor reception. Is that the master's order? The clogs of Tamiya are not the only ones. Is Rokurobei to shift for himself?" The girl, all confusion, made profuse apology as she hastened to repair the neglect. Kondo was easily mollified. "Bah! No wonder. Bring Tamiya near a woman, and all is confusion.... But Ito Dono?" – "This way, honoured Sirs: the Danna awaits the guests." They entered the sitting room, to find Kwaiba in a high state of anger and sulks. For some reason, error in transmission or date or other ambiguity, not a man of the guests had appeared. "The supper prepared is next to useless. We four can do but little in its dispatch. Not so with the wine; let every man do double duty here." He hustled around and gave his orders with some excitement; more than cordial with the guests who had not failed him. There was present one Kibei. Iemon had noted with curiosity his first appearance on this ground. What effect was this factor going to have on O'Hana's position in the household. He had been reassured on the physical point. Kibei was exceedingly ugly, a regular mask, and O'Hana was a woman to make much of physical beauty, as well as strength and ruggedness. He was a younger son of Inagaki Shogen, a *hatamoto* with a *yashiki* in Honjo and an income of three thousand *koku*. It was almost certain that Kwaiba would adopt Kibei. The negotiations had been long continued, and there was some hitch in the matter that Iemon could not make out. What he did realize was Kibei's hostility to himself. A noted fencer, making some sort of a living as teacher of the art, he was the last man with whom Iemon had any desire for a quarrel. Iemon was a coward, and the cold eye of Kibei sent a chill down his spine. Himself, he was always excessively polite in their intercourse.

Limited as to number the party tried to make up for the missing guests by liveliness. There was a dance by Kibei, drinking as substitutes of the absent, and competition in *uta* (poetry). Handing in his own effort – no mean one – Iemon left the room for a moment. As he came out on the corridor, and was about to return to the guest room, he found the maid O'Moto awaiting him with water and towel. A slight puckering frown came over Iemon's face at this imprudence. Said the girl pleadingly – "Danna Sama, deign to exercise patience. That of the mistress is sorely tried. The absence of the other guests, the pursuit of Kibei Dono, who only seeks to compromise her and secure her expulsion from the house, or even death at the hand of Kwaiba Dono, has driven her well nigh mad. A moment – in this room." Iemon drew back. – "A room apart, and in darkness! The age of seven years once passed, and boy and girl are never to be allowed alone together." He would have refused, but a sudden push and he was within. The *shōji* closed at once.

Kwaiba's voice called loudly – "Hana! Hana! What has become of the girl? There is no one to serve the wine. If the ugliness of Kibei drives her to cover, Tamiya's beauty should lure her out. Hana! Hana!" O'Hana slipped hastily from the arms of Iemon. Passing through the garden she entered the kitchen and snatched up a *sake* bottle from the stove. She did not notice that the fire had gone entirely out. She and Iemon entered the sitting room together, from different sides. Rokurobei looked sharply at Iemon. Kibei was engaged in hot talk with Kwaiba. Said Kondo – "Where have you been? Pressed by necessity? For such a lapse of time! nonsense! Is rice powder found in such a place? 'Plaster'? It does not leave the mark of a cheek on the sleeve." He laid a warning hand on Iemon, skilfully removing the telltale mark in so doing. "What has happened is clear enough. Fortunately Kwaiba and Kibei have got into a dispute over the merits of Heinai and Shosetsu as fencing masters; both of them dead as the long ago quarrels of the Toyotomi and Tokugawa Houses. Heinai was loyal, and Shosetsu a traitor; but Kibei tries the old man and officer by supporting the prowess of the latter. Besides the *sake* is cold and Kwaiba at start was in a very bad temper. He has thought for naught but his drink and disappointment. Cajole him by agreeing with him, but don't get into a quarrel with Kibei. He is expert with the sword, has a temper as ugly as his face, and would willingly engage in one. He don't like you...." He stopped. Kwaiba was speaking sharply. He had just taken the fresh bottle. "Cold as a stone! How careless you are." – "Not so," said O'Hana in some surprise. "It has just come off the stove." Kwaiba put the bottle in her hand, to her confusion. "O'Hana must have been asleep; or much engaged, not to note the difference." For the first time he looked sharply at her, then at Iemon. O'Hana often executed great freedom with him – "Asleep! Just so; and no wonder. Without guests the evening has been stupid enough. If Tamiya Sama had brought his wife with him it would have been complete." Kwaiba, Kibei, Kondo smiled at the sally. Iemon took the cue, and chose to resent the words. He said coldly – "O'Iwa certainly brings spice into everything she engages in. Her intelligence is unusual." O'Hana looked at him; then smiled a little, reassured. Passing behind him she stumbled. "Forgotten" – Iemon felt a letter thrust into his hand, which he passed quickly to his sleeve. Then he and Kondo rose to take their leave. The usual salutations followed. As if to compensate for the failure of the entertainment all joined in seeing them depart. Kwaiba was still grumbling and half quarrelling with O'Hana. O'Moto was engaged with Kondo Rokurobei. Kibei insisted on aiding Iemon; and Iemon did not dare to refuse his services in donning the *haori*. As he adjusted the awkward efforts of Kibei on one side, this amateur valet made a mess of it on the other. Besides, neither of them was any too steady on his feet. Then Kondo and Iemon set out in the rain. "*Sayonara! Sayonara!*"

The Plot Against O'Iwa

The following morning Iemon sat brooding, mind and tongue clouded by the drinking bout of the previous night. O'Iwa silently busied herself with his renovation. Rokurobei had delivered him over to her, decidedly the worse for wine and wear. He was somewhat astonished at the young man's easy discomfiture. Middle age with the Nipponese usually means the seasoned and steady toper. Regarding the matter as partly due to her own fault, and reassured by Kondo as to the events of the evening, O'Iwa heated the *sake* with all the greater care, serving it herself, chatting on the indifferent gossip of the neighbourhood. She spoke of the talk current as to Ito Kwaiba's adoption of an heir. "This man Kibei, his disposition appears to be as ugly as his face." With a little smile she added, "for the latter compensation is to be found in the first-named quality; a truth which he seems to disregard. What will become of O'Hana San?" For the first time since the night before the thought of the letter flashed into Iemon's mind. He put down the renovating morning draft, and on some excuse arose. His *kimono* lay neatly folded in the *hirabuta* (flat tray). Hastily he searched the sleeves. There was not a sign of the missive. With clouded brow he returned to the sitting room. A glance at O'Iwa made him feel ashamed. It had never come into her hands. He knew her well enough to be assured that he would have found it, scrupulously laid together with the tobacco pouch, nose wipe (*hanagami*), and divers other minor articles of daily use carried on the person. The whole affair perhaps was a dream. The more he considered, the more he became so convinced. His transports with O'Hana, their surprise, Kondo's rebuke – so far the evening was tolerably clear. It was only as to the final cups, the rising to depart, the standing in the cold night air, that the exact course of events became clouded. "Ah! It was all a vision. O'Hana never would have been so imprudent." There was a trace of doubt in his mind. He would clear it up at the fountain source – at Kwaiba's house and by the lips of O'Hana.

Kwaiba greeted him with almost boisterous cheerfulness. "Ah! Tamiya comes early; a flattering acknowledgment of last night's reception." To Iemon's deprecatory speech and apology – "Don't talk folly, after the manner of a country boor. Iemon San is a man of the world; and will give this Kwaiba credit for being the same. What does it amount to? A matter of a little too much wine.... Hana! Hana! The Master of Tamiya is present. Cut some bean paste, and bring tea. Heat the wine. Matazaemon was so sober an old dog that it is doubtful whether O'Iwa knows aught about the best remedy for past drinking." As Kibei entered – "There is the inventory of the Shimosa farms. Condescend to take a glance at the report of the *nanushi* (bailiff). Hana will aid." Thus dismissed, the two left the room. Kwaiba turned to Iemon – "A draught: no? Then Kwaiba will drink for both. For him it is a day of rejoicing. The coming of Tamiya is opportune. It was intended to send for him. Deign to aid this Kwaiba with counsel. The adoption of Kibei has finally been settled." The old man's exultation influenced even the indifference of Iemon's aching head. With well-simulated interest he said – "Naruhodo! Kibei Dono is indeed to be congratulated. As to our chief, since everything is to his satisfaction, Iemon is but too glad to speak his pleasure, to offer his congratulations." – "Nay! A little more than that, Iemon Uji. This Kwaiba would seek his aid in another matter of importance. Kwaiba is old. A woman no longer is an object to him. He cannot make a child. If O'Hana should give birth to a child great would be the discomfiture, knowing the truth. What is to be done in such a case?" He now was looking with direct inquiry into the face of

Iemon. The latter was much confused. He stammered – "Just so: so indeed. O'Hana San is truly an embarrassment. Doubtless she is also an obstacle to Kibei Dono. She...." Sneered Kwaiba – "Tamiya, though young, is wise. He grasps the situation at once. Deign, Iemon San, to take O'Hana yourself." Kwaiba raised his voice a little. Kibei brought O'Hana with him from the next room. She seemed alarmed and embarrassed. Said Kwaiba – "What have you there; the inventory? Ah! A letter: and there is no one to read a letter like Iemon San. Deign, Sir, to favour us. Iemon San alone can give the contents the proper inflection." He handed it to Iemon. A glance showed the latter that it was a letter from O'Hana, probably that of the previous night. His pocket had been neatly picked by Kibei. It was plain. He had been trapped. The pretended entertainment had been a plot in which the passion of O'Hana had been given full chance to range. Even the disinterested witness, the old fool Kondo, had been provided. He caught a curious, mocking smile on the face of the girl O'Moto, just then passing along the *rōka*.

Kwaiba allowed the silence to become oppressive. He seemed to await an incriminating outburst on the part of O'Hana, plainly on the verge of tears. However, the girl caught herself up. Instead she turned a calm, inquiring look toward the three men. Iemon alone looked down, his gaze on the letter the characters of which danced and waved before his eyes. Sharp as he ordinarily was, before this vigorous and astute old man, backed by the ruffianly prospective son with impertinent smile, the cowardice of Iemon deprived him of all spirit. His faculties were numbed. Kwaiba leaned over and removed the letter from his hands. "Since Iemon San will not read the letter, Kwaiba will try to do so; a poor substitute for the accomplished cleric." The old fellow seemed to know everything, as the tone of contempt indicated. He ran the scroll out in his hands – "Naruhodo! Ma! Ma! What's this? From some woman: a lascivious jade indeed!... Eh! Kibei Dono, apology is due your ears. This Kwaiba laughed at your suspicions." He threw down the scroll, as in a fury. Kibei picked it up. He began to read:

> *"Night is the source of pleasure, but greater that pleasure at sight of Iemon. The day comes when Iemon and Hana will be husband and wife, in fact if not in form. 'Ah! Day and night to be at the service of Iemon.' Thus does Hana pray gods and Buddhas. When distant from his side, even though the time be short, painful is its passage. Place this letter next to your very person. May that night come quickly, when the coming of Iemon is awaited. The connection with O'Iwa San is the punishment for sin committed in a previous existence. Condescend to dismiss her from your mind. View the matter wholly in this light. The spiteful brush (pen) refuses further service. Hard, hard, is the lot of this Hana. The honoured Master comes; the heartfelt wish is accomplished.*
>
> *With compliments,*
> *To Iemon Sama."*
> *Hana*

Kwaiba's rage grew and grew with the reading. At Iemon's name he sprang up and made a movement toward the stand on which reposed his swords. Laying a hand on the larger weapon he turned with a scowl – "Ah! This Kwaiba is old, but in vigour he is young. It is for Kwaiba to sport with the women. They are not to make a fool of him." Kibei sharply interposed. "Does Kwaiba Dono gain satisfaction by such a vengeance? To Kibei it seems a poor one. A matter so easily to be settled is not to be made a scandal in the ward. Deign, honoured Sir, so to regard it. To punish both at once with death is proper. But is it expedient? Condescend to hear the words of Kibei."

Kwaiba pulled himself up. It was as if someone had dragged him back. His rage departed. A cold malice took its place. He smiled blandly – "One does not quarrel over a harlot. Kwaiba spares their lives. Iemon shall take Hana home – as wife." – "As wife!" Iemon broke through his fear. "Surely the honoured *Kashira* is unreasonable. This Iemon is but the *muko* of Tamiya. To demand that O'Iwa San be discarded is going too far. Positively in this matter, though there have been love passages, the most intimate relation has never followed – now or in previous relations." – "You lie!" said Kwaiba coldly. "Furthermore 'Tis a matter not passing the period of last night. But that is not to the point. Against Matazaemon this Kwaiba has a grudge – as yet unsatisfied. Through O'Iwa San this shall be paid. With Iemon no harsh measures are adopted. Nay; Kwaiba comes to his aid. You, too, Kibei, shall assist.... Ah! For the ready consent, thanks. Ma! A delicious revenge is that gathered by Kwaiba. O'Hana the harlot takes the place of the Ojosan. And she loves Iemon! In our feasts Natsume and Imaizumi get the skin of the omelet; Iemon the centre. Then O'Iwa is to be driven out. To that Tamiya cannot object. He substitutes honey for garlic; O'Hana the flower for the ugly toad O'Iwa. Splendid! Splendid! But how? Ah! Here's Kondo, just in the nick of time. Rokurobei, aid us with your experience and influence. Aid us with Iemon, who would cleave to the O'Bake."

Put in possession of the facts Kondo was aghast. He had come to the parting of the ways; and under conditions which assured his participation in the plot. At first he turned on Iemon with bitter recrimination. "Oh! A virtuous fellow, who would drink a man's wine, lie with his woman, and then preach morality to a household! But the mischief is done. If not the paramour of O'Hana San, everybody believes it to be so...." Kwaiba held up his hands in well-simulated anger. Kibei and Rokurobei interfered. Iemon's last resistance was broken down. To talk? That is the business of a priest. Soon he was as eagerly engaged in the plot as if he had left the house in Samoncho for that purpose. Said Rokurobei – "What difficulty does the matter present? Set on Watanabe Goro to tempt and make love to O'Iwa. He is badly in debt. The handsome man of the ward everyone would suspect her fall. Surprised by Iemon, O'Iwa is driven out as unchaste. This Kondo stipulates that matters go no further. After all O'Iwa is innocent of offence. The husband's full rights are not to be excused. Neither she, nor Watanabe is to suffer injury."

Kibei laughed outright at the idea of a drawn sword in Iemon's hand. Iemon turned the contempt on to Kondo. Sneering, he replied – "The plan is worthless. O'Iwa is chastity itself. In the absence of this Iemon no man is allowed entrance to the house." Kwaiba knitted his brows – "Kakusuke! Kakusuke!" As the *chūgen* appeared – "Go yonder to the house of Akiyama Chozaemon San. Say that the Kumi-gashira would speak with Akiyama San." As the man departed – "Chozaemon is the man. For gossip and malice he is a very woman. Rejoice and he weeps; weep and he rejoices. If Akiyama cannot concoct some plan to get rid of O'Iwa, then no one can.... Alas! O'Hana and Iemon must die by the hand of this Kwaiba. Kibei will give his aid." The old man and Kibei got much enjoyment out of the cowardice of Iemon and the fright of O'Hana. But not for long. Akiyama Chozaemon, the one-time boy lover of O'Iwa; a long, lean, hungry-looking man, with long, cadaverous face and a decidedly bad eye, appeared with the *chūgen* Kakusuke close behind. The latter seemed a sort of policeman attending the none-too-willing Chozaemon. The latter's brow lightened at sight of the company. He owed Kwaiba money. Sending away the servant, Kwaiba unfolded the situation. Said Chozaemon – "Heigh! Tamiya takes the cast off leman of Ito Dono. Fair exchange is no robbery; Kibei Uji against O'Hana San. Iemon San goes into the matter with eyes wide open. The lady is an old intimate, it is said." This manner of approaching the subject was Chozaemon's way. He cared nothing for the scowls of Kibei nor the wrath of Kwaiba. He was needed, or they would not have called him to counsel. As for Iemon, he was grateful to Chozaemon; as neighbour, and for the insult to Kibei and Kwaiba.

Continued the mediator – "The obstacle of course is the O'Bake. O'Iwa is to be driven out. And Watanabe won't answer? Maa! Chastity in an O'Bake! It is a thing unheard of. 'Tis such, once of womankind, who seduce living men. Tamiya is now head of the House. O'Iwa once driven out, the property remains in his hands as its representative. She must be forced to leave of her own will. Good; very good. What is it worth to Kwaiba Dono?" – "Look to Iemon for commission," said Kwaiba roughly. "Nay! Nay!" mouthed Chozaemon. "Kwaiba is Kwaiba; Iemon is Iemon. The two are to be settled with separately. If Kwaiba Dono had gone to extremes at the start no question would have been raised. To do so now, with all present and after discussion, is out of the question. Kwaiba Dono wishes to adopt Kibei Uji; to get rid of O'Hana San. Iemon San has been neatly trapped. He must consent. O'Hana is a woman. She has no voice in the matter. All this is clear. But as to Chozaemon's labour in the affair; that it is which interests this Akiyama." He gave a sour reprimanding look at Kibei. Then he looked impertinently from Kwaiba to Iemon, and from Iemon to Kwaiba. Iemon in delight nodded assent. Chozaemon promptly turned his back on him and faced Kwaiba. At first the old man was very angry at the acuteness of Chozaemon. The sharp, free exposure did not please him. Then the idea of countering on this acuteness made him good tempered. He grumbled – "The ten *ryō* owing to Kwaiba at the New Year – principal and interest; such is the fee for a successful issue." Chozaemon held up his hands in pretended horror – "Pay back borrowed money! Is that expected by the Kumi-gashira?" – "Not 'expected,'" put in Kwaiba promptly. "With the seal of Akiyama San the return is assured." Chozaemon became thoughtful – "It is true. The last loan was under seal.... Too bad.... Well! Well! The conditions are hard. Submission is necessary. The debt will be forgiven?" – "Kibei and Iemon stand as witnesses," replied Kwaiba – "Then how is this?" said Chozaemon. All put their heads together. Akiyama Chozaemon went into details. Kwaiba pushed back his cushion; slapped his thighs. "Chozaemon, you are cheap at double the money. Just the thing! Eh, Iemon, Uji? Eh, Muko San?" All grinned a raptured assent.

The Plot Develops

For two days Iemon was maturing the preliminaries. He seemed unwell and out of sorts. The third day he did not get up at all. O'Iwa was properly anxious. Said she – "The change in the year is a sickly season. Condescend to take some drug. Allow Suian Sensei to be summoned." Iemon grumbled a dissent. She went on in her enthusiasm – "He is the very prince of doctors. See: here is a salve he recommends; for skin and nerves. O'Hana San, the beautiful concubine of Ito Sama, uses nothing else. He guarantees it on her praise, as means to remove blemishes of any kind or source." Iemon looked up quickly. The connection puzzled and did not please him. Perhaps he noted a puffiness about O'Iwa's face, remembered a repulsion toward marital usages. The women should leave the men to play their own game. He said gruffly – "Suian! A dealer in cosmetics and charms. Have naught to do with his plasters and potions; as cheats or something worse. As for O'Iwa, she is black as a farm hand from Ryukyu (Loo-choo). O'Hana is fair as the white *kiku*. Can the pastes of Suian Sensei change black to white?" Startled, O'Iwa looked round from the glass into which she was peering. She was taken by surprise. In their personal relations Iemon had always been more than considerate. For some weeks in secret she had been using this drug of Suian Sensei. In childhood O'Iwa had shown something of an epileptic tendency. This had worn off with time. Of late the recurrence had alarmed her. The drug of Suian, at the time anyhow, made her less conscious of the alarmed critical feeling which heralded the inception of the attacks.

Iemon gave her but time to catch the meaning of his insult. He went on – "Probably it is but a cold. Some eggs, with plenty of hot wine, will obviate ill effects. Deign to see that they are prepared." The channel of O'Iwa's thoughts changed. At once she was the housekeeper and nurse, and all solicitude to make him at ease. In the course of the meal of eggs with *sake* in came Natsume Kyuzo and Imaizumi Jinzaemon. "Ah! Iemon, pardon the intrusion. Probably the engagement of yesterday with Kwaiba Sama was forgotten.... In bed! A cold? But such is no treatment for the complaint. There should be a cheerful, lively atmosphere.... Ah! Here is the dice box. One can shake dice as well lying down as sitting. Deign to refresh the spirits with play as well as wine." Iemon saw to it that both were available. With surprise at first, misgiving afterwards, O'Iwa heated bottle after bottle of *sake*. The men did not pay the slightest attention to her presence. Absorbed in their game, there was but a rough call from time to time for wine, addressed to the air, a servant, anybody. At the end of the play Natsume rose to leave in high spirits. Imaizumi and Tamiya were correspondingly depressed. This was but a first day's procedure. Day after day, for the space of half the month, the play was repeated. Iemon had long since recovered. One day he stood with his hands shoved into the folds of his sash. He was very sober and sour. "Iwa, is there money in the house?" She looked at him in surprise. "Matters have not turned out at all well with Kyuzo and Jinzaemon. This Iemon is a hundred *ryō* to the bad. With spare cash at hand an attempt can be made to repair the loss."

O'Iwa prostrated herself before him. "May the Danna deign to consider. To Iwa this pastime of gambling seems a very ill one, particularly in a man of official rank. It is fraught with peril; and the offence once known rarely is pardoned. Condescend to hear and forgive the warning of this Iwa." She stopped a little frightened. Iemon was looking at her in greatest wrath and astonishment. "What! Is there argument from wife to husband? This insolence of behaviour crowns the insult of refusal. The very sight of your face is enough to make one sick at the stomach. Boors and *bakemono* are shut out at the Hakone barrier. But you – the guards have been put to sleep, and you have slipped through. Shut up! Get the money, or...." O'Iwa crouched at the *shōji*, in terror and surprise. The insulting words heaped on her pained and tortured. Now she felt the sharp sting of a hand forcibly applied to her cheek. Without a word she left the room. Returning she brought thirty *ryō* in gold on a salver. Timidly prostrate she presented it to Iemon. "Condescend to pardon Iwa. That she is ugly and incompetent she knows. Did not Iemon accept her?" The man stuffed the gold in his girdle. In reply – "No: Iemon was cheated by Kondo and Chobei. A plain woman – perhaps; but a monster, a worse than *rokurokubi*, was never thought of even in a dream. Compensation is to be found. Iemon likes gambling. He will gamble. Have a care to supply the needed funds; and don't interfere." Roughly he shoved her out of the way, and left the house.

For long O'Iwa saw nothing of Iemon; but she heard from him. In fact he was living in semi-secrecy at the house of Rokurobei. Now this messenger, then that, would come to O'Iwa. "If there is no money – sell something. The bearer will indicate. A supply must be found." Thus one thing after another left the house – to be stored in the godown of Kondo Rokurobei, to whose clever suggestion was due this way of stripping O'Iwa of all she possessed. With goods and clothes went the servants. In the course of a few weeks O'Iwa was living in one room, furnished with three *tatami* in lieu of the usual twelve in number. Hibachi, *andon* (night lamp), the single garment she wore, this was all she possessed in the house. Then at last she saw him. The light dawned on a cold snowy morning of early March. O'Iwa rose, opened the *amado*, and started her day. About the fourth hour (9 am) the *shōji* were pushed aside and Iemon entered. He looked as if fresh from a night's debauch. His garments were dirty and disordered. His face was sallow, the eyes deep set and weary, his manner listless. O'Iwa gave him the only cushion in the room. Seated before the *hibachi* (brazier) after some time he said – "A million pardons: the luck has been very bad.... Ah! The place here seems in disorder. It is not fit for a man to live in." He looked around as one waking from a dream. "No wonder: yet all can be restored. Iemon has surprised you?" Said O'Iwa timidly – "Matters are a little at odds and ends. O'Iwa needs but little; a stalk of *daikon* (radish) and a handful of wheat (*mugi*). Does the Danna remain here? If so...." There was a painful hitch in her voice, a puzzled look on her face. She had one *bu* in cash. In fact she was hoping for the monthly visit of Yosuke the farmer; if there was a farm any longer. She did not know.

"For the night," replied Iemon. "Sleep and food are the essentials of good play. All has been lost in the gambling houses of Shinjuku and Shinagawa, at the Nakanocho. Is there no money in the house?... Evidently not. Deign to secure some, no matter how." He took the silver *bu* she presented to him. "At least a bath and tobacco can be had. See to it that a meal is ready at even; not much, *sashimi* (sliced raw fish) and wine. Iemon would play, not eat." With this he rose. O'Iwa heard the sound of the closing gate. Long she remained, her face buried in her knees. In this gloomy situation what was she to do? She looked around. There was not a thing to sell; not even herself. Who would buy the ugly O'Iwa? An idea came into her head. In a moment she was in the street. Soon she stood at the door of her uncle, Yoemon. With this uncle and aunt she had but little to do. Matazaemon had been at daggers drawn with his brother, whom he accused of being a wretched miser, one acquiring wealth by very questionable means for a *samurai*. In old days Chobei had been a hired agent of Yoemon. The principal had escaped; the second had to leave Yotsuya and its neighbourhood. The Obasan (aunt) came out at O'Iwa's call. She greeted her niece with surprise. "Oya! Oya! Iwa is a stranger to this house. It has been heard that a splendid*muko* was received at Tamiya." The old woman looked at O'Iwa shrewdly, and not without kindness. O'Iwa took heart. She made answer – "It is true; of late matters have not gone well. Just now Iwa would ask the loan of a *shō* (1/5 peck) of rice, together with a *bu* to buy eels or *sashimi*. It is very rude indeed...." – "Very rude indeed!" said a harsh voice close by. O'Iwa shrank to the outer part of the doorway. The aunt fled to the inner part of the house. Continued Yoemon – "And what is Iwa doing at the house of Yoemon? That there is relationship between them this Yoemon does not recognize. Yoemon never exchanged look or word with his brother Matazaemon, nor does he desire to do so with the issue. Let the Tamiya of Samoncho look out for itself. A *muko* was taken without aid or advice of Yoemon. A stranger, one practising wayside divination, this fine fellow turns out a gambler and a debauched man, to the ruin of the House. Iwa can look to him; ignorant and foolish woman that she is. This Yoemon would contribute to the needs of a beggar before granting even a single *mon* to Iwa."

The grating rattled sharply as the angry old man pushed it to and let fall the bar. O'Iwa looked into the dark recess with pained and startled eyes. So much of a recluse she was learning that Iemon had long been the talk of the ward. She turned, and slowly took her way back to Samoncho. Here the reaction came. Strong was the inclination to laugh and weep; too strong for self-control. In alarm she ran to take from the closet the potion of Suian. Its effect was the opposite of what she expected – or perhaps it was taken too late. For an hour O'Iwa writhed, screamed, laughed in her agony. Then she sank into slumber. On awakening the sun was already well past the zenith. She sprang up in alarm. This meal to prepare – the duty of the wife – and not a step taken. It could not be helped. Just as she was, twisting a towel around her disordered hair, she started out to the place of one Kuraya Jibei of the Asakusa Kuramae no Saka. This man was a lender on the notes from the rice pensions of the *samurai* – a *fudasashi* dealer, as these men were called.

The distance was great. O'Iwa was tired out on her arrival. At the entrance the *kozō* or "boy" hailed her sharply. He waved her off. "No! No! Old girl, it won't do. Nothing is to be had here. Please come back the day before yesterday." He barred the way. Said O'Iwa, shrinking back – "Nothing is wanted of the honoured house. An interview with Jibei San, an inquiry to make. Such the request." Something about tone or manner, certainly not pity, made the fellow hesitate – "Jibei San! A beggar woman wants an interview with Jibei San! How about it?" – "Nothing to be had," answered the *bantō's* voice. "Tell her to read the white tablet hung before the entrance. It is all the house has to give." In speaking he edged around a little. O'Iwa raised the towel from her face. At once he was on his feet. "Ah! For long the honoured lady of Tamiya has not been seen. Many and profitable the dealings with Matazaemon Dono. Condescend to pardon this senseless fellow. He outrivals his companions in lack of brains. Deign to enter." The *kozō* was all apology – "Condescend wholly to pardon. Deign to have pity on the ignorance shown. With fear and respect...." Looking into O'Iwa's face he was overcome by his feelings. Bursting with laughter he fled to the front of the shop to stuff the dust rag into his mouth in mistake for a towel. This slight error restored his equanimity. The *bantō* looked after him with some fellow feeling and much anger. "He is half idiot. Condescend to disregard his rude speech and manner. After all he is but a *kozō*.... What can this Jibei do for the lady of Tamiya?"

"Knowing that the House has dealings with Jibei San, and there being necessity for three *shō* of rice, it is ventured to ask the loan." Thus spoke O'Iwa. Money, actual coin, was on the end of her tongue, but somehow she could not get the words out. Jibei was not particularly astonished. Since Iemon had taken charge of the affairs of Tamiya, its income was usually discounted well beforehand. Moreover, the rumour of Iemon's gambling was spreading among his connections. Neither Kwaiba nor Akiyama, nor the others engaged, were men to lose sight of the likelihood of fine pickings from the Tamiya. Jibei made prompt answer. "Respectfully heard and understood. It shall be sent.... Ah! It is required now? Matsu! Matsu! Put up three *shō* of rice for the lady of Tamiya. Its conveyance is to be provided. Place a *bu* in the parcel. The distance to Yotsuya is great. The *kago* (litter) men are exacting." O'Iwa's heart leaped with gratitude at the perspicacity of Jibei. He watched her departing figure as far as he could see it. Then he took out a ledger; and against the name of Tamiya he placed a question mark.

It was dusk when O'Iwa entered the house at Samoncho. She gave a start on finding Iemon glumly seated before the fireless brazier. "A fine hour for a woman to be gadding the street. And the meal! Unprepared: excellent habits in a wife!" "To the Danna apology is due. This Iwa is much in the wrong. But for the meal money had first to be secured...." – "Then there is money, or means to procure it? Where is it? How much?" – "Nay, the rice is here. This *bu* is enough to secure eels, *sashimi*, some delicacy...." She hesitated before Iemon's doubting glare. He was eyeing rice and money. The mark on the bag caught his eye. "Whence was this rice had? And this money? From Jibei, the *fudasashi* dealer? A visit paid in such garb? Truly the House is disgraced, not only by your ugliness, but by ill conduct. Who could remain in such a den?" O'Iwa threw herself in his way as he rose to leave the room. Clinging to his sleeve she pleaded for pardon, as only a woman can do who has done no wrong. There was an ugly look on Iemon's face as he turned on her. Frightened, she would have fled. Instead she could only crouch like a dog under the blows he showered on her. Then with a violent kick in the groin he rolled her over, and departed.

O'Iwa heard footsteps. Had Iemon returned? Despite the pain, she half sat up in her dread. Kondo Rokurobei appeared. The portly man held up his hands in horror and benevolence at what he saw. "But O'Iwa – what has occurred? Ah! Kondo has heard rumours of what is going on. The *tatami* (mats), screens, drawers (*tansu*), clothes-baskets – the house is completely stripped to satisfy the thirst for the money of others. Now he has descended to blows! Truly he is a miserable fellow." Kondo's voice grew loud in his wrath. "This must not go on. Rokurobei is responsible to Tamiya, to the ancestors. To be subject to a fellow like this will never do. A divorce is to be secured. Let him depart with his plunder. Let him have everything; only to get rid of him. He is husband, and head of Tamiya. But Kondo will be too much for him. A divorce shall be secured. Ito Dono, the ward chief, is to be interested in the affair. Pressure shall be put on Iemon to grant the letter of divorce." Indignation choked the worthy man. O'Iwa spoke slowly, with pain and effort. "Be in no such haste, Kondo Sama. Iemon has not been a good man. Much is known to this Iwa. He buys women at Nakacho. He buys *geisha*. He gambles. These are a man's vices. As to these Iwa has nothing to say. She is the wife, for two lives to maintain the house in good and ill fortune. A good wife does not look to divorce to rectify mistakes. With such remedy Iwa has nothing to do. But is not Kondo Sama the *nakōdo*? Was he not the mediator in the marriage between Iemon and Iwa? Deign to speak as *nakōdo*. Rebuke Iemon. Cause this gambling to be brought to an end." Rokurobei could hardly hear her to the end. His testy impatience was in evidence. He broke into protest – "This is complete madness; utter folly. You allow this fellow to ruin the House. He will dispose of the pension." – "The goods, the House, Iwa, all belong to Iemon; to do with as he pleases. Iwa is the wife. She must submit.... Ah! You refuse. Kondo Sama is no longer the friend of Iwa, to act as *nakōdo*." What had come into the soul of this gentle woman? Kondo in fright shrank back from the look she gave him – "A very demon! The mother, O'Mino, has returned to life. Oni! Oni! You are not human. Kondo assuredly will have nothing to do with O'Iwa, or O'Iwa's affairs." He left her helpless in the middle of her fit. Forgetting in his fright even his clogs, barefooted, he fled from the house in Samoncho.

Kwaiba's Revenge

Kondo Rokurobei went direct to the council of the conspirators. He found them assembled in the house of Ito. Kwaiba, Iemon, O'Hana, Chozaemon, Kibei, were drinking *sake*. Kwaiba as usual was bragging over his prowess in youth extended into age. O'Hana was laughing at him behind his back. Kibei was surly; yet his share of income was assured. Kwaiba roundly berated Iemon for lack of energy. "O'Iwa has been allowed to get the upper hand. Iemon is far too soft to deal with a woman who has been spoiled all her life." Iemon listened in silence, with a rather doubtful smile of acquiescence or contempt. In fact, knowing O'Iwa as he did, he had little confidence in Kwaiba or Chozaemon, or the methods they proposed. His own plan was maturing. Meanwhile in part it ran parallel. On this assembly burst the discomfited Rokurobei – "Ah! What an experience! The woman is a very fiend. A new pair of *geta*, bought but yesterday, and left at your house, Iemon Uji." Iemon looked at Kondo's frightened face and bare feet. Then he burst into a roar of laughter. Kwaiba was indignant. "Is the fright of Kondo San any license to bring his dirty feet on the *tatami*. Deign, good sir, to accept water for the cleansing. O'Hana San now is inmate of the house of Kondo; yet condescend for the moment to act the mistress here." This was part of the arrangement. With the goods of O'Iwa the person of O'Hana had been transferred to the charge of the honest Rokurobei. There Iemon had easy and decent access to the use of both.

Said Iemon – "What happened after this Iemon left Samoncho? Kondo Dono has been frightened." Kondo puffed and fumed as he cleansed his feet at the mounting step. He groaned – "Iemon Dono, you are certainly done for. Was it 'three years,' she said? Her face was frightful. This Rokurobei has no more to do with the affair. He goes no more to Samoncho. Alas! He will never sleep again. Oh! Oh! To be haunted in the next existence by such a rotten O'Bake." Said Kwaiba – "Did Iemon really beat her? He says he did." Answered Kondo – "She could barely move a limb. Of love for Iemon not a spark is left; but she clings to the honour of Tamiya, to the wife's duty to the House. There is no moving her. Rokurobei is suspect, as not doing his duty as *nakōdo*. Look to yourselves. If she ever gets suspicious of the real facts, has an inkling of the truth – look out for yourselves."

Kwaiba was thoughtful; Iemon was indifferent. None of them could think of aught but the venture already engaged in. A week, ten days, passed. In that time every effort was made to move O'Iwa to consent to a divorce. As *Kumi-gashira*, Kwaiba summoned her to his house. Before his kindly sympathy O'Iwa melted into tears. The scandalous treatment of Iemon had reached his ears. Why had he not heard of it before it reached such extremes? He looked indignation at his messenger, the one who had brought O'Iwa to his presence, Akiyama Chozaemon the neighbour of Tamiya, living not far off near the Ten-o. Said the ward head – "Kwaiba always took this Iemon, or Kazuma, for a scoundrel. A stranger, why bring him into the ward? But now he is master of Tamiya. In the place of the excellent, if obstinate, Matazaemon. Alas! The pension of the House is said to be hypothecated for five years. And the household goods; and separate properties of Tamiya – all gone?" O'Iwa nodded assent, and Kwaiba threw up his hands at such wickedness. At all events he counselled her to consider matters, to accept his aid. He would place her somewhere; in the country and far off from the ward in which Iemon as master of Tamiya in its degradation would always be an unpleasant sight and influence in her life; at least until Iemon could be expelled. With the fellow's past career doubtless this would happen before long. Meanwhile O'Iwa was to pass into one of the wretched, overworked, exhausted drudges on one of Kwaiba's Shimosa farms. From his chief's expressed views Chozaemon dissented. This was the one man O'Iwa distrusted. He had always shown dislike to her. In defense of her conduct Chozaemon was too clever to show any warmth. He was the subordinate making exact report to his chief. O'Iwa was completely taken in. This friendly neutrality aroused her every grateful feeling. Said Chozaemon – "Iemon is a coward. A *samurai* beats neither woman nor dog. If either are unfaithful to him, he kills the offender. Iemon's conduct has been thoroughly bad. Before the reproaches of O'Iwa San, beaten in argument he has retaliated by beating her to a jelly. Her face bears the marks of his violence. As to her body, my wife answers for it that it is a mass of bruises." – "Is that so?" said Kwaiba in deep sympathy. O'Iwa burst into tears. Kwaiba fumed with rage – "Truly Iemon is not a human being. He has the horns of a demon."

Then the priest Myozen, of the family temple, the Myogyoji of Samegabashi, appeared at the Samoncho house. To him O'Iwa looked for ghostly consolation against the ills of this world. Instead he merely chanted the old refrain, harped on the scandal brought on Samoncho by the continued bickering of the married pair. Husband and wife had mutual duty toward each other; but also there was a duty toward their neighbours. Iemon was irreclaimable.... This stranger! O'Iwa San should deign to take the active part herself; not afford this ill spectacle and example to the ward. Like most parsons he was convinced by the noise of his own voice, and spoke with the intense conviction of long rehearsal. O'Iwa heard him out with a curious chill at heart. The graves of her beloved *hotoke* (departed ones) were in the cemetery of Myogyoji. The temple had been one of the few generous features, almost extravagances, of Matazaemon. It had profited greatly by his donations. It was the honour of the House against the argument of the priest and the convenience of the neighbours; and all because a bad man had been brought into it. "What the revered *oshō* (prebend) has said reaches to the heart of this Iwa. Submission is to be an inspiration from the revered *hotoke*. Iwa will seek their counsel." Baffled, the priest left the house; veiled censure was on his lips; open disobedience and contempt on the part of O'Iwa.

Said Kwaiba – "Chozaemon has failed. At least this Kwaiba has saved his ten *ryō* – and gained one object. Kondo Dono, thanks for your kind hospitality to O'Hana San. Do you propose to adopt her?" Kondo made an emphatic gesture of protest and dissent. He said – "At least Kondo has the security of goods and money for his generous expenditures." – "Both of them belonging to O'Iwa San; just as Kwaiba holds the acknowledgment of Akiyama San." Chozaemon made a wry face. The prospect of pressure put on him, with all the added accumulation of the months of interest, was not a cheerful one. Said Kwaiba angrily – "Ah! Whoever would have suspected such obstinacy in the O'Bake; she who always was so yielding within her home and outside of it. She seemed to be such an easy mark. It was merely a matter of ordering her out. And now she baffles this Kwaiba of his revenge!" Iemon laughed outright. Kwaiba looked at him with surprise. Was this charlatan playing a double game? Said Iemon – "Fear enters at the words of the honoured chief. Pray condescend to be easy in mind. As yet Chozaemon has not failed. At least the question can be argued with the *Kumi-gashira*. It is left to these principals. Iemon is of better counsel." Then after a silence during which Kwaiba intently eyed him – "Tomorrow O'Iwa San leaves Yotsuya. Kwaiba Dono gets his revenge on the late master of Tamiya. Pray remember it, in favour of the present incumbent of the House." Said Kwaiba fervently – "Iemon would be a son to Kwaiba! Is it really true – that the O'Bake will be expelled the ward, in disgrace?" Iemon nodded assent.

On the following day O'Iwa had completed her ablutions. She arrayed herself in freshly washed robes. Then she took her place before the Butsudan. It was memorial day of the decease of the *hotoke*. Earnestly she prayed – "Deign, honoured *hotoke*, to have regard to this Iwa. The year has not lapsed since the hand of Iwa was placed in that of Iemon. Now the House is brought to ruin. No heir appears to console this Iwa and to continue its worship, to inherit its revenues. 'Take these in hand. Life lies before Iemon for their enjoyment. His revenue will be ample. Deign but to have the honour of the House in mind, the continuance of its line as object.' Such were the words of the honoured Matazaemon when in life. Unworthy has been the conduct of this trust by Iemon. But divorce is a scandal, always to be avoided by a woman. Return the love of Iemon to this Iwa. Deign, honoured *hotoke*, to influence his wandering passions toward this child of the House. Cause the husband to return to Tamiya, once more to uphold its rights and influence. Such is the prayer of this Iwa." She rose, placed the offerings, and struck the little bell with the hammer. As she did so a noise was heard at the entrance. Iemon, carrying fishing rod and basket, and followed by Natsume Kyuzo and Imaizumi Jinzaemon, burst into the room. All three were more or less drunk. Dumfounded O'Iwa looked from one to the other. Imaizumi carried a tub. Kyuzo knocked it from his shoulders. Then tumbled clumsily down on the cask. None of them had removed the dirty *waraji* (straw sandals) they wore. "Why do so in such a barn?" hiccoughed Kyuzo. "And this *sake*; Kyuzo found it without, at the kitchen door. Jinzaemon shouldered it. Whence does it come, Iemon San? Faugh! It smells as if the cask had been placed for the convenience of passers-by on the wayside. It stinks. That's what it does." He gave the cask a kick, knocking out the bung. The filthy liquid poured out on the floor.

Iemon appropriated the tub. He seated himself on it. "'Tis the fine liquor of Tamiya. All the house possesses. Iemon is hungry." Opening his basket he took out an eel. He began to skin it. A cry from O'Iwa arrested him. His wife sank down before him in attitude of prayer. "Importunate jade! What would you now? Further advice to a husband who wants but to get rid of the sight of an ugly face? Bah! This lump of a wench is neither good for child-bearing nor for house-keeping; she is not even a good *rusu* (care-taker)." His knife made a rip in the skin of the squirming animal. O'Iwa laid a hand on his sleeve. With a voice in which sobs mingled with the petition – "Today is a memorial day of the honoured *Hotoke Sama*. Deign to refrain from taking life in the house; nay, before the very *ihai* in the Butsudan. Such deed will cause pain to the *Hotoke Sama*; bring disaster on the House, perhaps on this Iwa and Iemon San." Iemon fairly roared as he sprang up from the tub – "What! You noisy slut! Is this Iemon to go without food because the *hotoke* dislikes the smell of eels?... Jinzaemon, can you cook eels?" Imaizumi had sought the *rōka*. His round featureless face showed his fright and indecision before this critical quarrel of husband and wife. Of all involved in the plot he was the most unwilling in performance of his role. But he answered according to rote – "Iya! Iemon Uji, the office of cook is a special one. Jinzaemon is no cook. He leaves that office to his wife. Moreover the cooking of eels is an art in itself." – "And the artist is here," chimed in the malignancy of Kyuzo. "O'Iwa San is noted for her skill." – "Right!" said Iemon. "Kyuzo and Jinzaemon have heard the refusal of O'Iwa. Cook this eel – or else Iemon pronounces the formula of divorce against the disobedient wife."

In silence O'Iwa rose. She went to the portable stove. With the bellows she stirred up the fire therein. She did not dare even for a moment to pray at the Butsudan. The skillet was on the fire. The eels were sizzling in the hot liquor. Suddenly Iemon made an exclamation. Taking a towel he grasped the handle of the vessel. The next moment he had forced down the hot pan and its contents on the head of O'Iwa. "Kiya!" With the single cry she fell over backwards, writhing in pain under the infliction of the scalding mess streaming over face, neck, and bosom. Imaizumi fled in dismay. Even Natsume Kyuzo protested. Seizing the arm of Iemon – "Iemon Uji, you go too far. Don't kill her." "Kill the O'Bake? It's impossible." Iemon spoke coldly. He was the one person of collected wits in the room.

Groaning with agony O'Iwa came to her senses. A man was leaning over her. Half blind as she was, she could recognize Chobei. His look was grave. His voice was reticent and confused. "What has been going on here, O'Iwa Dono? Ah! Chobei comes at a bad season. Ma! Ma! The house, too; stripped bare to the very boards, and the season still wintry. Truly this Iemon is a beast – a very brute (*chikushō*). What is Chobei to do? There is this matter of the honour of Tamiya." He wrung his hands as in great perplexity, glancing sideways toward O'Iwa. The first part of his speech she disregarded. Such talk and consolation were growing stale. That all should pity her caused no surprise. Her situation was not unusual. It was the last words which caught her ear. "The honour of Tamiya: Chobei San?" Chobei turned away; to put some peppermint in his eyes. Tears stood in them as he turned again to her. O'Iwa was alarmed. "What has happened?" She caught his sleeve, drew close to him. He answered – "Chobei cannot speak. To find O'Iwa San in such dreadful state renders it impossible to explain. Iemon San has gone too far." So he had, from Chobei's point of view and for his purposes. These young fellows never can keep within bounds; even in abuse of a woman. His resentment was extreme. O'Iwa insisted. Finally the resistance of Chobei was overcome. Iemon's name was posted at the Kuramae of Asakusa. He was in debt on every side. As the final blow, he had stolen the seal of Ito Kwaiba and forged an acknowledgment for twenty *ryō*. Kwaiba's enmity to Matazaemon was well known. He liked Iemon no better, and would pursue him to the end, force him to cut belly, and accomplish the official degradation and extinction of the Tamiya House (*kaieki*). "What is to be done?" He turned squarely to O'Iwa. She said – "Ito Dono has been kind to O'Iwa. Perhaps if request be made...." Chobei laughed. "Ito Kwaiba is always kind to a woman. It is not O'Iwa San whom he hates. But this is an affair between men. He secures vengeance on Matazaemon through Iemon and this official extinction of Tamiya. It is too tempting. He is not to be trusted. No hint of the deed must reach him. Is there no money at the command of O'Iwa San? The sum is but twenty *ryō*. Iemon brought this news to Chobei last night. He leaves Edo, to go in hiding, after ... after ... punishing the ... Well! Well! He is a wicked man. Chobei never suspected such wickedness. But Iemon is not the issue. He represents and can disgrace the Tamiya. There lies the issue. Has O'Iwa San no means, nothing in coin?" – "Less than a *bu*, sixty *mon*." She held out the coppers to Chobei.

Said Chobei with decision – "There is one resource left. There is the person of O'Iwa San. Deign to go into service at the pleasure quarter. Chobei is skilful. In seven days these wounds can be healed. Twenty *ryō* secured, the paper is taken up, the robbery of the seal is never discovered. We can laugh at Kwaiba's anger. All is for the Tamiya." He noted that O'Iwa was hesitating – "It is but as a pledge. The money is advanced on the person of O'Iwa San. A week, ten days, and other sources of loan will be discovered. This is the only measure Chobei can suggest. He has no means of his own to meet this debt." He smiled as at a thought – "Perhaps Kwaiba himself will pay his own debt!" He chuckled at the idea. "Why not make appeal at once?" repeated O'Iwa, grasping at any straw of safety from this resource, so horrible to the *samurai* woman. Said Chobei promptly – "Ito Sama knows perfectly well the state of Samoncho. Asakusa, Honjo, are far removed. An appeal for twenty *ryō* as surety money in applying for a situation would appeal to him; the other would not. Besides, thus far away he could not investigate closely, if he would. He could but say 'yes' or 'no.'" O'Iwa remembered what Kwaiba had said – the necessity of removing to a distance. The words and actions of these rascals dove-tailed admirably. A long silence followed. With exultation at heart Chobei saw her rise. She put out the fire, gathered together the few personal articles she still possessed. On seeing her struggle with the heavy rain doors he came to her aid. "For the time being accept the hospitality of Chobei's poor quarters. These wounds are to be healed." With full heart O'Iwa gratefully accepted. She took his hand as if to kiss it. Chobei hastily snatched it away. In his sleeve, the ink not twenty-four hours old, was the paper of the sale of O'Iwa to Chobei; her passing over to his guardianship, to dispose of as a street harlot, a night-hawk. The consideration? Five *ryō*: payment duly acknowledged, and of course nominal. The paper of transfer was in thoroughly correct form. Chobei had drawn it himself.

The Yotaka (Night-Hawks) of Honjo

O'Iwa's stay of nearly seven days at Chobei's house was one of the golden periods of her life. O'Taki received the Ojosan with humble joy. Iemon could not drop Chobei out of his life of prosperity. O'Iwa was soon brought in contact with the humble pair in adversity. Hers was a generous heart, and O'Taki could not look around her house without some indication of this kindness. Her sympathy with the wronged wife was great. A husband – thriftless, a gambler, inconsiderate – of such a one she had some experience. By the same means this lady was brought to her present pass. It roused her indignation. As to brutality; that was another matter. She squared her stout shoulders and looked derisively at the loose angularity of Chobei, his rickety physique. But the storm would pass. Ito Sama, Kondo Sama, Myozen Osho, all these were agreed. The Ojosan now out of his reach, without a home to go to, and only hostile faces met with in the ward, Iemon Sama would soon come to terms. Would the Ojosan deign to honour their humble home as long as she liked. She at once suppressed O'Iwa's rather futile attempts to aid in her rough household work. It had been the lady's part to direct her maids in their more repugnant tasks, and now brought right under her hand in this plebeian household. O'Iwa never had undergone the harsher lot of her mother O'Mino.

Chobei in his way was as kind as his wife. At once he devoted himself to the repair of his property. When O'Iwa produced the paste and lotion of Suian Sensei, as sovereign for the complexion, Chobei took them, smelled and carefully tasted, and finally put some of the paste on the end of the *hashi* or sticks to arrange the charcoal in the *hibachi*. A smell of garlic pervaded the room. He noted the puffy face of O'Iwa, the unnatural, almost ghastly, white of the skin where the wide pockmarks permitted it to be seen. Within the circles of these scars there was a curious striated effect, only seen at times in the efforts of artists to depict the supernatural, or of savages to frighten their foes. It gave a drawn cadaverous look to the lower part of the face. "There is more in it than *that*," mused Chobei. During her stay O'Iwa had one of her attacks – of nerves – in fact a true epileptic seizure. Chobei put an embargo at once on all remedies but his own. Cynically, he added – "But elsewhere there will be no Chobei. If the Okusama deigns to apply the drugs of Suian Sensei where she now goes, doubtless she will find early relief. At present they spoil Chobei's efforts." The clever rascal at once recognized his fellow in Suian, bribed to render O'Iwa more hideous than Nature had made her, to take away her womanhood and hope of an heir to the Tamiya. To poison her? That he doubted; although the ignorance of leech and victim might readily lead to such result.

Within the seven days O'Iwa San once more could show herself in public. It was now Chobei's part to carry the plot to completion. Iemon, at the proposition, had said – "Sell her as a night-hawk! An ugly woman like that no one will approach." – "'Tis Chobei's trade," said the pimp coolly. "In Yoshidamachi they have noses – over night. Between dark and dawn the member melts, becomes distorted, and has to be made. It has served its purpose. This is Chobei's affair. Provided that O'Iwa never again troubles the presence of Iemon Sama the object is attained." – "That is true. Do what you please. Kill her, if desired. O'Iwa in the Yotsuya; and Chobei feels the wrath of Ito Dono, of this Iemon." Unwillingly he signed the contract required by Chobei. He gave the latter a fee of ten *ryō* for the excision of this excrescence, and with a sigh of joy learned of the disappearance in company of the pimp and O'Iwa. Within three days carpenters and other workmen swarmed over the Tamiya in Samoncho. The master made ready for his return.

O'Taki had gone forth on a mission for Chobei. This would insure her absence for the greater part of the day. Said Chobei – "Deign, Okusama, to allow Chobei to prove his art. All his accomplishments have not been displayed." To pass off the ugly woman at night could be done. He was compelled to act by daylight; though relying somewhat on the dusky interior of Toemon's entrance and reception room. This Toemon was the chief of the guild which bought and controlled these unfortunate street-walkers, lowest of their class. Chobei sat down before O'Iwa. As if in an actor's room he was surrounded with a battery of brushes and spatulas, pastes, paints of all shades of greys, flesh colour, pinks – even reds. Under his skilful hands O'Iwa was transformed. To make her beautiful was impossible. He made her passable. The weather was cold, though spring was now close at hand. Chobei hesitated. The walk was a long one. His handiwork might fade or melt under the sweating induced by effort. Besides he had no desire for conversation. There were to be as few answers to curious questions as possible. In his house he had left the two women to themselves, and saw O'Iwa only when O'Taki was present. So he called a *kago* and gave the necessary directions. As the coolies moved off with their fair burden he trotted along in the rear, his project occupying his busy mind.

The place of Toemon was at Yoshidacho Nichome, in the centre of the Warigesui district. To the north was the canal of that name. To the south a second canal ditto; the second stream was the larger, fairer, and more pretentious South Warigesui. An equal distance to the east was the Hoonji Bashi, with the great temple of that name just across the bounding river or canal of the district. As the *kago* bearers ambled down the bank of the North Warigesui, O'Iwa thought she had never seen a more filthy stream than this back-water with its stale current. The bearers put them down at the canal. Chobei had some directions to give during the short walk of a couple of hundred yards to their destination. Said he – "For a *samurai* woman to engage in this business is a serious offence. After all the matter is mere form; a pledge to secure the return of the sealed paper forged by the husband. The wife performs her highest duty in saving the honour of the House. Is not that true?" There was a little sob in O'Iwa's voice as she gave assent. She felt different now that she was close at hand to the scene and crisis of her trial. Continued Chobei – "The agreement has been made out as with O'Iwa, daughter of Kanemon, the younger brother of this Chobei and green-grocer of Abegawacho of Asakusa. Deign to remember that the twenty *ryō* is needed to save a father in peril of default and imprisonment." – "The cases are not so different," whispered O'Iwa. "Just so," said Chobei. "Here is the place. Condescend to wait a moment, here at the entrance." Briskly he entered the house. "A request to make!" – "Ah! Is it Chobei San? The Danna Sama is absent for the day, at the office of the ward magistrate. Some drunkard considers that he has been robbed. The girl he accused was punished – perhaps unjustly. All the women of this house are honest." – "Beyond repair," laughed Chobei. "However, the other matter has been agreed on. The girl is here. An uncontrollable jade! The master has deigned to aid Chobei. Thanks are felt. Since she will run with the men, it is as well for Kanemon to get the profit of the business. If she breaks out – put a ring in her nose, and treat her as the farmers treat their cattle. Don't let her again bother home or Chobei. She will lie – of course. At Toemon's they are used to lies?" The woman Matsu laughed – "No fear as to that." She looked over the contract with care. "Ah! She is sold for life service; otherwise the twenty *ryō* would be a scandalous price. Is that her?... Um! Not a likely jade. Stand a little in the light.... This Matsu would never have closed the bargain without a view. But Toemon San has left no choice. In the scarcity of women, and his good-will to Chobei San, he would pay any sum. At twenty *ryō* she is a gem! You can come up here. Take! Haru! A new girl. Take her in charge and show her the house and its ways.... Chobei San, some tea." Chobei put a word into this running comment and invitation. As the girls were leading off the hesitating O'Iwa he said loudly and roughly – "Remember to obey the Okamisan (wife) in everything. Whatever she commands is right and must be done: no nonsense. Ah! Something forgotten: a moment please." He drew O'Iwa aside, seeing that she was on the verge of tears. Speaking gently – "Be astonished at nothing; be ignorant of everything. The house of Toemon in Honjo is not the drawing room of Tamiya in Yotsuya. Deign to remember that Chobei must play his part. Life is like an excursion in a pleasure boat. There are rough places to pass, some danger, and much refuse to get rid of. Condescend to have House and husband in mind. It is but for a week – or so." – "And Iemon San, the House; they will be secure?" – "That Chobei is assured of. See: he has the twenty *ryō* in hand. It is mere matter of securing the compromising paper and the return of Iemon. Some negotiations are necessary for that. In the future his behaviour will be much improved." He clinked the coin before her. As O'Iwa passed up the stairs he returned to the *hibachi* of the wife. The tea was a short course. Chobei was on needles while drinking it. He feared an outbreak from above in the course of O'Iwa's initiation into a vileness the depth of which she never even could suspect. "Yes: trade is good. Women are difficult to secure. The men prefer to have them in their homes, rather than to gain by their service elsewhere." In such professional talk of a few moments he quickly dispatched the refreshment, climbed into his clogs, and departed. O'Iwa had disappeared far into the depths.

Toemon and his wife were quarrelling. Said the woman – "Are you mad, to pay twenty *ryō* for such an ugly wench? No choice was given. This Matsu was to receive her. Chobei is a cheat." Toemon and the *bantō* drew O'Iwa under the light, much as if she were a bag of rice – "The clever rascal! From crown of the head to neck she is all made up. And perhaps elsewhere." – "At all events she is a woman." The *bantō* spoke as in doubt. "Never mind: we are great artists, too, if not so good at cheating as this Chobei. Twenty-six years! She's forty at least.... What may be your honoured age?" – "Twenty-six years," replied the distressed O'Iwa. The wife threw up her hands – "And she does not lie!... Haru! Kota! It is time to go out. The bell already strikes the hour of the dog (7 pm). Take Iwa to the reception room (*yoseba*). She is to learn the ways of the place; where to entertain her guests.... Come! Along with all of you!" Some ten or fifteen women had gathered in their array for their night's campaign. Paint, powder, plaster, disguised the ravages of disease among the hardened set of this low class house. O'Iwa accompanied O'Haru to what had been called the *yoseba*. The girl explained to her. Here was the place to bring and entertain any guest picked up on the street. They were not the degraded wretches who made the darkness of an alleyway the reception room for their lovers. It was to be remembered that the wine drunk not only profited the house, but paid in commissions for their own cosmetics and other little gratifications. On entering the place O'Iwa shrank back to the wall in horror; to shrink away in turn from the filth and obscenity to be seen on that support. She would have fled, but the entering crowd pressed her further in. It was a long room. The entrance formed a sort of parlour or place to sit. The rest of the apartment was divided longitudinally into little cubicula, rooms of the space of the one dirty mat with which each was furnished. A shelf contained its cynically filthy and suggestive furniture.

O'Iwa's disgust and terror was too obvious. O'Haru held on to her arm to prevent flight. The attention of the others was drawn to them. "Does the beauty want an apartment to herself? That is the privilege of the Oiran, the Go Tayu, the Kashiku. Ah! Sister dear; it is to be learned that this place is Hell – First Block. There is no 'second block' (nichome). One gets used to anything here; even to use a demon's horns for toothpicks." Thus spoke a hard-faced woman of some thirty odd, by her looks. Said the frightened O'Iwa in low tones – "Iwa has not come for this service. She is but a pledge. This redeemed, within the week she returns to her home. This place upsets one's stomach." Those present laughed loudly. "We all say that. The real reason for our coming is not to be told. Be assured that you must perform the service, or suffer. Condescend not to fall into the hands of the Okamisan. In anger she is terrible." There was a general movement of the women. Said O'Haru, drawing along O'Iwa by the hand – "Come! Make no trouble. A newcomer, you are sure to be successful and please Matsu Dono." O'Iwa resolutely held back. No matter what the suffering she would undergo it. Ah! A week in this place indeed was to be life in Hell. She called up the sight of the dismantled house, the figure of her grandfather, anything to strengthen her will to resist. O'Haru left the room. "Okamisan, the new girl refuses to serve. Haru makes report." The wife of Toemon leaped up from her cushion. Dressed in night clothes, a long pipe in hand, she rushed into the room. "What nonsense is this? Which slut is it that refuses the service of the house?... You! The ink on the receipt for twenty *ryō* paid for your ugly face and body is hardly dry.... Pledge? A week's service? You lie: as your uncle said you would lie. You are here for life service as a street harlot. Out with you!... No? No?" She was about to throw herself on O'Iwa, to cast her into the street. Then her passion, to outward appearance, cooled. She was the woman of her business, malevolent and without pity. "O'Kin! O'Kin!" The others now gathered around O'Iwa. O'Haru and the girl O'Take plead with her to obey. They tried to hustle her off by force. Said O'Haru – "Report had to be made. This Haru acted for the best. Truly such obstinacy deserves punishment. But Haru is filled with pity. Deign to obey. Go forth to the service. The result of refusal is terrible." O'Iwa shook her head – "O'Haru San is free from blame. Iwa is grateful for the kind words. To go out to this service is impossible." The woman O'Kin strode into the room; a big, strapping wench, and the understudy of O'Matsu in her husband's affections. "A new recruit?" She spoke in inquiry – "Yes: and obstinate. It is a matter of punishment in the *semeba*.... Now! Out with you all! No dawdling!" The irate woman turned on her flock. They fled like sheep into the open.

The Punishment

O'Iwa did not move. The two women approached and laid hands on her. Her yielding made no difference in the roughness of their treatment. Dragged, hustled, shoved, with amplitude of blows, she was already much bruised on reaching the place of punishment – the *semeba*, to use the technical term of these establishments "for the good of the community." During a temporary absence of the mistress, a ray of kindliness seemed to touch the woman O'Kin. She pointed to the square of some six feet, to the rings fastened in the rafters. "Don't carry self-will to extremes. Here you are to be stripped, hauled up to those rings, and beaten until the bow breaks. Look at it and take warning. Kin is no weakling." She shoved back her sleeve, showing an arm as hard and brawny as that of a stevedore. With disapproval she observed O'Iwa. The latter stood unresisting, eyes on the ground. Only the lips twitched from time to time. As the only person in the house, male or female, not to fear the Okamisan, O'Kin could only put down the courage to ignorance. She shrugged her shoulders with contempt. "A man would cause you no pain. The same cannot be said of Kin. You shall have the proof." Perhaps severity would be more merciful, by quickly breaking down this obstinacy.

The wife returned with the instrument of torture, a bow of bamboo wound with rattan to strengthen it. O'Kin took it, ostentatiously bent and displayed its stinging flexibility before the eyes of O'Iwa. The latter closed them. She would cut off all temptation to weakness. At a sign O'Kin roughly tore off the *obi*. A twist, and the torn and disordered *kimono* of O'Iwa fell to her feet with the skirt. She had no shirt. Thus she was left completely naked. In modesty she sank crouching on the ground. The cold wind of the March night made her shiver as O'Kin roped her wrists. Again the woman whispered her counsel in her ear – "When you get enough, say 'Un! Un!'" Detecting no sign of consent she took a ladder, climbed up, and passed the ropes through the rings above. She descended, and the two women began to haul away. Gradually O'Iwa was raised from the sitting posture to her full height of extended arms, until by effort her toes could just reach the ground. In this painful position the slightest twist to relieve the strain on the wrists caused agonizing pains through the whole body. "Still obstinate – strike!" shouted the wife. O'Kin raised the bow and delivered the blow with full force across the buttocks. A red streak appeared. O'Iwa by a natural contortion raised her legs. The blows descended fast, followed at once by the raised welt of flesh, or the blood from the lacerated tissue. Across the shoulder blades, the small of the back, the buttocks, the belly, they descended with the full force of the robust arms and weight of O'Kin. Every time the legs were raised at the shock the suspended body spun round. Every time the toes rested on the ground the bow descended with merciless ferocity. The sight of the torture roused the fierce spirit in the tormentors. O'Kin redoubled the violence of her blows, seeking out the hams and the withers, the shoulders, the tenderest points to cause pain. The wife ran from side to side, gazing into the face and closed eyes of O'Iwa, trying to detect weakening under the torture, or result from some more agonizing blow. O'Iwa's body was striped and splashed with red. O'Kin's hands slipped on the wet surface of the rod. Suddenly she uttered an exclamation. Blood was now gushing from the nose, the eyes, the mouth of O'Iwa. "Okamisan! Okamisan! It won't do to kill her. Deign to give the order to cease. She must be lowered." The wife coolly examined the victim. "She has fainted. Lower her, and throw salt water over her. The sting will bring her to." O'Kin followed the instructions in the most literal sense. She dashed the bucket of water with great impetus right into O'Iwa's face. "Un!" was the latter's exclamation as she came to consciousness. "She consents! She consents!" cried O'Kin with delight. The wife was decidedly sceptical, but her aid plainly would go no further at this time. Said she – "Leave her as she is. There are other matters to attend to than the whims of an idle vicious jade. She would cheat this Matsu out of twenty *ryō*? Well: time will show the victor." She departed – "to drink her wine, pare her nails, and sing obscene songs to the accompaniment of the *samisen*."

Tied hand and foot O'Iwa lay semi-conscious in the cold shed of punishment. At midnight the girls returned to this "home." They gathered around the prostate O'Iwa. From O'Kin they had an inkling of the courage displayed. They admired her, but none dared to touch her bonds. At last O'Haru San, unusually successful in her night's raid, ventured to approach the half drunk mistress of the house. "Haru makes report." She spread her returns before the gratified Okamisan. Timidly the girl added – "O'Iwa San repents. Deign to remit her punishment. She looks very ill and weak." – "Shut up!" was the fierce retort. Then as afterthought of sickness and possible loss came to mind. "She can be untied and sent to bed." – "And food?" – "She can earn it." The woman turned on O'Haru, who bowed humbly and slipped away. That night the girls contributed from their store to feed O'Iwa; as they did on the succeeding days and nights. The wife would have stopped the practice, but Toemon interfered. He meant to keep his dilapidated stock in as good repair as possible. He fed them pretty well. "The woman is not to be starved – at least too openly. The last case gave this Toemon trouble enough, and on the very day this epileptic came into the house, to bring confusion with her. Beat her if you will; but not enough to kill her." O'Matsu followed his words to the letter. One beating was followed by another; with interval enough between the torture to insure recuperation and avoid danger to life. These scenes came to be regarded as a recreation of the house. The other inmates were allowed to attend, to witness the example and fascinate their attention. But at last the Okamisan despaired. Amusement was one thing; but her hatred of O'Iwa was tempered by the desire to find some use for her, to get a return for the twenty *ryō* of which she had been swindled. Finally the advice of the *bantō* was followed. "The men of the house cannot be tempted to approach such an apparition. The other girls have not time to devote to making up O'Iwa as for the stage. They have not twenty *ryō* at stake, as had Chobei. Let her wash the dishes." Thus was O'Iwa "degraded" from her high estate as street-walker. Turned into a kitchen drudge she shed tears of joy. She almost forgot the matter of the pledge in this new and pleasant life. The time and the place, perhaps the drug she took, had done their work on the mind of O'Iwa. Iemon, the house of Samoncho, the *ihai* in the Butsudan, the pleasant garden – all were of the tissue of a dream amid a toil which deposited her on the straw wrappings of the charcoal and in a shed, thoroughly worn out at the end of her long day. The O'Iwa of Samoncho at this end of the lapsing year of service was dormant. But accidents will happen.

There was excitement in the house. Mobei, the dealer in toilet articles – combs, brushes, jewel strings – was at the grating. The women were clustered before the wares he exposed in his trays. This Mobei, as dealer in toilet articles (*koma-mono*) wandered all the wards of Edo, his little trays fitting neatly into each other, and wrapped in a *furoshiki* or bundle-handkerchief. His wares formed a marvellous collection of the precious and common place, ranging from true coral and tortoise shell, antique jewelry and curious *netsuke* of great value, to their counterfeits in painted wood, horn, and coloured glass. "Mobei San, long has been the wait for you. Is there a bent comb in stock?" – "Truly this Mobei is vexing. He humbly makes apology, lady. Here is just the thing.... How much? Only a *bu*.... Too high? Nay! With women in the ordinary walks of life it is the wage of a month. To the honoured Oiran it is but a night's trifling." The other women tittered. O'Haru was a little nettled at the high sounding title of Oiran. She would not show her irritation. Mobei continued his attentions. He laid before her and the others several strings of jewels, their "coral" made of cleverly tinted paste. "Deign to look; at but one *bu* two *shū*. If real they would cost twenty *ryō*." – "And Mobei has the real?" The dealer laughed. As in pity, and to give them a glimpse of the far off upper world, he raised the cover of a box in the lower tier. They gasped in admiration before the pink of the true coral. Hands were stretched through the grating to touch it. Mobei quickly replaced the cover. "For some great lady," sighed O'Haru – "Just so," replied Mobei, adjusting his boxes. He had sold two wooden painted combs and a string of horn beads in imitation of tortoise shell. He pocketed the hundred "cash," those copper coins with a hole in the centre for stringing. Then briefly – "The necklace is for no other than the Kashiku of the Yamadaya, the loved one of Kibei Dono of Yotsuya. The comb (*kanzashi*) in tortoise shell and gold is for the honoured lady wife of Iemon Dono, the *go kenin*. But Mobei supplies not only the secular world. This – for one who has left the world; for Myozen Osho of Myogyoji, the gift of Ito Dono. For the custom of Mobei the Yotsuya stands first in order." He took a box from his sleeve and showed them the rosary of pure crystal beads. Even in the dull light of a lowering day the stones flashed and sparkled. The women showed little interest. A priest to them was not a man – ordinarily.

He shouldered his pack. "Mobei San – a comb with black spots, in imitation of tortoise shell. Please don't fail me on the next visit." Mobei nodded agreement. Then he halted and turned. One of the women had called out in derision – "Here is O'Iwa San. Surely she wants to purchase. Mobei San! Mobei San! A customer with many customers and a full pocketbook." These women looked on O'Iwa's assignment to the kitchen as the fall to the lowest possible state. At sight of the newcomer Mobei gasped. O'Iwa on leaving the door of Toemon's house, *miso* (soup) strainers for repair in one hand, fifteen *mon* for bean paste (*tōfu*) tightly clasped in the other, came face to face with the toilet dealer, "The lady of Tamiya – here!" – "The lady of Tamiya!" echoed the astonished and curious women. Said O'Iwa quickly – "Mobei San is mistaken. This is Iwa; but lady of Tamiya...." Hastily she pulled her head towel over her face. In doing so the "cash" slipped from her hand. A *mon* missing meant no *tōfu*;

result, a visit to the *semeba*. In recovering the lost coin Mobei was left in no doubt. "'Tis indeed the lady of Tamiya. It cannot be denied." O'Iwa no longer attempted the impossible. She said – "It is Iwa of Tamiya. Mobei San, a word with you." The women were whispering to each other. "He called her '*shinzō*.'" Said O'Haru – "There always was something about her to arouse suspicion; so ugly, and with such grand airs. And how she endured the punishment! Truly she must be a *samurai* woman." The minds of all reverted to their master Toemon, and how he would take this news.

O'Iwa had drawn Mobei somewhat apart from the grating. With downcast face she spoke – "Deign, Mobei San, to say nothing in the ward of this meeting with Iwa." To Mobei's earnest gesture of comprehension – "Affairs had gone badly with Tamiya. Iemon San was misled into gambling by Natsume Kyuzo and Imaizumi Jinzaemon. He was carried away by the passion. It was no longer possible to stay in Samoncho. Worse conduct followed. In the kindness and advice of Ito Dono, of Akiyama and Kondo Sama, this Iwa found support. But she disobeyed. She would not follow the advice given. However, gratitude is felt by Iwa. One cannot leave this place, or long since she would have paid the visit of acknowledgment. A matter of importance arose. Chobei San came to Iwa's aid, and saved the situation. This place is terrible, but the consequences of not coming would have been more so. To Chobei gratitude is felt. It was the opportunity offered the wife to show her faith and courage." Now she looked bravely in Mobei's face. It was the toilet dealer's turn to show confusion – "Honoured lady, is nothing known?" – "Known?" answered O'Iwa in some surprise. "What is there to know? When this Iwa left Samoncho to be sure the house was cracking apart everywhere. The light poured in as through a bamboo door.... Ah! Have matters gone badly with the Danna in Iwa's absence?" Mobei shook his head in dissent. "Alas! Ito Sama, Akiyama or Kondo San, has misfortune come to them, without a word of condolence from Iwa? Perhaps Chobei San, in his precarious life...." The poor isolated world of the thoughts of this homely creature was limited to these friends in need.

Mobei had sunk on his knees before her. He raised eyes in which stood tears of pity and indignation. "The Ojosan knows nothing of what has occurred in Yotsuya? This Mobei will not keep silent. With the affairs of Iemon Sama, of Ito Dono and Akiyama San nothing has gone wrong. The absence of the lady O'Iwa is otherwise related. She has abandoned house and husband to run away with a plebeian, the *bantō* at the green-grocer's on Shinjuku road. Such is the story circulated." O'Iwa drew away from him as from a snake – then: "Mobei, you lie! Why tell such a tale to this Iwa? Are not the words of Ito Dono, of Akiyama Sama, of Chobei San still in Iwa's ears? What else has she had to console her during these bitter months but the thought of their kindness? This dress (a scantily wadded single garment), these bare feet in this snow, this degraded life – are not they evidences of Iwa's struggle for the honour of husband and House? Mobei, slander of honourable men brings one to evil. Mobei lies; lies!"

He seized her dress. The man now was weeping. "The lady of Tamiya is a saint. Alas! Nothing does she know of the wicked hearts of men. Too great has been the kindness of the Ojosan to this Mobei for him to attempt deceit. Deign to listen. This day a week; was it not the day to a year of the Ojosan's leaving the house in Yotsuya?" O'Iwa turned to him with a startled face. He continued – "A week ago Mobei visited Yotsuya. He has many customers there, not too curious about prices. Hence he brings the best of his wares. Coming to the house in Samoncho a feast was in progress. There were present Ito Dono, Akiyama Sama, Natsume and Imaizumi Sama, Kondo Dono; O'Hana San, of course. All were exceedingly merry, Iemon Dono poured out a cup of wine. 'Mobei! Mobei! Come here! Drain this cup in honour of the occasion. We celebrate the anniversary of the expulsion of the *bakemono*.

The demon is driven forth from the Paradise of Yotsuya. Namu Myoho Renge Kyo! Namu Myoho Renge Kyo!' This Mobei was amazed – 'The O'Bake.... What O'Bake?' – 'Why: O'Iwa San. A year since, with the aid of these good friends, and one not present here, Iemon freed himself from the clutches of the vengeful apparition. Our *Kumi-gashira* granted divorce in due form. The son of Takahashi Daihachiro – Yanagibara Kazuma – Tamiya Iemon no longer catches at sleep to wake in fear. Chief, deep is the gratitude of Iemon for the favour done by Ito Dono.' The Ojosan a *bakemono*! At these outrageous words Mobei felt faint. Receiving the cup, as in modesty returned to the *rōka* to drink, the contents were spilled on the ground. Ah! Honoured lady, it is not only that the Ojosan has been driven out. Her goods have been cleverly stolen by false messages of gambling losses. Stored with Kondo Sama they were brought back on the success of the wicked plot. The whole is a conspiracy of Iemon Dono with Ito Dono, with Akiyama, Chobei, Kondo, and others. They bragged of it, and told the tale in full before this Mobei, laughing the while. Why, lady! On the word of Chobei San the order of divorce was issued by Ito Dono. Within the month O'Hana San left the shelter of the house of Kondo Sama to enter the Tamiya as bride. Deign to look. Here is a jewelled comb reserved by Iemon Sama as present for O'Hana San his wife. Here is gift of Ito Dono to Myozen Osho for his efforts 'in the cause.'"

O'Iwa stood as one frozen. With Mobei's words the light was flooding into mind and soul. Step by step she now followed clearly the stages of this infamous conspiracy against her peace and honour. She had been fooled, cheated, degraded – and by Ito Kwaiba, the enemy of Matazaemon; by Iemon, son of the hereditary foe Takahashi Daihachiro. Mobei remained huddled at her feet, watching with fright the sudden and awful change in her face. The words came in a whisper. At first she brought out her speech with difficulty, then to rise to torrent force – "Cheated, gulled by the hereditary foe! And this Iwa lies bound and helpless! 'Tis understood! The end is at hand – Ah! The poison! The poison! Now it, too, rises; flowing upward to heart and head of Iwa. Accursed man! Accursed woman; who would play the rival and destroy the wife! The time is short; the crisis is at hand. Chobei's dark words become light. Hana would poison Iwa through this treacherous leech. Iemon would kill her by the foul life of this brothel – Gods of Nippon! Buddhas of the Universe! All powerful Amida, the Protector! Kwannon, the Lady Merciful! Deign to hearken to the prayer of this Iwa. Emma Dai-o, king of Hell, summon not the daughter of Tamiya before the dreaded throne for judgment – through the course of seven existences – until the vengeance of Iwa be sated with the miserable end of these her persecutors. May the sacred characters of the Daimoku, written on the heart of Iwa for her future salvation, be seared out as with hot iron. On Ito Kwaiba, Iemon, Akiyama Chozaemon, Chobei, all and everyone engaged in this vile plot, rests the death curse of Iwa. Against these; against Natsume, Imaizumi, Yoemon of Tamiya, lies the grudge of Iwa of Tamiya. Gods and Buddhas – grant this prayer!"

A violent hand was laid on the bosom of Mobei's robe. He screamed in terror at the fearful face bent over him. A broad round dead white swollen face, too sharp gleaming malignant dots darting flashes as from a sword between the puffed and swollen lids, froze him into a passive object. One of these lids drooped horribly down upon the cheek of the apparition. In the physical effort exerted, the slit of the mouth showed the broad black even teeth, which seemed about to clutch at his throat; as did the vigorous hand, the nails of which sank into his gullet. Framed in the mass of wild disordered hair Mobei was isolated as in a universe of space; left alone with this fearful vision. "Lady! Lady O'Iwa! Lady of Tamiya! This Mobei has done naught. Others have wronged O'Iwa San. Mobei is guiltless.... Ah! Ah!" With fright and pain he rolled over on the ground in a dead faint. Screaming and shouting the women Take and Kota rushed around and out to his rescue. O'Iwa San was now under the full control of her disorder. Takezo staggered back, her hands to her face to hide the horrible sight, to wipe from eyes and cheeks the blood streaming from the deep tears made by O'Iwa's nails. Kota from behind seized O'Iwa around the waist and shoulders. Sharply up came the elbow shot, catching this interloper under the chin. Neck and jaw fairly cracked under the well-delivered blow. Kota went down in a heap as one dead. A *chūgen* coming along the North Warigesui had reached the crossing. He thought it better to stand aside, rather than attempt to stop this maddened fiend tearing through space. At the canal bank there was a moment's pause. Then came a dull splash; as of some heavy body plunged in the water. With a cry the man hastened forward. Not a sign of anything could be seen. In this rural place no help was to be had, and he was little inclined to plunge at random into the foul stream. In haste he turned back to where a crowd was gathering around the prostrate Mobei, the groaning harlots to whom punishment had been meted out.

Chobei Gets the News

The *chūgen* stood over the toilet dealer now coming out of his half-trance condition. The eyes of the two men met and showed mutual astonishment. "Naruhodo! Mobei San! In a quarrel over his wares with the vile women of this district?" – "Kakusuke San! Ah! There is much to tell. O'Iwa San...." The *chūgen* of Ito Kwaiba was amazed attention. "This Mobei to his ill fortune, met with the lady of Tamiya. Her condition, her ignorance, was too pitiful. Learning all the truth from Mobei she inflicted on him this punishment. May it cease there! Namu Amida Butsu! Namu Amida Butsu!... Heavy the grudge against your master Ito Dono; against Iemon Sama, his wife O'Hana San, all in the plot against the Lady O'Iwa. 'To seven existences grant this Iwa opportunity to vent her anger. Everyone of the perpetrators of this deed shall be seized and put to death.' She invoked all the gods and Buddhas; Nay, the king of Hell – Emma Dai-o himself. Look to yourself, Kakusuke San. Deign to seek employment elsewhere." Kakusuke completed his task of raising the battered and scratched toilet dealer to his feet. "Mobei San, you have acted the fool; without doubt. Relate what has happened." Mobei did so in full detail. Kakusuke was thoughtful. "Much of this Kakusuke hears for the first time. A servant gets but snatches of the inside of such matters. Just now the mission has been from his master, Ito Dono, to the Inagaki *yashiki* near Hoonji; matter of transfer involved in the late adoption of Kibei Dono into the House of the Danna Sama.... So that scoundrel Chobei sold the lady of Tamiya to Toemon for a harlot. Alas! She deserved a better fate. One way or another they would kill her; and Chobei, his money in hand, abetted the crime. Where is this brothel?"

Surrounded by his women Toemon was listening to their excited statements. Takezo was crying with rage and pain, as she examined her fissured countenance before a toilet stand (*kyōdai*). Kota, brought back to consciousness, lay groaning in a corner. They were applying cold compresses to her broken jaw. Toemon looked up suspiciously as Kakusuke entered, supporting the lamed and maimed Mobei. "Look to this man's wares, scattered in the roadway; and to the man himself." He spoke roughly, and with authority. Toemon did not dare to resent his manner. With well feigned solicitude he addressed Mobei – "Ma! Ma! A terrible punishment. Your face has the blush of the plum blossom marked upon it.... O'Haru, run to the house of Wakiyama Sensei. Kota is badly hurt; his skill is needed. Stop at the drug store. Here is the 'cash' to bring salve for this good man's wounds. Alas! That a woman of Toemon's house should so maltreat others. When caught her punishment...." – "Shut up!" said Kakusuke. He had already taken his line of conduct in his master's interest. "How comes it that the Lady O'Iwa is found at the house of Toemon?" – "The Lady O'Iwa!" replied the brothel keeper in well-feigned surprise. Turning to Mobei – "It is true, then, what the women report; that Mobei San called the O'Iwa of this house 'Shinzo.' Who is this O'Iwa?" Said Kakusuke coldly – "The Lady O'Iwa is the granddaughter and heir of Tamiya Matazaemon, a higher *dōshin*. She is the wife of the *go-kenin*, Tamiya Iemon."

Toemon now was truly aghast. "Heir and wife of *go-kenin*! This Toemon had not the slightest inkling of her *status*. Chobei has juggled this Toemon most outrageously." He turned savagely on O'Matsu. "So much for stupid brutality. One must give you head, or have no peace. Why not treat the woman kindly, learn her story? Lies or truth that of all the women in the house is known. But O'Iwa San was a mark for malice. Chobei has lied. Between you the house is ruined. Since when were *samurai* women sold to life service? Fool! It means imprisonment, exile, to those implicated. This Toemon ends his days among the savage fishermen of Sado." He would have struck her. Kakusuke and the *bantō* interposed. The woman did not budge. Defiant, she stood with folded arms – "It was Toemon's arrangement to buy her in blind belief of Chobei. Why blame this Matsu? Since when were women exempt from service or punishment? The rule of the house is one or the other. How long has it been since O'Seki left the house – in a box; and Toemon had to make answer at the office." Then catching herself up in the presence of strangers – "Danna Sama, this is no time for a quarrel. Those of the house will say nothing; in their own interest. As for this worthy gentleman, the Lady O'Iwa was wife and heir neither of himself nor his master. Toemon San is grossly neglectful of courtesy due to guests. Leave Mobei San to this Matsu." She whispered in his ear.

Toemon had now recovered his balance. Kakusuke was a *chūgen*. He had an object in coming to Toemon's house, instead of making report at once to his master, to the outraged Iemon Dono. Of course Toemon misinterepreted this motive; and Kakusuke was quite ready to profit by his mistake. To the now courteous brothel keeper he was equally cordial. O'Matsu and her women carried off Mobei, to salve his wounds, regale him with fish and wine and good treatment, carefully to make inventory of his goods, and repack them with substantial diminution of purchases. What more could Mobei ask. His valued rosary, the necklace, the *kanzashi*, all the treasures were uninjured. His exchequer was palpably swollen, and more pleasingly than his phiz. His beating had turned out a good day's venture; and without misgiving he can be left in the careful hands of O'Matsu and her women. Meanwhile Kakusuke and Toemon sat over their wine. From the *chūgen* and toilet dealer the latter secured a complete view of his situation. It was bad, but not irreparable. As Kakusuke with due tardiness prepared to depart, the hospitable innkeeper had ample time to prostrate himself in salutation, meanwhile pushing over a golden *ryō* wrapped up in decently thin paper which permitted the filtering through of its yellow gleam. "Great has been the trouble and delay of Kakusuke San. Mark not this day in memory, good Sir." Kakusuke was equally polite in salutation – "Fear enters: thanks for the kind entertainment of Toemon San. This alone is to be kept in mind, mark of a day otherwise of but little import." These last words were a healing balm; and Toemon rejoiced.

With the departure of Kakusuke, the chief of the 'night-hawks' turned at once to his aides. "Take! Haru!... Ah! Kota is completely done up. You, Take, bear the marks of the day's encounter. Go to Asakusa Hanagawado. Chobei is to be brought here at once. The house must clear its skirts of this affair. If he refuses to come, put a rope about his neck and drag him here." The women bowed. At once they prepared for the street, a mission welcome enough under other conditions. O'Take was smarting from her wounds and not very willing to be an object lesson. O'Haru had in mind the fearful curse of O'Iwa, plainly heard by the women. Very willingly she would have had nothing to do with the affair.

Chobei was engaged at *go* with the metal dealer of his neighbourhood. The fish and wine were in course of preparation in the kitchen close by and under the skilled hands of O'Taki. The perfume, vinous and of viands, came to the noses of the competitors, to the disturbance of their game. Chobei had just made a profitable stroke. He had five *ryō* in hand, commission from the worthy *doguya* for the successful sale of a daughter to the Yamadaya of Nakanocho. This enterprising plebeian, having a son to succeed him in the business, had secured the necessary furnishing and adoption of a second son into the rival house of the ward, by means of the fifty *ryō* secured for the girl through the experience and clever tactics of Chobei. Many the compliments and congratulations exchanged by these excellent men and worthy representatives of their class as they tussled over their game of *go*. Profuse were the thanks of the metal dealer for past services and future feasting. It was with some displeasure therefore that O'Taki had her offices interrupted to respond to a loud and harsh – "Request to make!" sounded at the house entrance. Said she crossly – "Who is it?... Ah! O'Take and O'Haru San of Toemon Sama." Then in wonder – "Oya! Oya! O'Take San.... Your honoured face.... Has O'Take San gone to bed in the dark with the cat?" Answered O'Take, in no amiable mood – "It could well have been. Your man Chobei deals in such articles. There are the marks of O'Iwa's nails. As for Chobei, is the precious rascal at home?"

O'Taki heard her with rising rage – "O'Iwa? What has Chobei San to do with any O'Iwa and the house of Toemon San? Why call the man of Taki a scoundrel?" – "Because he is such. Nay, Okamisan, don't get angry." – O'Haru was speaking – "has your husband a brother in Abegawacho, a brother in need of twenty *ryō* and with a daughter who would do nothing but run after the men?" O'Taki was puzzled. "Chobei San has no brother, in Abegawacho or any other *chō*. Hence such brother has no daughter O'Iwa; nor are there children of his own, except the one born to him by this Taki, and a girl already sold...." A light was breaking in on O'Taki. Months before she had come home to find that the Ojosan had taken her departure. Explained Chobei – "At Yotsuya everything has been adjusted. Iemon Dono is established again with his wife. The Okusama will not come back to us. Deign to rejoice at the auspicious settlement of her affairs." Which O'Taki did; all the more as Chobei often was in funds in the successive days through Tamiya. Now she looked from one woman to the other, her fists clenched and working. Said the harsh voice of O'Take – "Chobei lied then; just as the Danna Sama thought. Nearly a year ago he brought to the house the daughter of his brother Kanemon. He sold her into life service as a night-hawk. For this she turned out to be worthless. O'Taki San knows our Okamisan. No matter how severely beaten, even until the blood came, O'Iwa would not consent to serve. Other means were tried, but the men of the house would have nothing to do with her. She was too ugly. Finally she was degraded into being the kitchen wench, to fetch and carry, and do the hardest and most nauseating tasks. At this downfall in her prospects like a very fool she rejoiced. Today she met the toilet dealer Mobei. He recognized her as the Lady O'Iwa of Tamiya in the Yotsuya. Drawn apart they spoke together. Suddenly she was transformed into a demon. Leaping on Mobei she tore and clutched at him. Kota and this Take ran to aid him. Kota lies helpless and with a broken jaw. Truly it might have been the kick of a horse she received. This Take is – as can be seen. The Lady O'Iwa disappeared toward Warigesui. A *chūgen* saw her leap in. Probably she has killed herself.... And now, O'Taki San, is not your man Chobei a scoundrel?"

Said O'Taki – "Rightly spoken; more than right. Wait here." Abruptly she entered the inner room. To Chobei – "You ... my fine fellow ... is this a time for *go*? Up and off with you; to accompany O'Take and O'Haru from Toemon's in Honjo. A pretty business is in preparation there." Said the embarrassed and enraged Chobei – "Wh-what does this rude entrance of Taki mean? Is not the master of the metal shop present? Is such language, such abruptness, to be used in his presence?" – "The Danna of the *doguya* is certainly present," coolly replied the woman. "It would be better if he was at home.... Honoured Sir, pray betake yourself there. This Chobei has business with Toemon Sama of Honjo, the brothel keeper and chief of the night-hawks, to whom he has sold for life service as a street harlot the Lady O'Iwa, wife of the *go-kenin* Iemon Dono and heir of Tamiya Matazaemon the *dōshin*. A man can be too clever – as this Chobei, who cheats his wife and all others. Do you be clever enough to take the hint and depart.... Off with you!" The *doguya* had sat in silence. His eyes were popping out of his head in frightened amaze. Chobei bounded up in a rage – "You huzzy – shut up! Would you publish the affairs of this Chobei to the world? Many a bridge is to be passed in the course through this world; and none too sure the footing. Money must be had to live and enjoy life. The result, not the means, is the important factor in its acquisition. Such rudeness to a guest! Vile jade, Chobei will...." O'Take and O'Haru had to interfere – "Fight it out later, Chobei San. This quarrel is no concern of ours. The sooner the master is seen, the better for Chobei San. His rage is great, and mounting. You have the contract? With that face the master; if you can." – "Just so! Just so! As for this wench – she shall have something to remember this Chobei by...." The worthy and trembling metal dealer took this remark as threat of renewed violence. "For the kind reception and entertainment: thanks. Jubei calls later." Nimbly he was on his feet. Diving under the *haori* into which Chobei was struggling he bounced out the front, leaving Chobei on the ground and floundering in the folds of his garments, from which issued most violent language. For the first time that day O'Take and O'Haru had something to amuse them. O'Taki refusing, they assisted Chobei to his feet and adjusted his robe. Then one on each side of him they set out for Honjo Yoshidacho. As parting salute to O'Taki, Chobei finished his sentence.... "Something to remember on Chobei's return." Her laugh in reply was so savage that the women turned to look at her. In fright they hastened off with their prize.

At Honjo the reception of Chobei called forth the whole house. The pimp entered the presence of Toemon with confident and jaunty air. "He has the contract?" said Toemon to the woman. O'Haru indicated a sleeve. The *bantō* and one of the *wakashū* (young men employes) grasped the arms of Chobei. The incriminating document was deftly removed by O'Haru and passed over to Toemon. "Now the fellow can neither produce it, nor play his tricks with it." He looked it over carefully; then placed it with his own copy. Chobei was too outraged and frightened to do more than squat and gasp as he looked around the circle of hostile faces. Without cushion he sat on the bare *tatami*, much as does a criminal at the white sand. Said Toemon severely – "For once Chobei has drunk hot water with this Toemon. Does he think to act thus with impunity. The younger sister of his brother Kanemon, 'a noted wench for the streets,' was brought here for life service; sold to Toemon for twenty *ryō*. Toemon does not intend that the price shall be too high for him. Chobei cannot lie out of his own contract. Toemon has it in his hands. Chobei has the twenty *ryō*. Toemon loses his money. Well and good: Toemon clears himself from the affair. The responsibility lies wholly with Chobei. Let him look to it." Chobei seized the moment when lack of breath in his anger halted the speech of Toemon. He would have lied, but Toemon again broke in. "Chobei has no brother. Chobei has no woman to dispose of on his own signature. The one he did have, the one he possesses, Toemon knows where to find. Toemon had a woman O'Iwa in his house. You sold the wife of a *go-kenin*, Iemon Dono of Yotsuya; a woman who was the heir of Tamiya Matazaemon the *dōshin*. The Lady O'Iwa is traced to the hands of Chobei. Settle the matter with those in office – *machibugyō, dōshin, yakunin* – when the affair comes to light...." – "Easily," burst in Chobei, once more himself. "Honoured chief, matters do not call for such earnestness. All this is mere froth and fury. It is true that Chobei has deceived the chief; but it was at the orders of those much higher. The lady of Tamiya was an obstacle. The sale was ordered by Iemon Dono himself; backed by Ito Kwaiba the head of the Yotsuya ward." – "Chobei, you lie," said Toemon. The words and advice of Kakusuke still rang in his ears. "Iemon Dono? Ito Dono? Who else will Chobei bring in as his bails? Such a man is not to be trusted. With this Toemon there is no more dealing. The guild is to be warned by a circular letter."

At this fearful threat all Chobei's jauntiness left him. His livelihood, his existence, were at stake. He prostrated himself before Toemon, dragging his body over the *tatami* to the *zen* (low table) at which was seated this autocrat of the night-hawks, this receiver of the refuse and worn-out goods of his greater brothers in the trade. Toemon harshly repulsed him with his foot. Chobei in despair turned to O'Matsu – "Honoured lady the chief is unreasonably angry. There shall be no loss of money, no harm suffered by the affair. Deign to say a word for Chobei." – "Since when has Matsu had aught to do with the affairs of the house? The women are her concern. She goes not outside her province." The pimp sought the feet of O'Take – "Condescend to plead for Chobei. His fault is venial. When no injury results, pardon follows. This is to cut off the breath of Chobei, of wife and child. Deign to intercede." The street harlot laughed. Her cracked voice was rough – "The commission of Chobei San has no attractions. This Take has had enough to do with the matter. Truly Chobei is a wicked fellow. Take would fare badly in such intercourse. Besides his company is too high flown. Officials! Samurai! Chobei San seeks and will find promotion in the world. Lodgings are preparing for Chobei Sama in public office – on the Ryogokubashi; of such he is assured." She drew away from him, harshly cackling. Thus he crawled from one to the other. It was "Chobei Sama," "Chobei Dono," in derision they would call him prince – "Chobei Ko." All stuck out their tongues at him. The young fellows of the house, several of them, stood round the entrance, ostensibly occupied, but with one eye on the scene. As Chobei sought the *bantō's* aid, the man raised a long lean leg and gave him a violent kick in the breast. Strong hands seized him as he rolled over and over to the edge of the platform, to land in the arms of the enthusiastic *wakashū*. The next moment, and Chobei was picking himself up out of the mud and snow of the street. The lattice of the house entrance closed noisily.

In his confusion of mind by force of habit Chobei turned round and bowed with ceremony toward the place of his unceremonious exit – "The time is inopportune. Chobei intrudes. He will call again." The opening of the wicket gate, the peering, scowling face of the *bantō* recalled the past scene to mind. With all the haste his tottering gait allowed Chobei sprang off northward to the Adzumabashi and home. As he sped, swaying along, his active mind was making calculations. "Ryogokubashi, the last home of the outcast beggar – other than the river which flows beneath it!" He shuddered at the prophecy. "Bah! One rascal loses; another gains. Toemon loses twenty *ryō*. From Iemon San ten *ryō* was the commission. Ito Dono gave five *ryō* and asked no questions. The total to Chobei sums up thirty-five *ryō*. For a year the affair of O'Iwa has fattened Chobei; with something still left." His foot struck a stone in the roadway. He looked up and around to find himself before the Genkwoji. About to enter on the maze of temple grounds and *yashiki* separating him from the bridge his gaze fell on the stagnant squalid waters of the canal. It was in the dirty foulness of this North Warigesui that O'Iwa had disappeared. Chobei pulled up short. A dead cur, copper hued, with swollen germinating sides and grinning teeth, bobbed at him from the green slime. Chobei slewed round – "A vile ending; but after all an ending. Iemon profits; Chobei gets the scoldings. Ah! If it was not that Ito Kwaiba is engaged in this affair; Tamiya should pay dearly. There is a double ration to share with Chobei – and not to be touched! Ito Dono is no man to trifle with. There was that affair with Isuke; and now, as he says, Iemon is a very son to him." A memory seemed to touch Chobei. His pace became a crawl. "Why hasten? Chobei rushes to the fiend – that demon Taki. Chobei would rather face O'Iwa than Taki in a rage." He laughed – "The attenuated hands of a ghost and the thick fist of Taki, the choice is not uncertain. From the lady mild and merciful there is nothing to fear. Evidently she has settled matters once and for all in the Warigesui. But at the tenement – there it is another affair. This Chobei will fortify himself against the shock. A drink; then another, and still more. The scoldings will fall on a blunted mind wandering in some dreamland. Time will soothe her rage. Tomorrow Chobei wakes, to find the storm has passed and Taki his obedient serving wench." Near the Adzumabashi, following his prescription against domestic enlivenment, he entered a grog shop; to turn his good coin into wine.

The quarter at Hanagawado in Asakusa was in an uproar. What had occurred was this – There was an old woman – 'Baba' in the native parlance for Dame Gossip – a seller of the dried seaweed called *nori* (sloke or laver), still called Asakusa *nori*, though even at that time gathered at Shinagawa, Omori, and more distant places. This old trot had returned, to make her last sales to the excellent metal dealer who lived opposite her own home in the *nagaya*, in which she lived next door to the Chobei, husband and wife. The tongue of the *doguya* was still in full swing of the recital, not only of his own experiences, but of the revelations of O'Taki. He was only too willing for this twenty-first time to repeat the tale to the *nori* seller, his good neighbour. The good wife and wives listened again with open mouths. The Baba was the most interested of them all. This choice morsel of gossip was to be gathered at the primal source, from the lips of O'Taki herself. She was all sympathy in her curiosity – ranging in the two cases of Chobei and wife on the one part, and the metal dealer and his insulted household on the other part. Away she stepped quickly from the assembly of ward gossips. At the door of Chobei's quarters she stopped – "Okamisan! Okamisan!... Strange: is she not at home? Is she so angered that no answer is given? However, this Baba fears no one.... Nesan! Nesan!" She passed the room entrance and went into the area. Glancing into the kitchen – "Oya! Oya! The meal is burnt to a crisp. It has become a soppy, disgusting mass. Nesan! Nesan! The rain falls, the roof window (*hikimado*) is open." She put down her empty tubs in order to play the good neighbour. The first thing was to close the window against the descending rain. Quickly and deftly she proceeded to wipe the moisture off the shining vessels, to put everything in order in O'Taki's usually immaculate kitchen. Women of this class are finicky housekeepers in their own homes. As the old wife became less engaged she began to hear strange sounds above. Someone was in conversation – and yet it was a one-sided queer kind of talk. The voice was threatening and wheedling. Then she heard a child cry. Surely O'Taki was in the upper room; and thus neglectful of her lord and household.

The old Baba went to the foot of the ladder and listened. "Nesan! Nesan!" No answer came, beyond the curious droning monotone above, varied by an occasional wailing cry of the child. It seemed to be in pain. Resolute, the sturdy old Baba began to climb the steps. At the top she halted, to get breath and look into the room. The sight she witnessed froze the old woman in horror to where she stood. A woman was in the room. She knelt over the body of the child, which now and again writhed in the hard and cruel grasp. The queer monotonous voice went on – "Ah! To think you might grow up like your father. The wicked, unprincipled man! To sell the Ojosan for a street whore, for her to spend her life in such vile servitude; she by whose kindness this household has lived. Many the visits in the past two years paid these humble rooms by the lady of Tamiya. To all her neighbours O'Taki has pointed out and bragged of the favour of the Ojosan. The very clothing now on your wretched puny body came from her hands. While Chobei spent his gains in drink and paid women, Taki was nourished by the rice from Tamiya. When Taki lay in of this tiny body it was the Ojosan who furnished aid, and saw that child and mother could live. Alas! That you should grow up to be like this villainous man is not to be endured.... Ah! An idea! To crunch your throat, to secure revenge and peace, security against the future." She bent down low over the child. Suddenly it gave a fearful scream, as does a child fallen into the fire. The Baba, helpless, could only feebly murmur – "Nesan! Nesan! O'Taki San! What are you about? Control yourself." She gave a frightened yowl as the creature began to spread far apart the child's limbs, and with quick rips of the sharp kitchen knife beside her dissevered and tore the little limbs from the quivering body. At the cry the woman turned half around and looked toward her. Jaws dripping red with blood, a broad white flat face with bulging brow, two tiny piercing dots flashing from amid the thick swollen eyelids, it was the face of O'Iwa glowering at her. "Kiya!" The scream resounded far and wide. Incontinently the old woman tumbled backward down the steep steps, to land below on head and buttocks.

Some neighbours, people passing, came rushing in. A crowd began to gather. "Baba! Baba San! What is wrong?" She could not speak; only point upward and shudder as does one with heavy chills. As they moved toward the stair a roar went up from the crowd in the street. O'Taki had appeared at the window, her face smeared with blood and almost unrecognizable. She waved a limb of the dismembered infant. The crowd were frozen with horror. As some shouted to those within to hasten the woman brandished the bloody knife. Thrusting it deep into her throat she ripped and tore at the handle, spattering the incautious below with the blood spurting from the wound. Then she fell backward into the room. When the foremost to interfere rushed in they drew back in fear at what they saw. The child's head was half knawed from the body; its limbs lay scattered to this place and that. The body of O'Taki lay where she had fallen. It was as if the head had been gnawed from the trunk, but the head itself was missing. Search as they would, it was not to be found. Meanwhile the news of these happenings spread rapidly. In the next block it was shouted that the wife of the pimp Chobei had gone mad and killed and eaten five children. A block further the number had risen to twenty-five. At the guardhouse of the Adzumabashi she had killed and gnawed a hundred adults.

These rumours were mingled with the strange tale of the old woman as to O'Iwa San. In time there were many who had witnessed the suicide of O'Taki, who were ready to swear they had seen the fearful lady of Tamiya. Chobei first learned of the affair by being dragged from the grog shop to the guardhouse of the Adzumabashi. Here he was put under arrest. Distressed and discomforted he stood before the ruin in his home, under the eyes of his neighbours. These stood loyally by him. As happens in ward affairs in Nippon the aspect of the affair not immediately on the surface was slow to reach official ears. Thus it was as to the Tamiya phase involved. Chobei had suffered much, and was in to suffer more. His fellow wardsmen were silent as to all but the actual facts needed for interpretation. The marvellous only filters out slowly. But they had their own way of dealing with him. The *kenshi* (coroner) made his report. Examinations, fines, bribes, the funeral costs, reduced Chobei to his worst garment. With this after some weeks he was permitted to go free. The house owner had turned him out. The wardsmen had expelled him. Enough of Kazaguruma Chobei – for the present.

News Reaches Kwaiba

Kwaiba was hard at it, practising his favourite arts. His *sake* cup stood before him, and from time to time he raised the bottle from the hot water, testing its temperature with skilled hand. He accompanied the action with a continual drone of a *gidayu*. Kwaiba by no means confined the art of *gidayu* recitation to the heroic tales usually therewith associated. His present effort was one of the suggestive and obscene *ukarebushi*, quite as frequent and as well received in the *gidayu* theme containing them. Kibei listened and applauded, with cynical amusement at the depravity of the impotent old man. Kwaiba had found an excellent bottle companion, and renewed his own former days in the "Quarter," with the fresher experiences retailed by Kibei. Said Kwaiba – "All has gone well. For half the year Kibei has been the son of Kwaiba. He has brought luck into the house." Kibei bowed respectfully. Continued the old man – "Iemon with his whore is fast destroying Tamiya by riot and drinking. Chozaemon is a fish in the net. The debt of ten *ryō* has doubled into twenty *ryō*, which at any cost he must repay. Kwaiba will make him cut belly if he don't. And Tamiya! Old Tamiya; Matazaemon! O'Iwa is paying his debt to Kwaiba by becoming an outcast, perhaps a beggar somewhere on the highway. If she shows her face in the ward, seeking 'cash' to keep life in a wretched carcass, this Kwaiba will send her to the jail, to rot as vagrant. But what did become of her? Iemon has never spoken." Kibei shrugged his shoulders. "A close mouthed fellow; too wise to talk of himself. He would but say that Chobei took the affair in hand." Kwaiba threw up his hands in horror and merriment. Said he – "'Tis rumoured the fellow is a pimp.But surely he could not dispose of O'Iwa in his line. The very demons of the Hell of lust would refuse all intercourse with her."

Just then Kakusuke presented himself. "Report to make to the Go Inkyo Sama. Inagaki Dono sends his compliments to Ito Sama. The papers of transfer are these; by the hand of Kakusuke." As he took the documents, said Kwaiba in answer to Kibei's inquiring look – "Your honoured parent has favoured this Kwaiba. The transfer is of farms in Kazusa for others in Shimosa. Thus all can be brought under one hand. A single *nanushi* (bailiff) can manage the whole property in the two villages." – "But the office...," objected Kibei. He had the *samurai* instinct against the slightest taint of failure in obligation. "Let Kibei San deign to follow in the footsteps of Kwaiba. The successor to the *nanushi* recently deceased is a child. Kwaiba is in no haste to provide a substitute pending majority. The right will lapse, and at majority the boy can be found occupation elsewhere, to no small gain in the revenue. Out of sight, out of mind. Kwaiba's present manager is unsurpassed; so is the income he manages to gather." He looked around in some surprise, seeing that Kakusuke still maintained his position, although dismissed. Then noting him closely – "What has happened, Kakusuke? Your colour is bad. Too cordial entertainment by the *chūgen* of Inagaki Dono? Or has Kakusuke seen a ghost?"

"Kakusuke has seen O'Iwa San; of Tamiya. Rather would he have seen a ghost; if indeed it was not a demon he saw." Kwaiba started – "O'Iwa! Where?" – "It was at the brothel of Toemon, chief of the night-hawks, at Yoshidacho in Honjo. Mobei the toilet dealer had suffered direfully at her hands. Meeting her unexpectedly, the fool let out all he knew of the happenings in the ward. In a rage she flew on him. 'To seven lives a curse on Iemon Dono, on Akiyama Sama, on Kondo Sama.'" – He hesitated; then added – "on the Go Inkyo Sama. Then in a straight line she flew off toward the canal. Did she drown herself? This Kakusuke could not ascertain. Going to the aidof Mobei, mauled and prostrate on the ground, the whole story was learned. Chobei had sold her for life to Toemon, to serve as a night-hawk."

Ito Kwaiba sat straight up. His idle braggart words of a few moments before came home to him. In Kibei he found no encouragement. After all Kibei was a *samurai*; harsh, but with the courage of his caste and profession. He spoke openly – "It was an outrageous deed. To sell a *samurai* woman to such a life! It stinks. This comes of bringing in a low dog (*yarō*) such as this Chobei. Did Iemon know of his intention?" He looked Kwaiba in the eye, but the latter met him squarely – "What Iemon knew or did not know, this Kwaiba knows not. But of this event he must know – and at once. Kakusuke, go in all haste to the house of Tamiya Sama. Kwaiba would consult with him." Kibei fidgetted and fumed. He walked up and down the room. Then abruptly – "Condescend to pardon the presence of Kibei. The honoured father having matters to discuss with the diviner – he finds no amusement in the counsellor." As he was withdrawing Iemon entered. Their greeting was cold to the extreme. Iemon knew that Kibei hated and despised him; as much as he, Iemon, hated and feared Kibei. Kwaiba called sharply to his genial son – "Pray be within call, if needed." He was glad to see the surly fellow's exit. In some things Kwaiba felt fear. The stiff courage of Kibei made him ashamed openly to air his weakness. He broke the news at once to Iemon. "Kakusuke has seen O'Iwa." Iemon looked at him curiously. Was Kwaiba frightened? Said the one-time priest – "What of that? She lives in Edo. A meeting with her is quite likely; at least for a man of the grade of Kakusuke." He smiled grimly – "But...," said Kwaiba. He plunged into the story of the *chūgen* in its full details. Iemon listened carefully. "Ah! She is likely to come here." – "Come here!" bellowed Kwaiba. "Just so," answered Iemon. "If she seeks vengeance on this Iemon, on Kwaiba, or the others, where else would she come than Yotsuya. We cannot run away." Kwaiba gasped at his coolness – "And Iemon Dono, does he open Tamiya to the presence of its ex-lady and mistress?" – "A beggar, an outcast, importuning Tamiya; the severed body will lie in the ditch, for the gatherers of offal to cast as food to the dogs on the moor. Fear enters, but – honoured chief, condescend to follow the example of Iemon."

The round eyes in the round face of Kwaiba stood out. He leaned over and touched Iemon's sleeve. In astonishment Iemon noted the fright depicted in his face. The blustering old man at bottom was an arrant coward. Two knaves should understand each other – as did he and Chobei. He felt that he had been gulled during the whole of his intercourse with this old fool. He should have bluffed; and not been bluffed. Said Kwaiba in lowered voice – "Kakusuke could see nothing of her. She disappeared into the waters of Warigesui. Suppose O'Iwa appears as a ghost, to take vengeance on Kwaiba...." He straightened up in astonishment and some anger at the derisive smile playing over the face of Iemon. Indeed Iemon was more than amused. Not at the circumstances, but at finding at last this weak spot in the man who had dominated him. Conditions, however, controlled him. It was fact that the physical O'Iwa might appear – to the distress and discomfiture of all concerned. They must stand together. He spoke with severity – "Rich and afraid of ghosts! Has not Ito Dono two spearmen when he goes abroad? When he has an interview with his lord does he tremble with fear? When the enemy in life, with all physical powers, is not feared; why fear a disembodied spirit deprived of all means of venting its wrath and spite? It is but the imagination which works havoc. None are more helpless than the dead. With them time and occasion has reached an end. If O'Iwa returns to Yotsuya, it will be in her own person. With O'Iwa, the beggar and night-hawk, our *Kumigashira* knows how to deal." – "Then Iemon knew the lot dealt out to O'Iwa." – "At first hand; from Chobei himself. The lean knave has prospered by the affair. Iemon had no such desire to see him, as to secure his costly presence at the dinner so unfortunately witnessed by Mobei.... But deign to call for wine; drive out these vapours with wine. Honoured chief, condescend to play the host to Iemon." Iemon's manner was not wholly natural, as Kwaiba could have detected if more himself. He felt immensely relieved. A priest – surely he was one to know all about the nature of ghosts; was one to speak with authority. Iemon was hardly to be regarded as in ecclesiastical good odour. But Kwaiba was easily satisfied. He, too, roared – "Wine! Wine! Bring wine!" As by magic Kibei appeared at the welcome sound. He disliked Iemon, but he liked wine. The servants bustled around. The wine was heated – again and again. A feast of fish – with more wine – followed. It was late when Iemon left the house, the only sober member of the party. Of his hosts, one was maudlin, the other asleep. The ample resources of Tamiya, if not of benefit to his person, in these past two years had given him the chance to harden his head; and he had grasped it.

Iemon by no means had all the confidence he displayed before Kwaiba. He was a priest, but environment influences everybody. There was a possibility – discountenanced by experience, but existing. As he walked slowly along Teramachi his thoughts strayed back into the past. "It was an ill bond between this Iemon and O'Iwa San. Without question she has drowned herself in the Warigesui. The body must be found and buried. Memorial services are to be recited, for one dying without relatives or friends (*segaki*)." The virtuous resolution was the outcome of his meditation and glances into the many graveyards passed in his progress through the temple-lined street. It was a beautiful street, with its overhanging trees, its open spaces populated by the many dead, its temples gorgeous in red and gilding amid the dark green of pine and cedar. Iemon on this night had to hasten his steps. Rain threatened. Gusts of wind came sharply from this side and that, driving the first drops of the coming storm. He reached home just as it broke with all its fury.

To O'Hana he would say nothing of Kwaiba's mission. On her remarking on the lateness of the hour, he made answer that the old man was out of sorts. Kibei was too robust a bottle companion for a man reaching toward his seventieth year. No matter how vigorous, Kwaiba's wine was showing on him. The two prepared for bed. O'Hana listened as the rain dashed in streams against the *amado*, as if trying to break its way in. She gave a little chuckle – "Who would have thought it!" – "What?" asked Iemon, perhaps a little tartly. He was nervous. O'Hana laughed – "That Iemon and this Hana should be where they now are. Their parting was on a night like this. Ah! At seeing a man weep Hana could have retired into a cave – forever. Only the fortunate accident of a drunken *yakunin* (constable) as guest enabled her to give warning.... And now! Once more united Iemon and this Hana live in luxury. Every wish is gratified. Thanks for the past which contained this meeting in its womb; thanks for the present in which happiness is secured:

'Losing one's way, again roads meet!
The hill of flowers.'"

A terrific gust struck the rain-doors. They bent and cracked before the force of the gale. The vivid white of lightning showed that one door had been forced from its groove. Iemon rose and replaced it. As he turned away suddenly the room was plunged in darkness. Said the voice of O'Hana – "The light of the *andon* has gone out. Oya! Oya! The lights in the Butsudan (altar) are lit. And yet this Hana extinguished them." Grumbled Iemon – "The wind has blown out the light in the *andon*. Doubtless a spark was left in the wick of the altar light. Fire is to be dreaded; great care should be taken in extinguishing the light." As he relit the light in the night lamp, O'Hana went up to the Butsudan to extinguish the lights there. She put her hand out to take one. A sharp scream, and she fell back in confusion and fright. "An *aodaishō* in the Butsudan! Help! Aid this Hana!" As she fled the snake with a thud fell on the *tatami*. Unrolling its six feet of length, it started in pursuit. Iemon stepped behind it and caught it by the tail. A sharp rap behind the head stunned it. It hung limp in his hand. "Hana, please open the *amado*." – "No, no: this Hana cannot; move she will not." – "Coward!" said Iemon. "Time comes when Hana, for generations in the future existence, will wander hill and dale in such form." – "Ara!" The woman was properly shocked at this speech, wicked and brutal as an imprecation. "Has the life of Hana been so foul as to deserve such punishment in a future life? Surely 'Tis not the priest of Reigan who speaks; nor Iemon." She could only see his lips move as he stood at the *amado*. "Evil was the connection between O'Iwa and this Iemon. Wander not as one unburied, but becoming a Buddha at once enter Nirvana. Namu Myoho Renge Kyo! Namu Myoho Renge Kyo! Wonderful the Law, wondrous the Scripture of the Lotus!" With the invocation he cast the stunned reptile far out into the garden. Returning, he said – "The *aodaishō* is the most harmless of snakes. The farmers keep it to destroy the rats which infest house and store rooms. How can Hana be afraid of snakes, living in this *yashiki* overgrown by weeds and grass, from roof to garden?" O'Hana did not reply in direct terms – "It is evil fortune to take a snake in the hand." – "Never mind such talk. It is the priest who speaks. This Iemon knows all about snakes. Go to sleep." She obeyed, knowing nothing about O'Iwa and the events of the day; yet her slumber was broken and restless. By morning she was in a high fever.

News from Kwaiba

Kwaiba was reported as ill; very ill. His friends and dependents who had to pay visits of condolence, spoke of this illness with awe and terror. To understand what follows something must be said of the past of this man. The actor, drawing on the presumed knowledge of his audience as to the story in the gross, can pass this over with a speech or two; a horror-struck gesture and allusion. Not so the *kōdan* writer, who perforce must lay before his reader all the *minutiae* of the case.

Ito Kwaiba did not brag when he spoke of his beauty as a boy, his handsome figure as a young man. These had brought him wealth and position; gained, it was whispered, in vilest service to his lord. In these days he had in his employ a *chūgen* named Isuke, or as some say Kohei. Engaged before the mirror Kwaiba was applying the paint and powder which of late had become necessary adjuncts to fit him to appear before his lord. A gesture of pain and discomfiture, and then Kwaiba turned irritably toward his satellite. "Isuke, you are a clever fellow. Kwaiba has needed no aids to his looks – up to recent days. Now paint and powder, all the armoury of a woman, or paraphernalia of an actor, hardly avail to conceal the blotches which disfigure Kwaiba's face and body. The voice broken and husky, the lightning pains in limbs and joints, these violet patches – in such state it soon will be impossible to act as attendant on his lordship's household service, as *kami-yakunin*. What disorder eats into the life and happiness of Kwaiba?"

For a time Isuke made no answer, beyond a bow at his master's acknowledgment of his cleverness, and in which he heartily concurred. He seemed engaged in a close contemplation of the end of his nose. "Hei! Hei!" It was all that Kwaiba could get out of him for the moment. Then noting the growing anger Isuke began with – "Condescend beforehand to pardon this Isuke. Though the anger of the Wakadono (young lord) is hard to bear, yet a faithful servitor should speak. Deign to step this way." He conducted Kwaiba to one of those small retired rooms, opening on an inner garden and common to every properly built house of any size in Nippon. He closed the few rain-doors, shutting out the light. Then fetching a piece of camphor, he set fire to it. When the thick yellow light flared strongly he took up a hand-mirror and passed it to Kwaiba. Kwaiba was frightened at what he saw. His face was dark as that of a peasant of Satsuma. Said Isuke – "The darkness is shown up by the light of the burning camphor. The colour is due to the poison circulating between the body and the outer skin. The white sunlight does not show up this symptom. But there is another test." Lighting a candle, he took a long steel *kanzashi* needle and heated it to redness. Holding the cold end by his head towel he grasped the arm of Kwaiba. The latter drew back, afraid. "Nay, it will give no pain," said Isuke. He thrust the hot length of the needle several inches under the skin. As far as Kwaiba was concerned he might as well have thrust it into the straw matting (*tatami*) at his feet. Isuke withdrew the needle and carefully pressed the arm. A brownish liquor oozed out; not blood. "The Danna has a nose – as yet." Kwaiba hastily applied his arm to that member. He turned his face to one side in disgust and horror – "Is this Kwaiba already dead and rotten? In such condition all is lost. Duty no longer can be performed. Service and income cease together. Isuke, there remains naught but to get out the mats. Kwaiba will cut belly."

Isuke examined him carefully and quizzically. Satisfied with his inspection, he said – "Deign to have confidence in Isuke. In former days he was not Isuke the *chūgen*. Son of a doctor of the Dutch practice at Nagasaki; gambling, wine, women have reduced Isuke to the state of a servant. Family and friends long since have discarded and cast him out. The severance of relations between parent and child was formal. Isuke owes naught of service or duty to any but his master Kwaiba. Here is his refuge. Deign to give Isuke three silver *ryō*. The disease is curable. Trust the matter to Isuke. *Soppin* (mercury) duly applied will remove the poison, and with it all the disastrous symptoms. The two hundred and thirty *tawara* of income are enjoyed by the Wakadono. Service can be performed; and Isuke preserves such a good master." Flattered and frightened Kwaiba at once handed over the money. Isuke disappeared to secure the drug necessary to the 'Dutch practice'. Baths and potions, potions and baths, followed in due course. The promises of Isuke were fulfilled. The fearful symptoms gradually were alleviated. In the course of six months Kwaiba was himself again; his position was assured to him. He heaved double sighs – of relief from the nightmare which had pursued him; of anxiety at the nightmare substituted for it.

Kwaiba was a rake and a gambler. So was Isuke. The two hundred and thirty *tawara* of income was saved to Kwaiba – and Isuke. Not long after the cure was thus assured Isuke disappeared. Kwaiba sighed gently, with relief at the departure of one who knew too much of his affairs, and with a scared feeling on losing the only 'doctor' in whom he had confidence. "These fellows come and go, like leaves on a tree. Isuke has grown tired, and deserted. Some day he may return. This Kwaiba is a good master." Isuke did return – in the form of a note from the Yoshiwara. Twenty *ryō* were needed to pay his debts to pleasure and gambling. Severely reprimanded, Isuke opened his eyes in astonishment. "Respectfully heard and understood: has the income been reduced? But that does not affect the share of Isuke. He keeps well within his limit." This was the first intimation Kwaiba had of Isuke's views as to his role of physician. In those days the doctor usually had the pleasure of performance, not of payment. Moreover with the great – like Kwaiba – performance was carried out at a distance; the pulse felt by the vibration of a string attached to the wrist, or at best by passing the hand under the coverlet. For a time Kwaiba's strange medical attendant devoted himself to his more prosaic duties of *chūgen*. Within ten days his master ransomed him from a resort in Shinagawa; price, ten *ryō*. A few weeks later he was heard from at a gambler's resort in Shinjuku. The note was peremptory – and for fifty *ryō*. Kwaiba lost all patience. Moreover, just then he held office very favourable for bringing this matter to an issue. But he must have Isuke; and have him in Yotsuya. As usual payment secured the presence of a repentant Isuke, full of promises of amendment. Kwaiba smiled, used soft words; and shortly after Isuke was confined to the jail on a trumped up charge of theft from another *chūgen*. Kwaiba, then acting as magistrate for the district, had full power. On notification he assured Isuke of a speedy release. This the unhappy man secured through a poisoned meal, following a long fast. He died raving, and cursing his master. No one heard him but his two jailers, who considered him crazy – this man of bad record.

Years had passed, but Isuke merely lay dormant in the mind of Kwaiba. Then came up the affair of Tamiya – the threatening curse of O'Iwa San. Iemon's counsel lasted but over night. With soberness and morning Kwaiba straightway showed the results of wrecked nerves and distorted imagination. Sleepless nights he now visited on his friends by an increasing irritability. The first few days of this state of Kwaiba were laughable. He spoke of O'Iwa San; not freely, rather with reticence. He made his references as of jesting expectation of her advent. Then he passed to boisterous tricks; springing out on the maids from dark corners or the turns in the corridors. Alarmed by these manifestations of the old man – not entirely strange, for he was a terror to the female element in his household – they soon noted that there was an unnatural wildness in his amusement at their discomfiture. Now he would talk of nothing but O'Iwa. From this hysterical mirth he passed to an hysterical fear. Afraid of visions of the Lady of Tamiya he stayed awake at night. To be alone appalled him. He would have others keep awake with him. He was now at the gibbering stage. "Night in the house of Kwaiba is to be turned into day. The day shall be the time for sleep. Lights! Lights! More lights!" He sat surrounded by his household, until the white light of dawn filtered through the spaces above the rain-doors. One of his women, her hair down for washing, met him unexpectedly in the corridor. With a howl of terror he started to flee. Then recognizing her, he flew on her and beat her almost to a jelly in his insane rage. People began to talk of the eccentricities of Ito Kwaiba – the honoured ward head.

Barely three weeks after Iemon's visit a violent scene occurred in the mansion of the *Kumigashira*. Shouts and screams, the smashing of screens and sounds of a terrific struggle were heard in Kwaiba's room. Kibei, who with the men preferred night for sleep, rushed in. He found the old man standing, stark naked and alone. His attendants had fled – to a woman. His pillow sword drawn, Kwaiba was dancing to this side and that. "Isuke! O'Iwa! Pardon! This Kwaiba is a wicked fellow! Isuke was poisoned by Kwaiba. O'Iwa San? Kwaiba sold her for a street whore. For seven lives they pursue him. Ah! A merry chase! But Kwaiba deals not with night-hawks. His game is higher. Away with the huzzy!" He had grasped in both hands the flower vase standing in the alcove (*tokonoma*). Kibei dodged, and catching him by a wrestler's hold, threw him to the ground. Kakusuke, just entering, was knocked flat by the heavy missile. Groaning, he rose, and with other servants came to the aid of the Wakadono. Kwaiba was overpowered and guarded during the remainder of the night.

With daylight he knew nothing of what had occurred; at least he made no reference to it, no response to the talk of others. His fear was now full on him. He babbled of nothing but Isuke and O'Iwa San. Now he was incapacitated, downright ill. There was no more turning of day into night, and *vice versa*. He was in the hands of his nurses. But to humour him Kibei marshalled the women. Their beds were made encircling that of Kwaiba in the midst. Kibei and Kakusuke were present. Thus they lay in this room brilliant with its scores of lanterns, its wax lights blazing on the lamp-stands. At the sides and in each corner were placed the scrolls of the holy *sutra*. Kwaiba in despair sought a sleep which would not favour him. "Someone walks in the corridor.... Namu Amida Butsu! Namu Amida Butsu!... Kibei! Kibei!" The appeal to the man would bring quicker response than that to the Buddha. Indeed there was a sound, as of hair rubbing across the paper screens, of someone or something trying to peer through the opaque material. There was a rattle and dash of rain. A gust swept through the corridor, the *shōji* slightly parted. Kwaiba gave a shriek – "O'Iwa! O'Iwa San! Ah! The bloated face, the drooping eyelid, the corpse taint in the air. It catches Kwaiba's throat. O'Iwa the O'Bake would force away Kwaiba the living. Ha! Ha!" A stronger gust, and the *shōji* dislodged from its groove whirled round and fell noisily into the room. Terror gave strength to the sick man. Kwaiba sprang madly forward. It was horrible to see the ghastly renovation of this tottering, flabby, emaciated man, who yet inspired the fear of a maniac's reckless strength. The frightened women huddled and crouched in the now darkened room, lit but by a single *andon* near the alcove. Was Kwaiba mad? As the men fought over the ruins of the *shōji*, in the darkness of the corridor, at first faint as a mist, then distinctly seen, the women were assured of the presence of O'Iwa. In long black robe, face wide and bloated, of a livid greenish tint, hair in wild disorder, bulging forehead, swollen eyeless lids, she stood over the struggling men. Suddenly she thrust the severed head she carried into the face of Kwaiba, leering horribly at him the while. With a yell he fell flat on his back. The braver entered with lights. All gathered round the unconscious Kwaiba.

This scene was the crisis of his disorder. The disease, once dormant, now fell on him suddenly and with full force. Perhaps these mental symptoms were its first indication. More annoying to his comfort, ulcers broke out all over his body. The itching drove the man nearly frantic. His mad scratching spread the sores. The boils developed. They ran with pus. So terrible was the stench that few would stay by him. The women fled the room in terror, driven away by the running stream of physical corruption, the continual babble of lewdness from the corrupt mind. He soon noted their absence. Kibei, attended by the sturdy and faithful Kakusuke, remained to nurse him. Suddenly said Kwaiba – "O'Hana, the harlot of Reigan; this Kwaiba would have talk and dalliance with her. Summon her hither. Let wine and the *samisen* be brought, a feast prepared. O'Hana! O'Hana!" He raved so for the woman that Kibei thought her presence would quiet him. A request was sent to the house of Iemon. Wishing her to know nothing of the affair of O'Iwa, Iemon had kept silence. He would have refused the mission – on the pretext of a quarrel with Kwaiba and Kibei. O'Hana showed herself unexpectedly obstinate – "It is to the favour of Kwaiba Sama that Iemon owes this Hana. She has a duty to the past, as well as to the present." With a snarl she turned on him, glowering. Iemon shrank back. He passed his hand across the eyes into which O'Iwa had just looked. He no longer opposed her going.

O'Hana was still weak from repeated attacks of the fever which had visited her ever since the night Iemon had cast forth the *aodaishō*. She said that the snake had bitten her. It was the poison, not fever, working in her. Iemon had laughed at her proposal to try the exorcisms of the priest. Behind the irritation aroused by his scepticism was that peculiar clinging of a woman to an old lover, to a man with whom she had been intimate. In the heart of O'Hana there still remained a strong leaning to the man who had removed her from the rapid and nauseating life of the Fukagawa brothel, which cast her into the arms of anyone who paid the price and raised his finger. With time and the old conditions probably she would have been as unfaithful to Iemon as she had been to Kwaiba. The latter showing his desire, she would have answered his call. Even before this disease-eaten swollen mass of dropsy, she showed but temporary repugnance. Leaning over him, almost overcome by the stench, with endearing terms she strove to rouse him to consciousness and recognition of her. It seemed fearful to have him die without the word of parting. Kibei aided her by raising the old man. The result was a horrible frightened stare in eyes made large by fever and delirium. Long he gazed at her. Said the woman – "'Tis Hana; Hana once the intimate of Kwaiba. Deign to take courage. This is but a passing affliction. With Hana as nurse recovery to health is assured." She laid her hands on his shoulders. In so doing her hair, come loose, fell down around her wan face. Kwaiba was as galvanized. With a howl the old man pushed her violently away. "Scrawny wench! What impudence to show your face here! Ah! To the last moment, waking and in dreams, she pursues this Kwaiba. I sold you. 'Tis true – I sold you for a night-hawk – to Toemon of Honjo. Does Kwaiba consort with wenches of such ilk?" Raising his fist he dealt her blow after blow, all the time shouting – "O'Iwa! O'Iwa! The O'Bake solicits Kwaiba. Broken loose from Hell and the waters of Warigesui she would force away Kwaiba. Help! Help! Aid for Kwaiba! Away with the O'Bake!" The old man again had broken into his mad fit. The shouts of Kibei brought Kakusuke. Kwaiba's hands were detached from the masses of O'Hana's hair. The wounds on her face were not so deep as those inflicted on her mind. At last the secret was out. In bare feet she fled along the muddy street toward the Samoncho house.

It was true that the vileness of the disease, the vileness of Kwaiba's tongue, had driven the women from attendance in the sick room to the remotest quarters of the house. But there was a deterrent even to their now limited service. All said the place where Kwaiba lay was haunted. Under press of necessity a maid had brought needed medicaments to the sick man's room. Putting down the light she carried on the *rōka*, she pushed open the *shōji* to enter the outer chamber. Her robe caught as she did so.

Turning to release it she gave a fearful shriek. Standing in the corridor, at the open screen behind her, were two tall figures robed in black. With dishevelled hair, broad white flat faces, bulging brows, eyelids swollen and sightless, yet they gazed through and through the onlooker and into the farther room. One creature, even more hideous with drooping lid and baldness extending far back, half moved, half fell toward the frightened maid. The woman's screams now were mingled with wild laughter. Kibei came rushing out, sword drawn, to find her in a fit of mad hysterics. Catching the drift of her broken phrases he went out on the *rōka*. There was no one there. *Haori* and *kimono*, hung up there to dry, rustled and moved a little in the draft. Had these frightened the woman? Kakusuke carried her back to her companions. Henceforth no one would enter that part of the building occupied by the sick man. Kibei as son, Kakusuke the old and faithful attendant, were isolated in their nursing.

Kibei noted the sick man's face. "Father, why the forehead so wrinkled? Is pain condescended?" Said Kwaiba – "'Tis the rats; they gnaw and worry at Kwaiba." – "Rats?" replied Kibei in some astonishment. He looked around. The *shōji* were tight closed. Kwaiba noted the inspection. He shook his head, and pointed to the *rama-shōji*, the ornamental open work near the ceiling. This could not be obviated. "Auntie (Obasan) is old and deaf. She sleeps; while rats, attracted by the foul sores of the scrofulous child, enter and attack the infant in its cradle. The child gets thinner and weaker every day; then dies. A terrible creature is the rat." So much for the opinion of Nippon. Kibei had brought a mosquito net. Its edges were weighted down with heavy stones. Thus the watchers could not be taken by surprise. Under its protection the sick man was saved from annoyance.

Said Kibei – "This illness is most tedious. Could not Kibei go to the Yoshiwara for a space? The letters of the Kashiku (*oiran*) accumulate. Kibei has nothing to give, and has given no explanation for not giving. What thinks Kakusuke?" Kakusuke was brave. Moreover he knew the Wakadono was brave. The prospect, however, of facing his old master in a crazy fit – and perhaps O'Iwa – had no attraction. He gave his advice – "The Go Inkyo Sama is in a very precarious state. He is now very weak. The worst may happen at any moment. For the Wakadono to be taking his pleasure at the Yoshiwara would arouse criticism in the ward; nay, even more than criticism. It would be held unfilial. Deign to reconsider the purpose." Kibei looked sourly at the swollen corruption which represented Kwaiba – "How does he hold on! His strength must be great." Kakusuke shrugged his shoulders – "The Go Inkyo Sama will not die easily. He has much to go through yet." – "In the name of all the *kami* and Buddhas, how has he come to such an end? He is a sight to inspire fear – in those who can feel such." Replied Kakusuke with sly look – "The Go Inkyo Sama has lived high, and loved beyond measure. The Wakadono does well to reconsider his purpose."

The night was passing. The two men, worn out by the continued watching and nursing, after vain struggle to keep awake had gone to sleep. Kakusuke was in the room with Kwaiba. In his slumber Kibei was back in the fencing room. The clash of the wooden swords (*bokken*), the cries of the contestants, rang clear in his ears. He woke to find rain and storm shaking and tearing at the *amado*. But it was the shouts of Kakusuke, standing at the *shōji*, which had aroused him – "Danna Sama! Danna Sama! Wakadono! At once! At once! Deign to hasten!" Kibei rushed into the next room. In fright Kakusuke pointed to the mosquito net. A figure stood upright within it, swaying, gesticulating, struggling. It was a figure all black and horrible. "Un! Un!" grunted Kwaiba. He was answered by a mincing, gnawing sound. "Father! Have courage! Kibei is here." He rushed at the heavy stones, to toss them to one side and enter the net. The swaying figure within suddenly toppled over in a heap. With his sword Kibei tore and severed the cording of the net. The black mass of rats scattered to the eight directions of space. On approaching Kwaiba a terrible sight met the eye. Eyes, ears, nose, chin, toes and fingers had been torn and eaten off. The lips were gnawed away and exposed to view the grinning teeth. A feeble groan – and Kwaiba had met his end. Neither Kibei nor Kakusuke dared to touch the foul body. In their panic the two men looked in each other's faces. "Namu Amida Butsu! Holy the Lord Buddha, Amida!" prayed Kibei, on his knees before the corpse. "Namu Amida Butsu!" answered Kakusuke.

In The Shadow of the Go Inkyo

Said a neighbour next day, on meeting his fellow-gossip – "Ah! Is it Goemon San? It is said the Go Inkyo is to be congratulated." Kamimura Goemon sniffed. He was a long man; with long face, long nose, long thin arms, long thin legs; a malicious man, who longed to give advice to his fellows which they much disliked to hear, and liked to see them writhe under the infliction. In fact this epitome of length rarely spoke in good faith or temper – "The Go Inkyo is to be congratulated? Escaping the troubles of this world, perhaps he has fallen into worse troubles in the next." At this unorthodox reply Mizoguchi Hambei showed surprise. Continued Goemon – "The Go Inkyo died a leper, eaten by the rats. Such an end hardly calls for congratulations." Mizoguchi gasped, with round eyes and round face. "Extraordinary!" – "Not at all," replied Kamimura, complacently tapping the palm of one hand with the elongated fingers of the other. "The Go Inkyo drove out O'Iwa San from Tamiya. He gave O'Hana in her stead to Iemon as wife. Hana the harlot! Cursed by O'Iwa in dying, he has met this frightful end. Akiyama, Natsume, Imaizumi will surely follow. As will all those involved in the affair." – "But is O'Iwa San really the cause of the death? The Go Inkyo in life was not the most careful of men in conserving health." This was timidly interjected by a third party. Kamimura suppressed him with a scowl – "Of course it is O'Iwa San. Has she not been seen? The women of the house answer for it. Only Kibei the sceptic, and Kakusuke who would face the devil in person, attempt to deny it." He threw up a hand. With unction – "Ah! It inspires fear. Small is the profit of wickedness and malice. He is a fool who indulges in either.... How cold it is for the time of year!"

Said the interloper – "But the congratulations have to be rendered all the same. It will be necessary to attend the all-night watch. How vexatious! Perhaps O'Iwa San will not appear. There is no getting out of it?" – "Certainly not," answered Kamimura. "The Go Inkyo was the head of the ward association. Twelve neighbours have been invited to the watch. At dawn the body is to be prepared. A pleasant undertaking, if all that is said be true! The viands will be of the best, the wine no worse and plentiful. None must fail to attend." He smacked his lips. The others likewise, but much less heartily.

It was an unwilling band which crawled in laggard procession through rain and mud and the length of the Teramachi to Kwaiba's house. A *dōshin*, the ward chief, a rich man, the mansion displayed all its splendour. The atmosphere, however, was oppressive. Kibei greeted the guests with heartiness, and accepted their condolence and gifts with lavish thanks and the cheerful face of him that profiteth by the funeral. Kakusuke was his main aid in connection with the Go Inkyo's last appearance. Occasionally a timid white-faced woman was seen, but she would flit away from the scene of these festivities, to seek the companionship of her panic-stricken fellows. Entering the funereal chamber the body was found, laid out and decently swathed so as to cover, as far as possible, the horrible nature of the death. On a white wood stand was the *ihai* in white wood, a virtuous lie as to the qualities of the deceased. It ran – Tentoku Gishin Jisho Daishi. Which can be interpreted – "A man of brilliant virtues, virtuous heart, and benevolent temperament." Screens, upside down, were placed at the head:

"Alas! The screen: the carp descends the fall." Akiyama, Natsume, Imaizumi, were the last to appear. The former had been composing a violent quarrel between his two friends – the long and the fat. Much recrimination had passed, and the usually peaceful Imaizumi was in a most violent and truculent humour. He glared with hate on Natsume, who now aided Akiyama in efforts to soothe his anger. On entering the assembly the looks of all were composed. "A retribution for deeds in the past world. Old; but so vigorous! The offering is a mere trifle. This Kyuzo would burn a stick of incense." Kibei extended his thanks and suppressed his smile as much as possible. He was breathing with full lungs for the first time in weeks. The storm was over; happiness was ahead; the clouded sky was all serene. "Thanks are felt. This Kibei is most fortunate: nay, grateful. Such kindness is not to be forgotten during life." – "The Inkyo an *hotoke*; Iemon Dono and O'Hana are the husband and wife not present?" The question came from someone in the room. "O'Hana San is very ill. Her state is serious. Iemon does not leave her." Akiyama answered for the truant pair. Kibei's joy was complete.

Akiyama, Natsume, Imaizumi were standing by Kwaiba's body. Kamimura slowly approached. The long man's face was longer than ever; longer, much longer than that of Natsume; and Kibei was not in the running. Goemon meditatively fondled his nose; on the pretence of concentrating thought, and for the purpose of relieving that member from the savour arising from Kwaiba's bier. This was no bed of roses – "Yes, the Inkyo is indeed dead." He sniffed. "Soon it will be the turn of all of you – to be like this;" another sniff – "of

Iemon and O'Hana, of Natsume and Imaizumi, of this Akiyama San." The latter gave a violent start. With hand to his nose also, he turned on the intruder. Continued Goemon – "A plot was concocted against O'Iwa San. Beggared and driven from the ward, deceived and sold as a street harlot, this death of the Inkyo is but the first in the roll of her vengeance. Kamimura speaks with pure heart and without malice. You men are not long for this world. Is Akiyama San reconciled? And...." He pointed a skinny finger at Kyuzo, then at Jinzaemon. "You show it. Your eyes are hollow; your nostrils are fallen in. The colour of the face is livid. You seem already to be *hotoke*, prepared to lie with the Go Inkyo." Akiyama found his tongue. He burst out in a rage – "The jest is unseemly. Kamimura San goes too far. It is true this Chozaemon gave counsel to Ito Kwaiba. Kyuzo and Jinzaemon took some part in what followed. But we acted on the orders of Ito Dono, of Iemon San. On the first will be visited any grudge." Goemon laughed harshly. He pointed to the corpse. "Here he lies. How did he die? Goemon does not jest, and the argument of Akiyama San is rotten. The master bids the servants to beat the snow from the bushes. The snow falls on them; not on him. How now Akiyama San?" Chozaemon turned away discomfited. All three felt very bad – in mind and body.

The bell of Sainenji struck the eighth hour (1 am). Just opposite, its clangour filled the whole mansion with a ghostly sound. In the depths of night this inert mass of metal seemed a thing of life, casting its influence into the lives of those present, rousing them to face grave issues. Noting the absence of Natsume, the round-faced, round-eyed, round-bodied Imaizumi followed after. Kibei came forth from the supper room, to find his guests all flown. "Where have they gone to, Kakusuke?" He looked around in amazement – "They were taken with pains in the belly. With this excuse they departed. Yotsuya is afflicted with a flux." The *chūgen* answered in the dry and certain tone of one unconvinced. Kibei shrugged his shoulders. "There is naught wrong with wine or viands?" – "Nor with the guests," replied Kakusuke. "They are cowards, who have caught some inkling as to the not over-nice death of the Go Inkyo." – "The latter day *bushi* are not what the *bushi* were of old; at least this brand of them. Ah! These wretched little bureaucrats; *bushi* of the pen. Two men to eat a supper prepared for twelve sturdy trenchers. Well: two are enough to wash the corpse. Lend a hand Kakusuke." – "Respectfully heard and obeyed," replied the *chūgen*.

The white dress for the last cover to the body was laid ready. Secured by Kwaiba many years before in a pilgrimage to the holyKoyasan, the sacred characters were woven into its tissue. Kakusuke dragged a large tub into the bathroom. Kwaiba's body was unswathed and placed in it. Kakusuke eyed his late master with critical and unfavourable eye. "Naruhodo! The Go Inkyo is a strange object. No eyes: nose, ears, lips gone; his expression is not a pleasant one.... Nay! The Wakadono is awkward. Throw the water from head to feet.... Take care! Don't throw it over Kakusuke. He at least is yet alive. The Wakadono is wasteful. More is needed. Deign to wait a moment. Kakusuke draws it from the well." He opened the side door and went outside. Kibei drew a little apart from the body. It stank. A noise at the sliding window (*hikimado*) in the roof made him look up. Oya! Oya! The face of O'Iwa filled the aperture – round, white, flat; with puffed eyelids and a sightless glare. With a cry of horror and surprise Kibei sprang to the door. As he did so slender attenuated hands groped downward. "Kakusuke! Kakusuke!" – "What is it, Wakadono?" – "O'Iwa: she looks down through the *hikimado*! She seeks the Inkyo!" Kakusuke gave a look upward – "Bah! It's the cat. Is the Wakadono, too, getting nerves? They are a poor investment." – "The cat!" Kibei sighed with relief. Nevertheless he kept his hand on his sword.

He turned round – to give a shout of surprise – "Kakusuke! Kakusuke! The body of the Go Inkyo is no longer here." As the astonished *chūgen* came running to look into the empty tub, both men nearly fell over in their wonder. The body of the Inkyo was whirling around the neighbouring room in execution of a mad dance. Followed by Kakusuke, his worthy son and heir sprang in pursuit. Invisible hands led Kwaiba and the pursuers into the darkness of the garden, into the rain and storm. Kibei heard the steps just in front of him. He pursued madly after them. "To lose his parent's body – this was against all rules of Bushido." Thus comments the scribe of Nippon. Kibei could commit all the moral and physical atrocities except – failure in filial conduct to parent and lord; the unpardonable sins of the Scripture of Bushido. Kakusuke soon lost his master in the darkness. Disconcerted and anxious he returned to secure a lantern. The wind promptly blew it out; then another, and a third. He stood on the *rōka* in the darkness to wait the return of the Wakadono. For the first time Kakusuke had noted failing purpose in his young master. He was more solicitous over this than over the strange disappearance of the Inkyo's body. Was the Wakadono losing his nerve; as had the O'Dono?

In time Kibei reappeared. To Kakusuke's inquiring glance – "Kibei pursued to Myogyoji; then up the hill. Here sight was lost of the Inkyo. The darkness prevented further search. A lantern is next to worthless in this gale. Kakusuke, go to the houses of Natsume and Imaizumi close by. They are young and will aid Kibei in the search." Kakusuke did not demur. Pulling his cape over his head, off he posted. He asked but to come across the Inkyo's body, in O'Iwa's company or not made no difference to this iron-hearted servitor. His mission was fruitless. The two men had expressed the intention of spending the night at the Kwaiba wake. Neither had as yet returned. Grumbled Kibei – "The filthy fellows! With this excuse to their wives they seek new pastures at Nakacho (Shinjuku), to spend the night in dissipation. 'Tis Natsume who is the lecher. Gladly would he wean Imaizumi from his barely wed wife." – "Or wean the wife from Imaizumi Sama! Wakadono, nothing can be done now. The dawn should be awaited." With these sage comments the *chūgen* squatted at respectful distance from his master. From time to time one or other arose, to look sceptically into the empty tub in which once had reposed the Inkyo's body. Finally both nodded off into sleep. At dawn – don, don, don, don, came a loud knocking on the outer gate. Kakusuke went out, to return with astonished face and portentous news. The dead bodies of Natsume Kyuzo and Imaizumi Jinzaemon had been found at the foot of the *bake-ichō*, a huge tree close by the guardhouse. Finger tip to finger tip three men could not girdle this tree. With the bodies of the men lay that of a woman. Two corpses, man and woman, were stark naked. Kibei's presence, as the successor to Kwaiba's office, was required.

He prepared at once to start for the Ōkidō. The tale was in time learned from the prolix Kamimura Goemon, who had witnessed part at least of the scene. As he was knocking at his door on the Shinjuku road, having just returned late from the watch at Kwaiba's house, rapid steps were heard in the street. A man, recognized as Kyuzo, passed, running at top speed. He dragged along by the hand a woman, the wife of Imaizumi. The two were nearly naked. Close in the rear pursued Imaizumi Jinzaemon, his drawn sword in his hand. They sped up the wide road. Goemon stepped out, to follow at a distance this flight and pursuit. At the *ichō* tree the fugitives were overtaken. The woman was the first to be cut down. Kyuzo turned to grapple with the assailant. Unarmed his fate soon overtook him. He fell severed from shoulder to pap. Having finished his victims Imaizumi seated himself at the foot of the tree, and cut open his belly. "Long had such outcome been expected," intoned the long-nosed man. The case needed no explanation. Others echoed the opinion of Goemon, who was merely many fathoms deeper in the scandal of the neighbourhood than most of them. It was agreed to hush the matter up. Reporting his own experience, to the astonishment of his hearers, Kibei, accompanied by Kakusuke, started down Teramachi toward Samegabashi. As they passed the Gwanshoji attention was drawn by a pack of dogs, fighting and quarrelling in the temple cemetery. A white object lay in the midst. With a shout the men sprang in. Tearing up a grave stick Kibei rushed into the pack, driving off the animals. There lay the body of Ito Kwaiba, brought hither by the hands of O'Iwa to be torn and mangled by the teeth of the brutes. Thus was it that the funerals of Ito Kwaiba, Natsume Kyuzo, and Imaizumi Jinzaemon took place in one cortege on the same day and at the same time. The postponement in the first instance – was it providential?

Tamiya Yoemon: With News of Kondo Rokurobei and Myozen the Priest

Tamiya Yoemon was stumbling home in all haste from the funeral of Ito Kwaiba. He was full of news for the wife, O'Kame. The neighbours could talk of nothing but the strange happenings in the ward, and details lost nothing in the telling; perhaps gained somewhat by the process. Most edifying was the reported conduct of the wife of the late Natsume Kyuzo, the observed of all observers at the funeral, the object of that solicitous congratulation which embodies the secret sigh of relief of friends, neighbours, and relatives at the removal of a prospective burden. Natsume had left behind him a wife, an old mother, an infant child, and huge liabilities. To administer this legacy – and perhaps to get rid of her mother-in-law – the wife had promptly and tearfully sacrificed her status, and sold herself for a term of years to the master of the Sagamiya, a pleasure house at Shinagawa post town. The sum paid – one hundred *ryō* – relieved the immediate future. The neighbours derided the ignorance of the Sagamiya in accepting the uncertain bail of Akiyama Chozaemon. If the lady behaved badly, small satisfaction was to be obtained of her security. "Ignorance is bliss." Let the Sagamiya bask in both and the beauty of the prize. Meanwhile their concern and admiration were for the lady destined to this post town of the crowded Tokaido, the stopping place of high and low, noble and riff-raff, entering Edo town. Of the inmates of the pleasure quarters, the harlots of Shinagawa, Shinjuku, Itabashi, were held in lowest esteem.

Arrived at his door Yoemon stopped short in surprise and alarm. To his loud call of "Wife! Wife!" answer there was none. Looking within he could barely distinguish objects through the thick smoke which filled the house. The last thing the Nipponese would do under such conditions, would be to throw open doors and panels. This would convert the place at once to a blazing conflagration. Where was the fire getting its start? Choking and spluttering Yoemon groped his way through the rooms into the rear. Wherever the fire was, it was not in the living rooms. The smoke was accentuated on reaching the kitchen. Here was a smell of burning rice, of Yoemon's dinner gradually carbonizing under the influence of an element other than the juices of his round stomach. Looking into the room, through the thickened haze he saw the flame of the fire brightening. O'Kame the wife could be made out, on her knees before the portable furnace. She was blowing a mass of slivers and brushwood into flame by the aid of a bamboo pipe. It was this stuff, green and partly wet, which gave out the choking acrid smoke. Yoemon was angered beyond measure at the sight of his ruined meal and expectations. "Kame! Kame! What are you doing? Have you gone mad? Ma! Ma! The dinner is being ruined. You are ill. Kame's head whirls with head-ache. Yoemon will act as cook. Go to bed – at once." At his peremptory speech the wife looked up into the face of the husband standing over her. She scowled at him in a way to cause fear. "Not a *shō* of rice; not a *mon*. Yoemon would give freely to a beggar, rather than confer a 'cash' on Iwa. Yoemon sells me as a street harlot." He started back in fright before the snarling distorted visage. The wife sprang to her feet. Pash! On his devoted head descended the hot iron pan with its content of stew. "Ah! Kame is mad – clean daft." With a wild laugh she seized the pot full of boiling rice and began to pour it into the drain. When he tried to stop her, he received the mess full in his bosom – "Mad? Not at all. This Kame never felt in better spirits. When grass grows in Samoncho we enter Nirvana. Ha! Ha! Ha! To hasten the happy time!" With a kick she knocked over the furnace. In an instant the *tatami* was in a blaze. Yelling like mad, shouting for help, Yoemon leaped from the house. O'Kame seized the burning brands in her bare hands, hurling them into this room and into that. Outstripping the old Yoemon, the younger men of the neighbours rushed in. The mad woman was soon overcome and carried from the burning building. Nothing else was saved. They took her to the house of Akiyama Chozaemon. Here she was tied hand and foot, and put in a closet. The old man Yoemon stood by in despair, watching the progress of events. Before the conflagration was extinguished his own and four other houses were destroyed. He was a ruined man; responsible for all.

Myozen the priest had just set foot on the slope leading up from Samegabashi to Yotsuya. A somewhat long retreat at Myohonji, attendance at the ceremonies held on the Saint's (Nichiren) birthday, had kept him in ignorance of recent events in Yotsuya. In the dawn of the beautiful day of earliest 3rd month (our April 13th) he had set out from Kamakura. Sturdy as were the priest's limbs, yet he was a little tired. He rested at the foot of the hill. Then his eyes grew big with astonishment. In the waning afternoon a funeral came wending its way downwards. But such a funeral! Two spearmen led the way. Then came a long train of attendants. Three catafalques followed, the first a most imposing bier. Then came the relatives. Kibei on horseback headed these. The women rode in *kago*. That it was a ward funeral Myozen had no doubt, both from its source and make up. He noted a parishioner in the cortege. "Kamimura Uji!" The long-limbed, long-faced, long-tongued man left the ranks and obsequiously greeted his spiritual father. At Myozen's question he expressed gratified surprise, and unlimbered his lingual member at once – "Whose honoured funeral this? Nay! It is a triple funeral; that of Natsume Kyuzo, Imaizumi Jinzaemon, the Go Inkyo, our ward-head. It is owing to this latter that there is such an outpouring of the ward, with attendance of barrier guards and firemen. Although the ending of Natsume and Jinzaemon was not edifying, that of our honoured once head gratified still more the public curiosity. Gnawed and eaten by the rats he died most horribly." He told of the eventful night. "Hence delay in the burial. The deaths of Natsume and Imaizumi were almost coincident. The body of the adulterous woman, rejected by both families, was cast out on the moor." He noted with satisfaction the great impression his tale made on the priest, as also the clerical garb and rosary held in hand. "Pray join the band. A little re-adjustment...." He bent down. With the baton he held in hand as leader of his section he carefully dusted the robes. Adjusting the folds he pronounced the results as most presentable. "The honoured Osho is ready to bury or be buried." Myozen took this remark in very ill form. He prepared to answer tartly, but curiosity overcame his weariness and ill temper. The procession was moving fast. He fell at once into line, with hardly an acknowledgment of Kamimura's courtesy, as this latter hastened forward to his place.

His neighbour in the procession explained. The nature of the deaths of the three men had aroused the feeling in the ward. Their connection with a conspiracy against O'Iwa San was now generally known. Without doubt it was owing to her vengeance that they had died as they did. Let them lie outside the quarter. The protest to Kibei was respectful but emphatic. A newcomer, he had made no great resistance. It was determined to bury them at the Denzu-In, close by the mound of the nameless dead of Edo's great fire of more than half a century before. Hence the direction of the cortege. As the cemetery of the great temple was approached the curiosity of Myozen, morbidly growing the while, became overpowering. The priest slipped from rank to rank. At the grave he stood in the very front. As long-time friend he besought a last glance at the dead. Those given to Natsume and Imaizumi called forth a careless prayer for each. The men hesitated before raising the cover concealing the body of Kwaiba. At Myozen's peremptory gesture they complied. He bent over and looked in. Frozen with horror, he was fascinated by those great holes for eyes, large as teacups, which seemed to fix him. Dead of leprosy, gnawed and torn by beasts, the face presented a sight unforgettable. The holes torn in the flesh twisted the features into a lifelike, though ghastly, sardonic grin, full of the pains of the hell in which Kwaiba had suffered and now suffered. A stench arose from the box which made the hardened bearers hold their noses and draw away. Yet the priest bent down all the closer. In his corruption the lips of the old man seemed to move. Did Kwaiba speak? Closer and closer: Myozen seemed never satisfied with this inspection. The poise and brain gave way. Priest and corpse met in the horrible salutation. With exclamation the attendants sprang forward. Myozen in a dead faint was carried apart and laid on the ground. Some priests of the hall busied themselves over him. Somewhat revived he was taken off to the residence quarters of the temple, and soon was able to return to his home. "Curious fool." Kibei was greatly angered. He was easily irritated in these days. The delay in the rites almost maddened him. Would old Kwaiba – his father Ito Inkyo – never be got out of men's sight? Out of Kibei's sight?

That night Myozen sat alone in his quarters. Somewhat shaken, he was ashamed and regretful at thought of his unseemly curiosity of the afternoon. The priests of Denzuin had regarded him with covert amusement and repulsion. He had noted one passing the sleeve of his robe over his lips. Myozen explained the incident by more than usual weariness. They condoled with him, and made horrified gestures of ill-disguised glee when they thought his attention was elsewhere. In his present privacy the scene at the grave came back to mind again and again. "Ah! Ah! If this Myozen had not looked. The Inkyo's face was terrible. Myozen cannot put it from mind." He glanced at the pages of the sutra lying before him. He turned them over. He knew they spoke of the horribleness of death; but what was the cold script to the actuality? It was no use, the attempt to read. Kwaiba's face interposed. "Oh! That salute! The very idea of that terrible salute, the contact with corruption!" He was as if plunged in an icy bath. He started nervously. It was but rain dashing against the *amado*, rattling and twisting in the gale. He could not sleep. That night he would watch. The fire was hot in the *hibachi* (brazier). He went to the closet to get some tea. On opening it he sprang back with a shout of alarm, to lean trembling and quivering in every limb huddled against the wall. "Namu Myoho Renge Kyo! Namu Myoho Renge Kyo!" One character of the wondrous formula secured pardon and safety to the believer in that paradise of Amida which Myozen was in no great haste to visit. Shivering as with a chill intently he watched the animal as it glided along the edge of the room, to disappear into the shadows. He shrugged his shoulders wearily. A rat had frightened him almost out of his wits! His heart beat tumultuously, almost to suffocation; then it seemed to cease altogether; to resume its wild career.

Hardly was he again seated, his hand on the kettle – don – don, don – don, don, don, don. Someone was violently knocking on the door. Myozen sprang up. Approaching the *amado* with silent step he eyed the bolts: "All secure." Snatching up a stake close by he jammed it in between floor and crosspiece. Leaning heavily on the panel he listened. "Myozen Sama! Osho Sama! Condescend to open; deign to give entrance! The storm nearly throws one to the ground. News! News for the Osho! A request to make!" Myozen held his ground against this outer temptation. "Who are you, out at this hour of the night and in such weather? Tonight Myozen does not open. Go away; return in daylight." – "But the honoured Osho Sama is needed. His presence is requested. Deign to open; at least to hear the message. The priest aids the afflicted." There was something in the voice he recognized, despite its terror. Regaining some courage he parleyed. The priest was for the consolation of the unfortunate. O'Iwa had been, was unfortunate. He could not open. "Who are you? Unless the name be given this Myozen holds no further talk. Tonight he is unwell, positively ill. Come at dawn and Myozen will receive you." – "Who? Does not the voice answer for the person? This is Tomobei, from the house of Kondo Rokurobei. Deign to open. The master needs and calls for the aid of the Osho Sama."

Voice and speech, the importance of Kondo in the life of Myozen, broke down his hesitation. Slowly he removed the bars. Tomobei entered, dripping with wet. He cast down his straw coat at the entrance. The man's eyes and manner were wild. He kept casting frightened looks into the wild welter of storm outside. When the priest would withdraw into the room he held him by the skirt. "What has happened?" commanded Myozen briefly. Replied Tomobei – "A terrible thing! Today the master was ready to attend the funeral of Ito Inkyo. The wife was engaged in putting the house *kimono* in the closet. O'Tama was playing on the upper *rōka*. She is but seven years old. Leaning far over to see her father leave, she lost her balance. Down she fell, to be impaled on the knife-like points of the *shinobi-gaeshi*. The sharp-pointed bamboo, protection against thieves, have robbed the Danna of his greatest treasure (*tama*). Deep into throat and chest ran the cruel spikes, to appear through the back. The sight inspired fear, so horrible was it. He could but call out – 'Tomobei! Tomobei!' All effort to detach the child, to saw off the points, did but make matters worse. It was necessary to fetch a ladder. When taken down she was dead. Alas! Alas! The Okusama is nearly crazed. The Danna Sama in his cruel distress does but rage through the house. 'Myozen Osho, he loved the child. Let Myozen Osho be summoned to say a prayer of direction, while yet the child spirit hovers hereabouts.' Such is the cry of the Okusama. Hence the presence of this Tomobei. Otherwise he would rather be scourged at the white sand than face the darkness in which O'Iwa San wanders abroad." Man and priest were weeping. The former in his fright and over the confusion and distress fallen on the household; the priest over the sudden and dreadful end of this child to whom the homeless one, the man devoted to the solitary life, had taken an unbounded affection as of a father. Great as was his terror, he forgot his own ills in the greater misfortune of the life-long friend. He remained bowed in prayer. "Namu Myoho Renge Kyo! Namu Myoho Renge Kyo! Oh! The wondrous law, the *sutra* of the Lotus!" He rose – "Myozen comes."

As they struggled through the storm, Tomobei kept up a nonsensical, running talk, full of the superstitious fear of the man of the lower classes. "Iya! The affair has been terrible, but misfortune is in the air.... What's that! Ah! Something passes by ... above. O'Iwa! O'Iwa!" He seized the priest's arm and clung to him in terror. Myozen's fears had all returned. He would have run away, but was too tightly held. "Where! Where!" He shrieked and whirled around toward Samegabashi. Tomobei held on tenaciously to his skirts. An object was bearing down on them in the dark. Close upon priest and man they jumped to one side. A cold hand was laid on the neck of the cleric, who squawked with fear. A howl answered the howls and mad cries and blows of the two men, who now threw themselves flat on the ground to shut out sight of the apparition. The beast sped down the hill. Discomfited, Myozen disentangled himself from the embraces of a broken water spout, which descending from the roof under which he had taken shelter, was sending its cold stream down his neck. Tomobei rose from the mud puddle in which he lay face downward. They gazed at each other. "A dog! A wandering cur!" Myozen eyed his once immaculate garments with disgust. How present himself in such a state! Tomobei read his thoughts and determined to keep a companion so hardly won. "There are present but the master and the Okusama, Tomobei, and Kiku; other company there is none.... Yes; the Ojosan." – "The corpse needs no company," said Myozen testily. In his disgrace and unkempt condition Myozen was unduly irritated at his child friend. The business was to be gone through. They were opposite the cemetery of Sainenji, on its western side. Said Tomobei – "A paling is loose. There is no need to descend the hill. This is no cheerful spot at this hour. Deign to sprint it, Osho Sama. In the time one can count ten the entrance at the rear is reached. Deign a spurt, honoured priest; deign to sprint." Myozen felt he was in for everything this night. With Tomobei he tucked up his robes to his hams, as if entering a race. Crawling through the bamboo palings into the haunt of the dead, at it they went – a mad spurt across to Kondo's house. Tomobei was the more active. He turned to watch the priest tripping over hillocks in the grass, knocking into gravestones hidden by the darkness. So near home, courage was returning. He burst into laughter at sight of Myozen madly hammering a battered old stone lantern of the *yukimidōro* style. The broad-brimmed hat-like object he belaboured as something naturally or unnaturally possessed of life, all the while giving utterance to anything but priestly language. Tomobei ventured back to his rescue. Myozen was quite battered and bleeding as the two rushed into Kondo's house.

The master was expecting them; but he threw up his hands as they appeared in the room. "Osho Sama! Tomobei! What are you about! Why rush into the room, clogs still on the feet? Deign to withdraw. The *tatami* are stained and streaked with mud.... Water for the feet of the Osho Sama! Tomobei, are you mad? Out with you: bring water to clean up this mess." In confusion the priest withdrew. His apologies were profuse as he reappeared – "Alas! Terrible the loss, and in such dreadful manner. Kondo Dono, Okusama, part at least of this grief Myozen would take on himself. Great is the sorrow at this end of one just beginning life." The wife received the condolence of the priest with a burst of weeping. Then she turned fiercely on the husband – "It is all the fault of Rokurobei. He was *nakōdo* for O'Iwa San in the marriage with Iemon. Turning against her, he took O'Hana into the house. Did she not spend her time in idling, and teaching the child the ways of her questionable life – 'how to please men,' forsooth?... Ah! Tama did have pretty ways. Though but of seven years, she danced, and sang, and postured as would a girl double her age. Now thus cruelly she has perished." Her mind, reverted to the child, again took a turn. "The plot against O'Iwa – with Ito Kwaiba, Iemon, Chozaemon – here is found the source of this calamity. O'Iwa in dying has cursed all involved. Now 'Tis the turn of Kondo and his unfortunate wife." She ended in another outburst of tears, her head on the mats at the feet of the priest. Rokurobei was tearing up and down the room, gesticulating and almost shouting – "Yes! 'Tis she! 'Tis she! The hateful O'Iwa strikes the father through the child. Ah! It was a cowardly act to visit such a frightful ending on one budding into life. O'Iwa seeks revenge. O'Iwa is abroad; and yet this Kondo cannot meet with her." Myozen was almost deafened with his cries and noisy earnestness. Truly to bring peace into this household, with division reigning between husband and wife smitten with fear of the supernatural, would be no easy matter. His priestly experience taught him the safest way to bring about his object.

"'Tis true; 'Tis true. But loud cries avail nothing. The aid of the Buddha for the deceased is to be sought." Apologetically he showed something of his condition to the wife. At once she rose. Outergarments were removed. Muddied undergarments were renewed. Myozen went into the mortuary chamber. The little 'Jewel' was laid out as in sleep. The wounded chest, the torn throat, were concealed by garments and a scarf-like bandage adjusted by a mother's sad and tender care. The incense sticks lay in clay saucers near the couch. "Oh, the wonderful Law! The *sutra* of the Lotus! Namu Myoho Renge Kyo! Namu Myoho Renge Kyo!" He looked long at the little silent figure. His eyes were full of tears as he turned and took the hands of the weeping mother who had followed him into theroom. Then for long he spoke in consoling tones. She was somewhat quieted when they returned.

Kondo Rokuobei was still moving restlessly about the room. Now he was here, now there; from the death room he returned to the company; from them he passed to the kitchen. The wife thought of the friend and priest. "Tomobei, go to the store-room and bring wine." Myozen was a curious mixture. His weak spot was touched – "Deign it, honoured lady, for all. Let the occasion be made seemly, but more cheerful. Cause not sorrow to the dead by an unmeasured grief. This does but pain the Spirit in its forced communion with the living. Death perchance is not the misfortune of subsequent existence in this world, but a passage to the paradise of Amida." He spoke unctuously; as one full informed and longing for its trial. His homily had no effect in moving Tomobei, who was flatly unwilling to perform the service ordered. "The wine...," broke in Kondo harshly. – "The go-down is at the end of the lot. The hour is very late, and the storm ... and other things ... it rages fiercely. This Tomobei...." – "Shut up!" roared his master, with easily roused anger. The maid O'Kiku (Okiku) timidly interposed – "There is a supply in the kitchen. This Kiku early brought it there, anticipating the need. Indeed the storm is terrible. One gets wet to the bone in traversing the yard." The wife caught the last words – "Aye! Wet and chilled the lost child spirit wanders, ringing its bell and vainly seeking aid and shelter; no aid at hand but that of the heartless hag in the River of Souls." At the thought of the little O'Tama in cold and storm she broke down. Crying bitterly, she crept from the room and laid down beside the bier.

The wine was served. Myozen drank. Then he drank again. His potations gave him confidence – for more drink – and recalled him to his functions. "Let us all pray. Namu Myoho Renge Kyo! Namu Myoho Renge Kyo! Wonderful the Law! Wonderful the *sutra* of the Lotus, explanatory of the Law by which mankind are saved, to enter the paradise of Amida. Be sure the wanderings of O'Tama will be short. Scanty is the power of the Shozuka no Baba. Soon shall the child sit upon a lotus. Early shall be her entrance into Nirvana. Namu Myoho Renge Kyo! Namu Myoho Renge Kyo!... Honoured master, let all join in. Command the servants to join in the recital of the Daimoku." Kondo waved a hand at Tomobei and O'Kiku, in assent and command. Vigorous were the tones of all in the responses. Myozen drank again. He pressed the wine on the others; drinking in turn as they agreed. The night was passing. It was the eighth hour (1-3 am). Said he – "Don't get drowsy. By every means avoid it. Now! A vigorous prayer." He raised his hand – "Namu Myoho Renge Kyo! Namu Myoho Renge Kyo!" But the responses were flagging. Said Myozen – "This will never do; at this hour of the night." He drank again – to find that the supply had come to an end. Kondo was nodding. Tomobei, if awake, was deaf to words. Myozen rose himself to fetch a new supply.

Kondo pricked up his ears. The temple bells were booming the hour watch in solemn unison. The rain splashed and pattered on the *amado*. A rustling, swishing sound was heard, close by, in the next room. Now it was as if a hand was passing along the screen. He sprang up, drawn sword in hand. His eyes were riveted on the *shōji*, anticipating an appearance. Then he laid a violent hand on the interposing obstacle and threw it back. A tall figure robed in black, with broad flat face and bulging brow, puffed eyelids in which were sunken little dots in place of eyes, hair in wild disorder framing the dead white face, stood before him. "O'Iwa! O'Iwa!" The lamp was knocked over, but not before he dealt the one fierce upward blow. Madly he sprang on the apparition and slashed away in the dark. "Kiya!" The cry rang loud. Kondo danced with joy, calling loudly for lights. "O'Iwa! O'Iwa! Kondo has slain the O'Bake, the enemy of his child! Rejoice with Kondo! The vendetta is accomplished!" In the darkness and confusion a groan was heard; then another, still fainter; then there was silence. Tomobei appeared with a light. He leaned over the long black robed body; to raise an alarmed face to his joyful master. "At what does the Danna Sama rejoice? What has he done? 'Tis Myozen Sama, the Osho Sama, who lies cut down. Dreadful has been the mistake of the Danna Sama. This is like to cost the House dear." – "Namu Myoho Renge Kyo! Namu Myoho Renge Kyo!" The sword had slipped from Kondo's hand, and in genuine grief he knelt beside the body of the unfortunate priest, seeking for some sign of life. Alas! Myozen had almost been cut in two by the upward sweep of the sword. From liver to pap was one gaping wound. He lay in the pool of almost all the blood in his body. Gathered around the corpse the four people eyed each other with terror.

Don – don – don, don, don, don. They sprang up in a huddled mass. The sound was at their very shoulders. "Someone knocks at the back door," said Tomobei. "Go open it," commanded Kondo. Tomobei flatly refused, and without respect, nay with insolence. Kondo picked up and weighed in his hand the bloody sword. Why mingle vile blood with good? Instead of cutting the man down he went himself and opened the half door at the top. A woman, dripping with water, her hair in wild disorder, her face white as chalk, stood outside in the storm. Kondo gave an exclamation of surprise – "O'Kame of Tamiya! How comes O'Kame here? It was said that Yoemon San had shut her up, as one gone mad." The woman smirked with satisfied air – "Kondo Rokurobei is seer as well as murderer. This Kame was bound and imprisoned; nay, almost divorced. Myozen, just dead at Kondo's hands, tomorrow was to pronounce the divorce. For so much, thanks to Kondo Dono. But O'Tama has died. Kame would condole with Kondo San; burn a stick of incense for O'Tama. Condescend to grant entrance." Said Rokurobei abruptly – "How knows O'Kame of the death of Myozen; who told her of the fate of O'Tama?" She laughed wildly – "Who? O'Iwa; O'Iwa is the friend of Kame. It was she who loosed the bonds. 'O'Tama of Kondo's house is dead. O'Kame should condole with the wife, the friend of this Iwa. Get you hence, for Kondo has murdered the priest.' ... So here we are; O'Iwa accompanies Kame. Here she is." She waved a hand into the storm and darkness. "Deign to give passage to the chamber where lies O'Tama. O'Iwa and Kame would burn incense to the darling's memory, to the little Jewel." With a roar Kondo seized the breast of her robe – "Vile old trot, off with you!" He gave her a violent push which sent her on her buttocks. The woman remained seated in the mud, laughing noisily. She held out two skinny arms to him. With a slam he shut the door.

He knelt by the priest's body, truly grieved – "Ah! O'Iwa is abroad. How has this mad woman knowledge of this deed? What was the offence of Myozen thus to deserve the hatred of Tamiya O'Iwa?" O'Kame had seen the priest enter, had stood in the wet listening to the wild talk of Kondo, had seen the bloody sword in his hand. Her mad brain had put riot and death together. The talk as to O'Tama she had overheard from her closet. Kondo thought of neither explanation. He was at odds with Akiyama, and had sent no message to his house. As he speculated and thought how best to compound matters with the temple, now grieved at the rash blow fallen on a friend, now aghast at the certain and heavy indemnification which would be exacted by the enraged clerics, an uproar arose outside. There were wild cries and a scream of pain. Then came a loud triumphant shout – "Heads out! Heads out! O'Iwa is slain! This Akiyama has killed the O'Bake. The incubus of the ward is lifted. Help!" Kondo sprang up and out of the house. Were the words true? Had another succeeded where he had failed? His lantern, the lanterns of many others, threw light on the place where Akiyama Chozaemon bravely stood ward over the prostrate body of the apparition. Returning late from Shitamachi he had entered the ward with shrinking terror. As he skulked along, with eyes on every dark corner, the figure of a woman was seen close by the eaves of the house of Kondo Rokurobei. As he approached she came forward laughing wildly the while. The light of his lantern fell on the ghastly white face, the disordered hair. In a spasm of fright he dropped the lantern and delivered his blow in drawing the sword. The cut was almost identical with the one delivered to Myozen the priest. The men there gathered looked into each other's faces, then at the body of O'Kame lying in their midst. The crowd parted, and Tamiya Yoemon appeared. Kondo Rokurobei and Akiyama Chozaemon stood by with bloody swords, their own skins without a scratch. They were self-accused.

The upshot of the affair was ruin for all. Matters in Yotsuya were coming to the official ears. Yoemon was forced to make charges against Akiyama; the more willingly as therein lay a chance to recoup his own losses through the wife he intended to divorce on the morrow. Kondo easily cleared his skirts of this offence, but was involved with the irate temple priests. All were entangled in the heavy costs of the law of those days. Of these three men something is to be said later.

Kibei Dono

Kibei was in great straits, financial and domestic. The death of Kwaiba had brought him anything but freedom. In Nippon the headship of a House is much more than the simple heirship of our western law. Relieved of his obligation in office the old man's hands were wide open to shower benefice or caprice on the most worthless. Endorsement for cash and goods to Natsume, Imaizumi, and Kamimura; donations to the temples of Teramachi and the Yotsuyazaka; favours in every direction except that of Akiyama Chozaemon, in the pursuit of whom Kwaiba found much amusement; all these items added to the very free living in his household had pledged deeply the ample revenue of two hundred and thirty *tawara*, and would have upheld the *samurai* trait of not knowing the value of money – if Kwaiba had been of that kind. Between Kwaiba and Kibei, the wild debauchery of the last year had brought the House to the verge of ruin. Kibei was aghast. Long since he had become deeply involved with the Kashiku Tamagiku of the Yamadaya in Edomachi Itchome of the Yoshiwara. The ugly fellow was madly in love with the beauty. On her he had poured out the treasures of the Ito House during the six months which preceded the illness of Kwaiba. During his prolonged absence from her the letters of the Kashiku had inundated the writing table of Kibei. Had he deserted her? Was all affection gone? Where now were the promises of ransom, the blood-sealed vow to become husband and wife, to assume the relation which endures for two worlds? Kibei sullenly read these lines; cursing Kwaiba and cursing himself. Ransom! With strict living for the next five years *he* might set matters straight and free the Tayu; and any day *she* might be bought by some rich country *samurai* or *gōshi* (gentleman farmer), or be carried off to ornament the *bessō* of some *hatamoto*. Kibei wiped the bitter saliva from his lips.

The domestic difficulties were accompaniment to these more important matters. In the large mansion Kibei was now alone. The tenth day had witnessed the flight of the last of the servants. The women had departed with the funeral, through fear, sacrificing wages and even such clothing as could not surreptitiously be removed. What woman – or man – could remain in a house which was the nightly scene of such fearful sounds of combat. Shrieks, wails, groans, came from the quarters once occupied by the dead Kwaiba. As to this there was no difference of opinion. The more venturesome had been favoured with actual sight of the scenes enacted. They had seen the old man as he was in death, pursued from room to room by two frightful hags, as gaunt, blear, sightless as himself. Dreadful were the cries of the dead man as the harpies fastened upon him, descending from above like two huge bats. These scenes took place usually at the eighth hour (1 am), not to cease until dawn. As for the men servants, they took their leave in the days following, asking formal dismissal (*itoma*) with recommendation to another House. They scented the approaching ruin of their present employer.

One day Kakusuke presented himself. Kibei looked up. He understood at once that the man had come in his turn to take leave. Kakusuke alone had remained with him. He was *chūgen*, stable boy, cook, maid; and did the work of all four without complaint. The change in his master was too marked. Kibei, in his turn, had become irritable, timorous as a girl, subject to outbreaks of almost insane rage. To Kakusuke the young man seemed to have lost all nerve. Kakusuke wanted to serve a man. As long as the Wakadono gave promise of redemption, of rising above his difficulties and emerging into a splendid career in which Kakusuke could take pride, the *chūgen* was ready to take the bitter with the sweet. To be maid servant and keeper of a man half mad had no attraction for this blunt-nerved fellow. He spoke plainly – "The Wakadono should deign to throw up the whole connection. Under the present conditions the ruin of the House is unavoidable. Condescend to return to the original House in Honjo Yokogawa. This course will be best. At least the Wakadono secures his own salvation. This is the advice of Kakusuke, grown old in experience of service in a *samurai* household. In naught else is there hope. As to himself, would the Wakadono condescend to grant dismissal." Long had been the intimacy between Ito Kwaiba and Inagaki Shogen. Kakusuke, the messenger between the two Houses, had watched this Fukutaro (Kibei) grow to manhood, had noted his prowess. It was with delight he had carried the documents which were to bring this new and vigorous blood into the home of his decadent master. This was the result. "A pest on these witches – and their craft!"

Kibei heard him out with growing anger. As the man's words gathered vigour and plain spokenness his hand wandered to his sword. He had a mind to cut him down then and there for his freedom of speech. More than half induced to recognize the truth of the indictment his better feeling halted him. With harsh and sardonic tone he gave unbelieving thanks for the implied reproof of the *chūgen*. The service of Kakusuke had been faithful beyond measure. It should have its proper reward. If others had chosen to depart as do those who run away, they had shown ignorance of this Kibei. From a drawer of the desk he took out a letter already prepared, a roll containing wages. He pushed the *zen* toward Kakusuke. This readiness, as if foreseen, hit the man hard. Respectfully he pressed the letter to his forehead, bowing with extended hands on the *tatami*; the money he did not touch. Finally he raised a timid questioning glance to his one-time master. Said Kibei jeeringly – "Kakusuke has given his advice. Is it part of his long experience that a servant should question the wages placed under his nose? Off with you! This Kibei would be alone; most willingly so." At the peremptory threatening gesture Kakusuke no longer hesitated. He had no inclination to be a victim of one of the mad outbreaks of the young man. Taking the roll humbly he backed out of the room. His steps were heard a few minutes later passing the entrance. Then the outer gate shut to with a clang.

For a long watch Kibei sat in meditation. He was as one who sleeps. Then he rose with decision. "'Tis the last chance. Kakusuke is right. The matter is to be brought to an end." Dressing for the street he left the house. He opened the big gate; then went to the stable, and saddled and bridled his horse. He led it outside, closed the gate, and mounting he rode forth, to go to Honjo Yokogawa and the *yashiki* of his father, Inagaki Shogen. Coming unaccompanied he was received with surprise and some discomfiture, as he was quick to note. He was very quick to note things in these days. Prostrating himself before his mother – "Kibei presents himself. Honoured mother, deign to pardon the intrusion. Fukutaro would solicit her pity and influence." The lady looked at him with amazement. "Fukutaro! What then of Kibei? Is some jest deigned at the mother's expense? It is in very bad taste.... But the face of Kibei implies no jest. Pray put the matter plainly. Why does her son come in petition to the mother?" Began Kibei – "The matter is most serious...." He went into the full details; from the time of his entrance into the Ito House, through the course of dissipation and illness of Kwaiba, down to the present ruined state of affairs. "All this is due to the curse of O'Iwa San, to this plot in which Kibei foolishly engaged." Of this he now fully felt the force. The events of the past weeks had wrecked him in mind and body. One disaster after another, in house and ward, had been visited on Kibei. The bitterness and dislike of the people toward Kwaiba was visited on his representative, who was held responsible. In his great mansion he lived alone. No servant would enter it to attend to his wants. Was he to cook and be valet for himself – and pose as the Kumi-gashira, the great chief of the ward! The position was an impossible one. Deign to use a mother's influence with Inagaki Dono. "Condescend to secure permission for the return of this Kibei to his original House, for the cancellation of the adoption."

The wife of Shogen sat frightened; at the tale, and at this radical way of finding an exit from the situation. The mother's heart was full of pity for the distracted son, whose haggard looks showed the strain of the past weeks. Besides she was a woman, and as such fully believed in and feared the curse of this dead O'Iwa, one who had died without funeral rites or prayer. "Fortunately the honoured father now is on the night watch at the castle. He is at home, drinking his wine. His humour is excellent. Wait but a moment." Leaving Kibei she went to the room of Shogen's light indulgence. The severe and conscientious nobleman was bending under the genial influence of the *sake*. "Kibei? He comes in good season. The heir of Kwaiba Inkyo has not favoured his real father of late. Ah! The boy was well placed. Kwaiba soon made way for him; and none too willingly, one can believe." He chuckled. Then noting his wife's troubled looks. "But there is something to tell." – "So indeed; none too pleasant." She went into the story Kibei had told her. "His fear of O'Iwa San is deadly. The House is ruined, with no profit in the connection. Deign to permit the cancellation of the adoption, his return to the House of his true parent." She stopped before the stern astonished look of the husband. Said he harshly – "Let him come up. Shogen answers Kibei Dono in person.... Heigh! Up here with you! For Ito Dono there is wine...." Kibei entered joyfully at his father's call. Success was in his hands. Once more he was to marshal his father's retainers and accompany him to the castle; once more be the habitue of the fencing rooms. "Honoured father, fear enters: for long this Kibei has not ventured into your presence." – "And need not for long again," thundered the old man. "What stuff is this for the ears of Shogen? Kibei would sever his connection with the Ito House. Kibei is afraid of a ghost! He fears a girl! A *samurai* wearing two swords shrinks from an encounter with a woman! Has Shogen no obligation toward his old friend Kwaiba? In more serious matters and in life Shogen would share Kwaiba's lot. Back with you to the house in Yotsuya! If this matter become known, both Kibei and Shogen will be the laughing stocks of Edo. At least keep such fears to yourself. Off with you! Shogen had wine for Ito Dono. For the fellow who would call himself – Fukutaro, he has none." With a kick he sent rolling the*zen* (table) with its burden of bottles and heating apparatus. In a rage he left the room.

Kibei's face was white as he raised it from the *tatami*. "Father has no experience of ghosts; he speaks at random and in anger. Terrible is the actuality." Said the mother, slowly and painfully – "He is the father; he is to be obeyed." Kibei was sitting upright. He nodded grave assent. Then suddenly he prostrated himself ceremoniously before the *shōji* through which Shogen had disappeared. He repeated the salutation before his mother. Then he rose – "Ito Kibei takes leave. May good health and fortune visit those of this House." At his exit the mother rejoiced. Severe had been the father's words, but they had brought the boy to reason. She wept and trembled at the reproof. Men had best knowledge of such affairs. She would pray at Reiganji, and have memorial service held for the peace of this O'Iwa in the next world. Then the curse would not rest upon her son.

On his appearance at the house entrance an *ashigaru* (foot soldier) led up the horse. Kibei waved him away – "For the present keep the animal in charge. With matters to attend to close at hand Kibei will use other conveyance." The man took the animal away. Leaving the gate of the *yashiki* Kibei walked the short distance to the Hoonji bridge. Here was a *kago* (litter) stand. "To Yamadaya in Yoshiwara." As the *kago* men went off at a trot – "Kibei has played and lost. How does the account yonder stand? Seventy *ryō* owed at the Matsuminatoya. For the rest, this Kibei can claim a night's attendance from the *kashiku*. If affection would not grant it, the huge sums bestowed in the past have a claim upon her. Then to end matters and die like a *samurai*. Tomorrow Kibei cuts belly." It was the debt which sent him direct to the Yamadaya, and not first to the tea house. Sitting over the wine all effort of the Kashiku to enliven him failed. Noting her discomfiture he smiled gloomily. Then in explanation – "The thoughts of Kibei go astray. The House is ruined. Ransom is impossible. This is the last meeting. Tomorrow Kibei cuts belly, and dies like a *samurai*." At first the girl thought he was joking. Then noting the wild look of despair in his eyes, she was frightened. Partly in disbelief; partly seeking to postpone this desperate resolve, to turn his thoughts and gain time for reflection; partly in that sentimental mood which at times affects this class of women – "Is Kibei truly ruined? Lamentable the fate of Tamagiku. Why not join him in death? But the idea is too new. Deign to postpone the execution for a space. Tonight shall be a night of pleasure with the Kashiku Tamagiku. With the morrow's darkness she dies with Kibei. Hand in hand they will wander the paths of Amida's paradise." She came close to him in service of the wine; put her arms about him, and drew him to her bosom; in every way cajoled and sought to comfort him, and corrupt his purpose. Consent was easy. The night was passed in love and wine. In the morning he left her.

Kibei was making his final preparations; writing directions which would benefit as far as possible the House in Honjo at the expense of that in Yotsuya. In the Yoshiwara a very different scene was taking place. With his departure the Kashiku sprang up. Hastily throwing a robe around her person she sought the room of the *yarite* – the bawd of the house. "The Kashiku! At this hour – what has happened?" – "Something of importance. This night Tama dies with Kibei Dono. The compact is closed, hard and firm." The astonished bawd had been rubbing the sleep out of her eyes. The last words brought her full awake – "Is the Kashiku drunk with wine? Is she mad? Truly it would seem so. And the bail? What is to become of the unfortunate? True it is Toemon of Honjo; and he has trouble enough already. He will never leave his prison." Tamagiku made a gesture of impatience – "This Tama has acted but to gain time. Can she have affection for such an ugly fellow? Was she to be the victim of some crazy outburst? Perhaps the day will bring better counsel; but the night's conversation does not augur it. His plans are most complete. The master must be seen. Deign to mediate; prevent the admittance of Kibei Dono as guest." O'Kayo the bawd nodded intelligence and assent. At once she sought the master of the house. "A dangerous guest," was his comment. "Send to the Matsuminatoya. They must be warned. We can look after ourselves." As an attendant of the tea house presented himself – "And the master, Teisuke San!" – "Is absent; this Tosuke represents him. He has gone to Edo. Perhaps the house will deign to look at a new inmate. A true Tayu! The daughter of Akiyama San of Yotsuya sacrifices her caste. But sixteen years, she is a jewel. Less than a hundred *ryō* will buy her. He is in great difficulties." Tosuke spoke with enthusiasm. The master of the Yamadaya answered promptly and with emphasis – "Accepted: let her be on hand in the course of the day. But Tosuke, there is another matter. Kibei Dono no longer can be accepted as a guest." He went into details. Tosuke drew a long breath. "A dangerous fellow! The Danna Sama never liked his presence. But he owes the house much money; seventy *ryō*." – "That is your affair," coldly replied the master of the Yamadaya. "This house answers not for the accounts of the tea-house. Previous notice has been given. Kibei Dono cannot be received as guest." – "That is not to be denied. He is most undesirable. But the seventy *ryō*! And the week's settlement to make with this house?" The Yamadaya had an idea – "It rarely passes a hundred *ryō*.... Five years is accepted? Then take thirty *ryō* and deliver this girl to the Yamadaya.... A true Tayu? If so the debt of Kibei finds payment." Tosuke agreed with joy.

At night the *kago* man set Kibei down before the Matsuminatoya. Teisuke, the *teishū* (host), regarded his arrival with mixed feelings. His coming meant something. Giving up his two swords, and once seated, Kibei's first act was to give thanks for past services. Calling for his account he produced the seventy *ryō* in its settlement. Prompt and profound were the humble thanks of the house for this unexpected liquidation. Kibei had secured the money by the transfer of obligations of Akiyama Chozaemon to the usurer Suzuki Sanjuro. Three hundred and fifty *ryō* immediately due against seventy *ryō* in cash satisfied even this shark. Teisuke was impressed. How deny such a guest? He would get rid of him, and profit both ways. Yamadaya now would promptly pay the additional seventy *ryō*due on the girl with whom they were so delighted. He had paid fifty *ryō* for her. At Kibei's call his order was prompt. "Tosuke, accompany Kibei Dono to the Yamadaya." Kibei's calm and collected manner reassured him. This man did not contemplate suicide.

With the appearance of Tosuke and Kibei at the Yamadaya there was a flutter. The Banto Matsuzo respectfully came forward. As Kibei came up to the *rōka* and shook off his *geta* he interposed. "Deign to wait, Kibei Dono. Matters have changed since morning. The Kashiku is very ill. She can see no one. Condescend to come another time. For one ill in body pleasure is no pastime. Pray consider; grant excuse for this one occasion." Kibei was surprised. He had left her perfectly well in the morning. Something in the *bantō's* face, in the massed position of the men standing by, apprised him of the truth. He was enraged at the lie and the insult. "Ill? That is very strange, when so well at morning. But it is immaterial. Kibei goes to the room." – "Impossible," was the firm reply of the *bantō*. "The Kashiku lies isolated from all. It is the order of the physician. Even those in the rooms around her have been ordered out. Pray forbear." But Kibei was obstinate – "Then a glass of wine at her bedside; Kibei has matters to impart." The *bantō* stuck to his post – "Wine! Amid the smell of drugs, the unseemly vessels of the sick room! Such could not be permitted." Kibei stretched out an arm. The *bantō*went flying a dozen feet. Kibei made a leap toward the stairway. But the bawd O'Kayo interposed her vinegary presence. She was brave; having the support of great numbers, of the whole household. "What rudeness! How inconsiderate your way of acting! You behave in very bad taste; with the roughness of an *ashigaru* (foot soldier). The Yamadaya does not entertain such miserable scamps. The Tayu is ill. This Kayo says it. Get you hence – to some coolie house. Return the day before yesterday." Kibei gave a yell – "Yai! You old bitch! The whole affair is plain to Kibei. Out of money, his presence is no longer desired. Ah! Kibei will have vengeance." Without arms, before the sullen determination of these plebeians, he felt his helplessness. An unseemly brawl, in which he would be worsted, must not be entered on. He must leave. In a towering rage he strode back to the tea-house. Tosuke tried to keep pace with him.

Said Teisuke in feigned astonishment – "Kibei Dono! What has happened?" Kibei did but stutter and fume. The *teishū* turned to Tosuke. This latter made answer for his charge – "At the Yamadaya they were very rude. Admittance was refused to Kibei Dono. The bawd O'Kayo told him to come back day before yesterday!" – "Very rude indeed! Were such things said? It is unpardonable. An explanation must be had with the house. Danna Sama, for tonight deign to leave this matter to Teisuke. Ample satisfaction shall be had for the outrage." Teisuke threw up his hands as with uncontrollable anger. Kibei paid no attention, but demanded his swords. Outwardly he had regained his self-control. The maid O'Moto looked with diffidence at her mistress. The woman was accustomed to such scenes. At her sign the girl brought the weapons, carefully wrapped up. She placed them before Kibei. Unrolling the cover he put them on. With scanty salutation he strode off. Teisuke watched him – "It would be wise for the Yamadaya to close early tonight, to take in their lanterns; nay, even to board up the front and take refuge in the store-house." Tosuke was in no hurry to face Matsuzo, the *bantō* of Yamadaya. Continued the easy old fellow – "Well, 'Tis their affair. They are as good judges as Teisuke; and they could have been more civil in refusal. At all events the house has seventy *ryō*, and Kibei Dono is sober. He will cut belly before dawn; and perhaps nothing will happen hereabouts." The old pimp went off to his inner room; to sit down before his wine about the same time that Kibei did the same in a cook shop opposite the great gate of Yoshiwara. Here he idled, barely touched his drink, and passed the time in bantering the maid servant. He was in a riotous humour. He would take her to wife – and sell her the next morning. "As they do yonder." But O'Kiyo was not of that kind. "There is a lover?" – "Of course!" In admitting it she blushed, somewhat offended at hint of suspicion that such was lacking. Jibed Kibei – "He will do the same. Better to be the wife of a *samurai*; even for an hour." In the end he frightened the girl a good deal, so boisterous was he. She had gone out to buy him a deep hat. With relief she saw him put it on and set forth into the darkness and the rain.

The eighth hour (1 am) was nearly ready to strike. The pleasure quarter was silent. Passersby were few. The occasional shuffling sound of *zōri* (sandals) could be heard behind the closed *amado*. Kibei smiled cynically as he recognized this mark of revolting passage from one room to another. In doubt he stood before the gate of the Yamadaya. How break in and kill them all? If Kibei had his way the Kashiku would keep her word. Just then a noise of voices was heard within, the falling of the bar. Several belated guests came forth. They were in the charge of O'Moto, the maid of the Matsuminatoya. Affectionate were the leave-takings with the quondam wives. "Condescend an early visit. This Haya lives but in the thought of Mosuke." – "Bunzaemon San, be faithful to this Hana. In his absence she is always ill. She receives no one." At this there was a roar of laughter from the others of the company. Bunzaemon answered with reproaches. Kibei followed behind. This fellow was somewhat lamed. He lagged behind. Kibei pulled his sleeve. Bunzaemon, the cit, turned in surprise and fear at sight of the *samurai* in his deep hat. Said Kibei – "Don't be afraid. Bunzaemon San has forgotten pipe, or purse, or something. He must go back to the Yamadaya." At the fellow's groping in his garments and failure to understand he grew impatient. "A friend lies at the Yamadaya. It is late, and they will not open at an unknown voice. Entrance somehow must be had. Deign to lend your aid." At last the fellow comprehended – "O'Moto San! A moment: my pipe…." – "Oya! The Danna Sama has forgotten his pipe?" The girl went back the short distance to the gate. She knocked and called. With sleepy tones the voice of Matsuzo the *bantō* was heard. The bar fell. The girl turned to look down the street toward her guests. She looked right into the face of Kibei. Dropping her lantern, with a smothered scream she fled.

Matsu, the *bantō*, looked with horror at the man before him. As Kibei threw off his hat he turned to flee. Tripping, he fell. Kibei drew him back by the leg. A blow cut him through the shoulder. As he rose staggering a second vicious side swing sent the severed head to the ground. The gate-man took the chance. Fleeing to the recesses of the kitchen, he swarmed up a post and hid himself among the rafters of the roof, amid the darkness of their shadows. Kibei turned back and carefully barred the gate. With the key at the girdle of Matsuzo he locked the bar chain. All was now ready for his visitation and search.

On the floor above they had a drunken guest in hand, trying to get him to depart. A *bantō* and several women formed the committee of expulsion. "Ah! Money gone, one's welcome is quickly worn out in this hell. But Jusuke does not budge. He fears not the whole pack of foxes…. Thanks: deep the obligation of this Jusuke, extending to the next life." A woman had picked up and restored his purse. "The bill is paid? An early start Tokaido way? Ah, true! Jusuke had forgotten." He was now all compliments and thanks. Then in a rage – "Oh! The huzzy! What is Jusuke's purse worth with nothing in it? Who has robbed the purse of Jusuke?" He was madly fumbling his tobacco pouch. A woman put his hand on the missing object in the folds of his girdle. He was mollified. As they moved to the head of the stairs – "Take care! Jusuke San, don't fall! Banto San, deign to aid the guest." Refusing all help the man lurched half way down the flight. Then he stopped, staring and looking before him. At the foot stood Kibei, bloody sword in hand. "Down with this Jusuke? But Jusuke cannot down. A fool blocks the way…. Fool, you block the way of Jusuke." – "Out of the road, drunkard!" The words of Kibei came between his teeth, half growl, half snarl. The man obstinately held his own. When Kibei would push past him – "Beast!" He struck the *samurai*. Kibei whirled the sword. The head rolled to the bottom of the steps. The blood bathed Kibei from head to foot.

His appearance was horrible. The women fled in all directions. The *bantō* covered their retreat. "Kibei Dono! Pray be reasonable. Control yourself!" Kibei made a step toward the women's rooms. The *bantō* was dreadfully frightened, yet bravely he interposed to save them. He shouted for aid; below and to the neighbours. Kibei reached him. A blow and he fell severed. Kibei gave a howl of joy. O'Kayo the bawd came out to ascertain the cause of the brawl. She turned livid with fear on recognizing Kibei. They were standing together in the sort of entresol or room at the head of the stairway. Only a large brazier separated Kibei from his vengeance. Its massiveness of three or four feet breadth baffled him. The woman was fleeing for life. As he strove to get within striking distance fear gave her wings. From one side to another she leaped and dodged. Kibei was hampered. He had to cut her off from stair and *rōka*. As he hesitated she discharged the iron kettle at his head. One implement followed another. In hurling the iron tripod ashes entered her eyes. At once Kibei leaped to close quarters. The first sword blow she dodged. As Kibei recovered she sprang by him and over the *hibachi*, seeking the safety of the stairs now open to her. Her night-dress caught on the handle of the brazier and brought her to the ground. Next moment she was severed from shoulder to midriff.

Methodically Kibei began his examination of the rooms. To most of the inmates this uproar was a mere quarrel in the house, the cause of which they neither knew nor cared to know. The first search was at the room of the Kashiku, close to that of O'Kayo the bawd. Her reception room was dark. Here the Kashiku's bed usually was prepared. The inner room, her dressing room, showed the dim light of an *andon*. Noting her absence from the usual place a hasty stride brought him to the *shōji*. As he violently shoved them apart a man rose from the bed in the room. A mere glance showed that this was no lover. As Kibei with drawn sword stood over him, he squatted on his hams, crouching and begging for life. To Kibei's astonishment he called him by name – "Deign, honoured Sir, to spare this Chobei. Be assured the Kashiku is not in this place. She lies tonight with the Danna of the house. Deign to seek her in his company." He pointed vaguely as he spoke, to give direction. Kibei laughed ferociously. From this source these directions were atrocious. He lowered the weapon – "Chobei! At this place and time! Well met, good Sir. Kibei is doubly grateful for what he has learned. Chobei and Kibei are fellows in fortune. Willingly Kibei leaves him to O'Iwa San and her mercies." His attentive gaze never wandered from the face of the one-time pimp. With a gesture of horror he rushed from the room. In fright Chobei rolled his head up in the coverlet, to keep out the vision evoked.

He continued his search – "Is it my little black fellow?" Such the greeting of one woman aroused from sleep. Trembling she rose at sight of Kibei. Harshly told to lie down, she gladly obeyed. Her quivering limbs already were nearly yielding as he spoke. In but one place did he encounter opposition. Pushing open the *shōji* of the merest closet of a room he came upon a girl whose face somehow was familiar. She was a mere slip of a creature to be called a woman. The undeveloped hips, the yet immature bosom, aroused his astonishment at finding her in such a place as inmate; that is, until the pure oval and beauty of the face caught his glance. As he entered she sprang up in alarm. Just roused from sleep she hardly knew where she was – "Father! Father! A man! A man is in the room! Help!" Kibei pushed her back on the bed. With his bloody sword he rolled over the bed-clothes. Then he made a move to get at the closet behind. Perhaps mistaking his action the girl sprang upon him. Kibei was startled at her mad energy. When he thrust her down she seized his hand in her teeth, sinking them deep into it. Pain and impatience – after all he was pressed for time – overcame him. Unable otherwise to shake her off he thrust the point of the sword into her throat and gave a vigorous downward push. Coughing up great clouts of blood, the girl sank back, dying on the *futon*. As he left the room remembrance came to Kibei's mind. He had seen her in Yotsuya. More than once O'Tsuru had served him tea in the house of her father, Chozaemon. How came she in this vile den? He took a step back to aid her if he could. She was stone dead.

The Tayu Nishikiyama now knew the cause of the disturbance. To the frightened page (*kamuro*) who came running to her – "Be quiet child. This is no time to lose self-control. Aid me in preparation." She dressed herself with the greatest care; "all in white, as befitted a lady in attendance on a nobleman." Then she took down her *koto* and struck the opening bars of an old and famous song – the "Jinmujo" (Inexhaustible Happiness) – said to have been sung by the famous Shizuka Gozen when she danced the Horaku, or sacred dance, before the Shogun Yoritomo at Kamakura Hachimangu. As Kibei turned into the corridor the voice of the Oiran caught his ear as she sang in accompaniment to the instrument. She was bending over the *koto* as the *shōji* were flung apart. Kibei, his hair hanging in disorder and framing a face ghastly white in contrast to the red streaks splashed over it and his garments, stood transfixed at the entrance. The Tayu looked up. With calm pose and courteous salute – "Kibei Dono, what manner of acting is this! Is not Kibei Dono the *bushi*? Truly madness has seized you, honoured Sir. This is Nishikiyama.... Deign to be seated. 'Tis Nishikiyama who serves Kibei Dono. What has been done cannot be undone. The last cup of wine in life is to be drained. Deign to accept it from these humble hands."

Kibei continued gazing on her. The unhappy man, his mind was opened to a flood of light. The hurricane of passion was passing. Slowly he advanced into the room. "Truly the Go Tayu is right. Kibei has gone mad; mad indeed!" He sank down on the cushion before her. At a sign the page placed the stand containing the bottle of cold *sake* before the lady. Skilfully the slender hands held it, gracefully poured it for the man doomed to death, taking this final cup served by her. Kibei raised it, drained it to the last drop. "The Kashiku: she is on this lower floor. Where lies she?" Nashikiyama noted the wild light returning to his eyes. She bowed her head before him – "The life of Nishikiyama is at the command of Kibei Dono. Her lips are sealed. Honoured Sir, how answer Kibei Dono's question?" For the moment he looked down. Then he rose – "Whose daughter can the Oiran be! Truly no lady in the land could show a higher courage, a finer courtesy. The final salute of this Kibei in life is to the Go Tayu." In grave ceremony it was performed. As he left the room the woman buried her face in her hands, weeping bitterly. In wonder and gratitude the frightened page extended her hands, her face hidden in the white robes of the Go Tayu.

Kibei trod this lower corridor with sombre tread. He would cut belly at the garden pond. With some surprise he noted an *amado* open at the end of the *rōka*. Voices were heard. Standing at the opening he saw lanterns. Some frenzied women had raised a ladder to the garden wall. They would thus escape, but the knife-like bamboo stakes prevented. Said a voice outside, and close to him – "The key to the gate: here it is." The Kashiku at a run passed by him. Kibei gave a shout. The frightened woman turned, recognized him, then sped on. In a few steps he was on her. The raised sword descended as she fell on her knees before him, in attempt to swerve its course. Through wrist and collar-bone, from neck to navel, the keen blade passed. Kibei threw the weapon aside. He leaned over her, his dagger drawn. Then he rose, holding by its tresses the head. For a moment he gazed on it. Slowly he walked to the pond in the centre of the garden. Carefully he washed the bloody trophy and placed it on the curbing. Confronting it he made reverential salutation. "Kibei keeps his promise to the Kashiku. With Tamagiku he treads the gloomy paths of Shideyama. Honoured lady – a moment and Kibei follows." Seated before the head reposing on the curb he opened his clothes. Thrusting the bloody dagger deep into his left side he slowly drew it across the belly; then made the upward cut. The body fell forward. Kibei indeed had kept his word.

Matters Ecclesiastical

Inagaki Shogen received the news at dawn, just as he was leaving the castle on completion of his night watch. The old knight smiled gravely, thanked the bearer of the message, and rewarded him with lavish hand. The *kago* bearers jolted on. The news had reached the train, and *chūgen* and spearman exchanged whispers. On arrival at the Inagaki *yashiki* his lordship made no motion to descend. The chamberlain raising the curtain gave a cry of horror. The old man lay stretched at the bottom of the little chamber. The dagger and the pool of blood told the tale. Shogen had followed the example of his son. He, too, now trod the paths of Shideyama.

With laggard tottering step Akiyama Chozaemon entered his house. Regardless of wife and the cushion she offered, of the hardly repressed tear in her salutation, he cast himself full length on the mats. He buried his face in his arms. The groans which issued from the prostrate body frightened the woman. "The honoured return; has other misfortune fallen on the House?" A shrug of the shoulders, a shiver; then the man half rose and faced her. She was startled at his expression. He was facing the most dreadful, not mere thought of ruin to him and his – "Suzuki San is liar and thief. Fifty *ryō* in hand the promise was for abstention. Now he demands twenty *ryō* more – the interest on the debt in full." His voice rose to a harsh scream. He laughed despairingly. "Seventy-five *ryō* interest, for the loan of a month; and that loan forced on this Chozaemon by Ito Kwaiba! Kibei has squandered everything. The loan comes back on the bail. If Suzuki holds the interest in hand, he allows the principal, three hundred and fifty *ryō*, to stand for the month. Unless he has the lacking twenty-five *ryō* by the fourth hour (9 am) tomorrow, complaint is laid at the office. As usual the interest is written into the face of the bond. The end is certain. This Chozaemon must cut belly or suffer degradation (*kaieki*)." He looked her over critically. The light of hope died out of his eyes – "Ah! If this Tsuyu could but be sold, the money would be in hand. But she is old and ugly. Pfaugh!..." How he hated her at this moment. Some half a dozen years older than Chozaemon the marriage had been arranged by the parents on truly financial principles. Mizoguchi Hampei was rich, and reputed stingy and saving. Just recently he had fallen into the Edogawa as he returned home late one night. Drunk and surfeited with the foul waters of the stream they had fished him out stone dead. Then it was learned that the old fellow of sixty odd years had several concubines, of the kind to eat into house and fortune. The reversion of the pension, of course, went to the House. In all these years Chozaemon had never received the dower of O'Tsuyu; nor dared to press the rich man for it, too generous to his daughter to quarrel with. The funds eagerly looked for by Chozaemon were found to be *non est inventus*. Probably, if alive, Mizoguchi would have argued that the dower had been paid in instalments. In his grave difficulties Akiyama could find no aid in his wife. She mourned her uselessness – "Willingly would Tsuyu come to the aid of House and husband, join her daughter in the bitter service. But past forty years.... 'Tis useless to think of it. Perhaps some expedient will come to mind." She brought out the arm rest and placed it near his side. Then she sat apart watching him. From time to time was heard the tap of her pipe as she knocked out the ashes. At last, overcome by sleep and seeing no sign of movement on the husband's part, she went off to bed, expecting that he would soon follow.

She woke with a start – "Father! Father!" The voice of O'Tsuru rang sharply in her ears. Dazed she half rose and looked around her. The daylight streamed through the closed *amado*. She had been dreaming. With surprise she noted her husband's absence. Had he gone forth? The cries of a bean curd seller were heard without – "*Tōfu! Tōfu!* The best of *tōfu*!" The palatable, cheap, and nutritious food was a standard meal in this house as in many others of Nippon. Akiyama was most generous in indulgence of his passions for gambling, wine, and the women of Shinjuku; and his household with equal generosity were indulged in an economical regimen of *tōfu*. The wife rose to answer the call of the street huckster. Her surprise increased as she found every means of exit bolted and barred, as during the night. The open sliding window in the kitchen roof caught her eye. Surely he had not departed that way! As she opened the back door a murmur of voices, as in the roadway or close by, struck her ear. The *tōfu* seller had his head turned away looking upward. At her call he turned quickly with apology – "Good day, honoured lady. A strange event! Ah! The honoured household still sleeps. All is silent.... Strange indeed! A man has hung himself on the big oak tree in the temple ground. Deign to look." He pointed to the big tree close by in the grounds of the Myogyoji. Sure enough: forty feet from the ground dangled the body of a man. It swayed gently to and fro in harmony with the movement of the branches. A hand seemed to grasp the heart of Tsuyu. The branches of the tree reached far over their roof. The open *hikimado*! With feeble voice she said – "My husband; he is strangely absent. Deign, somebody, to climb up and find out whether this man is – of the ward." The startled *tōfu* seller hastened to get aid. Several men entered the garden, quickly mounted to the roof, and thus reached the tree. Said the topmost fellow – "Ma! Ma! It is no pretty sight. He makes a hideous spectacle. The face is black as a rice boiler. The eyes stand out as if ready to burst. The tongue hangs out like a true guard (*hyōtan*). The grin onthe distended mouth is not nice to see. Ah! The rascal has used the merest cord to cut himself off. And he has nearly done so. The head is almost severed." He gave a shout – "Naruhodo! Why, its...." One close by silenced him. The men above looked down. They made signs to those below. The women gathered around O'Tsuyu as if to keep her from the sight. She broke away from them as the body was gently lowered to the ground. Her shrieks rang loud. They strove to detach her from the dead body of Chozaemon. The House ruined, daughter and husband taken out of her life in a single day; the blow was too crushing for a brain harassed by a life with this debauched worthless man. Her warders struggled with one gone clean daft. Years after men grown up from childhood in the ward looked with pity at the feeble ragged old mad beggar woman who crouched by the beautiful bronze dragon which ornaments the water basin of the Ten-o Jinja. They would drop in her hand a copper "cash," and drive off with rebuke the children who taunted and annoyed her – as they had done years before. Thus were mother and daughter – the innocent – involved in the father's crime against the dread Lady of Tamiya.

All these events created a tremendous stir in Yotsuya. Men disliked to go abroad at night. Women, to their great inconvenience were confined to the house. Two figures approaching each other in the darkness would be seen to hesitate and stop. "What's that – standing, slinking yonder by the wall? Alas! This Kinsaburo, this Genzaemon has evil fortune led him into the clutches of the O'Bake? O'Iwa! O'Iwa!" With that and mad cries they would fall on each other; at times only to exercise restraint after some injury had been done. Hence quarrels arose; feuds, started in all innocence, came into being. Women, as suspects, were chief sufferers. The local atmosphere was overcharged, nerve racked. And so from Honjo to Nakacho (Shinjuku), from Nakanocho (Yoshiwara) to Shinagawa, even in the nearer post towns of Kawasaki, Tsurumi, and Kanagawa the talk was spreading of the strange happenings in Yotsuya of Edo town. Katada Tatewaki, descendant of that Katada Samon who, as vassal of Gongen Samon (Iyeyasu) had had this Aoyama-Yotsuya district in fief, now first began his inquiries into the affair. The Katada had wide possessions elsewhere at the time of the grant. Samon had gifted much of his new fief as temple land, and on the old maps of the day this part of Edo is a blood red splash, indication of these many establishments. But the Katada influence still prevailed through the ward, indeed through the more than good will of the beneficiaries. Tatewaki's *yashiki* was at the top of Ushigomezaka. His modest pension of a thousand *koku* by no means represented the extent of his power. Iemon became frightened at the storm gathering against him. He was open to all suggestions of remedy for the cataleptic state into which O'Hana had fallen. The neighbour gossips suggested calling in the Daiho-in of Shiomachi. A service kept part at least of the money in the ward. They had their share in provision and consumption; the fifty *ryō* necessary were much to them – and to Iemon in his present circumstances.

The neighbours were assembled at Tamiya. Iemon went forth to greet the Daiho-in. With his attendant *kannushi* and train he presented himself at the entrance. Iemon was prostrate in salutation before the great man. – "Reverential thanks for the condescension. Deign to enter this unfortunate house." The Shinto priest was brusque, as is the way of the kind. Himself he was the *samurai*, with all the tone of official manner. "Ha! Ha! Salutation to all." He gave a comprehensive glance through the assembly and lost none of them in the process. He approached the couch of O'Hana. He opened the closed eyes, which stared fixedly into space as of one dead. He raised an arm upright from the body. Stepping aside, he squatted. Some moments passed. The arm remained rigidly upright. Satisfied, the Daiho-in signed to his attendants. Raising O'Hana they placed her in a sitting posture on a mat. Her hair was arranged in *ichōmage*. A *gohei* was placed between her hands. Then the Daiho-in began the recitation of the prayers and charms. The other priests gave voice at times in response. All present were awe-struck. The women hardly breathed, leaning eagerly forward. Their eyes took on a vacant stare, as if themselves mesmerized. The *gohei* began to tremble; then to shake violently. The woman's hair fell down in disorder around her face. All turned away their faces. Some women gave smothered cries. It was O'Iwa San who glared at them out of those eyes. The Daiho-in eagerly leaned close over O'Hana – "O'Iwa: where are you? What has become of your body? Be sure to speak the truth. Don't attempt to lie to the priest.... You don't know? Ah! you would be obstinate in your grudge. The charm shakes and quivers; it possesses O'Iwa.... You would rest in Samoncho ground? That is much to ask; particularly when the body is not in hand.... A substitute will do? Ah! Prayers?... For a year, at morn and night of each day? That is terrific. Consider the cost.... You care not for the cost! Only then will you cease to afflict the ward?... Very well: humbly this Daiho-in transmits the will of the dead."

Thus did the priestly mediator interpret to his gaping auditors the mumbling and cries given forth by O'Hana. The wild look faded from her eyes. She rolled over as in a faint. The priests raised her up. The Daiho-in turned to Iemon and the assembly – "The words of O'Iwa have been heard through this woman. O'Hana has been possessed by O'Iwa. Hence her trance.... Heigh! Water!" He began making passes over his patient – "The stage has passed. O'Hana no longer is possessed by O'Iwa. The wronged lady leaves O'Hana to peace. O'Hana is completely herself again. O'Iwa is all delusion. O'Hana believes this. She believes firmly. The Daiho-in tells her to believe. O'Iwa does not haunt O'Hana. O'Iwa has no ill will against O'Hana." He looked fixedly and with command into the eyes of O'Hana. His voice rang clear and authoritative. Then he began gently to stroke the back of her head, her neck and spine. "All is well?" "Hai! Hai! This Hana is completely restored. All is well." With a little sigh she sank back, to be laid on the cushions in a sleep which all wondered to see was most natural. Those present were in transports of delight. They buzzed approval as the Daiho-in addressed Iemon. "The Daiho-in has done his part. All have heard the words of O'Iwa San. The rest lies with the temple. Deign to receive these words. The Daiho-in returns." With his pack voicing loudly at his tail he left the entrance gate. The assembly streamed after. Iemon was left alone, biting his thumbs in helpless rage. He was aghast. "The old fox! What is to be done, pressed as Iemon is for funds? How is this Iemon to act? Refusal means the open hostility of the whole ward. It will turn against him. Ah! What a miserable old scamp. He did it all himself; he and his confederates. The gods descend from above; the Daiho-in shakes the *gohei* from below – and those fools believe, to the ruin of Iemon!"

Hence he would have postponed the costly appeal to the temple. Within the week a committee of the ward waited upon him. As if expecting them, Iemon gave ready compliance. With four or five other gentlemen he waited upon Shuden Osho, the famous priest of the temple of the Gyoran Kwannon. The Lady Merciful, Kwannon Sama, seemed the fitting deity to whom appeal should be made. A word is to be said as to this famous manifestation of the goddess. Told by Ryuo at length, of necessity here the account is much abridged. Gyoran Kwannon – Kwannon of the fish-basket – has several other names. She is called the Namagusai Kwannon, from the odour of fresh blood attached to the pursuit; the Byaku Kwannon, or the white robed; the Baryufu Kwannon, as wife of Baryu the fisherman. The image of the Byaku Kwannon exists. It is carved in white wood, stained black, with a scroll in the right hand, and holding a fish basket (*gyōran*) in the left hand. The story of Baryu, and of his connection with Kwannon, is of more moment.

In Morokoshi (China) there is a place called Kinshaden. Across the bay from Edo-Tokyo is Kazusa with its ninety-nine villages, one of which has the same name – Kinshaden. The fishing population of Nippon is a rough lot. From babyhood there is little but quarrelling and fighting between the bands which control the different wards of the villages. The relations between the people are very primitive. One of the important occupations is the *iwashi*, or pilchard, fishing. To pull in the nets loaded with the fish requires the united effort of the whole village population, men, women, even children. Among their toilers the people of Kinshaden noted a young girl of some sixteen or seventeen years; easily noted by the great beauty and attraction of face and figure, the willing readiness and wonderful strength she showed in her struggles with the weighted net. As she appeared several times at last some men went up to her – "Girl, you are a stranger here. For your aid thanks are offered. Who may you be; and whence from? Strangers, even in kindness, in Nippon must not conceal their names." The girl smiled. – "I come from Fudarakusan in the South Ocean.... Where is Fudarakusan? It is in India.... And India? It is in the South Ocean, the Nankai." To the wonder expressed at her coming such a distance of thousands of *ri* – "I come, I serve, for my husband." – "Your husband? Pray who may he be, in these parts?" – "Not yet is he chosen," answered the girl. "Come! The nets are drawn, the fishing ended for the day. I will ascend that rock; read the sutra of the Lady Kwannon. He who can first memorize it shall be my husband." Ready was the assent to such an attractive proposal – a beautiful helpmate in prospect, one endowed with surprising strength for her frail form, and who seemed to bring luck to the efforts of the village in the struggle for a livelihood. Even the Nipponese prejudice against strangers paled before such practical qualification.

The maid ascended to the rostrum. For three days she read and expounded the holy sutra of the Lady Kwannon. On the fourth day the fisherman Baryu – young, handsome, strong – felt sure that he could answer to the test. "Woman, descend! Today this Baryu will repeat the sutra, expound its meaning." With seeming surprise and merriment the girl obeyed. Baryu took her place. Without slip or fault he repeated the sutra, expounded the intricacies of its meaning. The girl bowed low in submission. "Condescend to admit my humble person to the hut of Baryu the fisherman. Tonight she pollutes with her presence a corner of his bed-chamber." Rejoicing Baryu at once took her to his home, where he would act the husband. At first gently she rebuked him. "These rough people of Kinshaden have regard to nothing! There is such a rite as marriage. Nine times are the *sake* cups to be drained between husband and wife. Thus is established this important relation. In the connection between man and woman there is such a thing as etiquette. This observed, the woman passes to the possession of the man. For the woman, second marriage there is none."

Thus were the decencies of the marriage bed taught to the rough fisherman. Near dawn Baryu awoke with surprise. His bed-fellow was in the last extremities. Dripping with sweat, she seemed to be melting away. Already she was unconscious. Then vomiting forth water she died. Baryu was tremendously put out. To lose a wife, who barely had been a wife; one so beautiful, so strong; this was extremely vexatious. "This won't do at all! Why has such a misfortune befallen this Baryu? O'Kabe (Miss Plaster) and O'Nabe (Miss Stewpan) endured without mishap the passage of their marriage night.... Hai! Hai!" in reply to a friend knocking at the door. "Baryu cannot go to the fishing today.... The woman? She has died. Baryu's wife is dead." Opening the door he retailed his experience to the wondering friend. As they talked, along came a priest most strangely dressed for this land. Approaching them he said – "Is this the house of Baryu?" At the fisherman's acknowledgement – "Has a girl come here?... Dead! Deign to let this foolish cleric hang eyes upon her." Baryu thought he would take his turn at questions. "And you; whence from?" "From Fudarakusan in the Nankai." "Get you hence, frantic interloper," broke in Baryu with grief and anger. "Enough has this Baryu heard of Fudarakusan. Baryu must needs observe his state as widower. The month must pass before he seeks a wife. And more than half its days remain! But look." Mollified by the humble attitude of the priest he went and raised the coverlet from the woman's body. He uttered a cry of surprise. "Oya! Oya! She has disappeared. There is naught here but a wooden image. Ma! Ma! what a curious figure – with scroll and fish basket, just as the wife appeared at the beach. This is what one reads of in books." He turned to the priest in wonder and as seeking explanation. Said the latter with earnest and noble emphasis – "Favoured has been this Baryu. The Kwannon of Fudarakusan of Nankai has shown herself before his very eyes. For the reform of this wicked people, to teach them the holy writing, she has condescended to submit to the embraces of the fisherman. Let not Baryu think of other marriage. For him has come the call to leave this world. Fail not to obey." Baryu rushed to the door, to catch but a glimpse of the departing form. All sign of the priest quickly faded. Baryu returned to the wooden figure lying where once had reposed the body of the beautiful girl. It was a most unsatisfactory substitute for the flesh and blood original. But Baryu made the most of it. He took his vow. He shaved his head, becoming a priest to recite and preach the sutra of the Lady Kwannon. Hence this Kwannon is known as the Baryufu Kwannon – wife of Baryu the fisherman. Hence she is called the Kwannon of the fish basket, in honour of the aid she brought the people of this village and land.

The Rites For O'Iwa San

Iemon fared as badly at the hands of the Buddha as at those of the Kami. Shuden Osho, as guardian of the sacred image of the Gyoran Kwannon, was a very great man indeed. After some delay the deputation from Samoncho was ushered into his presence, Iemon made profound obeisance and explained the cause of their presence. The visitations of O'Iwa to the district were causing the greatest public commotion. Not as a matter of private interest, but of public utility his interference was sought. If Iemon thought to abstract a copper 'cash' from the priestly treasury he made a gross mistake. Besides, the individual who disturbs the public peace suffers severely from official mediation, no matter what form this takes. Shuden inquired minutely as to the visit of the Daiho-in, of which he seemed to have heard. What information Iemon might have withheld, or minimised, or given a different complexion, was cheerfully volunteered by others, who also corrected and amplified any undue curtailing or ambiguity of their spokesman. Shuden listened to Iemon with a gravity and an expression hovering between calculation and jeering comment. He turned from him to the committee, giving great attention to those scholiasts on the text of the orator. He gravely wagged his head in agreement with the rival prelate, whose acumen he highly extolled. Memorial services were to be provided for a year. It was, after all, merely a form of restitution to the wronged lady. But also the wandering spirit of O'Iwa was to be suitably confined. Here lay the difficulty. Recitation of the sutra for seven continuous days; proper inhumation of the substitute beyond possibility of disturbance, would surely lay a spell on the enraged lady, and put an end to the curse of one dying an unworshipped spirit. For the burial a bamboo was to be provided – of length one *shaku* eight *bu* (one foot nine inches) between the joints.

With this notice Iemon and his companions withdrew. He was resigned to the payment of the fifty *ryō* necessary for the memorial services extending over the year. The inclusion in the bamboo was another affair. The finding of such was about as easy as the fishing for black pearls. He soon found that securing the substitute and securing the body of O'Iwa San for proper inhumation were kindred problems. After looking over all the bamboo which had drifted to Edo and was in the hands of the world secular – and most of it at surprisingly cheap rates – the committee was driven back on the religious world. They soon found that the article in question was kept in stock only at the Gyoran Kwannondo. Resorting to the priestly offices, Iemon felt convinced that the grave salutation of the incumbent official – they directed him to the treasury – concealed a derisive grin at his expense. He was sure of it when he learned that this rare object could be had – for another fifty *ryō*. The temple gave no credit; but Suzuki, the usurer who was one of the party, after some demur agreed to hand over the amount, which he had just received from Akiyama Chozaemon, the service bounty of the daughter O'Tsuru. With some reluctance the long nosed, long faced, long limbed Kamimura went security for the repayment on their return to the ward. With cheerful recklessness Iemon pledged the last chance of any income from the pension and resources of Tamiya for the next three years; so heavily was he in debt. Shuden on his part lost no time. With at least one member of the committee in attendance, to see that he played fair, for seven days vigorously was the sutra intoned by the loudest and most brazen of his subordinates, backed by the whole body of priests. Day and night a priest would slip to the side altar, to invoke the pity of the Buddha on the wandering spirit of the deceased lady in few pithy but hasty words, and to spend the rest of his vigil in a decent slumberous immobility.

The seven days accomplished, the procession formed. Six men in new uniforms – provided by Iemon – made pretence of great difficulty in carrying the long box (*nagamochi*). Four men carried the *sambo*, or sacred tray of white wood, on which rested the section of bamboo wrapped by the hands of Shuden himself in the sacred roll of the sutra of Kwannon. Officialdom of the ward was present. The citizens turned out *en masse*. For long Yotsuya had not witnessed such a scene. Within its precincts the *yashiki* of the great nobles were conspicuously absent; their long processions of spearman, *chūgen*, *samurai* and officials were only to be witnessed at times on the highway which leaves Shinjuku for the Koshukaido and the alternate and then little used Ashigaratoge road. Arrived at Samoncho the ground selected was inspected by Shuden. The bishop's eyebrows puckered in questioning mien. "Here there are too many people. Is there no other place?" They led him to another site. The wrinkle deepened to a frown – "Here there are too many children. Their frolics and necessities are unseemly. These would outrage the tender spirit. Is there no other place?" The committee was nonplussed. Iemon was in terrible fear lest all his effort and expenditure would go for naught but to swell Shuden's cash roll. A thought came into his mind. "There is no other open land, but the garden of Tamiya is wide and secluded. The wall prevents public access." People looked at him aghast. He was either mad with courage, or obstinate in disbelief in the power of O'Iwa San so plainly manifested. Shuden paid no attention to that surprised whispering. "Deign to show the way thither." Thus the procession took its course back to

Teramachi and through the gate of Tamiya. A spot was selected, just before the garden gate. It was open to the salutation and vows of passers-by, yet could be shut off from direct access toward house and public. At Shuden's order a hole was dug, just four *shaku* (feet) in depth. The Osho began the recitation of the sutra. The priests stood by in vigilant attention. As the last word reverberated on the bishop's lips they seized the sutra wrapped bamboo, slipped it in the long box – bum! the lock snapped. The congregation was tremendously impressed. For a decent time Shuden remained in prayer and meditation. "The charm is complete. O'Iwa no longer wanders, to her own penance and the disaster of men. Henceforth he who says she does so lies. Hearken to the words of Shuden. Admit none such to your company. Let not children make this place a playground. Shuden has given warning. Pollution surely follows. Their habits are unseemly, an insult to the dead. Even as to parents, those with infants on their backs are specifically to be excluded." He tied a paper covered with Sanscrit characters to a bamboo stick. This was placed on a white wood stake. On the stake he wrote kindred words, converting it into the counterfeit of a *sotoba*. Neither he nor any present knew what the words meant, or had care as to their ignorance of this essential of religion. Then he and his train gathered up their gowns and galloped out the gate, after practice and receipt of grave courtesy, so much did temple differ from shrine in its contact with secular life. The assembled multitude departed; much edified by the day's proceedings, and with low comment to each other on the dilapidation of Tamiya, its fall from the one time spruce and flourishing state. "Introduce a spendthrift in the door, and the wealth leaks from every crevice. The spirit of Tamiya Matazaemon must grieve at this sight. But why did he bring in as *muko* a stranger?"

Iemon could flatter himself on the efficacy of the divine interposition. The public mind was quieted. Nothing more was heard of O'Iwa San. Only the daily summons, on one pretext or another, to the ward office troubled him. The *yakunin* also made a practice of taking in Tamiya en route to performance of their various missions. This he knew was a practice as to men under observation. He went over his career as known to Yotsuya. There was nothing in it to call for question. Official censure does not rest its case on a ghost story. The famous investigation of Echizen no Kami (Ooka) into the Yaeume case of Yamada was matter of later days. Moreover, all his troubles were lightened by the state of O'Hana, the devoted object of unwavering affection. Ever since the Daiho-in had mesmerized her, impressed his will on her, the daily improvement could be marked. Now again she was her normal self; sadly thin and worn in spirit, a woman tired out, but yet the figure of O'Hana and in her right mind. To him she was the beautiful tradition of the past and just as beautiful as ever in actuality. Two weeks had passed since Shuden's experiment. One night, as the hour of the pig (9 pm) was striking, there came a knocking at the door. O'Hana rose from her sewing. "Danna, Kamimura San would say a word." Iemon made a gesture of annoyance. The long man had shadowed him, ever since entering on the engagement of bail. He went to the door and looked at his caller with amazement. Kamimura, his hair in confusion, was stark naked except for his wife's under cloth – and she was almost a dwarf. He stretched out a hand to Iemon, half in threat, half in begging. "Iemon Uji, a word: condescend to grant this Goemon ten *ryō*in silver, not in words. Suzuki the usurer has come on Goemon as bail of Iemon, in the matter of the exorcism. Today he stripped the house of everything. Wife and children, hungry and almost naked, lie on bare boards. When Goemon begged mercy, that he go to Tamiya, the wretched fellow jeered. 'Tamiya? Tamiya has but *hibachi* and three mats; the clothes worn by himself and wife. The house and land of Tamiya is but a reversion. Suzuki gets nothing at Tamiya but a lawsuit which would not pay the office fees. Kamimura is rich; his house is well supplied. One petition; and not only expenses, but the debt finds payment. Hence Suzuki troubles not

Tamiya.' With this off he went deriding me. Deign the loan, Iemon San. Condescend at least the shelter of clothes and food."

To the wretched fellow Iemon could make no reply. Ten *ryō*! Kamimura might as well have asked for ten thousand *ryō*. In house and land Iemon was secure. These belonged to the heirship of Tamiya as long as the House maintained its status. The pension was long mortgaged. The farms had disappeared. The trouble of Goemon pained him. He could only refuse; palliating the refusal with vague promises as to the near future. He would effect a loan. The debt of Suzuki repaid, all his goods would be restored to Kamimura San. Goemon took this talk at its real value. Shaking his fist he berated Iemon with violent words. "Ah! Shame is brought to the House of Kamimura, wretchedness to his family – and by this vile stranger. It is Iemon with his heartless wicked treatment of O'Iwa San, who has wrought distress and ruin to the ward. For Goemon there is neither food nor clothing? Wait! Time shall bring his vengeance on Iemon and his House." Iemon would have detained him; sought in some way to mollify him, at least get a hint as to how he purposed injury. Goemon shook him off as one would a reptile. With a wild laugh he went out naked as he was into the darkness.

He had no definite purpose in mind. However, as he passed the garden gate of Tamiya his eye caught the factitious *sotoba* standing white in the fitful moonlight. He stood stock still; then clapped his hands in mad joy and decision. Hastening to his home he sought out an old battered mattock and a rusty spade. Soon he was back at the garden gate. A blow and the bar fell. Goemon passed within. "She lies but four *shaku* deep. The task is quickly performed. None pass here at this hour." The dirt flew under his nervous arms. Soon he had the box out on the ground beside him. A peal of thunder; he must hasten, or stand a ducking from the coming storm. He laughed. What had a naked man to fear from getting wet? The clothes he wore would not spoil. Why did not man dress in a towel, as after the bath; its use, to wipe the moisture from the body. Now his eyes were fixed in curiosity on the bamboo staff before him. The first few drops of the rainstorm fell on his bare shoulders, but he disregarded them. "Naruhodo! How heavy it is! O'Iwa in life hardly weighed more. Lady of Tamiya – show pity on this Goemon. Iemon and O'Hana – those wicked voluptuaries – prosper and flourish, while Goemon is brought to beggary and starvation. Deign to visit the wrath of O'Iwa San on these vile wretches. Seize and kill them. Goemon sets O'Iwa free." He seized the mattock. Raising it overhead he brought the edge sharply down on the bamboo stake. At the moment there was a violent peal of thunder rolling off into a crash and rattle. The landscape was lit up by the vivid lightning. People uneasily turned over on their beds.

Shortly after dawn Iemon woke with a start. Don-don-don, don-don-don. There was a tremendous rapping at his door. O'Hana could hear but a whispered consultation going on without the *amado*. Iemon returned to the room. His face was white; his step tottered. Hastily he donned an outer robe. To her question he made scant reply, so agitated was he. His one idea was to keep from her what he had just heard. In the garden he found his wardsmen assembled. All were dumbfounded and aghast. They looked at each other and then at the broken bamboo tube. Close by lay the body of the man who had done the deed. Brains and blood had oozed from the hole in the skull in which yet stuck the pointed end of the mattock sunk deep within. Evidently the instrument had rebounded from the resilient surface of the bamboo. A by-stander pointed to the tiny fracture near the hard knot of the staff. It was a small thing, but enough to destroy all the past labours. Iemon went up to look at the body. "Why! 'Tis Goemon." To their questioning he told how Kamimura had called on the previous night, his rage at the inability of Iemon to aid him in distress. With hanging heads, eyes on the ground, and wagging tongues, all departed to their homes. Later the body of Goemon was borne to his house by neighbours. Iemon picked up the bamboo staff. Carrying it within he placed it in a closet. It was as costly an object as the house had ever held. He was in despair.

It was on that very day, at the seventh hour (3 pm), that O'Hana heard a call at the door. "A request to make! A request to make!" She recoiled from the sight presented. A beggar stood at the entrance of Tamiya. A dirty mat wrapped around his body, feet and arms emerging from bandages, making him like to some hideous insect with its carapace, his face wrapped in a towel, the effects of leprosy were hideously patent. – "What do you here? There is naught to be had. Pray depart at once." The answer was in tones the very harshness of which seemed to cause pain to the utterer – "The request is to Iemon Dono. Condescend to notify him." With fearful glance O'Hana shrank within, Iemon noted her nervous quivering. Promptly he was on his feet – "A beggar has frightened Hana? Such are to be severely dealt with." He went to the entrance. "A beggar, and such a fellow? How comes it entrance has been had to the ward? There is nothing for you here. If you would escape the dogs and bastinado, get you hence at once." The man did not stir from the spot on which he stood. Slowly he opened the mat held round his body (*komokaburi*), one of the coarse kind used to wrap round *sake*barrels. He was clothed in rags glued together by the foul discharges of his sores. He removed the towel from his face. The ghastly white and red blotches, the livid scars of the leper, the head with patches of scurfy hair ready to fall at a touch, startled even Iemon the priest. He would not have touched this man, expelled him by force, for all the past wealth of Tamiya. The intruder noted the effect produced.

"To such has the wrath of O'Iwa San brought this Chobei. Does not Iemon, the one-time neighbour Kazuma, recognize Chobei? And yet all comes through Iemon. Child, wife, means of life, all these have failed Chobei. In the jail robbed of everything, degenerate in mind and body, Chobei has found refuge at nights in the booths of street vendors; on cold wet nights, even in the mouths of the filthy drains. Fortunate is he when fine weather sends him to rest on the river banks. To seek rest; not to find it. O'Iwa stands beside him. When eyelids drowse Chobei is aroused, to find her face close glaring into his. Beg and implore, yet pardon there is none. 'Chobei has a debt to pay to Iwa. In life Chobei must repay by suffering; yet not what Iwa suffered. Think not to rest.' Some support was found in a daughter, sold in times past to the Yamadaya of Yoshiwara. There the child grew up to become the great profit of the house. The influence of the Kashiku was all powerful to secure entrance. For a night Chobei was to find food and a bed. But that night came Kibei San. He killed the Kashiku – crushed her out, as one would crush an insect. This Chobei nearly died; but Kibei left him to the mercy of O'Iwa. Her mercy!" He would have thrown out his arms in weary gesture of despair. The pain and effort were too great. He moaned. "Last night Chobei sought relief. Of late years the river has been spanned, for passers-by and solace of the human refuse. Standing on Ryogokubashi the dark waters of the river called to Chobei as they swept strongly by to the sea. A moment, and all would be ended. About to leap hands were laid on Chobei's shoulders. He was dragged back. Turning – lo! 'twas O'Iwa San. Another creature, still fouler than she, with sloping eyelid, bald head, and savage look, stood by. Said O'Iwa San – 'And Chobei would end all – with luxury before his eyes! Chobei dies not but with the consent of Iwa. Get you to Yotsuya; to Iemon and Hana, living in luxury and Tamiya. Aid will not be refused you.' And so she brought me here. Deign to hear the prayer of Chobei. Allow him to die in Yotsuya, upon the *tatami*; not on the bare earth, to be thrown on the moor for dogs to gnaw. Grant him burial in temple ground."

He changed his theme; the feeble quivering hands clasped his belly. "Ah! This pinching hunger. Double Chobei's suffering; of mind and body. Apply for alms or food, and the leper is repulsed. See! Two fingers remain on this hand. Count of the rest fills out the tale for but one member. O'Hana San, condescend a rice ball for this Chobei. You, at least, know not the pinch of hunger.... Ah! She still possesses some of that beauty and charm for which Iemon has brought ruin upon all." Before the horrible lascivious leer of this object O'Hana fled. Left alone Iemon spoke. He had been thinking – "Chobei has spoken well. From Iemon he is entitled to relief. Chobei shall die on his mat. But in such shape nothing can be done. Get you hence. Buy clothing fit to appear before men's eyes. In the bath wash that pus-laden body. Then come to Iemon. Relief shall be granted Chobei." Wrapping a *ryō* in paper he passed it to the leper. It was the last coin he possessed. O'Hana now returned with five or six rice balls savoured with salt. Fascinated, the two watched the horrible diseased stumps awkwardly shoving the food into the toothless mouth, cramming it in, and breaking it up so as not to lose the savour of a grain. "Until tomorrow," said Chobei. He picked up his stick. In silence the man and woman watched him. "Leaning on his bamboo staff he crawled away like some insect." O'Hana looked inquiringly at Iemon. He turned away his head.

Through the dusk Chobei crawled across the Ryogokubashi. The words of the woman O'Take had come true. He had a sense of being followed. He turned at the sound of footsteps. At sight of a *samurai* in deep hat, mechanically he stretched out hands and self in the roadway, begging an alms. The man drew apart, passing him in disgust and haste. Chobei went on. He had no aim. It was with surprise that he found himself, as often of late, on the embankment of the North Warigesui. He looked down on the foul place of O'Iwa's disappearance. "A foul ending; but after all an end. One night! One night's sleep! Deign, lady of Tamiya, to grant pardon and respite to Chobei. Just one hour of sleep." Carefully he adjusted his mat. Painfully he stretched himself out on it. "To die on the mat. Such was the word of Iemon." He felt his rags. "It was well he agreed. Chobei had other means to force compliance. Well, 'Tis for later use." A continued rustling aroused him. Someone was cautiously picking a way through the dry grass of the past winter, was creeping toward him. He half rose. Seeing that concealment was no longer possible, the man rushed on him. Chobei struggled to his feet, as one to fight for life. "Life is dear. Why kill Chobei the leper? Is he a test for some new sword? Deign to pardon. The flesh of the leper is too rotten. It defiles the weapon. Chobei has been the *samurai*; he knows.... Ah! Respite there is none. 'Tis Iemon! Iemon of Tamiya would kill Chobei!" He shouted and coupled the names in his despair. Fearful of discovery, of being overheard, Iemon did not delay. The gleaming weapon descended. Standing over the body Iemon showed uncertainty. He had some thought of search; even bent down over it. But he could not touch those foul rags. His nicety of feeling, almost womanlike – recoiled. Besides, what more had Iemon to do with the leper Chobei. Their account was closed. Should he leave the body where it was? Recognition might convey some danger, at least inconvenience. He looked around for means to sink it in these waters, and yet not handle its repulsiveness. A *shōyu* tub, old but fairly intact, lay upon the bank. It caught his eye. He rolled it up to the corpse. Gingerly he girdled the body of the dead man with his *tasuki*(shoulder cord). Now tight fast it clasped the roundness of the barrel. This he filled with stones, drove in the head, and with a shove sent it and its burden into the Warigesui. "That will hold him down. The rotten punk! Three days, and none could recognize him." Then he set off at rapid pace for Yotsuya.

Sanzugawa Bridgeless: The Flowerless Road Traversed by the Dead

It was the hour of the pig (9 pm) before Iemon reached the house in Yotsuya. To his surprise he found the *amado* still open on the garden. Someone was lying face downward on the *rōka*. It was O'Hana. To his alarmed inquiry as to what was wrong she answered in the voice of one trying to suppress great pain. "This Hana knows not. Opening a closet to get the spices used in preparing the meal, a rat sprang out. It scratched the face of Hana. Truly the pain is very great." She groaned, Iemon gently raised her. At the look on his face O'Hana said – "There is a mirror in the toilet set (*kyōdai*). Deign to get it for Hana." He did not get it – this dower gift once of O'Iwa – but tried to soothe her – "Let be: the wounds soon will heal. The pain will pass away." She shoved him aside and ran to the toilet stand. She took the hand-mirror to the solitary lamp lighting the room. Aghast she contemplated her features. One side of the face was completely discoloured. It was a dark red, almost black, with the mark of five fingers plainly visible, as if a hand had struck her. No rat had made this wound. O'Hana leaned over, her head resting almost on her knees. Iemon touched her shoulder – "Don't mind it. Truly the pain will pass with dawn. Hana...." He drew back from the scowling madness in the face raised to him – "Sa! Sa! Iemon! Iemon! Easily did you get hold of all my property, to waste it on O'Hana. 'Twas like grasping wet millet. Then, barbarous as you were, you sold me to the vile life of a street harlot. Ah! Vengeance!" In fright Iemon retreated. O'Hana, taking herself to be O'Iwa, all her madness had returned. She sprang up. Screens were beaten and torn to pieces. With the heavy mirror she turned on him, seeking vengeance for her imagined wrongs. Iemon narrowly escaped injury as he dashed in to grapple with her. He succeeded in dragging her away from the lamp. Thus did this wild battle rage in the half dark room. The fictitious strength of the ill woman gave out. He held her on the floor, as one subdued. As she relapsed into a sleep, almost of unconsciousness, he ventured to release her. Going to a closet he placed the mirror beside the bamboo stick; both hidden away.

All night he watched over her. Wearied out, with day he sought an aid readily given. The nurse, however, in alarm soon roused him. O'Hana was raving madly in a high fever. The woman could not restrain her. Her cries were terrible, but not more so than the speech from her lips – "O'Iwa, pardon! With the drugs of Suian this Hana would palsy O'Iwa's mind and body; poison the very springs of life, cut off all hope of issue. Ah! Vain the love of a man. All is granted him; body and goods. Iemon sells Hana for a street harlot. Out with him! Help!... Ah! Kwaiba aids – in all his rottenness. How horrible he is – huge vacant eye holes, the purple whitish flesh gnawed and eaten.... Ugh! He stinks!... Nay! 'Tis not Kwaiba. 'Tis Chobei: Chobei the leper, who would embrace this Hana. Iemon comes. There is murder in his eye – for Hana to see, not Chobei. Away! Away!... Again, there she comes!" She grasped the nurse's arm, and pointed to the just lighted *andon* which barely relieved the shadows of the darkening night; was it the woman's imagination? By the light, dimly outlined; sat O'Iwa San. Her hair hung down around face and body half turned aside. The bulging forehead, the puffed eyelids, were not to be mistaken. The woman shook off the sick girl's hand and fled the house. Iemon did not try to prevent her. He was as one paralyzed. He, too, had seen, and was convinced.

To watch through the night was the task of the anxious and wearied man. In the day a *yakunin* had come, with formal notice to attend next day the office of Katada Tatewaki Dono. His lordship had an inquiry to make. The summons was not to be disregarded, no matter what his own exigencies. O'Hana had dropped into a cataleptic state. As the eighth hour (1 am) approached he thought to clear brain and body by the rest of a few moments. His head had barely touched the pillow when sleep followed. The bell of Gwanshoji struck the hour. It roared and reverberated through Tamiya. Iemon awoke; an oppression like suffocation pervaded his whole body. Opening his eyes they stared into the wide white flat face of O'Iwa. Her eyes were now alive, darting gleams of fire deep from within the puffed and swollen lids. He felt her wild disordered hair sweeping his face as she swayed a little, still retaining her post and clutch on his bosom – "Iemon knows Iwa now! Hana knows Iwa now! Sworn to seize and kill both for seven births – come! Now it is that Iwa completes her vengeance." As she shook and pressed on him he came gradually out of his sleep. With a shout he cast her backwards. Springing up he grasped the sword at his pillow. Madly he dealt blow after blow on the body before him. To the groans he replied by fresh blows.

An uproar without called him to himself. Don – don – don, don, don, don. There was knocking at the gate. Iemon hastily trimmed up the wick of the lamp. He leaned over the body. O'Hana! The young man stooped over her, leaning on the gory sword. Great drops of cold sweat stood out on his forehead. A shout came from without. "In his lordship's name! Open, or force will be used." Why had the summons for the day been anticipated? The unhappy ravings of O'Hana flashed to his mind. Iemon no longer reasoned. A cunning insane light was in his eyes. Softly he made his way to the *amado* fronting on the garden. No one was without. In the rain and storm he might escape. Traversing the darkness he noted, however, the man posted at the gate in the rear. Springing on the roof of the shed he looked over into Teramachi. It was deserted. With the bloody sword he hacked off the sharp points of the bamboo stakes. They now aided his flight over the wall. He cast the weapon aside. In a few minutes he disappeared in rapid flight down the street. When Katada Tatewaki, accompanied by his men, at last broke down the stout resistance offered by the outer door of Tamiya he found the house empty, except for the dead body of O'Hana, lying in its pool of blood. She was still warm. He took it for mere murder, giving more urgent directions for immediate pursuit. Methodically he searched the house, down to the very rubbish pile. The seal of Tamiya was secured. This meant much. With sceptical smile he handled the broken bamboo stick found in a closet. He did not show the discovery to his men.

Where did Iemon go? The unhappy man himself could not have told what happened in the intervening days. He came to consciousness in the darkness of a spring night, just before the dawn. The stars were beginning to pale in the East. The landscape had the livid eerie light in which it is uncertain whether day or night is to be the issue. With surprise Iemon looked around him; then shuddered. The stagnant waters of Warigesui's filthy stream lay beneath him. He had found rest on the bank, at the very place where Chobei had died under his hand.

Iemon could go no further. His course was run. He knew it; but how end life? At heart he was an arrant coward. Determined to cut belly he drew the dagger he had kept with him. A shudder went through him at sight of the steel. Ah! Better the green slime of the waters below. He thrust the blade back into its scabbard. Moodily standing and gazing down, he gave an idle kick to a stone near by. Dislodged, it swayed, then rolled heavily down the bank, to plunge noisily into the stream, disturb its noisome depths. The effect was surprising. Following its course with his eye Iemon suddenly gave a yell of horror. Eyes starting from his head, arms raised high, he bent toward the stream. Hair standing on end he watched the hideous object rise to the surface. The face of Chobei, purple and bloated, the lips half gnawed and open in a fiendish grin, looked up at him. Down came the arms, and Iemon put hands over eyes to shut out the fearful vision. A horrid curiosity drove him again to view it. Was he mad? This time the barrel in its slow revolution brought to view the wide flat face, the bulging brow and heavy lids, the tangled, disordered hair of the drowned O'Iwa. Scream after scream of the now frantic wretch rang in the air. These waters! Seek death there! No! No! A thousand times – No! He turned to flee the place, but his legs refused the service. With fell purpose he ripped the blade from its scabbard, tore open his clothes to give the deadly thrust. As he raised the dagger invisible hands seized his arm. When he would release it, the other arm was seized. Everywhere these hands held him fast. He raged, tore, struggled madly to elude their grasp. Then, overcome, he fainted.

Katada Tatewaki from the top of the bank had been watching the struggle of his men. He came forward and looked down at the bound and helpless creature. "'Tis he: in very fact." On order a bamboo pole was fetched, and run between the bound hands and feet. Thus like some beast was Iemon conveyed to the nearest ward office. The formalities were few and soon over. To avoid chance of repetition of the scene they conveyed him as he was. Thus began the brutal progress across Edo in full daylight. People turned and stared after this escort of the man-beast. At a distance they took the burden as some savage bear, or perhaps one of those reputed '*tanuki*' so noxious in their pranks on humankind. Come closer it was seen to be a man. Any mad struggle to get free was treated to spear pricks applied with no great nicety beyond the avoidance of serious injury. Violent as were his struggles at times, it is doubtful if they could have walked him the long distance. For the days of his flight he had never rested; nor had these men in his pursuit. Yet he was unexpected game. The Yotsuya affair was taking a widening sweep. Tamiya Yoemon and Kondo Rokurobei were under examination. The death of a girl O'Haru at the brothel of Toemon of Honjo had unexpected effects. In the investigation which followed one of the women, O'Take, had made full confession. The pedlar Mobei had never left the house of Toemon; never escaped from the hospitality of O'Matsu. His goods had aroused her cupidity. The man died by poison, and was buried in the garden of Toemon's house. O'Haru knew of the deed. This knowledge was the girl's destruction. The wife and her substitute O'Kin hated O'Haru. Some remains of a first good looks, her youth, gave her power with the master of the house. The two women worked on his fears to gain consent for her destruction. A charge easily was trumped up, and she was dragged off to the cell of punishment. Under the hands of the wife and O'Kin she suffered so that she died in three days, not without letting her mate O'Take into the secret. Promptly the Honjo police were at work; not more prompt than was the woman O'Kin to disappear from Edo, almost a confession in itself. The rosary, found in the hands of the rector of the Reiganji, was easily traced through different mediators straight to O'Matsu herself. The man Toemon held out, and died under the torture. The woman confessed; and in her confession was comprehended the full story of O'Iwa's connection with Toemon's house. Of her no more need be said. She rotted and died in the jail. The girls were scattered to kindred houses. Two of the women, hunting their pray on Warigesui toward the *yashiki* quarter, had witnessed the murder of Chobei three nights before. The police had gone to secure the body. Tatewaki Dono was notified and had accompanied them. To the surprise of all Iemon, then the object of earnest search, was found on the spot.

The affair kept on spreading – to the very source of all these troubles. Katada Tatewaki in the course of procedure had transmitted the Tamiya case to the jurisdiction of the *machibugyō* of the North district of Edo town, Homma Iga no Kami. With greatest interest the two men in company poured over the innumerable documents now piling up in the case. Old Tamiya Yoemon proved easy game. He readily confessed all he knew. This brought in many witnesses from the wardsmen. It was not exactly what was wanted. The evidence was mostly mere hearsay and conjecture. In those days such testimony had a value not far below that of direct statement. All pointed the way to the real criminal, who after all was the star witness. Against Yoemon at first there was but little. However, in his rage against Iemon and Kondo Rokurobei – Akiyama was out of his reach – his tongue was too long. The faces of the magistrates grew serious as his connection with the money lender Suzuki was made plain. A *samurai* loaning money on interest! and pressing men to ruin for payment!! The stingy avaricious Yoemon appeared behind the usurer – until in time his own heavy losses had made him a borrower, and placed him in the hands of his once partner. Yoemon, together with the conspirators, was not allowed to participate in the forced restitution made by Suzuki. Nevertheless, at the time no great severity was shown the old man. He was remanded to the custody of his bail, to be kept confined to one room in the house.

The same leniency was shown toward Rokurobei. When he showed a disposition to be recalcitrant, to equivocate, Homma gave sign to the *dōshin*. Quickly the scourgers came forward with their fearful instrument, the *madake*. Made of bamboo split into long narrow strips, these tightly wrapped in twisted hempen cord to the thickness of a *sun* (inch), with the convenient leverage of a couple of *shaku*(feet), the mere sight brought Kondo to terms. As he entered he had seen them lead away a *heimin* (commoner) who had undergone the punishment. The man's back, a mass of bruised and bleeding flesh, was vivid to mind. At once he prostrated himself; made full confession. At last they were at the source. Kondo was a witness of the fact. He could and did tell of the inception and progress of the whole plot against O'Iwa San, the source of untold woe to Yotsuya. His story covered the period from the entrance of Iemon into the ward up to the discovery of the body of Kamimura Goemon. The role played by Kazaguruma Chobei was in part dark to him. Of the disposition of O'Iwa to the Honjo master of the *Yōtaka* he pleaded ignorance. Tatewaki Dono smiled as he counselled indulgence on this point. He knew.

Kondo, however, was sent back to the jail. He was unquestionably a principal. At last it was the turn of Iemon. The weeks had passed. The body had been carefully nursed back to vigour. The mind was in lamentable state. The ill-meant efforts of the jail authorities, the strengthening of the criminal in order better to endure the torture to the confession point, were somewhat baffled by the nightly visions of the wretched man. The two hags, O'Iwa and O'Mino; Chobei in his final stage of purple bloatedness; these were his nightly companions, to torment and harass him. Sleep! If he could but close his eyes to shut out these horrors! Instead they became more vivid. The jailors put him at the farthest corner of their ample premises. His fellow prisoners, such as were allowed daily exit to the yard, visited him with blows and foul insults for the disturbance he created in the night. But he was cunning withal. Trapped as he was, in his lucid moments he realized that there could be but little against him. O'Iwa? Not even in Tokugawa times was the supernatural cause of prosecution except at the hands of the vulgar. Nor in those days, any more than in these of Taisho *nengo*, was a wife legally protected against abuse of husband or parents-in-law. As for Chobei – he was dead. His own presence on the scene was no evidence against him as murderer. His only misgivings on that point lay in the confusion of mind as to the few days then covered. But who would blame a *samurai* for testing his blade on a beggar? What were beggars for? He knew nothing of the evidence given by Yoemon and Kondo; of the vile proof in the hands of Katada Dono. He had wholly forgotten the nurse who had listened to the wild ravings of O'Hana in her illness, broken sentences bearing so heavily and dove-tailing so nicely into the completed case. Owing to this woman Tatewaki Dono had not waited the appearance of Iemon at morning. Iemon also left out of account the characters of the two men before whom he appeared. Iga no Kami sat as judge in the case. Close beside him, a little in the rear, sat Katada Tatewaki, in whose jurisdiction the case had originated, and who was familiar with every stage. The four *dōshin* sat to one side and the other of these two men.

Homma and Katada were typical of their caste. Cold, callous, cruel, devoted rigidly to the formulae; of the *samurai* code, with strange exceptions granted to the virtues required of the common people – filial conduct and unswerving obedience to a superior – they were not men likely to regard with favour this intruder into their class. The name of *samurai* had been brought into contempt. Hence the serious character of the offence, the necessity of severest scrutiny. To the valued suggestion of Tatewaki, Iga no Kami nodded assent. Iemon thought of nothing but the murder of Chobei, the abuse of his wife O'Iwa, the conspiracy against her life and honour. The first question paralyzed his defence. Was he not the son of Takahashi Daihachiro? The whole terrible vista of the consequences of avowal appeared before him, once himself a *dōshin* and familiar with legal procedure. The family had suffered *kaieki* (deprivation of rights). It had been degraded from the caste. Properly speaking Iemon was an intruder into the *samurai* class. He was an impostor. His offence was against the suzerain lord, the Shogun. All the terrible penalties of treason hung over him. Tatewaki had been quick to note the opportunity to take this case out of the category of offence by a *samurai*. Iemon was a plebeian and a charlatan. He had insulted Government. At the stumbling denial quick order was given. A *yakunin* seized the rope and dragged down the head of Iemon. Others held him at the sides, to maintain the body rigid. Stout fellows, the pick of the jailors, came forward. With ferocious regularity the blows fell. Welts at once appeared. Soon the blood was trickling from the torn skin. There was no sign to mitigate the severity of the infliction. When at the seventieth blow the body collapsed in a faint the wretched man was a terrible sight. The attendants of the jail, witnesses of the full punishment of double the number of stripes, had rarely seen such severity exercised. The jailors hated this smooth fellow, this disturber of their peace. They kept a jail, not a madhouse. Their superiors showed no sign of the mercy of renewed questioning. Hence they would change the mad nightly ravings to the subdued groans of the punished.

The days passed and his body had healed, though movement caused pain and distress. Brought again before the judges at the very sight of the scourges he screamed out confession. Questioned as to the conspiracy against the caste, his fraudulent attempt to consummate marriage with a *samurai* woman – the actual fact or legality of it was ignored – his ill-treatment and sale of her; all these in terror he denied. Once he had looked upon banishment from Edo as the limit of his punishment. Now decapitation would be a merciful end. He strove to secure the favour of a quick and painless death. Again he was beaten almost to a jelly. He clung to his denial, so important was the issue. At the next appearance he was seized and dragged to a post fixed in the ground not far from the judge's seat. His knees were pressed down on the edges of the triangular bars. These formed a sort of grid, the edges of the bars being just enough blunted to avoid cutting the skin. None of the pain was spared, yet the prisoner remained fit for early future torture. The granite slabs were then piled on his knees. Each one weighed thirteen *kwan* (107 lb.). As the fifth slab was placed on the body of Iemon, the flesh assumed a reddish tint from the impeded circulation. Froth stained his mouth, mucus ran from his nose. A sixth, a seventh stone, were placed. "How now! How now!" The men pressed heavily on the stones. A *dōshin* bent over him, listening and waiting for sign of the important confession. The criminal was the one important witness of Tokugawa penal law. Without confession he was innocent beyond all other proof. As the eighth stone was placed Iemon began to vomit blood. The doctor raised his hand. The feet were showing signs of blackness, which rapidly spread upward. The man was in a dead faint. No confession had been secured.

Perhaps the examination was thus conducted out of some severity. Days passed. Whether or not the report of the physician was unfavourable, influenced by some means Homma had fear the man might die before a public retribution was secured. When Iemon again was dragged before his judges he had a terrible object lesson before him. A man was undergoing the torture of the lobster. Hands drawn up behind to the shoulders, the feet tightly bound across the chest, he was propped up on a mat. Properly conducted this 'effort to persuade' took place in the jail. Homma wished to try the effect of anticipation on Iemon. The prisoner looked quickly at the man under torture, then hung down his head. His lips were twitching with uncertainty. Homma struck hard – "Why deny the plain fact? Is justice so ignorant of the doings and whereabouts of a scamp. Kichitaro, or Kazuma the diviner, as he called himself, murders Chobei the pimp; a deed carried out before witnesses." A *dōshin* placed the document of the confession of the whores so that Iemon had no difficulty in ascertaining its title. "And why? Because of the agreement with Chobei to sell the woman he dared to call his wife. The proof? The seal of Tamiya, the document itself." At last Iemon looked up. The *dōshin* placed under his eyes the fatal contract with Chobei – agreement of exchange of the body of the woman in return for five *ryō* duly received. It had been recovered from the dead pimp's corpse. Carefully wrapped in oiled paper, Chobei had carried it – sewn in what he called his dress. Iemon unwilling to recognize past services, Chobei was sure to find it useful. Truly Iemon was young and impatient, and Chobei was double his age. With bitterness the survivor recognized this primal fact.

Iemon's eyes wandered from the paper to the thief under torture. The dark green of the body was rapidly changing. The doctor present gave a quick frightened sign. Skilful hands at once cast loose the bonds. Over toppled the body. Iemon noted the white, almost livid, colour of death. Restoratives were applied. All were busied with bringing the man back to life. Then he was carried off, expression so unlike that of a human being that the less hardened shuddered. Said Homma – "No confession yet?" He raised his hand to make a sign. Iemon knew the quickness of response. He almost screamed his appeal for further respite. The Law had triumphed. As Iemon put his thumb seal to the confession of guilt to insolence (*futodoki*) the magistrates rose and disappeared. "Futodoki" – they and he knew that it meant the death sentence.

Judgment was not delayed. The next day Homma, with Katada and an officer of the Shogun's household present, gave sentence. Yoemon and Rokurobei glared hate at Iemon who squatted with head bent to the ground. The sword – that now was his only hope. The first words of Homma showed that no mercy was to be dealt out in this case. Suzuki the plebeian merely suffered stripes and banishment from Edo. He had to make restitution to the amount of his property – such as was left after paying the huge fine to Government. Tamiya Yoemon and Kondo Rokurobei underwent degradation from the caste. There was no disposition to overlook the offence of usury. Beggary was to be the portion of Yoemon, the destitution of the outcast. For some years the senile old man, the virago of a woman once the wife of Kondo Rokurobei, were stationed at the Niomon, to attract and amuse the worshippers passing up to the great temple of the Asakusa Kwannon. Not for long could the woman hold her tongue. Abuse passed with the sun's height to blows, and the by-standers had to interfere and rescue the old man from the severe beating. It was to the profit, rather than disadvantage, of the temple. The pair were an added attraction. The priests left interference to those at hand. Then the old man disappeared; to ornament the highway with his corpse, or be cast on the moor, food for dogs and crows. Such probably was the end of Tamiya Yoemon. The woman had not been seen for some months. Her abilities as scold had attracted those qualified to judge; her transfer to the position of bawd in a low-class house of the neighbouring Yoshiwara soon followed.

Kondo Rokurobei fared tolerably well, considering his deserts. His confession had been a great aid in unravelling the case. He was not sentenced to cut belly. Degraded he heard with dismay the sentence of deportation and exile to the far distant island of Sado. At this savage place, subject to the hell of a Siberian winter and the intense heats of the summer, the once pampered man lived out his last days, few and evil. He who had passed the time idling with tea-cup, or *go*, or flower arrangement, and taking enjoyment in the freshness and coolness of his garden at the Yotsuyazaka, at fifty years now tried to lead the hard and dangerous life of the wild fishing population among whom he was unceremoniously cast. Such life was soon forbidden him. He was but in the road. Then he did such clerical duties as the village at times needed. A wife even was provided for him. The final blow was a palsy, cutting off all effort at making a livelihood. Beatings now took the place of food. The villagers laughed when they heard of the old man's fall from a cliff. They, too, would have acted as had the brothers of O'Nabe (stew pan). They took the word for the deed; and at the cliff foot near Negai they erected a wooden shrine to propitiate the spirit of "Jiya Rokuro."

The day of execution had come. When sentenced, bound as he was Iemon struggled forward to plead for mercy, respite from the barbarous punishment to be inflicted on the traitor. His reward was the cangue and bamboo saw – *nokogiribiki*; failing death by this, he was to be crucified. The attendants fell on him. Kicks and blows had little effect on the man frantic with terror. He almost reached the *rōka* at which sat Homma. Then madly struggling he was carried off to the jail. Said a *dōshin* – "His antics in the cangue will find small scope." The last clause of the sentence was due to the notorious unwillingness of any passer-by to give a cut. The punishment had lapsed since the days of the third Shogun, and was no more successful in Iemon's case. Placed in the cangue at the execution ground of Shinagawa a cut was made in each side of his neck. Smeared with blood the bamboo saw was placed on the cangue in inviting proximity to the head. For five hours people passed, with curious glances, but no movement to release the criminal. An Outcast butcher sidled up. The guards watched him with curiosity. Picking up the saw he made one pass. At the yell given by Iemon he dropped the implement and fled in terror, amid the laughter of guards and by-standers. Toward the hour of the sheep (1 pm) a *yoriki* with his *dōshin* appeared. On signal the cangue was removed. Inert limbs feebly twitching Iemon was bound tight to the double cross, his legs and arms stretched wide apart. This was raised, and again the hours passed in miserable waiting for a death which seemed to recede. If unconsciousness threatened he was given vinegar to drink as restorative. His fevered lips eagerly sought the fluid and prolonged his torture. In the spring light the days were long. As the sun was about to set the officer gave command. A *dōshin* came forward to the cross and made a sign. A guard thrust his spear upward into the belly of Iemon. The limbs made a movement, as in attempt to be drawn up. A guard on the other side in turn made a thrust. Others followed. For some moments they continued their sport, the reward of long waiting. The man was not yet dead. Impatient the *dōshin* gave the shaft of a spear a violent upward thrust. Its point appeared through the left shoulder. The head fell forward on the breast and hung limp. Iemon was dead.

These events could not be let pass without notice from either the pious or the timorous. Kyoho 2nd year 2nd month 22nd day (3rd April, 1717) the Inari shrine built to propitiate the fearful Lady of Tamiya was opened to worship with due ceremonies. It had been erected on the ground of the house once occupied by Matazaemon, facing on Teramachi and on the narrow street paralleling Samoncho to the East. It was almost opposite the entrance to the Shogwanji. At the family temple, the Myogyoji, on the Samegabashi side, a grave and stela was set up. With time, however, the opposition made itself felt. It was asserted that the Lady O'Iwa still walked the ward, inflicting pains and penalties on the inhabitants thereof. Triumphant reference was made to recent public disasters – of plague, pestilence, famine, and tax levies. The shrine was invitation for her presence. People had grown indifferent as the new paint grew old, then shabby on the once famous *miya*. Success lay with the opposition, and abolition of shrine and grave was easily enforced. It was but for a time. The ward was either equally, or more, unfortunate without the protection of its tutelary Inari shrine. Just when it was re-established cannot be stated, but in the late eighteenth century it was most flourishing. It was a favourite resort of *samurai* women, seeking consolation for unfaithful or brutal conduct of their husbands, and strength in the reputation for chastity of the famous Lady of Tamiya. In 1825 the third Kikugoro made Yotsuya famous by his presentation of the "Yotsuya Kwaidan" as written for the stage by Tsuruya Namboku (Katsu Byozo). In the first years of the Meiji restoration period Shunkintei Ryuo, the famous story-teller, heralded its renown in the Shin Yoshiwara. O'Iwa San became a feature of the Konharuko fête of that quarter. A grave was again erected to her at the Myogyoji. As she had no *kaimyō*, or posthumous name, the rector of the temple gave her that of "Tokusho-In Myonen Hisho Daishi," which can be interpreted – "She, pleasing of disposition and earnest in prayer; a woman of greatest brilliance." Let the reader not judge this composition harshly; or its truth.

The editor to the reproduction of Ryuo's story speaks of his difficulties. Placed in his hand for judgment he saw at once the power of the tale. But – how avoid incurring the divine anger of the Yotsuya Inari; how avoid being charged with the divine punishment? This question was solved by the publisher assuming the burden of both inflictions; under the spur of what *he* regarded as publication in inferior and untrue form. He answered these questions with a laugh – "Afraid? Not so: I, too, am human. Though the unusual is an object, yet I would not rejoice at incurring the divine anger by publishing what should not be published. Though the divine anger be incurred by publishing the Yotsuya Kwaidan, and the divine punishment be inflicted, yet who would not gladden the eyes and ears of the land? Hence in haste the true record is to be printed; owing to emission of unfounded stories. The true record being put forth, the people profit by it. How then is the divine wrath incurred by publication? Certainly not: the protection of the divine one is secured." The editor trusted in his argument; as does the present scribe.

More than once the remark has been heard as to these shrines of Nippon – "Their temples? Those dirty, shabby places, without architecture or interest, the haunts of snotty, ragged children?" The sun-helmeted gentleman and lady, or collection of their kind, rush them by in haughty contempt, and with some ridicule and ridiculous comment. Good Sir and Madame, you are passing history on the road. At this Kwogwanji, in its rather shabby guest hall, Kusonoki Masashige and his devoted followers spoke their last defiance and then cut belly. Kobe? It is noted as a place to take ship, and not be too long in doing so. This other, barely a mile from the Tokyo-Yokohama railway, is contemporary record of Nitta Yoshioka, who carved his bloody protest on the Ashikaga before he killed himself in the trap set by their treachery at this spot. Here behind the Koraiji near Oiso is a very shabby and tiny shrine nestled at the foot of the cliff. This had better be avoided. It is dedicated to the smallpox god. But more than history is neglected in the indifference and contempt shown these minor *miya*. A vein of thought inwoven into the minds of this strange people is instanced by this modest shrine of the Tamiya Inari. Wandering along the amusement quarter of some great city, a theatre is seen with a *torii* gorgeous in its red paint standing before the entrance. Within this entrance is a small shrine and a box for the practical offerings of cash or commodities. The theatre is decorated inside and outside with flags as for a festival (*matsuri*). Such is actually in progress. The representation is that of the Yotsuya Kwaidan. From manager and actor (even in the presentation of the figured screen of the moving picture) the malevolence of the O'Iwa Inari – the Fox-witched O'Iwa – is to be averted. Hence all the signs of worship as at her very shrine; hence the unwillingness of author or publisher to handle the story, at least in its full form. This is but a remnant of the fear of "black magic" still found and practised in Nippon. On the beach at Kamakura at times can be found straw chaplets with gaudy cloth attached to the centre; a copper coin, and rice offering are accompaniments. Or such will be found at the crossroads of town or village, or on the Yokohama Bluff. Or in times of epidemic in numbers they are laid on the wayside shrine of the god of measles or other disease. The latter disposition conveys its own warning; the others are *majinai* or charms by which it is hoped to transfer the disease to some other child, thus insuring the cure of the first sufferer. The coin has been rubbed on the body of the little patient. Dogs usually dispose of the food offering; and passing children are only too likely to pick up the nefarious coin. The road cleaner comes along at his rare intervals and sweeps the chaplet into the hole for refuse. It is to be regretted that the ignorance and malevolence indicated by these charms cannot as easily be gathered in and disposed of. With these remarks the Yotsuya Kwaidan and its tale of ill-fortune is brought to an end.

The Bancho Sarayashiki or The Lady of The Plates

The Yoshida Goten

WHEN PRINCE IYEYASU consolidated his power at Edo, more particularly on his becoming Sei-i-tai-Shogun, some provision had to be made for the great *daimyō* brought by the necessities of occasion to personal interview with their chief and suzerain. In the suburbs rose beautiful structures devoted to the entertainment of these *kyakubun* – or guests – as the greater *daimyō* were then termed. The Yatsuyama Goten, the Hakuzan Goten, the Kosuge Goten, the Yoshida Goten, other and elegant, if minor, palaces arose. Their first use disappeared with the compulsory residence of the *daimyō* under Iyemitsu Ko, but some were still maintained as places of resort and entertainment for the Shogun in his more relaxed moments. Others were devoted to the residences of favoured members of his family. Others were maintained for the entertainment of State or Church dignitaries, on occasion of particular mission from the court in Kyoto to that of Edo. Others were destroyed, or put to temporal uses, or their use granted to favoured retainers or church purposes.

One of the most beautiful of these was the Yoshida Goten in the Bancho. The site originally had been covered by the *yashiki* of Yoshida Daizen no Suke. One of those nobles favouring the Tokugawa against Ishida Mitsunari, as their designs became clearer with the years following Sekigahara, at the attack on Osaka castle he was found within its walls. Thus the "Overseer of the kitchen" fell under the wrath of his suzerain. Hidetada Ko was a man of much kind temperament, but he was a strict disciplinarian and a rough soldier. Whether or not the dishes furnished for his consumption and digestion had anything to do with the matter, there was serious cause enough. With many others the Daizen no Suke was ordered to cut belly, and his tribe suffered extinction – of rank and rations (*kaieki*). Such the reward of this turn-coat. His disappearance from the scene was followed by other removals. Daizen no Suke was head of the Koshogumi. With the confiscation of his *yashiki* site five other Houses of the 'company' were ordered to remove to other sites at Akasaka. Thus 2,500 *tsubo* of ground (24 acres) were obtained for the building of a new *kyakubun goten*. Erected on the ground of Yoshida's old mansion, now waste (更), it got the name of Sarayashiki. Time confused this character 更 with the events which there took place; and it was written Sara (皿) yashiki or Mansion of the Plates. Thus was the unhappy tale of O'Kiku written into the history of Edo and the Yoshida Goten.

The second daughter of Hidedata Ko, the Nidai Shogun, had been married to the lord of Echizen, Matsudaira Tadanao. At the time of the Osaka campaign Tadanao sulked. Prince Iyeyasu was very angry with him. However, when finally Echizen Ke did appear, he acted with such bravery, and to such effect in the campaign, that the old captain's anger was dispelled in his appreciation. To this connected House of the Tokugawa he thought to be liberal enough; not to meet the inflated scale of the ideas of Tadanao, who spent the next half dozen years in so misgoverning his lordly fief as to render necessary an adviser, planted at his side by his powerful cousin in Edo. In Genwa ninth year Tadanao rebelled – with the usual result to him who acts too late. He was suppressed, largely by the aid of his own vassals, and exiled to Hita in Bungo province. Here he shaved his head, took the name of Ichihaku. It was of no avail. Promptly he died. It seemed to be a dispensation of Providence – or dispensation of some kind – that exiles usually and early developed alarming symptoms; in the shortest possible time removing themselves and all cause of irritation to the overlord by their transfer to another sphere.

The Tokugawa Shogun was generous to his relations. The exit of Tadanao was promptly followed by the induction of his infant son Mitsunaga into his fief. However, for the child to govern the great district of 750,000 *koku* appeared to be a doubtful step. Its government actually being invested in the *daimyō*, it was not to be made a breeding ground for trouble through the action of subordinates. Hence the main fief with the seat at Kita no Sho (Fukui) was given to the uncle. Fukui today is a dull provincial town, and excellent stopping place for those who would have eyes opened as to the great wealth and wide flat expanse of these three provinces of Kaga, Etchu, and Echizen. Their lord was a mighty chieftain, entrenched behind mountain barriers; and the great campaigns, which figure in pre-Tokugawa history, were fought for a great object. The Maeda House, however, had had their wings clipped, and were confined to Kaga. The Matsudaira were established in Echizen. Etchu was much divided up. The reduction of the fief of Echizen Ke to 500,000 *koku* brought him within reasonable bounds, and he could well be left to ride with his hawks along the pretty Ashibagawa, or to take his pleasure outing on the crest of Asuwayama, the holy place of the city suburbs, and where Hideyoshi nearly lost life and an umbrella by a stray shot. Then would follow the return, the ride across the wide moat, its waters dotted with the fowl he went elsewhere to shoot, but safe within these precincts. Whether he returned to any better entertainment than that of the present day Tsuki-mi-ro or Moon viewing inn, one can doubt. He certainly did not have the pretty outlook from its river bordered garden front.

Sen-chiyo-maru, later Mitsunaga, was relegated to Takata castle in Echigo, with the minor income of 250,000 *koku*. Perhaps this fact, together with his youth, and the more entertaining expenditure of the income at an Edo *yashiki*, rather than in a mountain castle town, brought the Takata no Kata to the capital. Takata Dono, or the Takata no Kata, so named from the fief, is not known to fame or history under other appellation. She is said to have possessed all the beauty of her elder sister, the Senhimegimi, wife of Hideyori Ko, son of the Taiko, he who fell at Osaka castle. Furthermore, with the training of the *samurai* woman, the greatness of her position and personal attraction, she possessed all the obstinacy and energy of the male members of her family, with few of the restraints imposed on them by public service. Takata Dono frankly threw herself into all the pleasures she could find at the capital. Established in the Yoshida Goten, the younger *samurai* of the *hatamoto* quickly came under her influence. There was a taint of license in her blood, perhaps inherited from the father who was most unbridled in his passions. The result was a sad falling off from the precepts of Bushido in herself and her paramours. The Bakufu (Shogunal Government) was compelled to look on, so great was her power at the castle. In the earlier days sentence of *seppuku* (cut belly) was a common reward for open misconduct. A word from Takata Dono, and the disgraceful quarrels over her favours were perforce condoned; and her lavish expenditures on her favourites were promptly met. Alas! Alas! The up to date histories of Nippon sigh over and salve these matters. "They were the inventions of a later age; were not current in her life-time." Nor likely to be put too bluntly by those tender of their skins. But an old poem has come down to express the popular belief:

"Yoshida tōreba nikai kara maneku;
Shikamo kano ko no furisode de."

Somewhat irregular, like the lady's conduct, but which can be interpreted,

"Passing Yoshida, from above the signal;
Furthermore, the waving of long sleeves."

Of little deer (or dears) for the style of sleeve, the *kano ko*, can be read young deer. Bah! Was there not a 'parc aux cerfs' half way round the world? Nor were such confined to the capital cities of Edo and Paris.

The poem refers to the unbridled licentiousness the little lady developed on her translation from her provincial residence; though locally she had not failed to distinguish herself. What follows is part of the tales current. At the time the *himegimi* (princess) was thrown on her own devices in Takata-jo the *karō* or chief officer of the household was one Hanai Iki. This fellow owed his position entirely to his good looks and her ladyship's favour. This favour he met, not in the spirit of a loyal vassal, but in that of a professed and bold lady killer. As *karō* his attendance on her ladyship was constant and intimate, and it took no particular acumen to find out that the intimacy was of a more peculiar relation. Hence great was the undercurrent of comment, and regret at the unbridled conduct of the lady. None, however, dared to interfere with the caprices of one so highly placed; and the only means was to work on the decent feelings of Iki himself. Thus the tale was brought to his wife's ears. It is to be said that with her all jealousy was suppressed. It was for her to find the cure for her husband's unbridled conduct. As Hanai Iki was a mere official, and with no great claim to unusual or able services, it was hoped that his removal or reform in conduct would bring back the *himegimi* to a befitting conduct. There was no suspicion that her passion was a disease raging in her very blood, and that it was the man, not his personality she sought.

The wife first adopted the orthodox method of formal remonstrance. Without chiding, with a smile and great indulgence of one at no particular fault himself, she enlarged upon the subject in the service of the tea. "It is not a matter between Iki Dono and this Chiyo. There is no unseemly jealousy in the wife to bring forward the complaint. In fact the marital relation is not in question. As the husband pleases, so should the wife submit. But great is the talk aroused at these too private meetings with the *himegimi*. It is the House which is at stake. Its influence and prestige is threatened by a mere retainer. This in a short time can but lead to ruin. The caprice of a woman is well known. In some cooler moment the eyes of her ladyship will see another colour. The one to suffer will be Iki Dono, for now he has no other support but in his mistress. Deign to regain the confidence of the household, and no great harm can result beyond neglect. Honoured sir, you stretch out for what is far beyond reach; and in the end can but fail. Deign to be circumspect." If there was any tone of contempt and depreciation in the protest it was in the last few words. At all events the eyes of Iki were opened to the fact that it was sought to reach him through the wife's remonstrance. He expressed surprise and discomfiture at what he asserted had no real basis in fact. His office brought him in close contact with her ladyship; the more so as the management of the fief was in her hands. Matters were to be discussed which necessitated the exclusion of all others. However, if such was the talk of the palace, or even beyond its walls, he could but give thanks for the kindness of the remonstrance. Henceforth he would be more careful, and would trust to her good feeling to believe in his good faith.

With joy the wife heard what he said. With all good will she made herself the apostle of this explanation. No one believed her and facts soon belied words. Her ladyship, just entering on her passion, became more exigent in her calls for the *karō's* attendance. Iki now seldom appeared at his home. Long absences from the castle town, pressing business, any excuse to hand came to the alarmed ears of the wife. All the rumours gathered were sure to reach her in exaggerated form. Hanai Dono was the constant companion of her ladyship's wine feasts. He was her acknowledged paramour, and lived in the private apartments of the castle as in his own house. All talked – except the ladies in waiting of the *himegimi*. These were selected and trained by her; selected for beauty and trained to discretion. She would have no ugly thing about her; and all was to be for her use. Iki was handsome, and discreet. To her he was an object; as were the maids; the same apart from sex. He filled his role admirably, never introduced his favour with her ladyship into the public affairs of the House, or solicited for such personal advancement as made toward outward display. But circumspection of conduct never yet closed the mouth of gossip. There were those who were jealous of what he might do; and jealous of a favour they would gladly share themselves. The *himegimi* was the prize which all coveted, and which no one should possess to the exclusion of others.

Hence the buzz of talk rose loud, and the criticism stung the wife. She determined herself to learn the truth of these tales. Hitherto they were but the scandalous talk of people. Wife of the *karō*, naturally her ladyship did not require her attendance; but as such she had ready access and an intimate acquaintance with the palace routine. Her mind made up, she presented herself on some trifling pretext. Certainly in her manner there was nothing to arouse comment. Received in the inner apartments (*oku*), her plea, the introduction of a page into the service, was readily granted. On retiring she would speak with the superintendent of the *oku*, the old and experienced lady in waiting in charge of the *himegimi's* service. Thus she found the opportunity to wander the inner precincts, to disappear and to slip into the bed room of the *himegimi*. Here she stepped into a closet, pulled to the screen, and crouched down behind the heaped up quilts. For the companionship of her wandering lord she did not have long to wait; nor for proof of his inconstancy. Iki came into the room, holding by the hand and drawing after him one of palace ladies in waiting, Takeo by name. The girl was by no means unwilling. Her blushes and confusion added to the great beauty which made her the favoured attendant on the *himegimi*. Iki pressed her close and openly. The girl plead ignorance and inexperience. She was ashamed. Iki laughed. "Does not her ladyship set the example for others to follow? Deign...." The plea of his relations with the mistress came quite fit to the coarse feeling of Iki. Not so to the girl, who was warmed into some indignation, and drew all the more from him. He would persist; but just then her ladyship called from the next room – "Takeo! Takeo!" The voice was impatient, as of one in haste. Iki had time to thrust a letter into the girl's hand, which she quickly transferred to her bosom. All the boldness of O'Chiyo was at stake as the maid came to the closet. Close down she crouched; but Takeo had one eye on Iki, and only one careless eye on the heap of *futon*, of which she drew from the top. Iki made a grimace, for the benefit of the one he really loved. Her ladyship's appearance was received with the warm and flattering affection of the favoured lover; and O'Chiyo had proof positive that the relations of the two were kind indeed.

The suicide of the wife, the letter of protest she left behind, had more influence on the public than on the conduct of Hanai Iki. It simply removed the last restraint and means of reaching him. All now depended on her ladyship's infatuation. Old vassals sighed with joy when they heard of the proposed removal to Edo. As *karō* Hanai Iki would be left in charge of the fief. Not so: it was soon learned that his name headed the list of those transferred for household service. The grumbling was as open as it dared to be. The fief was to be contented with the service of two vice-*karō*; no great loss, except in matter of prestige in dealing with other Houses. The *karō* became a kind of male superintendent of the *oku*! But at all events the fief was rid of him. Nor was Iki particularly pleased. He had been feathering his nest in the material sense. The severance of the connection, without loss of esteem, meant to him a quicker consummation of his wishes with Takeo Dono, whom he would ask for as wife. Their relations had gone forward at a wild pace. Once thrown into the whirl of passion Takeo sought but to meet the wishes of her lover. The passion of the *himegimi* stood between them.

Established in Edo, at the Yoshida Goten, all went mad with content in their beautiful surroundings. The palace gardens were noted. A hint of the fine construction of the buildings is found today at the Kugyoji of Iinuma, built subsequently from the materials. For the use of the Shogun Ke in entertainment of his visitors, every art had been exhausted in its adornment. The screens were objects of beauty, and separated the large rooms with their fine pillars and ceilings of grained and polished woods. The *rama-shōji* were carved by Nature's handiwork, and the polished lacquer and brass reflected a thousand times the beauties roundabout. Whether the garden be viewed from the apartments, or both from the *tsukiyama* or artificial hill beside the little lake, it was a scene of balanced beauty, showing every nicety of man's hand in Nature's own proportion, and not guided into the geometrical designs of a carpet square or a surveyor's working table. Instead of the dry dullness of a provincial town, in which themselves they had to fill the stage to give it life and pompousness, Edo was close at hand, and they were part of, and actors in, the luxury and magnificence of the Shogun's court. It is not surprising that the *himegimi* returned to all this glitter and activity as one long banished from its seductions to a wilderness; added her own dissipation and lavish entertainment to the constant round of festivity and luxury rapidly supplanting the hard military discipline of the first Shogun's camp; a luxury itself to crystallize into a gorgeous rigid formalism, as deadly to the one not meeting its requirements as the lined and spotted beauty of some poisonous serpent.

The wine feast was at its height. The cup passed more freely in this chilly season of the year; and in the tightly closed apartments the warmth of association and the table's cheer were sought. The *himegimi* was more expansive than usual under the influence of the wine. Iki was positively drunk, and in his state over-estimated the condition of her ladyship. Takeo was serving the wine. Beyond stolen interviews of moments the lovers had found no opportunity for the longed for clinging of soul to soul, of person to person, during the night's long hours. The girl's hands trembled with passion as furtively she sought those of her lover in the passing of the wine cup. Iki was absolutely careless. Her ladyship too far gone to note his conduct? He seized the arms of Takeo and drew her to his side. The display of amorous emotion on the part of both was too open to escape notice. The *himegimi* rose to her feet as on springs. The beautiful flushed face took on a deeper tint as she scowled on the guilty and now frightened pair. Her breath came hard and with difficulty. Then reaching down she wound the long tresses of Takeo in her hand, and dragged her to her knee. Twisting and twisting, until the agony made the girl cry out, she berated her – "Ah! Wicked jade! Thou too have eyes for a man's person. Disloyal wench, would you aim to make the beloved of your mistress partner of your bed?... What's this?" From the girl's hand she tore the answer to the lover's plaint. The sharp eyes of her ladyship sought the maid's person. A nervous hand fumbled the folds of her *obi* (sash). "Ah! The treasure house is not far off. Such valued gems are carried on the person." Thrusting her hand into the gentle bosom the *himegimi* drew forth the guilty complement.

Wrote Iki:

"How act to drop the mask;
Many the pledges breathed in truth."

And the girl made answer:

"Ah! The night of meeting, love's consummation;
The hindrance, thing or person, object of hate."

The words were too plain. There was a certain savage tone of exulting wrath as the *himegimi* read out loud the contents of the missives. It chilled the hearts of those who heard her. She spoke: at first in low concentrated tones of bitter jesting hate. "Ha! Ha! Disloyalty goes beyond mere thought; would strike at the person of its lord. What lascivious slut is this, who thus would creep into the mistress' bed, to take her place?... Look up! Naruhodo! In that face is too much beauty. Vile huzzy, you would seek the favour of my lover. Hence forth neither he nor any man shall look on you, except with loathing." Close beside her was the *hibachi*, its burden of the hard burning charcoal from Ikeda now a bright cherry red. Dragging the girl to the brazier, twisting both hands more firmly in the long black hair, she forced her, face downwards, into the heated mass, pressing into the back with her knee. In terror the other girls looked away, or hid their faces in their sleeves. Before the towering anger of the princess none dared apology or intercession. The smell of burning flesh rose sickening. Takeo feebly moaned, and writhed a little under the nervous pressure of those delicate powerful hands. Then she was silent. The inhuman punishment had reached its end. Roughly her ladyship threw her aside, face upward on the *tatami*. Those who took a hasty glance turned away in horror from the face, black here, red and swollen there, the mouth filled with ashes, the eyes – one totally destroyed.

The *himegimi* was on her feet. "Iki – here with you!" In fear the man prostrated himself before the vision. "Not yet did the demon's horns sprout from her head; but the eyes injected with blood, the hair standing up to Heaven, converted her ladyship into a veritable demon." In slow and measured wrath she spoke – "Ah, the fool! Admitted to the favour of his mistress, the long continued object of her affection, with all at his command and service, he would sacrifice these for the embraces of a serving wench. Truly the man has gone mad with lust; or rather it is a man's face and a beast's mind. Thus before my very eyes he would dally with his whore and make me cuckold. Of such miscreants one feels no jealousy. Hate and punishment follow the insult." A quick movement backward and her halberd hanging at the wall was in her hand. The scabbard stripped from the shining blade was held over head. "Namu San! Holy the three sacred things!" Iki sprang to his feet, coward and fool he sought not to grapple with her, but to flee. The command of the *himegimi* rang sharp – "He is not to escape!" In this company of her maids, all *samurai* women, the discipline was complete. If they would not suffer the punishment of Takeo, they must respond. Whatever the backbiting and division among themselves, in her ladyship's service they would sacrifice life itself. Besides, more than one hated Iki with the heart-whole hate of neglected love and advances. Takeo had been more favoured than her companions, not through any fault of theirs in seeking this lady killer. Hence the alarm was quickly given. Iki was beset by this female army, everyone armed, himself with but his dagger. There was no outlet for escape. Then they came to close quarters. The boldest threw themselves on him. Dragged to the ground, bound fast, he was pulled and pushed into the garden. Breathless and dishevelled the female horde parted to allow the approach of the *himegimi* – "Such open insult and vile conduct is difficult to overlook. The disloyalty intended is past pardon. For this, too great the grudge." The keen blade flashed, and the head of Iki rolled some feet distant. Without a glance in the direction of the miserable Takeo, the princess took her way back to her apartment. At last some attention could be given to the suffering and disfigured girl. She was paying the penalty for her treachery and disloyal thoughts. The pains which followed were aggravated by neglect. The face and chest one mass of burns, the wounds soon became putrid. The stench was so frightful that none would go near her. They brought her food; then fled her presence in disgust. As she grew weaker, unable to feed herself, the pangs of starvation were added to her woes. The continued cries of agony grew feebler and feebler, became a mere low moaning; then ceased altogether. "Thus trifles lead to death, and lechery finds its punishment." The bodies of the guilty pair, thrown into the garden well, there found the only interment.

Her ladyship was not to escape. Following this scene her passions broke out of all bounds. She took no new lover; it was lovers. Men were beckoned to the Yoshida Goten as to a brothel – with waving sleeves from the upper story. For a night, for a week, for a month they would be entertained. The weaker sort soon displeased her, and were dismissed; to find their end in the well of the willow, the Yanagi no Ido, of the inner garden of the palace. It would seem as if some wicked demon had entered the person of Takata Dono, to lead her into this course of debauchery.

The Kojimachi Well

One day a toilet dealer came through the Bancho. The sun was already on its decline as he passed the front of the Yoshida Goten on his way to his home in Kanda. It shone, however, on a fellow who at once attracted the attention of the look-out maid. She gave an exclamation – "Ma! Ma! What a handsome man! Such a loveable fellow! Her ladyship...." Then a feeling of pity seemed to close her mouth. But further speech was useless. The *himegimi* lacked company for her night's feast. Herself she responded to the incomplete summons. A glance and – "Bring him here; without delay. Such a fine specimen is not to be allowed to escape." It could not be helped. At once the beauty, all smiles and gestures, with waving sleeves sought to attract the attention of the itinerant trader. The district was new to him, his sales had been poor. This summons was the direct favour of the Buddha. From this great mansion surely his pack would be much lighter on return. Timidly he approached the *samurai* at the gate, fearing harsh repulse. The officer, however, was very amenable, transferring him at once to the guidance of the maid already waiting close by. Thus was he brought to the women's apartments; to be surrounded by a bevy of the sex, of a beauty of which he had had no experience. They began looking negligently over his poor stock, and closely over his own person. Then – "'Tis at her ladyship's order that the summons is made. Come this way." At this unusual conduct in a *yashiki* he had some misgivings. His hesitation met with small consideration. The crowd of women surrounded him and pushed him forward, exercising a violence which astonished and paralysed resistance at being thus exalted above his sphere. Protesting he was taken to the bath. This office completed amid admiring comment, he was dressed in *hakama* (trousers) and blouse, of stuff perfumed and of silky softness, which made him feel as if he moved in some dream. Thus purified and arrayed he was led through a long range of magnificent rooms, the sight of which sent his heart further and further into his heels. Finally he was introduced into an apartment of no great size, but with dais and bamboo blind. Led before this, his guides drew apart and prostrated themselves in obeisance. The toilet dealer followed the excellent example.

The screen slowly rose and the Takata Dono appeared in all her beauty. At this period she was barely thirty years, in the full development of her charms. To the eyes of the poor toilet dealer it seemed as if Benten Sama, the goddess of love, was thus gravely regarding and measuring every line of face and body. Finally she seemed satisfied with this close inspection. A sign and the formality of the scene vanished. "Come closer.... The *sake* cup!" Anxiously wriggling himself to her very presence, she then questioned him as to age, business, habits. Her voice was as silvery gentle as her face was beautiful. Soon he found himself looking up into it with confidence, as well as with awed respect. The *sake* utensils brought, she condescended herself to fill the cup. This was filled again; and yet again. When the liquor began to show its influence her manner became more familiar. With a quick movement, which surprised him by the latent strength shown, she drew him close to her side, began openly to show her favour for him. "Such fine figure of a man is no such fool as not to know he can please a woman. The very trade leads him to study women's taste. Now sir: for test of your qualities...." But frightened the toilet dealer disengaged himself, and springing back a little he prostrated himself flat on the ground. "Deign not an unseemly jest. Close to the person of a great lady, such as is the honoured presence, the poor artisan finds but distress. His wares have no market amid this magnificence. Dependent on him for means of life are two aged parents. A bare subsistence is secured for them. Condescend his dismissal, that he may return to relieve their anxieties."

The speech met with but poor reception. Gentle was the laugh of the *himegimi*, yet a little wrinkle knitted her brow. She seemed to regard him in a somewhat strange light. "Have no misgivings as to their fate. An ample sum shall be sent to assure them against need. Meanwhile Nature and the occasion has furnished forth the toilet dealer – for the lady's toilet.... Now for the wine feast." In the scene of riot and merriment which followed the one thought of the unfortunate trader was to escape. There was no strict order in the banquet, no formality. The idea of the *himegimi* was to get the greatest pleasure out of everything to her hand, and all vied with each other, by song and art, with voice and musical accompaniment, by a minute attention to needs of host and guest to make the sensual effect of the scene complete. There was not a jarring element in the well trained bevy of women devoted to pleasure. The toilet dealer was free, yet bound. If he would seek occasion to leave his place, to move uneasily hither and thither in these wide rooms, as did the women with their carelessness and ease, always he found himself balked by their presence. Escape there was none. Soon he found himself again by her ladyship's side, to be plied with the wine until sense and caution gave way before the spell of the beautiful woman. To her it was an amusing game, a stimulant to her passion, the conquest of this reluctance in a man found to lack the brazenness and vulgarity of his caste. In the end he could but murmur at her feet that he was hers – to do with as she would. "Would that this dream could last forever! In this Paradise of the wondrous Presence."

The scene was changed. Her ladyship rose. In the company of a few of the women he was led still further into the recesses of the palace. Here he was arrayed for the night, amid the merry jesting and admiring criticism of his attendants. Accompanied to the bed chamber the *fusuma* (screens) were closed, and he could hear the fall of the bars in the outer passages. Submission now was easy, as inevitable, as taken by the storm of this woman's passion. With but short intervals of dozing she would draw him to her embrace, and intoxicate him with her caresses. "When the poison be taken – let the plate be full." With clearing brain, though under the spell of her beauty he never lost sight of the purpose to flee this doubtful snare. When at dawn she really slept, he rose toseek exit; to run into the ever vigilant guard. "Naruhodo! Truly an early riser the honoured guest. But all has been made ready. The bath is at hand. Deign to enter." Thus surrounded and compelled he began the second day. As the maid dressed him after the bath she broke out in admiration of his physical presence. "The handsome fellow! No wonder her ladyship was seized by the love wind." In the evening's entertainment he had proved himself no fool in interesting anecdote of the town, and a quaint and naive description of the view the lowly take of those who call themselves the great. Under the skilful questioning of one or other this simple fellow – of keen wit and observation – had shown a phase of life unknown to them, beyond the careless view afforded from between the blinds of the curtains of the palanquin. The vulgar boldness of his predecessors was conspicuously lacking, as was the tedious talk of war and discussion of court etiquette of noble and more formal guests. Not only her ladyship, but the maids thoroughly enjoyed him.

His astonishment and fearful protest at the gorgeous robe put on him turned them from pity to amusement. Said a bolder wench – "Take and enjoy the gifts of her ladyship as offered. The chance is not likely again to present itself. Put aside all thought of past; seek pleasure in the present, without regard to the future." Though spoken with a smile which showed the whole row of beautiful teeth, there was a menace in the words which came home to him. If he had had some suspicions of his whereabouts, he felt sure of it now. There were but rumours and suspicions, slanders of course, of which he seemed destined to prove the truth. The knowledge seemed to add dignity to his pose. He would await her ladyship's exit from the bath. Conducted to the garden he strolled its beautiful inclosure, noted the high roofs on every side. Standing by the *tsukiyama* he heard the shuffling of sandals. Turning he prostrated himself before the *himegimi*. Rosy, with sparkling eyes, long flowing black hair, regal presence, she was indeed the goddess Benten Sama in human flesh and blood. Without rising the toilet dealer made request – "Deign the honoured pity. To spend one's life in the service of the honoured Presence, this has been said; and for the words regret there is none. It is for those dependent. Condescend that no harm come to them, no distress from this visitation of gods and the Buddha. Willingly the price is paid for the delicious dream, no grudge felt for what is to follow."

The *himegimi* stopped short. For some time she was lost in thought. This man was keen enough of wit to know the price at which her favours were bought; brave enough not to flinch, or to make abortive effort to avoid his fate. Her whole experience brought feeling of disgust toward men, when once satiated. With this man the chord of pity was touched. The honoured sleeves were wet with the honoured tears as she made answer to the plea. Without slightest effort to deny her once purpose she consoled and reassured him. "It was determined, that granted favour you should never leave this place." Her brow darkened for a moment at the ominous words; than cleared radiant. "Those who enter here ascribe to their good fortune the pleasures they enjoy. Instead of modest gratitude they show the arrogance of possession. Purpose was first shaken by the filial love expressed for those who gave you being, the tender care and anxiety for their welfare. A man like you, one is assured of his faith and silence. At night you shall depart from here unharmed." She took him by the hand, and when he would show respect, with familiarity drew him along with her. Thus they walked the gardens, talking of varying subjects; she listening to his explanations and instances of life in the common world, and questioning him adroitly as to his past and future. Then the return was made to the inner apartments of the palace. From this stray honey bee the little lady sucked the last juices of its nature. The day was spent in the same riotous merriment and feasting. At the order of the *himegimi* he had withdrawn for the moment from her presence. When the maid came toward him, it was with expectation of another summons that he followed after. She took him to a little room. Here were his coarse garments and his pack. To these were added the gifts heaped on him by her ladyship. The change of garb completed suddenly the girl took him in her embrace, pressing the now soft perfumed hair and warm moist skin of his neck. "Ah! You lucky fellow! But know that silence is golden." With this she as suddenly seized his hand and led him swiftly along the dark corridor. At its end an *amado* was slipped back, and they were in the garden. To a postern gate she fitted the key. Pack adjusted he would turn to make salutation. Two slender firm hands laid on his shoulders sent him flying into the roadway. The gate closed with a sharp bang, and all sign of this fairy palace disappeared.

Every day the toilet dealer had prayed to *kami* and Buddha, made his offering of 'cash' at the favoured shrines, performed such pilgrimages (*sankei*) as his limited means and scanty time permitted. To this alone is to be ascribed his escape. Not so with others: to turn the page to a second instance – One day a maid from above called to the gate guard – "Stop that man!" – "Who?" The guard was at loss, not what to do, but whom to stop. Promptly the highway was roped off. None were allowed to move until inspection was made. As the plebeians lay prostrate with noses on the backs of their hands they marvelled and spoke to each other. "Truly a wondrous event! Some great rascal must have been detected. Thanks to the *kami* and the Buddhas the heart of this Tarobei is clean." – "And of this Jimbei. To pay the debt to the *sake* shop he has not hesitated to contract Tama to the Yoshidaya of

Yoshiwara." – "Well done!" quoth his friend. "Then credit at the Echigoya is good?" – "Deign to come and drink a glass of poor wine, to the pleasure and good luck of Jimbei." The edifying conversation was interrupted by call for inspection. All passers by but men were summarily motioned on. A maid stood by – "No, not this one ... nor this one ... nor that.... Ah! That big brown fellow, with huge calves. He is the man." At once the "big brown man" with enlarged pediments was cut out from the heap of humanity, with whispering fear and looks the others went about their business. "Truly his crime must be very great. Yet who would suspect it! He is not an ill looking fellow by any means." Others shook their heads as they went away, vowing never again to take this road to work, or home, or pleasure.

Before the *yakunin* the prisoner fell on his knees. "Deign the honoured pardon. Doubtless grave is the offence; but of it there is no remembrance. An humble wheelwright of Kanda, this worthless fellow is known as Gonjuro. It is work at Nakano which brings him hither." He turned from one officer to the other. They disregarded his prayers, and delivered him over to the maid, directing him to obey her orders, or suffer for it. In dumbfounded surprise and gathering confidence he followed after. Surrounded by the army of maids he more than readily submitted to their ministrations. The freedom of the bath, the donning of the gorgeous robe, pleased him beyond measure. To their quips and words of double meaning he made ready answer, meeting them more than half way with the obscenity of the Yoshiwara. "Tarobei is tricked out like an actor." At this all the greater was their merriment and boisterousness. Introduced into the presence of her ladyship, his first confusion at the magnificence of the surroundings was quickly removed by his cordial reception. The *himegimi* laughed at sight of him; laughed still louder at his uncouthness. Then she passed to more earnest measures; praised his thickness of limb, the sturdy robustness of neck and loins. To his apologies – she urged him not to be frightened or backward. Pushing the thick shock of hair back from his eyes he eyed her with growing comprehension. After all a woman was a woman. "'Tis no fault of this Tarobei. The *yakunin* compelled his presence. For such a noble lady he would make any sacrifice." He spoke with bold look and manner, thoroughly understanding now the nature of his summons at the caprice of some great lady. Had he not suffered equal good fortune with the beauties of Yoshiwara? He treated lady and maids with the same free familiarity and sportive roughness as if in one of his favoured haunts.

All the more was the *himegimi* amused at his extravagance. She made no sign of displeasure, and the girls made little resistance to the fellow's boisterous manifestations as he tousled them. Always her ladyship had eyes of the greatest appreciation on this splendid animal. The feast set before him he looked on with small favour. "What then tickles the palate of Juro?" She leaned toward him, her face flushed with this struggle to cage her latest prize. The silvery and enticing voice had for answer – "Take (bamboo); just plain boiled, with syrup and *shōyu*." Then timidly, as he sought her good will – "Just a little wine; two *go* (a pint) ... say five *go*." She laughed with good humour. His choice among this bevy of beauties at last had fallen spontaneously on herself. The conquest pleased her. Then he was well stuffed with coarse foods, hunted out of the supplies for the grooms and stablemen in the palace kitchen, with *sake* of a harsh and burning kind – "which had some taste to it." Indeed never had he drank such! The *himegimi* sipped a drop or two of the acrid liquor, made a wry face, and sought to bring the scene to its climax.

With the bath next day he was all grumbling and exigencies. The maids bore this with patience, and glances interchanged. Her ladyship had promised him breakfast to restore exhausted Nature – "And such was promised as that this Tarobei would never need another."

He roared his dissatisfaction. The hint was taken up at once. "This way: it is for the *yakunin* to carry out her ladyship's order, and to stop your gullet." The brusqueness of the *samurai* was poor exchange for the noisy amorous atmosphere of the inner palace. With indignation the worthy wheelwright obeyed the order to march ahead. "Ah! Just wait my fine fellow. A word to the lady of the mansion, and you shall learn the cost of insult to the man she favours. This *yarō* Gonjuro has no other wife. Her ladyship takes him as adopted husband." The officer winked and blushed a little at this very crude specimen. By this time he had led the man to the well curb in the inner garden. Harshly – "Now down with you. Favoured by the gods and Buddhas you cannot even hold your tongue. Ladies like not boasting of their favours. 'Tis now the time to express pity for you. Make ready!" Deftly he tripped him up, to send him an all fours. The sword flashed, and the wheelwright's head rolled on the ground. Just as it was the body was cast into the well.

Such was the fate of those who found favour with the *himegimi*. More and more suspicious became people of the strange disappearances traced to the precincts of the palace. Strange tales went around, to gather force with numbers. Kwanei 8th year (1635), whether for closer supervision of the lady or actual necessity, she was removed to the castle precincts, and there given quarters. Time doubtless it was, that tempered these crazy outbursts of the *himegimi*. She lived until Kwambun 12th year. On the 2nd month 21st day (12th September 1672) she died at the age of seventy two years. Grand were the obsequies of one so favoured by the Shogun. The *daimyō* went up in long processions to condole with the suzerain at the death of a rich aunt, and congratulate him on the possessions seized. On the 24th day the lord of the land sent lavish incense and a thousand pieces of silver, by the hand of Inaba Mimasaka no Kami Masamori, to Matsudaira Echigo Ke the son and heir, doubtless glad enough to get this much out of his lady mother's rich furniture and dower. From the Midai-dokoro, the Shogun's consort, by the Bangashira (Superintendent) of the women's apartments of the Shogunal palace, he secured another thousand pieces of silver. All was treasure trove toward the heavy expense of the imposing funeral. On the seventh day of the decease – the 27th day (18th September) – the obsequies took place at the Tentokuji of Shiba, where she was to rest, well weighted down by massive sandstone and an interminable epitaph – of which the posthumous name of Tenso-in can be remembered. The Shogun Ke was present in his proxy of Tsuchiya Tajima no Kami Kazunao.

The Yoshida Goten had shorter shrift than its once occupant. The *daimyō* were moving into *yashiki* under the compulsory residence edict. The *kyakubun* were still met at the outskirts of the city, but the many different palaces for their entertainment became superfluous. The main part of the Yoshida Goten was pulled down, and its magnificent timbers and decoration went to the equipment of the prior's hall of the Kugyoji of Iinuma. This great temple, situate one *ri* (2-1/2 miles) to the north of Midzukaido-machi, in the plain at the base of Tsukuba-san, is one of the eighteen holy places of the Kwanto, and under the charge of the Jodo sect of Buddhists. In former days the notice board was posted at the Chumon (middle gate), ordering all visitors to dismount from horse or *kago*. The *bushi* removed their swords on presenting themselves for worship. The temple itself is of moderately ancient foundation, being established in Oei 21st year (1414) by the two Hanyu lords, Tsunesada and Yoshisada, who built the castles of Yokosome and Hanyu, close by here in Shimosa. Grand is the *hondō* (main hall); and grand the magnificent old pines and cedars which surround it and line its avenues. These are set off by the girdle of the flowering cherry, famed among the ancient seven villages of Iimura. Moreover it was the scene of the early labours in youth of the famous bishop – Yuten Sojo; who solved so successfully the blending of the pale maple colour of its cherry blossoms that he gave the name *myōjō no sakura*, a new transcript of the "six characters." Here he grappled with and prevailed over the wicked spirit of the Embukasane. In later writers there is a confusion as to the tale of the Yoshida Goten. The palace material was used for the construction of the prior's hall. In the Genwa period (1615-23) the Senhimegimi, eldest daughter of Hidetada Ko the second shogun, cut *short* her beautiful hair and assumed the name of the Tenju-in-Den (as nun). The hair was buried here under an imposing monument; and later one of the ladies-in-waiting of the princess – the Go-tsubone Iiguchi Hayao. (The name of the princess Tsuruhime in *kana* is probably a later and mistaken addition.) Thus were the many adventures of the Takata Dono transferred to her equally well known and beautiful elder sister. The Senhime, wife of Hideyori, suffered and did quite enough herself for which to make answer. Meanwhile the site of the Yoshida Goten in the Bancho became more than suspected. Jack-o-lanterns, the ghosts of the victims of the *himegimi*, came forth from the old well to haunt and frighten passers-by. Nor were subsequent attempts to use it encouraging. Thus the ground lay idle and uncalled for, with no one to occupy it until the grant of a large tract in Dosanbashi as site for the *yashiki* of Matsudaira Higo no Kami compelled removal of several of the *hatamoto*. Among these were Okubo Hikoroku and Aoyama Shuzen.

The Sen-Himegimi (Princess Sen)

The Sen-*himegimi*, eldest daughter of Hidetada the second Shogun, figures little in our story; enough so, however, to necessitate the telling of one of the not least striking episodes in a life full of event. Married at the mature age of six years to the Udaijin Hideyori, son of the Taiko Hideyoshi and lord of Osaka castle, those childish years were the happiest of that period. Clouds were rising between Toyotomi and Tokugawa as the princess approached nubile years. On her the Yodogimi, mother of the Udaijin, visited the more personal effects of her resentment. For the growing girl it was a period of tears and affliction. In truth she well knew the weight of her mother-in-law's hand. So wretched was her life that there was some fear of her killing herself. A powerful influence in screening her in these later years was that of the famous Kimura Nagato no Kami. Shigenari and his wife Aoyagi were the guides and friends of the *himegimi* during this trying period; her councillors to forestall cause of the Yodogimi's wrath. Moreover the pleasant relations between the young husband and wife were an incentive to bear a burden patiently, which time might remove. Nevertheless the Yodogimi was inexorable. The night screens were set up in different chambers. When the Sen-himegimi made her escape from Osaka castle she was sixteen years old, and in all likelihood a virgin.

As to the stories of her escape from the besieged castle, then in the very throes of the final vigorous and successful assault by the three hundred thousand men surrounding it, these vary. According to one account Iyeyasu Ko, brows knit with anxiety as he watched his men pressing to the attack, thumped his saddle bow as vigorously as waning years now permitted – "The Senhime to wife, to him who brings her safe from the castle!" Not a man in his train moved. They looked at the blazing mass before them, the flying missiles – and staid where they were. Then came forward a Tozama *daimyō*, Sakasaki Dewa no Kami Takachika. Prostrating himself he announced his purpose to make the attempt. Making his way into the blazing pile of the burning castle he found the Senhime amid her frightened maids. Wrapping her up carefully he took her in his arms, and with great regard for her person, and none for his own, he sought her rescue. The last chance was through the blazing mass of the great gate. Just as he was about to clear it, down came the tottering superincumbent structure almost on their heads. The red hot tiles, the sparks like a fiery deluge, the blazing fragments of wood carried and tossed by the air currents, surrounded them as in a furnace. Nearly all the train perished in the attempt. Dewa no Kami succeeded in presenting himself before the Ogosho (Iyeyasu). Even the old captain could but turn with pity from the hideously disfigured man. The Senhime in all her beauty was saved. Bitter was her resentment against all – father, grandfather, their partisans – who had refused the gift of life to the young husband. Rescue or no rescue, she absolutely refused to carry out the agreement and become the wife of this – mask.

Other tales are less romantic. The most prosaic sends Dewa no Kami to Kyoto, on orders of Hidetada Ko. For the princess a second bed was to be found among the Sekke (the five great *kuge* Houses of the imperial court). The mission was not unsuccessful, but by the time the messenger returned Hidetada had changed his mind. Brusquely he offered her to Dewa no Kami. The Senhime got wind of these movements. Her resentment toward the Tokugawa House determined her hostile stand. She would not be an instrument to their advancement. Family relations were taken very seriously. It is to be remembered that her uncle Hideyasu, adopted into the Toyotomi, was so fiercely loyal to that House that his natural father, the Ogosho Iyeyasu, poisoned him, by his own hand and a gift of cakes, it is said. Those likely to hitch and hamper the movement against Osaka, such as the famous Kato Kiyomasa, found short shrift in the soup bowl. At all events the insult of refusal fell on Dewa no Kami. After all, by the most authentic tale, he seems to have deserved no particular credit. As to the actual escape from Osaka-Jo either of the following versions can be accepted. As suicide was the inevitable issue for the defeated, the Yodogimi, with some reluctance, had announced her purpose; and her intent to involve the *himegimi* in the fate of herself and son. This was but the ethics of the time; and was neither cruel nor unusual. It was thoroughly constitutional. Fortunately the fears of the Lady Dowager made her add – "the time is not yet propitious." She left the keep, intending to ascertain in person how matters went on outside, before going on with the ceremony inside. The maids of the Senhime at once surrounded her and urged flight. Overpowering any resistance, moral and physical, these energetic *samurai* women bundled their mistress well into *futon* (quilts). Then with no particular gentleness they lowered her over the castle wall. Others followed her – to destruction or better luck, without *futon*. Some twenty of them risked the descent. Horiuchi Mondo, a gentleman of Kishu Kumano, noticed the unusual group. They besought an aid for the princess he readily gave. Dewa no Kami happened to come on the scene, and promptly took the responsibility of the safety of the princess on his own shoulders.

Here the two versions join, for by the other Ono Shuri, captain of the defense and hence most seriously involved, sought the safety of his own daughter. The princess therefore was sent from the castle, under the care of his *karō* Yonemura Gonemon, to plead for the lives of the Udaijin and his mother the Yodogimi. Ono was careful to include his daughter in the train, and the *karō* followed his illustrious example. Dewa no Kami met the party outside the castle, and grasped the chance of being agreeable by escorting it to the camp of the Ogosho. Honda Sado no Kami here was in charge. His mission to the grandfather was eminently successful. Iyeyasu, overjoyed at the escape of the beloved grandchild, consented; provided that of the actual Shogun be obtained. All rejoiced, with little thought of Hidetada's harsh feeling. Perhaps the message expressed this; perhaps it was spoken to cover refusal, for he had deep affection for his children. But as in greatest wrath he made answer – "The thing is not to be spoken of. Why did she not die together with Hideyori?" The Senhime was safe enough now in his camp; and he did not purpose the escape of his rival Hideyori, to be a permanent danger to his House. The princess, worn out by many days of suffering, went to sleep in the shed which furnished her with quarters, and never woke until high noon on the following day. By that time she could choose between the tales of her husband's escape to Satsuma; or his suicide and her widowhood, the only proof of which was the finding of the hereditary sword of the Toyotomi House. She clung to the former story, despite the ascertained suicide of the Yodogimi, who hardly would have allowed the escape of the son and her own destruction. Thus disgruntled, later the *himegimi* was removed to Kyoto, fiercely hostile to all the Kwanto influence.

A word in conclusion as to the fate of the attendants, thus skilfully foisted on her. The daughter of Ono Shuri had escaped, with all the sufferings and passions aroused by family disaster. When subsequently the princess was removed to Edo she went in her train. They were companions in misfortune. In the hostile atmosphere she was taken with a consumption, long to undergo its torments. Overcome by homesickness she would return to former scenes, and worship at her father's grave. Permission was now granted. Yonemura accompanied the dying girl to the capital. Here Ono Shuri had lost his head in the bed of the Kamogawa (the execution ground). Here at Kyoto the daughter found her tortured end. Gloomy the old vassal prepared the funeral pyre of his mistress. As the flames shot high and wrapped the corpse, a woman's figure darted forward and sprang into the midst. Unable to distinguish the bones of his daughter from those of the honoured mistress, Gonemon placed the remains of both within the same casket, to rest at the last beneath the pines and cedars of the holy mountain of Koya.

On June 4th (1615) the castle had fallen. The date is important in connection with one of the current scandals. Later the Senhime was escorted down to Edo by Honda Mino no Kami Tadamasa, in whose train was his handsome son Tonosuke (Tadatoki). He is said to have been like enough in appearance to the Udaijin Hideyori to act as his substitute in the most intimate sense. The fierce little lady fell violently in love with him. By the time Edo was reached she ought to have married Honda, and in the passage of the months and days would have to. At all events this rather disproportionate marriage was early proposed to the council of the Bakufu, and after some discussion accepted. This decision was not reached until Genwa 2nd year 9th month (October 1616), or more than a full year after the fall of the castle. The failure to carry out the agreement with Dewa no Kami afforded ample reason for the extremity to which this latter's rage was carried. By all accounts he had lost a bride, the acknowledged beauty of the land, apart from the great influence of the connection. Perhaps his own hideous disfigurement was involved. He determined to lie in wait for the journey down to Himeji, Honda's fief; and kill or carry off the lady. The Shogun's Government got wind of the purpose. The lords were storming with wrath, and a public fracas was feared. All composition had been refused. Dewa refused to see his friend Yagyu Munenori, sent to him as messenger of greatest influence. Secret orders then were sent that Dewa no Kami must be induced to cut belly, or – his vassals ought to send his head to Edo. The Shogun's word and bond must be saved. The vassals knew their lord, and had not loyalty enough to act otherwise than to sever his head, as he lay sleeping off a drunken fit in broad daylight. It was against rewarding this disloyal act that Honda Masazumi showed open opposition to the council's decision; and Hidetada Ko himself disapproved enough not to inflict extinction (*kaieki*) on the family of the dead lord, the usual process. The continuance of the succession was permitted on the Shogun's order. All these matters were so public that little credit is to be given to the role assigned to Sakasaki Dewa no Kami in the event about to be described;

the issue of which was so unfortunate in the carrying out, that Sakasaki, in command of the bridal cortege and keenly feeling the disgrace, cut open his belly in expiation; and that the Government, to hush up talk as to attack on the train of the princess, put forward as explanation the proposed treachery and resultant death of Dewa no Kami.

As to the event itself: with greatest reluctance, uncertain as to her former husband's fate, the Senhime had been forced into agreement with the Honda marriage. From the Nishimaru (western) palace the bridal cortege took its way to the *yashiki* of Honda near the Hitotsubashi Gomon. Time was at a discount in those days, and by no means was the shortest route to anything taken. The procession filed out of the Sakurada Gomon, to circle with its pompous glitter the outer moat. All went very well. The *yashiki* walls bordering Tayasumura were slipping by. Then the steadily accumulating clouds poured forth their contents. It was a downpour, blinding in effect. The *rokushaku* of the Kurokwagumi – stout and tall palanquin bearers, "six footers" – floundered and staggered in the mud. The heavy palanquin came to the ground. Great was the rage of the princess at this unseemly precedent for such an occasion. "Rude ruffians! By this very hand this scum shall die!" *Te-uchi* was to be the lot of the miserable fellows prostrate in obeisance and seeking pardon in the blinding storm from the lady's dagger, menacing them from the open door of the palanquin. The Lady of Osaka was quite capable of carrying out her threat. Abe Shirogoro, later the famous Bungo no Kami, was equal to the occasion. With soft words he would soothe her. "Congratulations to the *Himegimi*! May her highness deign to accept the so happy augury of present ill luck bringing good fortune throughout a long and happy life. Deign to regard with future favour the words of Shirogoro." He got as near the mud as he dared in his respectful salutation. The lady's face softened. She was appeased.

Then she held up the hand, with the dagger still ready for action. Shirogoro sprang to his feet. Something else than storm was in progress. In the escort ahead there were other sounds than the rumbling and sharp crash of the thunder, the swishing of rain wind driven. The flashes of lightning showed that the cortege was the object of a most determined attack, which sought to make its way to the palanquin of the princess. Abe Shirogoro would have leaped forward, but the flashing eyes and presence of the *himegimi* held him to her nearer defence. The number of the assailants could not be ascertained in this darkness like to night. The tower of defence was Yagyu Tajima no Kami, greatest master of the sword in Nippon. He had the support of the younger Okubo, of Kondo Noborinosuke, of Mizuno Jurozaemon even then noted as expert with the spear. In general command was the beloved superintendent of the *hatamoto*, Okubo Hikozaemon. In daylight the affair would have been easy. But in this darkness they had to stand to their defence. That it was an attack by Osaka *rōnin*, enraged at the marriage of the princess, there was no doubt. But what their numbers? So far the defense was impregnable. There was nothing to fear. Three of the leaders of the *rōnin* lay on the ground. Their chief, visible in the lightning flashes, could not hope for success. It was the old and still active Hikozaemon, the *oyaji* (old chap), the hardened warrior of Iyeyasu, who scented out the threatening move. He sprang off into the dark wood, almost as the crack of the musket was heard. They would seek the life of the *himegimi* with deadly missiles! How contemptible; for great as yet was the scorn of such use. Vigorous was the old man's pursuit of a foe, seeking to ascertain his success and reluctant to flee. "Ah! Ah! Rascal! Just wait! Wait for this Hikozaemon!" The fellow did wait, a little too long. Noting the lessening darkness, the discomfiture of his train, he turned to flee in real earnest. As he did so, Hikozaemon, despairing of success, hurled his dirk. Deep into the fellow's shoulder it went. "Atsu!" Savagely he turned on the old man. Hikozaemon was skilled in defence, but stiffening with age. His opponent showed himself an able warrior. "Ah! Ha! 'Tis Hikozaemon Dono. With him there is no quarrel. Deign to receive a wound." The old fellow's sword dropped helpless under a sharp rap over the wrist from the back of the blade. This was enough for the man's purpose. With laughing and respectful salutation, of short duration, he turned to a more successful flight.

The storm cleared away, the cortege was re-formed; to enter in state the *yashiki* of Honda Sama. It was said that he got but a cold bride – one on whom only "the bed quilt lay light." Time, the ascertained fact of Hideyori's death, worked a change in the insanity simulated by the princess. Then she was so taken with her lord that she proved fatal to him. He died at the age of thirty-one years, was buried in his castle town of Himeji, leaving but one daughter as issue by the princess. The lady returned to residence at the Takebashi Goten, to be a disgruntling influence in her brother's court. But Honda Ke had not done badly. This consort made him a minister in the Shogun's household (Nakatsukasa no Tayu), a more likely promotion than one at the age of sixteen years, at this date of the Shogunate. From 10,000 *koku* his fief was raised to 150,000 *koku*; and he secured a wife so beautiful that his exodus to the houris of Paradise was a bad exchange. Meanwhile what was the cause of objection, thus expressed by force of arms, to the conduct and nuptials of the Sen-himegimi?

Shuzen Adolescens

The struggle between Toyotomi and Tokugawa was of that embittered character which follows from two diverse theories of political structure. The Taiko Hideyoshi, by force of military genius and constructive statesmanship, had assumed the pre-eminent position in the land. In doing so he had drawn to himself a sturdy band of followers whose whole faith and devotion lay in the Toyotomi. Such were the "seven captains," so conspicuous in the defence of Osaka-Jo in later years. Such were the doughty fighters Susukita Kaneyasu (Iwami Jutaro) and Ban Danemon. The latter unceremoniously shook off allegiance to his lord on the latter's treachery at Sekigahara, and turned *rōnin*. Such were great recalcitrant nobles thumped into complete submission, granted unexpected and favourable terms in their capitulation, devoted henceforth to the Toyotomi House, and of whom the Chosokabe of Tosa are representative. It is the fashion of modern historians to regard and speak of these brave men as irreconcileables and swashbucklers; thus tamely following after the Tokugawa writers of contemporary times, and imperialistic writers of today, to whom all opposition to the favoured "Ins" is high treason. As matter of fact, if men like the Ono were lukewarm and seeking their own advantage; if Obata Kambei Kagemori was a mere traitorous spy of the Tokugawa; Sanada Yukimura and Kimura Nagato no Kami, and in humbler sense Susukita Kaneyasu and Ban Danemon, if they had much to gain by the victory of their lord, yet were willing to endure hardship, face a defeat early seen, and accept the inevitable death which was meted out to him who refused the attempts at bribery and corruption of the victor. The "*rōnin*," of whom the then Tokugawa chronicles and captains spoke so contemptuously, were in the bulk not only "the outs," as opposed to "the ins," but they were too devoted to their party tamely to accept service with the enemy. Large were the bribes actually offered to Sanada and Kimura; and any or all of the seven captains could have made terms of advantage – to themselves.

"The scent of the plum, with the flower of the cherry;
Blooming on branch of willow 'Tis seen."

Iyemitsu Ko hung this poem on the flowering plum tree to which he gave the name of Kimura no Ume; a conscious tribute to the chivalry of Shigenari. And Okubo Hikozaemon risked life and favour in the destruction of the plant, and rebuke of the bad taste shown to men who had lost fathers, brothers, gone down before the deadly spear of the young captain.

The fall of Osaka-Jo decided the fate of the Toyotomi House. Not at once, for the rumour of the Udaijin's escape to Kyushu kept alive hopeful resentment in the minds of the scattered *samurai* whose captains had perished in the battles around Osaka, had died or cut belly in the final assault, or had lost their heads by the executioner's sword in the bed of the Kamogawa. Among those who found refuge in the hills of Iga was a certain Ogita Kuroji; a retainer of Nagato no Kami. This man gathered a band of kindred spirits, among whom his favoured lieutenant was Mori Muneoki, although he much leaned to the astonishing acumen of Kosaka Jinnai, a mere boy in years, but hiding in his short and sturdy form a toughness and agility, with expertness in all feats of arms, which discomfited would be antagonists. In the discussions as to future movements there was wide difference of opinion. Muneoki, the true partisan, proposed to rejoin Hideyori in Satsuma. "The prince is now harboured by Higo no Kami; Shimazu Dono of Satsuma, close at hand, will never permit the entrance of the Tokugawa into his borders. It is at Kagoshima-Jo that the prince will reorganize his party; and thither duty calls." But Kosaka Jinnai was equally positive in the opposite sense. He turned Muneoki's own argument against the proposal. The prince could well be left to organize the West. It was for others to see how affairs went in the North. Therefore the first thing was to hasten to Edo, to ascertain the position of Date Masamune and the great northern lords at this final triumph of the Tokugawa, when at last their jealousy and fear might be aroused to opposition.

Adventurous inclination, the desire to meet rather than run away from the enemy, turned the scale to Edo. Reluctantly Muneoki agreed. With Jinnai he proceeded, to learn the state of affairs as to the great northern House, so devoted to the new creed of Yaso (Jesus) as certain to be angry and alarmed at the savage persecution now entered on by the second Shogun. They returned to meet Ogita and the other captains at Odawara, and with unpleasant news. Masamune Ko, luckily for his would be interviewers, was absent at Sendai. However there was no difficulty in finding out that far from dreaming of further embassies to Rome from the Prince of Oshu, he had and was acting so vigorously that probably in no quarter of Nippon was the hostile and treacherous creed so thoroughly stamped out. The watch and ward of the north country was practically left to a loyalty of which the Tokugawa felt assured. Muneoki made this report with bitter joy, and Jinnai could not say him nay. Then the former carried out his first plan. He made his way to Kyushu, to learn the truth as to the Udaijin's fate. Assured of this he harboured with the malcontents of Higo and Hizen, to take his part and perish some years later in the Amakusa uprising.

Perhaps the tartness of Mori's criticism made his company unacceptable. Ogita preferred to follow the urging of Jinnai and his own inclination to observe how matters were going in Edo. Most of the company followed him, to establish themselves as best they could in the confusion of the growing town, rendered a thousand times worse by the settlement of the later troubles and the flocking of all classes to this eastern capital. Ogita set up as a doctor in Daikucho (carpenters' street) of the Nihonbashi ward, under the name of Gita Kyuan. His chief lieutenant, Jinnai, settled close to his leader in Kuremasacho, figuring as a physiognomist, of near enough relation to excite no comment in the companionship with the older man. His own years were disguised by an ample growth of hair and the past experience of an accomplished rascal. Jinnai could have passed himself off for a man of thirty odd years.

The house of a physiognomist was overrun with visitors, whom Jinnai knew how to sift, and who had no particular wish to encounter each other. Hence the presence of the leaders, with his own particular followers, Watanabe Mondo, Ashizuke Tosuke, Yokoyama Daizo, Hyuchi Togoro, excited no comment among the neighbours. The question of the marriage of the Senhime, the honoured widow of the Udaijin Ko, soon was stirring up a ferment in higher circles than these in Edo town. Sakai Uta no Kami and Doi Oi no Kami of the *rōjū* (council of state) were keen to urge the match. She was young, and they plead the cruelty of forcing celibacy on her. She was the centre of the ill disposed and most willingly so. The stern old soldier Aoyama Hoki no Kami took the opposite ground. It was for her to cut short her hair and pray for the soul of the husband perished in the flames of Osaka-Jo. Such was the precedent, and, he hinted with good ground, the disposition of the princess, then coquetting with Toshitsune lord of the great Maeda House of Kaga. Besides he knew that Kasuga no Tsubone, powerful influence in the private apartments of the palace, was urging on the match. The mere fact of her constant interference in the public affairs irritated Hoki no Kami beyond measure. He was acting through sentiment and conservatism. Kasuga and her allies were acting on political motives. They carried the day; to the great indignation of Hoki no Kami, and of an assistance he never dreamed of.

Among the band of *rōnin* the matter was discussed with all the greater heat and bitterness of purpose, inasmuch as they had to do so mouth to ear. Ogita expressed their feeling when he summed up the matter as an outrageous breach of chastity on the part of a princess, who could not positively know whether the husband was yet living, or really had died at Osaka – "Hence she is doubly guilty, of treachery and pollution of her living lord; or of shameful lechery in this open neglect of his memory and seeking another bed. Moreover to put her to death will strike terror into the partisans of the Tokugawa, and give courage to all the adherents of the cause, of whom thousands are gathered here in Edo. A display of vigour will maintain those inclined to the new service true to the cause." All rapturously agreed. The occasion of the marriage and procession was settled upon for the attack, in which the leaders and some eighty men were engaged. The result, as told, was disastrous to them. Watanabe and Ashizuke were killed by Tajima no Kami's own hand. Kondo Noborinosuke thrust his spear through the belly of Yokoyama Daizo. Jinnai brought off in safety the bulk of the party. Ogita had tried to bring down the lady princess by a gun shot. In the straggle with Hikozaemon he purposely did the old man as little injury as possible. Respect for the grand old warrior, an amused interest in one whose influence lay in plain speaking, held his hand. If Okubo Dono was entitled freely to express his opinion of the Shogun Ke, Kuroji took it as no insult to endure the same himself. He reached his home with a painful but not dangerous wound in the shoulder, to grunt over the infliction and this latest discomfiture.

His nurse was not at all to the taste of Kosaka Jinnai. O'Yoshi was a bare twenty-three years in age. She was a beauty and a flirt. Ogita indulged in the greatest expansion with her; as would the man of fifty years to the girl, a mistress young enough to be a daughter. The months and weeks passed following the attempt on the Senhime. The effort to hunt out the perpetrators had been given up in despair. The population of Edo as yet was too fluid and shifting to take very exact account of its movements. Doubtless they were *rōnin*, and had promptly scattered on failure of the attack. Then the constant attempts at incendiarism, in many cases successful, began to attract attention. The two *machibugyō*, together with the particular office for detection of thieves and incendiaries, were at their wits end to trace out this gang of fire bugs. One day O'Yoshi was just leaving the bath house in Daikucho called the Chosenya, when she met with an adventure. A young *samurai* coming along the street attracted her admiring attention. He was barely twenty years of age, of good height and commanding presence. In black garb and wearing *hakama*, his two swords tucked in his girdle, and his cue trimmed high, attended by a *dōshin*and several *yakunin*, the procession greatly flattered a woman's feeling. She tripped along, towel in hand, and her eyes anywhere but on her footing. Suddenly the strap of her clog broke. She was pitched forward, just able to keep her balance. The *samurai* trod sharply on the discarded *geta*. A cry of pain followed, and O'Yoshi was all discomfiture at sight of the blood staining the white *tabi* of the young lord. At once she was humble apology for her awkwardness, very badly received by the *dōshin* who scolded her most severely – "Careless wench! Such rudeness is not to be pardoned." He would have laid rough hands on her, but Aoyama Shuzen interfered. The woman was pretty, the injury painful, and he was young. "Don't scold her. It was by accident.... Don't be alarmed.... Ah! It hurts!..." He looked around, as seeking a place to rest.

O'Yoshi was very solicitous over the handsome young man. "Deign to pardon the careless action. Alas! The foot of the young master is sadly injured. My husband is a doctor, Gita Kyuan, of wondrous skill in the Dutch practice. Condescend to enter the poor house close by here, and allow drugs to be applied to the wound." Shuzen really was suffering inconvenience and pain from his wound. Besides, as attached to the office of the *machibugyō*, he sought all means of contact with the class whose offences were to be dealt with. He at once agreed. Ogita was absent when they entered. O'Yoshi tended the wound herself. The salve really had wonderful effect. Flow of blood and pain ceased. Cakes and tea, for refreshment, were placed before Shuzen. O'Yoshi entertained him with amusing talk of the wardsmen of Nihonbashi, not the most stupid in Nippon. She retailed the bath house gossip, and Aoyama carefully took in costume, manners, and the conversation of the beauty, which did not at all accord with her station in life. If she was connected with a doctor now, at some time she had been intimate with men of affairs in his own caste. He thanked her graciously and would have forced lavish payment on her. O'Yoshi was all pained surprise and refusal. That her reluctance was genuine he could easily see. "I am Aoyama Shuzen, and live in the *yashiki* at Surugadai. The kindness shown is not to be forgotten, and perhaps some day this Shuzen can serve his hostess." With compliments he took his leave. O'Yoshi watched the handsome youth well out of sight. She could not hear the remark of Shuzen to the *dōshin* – "A suspicious house; no frowsy doctor shows such favour to his dame. Dress, manners, language, betray contact with the *samurai*." The officer nodded admiring assent to his young lord's acumen.

Ogita Kuroji came limping home, to find O'Yoshi – Chosenburo Yoshi, as this adventure dubbed her – overflowing with her experience. At first he was rather pleased at such addition to his acquaintance. O'Yoshi was a bait to all but Jinnai, who would detach him from her. The others sought his favour to secure hers with greater ease. At mention of the *dōshin*, subordinate officials of the legal machinery, the official grade of the visitor, his brows knit. "Of official rank – that will never do! Deign Yoshi to be careful in relations with this man, if he should again appear. Engaged as is this Kuroji, the slightest hint, a suspicion, would be most disastrous." – "Then the affair of the Senhimegimi did not block matters? This Yoshi yet is to ride in palanquin, to be a *daimyō's* wife?" The tone was a little jeering, and the laugh as of one sceptical. With thoughts on this new love the reference to this futile scheming annoyed her. She would push this acquaintance to the full effect of her charms. Ogita took some offence. He spoke braggingly, but disastrously to the point – "Assuredly 'Tis Yoshi who shall be the lady of a *daimyō* of high place, not of a meagre fifteen or twenty thousand *koku*. Kaga Ke, Maeda Toshitsune, is grinding his sword. The great Houses in the west – Hosokawa, Bizen,

Kato, Mori, Satsuma, will follow him. Give them but the opportunity in the disorder of Edo, and the sword will be drawn. In a month, Edo, fired at a hundred points will lie in ashes. Then...." He stopped a little frightened. But she feigned the greatest indifference, teased him into opposition. Sitting down before the wine she got out of him the whole affair. Reverting to the accident – "But yourself, an accident has been deigned. Has another Yoshi encountered Kuroji Dono?" To the tender solicitude half laughing he made jesting answer. "A Yoshi with beard and wearing two swords. Today the contract was signed by all with the blood seal. The wine feast followed. The talk was earnest, some of it rash. Interposing in the quarrel, the dagger intended for the belly of one, was sheathed in the thigh of this Kuroji. A trifling flesh wound; well in a day or two, at present rest is needed." – "A dangerous affair; if it gives rise so easily to dispute." Such her comment. "Not so," answered the infatuated veteran. "They are too far in to withdraw." Before her eyes he unrolled the scroll. Her eye quickly ran along the crowded columns of the names – by the score. Here was indeed a big affair. Out of the corner of one eye she watched him put it away.

The salve Ogita Kuroji used for his wound had no such benefit as that offered Aoyama Shuzen; and perhaps O'Yoshi could have told the reason of its failure. By the next day the wound was inflamed enough to make movement difficult. Feeling the necessity of repair, Kuroji left all matters to his mistress, and sought early recuperation in complete rest. On plea of needed articles O'Yoshi was out of the house and on her hurried way to the Aoyama *yashiki* at Suragadai. The distance was short; yet her plan was already laid. Her dislike for the ageing Ogita was sharpened into hate by her love for the handsome young *samurai*. Close to the *yashiki* on pretext she entered the shop of a tradesman. To her delight she learned that the Waka Dono, Aoyama Shuzen, as yet had no wife. She had a hundred yards to go, and her purpose and ambition had expanded widely in that short distance. Her application for an interview with his lordship was quickly granted. She had often been subject of talk and comment between Shuzen and his subordinate officer. The *dōshin* happened to be present, and the attendant announced her at once. Passed to the inner apartment she found Shuzen as if he had been eagerly awaiting her coming for hours. Her reception was flattering. The ordinary salutations over they passed to most familiar talk, as of oldest friends between man and woman. When Shuzen would go further, and in love making press still greater intimacy, her refusal was of that kind which sought compliance. Said she with a smile – "Make Yoshi the wife of the Waka Dono and she will make the fortune even of one so highly placed as Aoyama Dono." To his incredulity and astonishment she would say no more. Shuzen now was determined not to let her go. He feigned consent, agreement to everything, with much regard for her, and small regard for the promotion at which he jested. Now they were in the very heigh-day of love. She resented his scepticism, and in the heat of her passion gave him everything – including the contract. His mistress by his side, seated in the confidence of an accomplished love affair he listened to her stream of revelation. This "doctor" and "husband" was neither doctor nor husband. His name was Ogita Kuroji, an Osaka *rōnin*. With Kosaka Jinnai and others of the same kidney he had been the head and front of the attempted rape of the Senhime. Shuzen knew enough to discount all the talk as to Maeda Ko, of the Hosokawa, and other great Houses. They were beyond his sphere. But here in his hands lay the web of a most important affair; so important that it frightened him a little. As his brows knit O'Yoshi too grew a little frightened; regretted that she had told so much all at once. She had babbled beyond measure in her transport. She had misgivings. Shuzen reassured her. For her to return to Daikucho would never do. A breath of suspicion, and Ogita's sword would deprive him of his mistress. Safe quarters were to be found in the *yashiki*. He called the *dōshin*, one

Makishima Gombei, and put her in his charge. The two men exchanged glances as she was led away.

The office of the south *machibugyō* was in a ferment when Aoyama made his report. All available *yakunin* were at once gathered. The list was carefully gone over with the minister for the month, Hoki no Kami. Despatched on their various missions the squads departed. To Shuzen was assigned the capture of Ogita Kuroji, leader of the conspiracy. This latter was chafing at the prolonged absence of O'Yoshi. Some accident must have happened to her. Then he remembered. She had gone to Hachobori. Here lived a sister, whose delivery was daily expected. Doubtless this commonplace event, yet surpassing in interest to every woman, detained her. A confusion outside attracted his attention. There was a crowd, and some disturbance. Hatsu! The people were being kept back by *yakunin*. "The thoughts of Kuroji were those of the wicked." At once he attributed their presence to himself. A look out at the rear and he quickly shot to the wooden bar. Between the bamboo of the fence men could be seen passing to and fro in numbers; and they were *yakunin*. He had been betrayed. The counsel of Jinnai came to mind, and he ground his teeth as he stood with drawn sword before the empty drawer of the cabinet. The scarlet of the *obi* of his false mistress flashed before his eyes. He had to die unavenged. "On his lordship's business! On his lordship's business!" The harsh voices sounded at the front. Those who would enter uninvited found themselves face to face in the narrow space with the old Kuroji, the man who had fought from Sagami to Tosa, from Chosen to Kyushu. The more incautious fell severed with a cut from shoulder to pap. A second man put his hand to his side, and rolled over to breathe his last in a pool of blood. Visions of 'Go-ban' Tadanobu came to mind. Kuroji would die, but he would leave his mark on the foe. Shuzen's men could make no progress, except to swell the death roll or their wounds. In rage their lord sprang to the encounter. Shuzen was young, but it is doubtful if the issue would have been successful with this man turned demon by the double injury and treachery. But Ogita amid this horde of assailants had suffered in his turn. In a parry his sword broke off short near the hilt. With a yell he sprang to close quarters, dealing Shuzen a blow with the hilt that sent him reeling senseless to the ground. Then, unable to accomplish more, and taking advantage of the respite caused by the rescue of his foe, he sprang to the ladder leading above. Once on the roof he saw that escape was hopeless. Already they were breaking into the rear. Men were approaching over the neighbouring houses. In the old style of ages past he waved them back with drawn dagger. There was no Shuzen to give command – "Take him alive!" They were only too glad to halt and let him do his will. Stripping to his girdle, before the assembled crowd he thrust his dagger into his left side and drew it across his belly. Then he made the cross cut through the navel. "Splendid fellow! A true *bushi*!" Admiring voices rose in the crowd. The body of Kuroji fell forward and down into the street. Thus he died.

This affair had ended in a way to redound greatly to the credit of Aoyama Shuzen. Others had not been so successful. Of nearly two hundred names only eighteen prisoners were secured. Shuzen stamped with impatience on learning of the escape of Kosaka Jinnai. He had learned much about him from the hate of O'Yoshi. "That man is the real leader of the band, the inspiration of Ogita Kuroji. Ah! Why could not this Shuzen be in two places at once!" Older officials bowed low, and smiled to themselves and each other at youth's self confidence. O'Yoshi now found short entertainment. Shuzen had no further use for the woman, for the means of his promotion. One day a *chūgen* led her to the postern gate of the *yashiki*, put a paper containing a silver *ryō* in her hand, and unceremoniously shoved her into the roadway. The gate closed behind her. At first she hardly comprehended the meaning of this treatment.

Then, as it filtered into her mind, her rage passed all measure. "Ah! The beast and liar! Yoshi was not fit to be the wife; nay, not even the female companion of this arrogant lord?" She had been juggled out of the secret of such value to him, then cast forth with the wages of a prostitute summoned to the *yashiki*. The woman was helpless. Broken in spirit she dragged herself off, to undergo a severe illness brought on by despite. Her foul role ascertained, friends and family would have nothing to do with her. Once recovered, she found herself deprived of all means of subsistence, even that of beauty, by her disease. Never more would she deal with the noble class, to be left with such a legacy. She would pray for the salvation of the man she had betrayed. On her way to the Asakusa Kwannon she passed the jail, then near the Torigoebashi. Stumbling along just here she raised her head, to confront the long line of rotting heads there set forth. Just facing her was that of her ex-lover Ogita Kuroji. It took on life. The eyes opened and glared fierce hate. The lips moved, and the teeth ground together. Then the other heads made measured movements. "Atsu!" With the cry she fell fainting to the ground, and it was difficult to restore her to consciousness. For several years the half crazed beggar woman sought alms near the jail, to act as guide and comment on the fresh heads exposed, until as nuisance she was driven off by the guard. Then the shameful swollen corruption of the body was drawn from the canal close by; thus to end on the refuse heap the treachery of Chosenburo no O'Yoshi.

The God Favours Shuzen

The influence of a House close to the person of the Shogun was no drawback to the close attention Aoyama Shuzen gave to official duty throughout his career. The Aoyama stood high in the council of the governing power. Even an old blunderbuss like Hoki no Kami could not shake this influence. When Yukinari tore the mirror from the hands of the young Shogun Iyemitsu Ko, berated him roundly for effeminacy, and dashed the offending object to pieces on the stones of the garden, this wanton treatment of the prince could not be overlooked. 'Invited' to cut belly by his intimates and opponents in the council (*rōjū*) he defied them, laid hand to sword, and swore they should join him in a 'dog's death'. The timely entrance of Okubo Hikozaemon prevented the unseemly spectacle of three old soldiers and statesmen enjoying the fierce and deadly pastime of one of the duels of Keicho (1596–1614). Hoki no Kami in his own way was right – and knew it; and he had the tacit approval of Hidetada Ko. The result was not *harakiri*, but the offending noble was consigned to the care of his brother. He and his were 'extinguished'; for the time being, and to the greater glory of his other relatives near the Shogun's person. Such was the rough discipline in Hidetada's camp of Edo. The second Shogun, now retired (Ogosho – *inkyō*), never lost the manners or the methods of the battle field.

The career of Aoyama Shuzen therefore was a steady rise in the Government service; in younger years attached to the immediate train of the prince, in greater maturity to the enforcement of the edicts through the legal machinery of the Bakufu. At this time he ruffled it bravely with the other young blades. The younger *hatamoto* on their part opposed to the *otokodate* of the townsmen the far more splendid *Jingumi* or divine bands. Yamanaka Gonzaemon knocked out several front teeth and inserted in their places gold ones. Hence the rise of the *Kingumi* or Gold Band. Aoyama Shuzen did likewise with substitution of silver. Hence the *Gingumi*. They were all of the Mikawa *bushi*; that is, drawn from the native province and closely affiliated to the Tokugawa House. Hence these *hatamoto* carried themselves high even against the greater *daimyō*, sure of support from their over-lord the Shogun. As for the town, they did as they pleased, seeking quarrels, distributing blows, and only restrained by wholesome reprisals of *rōnin* or the *otokodate* of the townsmen, who in turn relied on such *daimyō* as Date Ko and Maeda Ko, valued allies of the Tokugawa House, yet showing no particular liking for the encroachments of the palace clique on their own privileges.

The necessity of moving quarters was equally an embarrassment to Aoyama Shuzen and to his intimate and neighbour Okubo Hikoroku. Okubo suggested Honjo – "The water lies close by. Hence in winter the place is warm, in summer cool." – "And of mosquitoes swarms," interjected the practical Aoyama. "If the hillside be cold, it surely is no drawback to Hikoroku Uji." The one named made something of a wry face, and Aoyama smiled apart. He knew that Hikoroku was not so affectioned to the meetings of the Gaman Kwai as himself. However, smoothly – "This matter of the Yoshida Goten coming up offers fair opportunity. The failure of Endo Uji need not discourage Okubo Dono and this Aoyama." Both smiled a little. They could put palace influences better to work. "It is two thousand *tsubo*," said Shuzen. "Just the thing: moreover, it is close to palace duty. On this point Honjo is not in the running. Besides, the site has its own attraction. Of course Shuzen takes the well, in the division." Okubo interposed a lively objection, the shallowness of which Shuzen could detect. He humoured his friend's obstinacy. "Leave it to the lots." In haste the slips were prepared – "Hachiman, god of the bow and feathered shaft, grant your divine aid and bestow the old well ghost haunted on this Aoyama." Okubo laughed at his earnestness. "Aoyama Uji leaves this Okubo no resort but in the Buddha. Good fortune to Okubo, and may the will of the Lord Buddha be done.... Naruhodo! 'Tis yours after all. The shaft of the war god is stronger than the Buddha's staff." He took his disappointment so well as to be the more urgent in securing the transfer. This was granted, with expenses of removal.

Aoyama Shuzen superintended in person the preparation of his new residence. This was soon in readiness as little was to be done. Okubo took cash and construction. The former villa, fallen to Shuzen's part, needed mainly air and light, and repairs to its rotten woodwork. When it was time to think of the water supply Aoyama ordered the cleaning out of the old well. The workmen began to talk – "'Tis the old well of the inner garden, the Yanagi-ido of the Yoshida Goten. Danna Sama, deign to order exorcism made, and that the well be filled up and covered from men's sight." The Danna laughed at them, and was obstinate in his purpose. He took upon himself all the wrath of the disturbed and angered spirits. He hoped that they would not furnish material for more. To hearten them, he and his men descended to the level of the water. With headshakes and misgivings the chief ordered his men to the task – "Pfu! It stinks of ghosts, or something. Surely there will be dead men's bones for harvest; and perhaps those of the living. The old well has not seen its last ill deed." As for the dead men's bones, the well refuse was laid aside, and on Aoyama's order buried with no particular reverence in the bowels of the *tsukiyama* close by. "Let all the spirits of the place find company together," he jeered. The *yashiki* of Komiyasan in Honjo had its processions of marvels – dead men, frogs, *tanuki*, and fox – to shake its *amado* at night and divert the monotony of those who lived therein. The portentous foot perhaps he could not match, but he would share in this contest with ghostly visions. Chance had offered him the opportunity. All was prepared. Shuzen had established himself. Nightly with his camp stool he took his seat by the old well, to smoke his pipe and drink his wine – "Now! Out with you, ghosts! Here present is Aoyama Shuzen, *hatamoto* of the land. He would join in your revels. Deign to hasten.... What! The ghosts would rest this night?" Thus night after night passed with his jeering and no sign of the supernatural objects, not thus to be conjured. Time made the pastime stale – as stale as the waters of the Yanagi-ido which never furnished supply for the house or its tasks. Aoyama had the excuse of drinking wine. As for the household, the women would not even use the water for washing. They said it stunk too badly. In so far Shuzen failed.

It was about the time of his entrance on this new possession that more good fortune came to Shuzen. He was made the magistrate whose office covered the detection and punishment of thieves and incendiaries. It showed the estimation in which he was held, and satisfied both the vanity and the hard cold temper of Aoyama Shuzen. Looking to results, more than method, the selection was most satisfactory; if return of the number of criminals was the index assumed. Until a method attracted unfavourable attention by some scandal, only results were regarded by the Bakufu. But his household could not regard with any easiness a devotion of his lordship to the wine cup, which turned his court into a wine feast. Up to this time Aoyama Shuzen in all official duty had shown himself hard, unbending, callous, conscientious. Now the element of cruelty appeared, to develop rapidly with exercise until it was the predominant tone. Some illustrations are to be given from events occurring in these first three years of Shoho (1644–46).

Aoyama would show himself the strict disciplinarian. His chamberlain (*yōnin*) Aikawa Chudayu close beside him, his *dōshin* seated at either hand, he gave his orders and rebuke to the assembled constables. He scowled at them. Then with voice harsh from the contents of the big wine cup beside him he commanded – "Diligence is to be expected of all. He who fails to make many arrests shows sloth or ill will to his lord. Anyone against whom there is the slightest suspicion, even if he or she be abroad late at night, is to be brought to the jail. No explanation is to be allowed. There must be many arrests. Examination in the court is to follow; and many crimes, discovered under the torture, will be brought to punishment.... Heigh! Call up that old fellow there.... Who? That Ryusuke." At Shuzen's order Ryusuke forthwith came close to the *rōka*. "You, fellow ... what manner of man to act as constable are you? Days pass without a single prisoner being brought in. This jade, found in the street at the hour of the rat (11 pm) pleads excuse of illness and the doctor. This lurking scoundrel, seeking to set half the town on fire, pleads drunkenness as keeping him abroad. Thus many of these villainous characters, whores and fire bugs, find field for their offenses. No more of such leniency. Failure to arrest means dismissal from the service and punishment as an ill-wisher. Oldest and most experienced, the greatest number of prisoners is to be expected at your hands. Shuzen shows mercy. Your age remits the punishment, but dismissal shall afford example to the rest as to the wisdom of showing energy." Thus he cast forth without pity an ageing officer whose only offense was an experience which sought the mission of the night straggler, and allowed the harmless to go free. Ryusuke went forth from the office of the *bugyō* stripped of the means of living and of reputation, and assured of the unforgiving character of his lord. That night he cut belly, recommending his family to mercy. This was soon found – in debt and the debtor's slavery allowed by the harsh code. Thus was the jail kept full, with the innocent and a sprinkling of the guilty. No one dared to be lax; for life hung on salary, and on zeal the continuance of the salary. Moreover all revelled in the reward of the wine cup liberally bestowed for zealous service – and the more liberally as Shuzen took his turn with his big cup, every time he sent down the *sake* to his underling.

In Bakuracho lived one Zeisuke, a poor but honest fellow who made his living by peddling the smaller kinds of fish and the salted varieties, for his trifling resources allowed no larger outlay for his trays. In this way with greatest difficulty he managed to support an old mother, a wife, a young child. Locally he was known as 'Honest Zeisuke' for the not often found quality of representing the antiquity and character of his wares much as they were. When bad weather forbade the opening of the fish market, Zeisuke readily found some task at day labour by which a few *mon* could be secured, and for which his character for honest service recommended him. One night, when on his way homeward, he was passing the Asakusa Gomon just as the cry of fire was raised. Knowing the alarm of his aged mother Zeisuke at once bolted towards home. When all were running toward the fire this at once attracted attention. By the law it was the strict duty of the citizen to betake himself to his ward, and to be ready for service in preventing spread of the often disastrous conflagration. His action was noted by the ever present myrmidons of Shuzen. In a moment they were after him. Surrounded he was quickly caught. His explanation was not heard. "Say your say at the white sand, under the strokes of the *madake*," was the rough answer. Thus he was dragged off to the jail.

The next day Aoyama's first motion was to reward the captors with the wine cup. Harsh was the vinous scowl he cast on Zeisuke now cringing at the white sand. "Ha! Ah! A notable criminal; a firebug caught in the act, and attempting to escape. Make full confession. Thus much suffering is escaped, and the execution ground soon reached." Zeisuke had no confession to make, and to his explanation Aoyama turned a deaf ear. "Obstinacy is to be over-ruled." He made a sign. At once Zeisuke was seized. His head drawn downward two stout fellows now began to apply in rhythm the *madake* – strips of bamboo to the thickness of an inch tightly wound together with hempen cord, and making an exceedingly flexible and painful scourge. The blood quickly was spurting from his shoulders. Aoyama and his chamberlain sat enjoying the scene immensely. At the seventieth blow the peddler fainted. "A wicked knave! Off with him until restored." Then he settled himself for the day's pastime; for the torture had come to have the zest of an exhilarating sport. The cries of pain, the distortions of agony under the stones, or the lobster, or suspension, the noting of the curious changes of flesh colour and expression under these punishments, the ready assent to absurdly illogical questions, all this not only amused, but interested Shuzen. The naivete and obstinacy of the fisherman was just of the kind to furnish the best material. The fellow was sturdy of frame, and under skilled hands readily submitted to this dalliance for days without bending from his truth.

Meanwhile things went on very badly at the house in Bakuracho. The disaster of the arrest fell like a thunderbolt on the wretched little household. Day after day, hoping for the acquittal and release, one article after another went to the pawn shop. Reduced to absolute misery the house owner and the neighbours came to the rescue with a small sum raised among them. The long continued official suspicion affected even these toward the 'Honest Zeisuke', and their support grew cold. Then came the news that Zeisuke had died in the jail under the torture. Tearless, aghast, deprived of all support, the wife and mother long looked in each other's faces. Said the old woman – "Alas! Alas! Neither gods nor the Buddha exist. Faithful and devoted was Zeisuke to this old mother. Unfortunate in his life, he has been equally unlucky in death. What now is to be done!" She put her sleeves over the old and wrinkled face, and bending low concealed tears and a long farewell to the beloved in the person of her grandchild.

The wife was in little better case, but had to soothe this grief. A few coins remained. She would buy the necessaries for the evening meal. "But a moment, honoured mother. The return is quick. 'Tis but for the needed meal." Taking the child on her back she started off into the darkness. For a moment she turned to look at the mother. The old woman was following her with eyes tear dimmed in the sunken hollows. Thus they parted. For a moment the wife halted on the bridge over the Edogawa. The dark slimy waters were a solution, but she put it aside in the face of a higher duty. Soon she was on her way back.

To her surprise the house was in darkness. Surely a little oil was left in the bottom of the jar. She called, without getting an answer. In alarm she groped her way in the darkness, to stumble over the body of the old woman, lying limp and helpless. Something wet her hand. Now she was in all haste for a light. "Ah! Ah! The honoured mother! What has occurred? Has not ill fortune enough fallen upon the home of Zeisuke?" Alas! the hand was stained with blood. The old woman had intended the parting salute to be the last. Left alone she had bit off her tongue, and thus had died. Rigid, as one stupified, the wife sat; without tears, but thinking. Now she was left alone. But what as to the child? A girl too? Ah! There were enough of her sex in this hard world. She reached out a hand to the long triangular sharp blade close by. She touched edge and point of the *debabōchō* (kitchen knife) with the finger.

Here was the solution. Rapidly she loosed the child and lowered it to the ground. It took but a moment to open the little dress and expose the breast. Then knife in hand she leaned over it. As she did so the child opened its eyes, smiled, then laughing began to finger her bosom seeking sustenance. The feelings of the mother came over the woman. She put aside the knife to give the babe the breast. Alas! Starvation afforded but scant milk. Failing its supply the child cried peevishly. This last stroke of poverty was too much. The original purpose came back in full sway. With quick motion she put the child beside her and held it firmly down. The sharp pointed knife was thrust clean through the little body. A whimpering cry, the spurting of the blood, and the face began to take on the waxen tint. With the same short energetic movements the mother now sought her own end. Guiding its course with the fingers the knife was now thrust deep into her own throat. Both hands on the heavy handle she tore it downward; then fell forward on the mats. The wardsmen made report.

The Affair of the Asakusa Kwannon

Aoyama Shuzen stalked forward to his cushion near the *rōka*. Carefully adjusting his robes he scowled – most heavily; mainly at the almost boy crouched before him at the white sand. Expectant the *yakunin* stood by. Their leader stated the case against this outrageous criminal captured in the dead of night on the very steps of the Jizodo, in the very shadow of the great temple of the Asakusa Kwannon. The sacred structure, object of his nefarious design guarded his slumbers; the healing Yakushi Nyōrai, Jizo the god of youth and childhood, casting stony glances of benevolence through the closed lattices. "A most hardened wretch, an evident firebug, and probable thief; at once make full confession of the offence. Thus the torture is to be avoided, the punishment in so far mitigated." The voice was harsh and unrelenting, admitting of no explanation. The look accompanying it was without trace of pity, but full of the official scorn and dislike which would anticipate the turns and doubles of its quarry. The hare in this case but thought how best to meet this unforeseen and disastrous turn to events. He had heard much of the Yakujin – the god of disease and pestilence – under which pet name Aoyama Shuzen was known by a certain element of Edo town. He would tell the truth, with the certainty that in the effort enough lie would slip in to make out a good case.

The story at root was a simple one. Great of reputation for beauty and attraction in the Yoshiwara was 'Little Chrysanthemum' – Kogiku. In company with friends this Masajiro, second son of the wealthy Iwakuniya of Kanda Konyacho, (dyers street), had met and loved the *oiran*. He had been favoured in turn by the great lady of the pleasure quarter. Hence the displeasure of his father, who learned the fact by the unanticipated and unpleasant presentation of bills he thought had been settled long before by the diligence of Masajiro. Hence the preceding night, on the boy's return from dalliance with his mistress, he had been summarily turned out.... "Ha! Ah!" roared Shuzen. "A self confessed vagrant; a thief! Gentle the face and wicked the heart it conceals. Plainly a case for the jail and torture. The truth is to be learned. The scourges will bring it out. Make full confession...." A sign, and the attendants with their *madake* stood forward. In his terror Masajiro crawled toward the *rōka*. "Confession! Confession!" he bawled out. With grim smile Shuzen signed a halt. The *dōshin* prepared the scroll.

Yes: he had been turned out, but not as vagrant. The mother, so severe in the presence of the father, had fondled and wept over him. The Banto Shobei had grave and kindly words of admonition. All would be well, and forgiveness follow in time. He was to go at once to his nurse at Koshigeyatsu. Such effects as were needed would follow him. Money he was better without; beyond the little needed for the short journey. The father's anger was not to be aggravated. Soon he would enter for his night's draught, so haste was to be made. Thus he was bundled forth, to make his way in the darkness to the distant country village. The Baya's kind aid in the little conspiracy was assured at sight of her once ward. Overwhelmed with advice and woe he departed into the night, his step growing slower and slower with separation from his home. No money! That meant no Kogiku. The idea of never again seeing her face made his stomach turn. It did turn the direction of his footsteps, which now was toward the Yoshiwara.

Kogiku was overjoyed at sight of him. He had but just left her, and now returned to her side. What greater proof of love could she have? The favouritism of the Go-Tayu found favour for her lover's presence. Seated together she soon noticed his gloom, which all her efforts failed to lighten. Somewhat nettled she showed displeasure, charged him with the fickleness of satiation. Then he took her hands, and told her that this was the final interview. His dissipated life, the discovery of their relations, had so angered his father that under sentence of banishment from Edo he had come for a last look at her face. "What's to be done! What's to be done!" The lady wrung her hands in genuine grief over the handsome youth thus torn away. She had welcomed his presence as means of escape from her own difficulties. But a few hours before the master of the Uedaya had announced her sale and transfer to a wealthy farmer of Chiba. Ransomed by this country magnate she was to leave the gay life and glitter of the Yoshiwara, for a country life and the veiled hardships of a farm. In exchange for the twenty years of Masajiro – she obtained this settlement and a master passing fifty odd. She was in despair. The brilliant beauty, thus to sink in a few year's course into a farm wench, felt the sacrifice too great. Finding no aid in the boy lover, long she lay weeping, her head on his knees, hands pressed against her temples.

Masajiro was at no happier pass. "Up to the arrow point in love" his idea at bottom had been of a temporary separation. To find another Kogiku, a petted *oiran*, whose fame and beauty flattered any lover, was a stroke of good fortune not likely to occur. His own expression showed how little real idea of separation was in his mind. She noted it. Looking steadily in his face – "Constant the vows of this Kogiku, met by the love of Masa San. No matter how remote the prospect, the bond is that of husband and wife. With this old suburban drake Kogiku pollutes not her charms. Condescend to agree to a mutual suicide. Thus the obligation is avoided. Together the lovers pass to Meido (Hades) to wander its shades until the next and happier existence unites them in the flesh." In amazement and discomfiture Masajiro hung down his head. He would conceal the shock to his boyish timidity this proposal gave. His mind was full of such stories. He knew the earnestness of Kogiku. Then and there would she not draw her dagger to accomplish the deed? He was dreadfully frightened. Never would he have sought her presence, if such result had been anticipated. Now he must accompany her in death, or endure her grudge if successful in escaping her insistence. He temporized. Pointing to his plain disordered garb – "As to that – heartily agreed. But there is a seemliness about such procedure. A more befitting, a holiday costume, is to be sought. Then together, as on a joyful occasion, Masajiro and the Oiran will consummate the vows of husband and wife in a joint death." She looked him over, and was easily pacified by the evident truth and good sense. Again herself, in prospect of this avoidance of the unpleasant future she sought to entertain her lover with all the skill and charm she was so noted for. At midnight he left her, to secure an interview with Shobei on plea of forgotten needs; then he would return in more fitting garb.

His course lay through the now silent precincts of the great temple. More than the sun's circuit passed in these excesses, physical and mental, weighed upon him. He would rest a moment and consider his course amid the holy surroundings. Yakushi? The god was the physical healer in his theology and his services the strong and healthy youth did not need. Jizo Sama, or the six Jizo Sama, but a little way off? Probably the gentle divinity no longer regarded him as under tutelage. But the Lady Merciful – Kwannon Sama – why not make his petition to her? It was an inspiration, and earnest was the prayer which followed it – "Lady of Mercy, deign to regard with pity the unfortunate lovers. Grant that some exit be found for their woes, less harsh than the severance of the vital knot, offence to the Lord Buddha. Kwannon Sama! Kwannon Sama!... may the Buddha's will be done!" As he spoke a heavy object fell from above, to graze his shoulder and land at his feet. He stooped and picked it up. With astonished delight he noted the glittering coin within the bag. Ah! Ah! Away with all ideas of self destruction. Here was the means to escape the guilty consequence. Here was the ransom of Kogiku. He had shuddered at thought of return to the side of that woman, in death to wander the paths of Shideyama (in Hell) with the unhappy ghost – bald headed! Here now was the solution, in wine and the flesh and blood of the living long-tressed Kogiku, a very different person. His thought now turned to Yoshiwara. But – Naruhodo! Here was a second petitioner at this extraordinary hour. With amazement he saw a girl come flying across the tree and lantern dotted space before the great temple. There was something in gait and manner that he recognized, despite the deep *kōsō-zukin* concealing her features. From the shadow of the steps he sprang forward to confront her. It was so! The face beneath the *zukin* was that of O'Some the beloved of his brother Minosuke. The great dye house of the Iwakuniya sent much work to the minor establishment of Aizawaya in Honjo. His brother had such matters in his charge. At sight of Masajiro the face of the sixteen year old O'Some was dyed like unto the maple. "O'Some San! Here; and at this hour! Is it some visit to the shrine that in such haste...." In place of answer she wrung her hands and plead to be released. She must die. The river was not far off; there to end her woes. The scandal caused in the affair between herself and Minosuke had brought her to shame. Solemn had been the vows passed between them, tender the acknowledgments. By some retribution from a past existence thus she had found pollution with a beast. The heart yet was pure, and there was nothing to do but die. Deign forthwith to release her.

In his amazement he nearly did so. Alas! All these young girls, at least the desirable ones, wanted only to die. To become a divinity by death – *Shingami* – seemed to the feminine brain in youth the height of fashion. Very well: but he would seek to dissuade her. His pockets full of gold the present beauty of O'Some dimmed the past charms of Kogiku. She yielded to force and his urgency in so far as to accompany him to a refreshment stand just opening with the dawn. The mistress greeted them with kindness and affection. She showed them to an inner room. Here he urged his suit; flight and a home with the devoted nurse at Koshigayatsu. But O'Some was unwilling. She had been 'foxed' – herself was but a mere moor-fox. Deign to leave her to her own sad fate. It was the brother that she loved. Since she was deprived of him, she would seek the embraces only of the waters of the river. She urged and plead so prettily that her sadness and gloom entered into his own heart. She should be his companion. Kogiku in despite would join them. Thus the three together would find comfort in the shadow land of Meido. He gave up all attempt to persuade the girl. Briefly and almost harshly – "Be it so. Then we will die together. This Masajiro is under contract to die; and too tired to walk so far to find a partner. Condescend to await the night. Then we will take the shortest course to the river."

To this O'Some joyfully agreed. The day was passed in such harmless dalliance and favour as a young girl can show, who has had her own way; with a young man willing to dispense with thought during the intervening space of time before a not overly agreeable ending; and under the auspices of an honoured hostess fee'd by the glitter of coin into a consenting obtuseness. With the night they set forth in the rain. The river bank was not far off, but such vulgar plunge from the edge of the coarse promiscuity of Hanagawado was not to the taste of either. Then, as now, a ferry not far from the Adzuma bridge crossed to the pretty sounding "Eight hundred Pines." *Yashiki* then surrounded, a palace today covers the site. They watched the ferryman pushing off into the river's darkness. Then hand in hand they strolled up the bank of the stream, under the gloomy trees, seeking the favoured spot of their undoing. Suddenly O'Some stopped; sank at the feet of Masajiro. His hand sought the handle of the dagger. The weapon raised he was about to plunge it into the tender neck. Then a shout startled his ear. "Rash youths – Wait! Wait!" A powerful grasp was on his arm. With a shiver he came to consciousness. O'Some, the river, the bag of gold in his bosom, all had disappeared. He was lying on the steps of the Jizodo, surrounded by the *yakunin*. All had been a dream!

With open mouths the *yakunin* in the court looked at each other. Lo! They had nabbed a mere dreamer. How would his lordship take it? One more quick witted and thirstier than the rest answered for all – "Ha! Ah! A wretched fellow! Not only thief and firebug, but murderer also!" To the astonished and stammering protest of Masajiro there was the answering scowl of a very Emma Dai-O on the bench. "Miserable wretch! What is in the heart at best comes to the lips. This matter is to be sifted to the dregs, the witnesses examined. For offence so far disclosed he can take the lash. Then off with him to the jail." Masajiro, his back torn to ribbons and bloody with the fifty blows, was supported out of the court. Then the wine cup was condescended to the energy and acuteness of his captors. Enlivened by the morning's entertainment and his own big cup Aoyama Shuzen rose and departed.

Emma Dai-O gives Judgment

Great was the excitement and lamentable the experience of the Aizawaya. The matter of O'Some had been under discussion with the Iwakuniya. Beyond good words and cold courtesy little satisfaction could be obtained; nor could it be expected. The offence had been the work of a fox, and the jewel of a girl's reputation had been trodden in the mire. Returned to the saddened home, the nurse of O'Some was found awaiting them. At the news she had hastened from the country to console her old mistress and to take her one time charge in her arms. "Alas! Alas! Is the matter so beyond remedy? Surely with a good dower the Iwakuniya...." – "'Tis no such affair," answered the mistress, wiping away her tears. "As fact the girl is a wretched wench, disregardless of the parents. The little fool fell madly in love with the figure of the eldest son of the dye-shop. It seems that daily she made pilgrimage and prayer to the Ushi no Gozen, to the Gentoku Inari. What more malign influence could be invoked! One day Minosuke came on a mission to the shop. She followed him to the street, and for hours her whereabouts was unknown, until this return in disgrace. Accompanying him to Asakusa, there she exchanged vows and pillows with him at a convenient assignation house. Alas! On the return he was taken with a fit in the street. The prior of the Kido-ku-In, the great priest of the Shugenja (Yamabushi), was passing. His aid invoked, at once he recognized the rascal's disguise. Under the charms recited by the priest the true appearance was assumed, and a huge fox with a long tail darted away from the gathered crowd. No reputation has the girl gained by consorting with such a mate."

The nurse listened with amazed horror, turning first to the mother, then intently regarding the damasked face of O'Some, dyed red at the story of her shame. "Oya! Oya! Possessed by a fox! Alas! Truly it is almost irreparable. If it were mere defloration by the young master of Iwakuniya, that could be endured. But a fox mixed up in the matter.... Truly it would be well to take her off somewhere, to some hot spring in Idzu. There the influence can be removed, and O'Some San at least restored in mind." With this advice and gossip, with whispered consolation and laughing cheer – "'Tis no great matter after all; in the country – will be found girls a'plenty, quite as lucky or otherwise" – the kind and jovial dame took her leave.

The advice as to the hot spring seemed so good that preparations were under way in all haste. The straw baskets with their convenient deep covers to fit the larger or smaller needs of travel (*kōri*), the *furoshiki* or large square wrapping cloths, lay in the middle of the room, amid the pile of wraps and clothing for daily and more formal use. Skilled hands of maids and youths (*wakashū-kozō*) employed in the house were fast packing these latter into convenient parcels. Then to the hustle and bustle within the house was added the more unusual murmur of voices and tread of many feet without. The house owner (*ienushi*), accompanied by the head of the house block (*gumigashira*), entered in haste. Close at their heels followed the land owner (*jinushi*), the two bails (*jiuki* and *tanauki*). All looked with surprise and suspicion at these hurried preparations for departure. "Oya! Oya! This will never do. Honoured Sir of Aizawaya, the *yakunin* are now at hand from the office of Aoyama Sama. Your daughter in summoned to the white sand. Remove at once these signs of what looks like a flight." Eyes agog the frightened parents watched their neighbours and the servants hustle goods and parcels into the closets. They had hardly done so when the *dōshin*, followed by several constables, burst into the room. "The girl Some, where is she? Don't attempt to lie, or conceal her whereabouts." Eyes ferreting everywhere, the parents too frightened to move, the *yakunin* soon entered, dragging along the weeping O'Some. "Heigh! Heigh! The rope! At once she is to be bound and dragged before the honoured presence." Amid the bawling and the tumult at last the father found opportunity to make himself heard. He prostrated himself at the feet of the *dōshin*, so close to O'Some that the process of binding and roping necessarily included his own ample person. "Deign, honoured official, to forbear the rope. There is no resistance. The girl is very young, and ill. We accompany her to the presence of his lordship." Weeping he preferred the request. Iyenushi, Jinushi, Gumi-gashira, in pity added their own petition to the officer. This latter surveyed the slight figure of this fearful criminal. Besides, notoriously she had been foxed. He grumbled and conceded. "The rope can be forborne; not so as to the hands, which must be securely tied to prevent escape. The affair is most important. Delay there cannot be. His lordship is not to be kept waiting." Then he swept them all into his net. *Dōshin, Yakunin, Jinushi, Iyenushi, Gumi-gashira, Ban-gashira, Jiuki, Tanauki*, debtors, creditors, all and every in the slightest degree connected with the Aizawaya fell into the procession. But Edo town was growing used to these. 'Twas merely another haul of the active officers of the honoured Yakujin. "Kimyo Chorai" – may the Buddha's will be done, but spare this Tarobei, Jizaemon, Tasuke, or whoever the petitioner chanced to be.

Aoyama Shuzen stalked slowly forward to the *rōka*. Scowling he ran his eye over the crowd, taking in each and every. Then his eyes fell – first on Kogiku, the harlot of the Uedaya; then on the shrinking beauty of O'Some of the Aizawaya. Shuzen was improving in these days. The Ue-Sama (Shogun) spoke harshly of those retainers who made no provision for issue to support loyally the fortune of his House. Let him who would seek his lord's favour furnish forth such noble and lusty issue as in the Kamakura days, when Hojo Tokimasa, Wada Yoshimori Hatakeyama Shigetada, the Kajiwara, Miura, Doi, attended the hunting field of their suzerain followed by a dozen lusty heirs of the line – direct and indirect. Hence of late Shuzen had renewed his matrimonial venture, and taken to his bed a second partner. For side issue and attendance on his household affairs, his office was a fruitful field. The families of those condemned suffered with them, and the more favoured served in Aoyama's household, in all offices, from that of ladies in waiting to menial service – down to the *yatsuhōkōnin*. These latter, slaves for life, were more fortunate than their sisters *yatsu yūjō*, who were condemned to be sold for life service as harlots in the Yoshiwara. It was a hard law; but it was the law of the Tokugawa, of before the days of the ruling House. Shuzen profited greatly by it in the domestic sense. The harlot and the girl budding into womanhood would be acceptable addition to the companionship of his then bachelor existence.

His manner softened as he took his seat. His robes were more carefully adjusted. His cue bristled more erect. He was strikingly good looking. Dismissing all minor offenders he took up at once the great case of the day. The wretched Masajiro, his back bloodily marked by the scourge, was crouching in shame at the white sand before him. Shuzen gave him one savage glare, which added terror to his confusion before those once friends and relations. Then Shuzen began carefully and insistently to scan the faces of the girls. They were well worth attention. O'Some, sixteen and a beauty, had these aids to her other charms – a *kimono* of the fine striped silk of Izu, made in the neighbouring island of Hachijo by girls well fitted themselves to give grace to the beautiful tissue, an *obi* (sash) of fawn and scarlet into which was woven the shadowy figure, here and there, of a landscape – sketchy but suggestive. The belt which girded it within was of egg coloured crape, and the orange tissue broadened and hung down to add its touch of carefully contrasted colour. The hair was built high in the *taka-shimada* style, tied on top with a five coloured knot of thick crape. The combs and other hair ornaments were beautiful, and befitting the cherished daughter of the well-to-do townsman. Then Shuzen's look wandered to the harlot. Kogiku, Little Chrysanthemum, was noted in Edo town. Her beauty was more experienced, but hardly more mature than that of the town girl. Sedately she met the look, and without movement eyes plead smilingly for gentle treatment. She was dressed in a robe of gauzy water coloured silk. The sleeves were widely patterned – as with her class – but worked with rare harmony into the light grey colour of the robe. The long outer robe thrown over the inner garment (*uchikaku*) in these brilliant colours, in its tamer shades yet harmonized. Taken with the broad sash of the *obi* it made her rival the peacock in his grandest display. Her hair dressed high, was a bewildering harmony of the costly tortoise shell combs and pins (*kanzashi*) arrayed in crab-like eccentricity. The gold ornamentation glistened and sparkled amid the dark tresses. Truly Shuzen was puzzled in this claim for priority between the unrivalled beauty and the fresher and naiver charms of inexperience. Ah! Both should be the cup-bearers. But the sequel! Benten Sama alone could guide the lot.

It was ordered that the confession be read. Once more the judge, Shuzen carefully watched the faces before him of those most concerned. It was not difficult to detect amid the confusion of O'Some, the growing wrath of Kogiku, an unfeigned astonishment. With some satisfaction he noted this evident discrepancy in the plea. Suave, yet still somewhat harsh, he addressed O'Some. "The confession of this wicked fellow has been heard. What has Some to say in answer thereto." For a moment the girl raised her head to that of this Emma Dai-O. Then in confusion she half turned as seeking support – "Mother! Mother!" It was all she could say in her fright, and more than the mother could stand. She was the townswoman; self-assured in her way. She boldly advanced a knee. "With fear and respect: the girl is but of sixteen years, and the white sand has paralysed her thought and utterance. Deign, honoured lord, to pardon the mother's speech." Then she went into details as to the late unfortunate occurrence. With indignant looks at the crushed and unfortunate Masajiro, she gave her own testimony which rang with truth. "Well he knows all this matter. For the past six days the girl has not left home or parents caring for her afflicted body. 'Tis only this fellow Masajiro who claims to be the lover, to take the place of his brother Minosuke; a poor exchange in either case, with fellows who do but run after the harlots of Yoshiwara, to the bewitching of innocent girls." Tenderly she took the now weeping O'Some in her mother arms, and added her own tears to the soothing.

Shuzen slowly leaked a smile. He left the pair to themselves and turned to Kogiku. "And you?" Kogiku was not so easily confused. Readily she confessed to the contract between herself and Masajiro. "This affair of the rich purchaser from Kazusa came up suddenly. There seemed no outlet but suicide – if the dreary life away from Edo was to be avoided." Shuzen took her up harshly – "Bound to the Uedaya for a term of years then you would cheat your master out of the money he expended on you. This is theft, and most reprehensible. For such it is hard to find excuse." His roughness puzzled and frightened even the experience of Kogiku. She became confused. Shuzen was satisfied with the impression. He was unwilling further to delay his own prospects. Sending the matter over to the next sitting for final settlement he remanded all the accused – Masajiro to the jail and repeated scourgings for the lies contained in his confession; the girls to his own care. His experiences for the time being would largely condition the final judgment.

Shuzen was regular in his irregularities. Promptly, the case again convened, he gave judgment. There was none of the customary roughness in his manner. Even the official harshness was smoothed down. He dilated on the importance of the case, the necessity of making an example of this evident depravity of manners and morals affecting Edo town – "As for the girl Some, it is matter of question with whom she is involved, Masajiro or Minosuke; both well could be her lovers. Thus she has fallen under strange influences and been foxed. Such a girl is not to be allowed to wander at random. As act of benevolence henceforth charge is continued as in the present conditions. Kogiku is still more reprehensible. The attempt to cheat her master being so brazenly confessed is hard to overlook. Owing to her previous life perhaps the feelings have become blunted. The same benevolence and punishment is awarded to her – with hope of future amendment." The master of the Uedaya, crouching close to his head clerk made a wry face. The two men exchanged glances, and the clerk opened a very big round eye for his master to observe. The latter sighed. Continued Shuzen severely – "As for this Masajiro, he is not only liar, but would-be firebug and thief. What is harboured in the mind he would put into deed. It is but chance which has saved the life and purse of the passing citizen, and the sacred structures from the flames. To him the severest punishment is meet. However benevolence shall still hold its sway. Instead of the sword, banishment to the islands for the term of life, to serve as slave therein to the Outcast – such his sentence. To this judgment there is no appeal." Abruptly he rose. The weeping father and mother were baffled by the nonchalance of the daughter, who had no chance to give them comfort, but was at once removed in company with the willing lady of pleasure and experience. The huddled form of Masajiro was hustled roughly out with the kicks and blows to which he was becoming accustomed. Two or three years, under the rough charge of his new masters, were pretty sure to witness his body cast out on the moorland to the kites – or into the sea for fishes to knaw.

It was the *bantō* (clerk), faint with the hunger of long waiting, who led the parents into the first cook shop encountered on the way. Here over greens and cold water the father sighed, the mother wept apart, the clerk eyed biliously the meagre fare. Then in poured the company of Kogiku – a noisy, merry crowd. There were expressions of amused discomfiture, caught by the sharp ears of the clerk; suggestive references. He watched them; heard the lavish orders for food and wine – "Plenty of wine, and piping hot" – "Respectfully heard and understood." The waiting girls were at their wit's end. The feast in progress the *bantō* came boldly forward. "Honoured sirs, deign to note these parents here, deprived of their daughter. Your honoured selves have lost a girl of much value to your master. How is it then that you thus deign to rejoice? Plainly the grief of these must be out of place." The man addressed more directly looked him over coldly; then cast an eye on the distressed father and mother, at their meagre fare. His manner changed. He became more cordial. "Good sir, the affair is not to be taken thus! Sentence has been given, but...." He laughed – "it can be revoked. Already in the inner room the master is in consultation with the agent of Takai Yokubei San (Mr Highly Covetous), Aikawa Dono, – the honoured *yōnin* of Aoyama Sama. A round bribe, and the girl will be released...." The words were not out of his mouth when the father was on his feet. Led by the *bantō* he made the rounds of all – pimps, bawds, and bouncers – soliciting their influence – "Honoured gentlemen of the Yoshiwara, deign to interfere in the matter, to plead with the master of the Uedaya. House, lands, goods, all these are nothing if the cherished daughter be restored." He wept; and they took pity on his inexperience. The first speaker at once sprang up and went to the inner room. The master of the Uedaya cordially desired their presence. Added funds were no drawback to his own petition in the dealings with Yokubei San. The parents introduced he told them – "It is but a matter of cash. Kogiku, within the next three days, must be delivered to the *gōshi* of Kazusa, or else a large forfeit paid. She can kill herself on the day following. 'Tis no affair of the Uedaya. Add your gift of a hundred *ryō* to the bribe of the Uedaya, and Saisuke San, here present, can assure success. Aikawa Dono surely has not left the court. He awaits report, with as great anxiety as your honoured selves. As for the Tono Sama, he has had the presence of the girls for the six days, and will be all the more easily worked on. But from all accounts the honoured daughter had little to lose in the experience. She would make a splendid Go-Tayu." Seeing no sign of acquiescence he shrugged his shoulders, and continued to the honoured Saisuke San – "A most annoying affair: a hundred *ryō* to this shark, and only the premium and the debts of the *oiran* will be paid. But he will take no less?... Be sure she shall learn the use of the *semeba* (punishment cell) before she finds her new master." Saisuke San with slow smile made answer – "Be sure that by night she will be in your hands, ready for the experience."

Rejoicing the parents gave thanks, and betook themselves to their home. Half ruined, again O'Some would gladden their hearts. But the mother had an eye to the expense, and promised a reception hardly better than that awaiting Little Chrysanthemum. Why show favouritism? There was small difference between the two. But this the father energetically denied. Meanwhile Aoyama Shuzen was preparing for his wine feast, one of a pleasant succession extended over this interval. With misgiving and no pleasure he saw the entrance of Aikawa Chudayu. The chamberlain brought with him the account books. Shuzen's experience, however, noted past profit as salve to annoyance. He was a bitter hard man in domestic administration; cutting down food, and by fines the wages, of those more regularly employed in the household. This made the threatened loss of women serving by compulsion the more severe. Chudayu knew how to deal with his master. Affairs in the household were not going well, under the free indulgence of Shuzen toward himself and his pleasures. Besides he was about to deprive him of his new favourites. At a sign Kogiku and O'Some, already present by the lord's favour, withdrew. The younger girl had aged ten years in experience with this companionship of the week. Chudayu watched them depart. Then sighed heavily. "Ah! Ha! So it's *that*." Shuzen moved testily, as sharply he regarded his satellite. "Acting under the instructions of your lordship, the box of cakes has duly been received from Saisuke. The affairs of the household require a large sum. Her ladyship's confinement is to be considered, the entertainments required by custom for the expected heir. To return the gift means to your lordship – the sacrifice of two hundred *ryō*. May the Tono Sama deign to consider a moment. Such double good fortune is rare – and the messenger waits upon this trifling sacrifice of a pleasure for which substitutes easily can be found." He drew the *furoshiki* from the box. Shuzen sighed; but did not hesitate. "Hasten Saisuke off at once; with the exchange." He placed the box in a closet close by. "As for the wine feast, Chudayu shall be the cup-bearer. Shuzen is in an ill humour." He had an ugly look. Chudayu, however, did not draw back. Leaning forward with a smile – "This Chudayu would make report, to the pleasure of the Tono Sama." – "Of what?" asked Aoyama, in some surprise at his chamberlain's earnest manner. "Of the whereabouts and close proximity of Kosaka Jinnai." – "Ah!" The tone of voice had the depth of years of expectant hate.

Kosaka Jinnai

When Takeda Shingen swept down upon the lower provinces in 1571, fought a rear guard action at Mikatagahara, in which he nearly extinguished Tokugawa Iyeyasu, with a taste of the latter's remarkable powers of recuperation, he went on to his real aim of a trial of strength with the main Oda forces in Mikawa and Omi. The great captain lost his life by a stray bullet before Noda castle. His death for long kept secret, until the northern forces had withdrawn into the fastnesses of Kai, the war languished, to be renewed with greater activity under the rash and ignorant leadership of his son. Katsuyori and his tribe cut belly at Temmoku-zan, the last and successful bid of Iyeyasu against his former enemies. Then the Tokugawa standard was planted from Suruga to Mikawa, and Iyeyasu became indisputably the first of Nobunaga's vassals – and one never thoroughly trusted.

Among the twenty-four captains of Takeda Shingen was a Kosaka Danjo no Chuden. His son Heima inherited the devotion, as well as the fief, of the father. Unlike many of the Takeda vassals in Kai he clung to Katsuyori Ko through all the bad weather of that unlucky prince. Kai was no longer a safe place for vassals true to the native House. Better luck could be assured with the old enemies, the Uesugi in the North. But Heima would not seek other service than that of his once lord. He only sought a place to live.

When the ex-soldier appeared with his wife in the village of Nishi-Furutsuka at the base of Tsukuba, the people thereabouts had more than strong suspicion that he who came so quietly into their midst was not of their kind. However his presence was accepted. His willingness to take up farm labour and another status, to become a *gōshi* or gentleman farmer, his valued aid and leadership in the troubled times which followed, were much appreciated. The year 1599 found the old fox Iyeyasu Ko planted in Edo castle; and Jisuke, as Heima now called himself, leaning over the cradle of a boy just born – a very jewel. Jisuke's wife was now over forty years in age. Hence this unexpected offspring was all the dearer. In the years there had been losses and distress. The new-comer surely was the gift from the Kwannondo nestled on the slopes of the mountain far above the village. To the Lady Merciful many the prayers for such aid.

The child grew and prospered. A farmer's boy, yet he was the *bushi's* son; made plain in every action. Under the tutelage of the priests of the neighbouring Zen temple he learned all that they chose to teach, far outstripped his fellows, and in class room and in sport was their natural leader. Sport was the better test. With years Jinnosuke tired of the clerical teaching. The leader of the village band he was its mainstay in the wars with boys of rival hamlets thereabouts. These were soon driven away, and their own precincts invaded at will. The mountain became distinctively the property of Jinnosuke and his youthful companions, whose whole sport was devoted to mimic warfare. Their leader, thus unchallenged, became more and more reckless; more and more longed to distinguish himself by some feat beyond mere counterfeit war. One day, under his direction, in the storming of the hill which represented the enemy's castle, much brushwood and dried leaves were gathered. "Now then! Set the fire! The foe, blinded by the smoke, perishes under our blows. On! On!" The other children eagerly obeyed. The blazing mass towered up and up. The trees now were on fire. The wind blowing fiercely drove the fire directly on to the Kwannondo, which stood for the citadel of the besieged. Soon the temple itself was in flames. Greatly excited the boys swarmed amid the smoke and confusion as if in real battle. "Now – for the plunder!" At Jinnosuke's order the furniture of the temple was made the object of loot, heaped up at a safe distance for future division.

Thus engaged loud shouts met their ears. In fright the band of youngsters turned to meet the presence of the enraged incumbent, the *dōmori*. The temple was his charge and residence. His small necessities were supplied by visits to the villages below. "Oi! Oi! wretched little villains! Thus to fire the temple in your sport is most scandalous. Surely your heads shall be wrung off – one by one. Terrible the punishment – from Heaven and the Daikwan." The boys in confusion began to slink away. Then the voice of Jinnosuke rose above the tumult. "On! On! This priest stinks of blood. Be not cowards! The commander of the castle would frighten with words. 'Tis he who is afraid. It is his part to cut belly in defeat and die amid the ruins." In a trice the whole pack had faced around. Boldly with staves they set upon the priest. Numbers brought him helpless to the ground. There was a large stone lying close by. Heaving it to his shoulder Jinnosuke stood over the prostrate man. "According to rule the matter is thus to be conducted. This fellow is to be given the finishing stroke; then buried in the castle ruins." He cast down the heavy block with all his force. The priest's brains were spattered on the ground. Under the direction of Jinnosuke the body with feebly twitching limbs was thrown into the now blazing mass of the temple. Then forming in line, and raising the shout of victory, the youthful band of heroes marched off to the village. Under pain of his displeasure – which meant much – Jinnosuke forbade any bragging or reference to the affair. Wisely: a day or two after a peasant came on the scene. In fright the man hastened to make report. At once buzz was most tremendous. Was it accident or the work of thieves, this disaster? Said one man sagely – "The *dōmori* was a great drunkard. Deign to consider. The temple furniture is untouched. Thieves would have carried it off. He carried it out to safety, to fall a victim in a further attempt at salvage. The offence lies with the priest, not with the villagers." The report pleased all, none too anxious to offend the bands of robbers ranging the mountain mass and the neighbouring villages. Thus report was made by the village council to the Daikwan's office. The temple authorities had a severe reprimand for allowing such a drunkard to be in charge of the shrine. Jinnosuke stuck his tongue in his cheek. "Trust to the valour and skill of this Jinnosuke. These constables are fools." But his companions were a little frightened with this late exploit. Their numbers fell off. Many of them now came to the age fit for farm work. Jinnosuke was not long in finding substitutes in the real thieves who haunted the neighbourhood. Their spy, and often engaged in their raids, yet in his own district he was only known as a bad and dissipated boy.

Something of this had to come to the ears of Jisuke; but not the full extent of his son's wickedness. He sought a remedy for what he thought mere wild behaviour. Now in the town, years ago, there had lived a poor farmer and his wife; "water drinkers," in the local expression for bitter poverty. The man laboured at day tasks, and the wife laboured as hard with him, bearing her baby girl on her back. Jisuke aided as he could, and as was his wont, and when the pair were taken down and died with a prevailing epidemic disease, it was Jisuke and his wife who took the child to themselves, to bring her up as their own. O'Ichi San grew into a beautiful girl, and at this time Jisuke and his wife trusted to her favour and influence to bring Jinnosuke to the sedateness and regularity of a farmer's life. The girl blushed and looked down as she listened to what was more than request, though put in mildest form. "One so humble is hardly likely to please the young master. Filial duty bids this Ichi to obey, and yield her person at command." The mother was more than gratified at the assent and modesty – "Dutiful you have always been. We parents have no eyes. The whole matter is left to you. If Jinnosuke can be taken by your person, perchance he will devote his time to home and the farm work, now so irksome to his father. Where he goes in these long absences is not known; they can be for no good purpose." Thus the arrangement was made. The girl now busied herself about and with Jinnosuke. She was the one to attend to all his comforts, to await his often late return. Thus used to her he soon began to look on her with anything but brotherly eyes. Was she not the daughter of old Tarobei, the water drinker? He knew the story well. Thus one night he took O'Ichi to himself. She pleased him – as with the parents. No objection was anywhere raised to the connection; a village of Nippon has cognizance of such matters; and in short order public notice was given of the marriage.

The influence was not of long duration. With his wife's pregnancy Jinnosuke disappeared. From the age of thirteen years he had been hand in glove with all the rough fellows of the district. These were stirring times in the south. There was something to pick up. After all was not he a *samurai's* son. Jinnosuke was too late for action. Although but seventeen years old his short sturdy and astonishingly active frame and skill with weapons was a welcome addition to the band that Ogita Kuroji had gathered after the fall of Osaka-jo. Now Jinnosuke figured as Kosaka Jinnai. Here first he came in contact with the law and Aoyama Shuzen. On this failure he betook himself at once to the disguise of his native village; to enter it as quietly as if he never had left it, to find himself the father of a baby girl, Kikujo, and to procreate another on his patient wife. But before this second girl, O'Yui, was born Jinnosuke, as the village still knew him, had again disappeared. This was in strict accordance with his principle, of which something is to be said.

Of these Osaka *rōnin*, determined not to take another master, there were three Jinnai. In council over past failure, said Tomizawa Jinnai. "The ambition of this Tomizawa?" He laughed. Jinnai was no distinctive term in this gathering. "It is to collect all the beautiful costumes of Nippon." – "Admirable indeed!" chimed in Shoji Jinnai (or Jinemon, as he called himself). "But why stop at the surface? As you know, the ambition of this Shoji had long been to see gathered together all the most beautiful women of Nippon. And you, Kosaka?" – "To see all distinction done away with between other men's property and my own." – "Splendid indeed! But don't poach on our ground." The two others clapped their hands and laughed. Kosaka Jinnai did not. "Well then – to put the matter to the test," said he callously. Tomizawa Jinnai forthwith took up the collection of old clothing and costumes of divers sorts. He can be said to be the ancestor of the old clothes trade of Edo – Tokyo; and the Tomizawacho at Ningyocho no Yokocho, the place of his residence, is his memorial. To this day it is a centre for old clothes shops. Shoji Jinnai pressed the petition he had once put in (Keicho 17th year – 1612) as Jinemon before being finally convinced of the righteousness of a Tokugawa world. He was lucky enough to find oblivion and reward in the permit for a harlot quarter. As its bailiff (*nanushi*) he assembled three thousand beautiful women for the service of the Yoshiwara, then at Fukiyacho near Nihonbashi, and of which Omondori is the chief relic. Kosaka Jinnai, under such encouragement and auspices, betook himself more vigorously than ever to robbery; enhanced by a mighty idea which the years gradually brought to ripeness in his mind. From being a sandal bearer Hideyoshi the Taiko had risen to rule. He, Jinnai, would emulate the example and rise to rule from being a bandit. He was not, and would not be, the only one of the kind in the political world. Hence his wide travels through the provinces, his seeking out all the most desperate and villainous characters, for he had "trust" in few others, his weaving together of a vast conspiracy of crime, not to be equalled in any time but the closing days of the Ashikaga Shogunate – and that not so far off. Of this period of Jinnai's life there is a tale to relate.

A Matter of Pedestrianism

Up to the very recent days of Meiji the precincts of the Shiba San-en-zan Zojoji, now known more particularly as the most accessible of the burial places of the Tokugawa Shogun, were an excellent example of the old monastic establishments. The main temple with its wide grounds was completely girdled by a succession of halls or monastic foundations, some of which were famed through the land for their theological teaching of the principles of the Jodo sect. Conspicuous among these were the Tenjingatani and the Mushigatani, seminaries widely sought for the erudition of the professors. In all nearly three thousand students attended the halls, with an eye to an ecclesiastical future.

On the dawn of a cold winter morning a priestly clad man, a *shoke* or one of the lowest clerical order, mainly notable for the vastness and robustness of his proportions, could have been seen leaving the gate of the Tokucho-in. His size alone would have attracted attention, for the mouse coloured *kimono*, the white leggings and mitts (*tekkō*), the double soled *waraji* (sandals) fastened on a pair of big feet, were usual travelling equipment of his kind, made sure by the close woven *ajiro* or mushroom hat covering his head; admirable shelter against heat in summer, and a canopy – umbrella like – against falling snow in winter. By somewhat devious route he strode along a narrow lane, crossed the Gokurakubashi and halted before the Chumon on the broad avenue leading up to the temple. A glance thither satisfied him for a leave-taking, which yet displayed some sentiment. A few moments carried him without the entrance gate, and but few more saw him crossing Kanesujibashi, evidently on some long tramp, if the steady swing of a practised walker, in no haste and conserving his strength, is any test.

The road in those days passed through a long succession of village houses, the *chō* of Shiba village, broken very occasionally by a *yashiki* wall. It was not until he reached the barrier at Takanawa, Kurumacho, that he came full out on the bay just lighting up with the coming day – a beautiful stretch of water, now spoiled by the ugliness of the railway and the filling in which has turned the haunt of thousands of wild fowl into a prairie, soon to be covered by hideous factories and other sites of man's superfluous toil. Close by the little saddle at Shinagawa, now a railway cutting, a stream came into the bay from the west. On the bridge the priest Dentatsu stopped for a moment. Throughout, from the time of leaving Kanesujibashi, he had had a feeling of being followed. Now he determined to get a good look at his pursuer, it was not particularly satisfying. "Iya! An ill looking chap – with an eye like a knife." The object of these remarks had halted with him, at the further side of the bridge. He was contemplating the water with one eye, the priest with the other. A short sturdy man of forty odd years, Dentatsu noted the good but thin upper garment, the close fitting leggings, the well chosen *waraji*, the copper handled dagger in his girdle. Furthermore he noted a cold decision in the glance of the eye that he liked least of all in the fellow's equipment.

This was a man he would not choose for companion – "Bah! Short Legs, this Dentatsu will soon leave your stumps in the rear. A little speed, and this doubtful fellow is left behind beyond hope." So off started his reverence at the full pace of his huge legs and really great endurance. Through Omori and Kamata, crossing in the same boat at the Rokugo ferry, through Kawasaki and Tsurumigi – totsu-totsu-totsu the stranger's legs kept easy pace with those of the priest. "A most extraordinary fellow," thought Dentatsu. "He moves as on springs. It would be well to settle matters at once with him." Halting he waited for this pursuer to close up the few score feet maintained between them. His frowning manner had a genial greeting. "Ah! Ha! Truly the Go Shukke Sama is no mean walker. But even then company on the road is good. From the Zojoji; by that *kesa* (stole), dress, and carriage? Probably the honoured priest has a long journey before him – to the capital?" Dentatsu duly scanned his company – "To the Chion-In, the parent temple, and none too fond of companionship on the road. Deign, good sir, to spare yours; with such short legs the task of precedence would be out of the question. Drop the useless effort of this pursuit, which becomes an annoyance."

Dentatsu's manner was truculent, his grasp on his stick even threatening. The fellow met this rough greeting with the suavest determination. "Oya! Oya! Naruhodo, Go Shukke Sama! A very rude speech indeed! After all the highway is free to all, and I too travel the Tokaido toward the capital. Deign to grant your company and the entertainment will be all the better. Don't be deceived by length, or lack of length, in one's legs. The promise will be kept not to detain you.... That you came from Zojoji is plain from your garb, if you had not been seen to turn into Tokaido from the temple avenue.... I too travel Kyoto way.... See! In our talk already Hodogaya town is passed. This climb.... here is the top of the Yakimochizaka. The mark stands here to bound Sagami and Musashi. Ha! Ha! The Go Shukke Sama has splendid legs, but he is handicapped by his weight. Surely it cannot be less than two thousand *ryō* in coin that he carries in the pack on his shoulders. That contains no bills on the Shoshidai (Governor) of the capital."

Ah! The matter now was fully lighted. The fellow then had known his mission from Zojoji to the parent temple, to remit this sum to the capital. Dentatsu had not anticipated difficulty so early in his journey, nor did he much care for the contest which was offered him. He judged the man by his legs, and these were almost miraculous in swiftness, activity, and strength. "Alas! A dangerous fellow indeed. The luck of this Dentatsu is bad. What now is to be done?" The cold sweat at his responsibility gently bedewed his forehead. Yet Dentatsu was a brave man. The tradesman – or robber – laughed lightly. "Don't look so queer, so put out, honoured Shukke Sama. Truth is told in saying there is business on Tokaido. Even if highwayman, the last thing thought of would be to meddle with the funds of the honoured Hotoke Sama (Buddha). Be reassured; and as such be more assured in having a companion. The coin? Pure guess, and from the small size of the parcel and the evident difficulty found in carrying it. It weighs too much on one shoulder. Trust not only the thief, but the trader to know the signs of cash.... You would breakfast at Totsuka town? Did they send you forth with empty belly? Surely the monastery kitchen has no such reputation for stinginess among the vulgar." His manner was so reassuring that Dentatsu gained confidence in him and his profession. Gladly now he accepted this failure to relieve him of his precious burden, and this offer of company. He resented however the reflection on the monastery kitchen – "Not so! Nor is this foolish priest so at odds with the cook as not to find a bit of mountain whale (flesh) in the soup. Repletion is the aim and object of a monastic existence." – "Ha! Ha! Ha!" laughed the fellow. "Yet the honoured Shukke Sama would breakfast so close to Edo town! Good sir, deign to leave the matter to me. Both are in haste – you to the capital; I almost as far.... This Fujisawa is a wondrous place. As priest you know its temple and its wandering prior, the precious relics of the Hangwan, but the woman Terute of course the priest despises; yet Oguri owed much to her – life and success in his vendetta. Besides in a copse, just over yonder hill, is the shrine of the other Hangwan – Yoshitsune. A prayer to his head there buried brings success in warlike adventure, no great affair for cleric or tradesman.... Already the Banyu ferry is close at hand. Surely if we would reach Sumpu (Shizuoka) this day there can be no lunching short of Odawara town."

Dentatsu would have stopped short, if such halt had not involved the rapid disappearance of this elastic and now entertaining companion. As it was both had to slow pace to let him get breath taken away by pure amazement. "Odawara town! Sumpu before night! Tradesman, have you gone mad? To Sumpu it is full forty-eight *ri* (120 miles). You talk like a fool. Who is there, to walk such a stage in a day?" – "The honoured Shukke Sama and this tradesman. In talk and argument the ground flies under the feet of such walkers, and the promise to keep pace will be maintained. Just see – this is Kodzu town; yonder the waters of Sakawagawa. 'Tis early yet, but time can be spared for food. For exercise belly timber is needed. A good lining of wine and food to the inwards is the tonic to more talk and exertion. Now in with you, to this broad space leading to the castle – the keep of Okubo Kaga no Kami, with his hundred thousand *koku* and the trust of the suzerain worth all his other honours. Ah! Here is the eight roofed Minoya, best of its kind in the town. And what a town. Between wine, food, and singing girls, one loiters as long as a second Odawara conference; at times to one's ruin.... Ah! Ha! A stop for the mid-day meal. Nēsan, no more delay than needed. Speed is urgent, yet food and wine of the best. The honoured Shukke Sama is affected toward vegetable food.... What! The Buddha called wine *hannyato* – hot water bringing wisdom? Nēsan, the honoured Shukke Sama is a man of sense, no ascetic when unsatiated – or on a journey. He would wear out belly and *waraji* (sandals) on the same service. Fish boiled with a little salt, *sashimi* (sliced raw fish) – and *don't* forget the *kamaboku* (fish paste). Two bottles for each, with as much more heating. Bring a large bowl, empty. Never mind the change.... And now, honoured Shukke Sama, deign at least to the uninitiated the basis of this wondrous argument." Dentatsu could not take offence at his merry humour. Himself he smiled, as he poured from the second bottle of the wine. "Yes; the Buddha has called wine *hannyato*, thus permitting its use to the initiated; just as stronger foods, properly labelled, are fit for the belly. Thus by the mouth is purified what goes into the belly. If the mouth can perform lustration in the one case, it can do so by its exercise in another and more intimate fashion." The fellow was immensely pleased. Leaning over he had drunk in the countenance of the priest in the course of his argument – "Naruhodo! A big body: 'twas feared the mind would be small. Deign, honoured sir, to wait a moment; a purchase to make...." Off he bolted with the *domburi* or large bowl, something of a mystery to the priest. It was soon solved by his reappearance with the vessel filled with the small salted squid *(ika)*. "There! Honoured Shukke Sama, sample the best of Odawara town, noted for *kamaboku* and its small fish-salted; and of these the *ika* is unsurpassed." As they drank the wine, urged on by the savoury relish, he gave few and brief directions. The food was wrapped up by the *nēsan*, several bottles of wine put in the package, for use in a journey that must be pressed. "Now – the bill; for you, *nēsan*, what is left over. Honoured Shukke Sama, a gentle pace for the time being. The belly full, one loiters to let it do its work. From here to Yumoto is a *ri* (2-1/2 miles), of most gentle rise. And what a pretty scene; the valley narrowing to its clinging hills hiding the strange and beautiful scenes beyond, yet which cause a little fear even to the stoutest hearts. This river seems alive, twisting, and turning, and pouring in multitudinous and minute falls over the rounded boulders. The greater falls are naught else – on the larger scale. All day one could watch the twists and turns of one spot in a rivulet, white, green, almost black, yet never the same.... Note how the pass narrows. This is Hata, beyond is the monkey's clinging hill – well named. More than one rock from the steep above has torn away the traveller's grasp and crushed a skull as if an egg shell." They breasted the steep hills through forest, came out on the gentler upper slopes covered with the long bamboo grass through which could be seen the rough heaped up surface of volcanic debris. The trader came to a halt. "A request to make."

"Ah! Now the fellow's mask is off – in this lonely spot.... He shall have a tussle for it." Dentatsu was as much enraged as scared. Grasping his staff he faced the townsman with harshness and visible irritation. Said the latter testily – "Put off the honoured scowl. Truly the distrust of the Shukke Sama is most uncomplimentary. But – as priest of Zojoji, and on its mission, there is a passport. Women or guns with such, and those unfurnished, cannot pass the barrier. I am unfurnished." Dentatsu showed his amazement – "Yet you would journey to the capital! And...." – "Started in great haste, without time even for equipment, as can be seen – in a way. Deign to grant the request of entering in 'companion.' With this favour all will be well, and the obligation greater." Said the priest gravely – "True: and companions for the day, breaking food together, it is no great matter. But a townsman as company – the barrier guards would certainly make question." – "Write the matter in; write the matter in. They shall have answer.... For whom? The name is Jimbei, of Kanda ward; but just now a servant of Zojoji. Jimbei will be a credit to the honoured Shukke Sama. Write it in." His manner was so peremptory that the priest drew forth his writing materials. With one hand grinding his tablet of ink, with one eye watching Jimbei, he saw him disappear into the bushes. With misgiving the characters were added to the passport, a gentle forgery easy to the cleric in mind and hand. Who would not cheat barrier and customs, and feel all the better for the deed? To the misgivings were added a gasp of astonishment. From the bush appeared Jimbei clad in full raiment of a temple servant, carrying pole and the two boxes (*ryōgake*) on his shoulders, and so like to the role that Dentatsu felt as travelling in the style of his betters. "But ... in this lonely place how effect such change? How...." Jimbei quietly removed the document dangling from his fingers. "How – and why – and which

– and where – all these are for later explanation. Time presses if Sumpu is to be reached at night. Jimbei answers for the credit of the Go Shukke Sama. Now, honoured sir – down the hill with you." They were standing on the crest overlooking the lake far below. Jimbei set the example by starting off at a rapid pace. Never had priest better attendant, or one more skilled in dealing with barrier curiosity. He was loquacious, without giving information. The matter was clear, and Jimbei gave hint as to the mission and the burden. Dentatsu was given early clearance. At the top of MukOsaka Jimbei loyally restored to him the precious burden until then assumed. "Now, sir priest, be assured of Jimbei Dono's good faith. The favour has been great. The acknowledgment shall be as great. In this life the Go Shukke Sama and this Jimbei are bound in brotherhood." If Dentatsu felt grateful, he also felt a little chilled.

"A wonderful fellow! Such legs on such a small body have never been seen.... Nor such an eye. This man is as much brains as bulk. Every member is intelligence – Extraordinary!" He kept this opinion to himself. Aloud – "This Dentatsu admits his inferiority. He is worn out. Since Jimbei balks Mishima town, from there onward this foolish priest takes nag or *kago*." Was he speaking truth, or trying to get rid of him? Jimbei stopped and observed him keenly. Bah! His was the master mind over this poor cleric. "The Shukke Sama already has had test of Jimbei's wit and talk. Deign not to spit folly. Leave the matter to Jimbei, and be assured that the passage of time and space will go unobserved." Nor did the priest find it otherwise. The leagues passed on apace. At this rest shed they stopped awhile for tea, and to consume provision. At another Jimbei halted to order *sake* for himself and companion. The sun was far down as the ferrymen landed them on the further side of the Fujikawa. Okitsu? Mio no Matsubara? No indeed: passing under the walls of the Seikenji, Jimbei spoke with enthusiasm of the place famed for eatables – Sumpu town. Totomi-wan, Suruga-wan, furnished the fish, unsurpassed; the *tai* (bream) of Okitsu, famed for *sashimi* – all these, including the best *sake* in Nippon. Dentatsu sighed with weariness and anticipated pleasure of the table set. Passing through the darkness of full night the mass of a castle bulk could be made out. Then they came into the blaze of such light as a large provincial town afforded. Said Jimbei, with some exultation – "Sumpu town, and its inns of note. Eh! Honoured Shukke Sama!"

The Affair of Kishu Ke

Jimbei, as of one born and bred in the town, at once led his companion off from the castle precincts. The many lanterns hung out in the narrow streets showed this Jinshukucho to be the lodging quarter of the town. Approaching the entrance of one more conspicuous – "The Yorozuya.... Ah! Shelter for the night." The maids kneeling at the entrance chorused their welcome. Keenly they took in the prospective guests, garb mainly, possessions less conspicuous. All Nipponese travel light, and tea money is to be judged by outward appearance. "Deign to enter;" the usual mechanical and none too enthusiastic greeting. Jimbei was at home – "And the eight mat room over looking the street?... Oh! Nēsan is without memory." The girl, a little puzzled, admitted the defect and made apology. Alas! The room had been taken for one of the train of Kishu Ke. They were *samurai*, on their lord's business, and would have no near neighbours. Another room of size and suitability was available. "Honoured Shukke Sama, water for the feet." Deftly he stripped off the sandals of Dentatsu, acted the servant to perfection, and attended to his own purification with practised swiftness. Then under the guidance of the maid the room was sought. The host appeared almost as soon with the inn register. "Dentatsu, *shoke* of Jojoji; one companion – from Mishima this day." With grave face

Jimbei made the entry; and Dentatsu gave all the approval of an outraged weariness.

"And now – the bath? Nēsan, the Danna Sama is large of body and liberal of needs. No vegetation as repast for him. Just a...." Jimbei went into a huge order of food and wine to repair their tired bodies. The girl sighed in relief – "The honoured *bōzu*-san (sir priest) is most considerate. He asks but what is easily supplied." To Jimbei's supposed inquiry – "To furnish out of the usual course is never easy. The honoured priests often give trouble." A serving man stuck his nose within the *shōji*. "For the honoured guests the bath...." – "Danna, the bath." The girl stood expectant. Following her guidance the weary Dentatsu, under the manipulation of his more active companion, underwent this partial renovation. Before the *zen*, well covered with the eatables, Dentatsu sighed – "Ah! Ha! This Dentatsu is weary beyond measure. Tomorrow he will rest here. The distance...." Jimbei cut him short – "The Danna deigns to jest. The rest of a night, and all the weariness departs. Wine and food, sleep, will show the folly of such thought. Besides, the temple's important affair...." Dentatsu did not seem to be so solicitous concerning temple matters as his attendant. Jimbei gave him little chance to show it. He prattled and talked, had much to ask of *nēsan*. This shortly, and as decided – "With an early start let the beds be laid at once." Off he dragged the unwilling Dentatsu. When they returned from preparation for the night the beds were laid. Dentatsu tumbled incontinently into one, and in a moment was snoring. Jimbei sat smoking, watching him and the girl making the final preparation of the chamber for the night. As she passed close to him suddenly he seized her and drew her down to him – "Ara! Danna, this won't do at all. A maid in the inn, such service must be refused. Condescend to loosen." But Jimbei did not let her go. He drew her very close. – "Ha! Ah! Indeed one is much in love. However don't be alarmed. It is another affair. The Go Shukke Sama has a little soul in a big body. He is wearied beyond measure; yet the temple affairs require an early start. Deign to call us at the seventh hour, but be sure to say it is the sixth. Is it agreed?... For a hair ornament." The maid understood the coin and the innocent deception. Dimming the night light she took her departure. An inn of Nippon never sleeps.

Dentatsu was aroused, to find the lamp still burning brightly in the room. The maid, somewhat frightened, was vigorously shaking him. "Oya! Oya! To shake up such a big Danna, 'Tis terrific. He may deign to bestow a beating." Said Jimbei, with calm philosophy – "For the *kerai* to inconvenience his master is not to be permitted. You are of the inn service. Hence not to be reproved by strangers. It is your function to arouse." – "The sixth hour!" grumbled Dentatsu. He rubbed his eyes as one who had just gone to sleep. Jimbei carried him off to the cleaning processes of early morn. The return found the table laid with the meal. With quietness and despatch Jimbei settled all matters with the aplomb of the practised traveller. Before he was well awake Dentatsu found himself following after through the dark streets. "Surely the maid has mistaken the hour. 'Tis yet the darkness of night." – "Not likely," interjected Jimbei, as swiftly he urged him on. "The girl sees to departure every day in the year. It is the darkness of bad weather, and all the more need for haste." He looked around in surprise. They had reached the ferry at the Tegoe crossing of the Abegawa, at the edge of the town. "Naruhodo! Not a coolie has yet appeared. There is no one to carry us across the river. How now! Has the girl really mistaken the hour?... Return? Why so? That would be to look ridiculous, and the woman is not worth scolding. However, this Jimbei knows...." With misgiving and protest Dentatsu followed him a little up stream, toward the Ambai-nai or Nitta crossing. Here the broad middle space is usually left bare of flood. Jimbei began to strip.

"Naruhodo! Townsman, surely the crossing is not to be trod without the practised guidance of the coolies? This Dentatsu budges not a step...." – "Deign to be silent," was the reply. Jimbei was already in the water; with the priest's luggage and his own. With fright and interest Dentatsu watched him feel his way through the stream. Surely he was a most surprising fellow. On the other bank doubtless he would disappear at once. The big legs of Dentatsu trembled under him. He had thoughts of entrance, but the impossibility of overtaking these legs of quicksilver prevented him. "Ora pro nobis"; these departing treasures. No! Now he was returning. "Now, Go Shukke Sama, up with you." He made a back for Dentatsu, but the big man backed away. "Jimbei! Are you mad? Is Jimbei one to carry the big...." – "Body in which is lodged such a small soul? Be sure, sir priest, this Jimbei easily could shift double the weight. Up with you!... Don't put the hands over my eyes. A little higher: that's it." Off he started into the flood. The first channel was easy; barely to the thigh. Dentatsu walked across the intervening sand, with more confidence and not a word of doubting protest. Again, and readily, he mounted this surprising conveyance. The second attempt was another affair. The river flowed swift. The legs of Dentatsu were wound around the neck of Jimbei, now in water to his chest. He looked in fright and some pleasure at the waves, flicked here and there with white. Jimbei halted – "A fine sight, sir priest. Note the deep blue. It shows depth, yet this is the ford. Just below it runs far over man's head, with swift undercurrent. He who once is caught in it rises not again until the crossing is reached, far below." Said Dentatsu, scared and annoyed – "Why loiter then in such a dangerous place?" – "Because just now the world is Jimbei's world." The tone of voice, the look up he gave, froze the soul of Dentatsu.

"Just consider, sir priest. A movement, and the honoured Go Shukke Sama is food for fishes. His disappearance accounted for, his luggage, the two thousand *ryō* of the temple, pass to Jimbei as his heir, and none to make report. The honoured Shukke Sama, is he prepared?" Dentatsu was no fool. This man was in earnest for the moment. With all the calmness of a desperate position he made terms – "Life is everything. Deign to place this foolish priest on solid ground. Jimbei takes the coin, goes unscathed, without word now or hereafter. The priest's word for it – and surely Jimbei fears not for himself." He clung fast to Jimbei's neck. The latter had gone off into a most outrageous peal of laughter which almost shook his freight from the perch aloft. Then slowly and carefully he proceeded into the shallows, set down his charge on the further bank – "A magnificent compliment: but no more of this. Perhaps now the Go Shukke Sama will have trust in Jimbei, submit to his guidance. For once in earnest, the escape was a narrow one.... Ah! Ha! Ha! Ha! How scared!" Dentatsu did not deny it – "More than frightened; thoroughly scared." He scanned his companion. "A most surprising fellow! Surely...." He was perplexed. But Jimbei paid no attention to his questioning deferential manner. He was plainly the master – "Come now! All haste is to be made." Urging the pace soon they were amid the hills. The white light of dawn was approaching as they were reaching the top of a difficult climb. "The Utsunoya-toge (pass)," said Jimbei. A peculiar vibration in his voice made Dentatsu look at him with surprise. His mouth was set. His eyes shone colder than ever. Every faculty of the man was awake and alert. Silent he halted, put down the pack on the steps of a little wayside shrine, drew out his pipe to smoke. "Beyond is the Tsuta no Hosomichi, running along the mountain side for some *chō*; the 'slender road of Ivy,' for it is no wider than a creeper." – "A bad place!" mechanically murmured Dentatsu. "A very bad place!" was the grave reply.

Then the sound of steps was heard. A man, puffing, came up on the run. He addressed himself with respect to Jimbei – "Honoured chief, they enter on the pass." – "Good: now – vamoose; but be at hand." The man saluted, to Jimbei and the priest, and disappeared in the direction whence he came. "Vamoose? Vamoose? What and why this word vamoose?"

– "Shut up!" was the emphatic reply of Jimbei. His eye turned to wayside shrine, close by at the summit of the pass. "Now, in with you, sir priest. No word or motion, if life be valued.... In with you." Dentatsu looked him all over. In resentment? If he felt it, he did not dare to show it. Mechanically he turned and huddled himself within the grating. Jimbei forced it in on him, for the space would but hold the big body of the priest. He had hardly done so when another man came running up, almost breathless – "Chief! They are at hand." – "Good: vamoose." – "Again 'vamoose'", grumbled Dentatsu openly. "Why such strange words; and at least why not explain them?" – "Ah! Ha! A noisy priest; these clerics can do nothing but clack, clack, like a parcel of geese or women. Even the best of them – who thus consorts with Jimbei. Remember, Bozu – silence, or the Go Shukke Sama finds Nirvana – not Gion; or was it Chion." With a silent ferocious laugh, or expression of such, he disappeared into the bushes.

But few moments passed. Dentatsu wriggled uneasily in his robes, the only motion space permitted. Then was heard the merry sound of bells. A pack train appeared; or rather two horses, one as carrier. A *samurai* rode in front; another followed on foot. Four or five grooms were in attendance. Close by the shrine, at the top of the ascent, they halted to get wind after this last steep pull. "What a splendid sight! Naruhodo, Gemba Dono! The sun rises from the bosom of the waters. How blue they seem! The hills take shape in the dawn's light. Truly the start, so inconveniently early, is repaid in part. One could stay here forever ... what call you this place?... Tsuta no Hosomichi? And the resort of highwaymen. But the *samurai* has his sword. Such fellows are not of the kind to trouble. Much more so a *tanka* couplet to celebrate the beauty of the spot." He laughed, and his companion swaggered to the front of the shrine, with that peculiar hip motion of his caste. Dentatsu held his breath. The grooms chanted the few lines of a song – "The eight *ri* of Hakone – the horse's pack; the Oigawa – its wide flood, not so." Slowly they rose to follow the masters. He who walked preceded. The pack horse followed. The rider was well engaged in the narrow way. The grooms were preparing to follow. Then a man burst forth from the bushes at the roadside. "Atsu!" The *samurai* had but hand on his sword hilt when his assailant had cut deep into shoulder and pap. His companion tried to turn. Then Dentatsu saw the animal he rode stagger and fall. The rider had but time to throw himself to the ground. Before he could rise his head rolled off a dozen paces, then bounded down the steep slope. Striding over the body smoking in blood, Jimbei grasped the rein of the pack horse. The grooms, who had looked on eyes agog, took to flight down the pass as they had come. The whole affair had not taken two minutes.

Gasping with fright Dentatsu allowed himself to be dragged from the shrine. "Ah! Ha! Ha! A surprising fellow! Such activity was never shown by man. Truly Jimbei is of the hobgoblin kind." Jimbei was once more transformed. His costume of priests' attendant had been resumed. The carrying boxes, now much heavier, were ready to shoulder. Gravely he indicated the burden. "Four thousand *ryō* there; a thousand *ryō* to be carried elsewhere. But now there is need for great haste. Neither Jimbei nor the Go Shukke Sama is to be found in these parts. On with you, sir priest." – "Ah! Jimbei! Jimbei! A strange fellow indeed! What manner of company has this Dentatsu fallen in with?" – "This is no time for questions – or answers," was Jimbei's stern reply. "The relation evidently is for life. Jimbei recognizes it.... Yes, the crest is that of Kishu Ke; the money, funds remitted to his treasury. Hence all the greater need to hasten." Speed they did, by paths and shorter ways unknown to Dentatsu as frequent traveller of this road, and which spared the Hamana bight and rest at the tea sheds of the Tokaido. Fright urged on Dentatsu without protest; settled purpose hastened Jimbei. Thus Yoshida post town was reached in good time to inn, for the priest was half dead with fatigue.

Jimbei surveyed his charge, critically and with much kindness, as one does what has been of greatest use to him. "Not a step further can this Dentatsu go." It was not refusal; it was plain assertion of fact; and Jimbei agreed. "There is no longer need for haste. Two, three days stoppage, with the best of food and wine shall be the reward of the honoured Shukke Sama. Nay, until thoroughly restored." They had come from the bath and were seated at a table loaded with wine and food. Dentatsu prepared to eat. Just then the landlord stuck his head in between the *shōji*. His face was anxious and frightened. "Regret is felt. On Utsunoyama, at the crossing of the pass, the honoured money train of Kishu Ke has been held up and robbed. 'Tis a great affair; by some notable robber! At Yoshida none are allowed exit or entrance during the next six days. People and strangers are to undergo strict examination. Deign the honoured pardon, but ... after all the charges are to be met for the detention." The morsel then being conveyed to the mouth of Dentatsu stopped short. A warning look from Jimbei nearly made him choke. The townsman was all suavity and glee – "How fortunate! The honoured Shukke Sama, foot sore, would rest several days. And at no expense! The generosity of Matsudaira Ko passes measure. Are we not lucky, Danna?" To the host – "So it makes no difference. But at this distance...." The host shrugged his shoulders. "It would seem so; but the order is official. The notice came by boat from Oigawa. The whole Tokaido is up – from Yoshida to Numazu town." – "And why not to Edo and the capital (Kyoto)," Jimbei laughed. The host laughed too. Well satisfied with his guests' satisfaction he withdrew. Dentatsu did but blink.

The meal removed Jimbei sat in apparent thought. "A boat – and Yoshida! Who would have thought it? Ah! The wicked are not to escape punishment. Three feet nearer Heaven – on a stake; and one's belly full of wind holes – from the spears. Go Shukke Sama, the crime was a dastardly one. Five thousand *ryō*! Surely it means crucifixion on the embankment. We will furnish poles for plover – to roost upon." Dentatsu made a sign of frightened repulsion. He could not speak. Jimbei seemed to catch an idea. "Nēsan! Nēsan! keep the honoured Shukke Sama company over his wine. There is a purchase to make.... By the house? No such trouble asked. It is for *waraji*, with cloth in front and rear, indispensable.... Not found here? Nay, these eyes saw them on entering the town. Someone will get ahead in the purchase – with great regret. The place was seen, but not knowing the streets it is not to be described." When the girl carried out the dishes, to bring in more wine, Dentatsu raised heavy reproachful eyes – "Then Jimbei would run away, leave the priest in the lurch." He cast a look at the hateful *ryōgake*, stuffed with recent spoil. Jimbei froze him into silence – "From the town there is no escape. Leave the matter to Jimbei. Drink: even if the liquor chokes." – "A means of escape will be found?" – "Truly a big body and a cowardly heart. Why, man this but a difficult place. Jimbei leaves, to find an exit." – "Just so!" was the gloomy answer of the priest. He put his head in his hands. Meanwhile Jimbei betook himself to the front. To avoid annoyance he borrowed an inn lantern. With its broad mark of "Masuya," the name of the inn, he sallied out into the darkness.

He was gone nearly a whole watch. Dentatsu, assured of his desertion, was in despair. He had relied on the fertile mind of this scamp. Ah! What a predicament this fellow had got him into. Then the voice of Jimbei sounded at his shoulder. Dentatsu almost leaped up. Instead he gulped down the *sake*, until then barely touched, to the maid's great astonishment. "Surely the Danna Sama must be ill." – "More likely tired, than unwell. But the wine will make it pass. The *waraji*? Here they are." He laughed as he drew them from his bosom. The girl was all astonishment. They were just as described; such as were never seen west of Hakone. Truly a sharp-sighted guest! When alone Jimbei spoke briefly – "Take courage. The matter is arranged." Said Dentatsu, heavy-eyed – "The mission settled? Has some other lost his life at Jimbei's hand?" Jimbei laughed; then frowned. "Neither blood nor coin does Jimbei spill for mere pastime. He has purpose." He handled the *waraji*. Said Dentatsu in some amaze – "Where did you get them?" – "In Odawara." – "Has Jimbei been to Odawara?" – "Just so: but not now. Jimbei is no Tengu Sama. Did not the Go Shukke Sama take food at Odawara? This kind are only found there; and pretexts are always needed to range a town in darkness. The mission is performed. Be assured that before day these very people will urge departure.... How so? Jimbei is not without friends; and has done his own part as well. The train is laid, and in all quarters of Yoshida town the fire will break out. The wind blows strong, and ... 'Tis them or us." His look was so cold as to freeze. Dentatsu, in ecstasy of gratitude did but seize his hands and murmur – "Wonderful man – truly a great captain!" For the first time Jimbei looked a genuine benevolence.

Dentatsu pushed the covers partly away and sat up in bed. Severe had been the chiding of Jimbei – "Honoured Shukke Sama, such conduct will never do. Fortunate it is that the event is postponed but an hour or so. Nēsan surely is amazed at the sudden abstinence of the Go Shukke Sama from food and drink. Moreover there is work to be done. The body unnourished, it gives way. Deign to rest. Be assured the urging will come from others." These the final words before the townsman-bandit had himself dropped off into soundest slumbers. Dentatsu watched him, with confidence and some awe. Smoothed out in sleep and under the influence of some pleasant dream, Jimbei was as harmless looking as one of the doves in the temple of the war god Hachiman. He leaned over and would wake him. "*Urusai!* Annoying fellow! Ah! This *bōzu* is part hare, part ass, part swine. When not braying, he is stuffing, or ears up in fright. Deign to rest, honoured priest. Legs and body will soon have enough to do." Again he turned over; and again the snores rose loud. Dentatsu could not sleep. He lay awake, listening to the diminishing sounds of inn life.

The temple bells were striking the sixth hour. The sound was a strange one. The strokes of the hour ran into one continued roar. Jan-jan-jan – pon-pon – gon-gon – cries of men, the racket of wooden clappers and of drums, were now added to the uproar. For a few moments Dentatsu stood the increasing excitement. Through the cracks of the closed *amado* he could see a reddish glare, becoming brighter and brighter. He sat up and roughly shook Jimbei by the shoulder. "Oh! This rascally cleric. Nothing will satisfy his stupidity, but to carry it to extremes. Honoured Shukke Sama, wait the urgency of others; don't supply it. We at least lack not preparation.... Ah!" The *shōji* were thrown hastily back. The host of the inn appeared, his face pale and lips trembling. "Honoured guests! Still in bed? Deign at once to flee. The town is in a blaze. Every quarter has its conflagration which walks apace; and in this gale hopeless to overcome...." – "Don't talk folly," sleepily answered Jimbei. "Is not the town in ward for these six days. Why disturb oneself? Let all burn together?" The host wrung his hands – "Honoured sirs, the blame and punishment falls on this Masuya if injury befall its guests. All lies wide open. Deign at once to leave.... Naruhodo!" His mouth was wide open. Jimbei and Dentatsu rose as on springs, full clad, *waraji* on their feet. The way "lies wide open." This was the watchword to Jimbei. "Edokko (sons of Edo) always are ready, and need no urging." With this genial explanation he and Dentatsu shouldered past the astonished landlord. If the latter would have had suspicions they were thwarted or postponed by the cries which rose below.

His own main house was now in flames. Hands to head in this confusion of ideas he abandoned all thought of his guests and rushed down below. As if in his own home, with no guide but the outer glare Jimbei passed to the inn rear. In the darkness of the passage he had stopped, leaned down and struck a light. The precious *ryōgake* on his shoulders, with the priest he took to the fieldpaths in the rear of the town. The ground was level; the land rich rice field with its interspersed and picturesque clumps of trees and bamboo, its verdure bowered villages. From time to time they looked back at the sky, flaming red, and in its darker outer parts a mass of glittering flying sparks "like the gold dashes on aventurine lacquer ware."

For two days they had lain at Okazaki town, Dentatsu incapable of movement after the mad run along the classic highway in the darkness of that fearful night. As refugees from the stricken town they met with kind reception. The greater part of Yoshida town lay in ashes; and so great the disaster, so unsuspected the cause, that men looked rather to the hand of Heaven than of human kind for the source of such punishment. Jimbei spoke gravely as the two stood on the long bridge leading to Yahagi across the river. "The luck of one, the misfortune of another – 'twas the life of the Go Shukke Sama and of this Jimbei against the lives and fortunes of those wretched people. And is there aught to outweigh life?" The priest nodded a lugubrious and pleased assent to this plain doctrine. "It is just as well the host of Masuya lost life as well as goods. He might have made plaint, and had too long a tongue.... Jimbei could not foresee such weakness in so huge a body." He looked Dentatsu over with a little kindly contempt. "And so the honoured Shukke Sama would ask the name of this Jimbei? Honoured sir, the favour of your ears – for Kosaka Jinnai, son of Heima of that name, descendant of the Kosaka known to fame in service with Shingen Ko of Kai. Times have changed, and misfortune driven Jinnai to seek revenge for his lord's undoing." He mocked a little; the tone was too unctuously hypocritical. Then abruptly – "Sir priest, here we part. Your way lies ahead to Gifu town. Delay not too much, until the lake (Biwa-ko) is reached. Travel in company, for Jinnai, though his men are numbered by the thousand, controls not all the craft. A priest can scent a true priest. Seek out your kind.... Ha! You make a face.... Here: two hundred *ryō*. The monastery is none too generous, and would have you live – abroad. *Sutra* and prayers are not amusing. By face and years the honoured Shukke Sama loves the sex as well as the best of his kind. The very shadow of a monastery is prolific. More merriment is to be found with the girls of Gion than with those who dance the *kagura* (sacred dances) at Higashiyama. Besides, these are for your betters. If further off – seek Shimabara (the noted pleasure quarter). Go buy a Tayu; the funds are ample and not to be hoarded.... There need be no hesitation. 'Tis money of no thief. The prince robs the public; and Jinnai robs the princely thief. No trader ever has hung himself from the house beam for act of Jinnai; and more than one owes credit and freedom from a debtor's slavery to his aid."

It was with thanks, the parting with a man famed by deed before one's eyes, that Dentatsu slowly passed on to the bridge. From its further end he could see the road leading into the Nakasendo hills. Long he waited until a diminutive figure, hastening along it, appeared from time to time between scattered houses on the outskirts of Okazaki town. Then in earnest he took his own way, partly impelled by fright and anxiety at loss of his companion and being thrown on the resources of his own wits. He felt for a time as a blind man deprived of his staff. It was years after that Yoshida Hatsuemon, he who died so bravely at Osaka, accompanied Marubashi Chuya to the new fencing room opened at Aoyama Edo by the teacher of the *yawatori* – a new style of wrestling introduced from

Morokoshi (China) – of spear exercise (*sōjutsu*), of jujutsu. Marubashi Chuya had tried the new exponent of these arts, and found him master in all but that of the spear, in which himself he was famed as teacher. At this time (Shoho 3rd year – 1646) the crisis of Jinnai's fate and the conspiracy of the famous Yui Shosetsu were both approaching issue. To his amazement Hatsuemon recognized in Osada Jinnai the one time Jimbei of the days when he had journeyed the Tokaido in priestly robe and under the name of Dentatsu. The recognition was mutual, its concealment courteously discreet on the part of both men. Shosetsu appreciated the merits, the audacity, and the certain failure ahead of Jinnai's scheme. The better remnants he would gather to himself. Yui Shosetsu Sensei aimed to pose as a new Kusunoki Masashige, whose picture was the daily object of his prayers and worship. All was grist to the mill of his designs; but not association with such a chief – or lieutenant – as Kosaka Jinnai. Forewarned Marubashi and Yoshida (Dentatsu) held coldly off and sought no intimacy. Thus watched by keen wits of greater comprehension Jinnai rushed on his course into the claws of Aoyama Shuzen and the meshes of the Tokugawa code for criminals of his class.

If Old Acquaintance Be Forgot

Thus Kosaka Jinnai, under the name of Osada, at the beginning of Shoho 2nd year (1645) was established at Aoyama Harajuku-mura. For a gentleman of such abilities his pretensions were modest. It is true that he hung out a gilt sign before his fencing hall, with no boasting advertisement of his qualities as teacher. Yet his fame quickly became such that students flocked to him by the score. In a few months, on plea of being over-stocked, he was turning away all who would seek his instruction. Some he could not refuse – retainers of *yashiki* in his vicinity. But the generality of his disciples were a very rough lot; and this finer quality of his flock were carefully segregated, came and went at their appointed time apart from the common herd; and as matter of fact profited much from their teacher, and knew very little about him. Which was exactly the aim of Jinnai. This was remembered of him later.

There is but one domestic episode connected with this period, so short and purposely obscure in its duration. About the time of his first establishment a villager, on visit to Edo town, chanced upon the practice hour of Jinnai. The years had passed, yet the rustic had no difficulty in recognizing in the Sensei the one time Jinnosuke. When later he sought a more personal interview the great man was found courteous but freezing cold in the reception. The news from Tsukuba district was of that mixed character not to afford any exuberant pleasure. His reputation for bad company had gone abroad, though no great deeds of wickedness had been attributed to him. With the devotion of a daughter his wife had nourished the old folk, brought up her two daughters. On her shoulders during all these years had rested the management of these small affairs. The girls grew toward womanhood. When O'Kiku was in her seventeenth year Jisuke had died – unconsoled at the ill turn fortune had played him in this unfilial son. These grandparents had lingered out the years, crippled and helpless, urging a re-marriage on O'Ichi – always refused on the plea that such relation was for two lives. Jisuke Dono had united them, and he alone could separate her from Jinnai. She sought no second relation herself and plead against it; and Jisuke would not force it on this filial daughter, who thus would block the disinheritance of the son. Thus the farm stood, ready for the master on his return. Truly the whole village wondered, and admired her filial conduct.

To most of this Jinnai listened with indifference. "These girls – their looks and age?" Replied the man – "O'Kiku now is seventeen years; O'Yui Dono has fifteen years. Truly they are the village beauties, and rarely found in such life, for they would spare the mother all labour." He spoke with enthusiasm. "Then the mother lives?" The man shook his head – "The grave mound yet is very fresh. When she died she spoke no word of Jinnosuke Dono." Boldly he looked in rebuke at the unfilial man. Jinnai, if anything, showed annoyance. The old woman alive would have kept the inconvenient wife – the three women – at the distance of Tsukuba's slopes. His plans admitted of no possible descent on him at Aoyama Harajuku. Briefly he made request for the favour of bearing a message. Gladly the mission was accepted. With a discouraging cordiality in the leave taking the old acquaintance took his way back to the village. With something of a flutter O'Ichi opened and ran out the scroll he brought – "Unexpected and gratifying the meeting with Tarobei San. The news of the village, not pleasing, is subject of condolence. Deign to observe well the instructions here given. The time will come when a summons to Edo town will be in order. At present the establishment is new and tender, and stands not the presence of strangers to the town. Condescend to show the same care in the present as in the past. The farm and its tenure is left to the hands of Ichi. As for these girls, look well to their care. They are said to be handsome and reputed the daughters of this Jinnai. Obey then his command. These are no mares for the public service, or for the private delectation of some rich plebeian. Service in a *yashiki* need not be refused, and jumps more with the plans and purposes of Jinnai. Keep this well in mind, and await the ripeness of time. With salutation...." Such the cold greeting through the years. "Reputed the daughters of this Jinnai." Ah! He thought and knew the years turned the beauty Ichi into the worn and wrinkled country hag of nearly forty years, only too ready to market her girls for her own necessities. She was ill and worn in her service. Here Jinnai was to be recognized. He was the man of his caste, with contempt for the plebeian he turned to his uses, but who must have no intimate contact with him or his.

Edo town was in a turmoil. North, East, South of the town the lives and purses of men who walked were at hazard. Plainly some band was operating in these quarters of the town. Aoyama Shuzen was hard put to it. His arrests, outrageous and barbarous, increased with his difficulties. Some specimens have been instanced. His bands of *yakunin* lay out in a wide net around the threatened quarters of the city. On the outskirts of Honjo a country mansion would be fired and plundered. In Okubo a temple (the Jisho-in) was clean gutted of its treasury – without notice to its neighbours. Not a sign of the spoil could be traced until the Shoshidai of Kyoto sent as present to the suzerain a most valued hanging picture (*kakemono*) of Shubun, picked up for him in Osaka town, and worthy of being seen by the eyes of Edo's ruler. Murder and rape were the common accompaniments of these crimes, the doers of which left no witness, if resisted. *Tsujikiri*, cutting down wayfarers merely to test the value of a sword blade, found revival. Such murders in the outward wards of the city were of nightly occurrence. Yet they all centred in Aoyama's own precinct; starting forth from the fencing hall of Osada Jinnai. What a band they were! At this long distant date the names read with that tinge of the descriptive which such nomenclature gives – Yamaguchi Chiyari, Kanagawa Koni, Sendai no Okami, Okayama Koshin, Kumamoto Kondo, Tsukuba Ende; their great chief being Kosaka Jinnai.

The eleventh month (December) was closing its first decade. The wine shop at Shiba Nihon Enoki was celebrating a first opening, a feast in progress for some hours, and to be maintained for the few ensuing days. The enthusiasm was at its height, and the wine flowed like water. Some few guests, who could, tottered home at midnight. Clerks and domestics – there is little difference in Nipponese practice – shut up the premises as well as their drunken state permitted. Those who had still some trace of sobriety proceeded to guzzle what was left in the opened casks. When the hour of the ox (1 am) struck, not a man in the place knew front from rear. They lay sprawled out dead drunk – as were some of the women. This was the hour watched for and chosen by Jinnai. Such of the females as could give the alarm were bound and gagged by the masked invaders. Then they gutted place and store-houses. With bending backs they betook themselves over the hills the short distance to Harajuku. Here Jinnai, in the unwise benevolence of the bandit chieftain, gave rein to the licentiousness of these favourites of his mature age, to these lieutenants and agents in the great movement for which all this loot was gathered. The circuit was formed. The heads of wine barrels just stolen were broached. The grizzled, tousled member who officiated as cook, and as such had been left behind to his own offices, produced the feast of fish and delicacies in celebration of the great deed and accomplishment. "Now is the turn of this company," said Jinnai in pleasant reference to the victims of the raid. "A real banquet of extreme intoxication. Alas! We have no *tabo*.... Too dangerous a loot," commented Jinnai amid the roar of laughter and approval. "Use and abuse go together; and the necessity to slit the throats of such chattering parrots. For this company the remains would give trouble, and might bring unexpected visitors about our ears. Be virtuous – and spare not the wine." The advice was followed to the letter. Soon the house of Jinnai was a match for that of the looted wine shop.

With the light of the December dawn a metal dealer (*doguya*) was trudging his way over the sifted cover of an early snow fall. He lived thereabouts; often had had small jobs of mending the weapons and implements of this sturdy establishment of Jinnai, hence had some good will to its owner, which was more than could be said of most of the neighbours. To his surprise he noted the wide open gate to Jinnai's entrance, the many tracks leading within. Strange sounds were heard. He would venture on a look. "Oya! Oya!" The man stood stock still, half in fright and half in a wondering concupiscence of curiosity, as he took in the riotous vision of the fencing hall. Some twenty men lay scattered in different postures – all dead drunk. The noise arose from their wide open snoring mouths and nostrils. A score of wine casks lay tumbled, the liquor spilled on the *tatami*. Mingled with the remains of food and vomit were stained cups and dirty plates. More suggestive to his frightened eyes was the heap of packages laid out at the side. Some of them had been opened, and displayed the varied assortment of the contents. Most conspicuous was Jinnai, who had gone to sleep with the bag of all the coin found in the wine shop as pillow. Ah! Ha! The scene needed no interpreter. This was a mere band of thieves, the house their den. The man stole to the kitchen. He knew his ground, and that in these bachelor quarters no women would be stirring. Jinnai was a misogynist – on business principles. Hearing a stir he would have fled at the rear, but the body of the drunken cook, the intermediary of their dealings, lay square across the exit. Fearful he made his return. As he passed out the front – "Alas! Alas! What is to be done? The Sensei, so just and prompt in his dealings, so kind in his patronage, is a mere thief. Report is to be made. As witness this Sentaro will send the Sensei to the execution ground. But the honoured mother – no trouble is to be brought on her. By other discovery ... and perchance someone has seen this entrance! What's to be done? What's to be done?" He did one thing in his perplexity. He shut the outside door, closed fast the big gate, and departed by the service gate. Thus no others should intrude on this rash man; and likewise Jinnai had no inkling of his visit. Then the *doguya* fled to his home, so blue in the face and overcome as to frighten the household. They gathered round the unhappy man with hot water to drink as restorative. "Had he seen a ghost?"

All day he pondered. Then he told his story to Aikawa Chudayu. The officer was indebted to Sentaro; for many a hint in his operations. "Deign somehow, honoured *yōnin*, that the Sensei be allowed to escape. For this Sentaro to appear as witness will bring down the curse of one sure to be visited with execution. Condescend this favour." Chudayu looked on him with approval, but shook his head in doubt – "Never mind the curse of one dead. The service to the suzerain is most opportune. Thus surely there will be reward, not punishment. For the present you cannot be allowed to leave, but the mother shall suffer no anxiety. There is much serious matter against this man; perchance no testimony will be called for.... Strange he should be caught thus; on both sides, and in accordance." He looked over the scroll he held in his hands, and with it took his way to his master's apartment. Thus it was he could spring on Shuzen the greater affair concerning the long missing man. Making his report of the tale of the *doguya* he passed over the scroll he held in his hand – "The fellow is caught in both quarters. There are three of these *rōnin*, most intimate. Of this Marubashi Chuya little favourable is known, but he has the support of Yui Sensei, the noted master of the Ushigome Enoki fencing room, and favourite of all but Hida no Kami, whom he would rival in attainment. Shibata Saburobei and this Kato Ichiemon seem honourable men, of clean lives and reputation beyond the fact of being *rōnin*. All experts at arms they live by teaching one form or other of the practice. Curiosity led Chuya to the encounter of this Osada at his fencing hall, to find him more than his match at everything but his favourite art of the spear. But here lies the point. Later he returned, in company with a one time *shoke* of the Zojoji. As Dentatsu the priest had met with Jinnai, and nearly suffered at his hands. In what way he did not say, but told Chuya that the man's real name was Kosaka – of the stock of Kosaka Dansho no Chuden of Kai; of him your lordship already has had experience in early days. At last he comes into the net and under such fair terms."

Aoyama did know his man; even after all these years. He had ripened much. Why not Jinnai? He would have gone himself, and chafed at not doing so; but his satellites showed him the lack of dignity in such procedure. The magistrate in person to take a common thief! Darkness offered chance of escape; so with dawn a host of *yakunin* was sent under a *yoriki* and several *dōshin*. Aikawa Chudayu himself volunteered. Jinnai and his men were not yet up. On the previous day awaking amid the unseemly debris of the night's debauch, with no clear recollection of its progress and ending, the chief's first alarm had been dissipated by finding the outer gate locked. The unbarred wicket was attributed to an oversight which hardly would attract notice from the outside. Indeed he had not been the first to rise and take tale of his companions, to ascertain which one had occasion to open it and go without. With such a chief few would admit negligence. The day passed without notice. Confidence was restored. Now from the outside was heard a hum of voices. "On his lordship's business! On his lordship's business!" The cries came together with an irruption of *yakunin* into the entrance hall, Jinnai and his men promptly sprang to arms. A scattered fight began, with none too great stomach of the officers before the stout resistance offered. It was no great matter to reach a ladder to the loft. Jinnai was the last man up. The more daring to follow was laid low with an arrow shot from above, and the ladder disappeared heavenward. Panels now were thrust back, short bows brought into use, and almost before they had thought to fight or flee the constables had five of their men stretched out on the *tatami*.

Before the shower of missiles they could but retreat. At the request for aid Aoyama Shuzen was in a rage. There was now no preventing his departure. Mounting his horse off he rode from Kanda-mura toward Harajuku-mura. But it had taken some little time for the messenger to come; and more for Aoyama with his staff to go. Meanwhile much had taken place. The ward constables had joined the *yakunin* of Shuzen. The place completely surrounded, *tatami* were taken from the neighbouring houses for use as shields against the arrows. Then on signal a concerted rush of the hardiest was made. Pouring in, with ladders raised aloft; tumbling each other into the ditches, in the confusion pummelling each other with mighty blows, and in consequence securing stout whacks from the enraged recipients; the unlucky constables were soon indistinguishable in their coating of mud and blood. The outrageous ruffians, however, were soon tumbled from the posts of vantage and precise aim by well directed thrusts. A dozen men poured up the ladders and through broken panels into the loft above. Here in the uncertain light they hesitated. The figures of the foe could be seen, armed and ready for an arrow flight. Then a shout was raised from below. Stifling smoke poured up from every quarter. The scene was illuminated by the blazing figures of the archers, for these were old armour and weapons, lay figures stuffed with straw and meant but to gain precious moments of respite. The *yakunin* now had themselves to save. The retreat was as disorderly as at their first advent, but their rear was not galled by aught but flying sparks and burning timbers. Discomfited they watched the blazing mass of Jinnai's once establishment; watched it until it was a mere mass of ashes and charred beams.

Jinnai had been long prepared for such an adventure. The *yakunin* at first driven back he followed his company through the tunnel leading to beneath a subsidiary shrine in the grounds of the neighbouring temple of the Zenkwoji. Here he dismissed them, with hasty division of the raided coin, and instructions to their chiefs to meet him at the festival of the Owari no Tsushima in the fifth month (June). Himself he would go north, to give notice and gather his recruits. Thus exposed at Edo, the great uprising now must centre in Osaka. They scattered to their different courses; and thus Jinnai failed to meet the enraged Aoyama Shuzen, now present on the scene. But even the harsh discipline of their master had to yield to the piteous appearance of his men in their discomfiture. Aikawa Chudayu bent low in most humble apology. They had underestimated the man, had virtually allowed him to escape – "Naruhodo! The figures were of straw, and no wonder yielded so readily to the spear. Only the sight of the flames rising amid the armour betrayed the deceit in the gloom of the loft. Deign to excuse the negligence this once." A *dōshin*, an old and experienced officer, spoke almost with tears. Aoyama gave a "humph!" Then looking over this mud stained, blear eyed, bloody nosed, ash dusted band of his confederates he began to chuckle at the battered and ludicrous composition. All breathed again. But when he had re-entered his *yashiki*, and was left to himself, without concubine for service, or Jinnai for prospective amusement, then indeed he stamped his feet, his belly greatly risen. Alas! Alas! How could Yokubei Sama find a substitute for the one; and secure the real presence of the other?

The Shrine of the Jinnai-bashi

It was one of those small Fudo temples, tucked away on a shelf of the hillside just above the roadway, embowered in trees, with its tiny fall and rock basin for the enthusiastic sinner bathing in the waters of this bitterly cold day. The whole construction of shrine, steep stone steps, and priestly box for residence, so compactly arranged with the surrounding Nature as to be capable of very decent stowage into a case – much like those of the dolls of the third or fifth month. The nearest neighbour was the Shichimen-shi – the seven faced Miya – in this district so dotted even to day with ecclesiastical remnants, from Takenotsuka to Hanabatakemura on the north edge of Edo – Tokyo. However it was not one of their resident priests who stood at the *rōka* of the incumbent cleric seeking a night's lodging. The kindly oldish *dōmori* (temple guardian) looked him over. Nearly fifty years of age, two teeth lacking in the front, his head shaved bald as one of the stones from the bed of the Tonegawa, a tired hard eye, thin cruel and compressed lips added nothing to the recommendation of the rosary (*juzu*) and pilgrim's staff (*shakujō*) grasped in hand; and indeed the whole air of the man savoured of the weariness of debauch, and of strife with things of this world rather than of battles against its temptations. Yet the wayfarer was greeted with kindness, his tale of woe heard. His own quarters – a flourishing tribute to the mercies of the eleven-faced Kwannon, with a side glance at Amida – had gone up in smoke the day before. Naught remained but the store-house, with its treasure of *sutra* scrolls and hastily removed *ihai* of deceased parishioners. The disaster was not irreparable. His enthusiastic followers already sought to make good the damage. Himself he would find aid from the cult in Edo.

Kosaka Jinnai, for the unfortunate cleric was none else, seated himself in the comfortable quarters of the *dōmori*, to earn his shelter by a talk which in interest richly repaid the meagre fare, and made amends for no prepossessing exterior. On his pleading weariness the *dōmori* got out *futon* and spread a couch for the guest. This suited Jinnai's real purpose, which was not to loiter close to Edo and Aoyama's claws, but to push on that night toward Tsukuba and old friends, and recent ones he knew he would find on its none too savoury slopes. But Heaven does not permit the wicked a continued license in ill deeds. The weariness and indisposition pleaded, in part genuine, rapidly grew worse. The chilled feeling passed into its palpable and physical exposition. With alarm the *dōmori* watched the progress of this ailment. His hot drinks and solicitude would not produce the needed perspiration. Instead the chill was followed by high fever and delirium. The medical man, summoned from the village, was taking leave – "A plain case of ague from Shimosa's swamps. Is he friend or relative of the honoured Shukke Sama? No?... Alas! A case of resting under the shade of the same tree; of drinking from the same stream. Deign to have a care with this fellow. He says strange things, and raves of robbery and strife – 'I am Kosaka Jinnai; the famous Jinnai.' Truly you are to be pitied at being saddled with such a guest. Doubtless it is affliction for some deed committed in a previous life, a connection of two worlds between the honoured Shukke Sama and this doubtful guest."

The *dōmori* was an old and foolish fellow; but still able to catch the warning tone and manner of the leech. With anxiety he went to his guest. Jinnai was sleeping under influence of the draught administered, and on the word of the medical man was insured for some hours unconsciousness under the drug. Placing food and drink close to hand, out into the darkness went the sturdy old chap. The day saw him at Harajuku-mura, wandering around the site of ashes and charred beams of the late conflagration. No sign of renovation was there found. For satisfaction and a meal he turned to the benches of a near-by eating shed. His inquiries confirmed his own fears and aroused the suspicions of others. "Truly the honoured Bozu San must live far from this part of Edo. These ruins are of no temple. Here stood the fencing room of one Osada Jinnai, a *rōnin*. This fellow turned out to be a famous bandit and escaped criminal; no less a person than the Kosaka Jinnai engaged in the attempt of years ago to carry off or slay the Tenju-in-Den of the suzerain's House. Heaven's vengeance long since visited the others. Now Aoyama Dono seeks this fellow. Is he friend or relative that thus inquiry is made?" The *dōmori* in fright cut short his meal and questions. Paying his scot he made off in a hurry. Soon after one of Shuzen's spies passing, he was informed of the matter. Then the hue and cry was raised through the ranks to find this suspicious cleric.

From Jinnai the *dōmori* got little satisfaction on return at dark. He found him sitting, with natural and restored presence, smoking, and measuring him with the cold cynical glance which froze the marrow in his spine. "Ha! Ah! The honoured Shukke Sama wanders far and long." The priest did not attempt to conceal fright or mission – "Honoured guest, the poor quarters of this foolish cleric are open to the afflicted of his kind. But Kosaka Dono, deign at once to remove from here. Already the *yakunin* are on the trail. Yourself, in the mad fits, you make no concealment of name and exploits. Found here, discredit is brought upon the Buddha, and ruin to this his follower. Condescend at once to seek other quarters." He looked earnestly and pleadingly at the bandit chief, with squawking groan to lower his head almost to the *tatami*. Jinnai's eye went through him in his cold wrath – "Be assured of it; that I am Kosaka Jinnai; and hence one without fear. Let the *yakunin* come – to their own destruction. These quarters just suit this Jinnai – for the time. Cowardly and foolish cleric, you would prattle and bring trouble on yourself with that wheel of a tongue. Then get you hence. This Jinnai undertakes the charge and exercise of the weapons of the furious god. Bah! They are but of wood." To the horror of the priest he gave the wooden Fudo which adorned the chamber such a whack that the unfortunate and flawed divinity parted into its aged fragments. "What! You still delay!" A hand of iron was laid on the old fellow's neck. Jinnai bent him to the ground. He looked around for implement. None was better to hand than part of the outraged god. Holding firm his victim, and raising his robes, a vigorous hand applied to the priest's cushions such a drubbing as he had not had since childhood's days. Then grasping him neck and thigh Jinnai cast him out onto the *rōka* and down the steps which led to it. The old fellow heard the *amado* close tight with noise. Thus the unwilling god entered on the service of this new satellite.

The hue and cry was loud. In the cold of the night the *dōmori* wandered, afraid in his shame and trouble to approach parishioners; afraid in the chill outside air to sleep. A hail came to his ears – "Sir priest, have you not dropped coin?" Ah! Here was a stranger; and his tale he did unfold. Parlous his case; and for him the sky was upside down. "Most lucky! At our place today a prayer of *hyakumanban* (memorial service) is to be held. Food, sleep, and counsel, wide enough for this weariness and distress are offered. Deign to go in company." Thus the spy led him to his officer, a *yoriki* established at Fuchiemura in the attempt to net this desperate fellow. With joy the news of Jinnai's close proximity was heard. Entrusting the tired and barely conscious priest to the village head-man, officer, *dōshin*, and *yakunin* set out. Jinnai had overrated his capacity. Again the fit was strong on him. He shook and shivered, helpless under the weight of every covering he could find, and dared not move or turn in fear of the chill aroused. Then at the outside came the shout – "His lordship's business! Make no resistance; submit at once to the rope, in hope to secure grace." The *yakunin* roughly broke down the doors of the priest's house. They found Jinnai on foot. Growled he – "You are not the kind to face Jinnai. A rush – to freedom; with such of you as stand for carrion." He boasted overmuch. His fit was too strong even for such iron resolution. The crisis of the fever was at hand, and his legs bent under him. A shove from behind sent him weakly sprawling in a heap. Then they all fell on him, bound him hand and foot, and carried him to the village.

The cortege halted on its way to Edo town. Loud had been the lamentation of the unfortunate *dōmori*. He was a ruined priest. At best a witness, perhaps to be regarded and tortured as the accomplice of this desperate villain; jail or the execution ground awaited him. He plead with this one and with that. With sympathy they heard, but in stolid silence. The spy, who had accosted him, knew the old man well – holy, pure, somewhat simple and guileless of mind, he was object of reverence and gentle derision of the parishioners who sought his service in every trouble. The man spoke to the *dōshin*, explained the matter. The *dōshin* took him to the *yoriki* seated beneath a tea shed. The officer nodded; then called for the report. "There is an error of transcription." Thus he altered the characters 辻堂 to 辻捕. Instead of *tsujidō* a cross road temple, now it read "taken at the cross roads" – "Call the old man here." To the priest – "Through no fault of yours has this man visited you. Be better advised as to other guests.... But now – take this coin. This man's course is run. He surely will be ordered to the execution ground. Great has been his wickedness, and his grudge is not to be visited on others. Prayers are to be said for his soul in the next world. The *dōmori* of the Fudo, his zeal and honesty, his purity of heart and manners are vouched for by those who know. Pray for him.... Now – get you hence!" He put a gold *koban* in the priest's hand, allowed the joyful reverence, and cut short the protests of inconvenient gratitude. The *dōshin* shoved him off to the rear. The friendly spy carried him apart and pointed to a path running through the fields behind the houses of the hamlet. None cared to observe his departure. Thus Jinnai came to Edo, minus his ghostly purveyor.

First carefully was his body nourished for the coming entertainment. With clement genial smile Aoyama Shuzen claimed the acquaintance of this one time antagonist. As to the past and recent events there was no doubt. Aoyama had hazy, but little confirmed, ideas of greater objects; knowing as he did the early nature and history of Jinnai. But the Tokugawa were now so firmly seated. Confession was to be secured in the first place, to legalize the execution; and information in the second place, if such existed. Of confession there was none; not even answer. Jinnai closed tight his lips in scorn. Then first he was scourged; the scourging of he who is already condemned. The stout fellows stood forward with their *madake*; those thin slips of rattan, two feet in length, wrapped into a bundle an inch in thickness with stout hempen cord. Ah! How flexible and painful! As they laid on quickly the welts and bloody stripes appeared. At the hundred and fiftieth blow the medical man and legal procedure demanded forbearance. He was removed. "Cure his back!" roared Shuzen. "Rub salt into the cuts. Next time the tender surface will force at least words from his lips." But he underestimated his man. Bound to a stake, with arms behind, kneeling on the sharp grids, Jinnai hugged the stones – five, six, seven – Chudayu leaped down to aid the *dōshin* in pressing down the weight of nearly eight hundred pounds resting between chin and doubled hams. The body of Jinnai grew lobster red, his lips were tinged with bloody foam and gouts appeared. The hours passed. The black colour of the feet rose upwards. Then the sign was given and the man taken away in a dead faint, without the utterance of word or groan.

Thus the game went on. Now it was the lobster. Aoyama would not go to the prison, nor miss the sight. For a whole morning with curiosity he watched the progress of the torture. Jinnai lay on a mat. Arms pulled tight to the shoulders and behind the back, the legs drawn together in the front and dragged up to the chin. The body at first had the dark red of a violent fever, but the sweat which covered it was cold as ice. Then the colour darkened to a purple, changed to an ominous blackish green. Suddenly it began to whiten. In alarm the doctor ordered relief. With wrath Shuzen rose from his camp chair close by; still no confession.

What was suspension to this? Jinnai hung limp as a dangling fish from the beam. Arms drawn behind his back and upward to the shoulders, a weight added to the feet made any movement of the limbs agony to the whole body. It was a sort of prolonged crucifixion. When blood began to ooze from the toes again removal was ordered. Of the latter part of the torture Jinnai knew little. He was unconscious. This hardy body of his was adding to his torments. Even Shuzen could not help admiring this obstinate courage. He would try one other means – flattery; genuine in its way. "Useless the torture, Jinnai, as is well known with such a brave man. But why prolong this uselessness? Done in the performance of official duty, yet it is after all to our entertainment. Make confession and gain the due meed of the fear of future generations, their admiration and worship of such thorough paced wickedness. Surely Jinnai is no ordinary thief. Shuzen never can be brought to believe him such." He spoke the last somewhat in scorn. At last Jinnai was touched with anger. He opened eyes, and, for the first time, mouth – "Aoyama Dono speaks truth. But why regret past failure? My followers? They number thousands. Why rouse envy or show favour by giving name of this or that lusty fellow? The object? As to that exercise your wits. Fat wits; which in these twenty years could not hunt out this Jinnai. Ah! 'Twas but this unexpected illness which played this evil trick; else Jinnai never would have faced Shuzen; except sword in hand. This Jinnai is a thief, a bandit; the tongue grudges to say. Such is his confession. Not a word more – to Aoyama Uji." He closed his eyes and mouth. Enraged at the failure and familiarity Aoyama shouted out – "The wooden horse! The water torture!" They mounted the man on the sharp humped beast. Lungs, belly, abdomen wide distended, in every physical agony, his body could but writhe, to add to the torture of his seat as they dragged down on his legs. Eyes starting wildly from his head, gasping for air, the unfortunate wretch was given the chance to belch forth the liquid. "Atsu!" The cry was between a sigh and a yelp of agony. Then he fainted. With chagrin at his failure Aoyama Shuzen put official seal to the confession bearing the thumb print of Kosaka Jinnai. Thus ended this phase of the contest between the two men.

Jinnai's body was too racked by the torture for immediate sentence. When he was brought in the court Aoyama Shuzen had another wicked surprise to spring upon him. Jinnai's rejuvenating eye noted the band of peasants, the two beautiful girls brought captive in their midst. He knew at once who they were; even if the viciously triumphant look in Shuzen's eyes, the piteous fright and affectionate sympathy in theirs, had not enlightened him. The presence of O'Kiku and O'Yui was due to an ill freak played by fortune. In the fall of the year an illness of the mother – cold? – came to its end and herself with it. What was to be done with farm and girls? To the villagers this question was of serious debate. Of one thing they were in dense ignorance. Three years before a new farm hand appeared in Jisuke's household, and men could well wonder at the favour he found with the old man. With some misgivings they had warned him against recklessly introducing a strange *muko*, without first consent of the village. Jisuke assured them against what was actual fact. Wataru Sampei was a *samurai*, of *samurai* stock, and liegeman to his own old masters of Kai province. It was with the consent and approval of the dying man that O'Kiku was united to him. The household in Nippon is adamant in its secrets to the outside world – and that against the most prying curiosity anywhere found. O'Kiku lay in of her child and nursed the babe in her own nurse's house. Thus in full ignorance the council met to consider the request made by the girls to communicate with Jinnai – Osada Sensei – at the famous *yashiki* of Aoyama.

Most of them were ready to consent. Then rose one Jinemon, smarting under the sense of having fields adjacent, coupled with flat refusal to his son of the simple girl O'Kiku. He suspected this virginity of nearly twenty years; and with an ill turn to this obstacle might do himself a good one. "Take heed, good sirs, what counsel ye come to. News fresh from Edo couples the name of Osada Sensei with Kosaka Jinnai; makes him out a violent bandit and would be ravisher years ago of the Tenju-in-Den. Surely his fate will be hard. Send them to the *yashiki* of Aoyama – but to that of Aoyama Shuzen Dono. Thus their request is met; and no blame incurred. The honoured *bugyō* (magistrate) answers for the district (Aoyama), and the girls will not suspect the destination. Otherwise, look well to yourselves. Aoyama Sama is known as the Yakujin. Great his influence in Edo, and sour his wrath as that of Emma Dai-O. It will fall heavy on you." This intimation, that he would do what they would avoid, soured all the milk of human kindness. Wataru Sampei, departed in all haste to Edo, returned in fright to announce his discovery of the state of affairs. The father Jinnai then was undergoing the harsh tortures of Shuzen. He found the farm in charge of Jinemon and his son; the two girls already sent in all ignorance to the *yashiki* of Aoyama. Receiving a harsh dismissal he dared not punish, from the house and tears of the old nurse he received as if by theft his infant son. With him he took his way to Edo; to establish himself as gardener at Honjo Koume; or at Narihira, some say.

In daily rounds of the jail the *dōshin* stood over Jinnai. In three days this man was to go to Torigoebashi. Here he was to be crucified and speared – "with many spears" ran the sentence, to indicate the prolongation of the torture. "Jinnai, you have shown yourself brave, have refused to name even one associate. The time passes. Perhaps some wish, not incompatible with duty, comes to mind." Jinnai opened his eyes at the unexpected kindly tone and words. It was as if one soldier looked into the eyes of his compeer on the battle field, as well could be the case with this man older and of more regular experience than himself. The answer came with the measured slowness of an earnest thanks and appreciation – "The offer comes from a kind heart, shown on previous occasions.... There are women held here." He hesitated. "Deign the last cup of cold water at their hands." The officer did not refuse. O'Kiku and O'Yui knelt beside the couch on which lay the broken body of the father. Said Jinnai – "The end is most unseemly; words grudge to speak that mere accident thus should determine the fate of Kosaka Jinnai; he who sought to determine the fate of Tokugawa Ke. A dagger would have secured the fitting ending, that you two should not bear the public service of the town, a certain fate. This remedy Jinnai now forbids. With life changes occur; old scores are wiped out. Hearken well: live with patience; serve well to the hour. Now the last cup of life is to be drained; this first meeting brought to an end." Tears running down her face O'Yui, mere child budding into womanhood, presented to her sister the vessel never used as yet and filled with the cold liquid. From the hand of O'Kiku it was accepted. Jinnai drank, looked long and earnestly into the face of both, then with a wave of the hand dismissed them. He had had his say. The hardness of the man returned, and all his courage with it.

Three days later – Shoho 2nd year 12th month 1st day (17th January 1646) – the procession was formed to move to the execution ground at Torigoebashi. The assembled cits marvelled at sight of the man and rumour of his extraordinary wickedness. There was a concentration of mind and energy in the face of Jinnai, which under any condition would attract attention. The centre of the scene, he bore himself splendidly. Despite the pain he suffered no incapacity was pleaded. Thus he forced nature. The costume of the famed robber at this noted execution in Edo's annals? He wore – "a wadded coat (*kosode*) of fine silk from Hachijo in Izu, and that of quintuple stripe. The *obi* (sash) was seamless and of a purple crape. Into brick coloured leggings was twisted bias white thread, and his straw sandals (*waraji*) matched them." The jail had given to a naturally fair colour a somewhat livid greenish tint, rendered more commanding and terrible by the piercing cold eyes. Those far off said – "How mild looking! How tranquil!" Those near at hand shuddered and were glad at the removal of such wickedness. The *yoriki* – informed of the purport – let him speak. Jinnai turned to the crowd. His voice reached far. "Brought to contempt and a punishment words grudge to mention, this Jinnai holds not evil thoughts against those who carry out the law. The ill fortune of unexpected disease made capture easy, and has brought about this vile ending. Hence on death Jinnai will not leave this place; but as an evil spirit remain to answer those who pray for relief from the mischance of this ill disease. Those afflicted with *okori* (malaria) shall find sure answer to their prayers. Held now in no respect, this later will be bestowed. The last purposes of those about to die are carried out." He ceased speaking. A sign and he was stripped and raised on the implement of torture: キ – ill described as a cross. For hours he hung, revived from time to time with vinegar. Then signal was given for the end. First one, then another, *yakunin* thrust a spear into his belly, seeking least injury and greatest torture. As he approached the utter prostration of a dissolution the *yoriki* gave sign. The spear point thrust into the vitals showed through the left shoulder. And Jinnai died.

To the north, just beyond the present Torigoebashi, is the Jinnaibashi, relic of this episode. On the north, close by the Torigoe Jinja stands the shrine to Jinnai, the god granting cure to sufferers from ague. No mean resort is it; nor modest the offerings of wine to his service. There it has endured through these hundreds of years. Jinnaibashi, Jigokubashi (Hell Bridge) is a relic of the place of execution soon abandoned. After the fifth year of the period the jail was removed to Temmacho; the execution ground to Kotsukabara.

A Winter Session

Aoyama Shuzen was in conference with Chudayu. Preparations were to be made. It was with something like dismay that the members of the Endurance Society received the missive –

> *"At this season of the great heat your honoured health is matter of solicitude. More and more may it thrive. Hence the condescension of the honoured (your) litter is requested on the coming sixteenth day. The wish is expressed to offer a cup of inferior wine. With fear and respect:*
> *To...."*

Alas! Alas! If they could have but reached the ceremonies of the New Year. This rascal Aoyama would have been too occupied with the official visits to press his right to a meeting in the season of extreme cold (the *tai-kan*). But now – on the 16th day of the 12th month (2nd February): Ah! Ha! He was a wicked fellow. The grudge properly lay against Kondo Noborinosuke who had sweated the juice out of them in the intense heat of the hot season. Now Aoyama proposed to freeze it on the surface of their bodies. But to refuse was out of the question. Charged with weakness and effeminacy one would be laughed at as a fool; be unable to show his face. After all perhaps one could escape the ordeal with life.

The 15th day, on which the invitations were issued, was threatening. The 16th day fulfilled the promise. Cold blew the blasts down from snow clad Tsukuba, with full sweep across the Shimosa plain. As it caught the unfortunates crossing the Ryogokubashi in their progress toward the Bancho, they shook and shivered with more than anticipation. An occasional flake of snow heralded the heavier fall. At the *yashiki* of Aoyama all was in readiness to welcome the guests. Shuzen stood at the house entrance to greet them. With thin open silken robe thrown over his *katabira* or summer robe, lacking shirt, and wearing the wide woven grass cloth *hakama* (trousers) which sought every breeze, he carried a fan in his hand. The *kerai* met the guests with ice cold water for such as cared to dip the hands – and none dared refuse. Shuzen fanned himself vigorously; and his guests were zealously supplied with fans, or the heat inspired by their progress was dissipated in the draught raised over them by energetic hands. The door-man (*toritsugi*) monotonously sang out the new arrivals – "Abe Shirogoro Sama, Kondo Noborinosuke Sama, Okubo Hikoroku Sama, Yamanaka Genzaemon Sama, Okubo Jizaemon Sama, Endo Saburozaemon Sama, Kanematsu Matashiro Sama, Okumura Shuzen Sama..."; and Shuzen had greeting for all. "Ah! Ha! Such terrific heat! Not for sixty years has such been experienced. An old fellow in the *yashiki* will answer for it. But be sure all has made ready for comfort. Truly the honoured presence in these dog days in a gratification. The viands, the drink, all have been carefully cooled. Deign to come within, to a cooler place, away from this desolating heat. Condescend to notice how the very leaves have been withered off the trees."

With inward groans, their teeth chattering and their bodies shivering, they followed this merciless fellow. "Ha! Ha! For tobacco there will be fire in the braziers. At least one's fingers are assured of warmth." They smirked at the anticipated pleasure. Warm fingers and the heated *sake*! But – Oya! Oya! Bare were swept and wide open thrown the rooms. Screens (inner and outer) had all been taken away. From the garden came the cold blast, blowing icily through this wide bare space. For cushions – the straw *zabuton*; for fire in the braziers – punk! Explained Shuzen in all kindness and suavity – "Fires in the braziers in this heat were too terrific even to think of; so punk (*hinawa*) has been substituted.... No need for thanks; the mere duty of the host. And now – no ceremony: off with the garments of all. A middle cloth answers purposes of decency. Deign the trial. Here is cold water to cool the heated body." Promptly he stripped to the skin. The *kerai* were bringing to the verandah black lacquered basins filled with water in which ice floated. Before this terrific fellow there could be no hesitation. They followed his example in being soused from head to foot. In the wiping – "Let the rag hang loose. Don't wipe with knotted towel. Stupid fellows! The cool wetness clinging to the skin gives a shiver of delight." Thus shouted Shuzen to his officiating satellites. Then all the guests took seats. The mucous was running from the noses of the old fellows who had fought campaigns at Odawara, Sekigahara, Osaka. Aoyama noted it with delight; and even Kondo felt a grudge against him, yet was compelled to laugh.

The viands were brought – to send a chill down the spines of all; macaroni in cold water (*hiyamugi*), and the equally heating sea ear in frozen salt water (*mizugai*). Shuzen urged the latter, as better fitted for the season. As piles of *sashimi* (sliced raw fish), resting on neat beds of shaven ice, were brought eyes looked to heaven – to hide the expression. When the wine appeared, the bottles immersed to the neck in tubs filled with salted ice, the more recondite parts of the room echoed groans. Even Shuzen smiled with complacence. He felt he had scored success. It was Endo Saburozaemon who showed no sign of discomfiture. "Naruhodo! Aoyama Uji, in this great heat how explain a thing so strange? Deign, honoured sir, to look. This white substance falling from the sky; if it were not so hot, one would call it snow." Said Aoyama undisturbed – "Not so, Endo Uji. It is but from wild geese fighting in the sky, their feathers; or perchance *kanro* – the sweet dew which falls from heaven when a virtuous lord condescends to rule. Who more virtuous than the honoured suzerain?" All bowed in heartfelt enthusiasm and respect. Then said Saburozaemon – "'Tis a thing to note closer at hand; a stroll in the garden, to seek its coolness in this heat." He leaped down into the fast accumulating snow.

Others too stole away, at least to get protection from the outrageously cold blasts of the exposed rooms, and the further exactions to be anticipated from the ingenuity of their host. Growled Kanematsu – "It is the value of one's life risked with such a fellow as Aoyama. Where Kanematsu sits the snow drifts in on his shoulders. He is without consideration or mercy."

– "For any: his women must find service in such a *yashiki* a substitute for the torments of Emma Dai-O." – "Not so," sneered Kondo. "Even the wife is but a wooden figure; much like Kondo's fingers." An idea seemed to come to him. He left them for the time being. The others stood sheltered from the wind, to talk and shiver, Endo joined them from his garden stroll. Seeing Kondo on his return, said Abe Shirogoro – "Eh! Naruhodo! The smile of pain relieved! Kondo Uji, has he found means to unbend, to thaw out those fingers? Ha! The rascally fellow knows the way about. There is hot water at hand. Deign to give the hint, Kondo Dono." Kondo leaked a smile, then snickered – "It was but an idea. Hot water in this *yashiki* on such a day there is none. But it is always to hand for the effort. The fingers of Kondo were turning white, were in danger, and so...." He held out his fingers for inspection. Abe looked with envy. "They fairly steam!" Then suddenly putting his fingers to his nose – "Oh! Oh! The filthy fellow! Kondo Uji! Deign to wash your hands. Indeed hot water is always carried on one's person. But...." All grasped their nasal members and protested. Noborinosuke laughed outright, and submitted to the ablution. Abe in malice gave the hands a copious libation. For the nonce his fingers had been saved and Kondo was satisfied with the outcome.

A woman dressed in the summer garb for service came from a room close by. The opening and closing of the *shōji* gave Endo Saburozaemon a glimpse. At once – "This way...." His tone commanded attention. Abe Shirogoro, Kanematsu Matashiro, Okubo Hikoroku followed him. It was the maids' sleeping room they entered. "Are! Are! Have not the honoured sirs made a mistake? Deign to return to the other apartment. This is the maids' dressing room." – "And in no better place can one be," grumbled Shirogoro. His eyes took in the room with avid curiosity. Here the girls quickly slipped into winter garb, until called to the banquet hall for service. But it was not the glimpse of shoulders of the one so engaged at the moment, as the brazier covered by a quilt and placed in the centre of the room. From this the girls had emerged in confusion. Said he reprovingly – "Eh! Eh! In this great heat to have a brazier – it is more than out of season. Surely it is against the order of the master of the house." The girls, uneasy and at a loss, had but for answer – "It was the idea of O'Kiku...." The beauty, still flushed with the suddenness of her effort, came forward smiling. The attention of all was riveted. A little taller than the average of her sex, very fair of skin, the sparkling eyes in the pure oval of the face framed in tresses reaching almost to her feet, the tiny feet and long fingers appearing from the edge of the robe, the incomparable poise of head and neck, this woman was a beauty, to be rivalled by few in Edo town. The voice too was as musical as were her words to the frozen men – "It is but a water *kotatsu*; so that one can be cooled in this extreme of heat.... Within? Ice – of course. Deign to enter." The suppressed groan of Abe was cut short. He looked fixedly at the bright laughing face before him. The smile was pained and stereotyped, but the sympathy was evident. He understood. "Ho! Ho! Endo, Kanematsu, Okubo, deign to try this delicious coolness. Ah! Ha! This water *kotatsu* is a splendid idea. In this great heat it restores one to life. Truly Kiku is as clever as she is beautiful; one apart from all the others." The men crowded together under the *kotatsu* – "More ice! More ice! The *hibachi* grows warm." Laughing O'Kiku brought the necessary supply with the tongs, blew it into life with a little bellows.

All the time Endo observed her closely. To Abe – "Truly she is a beauty.... Your name is Kiku.... And age?... Twenty years only!... So Kiku is sempstress in the house of Aoyama Uji. So! So!" He and Abe regarded her attentively. They praised her beauty. The crimson blush spread over face and neck, adding to her charm. Thoroughly warmed the men left the room. Said Endo – "Oh, the liar! This Aoyama poses as a misogynist, takes a wife – perforce, and charges those of us who like women with effeminacy. Okubo, how about this Kiku.... The Sempstress?

Oh, you stupid fellow! Why – there is no more beautiful woman in Edo. She is the mistress of Aoyama; who deceives and mocks us all. And now – to bring him to open shame." Aoyama Shuzen, quick to note their absence, and the return so refreshed, was much put out. "Where have these fellows been?"

Endo Saburozaemon was not slow in the attack. "Truly, Aoyama Uji, words do not fit deeds. Are you not a bit of a rascal?" – "Why so?" was the calm reply of Shuzen, always ready to a quarrel. "You pretend to hate women; you charge us with effeminacy who have wives; and take your own but on compulsion. Yet in this very house there is not only a wife, but the most beautiful woman in Edo for concubine." Shuzen's astonishment was too manifest. "Who?" said Endo, with some misgiving that he had missed fire. "This Kiku; would you deny it?" – "Surely so," was Shuzen's assured reply. Then seeing the curiosity of those around he added with courtesy – "This Kiku is a slave girl, a criminal under judgment, a *yatsu-hōkōnin* by favour. Would you know about her? She is daughter to the robber Jinnai, not long since put to death. The law may be harsh, yet it condemns the line of such men to extinction, and sends their issue to the execution ground. Whether through good will, or mistaking the Aoyama Harajuku, the resort of this Jinnai, for this *yashiki*, the villagers brought the two girls Kiku and Yui from near Tsukuba. In pity one was taken into the life service of the *yashiki*. For his business Jinzaemon of the Yoshiwara Miuraya considered the younger Yui as more fitting. To him she was bound as *yatsu-yūjō*.... Husband? No: and thus all posterity of the robber is stamped out. Yui serves for life as harlot in the Yoshiwara, with no recognized issue. Kiku serves for life at the *yashiki*. The case is a pitiable one." All present echoed what he said. "It is the offence, not the person, which is to be hated. Truly it is a hard lot." They were curious to see her. Said Shuzen – "Surely she has been rated too high, but – summon Kiku here." As the girl stood in the midst for all to observe, blushing and panting a little with fright at all these eyes upon her, there was no gaze more intent than that of Aoyama Shuzen. The pity expressed and the praises lavished reached his ears. He studied her from head to foot, heard the caustic criticisms – "Such a beauty, and a serving wench! Aoyama is a fool."

The Tiger at the Front Gate; the Wolf at the Postern

Thus it came about that O'Kiku was an inmate of Aoyama's *yashiki*. He had told the tale, the fatal error drawn by the mother from the peasant's message. It was her own deed. Thus "evil seed produces evil fruit. In one's posterity is punishment found." All knew Kiku's story. Promptly with her appearance in the household she was named Shioki – O'Shioki San, O'Shioki San; when not addressing her these companions called it to each other for her to hear. Shioki? It means 'the execution ground'.

A flower blooms but to wither; and this flowering branch was to be tended by the master's hand. Now she was faced with a new and terrible danger. O'Kiku was quick to note the state of Shuzen's household. Of the *koshimoto*, two were the favoured concubines during the incapacitation of the wife. The lowliness of her own position – menial servant and mere serving wench – would seem to protect her. Moreover she was not brought into contact with the house master. But after all she was the *bushi's* daughter, brought up by a mother trained from youth at the hand of the *samurai* grandmother. Thus dragged out into the light by indiscreet curiosity the tiger's eye had fallen upon her. Shuzen marvelled at his stupidity, his oversight. This woman was indeed a beauty, the concubine for long sought, and to hand free of her charms. He stood adjusting his robes; then lost in thought. There were obstacles – in the girl's position. But that night O'Kiku was ordered to serve the wine. The intelligence and training, corresponding to the outward physical charms, aroused in him a very fury for possession. Abrupt, blunt, overbearing he approached her in the coarsest way – "Kiku, first pity and now love has seized upon the heart of Shuzen. With women all his relations have been those of cold formality – the business of connection or the necessity of an heir. Now an entirely different feeling is aroused. The very sight of Kiku's figure inspires fondness, an exclusion of all others of her sex. 'Tis Kiku alone who remains the object, all others are mere lay figures. You are a woman, and by nature know of such things. Is not this truly love? Consent to become the concubine of Shuzen. Let this very night seal the union."

He attempted to draw her close to him, but she shrank away in confusion and fright. Shuzen was amazed – "What! You refuse?... Ah! Then it is hate of this Shuzen which is felt. Most unreasonable hate, for he acted but as *bugyō* of the land. It is a disloyal hate." In his mad and thwarted lust his lips trembled. The girl humbly remained prostrate – "Condescend the honoured forbearance. Such could not be the case. Great the favour of Heaven, of your lordship as its agent, in saving this Kiku from the final punishment, the coarse assault of menials. But deign to consider. Kiku is the daughter of Jinnai. She is a reprieved criminal in the land, can be naught else but of lowest status. Kind the honoured words, great the gratitude inspired; but is not the summons unseemly. Deign forbearance; add not to the offence of Kiku." In her mind was the last scene with her father Jinnai; the tortured, distorted, suffering body of the condemned bandit. Pollute her body with this man who had thus played with the one to whom she owed life and duty; to the man who had sent the father to the execution ground? She would have used her dagger first on herself, rather than on him. His words did inspire uncertainty. He was the officer in the land, the representative of the suzerain, hence guiltless. But that made not the idea of his embraces less repulsive, though she wavered in thoughts of vendetta – between filial duty and loyal service to the suzerain. Her attitude puzzled Aoyama. The unusualness of his proposition he put aside. Her claim to loyalty, in his hopes as the successful lecher, he was disposed to accept. Was there not something deeper?

Then the battle began between them, to last for those weeks of the winter months. Force matters he would not. There was a zest in this pursuit, far apart from any mere sensual gratification. The desire he felt for her person was all cruel. It was joined to the desire to humble her, to force her to consent by her own lips and motion and against reason, to grant the gift of herself even if unwilling. There was an enjoyment in soiling the body and mind of this beauty. Thus with refusal love began slowly to turn to a hatred full of malice. One night Aikawa Chudayu was present. O'Kiku as usual served the wine. Shuzen turned to him impatiently – "The speech of the overlord is without effect. Chudayu, try your hand, and bend Kiku to consent to my wishes, to become my concubine." Shamed before the whole household? O'Kiku had grown used to this grossness in the determined pursuit of Shuzen. Now openly addressed before the chamberlain and others she looked down; a little flushed, and hearing with astonishment the words which came from such a quarter. Chudayu spoke slowly; addressed her with a severity of tone which belied his intent. "O'Kiku Dono, why are not thanks given for such condescension on the part of the Tono Sama? Apart from his rank is not the experience of his fifty years, on the battle field of war and love, to count in his favour? Most imposing and strong his figure, despite his age. All bow in respect before the lines marked by the wisdom of years in his lordships face. Why refuse to follow the example of the other women of the household – and share with them? These are indeed *koshimoto*; your promotion to the position, from the vilest status, but a caprice and kindness. You should obey the order of the Tono Sama. His face alone would inspire fear. All regard it with awe, as if in contemplation of that of Emma Dai-O. And who refuses to obey the mandate of the king of hell? Answer – who?" He leaned far over toward her. O'Kiku looked at him; then hid her face in her hands.

These were not her only trials in this Jigoku *yashiki* (Hell mansion). There was her ladyship to take into account. Says the proverb of the Nipponese – "dabble in vermilion, and one is stained red." Contact with Shuzen had developed all the harsher traits in this stern *samurai* dame. She despised the former character of her husband, and now was mad with jealousy at his unrestrained lechery. However there was some consolation in this new pursuit. Promiscuous in his intercourse with all and every other of her household, she could do but little. These were women of more or less position. Now he threatened to turn all devotion in the one direction of this beautiful girl, to condescend to a serving wench.

"The Rangiku [Caryopteris mastachantus]: it has a fox's shape."

Thus sneered her fellows. O'Kiku now was punished as scapegoat for all the others. The natural harshness of her ladyship's character turned to barbarity. This 'slave' – O'Shioki – in no way could satisfy her. The slightest fault, of self or other, was visited on O'Kiku. One day her ladyship in her rage seized her and dragged her by the hair over her knees. A short baton of bamboo was to hand, and with this before all she put the girl to the shame of childhood's punishment, and with a malice and heartiness of will and muscle which left O'Kiku lame, and thus victim in other derelictions of duty. This so pleased the *okugata* that it became a favourite pastime, whenever the girl was at hand and her own arm had rested. She would have starved her, but the rest contributed of their store out of mere fellowship. Her ladyship recognized the uselessness. She did not dare deface her beauty. Believing in Shuzen's love her vengeance was confined in its exercise. With despair she regarded her bloated disfigured person, the wan faded aspect due to her advanced pregnancy. Ah! If she could but fasten some offence upon her. She would bring about this interloper's death. With delight she noted the signs of dislike and malice in Shuzen. Surely the tales were true that the beauty was holding out for the price of her charms. It should be a case where beauty would not secure pardon.

It was at this time that, with Shuzen's consent, she put O'Kiku in charge of ten plates condescended in trust to the House by the Toshogu (Iyeyasu). It was a bid of Shuzen, the mark of the conferrence of position as *koshimoto* in his household. Only in the madness of love – or lust – would he have risked such impropriety. The regular time for counting had arrived. O'Kiku carefully replaced the beautiful objects, marked with holly hock crest, into their lacquered box. Again Shuzen importuned her with his suit. Then in vexation – "Ah! Truly a rebellious and wicked grudge is held by this Kiku. Attempt at denial is useless, it is not only rebellion against the master, but against the decree of the master of all. Decide at once. Either be the concubine of Shuzen; or suffer the sword cut." Again she plead with him, and Shuzen's eyes opened wide with astonishment. "Condescend the honoured hearing. Kiku has plead as one no longer of this world. 'Tis true. But before now she has already taken the vow of two worlds." – "What!" said Shuzen in amazement. His mind lighted up as she proceeded – "It is true. Under guise of farm hand at the village lived Wataru Sampei, a *samurai* and *rōnin* of the Takeda House of Kai. By him there is a child – now three years old. Alas! The father lives in direst poverty. Twice in the month – the 15th day when the festival of the Ichigaya Hachiman shrine is held, the 25th day when that of the Hirakawa Tenjin Sama is held – with the child Jumatsu he is to pass. A wave of the hand – 'Is it Kiku?... Is it mother?' The relationship longed for and regarded as enduring to the whiteness of the hair thus is reduced to the wave of a hand. The chaste wife suffers not the embrace of two men. Oh! Husband! Son!" Weeping O'Kiku hid her face in her sleeves as she made her plea.

Harsh and triumphant was the voice of Shuzen as he pressed on this newly discovered weakness. "Then you lied; Jinnai lied, in calling you a maid. This Sampei and Jumatsu rightly are gallows-birds, doomed to the execution ground. Shuzen has but to say the word. Seized they are put to the torture; the child to know the bitterness of the scourge. Such a tiny body will be cut to ribbons. Listen well! Obey the command of this Shuzen. 'Tis the choice between the jewelled palanquin of the favoured mistress, or torture for these two. The kind offices of the bed for Shuzen, or the rottenness of the jail for these two criminals. The gift of Kiku's chastity secures for them oblivion.... You would ask time? Tomorrow night, after the counting of the plates, the answer will be received." He ceased – to turn to Chudayu, who for a little time had stood by, as one waiting on a matter of business. O'Kiku, face white and drawn, tottered away to her room.

She had played false, and at a cast lost all. Gloomy, the long hair framing the distraught and unhappy face, she sat. "Unhappy the lot of this Kiku. The sisters left without a father's sanction, to witness the shadow on the mother's life; to know that father but as criminal ready to be sent to the execution ground; and now, by rashness of the tongue, to condemn husband and infant son to such a hideous fate! Remedy there is none. Perchance the life of this Kiku in sacrifice for both arouses kindness to pardon; or at least secures them in ignorance." Now she was all decision. Rapidly she loosed the girdle of her sash. The safety of her beloved was at stake, and no father's command held. The feet bound she seated herself before the mirror, took up the dagger and felt its keen point, then the morbid soft flesh of the neck. As she raised her arm it was seized at her side. Noiseless Chudayu had entered and acted in prevention. With a grunt he bent down and severed the sash cord which restrained her. Then holding the dagger daintily he spoke his will – "Is not this madness, O'Kiku Dono? The Tono Sama has issued his summons, and the heart does not conform. The secret thought is known to this Chudayu. Turn therefore to a friend. Safety is not to be sought by the drastic method of the steel. Look to flight. Chudayu aids – nay goes in company. Against him there can be no grudge. If Sampei and this boy exist, they are not to be met within the *yashiki* of Aoyama Shuzen – either by submission and riding in the jewelled palanquin, or by the argument of the dagger. It is an easy matter for Chudayu. An error confessed in conducting of the accounts, and with purse well lined with the gold of Shuzen this *yashiki* is abandoned. O'Kiku Dono goes in company. Between the two known connection there is none, and without the wife this Sampei and Jumatsu go unharmed. In the relationship with Jinnai the link is missing and Edo too wide a mark to pick them out. So much can Chudayu answer for."

"Ah!" At times a Buddha is met in Hell itself. With astonishment and reverence O'Kiku regarded this saintly apparition. Noting the impression made Chudayu sat close by her. A little disturbed and restive she moved away. "The words of Chudayu Dono are more than kind; never to be forgotten in this world. By such means are Sampei and Jumatsu really to be saved?" – "Most assuredly," was the smooth reply. "Chudayu acts at once. Deign but the required pledge...." – "The pledge?" O'Kiku spoke now with misgiving filtering into a sinking heart. Said Chudayu with impatience – "Pledge: don't feign innocence, O'Kiku Dono. Does Chudayu sacrifice all for the mere amusement of the affair. Amusement there is indeed for him. O'Kiku must consent to accept this Chudayu. Deign to change ox for horse. Failing Sampei, it is to Chudayu she grants her favours. This is to be agreed – and right now, as pledge, a proof offered of her sincerity." Now there was no mistaking the words in invitation made plain by eye and gesture. She wrenched away the detaining hands laid upon her; sprang up. "Ah! Villainous man! You would rob your lord, deceive and betray this Kiku. Such speech is pollution to the ears; the touch of such a creature is loathsome. Chudayu has the weapon of Kiku; but Kiku can still cry out and bring the household about your ears. Beast – away from here!" Armed as he was Chudayu was afraid – "'Pollution' – 'beast'? Ha! The woman's thought rises after all to the surface in her hate. For this you shall pay. Just wait." He left the room in haste, to betake himself at once to the apartments of the *okugata*. O'Kiku crouched on the *tatami*, her eyes wide open, fastened on the texture of the straw surface, saw nothing but this new and terrible position. She could not die; she could not live; and yet the tiger was at the gate, the wolf at the postern.

A maid came to summon her to Shuzen's presence. Knowing her position, her feelings, the solidarity of sex had veered to kindliness for this unwilling rival. The girl was shocked at sight of her. "O'Kiku Dono! Tis but for the counting of the plates – as usual." She aided her to don the ceremonial costume. In all the magnificence of her apparel, with hair dressed high, she followed after the girl. In her beauty a splendid sight, in her heart "she was as the sheep going to the butcher." Her ladyship sat close beside Shuzen. Other *koshimoto*, with Chudayu and several retainers, were present. Despite the customary nature of this vicarious reverence to the spirit of the Tosho Shinkun (Iyeyasu) there was an oppression, a suppressed interest, which seemed to fasten every eye on O'Kiku as slowly and gracefully she bore the box before her lord, made salutation. "Open;" the word from Shuzen's lips came dry and harsh – "One" – "Um" – "Two" – "Um" – "Three, four" – "Um" – "Five" – "Um" – "Six, seven" – "Um" – "Eight" – "Um" – "Nine.... Oya! Oya!" Then in fright – "What shall I do!" With horror O'Kiku gazed at the fragments of the tenth plate lying at the bottom. Shuzen, all moved by his wrath and excitement, leaned forward. The holly hock crest ground to powder was almost indistinguishable. Hardly able to believe her eyes O'Kiku mechanically began to finger the pile of porcelain – One, two, three ... they followed up to nine.... "What shall I do!"

The malice and ferocity of Shuzen's tone sent a thrill through those present – "Vicious jade! This is a sample of Kiku's hatred to this Shuzen, through him of her disloyalty to the revered House. What explanation can be offered? What expiation?" Slowly and in despair O'Kiku raised her head. She caught the triumphant glance passed between the *okugata* and Chudayu. All was illuminated. This was Chudayu's threatened vengeance. As of one dying her voice – "This is not the deed of Kiku. Daughter of the criminal Jinnai she holds no grudge against lord or suzerain; would but pray in this world for oblivion of those offences in a future existence. Deign, my lord to believe this Kiku. Malice acts here. But a short time ago Chudayu...." The man sprang forward – "Lying hussy!... Tono Sama, this woman would save herself by slander. Plain has been her ill feeling against the honoured lord in refusal to obey his summons. Here lies the proof of ill intent and rebellion against the suzerain's House. Surely there is no punishment for such but death!" – "Surely there is no punishment for this but death!" The harsh voice of the *okugata* was heard in repetition.

Shuzen spoke – "'A twig broken on the flowering branch of plum, and the whole is to be cut off.' Such the words of Kuro Hangwan Yoshitsune. Kiku, you are a vile, treacherous woman; undeserving of Heaven's favour and the kindness shown by Shuzen. Now you lie – with the fancy tale of child and husband, in order to escape the bed of Shuzen; with slanderous insinuation to throw your crime against others.... Here!" At the command the *kerai* came forward and dragged her within reach. Shuzen seized a hand. "Ten the plates: one broken, the tale destroyed. Apology is to be made. Make full confession. No? For the one, ten are due." There was a *hibachi* close by his side. He dragged her arm over the brazier, drew his dagger – "One." At the middle joint the finger fell severed into the ashes. "Two" – "Two," faintly answered O'Kiku. "Three" – "Three" – "Four" – "Four" – "Five" – "Five." Shuzen laughed. "Kiku cannot hold grudge as being maimed. The stumps remain." Chudayu sprang forward at Shuzen's sign. Roughly holding the bleeding stumps he pressed them into the harsh cautery of living coals. A suppressed wailing cry from Kiku, a shuddering and turning away of the frightened women; her ladyship laughed out loud. Kiku raised her head and gave her a long look. Shuzen grasped the other arm. The punishment went on. "Six.... No confession?" One by one the remaining joints fell. Only the thumb remained. Like a demon the *okugata* sprang forward. She snatched away the keen weapon, and pressing down the edge of the blade triumphant raised the severed digit torn away to the wrist. Shuzen himself rose in astonishment at the act. All were in a wild excitement. The violent woman strove to shriek, but choked in her rage and utterance. They surrounded her and bore her off to her own apartment.

A wave of the hand and all but Chudayu had departed. Shuzen was divided between his hate and the certainty of having been deceived. Besides, only the body was maimed, and in the malice of his heart he would soil this woman's soul. He leaned over the helpless figure. "Your own deed, Kiku: make confession and submission. There is yet life to plead for. Ha! 'Tis true. Vicious wench, you would seek the destruction of Shuzen by temptation; the grudge is to be carried to the end." From far off came the answer – "Alas! To this Kiku are imputed the wet garments. A lie destroys her to whom life is displeasing. Aye! The grudge is to be carried to the end. Against this treacherous Chudayu, against Aoyama and his House the grudge. Remember well!" In fury Shuzen sprang to his feet – "Chuudayu, take hold of this woman. Out with her to the garden!" With practised hand the chamberlain bound hands and feet. Then following after Shuzen he dragged her through the snow to the old well. "'Tis here," said Shuzen briefly. Removing the bucket the rope was tied under the arms of O'Kiku. "Your own act and deed, Kiku. In your punishment apology is made to the suzerain House. Go join your father Jinnai at the Yellow Fountain (Kwosen) in Hell.... Chudayu, kill her by inches." Seeing the chamberlain's hesitation Shuzen gave the body a push. Swift the descent. The splash of the water was heard. "Heave up!" With eager energy Chudayu brought O'Kiku to the curb. "No confession yet?" – "Aye! Grudge the last thought; grudge against Chudayu; against this Aoyama, him and his." The long wet hair hanging about the chalk white face, the bulging glaring eyes, the disordered saturated garments of the half drowned girl, were too much for Chudayu. The man now was struck with fright. He sought to save her. "Tono Sama, is not the purpose satisfied? A request...." – "Coward! Are you afraid of the ghost? Surely Kiku will visit the couch of Chudayu – as perhaps to his desire." But Chudayu now openly was afraid and not ashamed. "Deign to spare her, Tono Sama.... O'Kiku Dono, this is no affair of Chudayu. As ghost deign to haunt the Tono Sama. 'Tis the Tono Sama who kills you." He plead; but inexorable the whispering voice – "The grudge! Against Chudayu...." Then in terror Chudayu sought the end – "Ah! Vile bitch!... Tono Sama, deign to cut short the curse, and with it the breath of this hussy." – "Your act and deed, Chudayu...." Shuzen took up the rest of the sentence. "Pass your sword into her belly, Chudayu; the lord's order." Chudayu hesitated. Then looking away he thrust – once, twice. There was a squishing sound, as of steel entering something soft. A heart rending scream rang through the air. It was like the ripping apart of silk. Shuzen stepped to the curb, looked into the agonized staring eyes. Then he gave the final thrust of his dagger into the windpipe, and cast the weapon to Chudayu to cleanse. As if an automaton the man went through his task: brought the heavy stone to bind into the long trailing garment. Seeing his helplessness Shuzen shrugged his shoulders with contempt. With his dagger he severed the rope. *Dobun!* A final splash of water at the end.

Chudayu Wins His Suit

Chudayu's legs bent under him. "Ah! My lord! O'Kiku grasps my neck!" A cold hand laid upon him he shrieked in fear. Shuzen turned – "Fool! 'Tis a clod of snow from the tree above, fallen on your collar. Off with you to bed. Truly in these days such fellows are good for nothing." Off he strode to the *rōka*. For a moment he looked out – on the heavy flakes coming down like cotton wadding, at the figure of Chudayu staggering like a drunken man to his quarters. With a laugh he closed the *amado*, seated himself before the heated wine. Yet the woman would not get out of his thoughts. "What a fool! A matter of no import would have given her position with others and influence with this Shuzen.... Ha! Ha! How frightened was Chudayu! It is not the shadowy fingers of the dead which do good or ill, but the flesh clad muscles of the living. As to your ghosts...." He snapped his fingers and drank wine in derision. Thus he spent the early hours of the night.

"What's that!" He put the bottle down at the sound of voices in excitement, of running feet. Soon an officer appeared. The *okugata* was threatened with premature delivery. A physician was to be had at once. Shuzen shrugged his shoulders with indifference. Five months – seven months – nine months – what a matter to trouble a man with! So angry was he that they dared not tell him more. Matters were going very badly with her ladyship. In her delirium she raved over the past scene of the punishment. The tortures of this present delivery were added to an hundred fold by the disorders of the over-wrought brain. Then the child was born. The assembled women whispered to each other. A very monster had seen light: perfect in its main parts, but with the face of Emma Dai-O as a foetus – with the fingers lacking on the hands. They dared not let the sick woman see it. She detected their confusion, asked to see the child. She grew more and more excited with refusal, and they were at a loss what to do. Finally the child was brought, to her distress and confusion. Then – as from the ceiling – "Shame on the House of Aoyama Shuzen. A maimed child, a monster is born as its issue." And the voice began to count, followed by the moving lips of her ladyship – "One" – "One" – "Two" – "Two" – "Three" – "Three" – monotonously it went on to – "Nine.... Ah! What shall I do! One is missing. Wa! Wa!" So lamentable the crying voice that a chill went to the hearts of all. Again the count went on; again the failure and the lamentable cry and weeping. Her ladyship sat up. They strove to restrain her, but in her madness she shouted back in answer to the counting – "One, two, three, four, five, six, seven, eight, nine.... Ha! One is missing! Vile slut! Thus to maim the child in malice." She raved and tore at the covering. From the disordered hair streaming around face and bust looked out at them the wan face of O'Kiku. In disorder the women fled. Driven back by the necessity of their duty they found her lying dead in a pool of blood. As for the maimed and deformed monster, he took well to the nurse's breast. Such they always do.

Where was Chudayu in all this confusion? Shuzen had men hunting him high and low. Angered at his absence, his own dislike and suspicion of him as possible rival grew with the night and the hours, rendered bitter by these household scenes. He would settle matters with Chudayu. "Yokubei" he had heard him called; and covetousness turns not only to gold and such like. As fact Chudayu had good excuse for absence. Much out of sorts he had betaken himself to his own rooms and the care of the old woman in charge, his only female companion in lieu of wife. Ah! What weather! The snow changed to sleet and rain drove into and chilled to the marrow those out in the storm. The *baya* (old woman) at his entrance was all astonishment – "Danna Sama! The garments are wet through. Condescend at once to make a change." Gruffly Chudayu accepted her aid. Stripping off first one and then another of the outer garments he too grumbled in his turn – "What a fool the woman was! To lose life against the sacrifice of such a trifling thing. Ah! She was a maddening beauty; of the kind to drive the blood to boiling heat. Never again.... What's that?" Pon-pon: the sound of someone knocking ashes from a pipe into the receiver came from the inner room. The *baya* was laughing – "Ha! Ah! The Danna Sama is a sly one. He is the one to make friends with the beauties. The lady regretted the Danna's absence, said that she would wait the honoured return.... Who? 'Tis she so sought by the Tono Sama himself; and who instead favours the Danna. O'Kiku Dono...." Before the wild stare of Chudayu, the clutch on her wrist, the old woman stopped in fright. Then from within came the counting – "One, two, three, four, five" – "Six," Chudayu mechanically joined in. "Seven" – "Seven" – "Eight" – "Eight" – "Nine" – "Nine" – the words were followed by the chilling lamentable wail of a soul in agony. "What shall I do! What shall I do!" With a yell Chudayu dashed to the *shōji* and threw them back. No one! With astonishment and terror the old woman gazed at him as seeking an explanation which did not come. "The lights in the Butsudan! Namu Amida Butsu! Namu Amida Butsu! Praise to Amida, the Lord Buddha!... Wine! Wine, and much of it; very hot!"

He sat, his head in hands, watching the flickering light in the altar stand. "Ha! 'A woman and a man of small comprehension: these are hard to govern.' Koshi (Confucius) says it. This Chudayu has played the fool to the Tono Sama's extravagances." The bell of Gekkeiji began to strike the hour of the watch. It came clear and mournful across the snow. "How like a woman's nature," says the native scribe. "One" – "One" – "Two" – "Two" – "Three" – "Three." ... Chudayu went on, mechanically following the blows hammered into his brain. Then came the heart rending hopeless wail which chilled his very soul. The old woman in amazement and pain gave a howl as the hot wine ran over hands and fingers. Chudayu on his feet stupidly gazed at the bottle rolling to the end of the room. "'Tis of no import," he muttered. "Now – to get hence. Close up all. Tonight Chudayu returns not." – "But Danna Sama! Condescend to consider! The Danna Sama is not himself. Truly he will be ill. Deign the honoured couch." The couch in that room! He shuddered all over. The old woman wrung and wiped her scalded fingers, and would persuade him to seek rest. She simpered in her blandishment. "Where could she possibly have gone, for *baya* saw no exit? Perhaps the lady comes again; and in the *yashiki* there is no greater beauty than O'Kiku Dono. Fortunate the Danna...." Truly she thought him gone mad. "Shut up!" roared Chudayu. His eyes blazing under the heat of the quantity of his hot stimulant he thrust her, a heap huddled into a corner of the room. Trembling hands adjusted what garments he could lay eyes upon. Over all he threw a long wool cloak with hood and eyelets against the snow. Turning to the entrance he glowered at her, hand on his dagger – "More words of that vile jade, and *baya* joins her own beneath the stone. This Chudayu goes to Nakacho, to a public woman. If that O'Bake comes again.... Ha! Ha!... Let her lie with Baya.... Why! She's not even rotten yet!" He left the old woman stupefied and quaking, himself to leap out into the storm and darkness.

Outside the gate he had a shock. In the shadow he ran into a woman standing by, who turned at his greeting. O'Kiku's face? With clenched fist he would have struck, but the vision faded. "Truly the *baya* is not wrong. Chudayu is mad, or drunk." His knuckles had near encounter with the brazen crest fastened into the post. This brought him to himself. Rapid was his descent of Gomizaka. At its foot was a *kago* stand. "The Danna Sama from the Aoyama *yashiki* – he condescends the *kago*. One all closed? The Danna Sama will lie as snug as in a *koshi* (*kwanoke* = hearse)." Chudayu took the joke badly. The fellow sprawled on the ground under the blow – "Is this a funeral procession? Truly the night itself is bad enough

– without the joke." – "A scurvy knave," humbly explained the *kago* chief. "A country recruit, just to hand. Deign to pardon his impertinence." He edged the fellow off, called up another man – "The Danna stands not on the fare? Truly 'Tis such a night as rarely has been seen. With wind and sleet the men can barely stand. But the Danna is in haste. Surely a woman is at the journey's end.... Not a palanquin but with mats." Chudayu was neatly bundled into the litter. The mats were lowered at the sides and covered with oiled paper. "To Nakanocho; and at good round pace." He hardly heard the functionary's words. "Ah! How she hated this Chudayu! How she glared into the Tono Sama's eyes as he dealt the blow into her pap!... A vicious jade; yet a beauty. Where could such beauty be encountered? May the *kami* (gods) grant Chudayu the same good fortune this night!" More pleasing vision soothed him. He was filled with hot wine and fast grew dazed and sleepy. The gentle motion of the *kago* rocked him as in a cradle. Yet he could not get sleep. Her voice was in his ears; without, in talk with the *kago* men? He raised a corner of the mat. With surprise – "Heigh, *kagoya*! What place is this?" He was passing the moat on his right not left; the hill sloped down, not up toward Nakano (Shinjuku). "Danna Sama, it is Suidobashi." – "Suidobashi! And does one go to Nakanocho by Suidobashi? Knaves! About with you, and to the right course as directed."

The men, after their kind, grumbled; but to themselves; and in a way their fare should hear. "Naruhodo! What a beast of a night is this! Mate, it is to Nakanocho; but Nakanocho whither? The Danna Sama is testy. He is not to be questioned. He might give a cut. Jubei is lucky. He has changed head for rear. A care there! A care there! What? Again around? What a night, and what a Danna to deal with!" The unconscious Chudayu was borne onward. Again the vinous fumes passed off. To his amazement be saw the water on the left; but not what he sought. "Heigh! Heigh! *Kago* men, whither now? What place yonder?" – "Yanagibara, Danna Sama." Chudayu's voice was big with wrath. "True *kago* men as guides! Does one go to Yanagibara to go to Nakanocho of Shinjuku." – "Oya! Oya! The Danna always tells us to go this way, that way. Nakanocho, Nakacho – is it Yoshiwara, or Fukagawa, or Naito Shinjuku towhich the Danna goes? 'Tis but the lady at the pole who has a clear head and forces us to go this way.... Danna, never mind the fare money. Condescend to alight. It is a hard night; too hard for such a baffling task.... Here is your pretty friend again!"

Chudayu raised the mat and looked out. Vaguely outlined in the again whirling snowy darkness stood O'Kiku. With wild cry he sprang out, sword drawn. The *kago* men dropped the litter and took to their heels. Dazed Chudayu looked around him. Ah! He was drunk with wine, and visions haunted him. Yanagibara? Let it be Yoshiwara then. Stalking through the Omon he made his way to the Nagatoya, a tea house at which he was known. "Oya! The honoured Danna Sama of the Bancho *yashiki*. In good season Aikawa Dono; the lady awaits the honoured *buke-sama*." – "A lady waiting? Fool! Who brings a woman to this market where he comes to purchase?" The *bantō* (clerk) of the tea house insisted. "Aikawa Sama, is it not fact? She is barely of twenty years; outstripping in beauty the greatest of the Go Tayu.... Her name? O'Kiku San...." In his amazement the man rose from his kneeling salutation, craned his neck to watch the flying figure of Chudayu disappear. Perhaps the Danna had gone mad. Surely he was mad; and not one to come on foot on such a night and all the way from the Bancho. He sighed at loss of such an eager customer.

Chudayu walked into the first tea house to hand when he had stopped for breath. A first visit, his tea money (*chadai*) was munificent. Such a customer deserved good treatment from the Izuzuya. Hence the attendant guided him to the Miuraya, where was bespoken the presence of the brilliant *oiran* O'Yodo. The hour was late. The *oiran* was detained. Chudayu was sleepy and demanded his room. Hardly had he taken to his couch to await her presence than he was asleep. Leaving her other guest O'Yodo pushed open the *shōji* and entered. She deserved her reputation for beauty. A splendid girl, for she was not more than woman yet. A little tall for her sex; fair and with but little powder, an oval face, long trailing hair, and shapely hands and feet for all this business. *Batan-batan* the sound of the *zōri* (sandals). She dropped these on the outside. The stranger was asleep. Sitting beside him she gathered the folds of her crape night robe about her bare feet. With a deft touch she adjusted the knot of the pink sash which confined it; then turned attention to the long silver chased pipe and the face of the sleeping man. Some feeling was aroused she could not understand. There was much she did not yet understand in this bitter toil of hers.

Chudayu began to speak; at first in halting and broken sentences; then in a continued flood – "Ah! Ha! That look of hate! Chudayu acted most foully. 'Twas he who took the plate, to secure his safety and O'Kiku's death. Deign to pardon. It was not Chudayu; 'twas the Tono Sama who dealt the fatal blow.... What? The suffering?... Ah! But the suffering of mind.... Now she begins – one – two – three – four – five – six – seven – eight – nine.... Kiya!" The shriek rang through the room, bringing O'Yodo to her feet. Crouched beside the *andon* was outlined vaguely the figure of her sister O'Kiku. "Nēsan! Here! And what...." At the words she turned to meet the wide open frighted gaze of Chudayu. The matter of fact, gentle tones calmed him. "A first meeting with the honoured guest. Deign to pardon the awkwardness of Yodo." Chudayu came out of his sleep reassured. He had dreamed; a frightful dream. She told him so, and pressed him curiously as to why he had called out. "The honoured *samurai* (*buke-sama*), who then favours Yodo?" He spoke, as being again himself – the military man, and no less a person than the chamberlain of Aoyama Shuzen Sama, *hatamoto* with a *yashiki* in the Bancho. "Perhaps then a serving maid called O'Kiku is known to the honoured sir." Again Chudayu's doubts were raised at evident resemblance – to be reassured. "No kin: we knew each other well in early life. The father was a great criminal, and O'Kiku, it was heard, was condemned to be a slave for life. Entered in this business nothing has been seen of each other. She is well – in mind and body?" The question was timid, and Chudayu did not notice the unnatural eagerness. "In Kiku's place mind and body are assured their lot; to undergo no change." Captivated by this beauty he was now eager for his good fortune. Reluctant and with misgiving she allowed him to draw her close.

Sampei Dono

He was poor; coarsely and scantily clad as he came on his return through the darkness and snowflakes now coming down wet and moist, whirling and twisting under the increasing gale and gradually turning into a penetrating chilling sleet against which the straw raincoat was poor protection. In this guise Wataru Sampei was the gardener, making a precarious living at which his skill was accidental and vicarious. In his shabby home he was the *samurai*, his two swords treasured, carefully wrapped and put away in the closet; struggling to live in order to bring up this boy Jumatsu in his own cult, to better times and retribution on the upstarts from the South. This night too had been part of his *samurai's* duty, in its *sankei* or pilgrimage to the Asakusa Kwannon. O'Kiku believed in efficacy of prayer to the goddess of mercy. A hasty word, implied rather than spoken, as to a passer by during the first sight of her, and the gesture of acquiescence on his part who had little faith. But the gesture was as strong in its obligation as an oath written and signed in blood.

On approaching his home with surprise he noted a woman by the door. She seemed to be in the act of coming or going. Surely he could not mistake that figure; nay, throwing the light of his lantern ahead a glimpse of the white wan face startled him. His heart leaped within him – "Is it Kiku? How comes the wife here at this hour? How has exit from the *yashiki* been permitted?" But the woman answered not. Instead she moved away from him, into the darkness. More and more astonished Sampei called after her and followed. Always she eluded him. Thus he was led away two hundred, three hundred yards. There she was, halted beneath the willow tree on the river bank. His pace broke into a run. Now she did not move or attempt to elude him, but as he came up the figure was but a stela to point the way to a near-by shrine. Sampei passed his hand over his brow. Kiku was too much on his mind; this forced widowerhood with charge of a toddling boy. Ah! If pity and affection would but allow him to transfer the child to others! Better would it be for both. But how face the mother without the child – and then, the lot of one's favoured child in the house of strangers and under their cold glances? Sampei himself could not part with Jumatsu. Easy was it for him to cut belly – and leave mother and child in this desolate condition. Meanwhile his uneasiness of mind at their present outlook was driving him to delusions.

Taking off his wet outer garments he stole into the bedroom. Now it was very late in the night; he would not disturb the child. To his surprise he found him sitting up on the quilts, shivering and weeping. "Bochan! What's gone wrong?" He took the child's hands, anxious to note any sign of distress or fever. But Jumatsu made answer in his turn – "Mother has just been here. She was crying. She said – 'Bo, the parting is for long. Never again will the mother be seen. Grow up, Bo; grow up to be a fine man.' Then she cried more than ever." A hand seemed to grasp the heart of Sampei – "Mother here, Bochan!" Surely the child could not lie, even make up the story at this age, so fitting into his own uneasy vision. Continued the little fellow mid his tears – "It was not her fault. Someone broke the holly hock plate and charged mother with the crime. Then the Tono Sama killed her. He wanted her for his concubine; and so came to hate her and easily took the tale. It was not her fault. She said this – then went away." – "Whither?" Sampei's tone was so abrupt and harsh to startle the child into quiescence. He pointed to the house altar on its stand – "Mother just went away; into the Butsudan.... And she hasn't come back – to Bochan." He ended in a wail and childish weeping. Ah! The hands now grasping at Sampei were of ice. Slowly he approached the Butsudan. Startled he saw the snow within it. This wild tale was taking the hold of certainty on his mind. He lit first one light, then the other in the altar stand. Then sharply of itself rang the little bell. A cold sweat stood out on Sampei's body – "Namu Amida Butsu! Namu Amida Butsu!" Earnest the prayer for some departed soul. Unconvinced, yet feeling the truth of the impression he passed the night with eyes wide open. With dawn he would go forth to make inquiries at the Bancho *yashiki*. This would be the fifteenth day. Anyhow Kiku would be expecting him.

He set out early, carrying the boy on his back. Humbly and with experience of such places he approached the gateman. "An inquiry to make." – "What is it?" – "At this *yashiki* is there not a woman labouring, one O'Kiku?" The man eyed him with the contemptuous tolerance of him who knows – "Woman labouring? In the *yashiki* there are two score and more. Of Kiku more than one; although those of the men's quarters have nothing to do with such matters. Perhaps the slave girl Kiku is intended.... See her! Good fellow, are you mad? One under condemnation is not to be seen.... You have come far? Even if you had come from Oshu or Kyushu you could not see her.... But all the way from Honjo; it's too bad." The man looked at him with more benevolence. After all he had some heart, and many distressed people came to this *yashiki*; entered into it. "Are you thirsty?... No? In that case entrance there is none; although the water of the well in the *yashiki* is said to be superior to all other, sovereign to cure thirst.... Ah! You have been dying with thirst all night. Your tongue cleaves to the roof of the mouth. Then the case is altered. For the silver thanks are felt. Just enter. Perhaps some maid will come to the well to draw water. Perhaps this Kiku herself. One so ready – of tongue – can easily excuse his presence and this Yozaemon, if there be question."

With humble thanks and joy Sampei followed the instructions. The well was at the corner of the larger paved space and from it he could see into the inner garden and the greater privacy of the establishment. Here he could note more life at this early hour, and even the stir of excitement. People were running to and fro as under some unusual stimulus. Slowly he drank, delayed as long as he could, unnoticed and unquestioned. He could not thus act too long. Indeed as he moved off a foot soldier (*ashigaru*) passing asked his business. He gave excuse as on mission to a servant, whose name he picked up from one just gone by. As the man had taken a message outside his answer was a safe one. Sharply the *ashigaru* repeated the fact of absence, and Sampei had no excuse not to leave. The excitement now was spreading to the front quarters of the *yashiki*. Fragments of talk showed him that his visit was most inopportune. Her ladyship had just died, and the household was in a buzz. When he would again speak to the gateman, the functionary's manner did not encourage it, Sampei took the hint of his cold unrecognizing eye and bowed in humble acknowledgment to all in going out the gate. "Chudayu Dono – where is Aikawa Sama to be found?" – "The honoured chamberlain? He left the *yashiki* last night in the other watch. There has been no return during this of Yozaemon." So much he caught in passing.

Slowly Sampei passed down the Gomizaka and along the moat of the castle. It was with greatest reluctance he left this place. The child began to whimper. "*Otosan* (father), this Jumatsu is hungry." The little fellow's whimper turned to genuine tears. The father heartened him. Just ahead, on the Kudanzaka, all that should be remedied. Of the number of small shops Sampei noted the sign of the Kikkyoya – the House of the Full Well Bucket. Bending under the curtain strips hanging at the front he entered the cook shop. "Deign to come up here.... For food? Of the best: clam soup, a stew of vegetables and fish, hot boiled *tōfu* ... and *sake*, none better." The place did not promise much despite the advertisement. Avoiding the doubtful stew Sampei ordered wine for himself and hot boiled bean paste (*tōfu*) for Jumatsu. As he fed the child, and at opportunity sipped his wine, a blind shampooer entered; in this tiny place to take a seat close by. Apparently he was well known thereabouts. In bringing wine the host sat down beside him to talk – almost into the ear of Sampei. – "Toku no Ichi San, you are early abroad. Does illness or luxurious idleness summon the honoured *Amma San* to the couch?... But yourself, you do not look well. Work late into the night goes not with early rising. This is going to excess." The man coughed and drank, turned his sightless eyes on Sampei. What he said made this latter all attention.

"It is no early call brings out this Ichibei. Ah! What a night this last!" – "Truly so," replied the matter of fact host. "And no sign of the storm's cessation." He looked out for a moment on the flakes of snow, again coming down thick and heavy. "Drink your wine, Ichibei Dono. In truth you are as white as yonder falling flakes which you do not see. And 'Tis said your kind cannot see ghosts." – "See them; no. To those whose eyes are darkened by the night of blindness the gods have granted grace against such visions. But alas! Other faculties have been sharpened. He who cannot see, can hear. Listen Jirobei San. Last night this Ichibei was called to the *yashiki* of Okubo Sama. The *okugata* was in pain and needed his treatment for the limbs. It is a kindly house, one good to go to. The storm kept Ichibei in the *yashiki*: Food and the mat was granted, for his lordship would not send a cur, once granted shelter, out into storm and darkness. But next door it is very different. Here is the *yashiki* of Aoyama Shuzen

Sama – the Yakujin of Edo. Jirobei San knows of him. His lordship took the *yashiki* for the old well of the Yoshida Goten. 'Tis said at nights he takes wine and pipe, sits by the well, and in his hardiness and defiance of weather and season challenges the ghosts to appear. Last night.... Ah! The scene rung into the ears appears before the eyes even of the blind. It was the sound of blows – as of a wet cloth striking bare flesh. A woman plead for mercy. 'Vile wench.... Kiku.' These words were heard. Then such a scream – 'Kiya!' as of rending silk – that yet it rings into the ears of this Ichibei; to banish sleep and peace of mind for the rest of the night. What could it be? Had the ghosts appeared? Or had some maid displeased the Tono Sama, and hence suffered death at his hand (*te-uchi*)? He is not one to spare suffering.... Ah! How she suffered! All night Ichibei has lain awake and suffered with her. It seems as if her cry never would depart from these ears. With dawn I fled – without food, and doubtless to the astonishment of all. Feeling faint, your shop offered refreshment." – "Another bottle?... O'Kabe! At once: for Toku no Ichi San.... Honoured guest, thanks. Deign again the honoured patronage. Sixty *mon* the price, *sayonara*."

Sampei paid the scot, and with Jumatsu carefully wrapped up against the storm passed out into the open air. Now he was himself again; the *samurai* of Kai, with the old traditions of his province and his liegeship to the great Takeda House. Against this Aoyama double was the vendetta – for Jinnai, for his wife Kiku. His ears had drunk in the convincing tale of the blind shampooer. His decision was as ready. His steps now were bent to the Miuraya in the Yoshiwara. At his name the *bantō* expressed surprise. "The *oiran* was about to send a message; most opportune the honoured coming. Deign for the moment to wait." Related to their great attraction Sampei had every attention. Shortly the sound of *zōri* was heard, and O'Yui entered the room. Jumatsu viewed her beauty and splendour with grave approval, astonishment, and fear. "Obasan (auntie)? But she is young; beautiful, just like mother. Oh! Just like the pictures of the great Tayu." The two elders listened, preoccupied and with pained smile. "What book; and where seen?... Oya! Oya! In the priest's room at the Fukuganji? That should not be. Priest and *oiran* are not of kin." O'Yui's laugh was so silvery that Jumatsu in admiration pressed close to her knee. Clasping him she spoke to Sampei. Ah! How great was her anxiety. As she told her tale the heart of Sampei was filled with wrath and certainty – "This Chudayu is such a strange fellow. The weather still holds him to the place. Hence by good luck it was possible to ask for a consultation. Has not some injury befallen the person of Nēsan? The ravings of this man in his drunken sleep, the vision of the sister, the face and garments all dyed with blood, cannot these find confirmation or disproof? In the embrace of this man Yui shudders." She wept.

With growing weight and terror at heart she noted the increasing gloom of Sampei's face. "Kiku is no longer of this world. It is true. Herself she told the tale to Jumatsu. At the *yashiki* all is confusion with the death of the lady of the House. By accident Jumatsu's vision is corroborated by the blind shampooer, led into the cook shop of Kudanzaka by the same hand which led Chudayu to the arms of the *oiran* O'Yodo. The evidence is complete for this Sampei. Tonight – at the first opportunity – Sampei kills this Aoyama Shuzen; then cuts belly. As for Chudayu, Kiku has brought him to O'Yui San. Deign to accept the charge. Last night he has been the lover, and the chance of the weather and the charms of O'Yui have kept him here. Let the coming night be his last." He put a restraining hand on the sleeve of O'Yui. In vengeance at once she would have rushed off to poniard this obscene fellow. Be once more the object of his embraces? Alas! Hers indeed was "the bitter toil," which led her to the arms of this scoundrel dripping with a sister's blood. But she listened to the cold and cautious counsel of Sampei, and nodded comprehension and assent. When she re-entered the room where Chudayu was drinking and roistering there was not a sign of any emotion. Once again she was the harlot, to charm and inveigle him into remaining with her. Ha! Ha! The gods had granted his prayer. "Kiku? She was a beauty – and the impression of childhood would be corroborated by her later appearance. But even thus she is a faded old woman to the honoured *oiran*. A bag of bones!" He roared with drunken laughter; and O'Yui fingered the handle of the dagger in her bosom, in frenzy at the vile jest. "Come now! Kiku has been the object of Chudayu's love. He confesses it. But now – away with such an O'Bake. He seeks the greater solace of O'Yodo's arms." The wine nearly choked him. His eyes stood out. He gasped and choked. Anxiously the *oiran* nursed him back to breath.

Late that night he had gone to bed very drunk. The ninth hour struck (1 am). O'Yodo, who had sought temporary excuse, entered. Chudayu again was dreaming, horribly. Ah! This vision would never pass. O'Kiku was standing by him. At first faint, then loud came the voice, and Chudayu counted with her – "One" – "One" – "Two" – "Two" – "Three" – "Three".... On went the count. Now she was astride of him, pressing him down, throttling him. "O'Kiku Dono! It was not Chudayu. The treachery was his; but the Tono Sama gave the blow." He writhed and struggled in his sleep. Then O'Yui dealt the thrust, straight downward. "Yai! Yai! Ah!" The scream rang out, startling all around. Alas! A little misdirected the dagger glanced from the bone and pierced the shoulder. As the man rolled her off the girl made one desperate effort. Deep she thrust the blade into his right side, ripped it up and side ways. "Kiya!" Chudayu staggered and rolled over, hands to his side to hold in the severed liver and guts. When she would strike again her hands were held. The bawd (*yarite*), aroused and passing, saw the shadow of the raised dagger. The *bantō* had come to her aid. While some sought to aid the desperately wounded man, others drew away O'Yodo, again the woman and overcome with tears of regret at her failure.

Jinzaemon of the Miuraya questioned her. Was it *shinjū* – a mutual suicide to insure happiness together in the next life? Had she really known the man before, and not pretended new acquaintance? Then, without mention of Sampei, she told the story of her vision, her certainty that inquiry would establish the truth of its accusation. Jinzaemon had no recourse. The Yoshiwara *bugyō*, with *dōshin*, was soon at hand. "To kill a man on such evidence...." But before applying torture he would question the victim. Chudayu's case was hopeless. The liver was almost severed. Death was but a matter of an hour or two. During that time his ravings in delirium, his confession in lucid moments, added a new and momentous phase to the case in corroborating the tale of the*oiran* as to the strange vision. The *bugyō* did not dare to go further. He must consult those higher in authority. A *hatamoto* of the land was involved; one just favoured with appointment as *tsukaiban* (staff officer) to the suzerain. The *machibugyō* himself had no power in this case. Hence the affair – its nature and its proof – must be submitted to the *waka-toshiyori*, the officer of State in immediate charge of the *hatamoto*, their control and interests. Meanwhile the affair must be smothered and strict search made for the recent visitor Sampei, who had completely disappeared. Jumatsu readily was traced to the care of the house master (*iyenushi*) at Koume. His tenant, on plea of business in Kai, had left the child with him. Thus they went astray, and thus failed to act. Meanwhile Shinano no Kami at last determined to send for and question Aoyama Shuzen. The seventh day following the retribution was reached – to the great enlightenment of these puzzled magistrates.

Aoyama Wins his Suit

Aoyama's *yashiki* blazed with light. The guests looked around, at the many lamps, the waiting-women in dainty attire, the ornament of service and of substance; and then looked into each other's faces. The unseemliness of the thing was on the minds of all these dozen to twenty gentlemen. The body of the wife had hardly been carried from the house to the funeral pyre. It was true that grief was to be given no display in the *samurai* code. The new promotion offered excuse for its celebration. But on the whole this feast seemed an indecent exhibition of rejoicing. "Aoyama Uji is not the Shuzen of old. What has got into the man this past month?" Thus Okumura Shuzen spoke of his namesake. "Bah! It is the shadow of Kiku, the 'sewing girl'. Aoyama rejoices in thus replacing old material. May he get a better heir on her than his last. 'Tis said to be a monster!" Endo Saburozaemon whispered, half in jest and half in a savage earnest of disapproval.

Okubo Hikoroku first broached the matter openly at table. "Aoyama Uji, is this not a strange meeting? Here we are, all members of the Gaman Kwai; as *hatamoto*, men close to the suzerain's knee and ready for the call to battle. But this – with the glitter of apparel in substance and women, it is show and feast for *kuge* (court nobles), a meeting to view the moon and its light upon the snow. Deign to explain." Aoyama smiled. He might have made some formal excuse for this eccentricity. Saburozaemon spoke out for him – "Don't be obtuse, Okubo Uji. The one lacking here is the cause of the feast. O'Kiku Dono still delays. Is it not so, Aoyama Uji?" He spoke with cold certainty, a curious intonation in voice. Aoyama was black with a fury about to burst forth when Okubo sprang up. He looked around. "Just so! Wait but a moment. We'll have her here." Aoyama was turned aside, and would have detained him. "Hikoroku Dono, it is useless. Kiku is not in the *yashiki*." To the dubious look of astonishment – "It is fact. She was a vile disloyal woman. Breaking the holly hock plate, the trust gift of the Toshogu, this Aoyama put her to death. This shall be apology to the suzerain's House." Okubo sat down again in pure amazement – "For what is said one feels regret. The apology is made; but surely...." Endo Saburozaemon laughed outright. He seemed with intention to egg him on. Okubo turned indignantly. "Why laugh, Endo Uji? Is the life of a human being to be put against a piece of porcelain?" – "Saburozaemon laughs at your credulity, Okubo Dono. It is but a ruse to put us from the search. Kiku certainly is not far off."

Okubo danced up in a fury. This time he was not to be kept. "'Tis true! But the badger's lurking hole, the place where he keeps her, is known. Soon she shall be here." Defying Shuzen's wrath he and Endo left the room. Okubo was ahead. Throwing open the *shōji* of the maid's room he looked within. Ah! Standing by the closet in the dim light was the figure of O'Kiku. "Kiku, why are you here, not joining in the feast? The beauty and the lady, whose love seduces so stern a man as Shuzen to soft ways, is not to neglect the guests. Come to the banquet hall." He seized her sleeve. Said Saburozaemon from the *rōka* – "Whom do you address, Okubo Uji?" He looked around the room. "There is no one here.... Kiku? You grasp a garment hanging on the clothes rack." It was true. Dazed and somewhat upset Okubo returned to the banquet room. Aoyama met defiantly the hard look of Endo, the inquiring question of Okubo – "Is it true Aoyama? Did you really value a human life against a plate, and kill her?" – "It is plain fact," was the answer.

Again the strange looks passed between the guests. Some shrugged their shoulders. Others looked at him and whispered. Some laughed, with glances at the frightened faces of the waiting women. "It's not to be believed," said the emphatic tones of Okubo. Suddenly a breath seemed to go round the room. Everylight went out; except the one before Hikoroku.

Dimly outlined by Shuzen's side could be seen the figure of O'Kiku. The wan face amid the long disordered dangling hair; the gore smeared face, and neck, and bosom, sent a thrill and shudder through those present. At the exclamations Shuzen turned. He saw her – "Vile jade! You too would reproach Shuzen. A cut for you!" He sprang up, dagger in hand to cut her down. Then followed a wild scene with the raving man. The maids sought to avoid death; happily with success beyond trifling injuries, for sight of a woman made him frantic. Surrounding Shuzen the men drew him on. From behind Okubo, Okumura, Endo rushed upon him. Overpowered he was secured. With the madness of the host the banquet came to an end. As they left Okubo said to Endo Saburozaemon – "Really Endo Uji, why so rough in speech with Aoyama? With those of one band quarrels are not to be sought." – "Nor will be," answered Saburozaemon with a slight tinge of contempt. Then he added slowly – "There is a strange affair in Yoshiwara. The chamberlain of Shuzen, one Chudayu, is involved; and Shuzen with him. This matter of Kiku threatens grave issue with the *waka-toshiyori*. It is said that the two murdered the woman – because both wanted her for concubine." He laughed harshly – "Why tell these facts to neighbour Okubo?" Said Hikoroku, with his blunt truth – "The sounds and sights from Shuzen's *yashiki* are not always pleasant. There are tales in the household of a night – that on which Shuzen's wife died. All there was in confusion. It is for fellow-members to protect the reputation of each other." Endo was rebuked in turn.

Shuzen was himself again. With the passing of the wine, the guests, the confusion, he was the cold, collected, dreaded master of a few hours ago. Respectfully the *kerai* withdrew. Left to himself he pondered the events of these hours. He recognized and measured the concentrated dislike expressed in the words and actions of Endo Saburozaemon, egging on Okubo, irritating himself to desperation. To Shuzen it was a question as to just what was meant. At his age even in his caste men did not seek each other out to draw the sword. The issue was much more serious, involving disgrace. He would like to get at the inner motive of this fellow's action. How invaluable the aid of Chudayu, who knew the ins and outs of the *yashiki* of all Edo, and particularly of his lord's intimates. But he had disappeared – as if the earth had swallowed him. Shuzen had condoned too many instances of the chamberlain's free use of his lord's funds, to come upon him harshly for any peculation. The man had been useful in many dubious actions; in bribery, solicitation, pimping, as a useful and facile witness. Chudayu would worm himself to the bottom of this matter in short order.

Thus he went to rest. Despite disordered brain his sleep was sound. It was Gekkeiji's bell striking the ninth hour (1 am) which roused; or else the throat fouled and dried his mouth. He was parched beyond measure; his tongue seemed to fill the whole cavity. Impatiently he called – "Heigh there! Water! Is there no one to attend?" – "At the lord's service...." The gentle tones of a woman made answer. She knelt at his pillow. The water pitcher was offered. He took it and drank greedily. Then – "What maid is this? Does she seek Shuzen's bed? He is in no humour for such favour." And the girl wailed in answer – "Ah! Ah! Harsh his lordship's tone, harsh his words. Has not long since his command been issued? The fault lies not with Kiku. A lying officer stands between the Tono Sama and his handmaid." Shuzen sat bolt upright, glaring. Framed by the long trailing hair there appeared to his eyes the wan, blood smeared face of O'Kiku. With a yell he was on one knee – "Wretched woman! Does Kiku still pursue and solicit Shuzen? Make ready! Again a cut!" He sprang to his feet, grasped and drew the pillow sword. With smothered cry of terror and anguish the figure turned to flee; but he cut her down from shoulder to pap. As he did so the *shōji* were flung wide apart. The moonlight from the opened *amado* flooded the room and lighted up the intruder.

Rage and hate growled in the tones of Shuzen – "A bandit thief and doubtful fellow, thus to push himself into the presence of a *hatamoto* of the land! Fellow, name yourself: who thus by night breaks into Shuzen's presence, intrudes upon his pleasure." Harsh and insulting the laugh of Sampei. He pointed with his drawn sword to the bleeding prostrate corpse of the unfortunate waiting maid, cut down by Shuzen in belief of the apparition of her namesake. "More than one Kiku harbours in the lair of Aoyama. Would he slay them all in sacrifice to his lust? Wataru Sampei comes to ask account of his wife Kiku, daughter of Jinnai, *rōnin* of Takeda Ke of Kai, as is himself. Now – to the contest! God of the bow and feathered shaft, favour this Sampei!" – "Favour this Shuzen!" Both men made invocation almost in the same breath as they sprang at each other. Sampei was pushed on by rage and vengeance; Aoyama by a savage joy in combat. Here was a worthy antagonist, a true taste of old of the battle field. If Sampei was the younger man, he was also in worse training than Shuzen; and in his poor condition hardly a match for the practised soldier. However Shuzen was compelled to admire a resourcefulness in parrying his own fierce attack, the beauty of his enemy's Muramasa blade, which seemed itself to act and seek his life. "Shuzen's prize – the sword of Sampei!" He shouted in exultation. Sampei was forced back to the *rōka*. At the sill he tripped and fell. "Now off with you – to Meido and the Yellow Fountain, to join wife and parent thief." Shuzen in joy swung high his blade for the fatal blow. Sampei without sword was helpless at his feet. But the blade did not descend. Shuzen's arm was held fast. By the outraged wife, O'Kiku, as later tradition would assert? At this pass Sampei used his dagger. Plunged straight into the belly of Shuzen with it he disembowelled him. Abandoning hold on his weapon, with a screech Aoyama fell, twisting and writhing in the pool of his blood. When the *kerai*, roused by the disturbance, the shouts and the clashing of swords, fell on Sampei, to disarm and make short work of him, the *karō* Makishima Gombei prevented them. With difficulty he dragged Shuzen's sword out from the deep cut it had made in the beam of the partition. "Stain not good weapons with the blood of a rascal and thief, who shall undergo the torture and the disgrace of the execution ground. Be sure his lordship will be well avenged. It is better so."

Thus with bitter regret Sampei found himself avenged, but still in life. The next day, with the presence of the messengers from Shinano no Kami, the situation changed. With the report from Makishima was demanded the person of Wataru Sampei, whose story fitted into present evidence obtained. Deeper and deeper went the investigation into Aoyama's house affairs. Here was great disorder – harshness, lust, ill discipline. On this latter charge – lack of discipline – official displeasure gladly fell. The tale of the monster, obviously unfit for any service to the suzerain, came out. The *kaieki* of the House – deprivation of rank and income – followed. As far as posthumous action could disgrace, so far did Shuzen suffer.

Much better was the fate of Sampei. The case of the Bancho *yashiki* no longer could be hid under a bushel. It was the affair of a *hatamoto*, so hated by the *daimyō*. Satsuma no Kami sought and obtained his charge. During the weeks which followed Sampei was the object of respect and solicitude of those who had the care of him. As *rōnin* of the Takeda House this was all the greater in this *yashiki* where the Tokugawa were held in no great affection. The breaking into the *yashiki* of a *hatamoto*, the slaying of its lord, could not be condoned. The official world was glad to combine this with the lack of discipline decision. When the inevitable order came to cut belly it was a chamberlain of Satsuma no Kami who acted as *kaishaku* (second); and Sampei knew that to this man would fall the possession and adoption of his little son. Thus came he to his end, and his House into this brave heirship. Thus was disappointed the malice of Shuzen, in his last breath denouncing his slayer as the husband of O'Kiku. Announced Horibe Izumi no Kami, the *machibugyō* who made final disposition of the case – "Between Sampei and Kiku no marriage being proved, the issue belonging to the man, the child Jumatsu is held sinless; for the woman Yui detention for further examination of conduct and condition." This examination never came; nor was intended to come. For some months she was detained in the *yashiki* of Horibe Sama. Then the third Shogun died; a general pardon followed of all ordinary offenders. Under this order she was released, and the Miuraya had the hint or good sense not to press for renewed service. A nun, she cut off the long and beautiful hair, to pray in this world for the souls of father, sister, he who had acted as more than brother in the vengeance taken. Thus through the long years to her final and irrevocable release without any earthly condition.

The Sarayashiki

Again the site of the Yoshida Goten lapsed to waste land. Through the years stood the *yashiki* of Aoyama Shuzen, in wall and roof and beam gradually going to rot and ruin. Passing by on nights of storm wayfarers saw most frightful visions – the sports and processions of spectres issuing forth from the old well of the one time inner garden. Their wailing cries and yells were heard. Conspicuous among them was the sight of the unfortunate Kiku, her wan face framed in the long rank disordered hair; the weird beauty frightful in its expression of horror, as with the stumps of fingers she counted – "One, two, three ... four, five, six ... seven, eight, nine." Then came the haunting fearful cry – "Alas! What's to be done? One lacks. Oh! Oh!" Sight, sound, glare went to the hearts of the stoutest witnesses. Soon the ill fortune of those thus favoured with the vision of the Lady of the Plates was rumoured abroad. Wounds, money losses, even death fell on them or on their households. Men no longer were curious. They fled the neighbourhood of this ill omened gap in Earth's surface, unseemly exit for these foul spirits. On nights of rain and storm none passed that way. Even by day the children were rebuked and forbidden to approach the well.

Many are the stories as to the place. To instance one of these: It was Hoei third year (1706) – the approach of winter in this tenth month (November). Then came to Edo town a wandering pilgrim (*shugenja*) and his wife. Tramping the land all summer to Nippon's varied shrines and sights, now they were on the return to their home in Michinoku (Oshu). Much had they heard of Edo, capital seat of Nippon's great lord. Every day busied with its sights they returned wearied to their inn in the Shitaya district. This day they had wandered far. Returning from Renkeiji of Kawagoe they passed the Naito Shinjuku quarter. Almost as great, if of different kind, was the woman's curiosity at sight of the caged beauties, waiting the summons of those far better supplied with cash than her own spouse. Finally in indignation she dragged away the loiterer; and muttering rebuke followed after the jingle of the rings on his pilgrim's staff. They were passing through the Go Bancho, along the long stretch of *yashiki* wall. From a postern gate came forth a woman. The light of her lantern fell on the man and his equipment – "Oya! Oya! Good fortune indeed: honoured *shugenja*, a moment's stay. Tonight a memorial service is to be said for the mansion's lord. Condescend to enter and grant service." Willingly husband and wife heard the invitation to rest their wearied bodies. Passing through the garden water was supplied to wash the feet. Then they were seated before an ample feast fit for their kind; of glutinous rice balls coated with the sweet bean paste (*botamochi*), of macaroni the savour of which tickled the nostrils, *sake* followed, in generous quantity and of quality to match.

Said the girl – "It is an all night service that is requested. Deign to undertake the watch and prayer. Ample shall be the reward." Prostrate the *shugenja* spoke his thanks. The Butsuma, or room containing the little shrine, was close at hand. Seating himself, his woman just behind, he bowed and made reverence. "Thanks for the honoured entertainment so generous and excellent. May the honoured spirit find rest, at once entering Nirvana ... and now, the Hannya Shinkyo – *Sutra* of the divine intelligence." He began the recitation, accompanied by his wife. Both intoned the *nembutsu* – "Namu Amida Butsu! Namu Amida Butsu! Praise to Amida the Lord Buddha!" Again the recitation of the *Sutra* was begun. The hours of the night advanced. Man and wife became more and more drowsy; slower and slower came the words of the sacred writing. Then the man nodded off to sleep; as long before had the wife. The hour of the ox struck at Gekkeiji, filling this whole district with its heavy boom. The man woke with a start. What fearful shriek was that? Close by in the next room a woman's voice began counting. But such a voice! "One, two, three...." on it went to "nine.... Ah! Woe is me! One lacks. What's to be done!" Shrill, blood chilling the cry of anguish which followed. Curiosity overcame terror. The man stole to the screens and gently opened the merest slit. Over his shoulder looked the startled wife.

A shudder went through both at the sight. Wan, frail, the beautiful anguished evil face of a girl could be seen through the long tangled hair framing it. Slender to the emaciation of great suffering she knelt before the pile of plates she was counting – "One, two, three, four, five, six, seven, eight, nine...." The wild chilling scream froze man and woman. For at the moment in sprang another female, in whose worn emaciated face and figure was displayed such concentrated evil passion of hatred and jealousy as rarely to be seen on human being. Like the flying hateful god Idaten she sprang upon the girl, grasped her long black hair, and hurled her to this side and that. Helpless the victim held up the bloody stumps of fingers. Now the face was seen to be dyed in blood, the garments dyed red with blood, the girl again agonizing in a pool of blood. With horror the pilgrim and the woman hid their faces. The man's hands trembled as he struck the bell and intoned the holy recital. Thus in a daze, amid the counting, the cries and shouts, the weeping and the wailing, he went on. The cry of the cock was heard. As if by magic all the wild sounds ceased. The wanderers looked around in amazement. The altar was the stone curb of a well. The *yashiki* and its magnificence stood close by; but the building was roofless and in ruins. Chilled to the bone, half dead and half mad with fright, the two fled – to reach their inn.

At their tale host and those assembled shook their heads. "It is the Sarayashiki of the Bancho, the well that of the old Yoshida Goten, whence ghosts issue; unless by good fortune the vision be a trick of fox or badger. Honoured Sir, have prayers said to avoid ill fortune." But a merry, foul, cynical old fellow – peasant turned townsman – twinkled in his laughter. "Then O'Kiku San has favoured the *shugenja* and his spouse with feast and gifts?" – "'Twas very strange," naively replied the pilgrim. "Copious and splendid the entertainment. Of the reality there can be no doubt. This Jubei did not feast in a dream on those dainties." The host and other auditors broke into coarse laughter – "Feast! The *botamochi* was of horse dung, the macaroni was earth-worms, the wine – was urine." All roared in their great joy. The unfortunate pilgrims, much put out, made gesture of discomfiture and fright. Said the peasant-townsman, in sly hit at the host – "Perchance O'Kiku brought the viands from near-by inn or cook shop. Surely these furnish little better." Laughing he left the now angry innkeeper to aid his wretched guests, writhing and retching in all the pains, actual and imagined of such a feast.

Command went forth to the holy man – and from the Shogun Ke himself. A halt must be brought to these unseemly proceedings so close to the suzerain's dwelling. These priests of the Dendzu-In, in the shadow of whose temple rested so many of the Tokugawa dead, were famed for learning and for piety. The founder of the Hall, Ryoyo Shonin, had set to his successors this standard as necessary accomplishment, bequeathing to them perhaps the ability to meet the demand of his title of Mikatsuki Shonin. Between his eyes was a mole in shape like to the crescent moon of the third day. Hence the appellation and its meaning application; for as the moon waxed to its full, so did the Shonin with advancing years wax great in learning, and throw his increasing light upon mankind. Of this first prior there is a tale. It was the period of the Ashikaga wars, and the Shonin, for safety and on business of his order, was resident for the nonce at Asonuma in Kotsuke province. As he prayed and wrought in the night, without rose violent sound of fighting and disturbance. Rising he looked forth. Two bands of men at direst odds displayed the greatest cruelty to each other. But what men! Emaciated to flesh and bone, weird and unhappy of face, the Shonin saw that these were not of this world. His determination was at once taken. Rosary in hand and intoning the *nembutsu* he stepped forth. The strife parted before him; its actors were prostrate in his presence. "What means this fierceness of battle?" asked the prelate. "Surely ye are not of the world, thus without mercy to strive to do such pitiless cruelty." – "Not of this world," said one raising his head; "but no more cruel than men in the flesh. In the Gempei wars, fighting we lost our lives. Our bodies tumbled promiscuously into one common ditch, without rites or worship, the grudge still continues through the decades. Deign, honoured priest, the aid of prayers of one so holy, for the rest of all." Gladly the prior grasped the opportunity – "For such surely is the charm of the Sacred Name – the paper with the sacred characters of the Nembutsu, Namu Amida Butsu. Not this ignorant foolish cleric, but the vow of the Nyōrai, Amida, relieves you from the Hell of fighting (Shurado). Deign to accept the charm and enter Nirvana." Gladly the outstretched hands received it. Then all vanished in a mist. On the following day with discretion and modesty the prior told his experience to his open mouthed and credulous disciples. An ancient man of the place was found to point out where tradition placed the burial and its mound. The bones found on digging were sorted, and with rites found burial. Never after were prior, disciples, or villagers troubled with these visions. But the prior's reputation took an upward bound, to the credit of his sect.

Thus it was with his successor – himself a true Mikatsuki Shonin in the illumination of his learning – "From his youth he had abandoned the world, and all the scripture had passed under his eyes. At eighteen years he knew all the *sutra* and the doctrines of Shaka (Sakyamuni), and books whether exoteric or esoteric. Moreover he understood thoroughly astrology and almanacs, the poetry of Morokoshi (China) and Nippon, and instrumental music. Truly once heard he knew ten times, so clever he was." It was to this Saint, in his eighty-second year, that the order came to lay the ghost of O'Kiku, to dispel the disorderly spectres of the well of the Yoshida Goten. "A difficult, nay a severe task; but one well within the power and mercy of the Buddha. Tonight we go forth to the attempt. Let all exert themselves." His subject clerics bowed low – "Respectfully heard and obeyed." They liked it not. The nights were cold; the place noted for bad company, and bad weather. But the order of their head was not to be disobeyed.

With the first watches of the stormy night the Shonin and some thirty priests were assembled about the well curb. Earnestly the Shonin read the sacred writing. Vigorously his followers made the responses. Louder the voices and greater their confidence as the night progressed without sign of visions. Then said the Shonin – "Surely great is the efficacy of the *sutra*. Namu Amida Butsu! Namu Amida Butsu! All evil visions and spectres vanish; to seek the peace and oblivion of Nirvana. Let the event prove the efficacy of the charm." – "Namu Amida Butsu! Namu Amida Butsu!" Loud the voices of the priests, but now in terror. The bell of Gekkeiji was striking the hour of the ox (1 am). Crouching and shivering they saw the spectral lighting up of the well. The blue glittering points began to dot its mouth. Then swarms of spectres began to pour forth, obscene and horrible. Among them appeared the ghost of O'Kiku. Stricken with fear the priests stopped all reading of the holy writ. Flat on their faces, their buttocks elevated high for great concealment, they crouched in a huddled mass. "Namu Amida Butsu! Namu Amida Butsu! Spare us, good ghosts – thus disturbed most rudely in your nightly haunt and revels. Ha! Ah! One's very marrow turns to ice. No more! No more! Away!" But the Shonin held firm. Surrounded by the jibing menacing mass of spirits, steadily and without fear he hung on to his scroll, read the *sutra*, intoned the *nembutsu*. One by one his company stole away; as did the spectres with approaching dawn.

He did not reproach his flock. Said the prior to the shamed assembly – by daylight: "Surely this is a very difficult undertaking. This curse of the dead is no ordinary one. It is a soul without light, of some highly debauched sinner, of some woman vowed to eternal hate. Deep the malignancy; but deeper yet the efficacy of Mida's vow. Seven nights will do it. Let all make every effort." He looked around, with trace of gentle rebuke – "We are men who have left the world (*shukke*). Why then fear the dead; when ye are part and parcel of them? Perhaps greater company is needed." He sought it from his fellow priors. From Shiba to Asakusa they swarmed. With fifty, with seventy, with a hundred and seventy priests, all reciting the *Sutra*, intoning the *nembutsu*, the noise and confusion rose high above the sound of storm and spectre. Sleep was banished far and wide thereabouts. But this could not last. "One, two, three, four...." with the counting of the plates the chilling heart rending shriek, the wail of the unhappy girl, the stoutest volunteers quailed and with their hands shut out the spectral vision. These volunteers disappeared with the second week of recitation entered on by the Shonin. Even his own band began to fail him. They sent substitutes, in the shape of the temple servants, the lowest grade, the Shoke Sama. When a third week was announced, as sure to accomplish the exorcism, there was open rebellion. It was with sadness and admiration that the Shonin saw his band thus reduced to a few faithful men, the oldest of his flock, almost as old as himself – and these deaf, blind, and almost dumb. "Ah! It is a tremendous affair. Deep the malignancy of this curse. This foolish priest has overrated his reputation with the Buddha. Great the discredit to the sect and temple at the wide heralded failure." He felt as ill and out of sorts away from the presence of the vision, as did his disciples in its presence. He was old and foolish and over-confident.

The prior slept on his cushion, his robes still wet with the storm and rain of the previous night. Then came a woman, dressed in sombre garb. Approaching the sleeping priest she wrote upon his sleeve the character *ki* 機, bowed reverently, and disappeared. He awoke seeming to hear her footsteps. How clear was this dream! The character *ki*, what did it portend? The Buddha would not fail his priest. Taking himself to the altar he prostrated himself before the seated figure. Then he prayed. And as he prayed – perhaps resumed his nap – wonderful to say again the character 機 appeared, this time on the Buddha's sleeve. The Shonin rubbed his eyes. Was he awake or dreaming? He did not know. '*Ki*', the chance, the opportunity that the successful man in every undertaking grasps, where others fail. He must apply it to his own calling and the crisis. They exercised their brains; he was reputed to be well furnished. This next night was the last of the third seven days. Failing favourable issue he would take up his staff and depart to other place, never to reappear in the beloved precincts of his hall. Thus inspired he thought and thought. The grave, kindly, piercing eyes became brighter and brighter. Then his monks came running in surprise and alarm. The reverend prior was laughing – not in merriment, but with the joy of him who has found the successful issue to be so plain and easy.

This last and critical night in storm and riot proved to be the worst of all. Said the Shonin with grave kindness – "This night the Shonin goes; others need not accompany." All rejoiced – until they saw his preparation to face the rain and cold. Then they weakened, and all plead to accompany him. Splendid the train assembled around the well curb. Again the reading of the *sutra* began, the intonation of the *nembutsu*. Again the clerics cursed their ill timed enthusiasm, which brought them out in the storm and to such unseemly company. Again the ghosts issued forth from the old well in their obscene riot. Jeering, menacing they swarmed around the frightened priestly band. Immoveable the prior. Natural and supernatural seemed to hang on the issue between priest and spectres. The figure of O'Kiku, wan, sad, malignant appeared. She counted – "One, two, three, four, five, six, seven, eight, nine...." – "Ten!" shouted the Shonin, extending the Junen. "Ara! What joy! None lack. Ah! By the Shonin's virtue this Kiku secures Nirvana. Gratitude and obeisance are due." With the words the figure faded, the spectres disappeared, the storm rumbled and passed off rapidly to the distance, and the stars shone out on the cold clear sky of a perfect fall night with its studded firmament.

Thus did the Shonin find the secret in the *ten* repetition of the sacred formula – the *ju* nen. On her finger stumps O'Kiku counted – counted as does the successful man in the business of life. But O'Kiku was maimed. The thumb was lacking. Hence the tale went but to nine. The missing factor once supplied her count found completion. Long had been accomplished her vow of indignant vengeance, but still the plates remained to count for her own release, and this she could not effect. Great was the reputation thus acquired to priest and temple.

Legends of the Sea

Introduction

AS AN ISLAND NATION, it is only natural that the sea holds much significance for Japan. In bygone years, on the last day of the Festival of the Dead the sea would be covered with countless *shōrōbune* (soul-ships), for on that day, called *Hotoke-umi*, which means Buddha-Flood, or the Tide of the Returning Ghosts, the souls go back to their spirit world again. No superstitious human being would dream of putting out to sea amid such sacred company, for the sea that night belongs to the dead; it is their long pathway to the realm where Emma-O reigns supreme. It sometimes happened, however, that a vessel would fail to come to port before the departure of the soul-ships, and on such occasions it is said that the dead would arise from the deep, stretch forth their arms, and implore that buckets may be given them. Sailors would present the ghosts with one that has no bottom, for if they gave the dead sound buckets, the angry spirits would use them for the purpose of sinking the vessel.

"The legend of Urashima," wrote Professor B.H. Chamberlain in *Japanese Poetry*, "is one of the oldest in the language, and traces of it may even be found in the official annals." Indeed, the popular version, which we give in this section, was included in standard school reading books in the first half of the twentieth century and has become one of the 'core' fairy tales of Japan. In that tale we are taken to the Dragon Palace, while elsewhere in this section we encounter a Serpent God, the spirit of a magical abalone and a 'shark person'.

Urashima and the Tortoise

ONE DAY URASHIMA, who lived in a little fishing village called Midzunoe, in the province of Tango, went out to fish. It so happened that he caught a tortoise, and as tortoises are said to live many thousands of years, the thoughtful Urashima allowed the creature to return to the sea, rebaited his hook, and once more waited for the bite of a fish. Only the sea gently waved his line to and fro. The sun beat down upon his head till at last Urashima fell asleep.

He had not been sleeping long when he heard someone calling his name: "Urashima, Urashima!"

It was such a sweet, haunting voice that the fisher-lad stood up in his boat and looked around in every direction, till he chanced to see the very tortoise he had been kind enough to restore to its watery home. The tortoise, which was able to speak quite fluently, profusely thanked Urashima for his kindness, and offered to take him to the *ryūkyū*, or Palace of the Dragon King.

The invitation was readily accepted, and getting on the tortoise's back, Urashima found himself gliding through the sea at a tremendous speed, and the curious part about it was he discovered that his clothes remained perfectly dry.

In the Sea King's Palace

Arriving at the Sea King's Palace, red bream, flounder, sole, and cuttlefish came out to give Urashima a hearty welcome. Having expressed their pleasure, these vassals of the Dragon King escorted the fisher-lad to an inner apartment, where the beautiful Princess Otohime and her maidens were seated. The Princess was arrayed in gorgeous garments of red and gold, all the colours of a wave with the sunlight upon it.

This Princess explained that she had taken the form of a tortoise by way of testing his kindness of heart. The test had happily proved successful, and as a reward for his virtue she offered to become his bride in a land where there was eternal youth and everlasting summer.

Urashima bashfully accepted the high honour bestowed upon him. He had no sooner spoken than a great company of fishes appeared, robed in long ceremonial garments, their fins supporting great coral trays loaded with rare delicacies. Then the happy couple drank the wedding cup of *sake*, and while they drank, some of the fishes played soft music, others sang, and not a few, with scales of silver and golden tails, stepped out a strange measure on the white sand.

After the festivities were over, Otohime showed her husband all the wonders of her father's palace. The greatest marvel of all was to see a country where all the seasons lingered together. Looking to the east, Urashima saw plum- and cherry-trees in full bloom, with bright-winged butterflies skimming over the blossom, and away in the distance it seemed that the pink petals and butterflies had suddenly been converted into the song of a wondrous nightingale. In the south he saw trees in their summer glory, and heard the gentle note of the cricket. Looking to the west, the autumn maples made a fire in the branches, so that if Urashima had been other than a humble fisher-lad he might have recalled the following poem:

"Fair goddess of the paling Autumn skies,
Fain would I know how many looms she plies,
Wherein through skilful tapestry she weaves
Her fine brocade of fiery maple leaves:
Since on each hill, with every gust that blows,
In varied hues her vast embroidery glows?"

It was, indeed, a 'vast embroidery', for when Urashima looked toward the north he saw a great stretch of snow and a mighty pond covered with ice. All the seasons lingered together in that fair country where Nature had yielded to the full her infinite variety of beauty.

After Urashima had been in the Sea King's Palace for three days, and seen many wonderful things, he suddenly remembered his old parents, and felt a strong desire to go and see them. When he went to his wife, and told her of his longing to return home, Otohime began to weep, and tried to persuade him to stop another day. But Urashima refused to be influenced in the matter. "I must go," said he, "but I will leave you only for a day. I will return again, dear wife of mine."

The Home-coming of Urashima

Then Otohime gave her husband a keepsake in remembrance of their love. It was called the *Tamate-Bako* ('Box of the Jewel Hand'). She explained that he was on no account to open the box, and Urashima, promising to fulfil her wish, said farewell, mounted a large tortoise, and soon found himself in his own country. He looked in vain for his father's home. Not a sign of it was to be seen. The cottage had vanished, only the little stream remained.

Still much perplexed, Urashima questioned a passer-by, and he learnt from him that a fisher-lad, named Urashima, had gone to sea three hundred years ago and was drowned, and that his parents, brothers, and their grandchildren had been laid to rest for a long time. Then Urashima suddenly remembered that the country of the Sea King was a divine land, where a day, according to mortal reckoning, was a hundred years.

Urashima's reflections were gloomy in the extreme, for all whom he had loved on earth were dead. Then he heard the murmur of the sea, and recalled the lovely Otohime, as well as the country where the seasons joined hands and made a fourfold pageant of their beauty – the land where trees had emeralds for leaves and rubies for berries, where the fishes wore long robes and sang and danced and played. Louder the sea sounded in Urashima's ears. Surely Otohime called him? But no path opened out before him, no obliging tortoise appeared on the scene to carry him to where his wife waited for him. "The box! the box!" said Urashima softly, "if I open my wife's mysterious gift, it may reveal the way."

Urashima untied the red silk thread and slowly, fearfully opened the lid of the box. Suddenly there rushed out a little white cloud; it lingered a moment, and then rolled away far over the sea. But a sacred promise had been broken, and Urashima from a handsome youth became old and wrinkled. He staggered forward, his white hair and beard blowing in the wind. He looked out to sea, and then fell dead upon the shore.

The Land of the Morning Calm

WE GIVE HERE a picturesque legend of Japan's first invasion of Korea (known in the West sometimes as The Land of the Morning Calm).

One night the Empress Jingo, as she lay asleep in her tent, had a strange dream. She dreamt that a spirit came to her and told her of a wonderful land, a land in the West, full of treasures of gold and silver, a dazzling land, fair to look upon as a beautiful woman. The spirit informed her that the name of this country was Chosen (Korea), and that it might belong to Japan if she would set out and conquer this wealthy land.

The next day the Empress Jingo informed her husband about her dream; but the Emperor, a stolid, matter-of-fact man, did not believe in dreams. However, as his wife persisted in thrusting upon him what he deemed to be a foolish scheme, he climbed a high mountain, and looking toward the setting sun saw no land in the West. When the Emperor had come down from the mountain, he informed his wife that he would on no account give his consent to invade and conquer a country which simply owed its existence to a disordered dream. But the Gods were angry with the Emperor, and shortly after he had uttered his prohibition he died in battle.

The Gift of the Dragon King

When the Empress Jingo became sole ruler she was determined to go to this country she had heard about in a dream; but as she was resolved to make her expedition no puny and tame affair, she called upon the Spirit of the Mountain to give her timber and iron for her ships. The Spirit of Fields gave her rice and other grain for her army, while the Spirit of Grass presented her with hemp for rope. The Wind God looked favourably upon her scheme, and promised to blow her ships towards Korea. All the spirits appeared in compliance with the Empress Jingo's wishes except Isora, the Spirit of the Seashore.

Isora was a lazy fellow, and when he finally appeared above the waves of the sea, he did so without gorgeous apparel, for he was covered with slime and shells, and seaweed adorned his unkempt person. When the Empress saw him she bade him go to his master, the Dragon King, and ask him to give her the Tide Jewels.

Isora obeyed, dived down into the water, and presently stood before the Dragon King and made his request.

The Dragon King took out the Tide Jewels from a casket, placed them on a great shell, and bade Isora promptly return to the Empress Jingo with this precious gift.

Isora sprang from his master's palace to the surface of the sea, and the Empress Jingo placed the Tide Jewels in her girdle.

The Voyage

Now that the Empress had obtained the Jewel of the Flood-Tide and the Jewel of the Ebb-Tide she had three thousand ships built and launched, and during the tenth month she started on her great expedition. Her fleet had not proceeded far when a mighty storm arose, so that the vessels crashed together and were likely to sink to the bottom of the sea. The Dragon King, however, commanded great sea-monsters to go to the rescue; some bore up the ships with their great bodies, others pushed their heads against the sterns of many vessels, thus propelling them through a heavy sea which had very nearly driven them back whence they came. Powerful dragon-fishes lent their aid to those pushing and snorting in the rear by holding the ships' cables in their mouths and towing the vessels forward at a surprising speed. Directly the storm ceased, the sea-monsters and dragon-fishes disappeared.

The Throwing of the Tide Jewels

At last the Empress Jingo and her army saw the distant mountains of Korea loom out on the horizon. On nearing the coast they perceived that the whole of the Korean army stood upon the shore with their ships ready to be launched at the word of command. As soon as the Korean sentinels perceived the Japanese fleet, they gave the signal for embarking, and immediately a great line of war-vessels shot out over the water.

The Empress stood watching these proceedings with unruffled calm. She knew that the victory or defeat of her army lay in her power. When the Korean vessels drew near to her fleet she threw into the sea the Jewel of the Ebb-Tide. Directly it touched the water it caused the tide to recede from under the very keels of the Korean ships, so that they were left stranded upon dry land. The Koreans, suspecting no magic and believing their stranded condition to have been the result of a tidal wave and, moreover, that the Japanese vessels would succumb to the back-wash, sprang from their vessels and rushed over the sand. Now the Japanese bowmen twanged their bow-strings, and a great cloud of arrows flew into the air, killing many hundreds of the enemy. When the Koreans were quite near the Japanese vessels, the Empress flung forth the Jewel of the Flood-Tide. Immediately a great wave rushed over and destroyed nearly the whole of the Korean army. It was now an easy matter for the Japanese to land and capture the country. The King of Korea surrendered, and the Empress returned to her own kingdom laden with silk and jewels, books and pictures, tiger-skins and precious robes.

When the Tide Jewels had been thrown by the Empress, they did not lie long on the bed of the ocean. Isora speedily rescued them and carried them back to the Dragon King.

Prince Ojin

Soon after the Empress Jingo's return she gave birth to a son named Ojin. When Ojin had grown into a fair and wise little boy, his mother told him about the wonderful Tide Jewels, and expressed a wish that he, too, should possess them in order that he might bring honour and glory to Japan.

One day the Prime Minister, who was said to be three hundred and sixty years old, and the counsellor of no less than five Mikados, took Ojin with him in a royal war-barge. The vessel skimmed over the sea with its gold silk sails. The Prime Minister in a loud voice called on the Dragon King to give young Ojin the Tide Jewels.

Immediately the waves about the vessel were churned into foam, and amid a great thunderous roar the Dragon King himself appeared with a living creature of dreadful countenance for a helmet. Then out of the water arose a mighty shell, in the recess of which glittered the Tide Jewels. After presenting these jewels, and making a pretty little speech, he returned to his great green kingdom.

The Slaughter of the Sea Serpent

ORIBE SHIMA had offended the great ruler Hojo Takatoki, and was in consequence banished to Kamishima, one of the Oki Islands, and forced to leave his beautiful daughter Tokoyo, whom he deeply loved.

At last Tokoyo was unable to bear the separation any longer, and she was determined to find her father. She therefore set out upon a long journey, and arriving at Akasaki, in the province of Hoki, from which coast town the Oki Islands are visible on a fine day, she besought many a fisherman to row her to her destination. But the fisher-folk laughed at Tokoyo, and bade her relinquish her foolish plan and return home. The maiden, however, would not listen to their advice, and at nightfall she got into the lightest vessel she could find, and by dint of a fair wind and persistent rowing the brave girl came to one of the rocky bays of the Oki Islands.

That night Tokoyo slept soundly, and in the morning partook of food. When she had finished her meal she questioned a fisherman as to where she might find her father. "I have never heard of Oribe Shima," replied the fisherman, "and if he has been banished, I beg that you will desist from further search, lest it lead to the death of you both."

That night the sorrowful Tokoyo slept beneath a shrine dedicated to Buddha. Her sleep was soon disturbed by the clapping of hands, and looking up she saw a weeping maiden clad in a white garment with a priest standing beside her. Just as the priest was about to push the maiden over the rocks into the roaring sea, Tokoyo sprang up and held the maiden's arm.

The priest explained that on that night, the thirteenth of June, the Serpent God, known as Yofune-Nushi, demanded the sacrifice of a young girl, and that unless this annual sacrifice was made the God became angry and caused terrible storms.

"Good sir," said Tokoyo, "I am glad that I have been able to save this poor girl's life. I gladly offer myself in her place, for I am sad of heart because I have been unable to find my father. Give him this letter, for my last words of love and farewell go to him."

Having thus spoken, Tokoyo took the maiden's white robe and clad herself in it, and having prayed to the image of Buddha, she placed a small dagger between her teeth and plunged into the tempestuous sea. Down she went through the moonlit water till she came to a mighty cave where she saw a statue of Hojo Takatoki, who had sent her poor father into exile. She was about to tie the image on her back when a great white serpent crept out from the cave with eyes gleaming angrily. Tokoyo, realising that this creature was none other than Yofune-Nushi, drew her dagger and thrust it through the right eye of the God. This unexpected attack caused the serpent to retire into the cave, but the brave Tokoyo followed and struck another blow, this time at the creature's heart. For a moment Yofune-Nushi blindly stumbled forward, then with a shriek of pain fell dead upon the floor of the cavern.

During this adventure the priest and the maiden stood on the rocks watching the spot where Tokoyo had disappeared, praying fervently for the peace of her sorrowful soul. As they watched and prayed they saw Tokoyo come to the surface of the water carrying an image and a mighty fish-like creature. The priest hastily came to the girl's assistance, dragged her upon the shore, placed the image on a high rock, and secured the body of the White Sea Serpent.

In due time the remarkable story was reported to Tameyoshi, lord of the island, who in turn reported the strange adventure to Hojo Takatoki. Now Takatoki had for some time been suffering from a disease which defied the skill of the most learned doctors; but it was observed that he regained his health precisely at the hour when his image, which had been cursed and thrown into the sea by some exile, had been restored. When Hojo Takatoki heard that the brave girl was the daughter of the exiled Oribe Shima, he sent him back with all speed to his own home, where he and his daughter lived in peace and happiness.

The Spirit of the Sword

ONE NIGHT a junk anchored off Fudo's Cape, and when various preparations had been made, the Captain, Tarada by name, and his crew fell asleep on deck. At about midnight Tarada was awakened by hearing an extraordinary rumbling sound that seemed to proceed from the bottom of the sea. Chancing to look in the direction of the bow of the vessel, he saw a fair girl clad in white and illumined by a dazzling light.

When Tarada had awakened his crew he approached the maiden, who said: "My only wish is to be back in the world again." Having uttered these words, she disappeared among the waves.

The next day Tarada went on shore and asked many who lived in Amakura if they had ever heard of a wondrous maiden bathed, as it were, in a phosphorescent light. One of the villagers thus made answer: "We have never seen the maiden you describe, but for some time past we have been disturbed by rumbling noises that seem to come from Fudo's Cape, and ever since, these mysterious sounds have prevented fish from entering our bay. It may be that the girl you saw was the ghost of some poor maiden drowned at sea, and the noise we hear none other than the anger of the Sea God on account of a corpse or human bones polluting the water."

It was eventually decided that the dumb Sankichi should dive into the sea and bring up any corpse he might find there. So Sankichi went on board Tarada's junk, and having said farewell to his friends, he plunged into the water. He searched diligently, but could see no trace of corpse or human bones. At length, however, he perceived what looked like a sword wrapped in silk, and on untying the wrapping he found that it was indeed a sword, of great brightness and without a flaw of any kind. Sankichi came to the surface and was quickly taken aboard. The poor fellow was gently laid on the deck, but he fainted from exhaustion. His cold body was rubbed vigorously and fires were lit. In a very short time Sankichi became conscious and was able to show the sword and give particulars of his adventure.

An official, by the name of Naruse Tsushimanokami, was of the opinion that the sword was a sacred treasure, and on his recommendation it was placed in a shrine and dedicated to Fudo. Sankichi faithfully guarded the precious weapon, and Fudo's Cape became known as the Cape of the Woman's Sword. To the delight of the fisher-folk, the spirit of the weapon now being satisfied, the fish came back into the bay again.

The Love of O Cho San

IN THE ISOLATED HATSUSHIMA ISLAND, celebrated for its *suisenn* (jonquils), there once lived a beautiful maiden called Cho, and all the young men on the island were eager to marry her. One day the handsome Shinsaku, who was bolder than the rest, went to Gisuke, the brother of Cho, and told him that he much desired to marry his fair sister. Gisuke offered no objections, and calling Cho to him, when the suitor had gone, he said: "Shinsaku wishes to become your husband. I like the fisherman, and think that in him you will make an excellent match. You are now eighteen, and it is quite time that you got married."

O Cho San fully approved of what her brother had said, and the marriage was arranged to take place in three days' time. Unfortunately, those days were days of discord on the island, for when the other fishermen lovers heard the news they began to hate the once popular Shinsaku, and, moreover, they neglected their work and were continually fighting each other. These lamentable scenes cast such a gloom upon the once happy Hatsushima Island that O Cho San and her lover decided that for the peace of the many they would not marry after all.

This noble sacrifice, however, did not bring about the desired effect, for the thirty lovers still fought each other and still neglected their fishing. O Cho San determined to perform a still greater sacrifice. She wrote loving letters of farewell to her brother and Shinsaku, and having left them by the sleeping Gisuke, she softly crept out of the house on a stormy night on the 10th of June. She dropped big stones into her pretty sleeves, and then flung herself into the sea.

The next day Gisuke and Shinsaku read their letters from O Cho San, and, overcome by grief, they searched the shore, where they found the straw sandals of Cho. The two men realised that the fair maid had indeed taken her precious life, and shortly after her body was taken from the sea and buried, and over her tomb Shinsaku placed many flowers and wept continually.

One evening, Shinsaku, unable to bear his sorrow any longer decided to take his life, believing that by doing so he would meet the spirit of O Cho San. As he lingered by the girl's grave, he seemed to see her white ghost, and, murmuring her name over and over again, he rushed toward her. At this moment Gisuke, awakened by the noise, came out of his house, and found Shinsaku clinging to his lover's gravestone.

When Shinsaku told his friend that he had seen the spirit of O Cho San, and intended to take his life in order to be with her for ever, Gisuke made answer thus: "Shinsaku, great is your love for my poor sister, but you can love her best by serving her in this world. When the great Gods call, you will meet her, but await with hope and courage till that hour comes, for only a brave, as well as a loving, heart is worthy of O Cho San. Let us together build a shrine and dedicate it to my sister, and keep your love strong and pure by never marrying anyone else."

The thirty lovers who had shown such unmanly feeling now fully realised the sorrow they had caused, and in order to show their contrition they too helped to build the shrine of the unfortunate maiden, where to this day a ceremony takes place on the 10th of June, and it is said that the spirit of O Cho San comes in the rain.

The Spirit of the Great Awabi

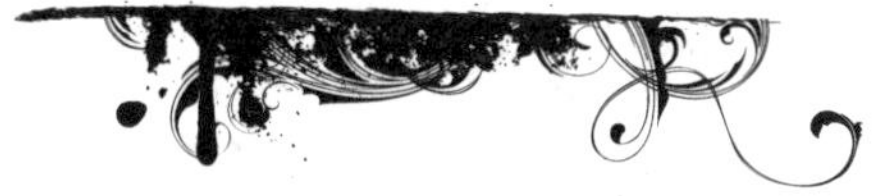

THE MORNING AFTER a great earthquake had devastated the fishing village of Nanao, it was observed that about two miles from the shore a rock had sprung up as the result of the seismic disturbance and, moreover, that the sea had become muddy. One night a number of fishermen were passing by the rock, when they observed, near at hand, a most extraordinary light that appeared to float up from the bottom of the sea with a glory as bright as the sun. The fishermen shipped their oars and gazed upon the wonderful spectacle with considerable surprise, but when the light was suddenly accompanied by a deep rumbling sound, the sailors feared another earthquake and made all speed for Nanao.

On the third day the wondrous rays from the deep increased in brilliance, so that folk standing on the shore of Nanao could see them distinctly, and the superstitious fishermen became more and more frightened. Only Kansuke and his son Matakichi had sufficient courage to go fishing. On their return journey they reached the Rock Island, and were drawing in their line when Kansuke lost his balance and fell into the sea.

Though old Kansuke was a good swimmer, he went down like a stone and did not rise to the surface. Matakichi, deeming this strange, dived into the water, almost blinded by the mysterious rays we have already described. When he at length reached the bottom he discovered innumerable *awabi* (ear-shells or abalone), and in the middle of the group one of vast size. From all these shells there poured forth a brilliant light, and though it was like day under the water, Matakichi could find no trace of his father. Eventually he was forced to rise to the surface, only to find that the rough sea had broken his boat. However, scrambling upon a piece of wreckage, with the aid of a favourable wind and current he at last reached the shore of Nanao, and gave the villagers an account of his remarkable adventure, and of the loss of his old father.

Matakichi, grieving sorely over the death of his parent, went to the old village priest and begged that worthy that he would make him one of his disciples in order that he might pray the more efficaciously for the spirit of his father. The priest readily consented, and about three weeks later they took boat to the Rock Island, where both prayed ardently for the soul of Kansuke.

That night the old priest awoke with a start and saw an ancient man standing by his bedside. With a profound bow the stranger thus spoke: "I am the Spirit of the Great Awabi, and I am more than one thousand years old. I live in the sea near the Rock Island, and this morning I heard you praying for the soul of Kansuke. Alas! good priest, your prayers have deeply moved me, but in shame and sorrow I confess that I ate Kansuke. I have bade my followers depart elsewhere, and in order to atone for my sin I shall take my own wretched life, so that the pearl that is within me may be given to Matakichi." And having uttered these words, the Spirit of the Great Awabi suddenly disappeared.

When Matakichi awoke next morning and opened the shutters he discovered the enormous *awabi* he had seen near the Rock Island. He took it to the old priest, who, after listening to his disciple's story, gave an account of his own experience. The great pearl and shell of the *awabi* were placed in the temple, and the body was reverently buried.

The Jewel-tears of Samebito

ONE DAY, while Totaro was crossing the Long Bridge of Seta, he saw a strange-looking creature. It had the body of a man, with a skin blacker than that of a negro; its eyes glowed like emeralds, and its beard was like the beard of a dragon. Totaro was not a little startled at seeing such an extraordinary being; but there was so much pathos in its green eyes that Totaro ventured to ask questions, to which the strange fellow replied:

"I am Samebito ('shark person'), and quite recently I was in the service of the Eight Great Dragon Kings as a subordinate officer in the Dragon Palace. I was dismissed from this glorious dwelling for a very slight fault, and I was even banished from the sea. Ever since I have been extremely miserable, without a place of shelter, and unable to get food. Pity me, good sir! Find me shelter, and give me something to eat!"

Totaro's heart was touched by Samebito's humility, and he took him to a pond in his garden and there gave him a liberal supply of food. In this quiet and secluded spot this strange creature of the sea remained for nearly half a year.

Now in the summer of that year there was a great female pilgrimage to the temple called Miidera, situated in the neighbouring town of Otsu. Totaro attended the festival, and there saw an extremely charming girl. "Her face was fair and pure as snow; and the loveliness of her lips assured the beholder that their very utterance would sound 'as sweet as the voice of a nightingale singing upon a plum-tree.'"

Totaro at once fell in love with this maiden. He discovered that her name was Tamana, that she was unmarried, and would remain so unless a young man could present her with a betrothal gift of a casket containing no fewer than ten thousand jewels.

When Totaro learnt that this fair girl was only to be won by what seemed to him an impossible gift, he returned home with a heavy heart. The more he thought about the beautiful Tamana, the more he fell in love with her. But alas! no one less wealthy than a prince could make such a betrothal gift – ten thousand jewels!

Totaro worried himself into an illness, and when a physician came to see him, he shook his head, and said: "I can do nothing for you, for no medicine will cure the sickness of love." And with these words he left him.

Now Samebito gained tidings of the sickness of his master, and when the sad news reached him, he left the garden pond and entered Totaro's chamber.

Totaro did not speak about his own troubles. He was full of concern for the welfare of this creature of the sea. "Who will feed you, Samebito, when I am gone?" said he mournfully.

When Samebito saw that his good master was dying, he uttered a strange cry, and began to weep. He wept great tears of blood, but when they touched the floor they suddenly turned into glowing rubies.

When Totaro saw these jewel-tears he shouted for joy, and new life came back to him from that hour. "I shall live! I shall live!" he cried with great delight. "My good friend, you have more than repaid me for the food and shelter I have given you. Your wonderful tears have brought me untold happiness."

Then Samebito stopped weeping, and asked his master to be so good as to explain the nature of his speedy recovery.

So Totaro told the Shark-Man of his love-affair and of the marriage-gift demanded by the family of Tamana. "I thought," added Totaro, "that I should never be able to get ten thousand jewels, and it was that thought that brought me so near to death. Now your tears have turned into jewels, and with these the maid will become my wife."

Totaro proceeded to count the jewels with great eagerness. "Not enough! Not enough!" he exclaimed with considerable disappointment. "Oh, Samebito, be so good as to weep a little more!"

These words made Samebito angry. "Do you think," said he, "I can weep at will like women? My tears come from the heart, the outward sign of true and deep sorrow. I can weep no longer, for you are well again. Surely the time has come for laughter and merrymaking, and not for tears."

"Unless I get ten thousand jewels, I cannot marry the fair Tamana," said Totaro. "What am I to do? Oh, good friend, weep, weep!"

Samebito was a kindly creature. After a pause, he said: "I can shed no more tears today. Let us go tomorrow to the Long Bridge of Seta, and take with us a good supply of wine and fish. It may be that as I sit on the bridge and gaze toward the Dragon Palace, I shall weep again, thinking of my lost home, and longing to return once more."

On the morrow they went to the Seta Bridge, and after Samebito had taken a good deal of wine, he gazed in the direction of the Dragon Kingdom. As he did so his eyes filled with tears, red tears that turned into rubies as soon as they touched the bridge. Totaro, without very much concern for his friend's sorrow, picked up the jewels, and found at last that he had ten thousand lustrous rubies.

Just at that moment they heard a sound of sweet music, and from the water there rose a cloud-like palace, with all the colours of the setting sun shining upon it. Samebito gave a shout of joy and sprang upon the parapet of the bridge, saying: "Farewell, my master! The Dragon Kings are calling!" With these words he leaped from the bridge and returned to his old home again.

Totaro lost no time in presenting the casket containing ten thousand jewels to Tamana's parents, and in due season he married their lovely daughter.

Legends of Buddha & Buddhism

Introduction

THE FIRST LEGEND HERE is obviously not of Japanese origin. The priests of Buddhism in Japan knew that the success of their religion lay, not in sweeping out the old gods of Shinto, but in adapting them with infinite cleverness to the needs of their own teaching. In this case Japan has borrowed from India and in a minor degree from China, if we may look upon the dragon as originally belonging to the Celestial Kingdom. We insert it here because it often enters into a priest's discourse, and has a decidedly Japanese setting. The other two legends given in this chapter are strictly Japanese.

Legend is nearly always elemental. Divinities, irrespective of their austerity, are brought down to a very human level. It is a far cry from the complex teaching of the Lord Buddha to the story of Amida Butsu and the whale. One can trace in that legend an almost pathetic desire to veil the greatness of Buddha. The gigantic size of the Daibutsu is not really in keeping with that curious love of little things which is so characteristic of the Japanese people. There is a playful irony in this story, a desire to take down the great Teacher a peg or two – if only to take him down in stature a paltry two inches!

The Legend of the Golden Lotus

THE LORD BUDDHA, having concluded his holy meditations upon Mount Dan-doku, slowly walked along a rocky pathway on his way to the city. The dark shadows of night crept over the country, and there was profound stillness everywhere.

On nearing his destination the Lord Buddha heard someone shout: "*Shio-giyo mu-jiyo*!" ("The outward manner is not always an index to the natural disposition.")

The Lord Buddha was delighted at these words, and desired to learn who had spoken so wisely. Over and over again he heard the same words, and, drawing to the edge of a precipice, he looked down into the valley beneath, and perceived an extremely ugly dragon gazing up at him with angry eyes.

The Holy One then seated himself upon a rock, and inquired of the dragon how he had come to learn one of the highest mysteries of Buddhism. Such profound wisdom suggested a store of spiritual truths yet to be revealed, and the Lord Buddha, therefore, requested that the dragon should give utterance to other wise sayings.

Then the dragon, having coiled himself round the rock, shouted with a great voice: "*Ze-shio metsu-po*!" ("All living things are antagonistic to the law of Buddha!")

After uttering these words the dragon was silent for some time. Then the Lord Buddha begged to hear yet another sentence.

"*Shio-metsu metsu-i*!" ("All living things must die!") shouted the dragon.

At these words the dragon looked up at the Lord Buddha, and upon his dreadful countenance there was an expression of extreme hunger.

The dragon then informed the Lord Buddha that the next truth was the last, and so precious that he could not reveal it until his hunger had been appeased.

At this the Holy One remarked that he would deny the dragon nothing so long as he heard the fourth truth revealed, and inquired of the dragon what he demanded. When the Lord Buddha heard that human flesh was what the dragon required in exchange for his last precious fragment of wisdom, the Master informed the dragon that his religion forbade the destruction of life, but that he would, for the welfare of his people, sacrifice his own body.

The dragon opened his great mouth and said: "*Jaku-metsu I-raku*!" ("The greatest happiness is experienced after the soul has left the body!")

The Lord Buddha bowed, and then sprang into the gaping mouth of the dragon.

No sooner had the Holy One touched the jaws of the monster than they suddenly divided into eight parts, and in a moment changed into the eight petals of the Golden Lotus.

The Bronze Buddha of Kamakura and the Whale

THE GREAT BRONZE BUDDHA of Kamakura, or the Daibutsu, is undoubtedly one of the most remarkable sights in Japan. In its sitting posture, it is fifty feet high, ninety-seven feet in circumference, the length of its face eight feet, and as for its thumbs they are three feet round. It is probably the tallest piece of bronze in the world. Such an enormous image naturally created a considerable sensation in the days when Kamakura was a flourishing city, laid out by the great General Yoritomo. The roads in and about the city were densely packed with pilgrims, anxious to gaze upon the latest marvel, and all agreed that this bronze image was the biggest thing in the world.

Now it may be that certain sailors who had seen this marvel chatted about it as they plied their nets. Whether this was so or not, a mighty whale, who lived in the Northern Sea, happened to hear about the Bronze Buddha of Kamakura, and as he regarded himself as being far bigger than anything on land, the idea of a possible rival did not meet with his approval. He deemed it impossible that little men could construct anything that could vie with his enormous bulk, and laughed heartily at the very absurdity of such a conception.

His laughter, however, did not last long. He was inordinately jealous, and when he heard about the numerous pilgrimages to Kamakura and the incessant praise evoked from those who had seen the image he grew exceedingly angry, lashed the sea into foam, and blew down his nose with so much violence that the other creatures of the deep gave him a very wide berth. His loneliness only aggravated his trouble, and he was unable to eat or sleep, and in consequence grew thin. He at last decided to chat the matter over with a kindly shark.

The shark answered the whale's heated questions with quiet solicitude, and consented to go to the Southern Sea in order that he might take the measurement of the image, and bring back the result of his labour to his agitated friend.

The shark set off upon his journey, until he came to the shore, where he could see the image towering above him, about half a mile inland. As he could not walk on dry land he was about to renounce his quest, when he had the good fortune to discover a rat enjoying a scamper along a junk. He explained his mission to the rat, and requested that much-flattered little creature to take the measurement of the Bronze Buddha.

So the rat climbed down the junk, swam ashore, and entered the dark temple where the Great Buddha stood. At first he was so overcome by the magnificence he saw about him that he was uncertain as to how to proceed in carrying out the shark's request. He eventually decided to walk round the image, counting his footsteps as he went. He discovered after he had performed this task that he had walked exactly five thousand paces, and on his return to the junk he told the shark the measurement of the base of the Bronze Buddha.

The shark, with profuse thanks to the rat, returned to the Northern Sea, and informed the whale that the reports concerning the size of this exasperating image were only too true.

'A little knowledge is a dangerous thing' evidently applies equally well to whales, for the whale of this legend, after receiving the information, grew more furious than ever. As in a story familiar to English children, he put on magic boots in order to travel on land as well as he had always done in the sea.

The whale reached the Kamakura temple at night. He discovered that the priests had gone to bed, and were apparently fast asleep. He knocked at the door. Instead of the dismal murmur of a half-awake priest he heard the Lord Buddha say, in a voice that rang like the sound of a great bell: "Come in!"

"I cannot," replied the whale, "because I am too big. Will you please come out and see me?"

When Buddha found out who his visitor was, and what he wanted at so unearthly an hour, he condescendingly stepped down from his pedestal and came outside the temple. There was utter amazement on both sides. Had the whale possessed knees they would assuredly have knocked together. He knocked his head on the ground instead. For his part, Buddha was surprised to find a creature of such gigantic proportions.

We can imagine the consternation of the chief priest when he found that the pedestal did not bear the image of his Master. Hearing a strange conversation going on outside the temple, he went out to see what was taking place. The much-frightened priest was invited to join in the discussion, and was requested to take the measurement of the image and the whale, and accordingly began to measure with his rosary. During this proceeding the image and the whale awaited the result with bated breath. When the measurements had been taken the whale was found to be two inches longer and taller than the image.

The whale went back to the Northern Sea more utterly vain than ever, while the image returned to its temple and sat down again, and there it has remained to this day, none the worse, perhaps, for finding that it was not quite so big as it imagined. Dealers in dry goods and dealers in wood and iron agreed from that day to this to differ as to what was a foot – and the difference was a matter of two inches.

The Crystal of Buddha

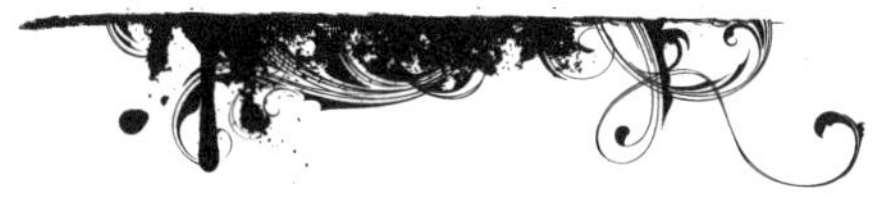

IN ANCIENT DAYS there lived in Japan a great State Minister named Kamatari. Now Kamatari's only daughter, Kohaku Jo, extremely beautiful, and as good as she was beautiful. She was the delight of her father's heart, and he resolved that, if she married, no one of less account than a king should be her husband. With this idea continually in his mind, he steadfastly refused the offers for her hand.

One day there was a great tumult in the palace courtyard. Through the open gates streamed a number of men bearing a banner on which was worked a silken dragon on a yellow background. Kamatari learnt that these men had come from the court of China with a message from the Emperor Koso. The Emperor had heard of the exceeding beauty and exquisite charm of Kohaku Jo, and desired to marry her. As is usual in the East on such occasions, the Emperor's offer was accompanied with the promise that if Kohaku Jo should become his bride he would allow her to choose from his store of treasures whatever she liked to send to her own country.

After Kamatari had received the envoys with due pomp and ceremony, and put at their disposal a whole wing of the palace, he returned to his own room and bade his servant bring his daughter into his presence.

When Kohaku had entered her father's room she bowed before him and sat patiently on the white mats waiting for her august parent to speak to her.

Kamatari told her that he had chosen the Emperor of China to be her husband, and the little maid wept on hearing the news. She had been so happy in her own home, and China seemed such a long way off. When, however, her father foretold more happiness in the future than she had ever had in the past, she dried her eyes and listened to her parent's words, a little amazed to hear, perhaps, that all China's treasures were to be laid at her own small feet. She was glad when her father told her that she would be able to send three of these treasures to the temple of Kofukuji, where she had received a blessing when a little babe.

So Kohaku obeyed her father with not a little misgiving, not a little heartache. Her girl companions wept when they heard the news, but they were comforted when Kohaku's mother told them that some of their number would be chosen to go with their mistress.

Before Kohaku sailed for China she wended her way to the beloved temple of Kofukuji, and, arriving at the sacred shrine, she prayed for protection in her journey, vowing that if her prayers were answered she would search China for its three most precious treasures, and send them to the temple as a thank-offering.

Kohaku reached China in safety and was received by the Emperor Koso with great magnificence. Her childish fears were soon dispelled by the Emperor's kindness. Indeed, he showed her considerably more than kindness. He spoke to her in the language of a lover: "After long, long days of weary waiting I have gathered the 'azalea of the distant mountain', and now I plant it in my garden, and great is the gladness of my heart!"

The Emperor Koso led her from palace to palace, and she knew not which was the most beautiful, but her royal husband was aware that she was far more lovely than any of them. Because of her great loveliness he desired that it should be ever remembered throughout the length and breadth of China, even beyond the bounds of his kingdom. "So he called together his goldsmiths and gardeners," as Madame Ozaki writes in describing this story, "and commanded them to fashion a path for the Empress such as had never been heard of in the wide world. The stepping-stones of this path were to be lotus-flowers, carved out of silver and gold, for her to walk on whenever she strolled forth under the trees or by the lake, so that it might be said that her beautiful feet were never soiled by touching the earth; and ever since then, in China and Japan, poet-lovers and lover-poets in song and sonnet and sweet conversation have called the feet of the women they love 'lotus feet'."

But in spite of all the magnificence that surrounded Kohaku she did not forget her native land or the vow she had made in the temple of Kofukuji. One day she timidly informed the Emperor of her promise, and he, only too glad to have another opportunity of pleasing her, set before her such a store of beautiful and precious things that it seemed as if an exquisite phantom world of gay colour and perfect form had suddenly come into being at her very feet. There was such a wealth of beautiful things that she found it very difficult to make a choice. She finally decided upon the following magical treasures: a musical instrument, which if one struck would continue to play for ever, an ink-stone box, which, on opening the lid, was found to contain an inexhaustible supply of Indian ink, and, last of all, "a beautiful Crystal, in whose clear depths was to be seen, from whichever side you looked, an image of Buddha riding on a white elephant. The jewel was of transcendent glory and shone like a star, and whoever gazed into its liquid depths and saw the blessed vision of Buddha had peace of heart for evermore."

After Kohaku had gazed for some time upon these treasures she sent for Admiral Banko and bade him safely convey them to the temple of Kofukuji.

Everything went well with Admiral Banko and his ship until they were in Japanese waters, sailing into the Bay of Shido-no-ura, when a mighty tempest whirled the vessel hither and thither. The waves rolled up with the fierceness of wild beasts, and lightning continually blazed across the sky, to light up for a moment a rolling ship, now flung high upon a mountain of water, now swept into a green valley from which it seemed it could never rise again.

Suddenly the storm abated with the same unexpectedness with which it had arisen. Some fairy hand had brushed up all the clouds and laid a blue and sparkling carpet across the sea. The admiral's first thought was for the safety of the treasures entrusted to him, and on going below he discovered the musical instrument and ink-stone box just as he had left them, but that the most precious of the treasures, Buddha's Crystal, was missing. He contemplated taking his life, so grieved was he at the loss; but on reflection he saw that it would be wiser to live so long as there was anything he could do to find the jewel. He accordingly hastened to land, and informed Kamatari of his dreadful misfortune.

No sooner had Kamatari been told about the loss of Buddha's Crystal than this wise minister perceived that the Dragon King of the Sea had stolen it, and for that purpose had caused the storm, which had enabled him to steal the treasure unperceived.

Kamatari offered a large reward to a number of fishermen he saw upon the shore of Shido-no-ura if any of their number would venture into the sea and bring back the Crystal. All the fishermen volunteered, but after many attempts the precious jewel still remained in the keeping of the Sea King.

Kamatari, much distressed, suddenly became aware of a poor woman carrying an infant in her arms. She begged the great minister that she might enter the sea and search for the Crystal, and in spite of her frailty she spoke with conviction. Her mother-heart seemed to lend her courage. She made her request because, if she succeeded in bringing back the Crystal, she desired that as a reward Kamatari should bring up her little son as a *samurai* in order that he might be something in life other than a humble fisherman.

It will be remembered that Kamatari in his day had been ambitious for his daughter's welfare. He readily understood the poor woman's request, and solemnly promised that if she carried out her part faithfully he would gladly do his.

The woman withdrew, and taking off her upper garments, and tying a rope round her waist, into which she stuck a knife, she was prepared for her perilous journey. Giving the end of the rope to a number of fishermen, she plunged into the water.

At first the woman saw the dim outline of rocks, the dart of a frightened fish, and the faint gold of the sand beneath her. Then she suddenly became aware of the roofs of the palace of the Sea King, a great and gorgeous building of coral, relieved here and there with clusters of many-coloured seaweed. The palace was like a huge pagoda, rising tier upon tier. The woman swam nearer in order to inspect it more closely, and she perceived a bright light, more brilliant than the light of many moons, so bright that it dazzled her eyes. It was the light of Buddha's Crystal, placed on the pinnacle of this vast abode, and on every side of the shining jewel were guardian dragons fast asleep, appearing to watch even in their slumber!

Up swam the woman, praying in her brave heart that the dragons might sleep till she was out of harm's way and in possession of the treasure. No sooner had she snatched the Crystal from its resting-place than the guardians awoke; their great claws extended and their tails furiously lashed the water, and in another moment they were in hot pursuit. Rather than lose the Crystal, which she had won at so much peril, the woman cut a wound in her left breast and forced the jewel into the bleeding cavity, pressing her hand, without a murmur of pain, upon the poor torn flesh. When the dragons perceived that the water was murky with the woman's blood they turned back, for sea-dragons are afraid of the very sight of blood.

Now the woman sharply pulled the rope, and the fishermen, sitting upon the rocks far above, drew her to land with ever-quickening speed. They gently laid her upon the shore, and found that her eyes were closed and her breast bleeding profusely. Kamatari at first thought that the woman had risked her life in vain; but bending over her he noticed the wound in her breast. At that moment she opened her eyes, and, taking the jewel from its place of concealment, she murmured a few words about Kamatari's promise, then fell back dead with a smile of peace upon her face.

Kamatari took the woman's child home and looked after him with all the loving care of a father. In due time the boy grew to manhood and became a brave *samurai*, and at Kamatari's death he, too, became a great State minister. When in later years he learnt the story of his mother's act of self-sacrifice he built a temple in the Bay of Shido-no-ura, in memory of one who was so brave and true. It is called Shidoji, and pilgrims visit this temple and remember the nobility of a poor shell-gatherer to this day.

Tales of Kobo Daishi

KOBO DAISHI ('Glory to the Great Teacher'), who was born AD 774, was the most holy and most famous of the Japanese Buddhist saints. He founded the Shingon-shu, a Buddhist sect remarkable for its magical formulae and for its abstruse and esoteric teachings, and he is also said to have invented the *Hiragana* syllabary, a form of running script.

In the *Namudaishi*, which is a Japanese poem on the life of this great saint, we are informed that Kobo Daishi brought back with him from China a millstone and some seeds of the tea-plant, and thus revived the drinking of this beverage, which had fallen into disuse. We are also told in the same poem that it was Kobo Daishi who "demonstrated to the world the use of coal." He was renowned as a great preacher, but was not less famous as a calligraphist, painter, sculptor, and traveller.

'A Divine Prodigy'

Kobo Daishi, however, is essentially famous for the extraordinary miracles which he performed, and numerous are the legends associated with him. His conception was miraculous, for when he was born in the Baron's Hall, on the shore of Byobu, a bright light shone, and he came into the world with his hands folded as if in prayer. When but five years of age he would sit among the lotuses and converse with Buddhas, and he kept secret all the wisdom he thus obtained. His heart was troubled by the sorrow and pain of humanity. While on Mount Shashin he sought to sacrifice his own life by way of propitiation, but he was prevented from doing so by a number of angels who would not allow this ardent soul to suffer death until he had fulfilled his destiny. His very games were of a religious nature. On one occasion he built a clay pagoda, and he was immediately surrounded by the Four Heavenly Kings (originally Hindu deities). The Imperial Messenger, who happened to pass by when this miracle took place, was utterly amazed, and described the young Kobo Daishi as 'a divine prodigy'. While at Muroto, in Tosa, performing his devotions, we are told in the *Namu-daishi* that a bright star fell from Heaven and entered his mouth, while at midnight an evil dragon came forth against him, "but he spat upon it, and with his saliva he killed it."

In his nineteenth year he wore the black silk robes of a Buddhist priest, and with a zeal that never failed him sought for enlightenment. "Many are the ways," he said; "but Buddhism is the best of all." During his mystical studies he came across a book containing the Shingon doctrine, a doctrine that closely resembles the old Egyptian speculations. The book was so abstruse that even Kobo Daishi failed to master it; but, nothing daunted, he received permission from the Emperor to visit China, where he ultimately unravelled its profound mysteries, and attained to that degree of saintship associated with the miraculous.

Gohitsu-Osho

When Kobo Daishi was in China the Emperor, hearing of his fame, sent for him and bade him rewrite the name of a certain room in the royal palace, a name that had become obliterated by the effacing finger of Time. Kobo Daishi, with a brush in each hand, another in his mouth, and two others between the toes, wrote the characters required upon the wall, and for this extraordinary performance the Emperor named him Gohitsu-Osho ('The Priest who writes with Five Brushes').

Writing on Sky and Water

While still in China Kobo Daishi met a boy standing by the side of a river. "If you be Kobo Daishi," said he, "be honourably pleased to write upon the sky, for I have heard that no wonder is beyond your power."

Kobo Daishi raised his brush; it moved quickly in the air, and writing appeared in the blue sky, characters that were perfectly formed and wonderfully beautiful.

When the boy had also written upon the sky with no less skill, he said to Kobo Daishi: "We have both written upon the sky. Now I beg that you will write upon this flowing river."

Kobo Daishi readily complied. Once again his brush moved, and this time a poem appeared on the water, a poem written in praise of that particular river. The letters lingered for a moment, and then were carried away by the swift current.

There seems to have been a contest in magical power between these two workers of marvels, for no sooner had the letters passed out of sight than the boy also wrote upon the running water the character of the Dragon, and it remained stationary.

Kobo Daishi, who was a great scholar, at once perceived that the boy had omitted the *ten*, a dot which rightly belonged to this character. When Kobo Daishi pointed out the error, the boy told him that he had forgotten to insert the *ten*, and begged that the famous saint would put it in for him. No sooner had Kobo Daishi done so than the Dragon character became a Dragon. Its tail lashed the waters, thunder-clouds sped across the sky, and lightning flashed. In another moment the Dragon arose from the water and ascended to heaven.

Though Kobo Daishi's powers of magic excelled those of the boy, he inquired who this youth might be, and the boy replied: "I am Monju Bosatsu, the Lord of Wisdom." Having spoken these words, he became illumined by a radiant light; the beauty of the Gods shone upon his countenance, and, like the Dragon, he ascended into heaven.

How Kobo Daishi Painted the Ten

On one occasion Kobo Daishi omitted the *ten* on a tablet placed above one of the gates of the Emperor's palace. The Emperor commanded that ladders should be brought; but Kobo Daishi, without making use of them, stood upon the ground, and threw up his brush, which, after making the *ten*, fell into his hand.

Kino Momoye and Onomo Toku

Kino Momoye once ridiculed some of Kobo Daishi's characters, and said that one of them resembled a conceited wrestler. On the night he made this foolish jest Momoye dreamed that a wrestler struck him blow upon blow – moreover, that his antagonist leapt upon his body, causing him considerable pain. Momoye awoke, and cried aloud in his agony, and as he cried he saw the wrestler suddenly change into the character he had so unwisely jeered at. It rose into the air, and went back to the tablet from whence it had come.

Momoye was not the only man who imprudently scoffed at the great Kobo Daishi's work. Legend records that one named Onomo Toku said that the saint's character *Shu* was far more like the character 'rice'. That night Onomo Toku had good reason to regret his folly, for in a dream the character *Shu* took bodily form and became a rice-cleaner, who moved up and down the offender's body after the manner of hammers that were used in beating this grain. When Onomo Toku awoke it was to find that his body was covered with bruises and that his flesh was bleeding in many places.

Kobo Daishi's Return

When Kobo Daishi was about to leave China and return to his own country he went down to the seashore and threw his *vajra* across the ocean waves, and it was afterwards found hanging on the branch of a pine-tree at Takano, in Japan.

We are not told anything about Kobo Daishi's voyage to his own land; but directly he arrived in Japan he gave thanks for the divine protection he had received during his travels. On the Naked Mountain he offered incantations of so powerful a nature that the once barren mountain became covered with flowers and trees.

Kobo Daishi, as time advanced, became still more holy. During a religious discussion the Divine Light streamed from him, and he continued to perform many great marvels. He made brackish water pure, raised the dead to life, and continued to commune with certain gods. On one occasion Inari, the God of Rice, appeared on Mount Fushime and took from the great saint the sacrifice he offered. "Together, you and I," said Kobo Daishi, "we will protect this people."

The Death of Kobo Daishi

In AD 834 this remarkable saint died, and we are told that a very great gathering, both lay and priestly, wept at the graveyard of Okunoin, in Koya, where he was buried. His death, however, by no means meant a sudden cessation of miracles on his part, for when the Emperor Saga died "his coffin was mysteriously borne through the air to Koya, and Kobo himself, coming forth from his grave, performed the funeral obsequies." Nor did the wonders cease with this incident, for the Emperor Uda received from Kobo Daishi the sacred Baptism. When the Imperial Messenger to the temple where Kobo Daishi was worshipped was unable to see the face of this great saint, Kobo "guided the worshipper's hand to touch his knee. Never, as long as he lived, did the Messenger forget that feeling!"

Shodo Shonin

SHODO SHONIN was the founder of the first Buddhist temple at Nikko, and the following legend is supposed to have led to the construction of the sacred bridge of Nikko.

One day, while Shodo Shonin was on a journey, he saw four strange-looking clouds rise from the earth to the sky. He pressed forward in order to see them more clearly, but could not go far, for he found that his road was barred by a wild torrent. While he was praying for some means to continue his journey a gigantic figure appeared before him, clad in blue and black robes, with a necklace of skulls. The mysterious being cried to him from the opposite bank, saying: "I will help you as I once helped Hiuen." Having uttered these words, the Deity threw two blue and green snakes across the river, and on this bridge of snakes the priest was able to cross the torrent. When Shodo Shonin had reached the other bank the God and his blue and green snakes disappeared.

Kato Sayemon

KATO SAYEMON lived in the palace of the Shogun Ashikaga, where he had his separate apartments, and as there was no war at that time, he remained contentedly with his wife and concubines. Kato Sayemon was a man who loved luxury and ease, and he regarded domestic peace as the greatest of all earthly blessings. He honestly believed that among all his smiling, courteous women there was nothing but harmony, and this thought made life particularly sweet to him.

One evening Kato Sayemon went into the palace garden and was enchanted by the ever-moving cloud of fireflies, and he was scarcely less pleased with the gentle song of certain insects. "What a charming scene," murmured Sayemon, "and what a charming world we live in! Bows and smiles and abject humility from my women. Oh, it's all very wonderful and very delightful! I would have life always so."

Thus voicing his thoughts in this self-satisfied manner, he chanced to pass his wife's room, and peeped in with a loving and benevolent eye. He observed that his wife was playing *go* with one of his concubines. "Such polite decorum," murmured Sayemon. "Surely their words are as sweet as honey and as soft and fair as finely spun silk. But stay! What strange thing is this? The hair of my wife and the hair of my concubine have turned into snakes that twist and rear their heads in anger. All the time these women smile and bow and move their pieces with well-ordered charm and grace. Gentle words come from their lips, but the snakes of their hair mock them, for these twisting reptiles tell of bitter jealousy in their hearts."

Sayemon's beautiful dream of domestic happiness was for ever shattered. "I will go forth," said he, "and become a Buddhist priest. I will leave behind the hot malice and envy of my wife and concubines, and in the teaching of the Blessed One I shall indeed find true peace."

The next morning Sayemon left the palace secretly, and though search was made for him, he could not be found. About a week later Sayemon's wife reduced the establishment and lived quietly with her little son, Ishidomaro. Two years went by and still there came no news of her husband.

At length Sayemon's wife and child went in search of the missing man. For five years they wandered about the country, till at length they came to a little village in Kishu, where an old man informed the weary and travel-stained wanderers that Sayemon was now a priest, and that a year ago he lived in the temple of Kongobuji, on Mount Koya.

The next day the woman and her son found that at the temple of Kongobuji no women were permitted to enter, so Ishidomaro, after carefully listening to his mother's instructions, ascended the mountain alone. When the boy, after a long and arduous climb, reached the temple, he saw a monk, and said: "Does a priest called Kato Sayemon live here? I am his little son, and my good mother awaits me in yonder valley. Five years we have sought for him, and the love that is in our hearts will surely find him."

The priest, who was none other than Sayemon himself, thus addressed his son: "I am sorry to think that your journey has been in vain, for no one of the name of Kato Sayemon lives in this temple."

Sayemon spoke with outward coldness, but within his heart there was a struggle between his religion and love for his son. Knowing, however, that he had left his wife and child well provided for, he yielded to the teaching of the Lord Buddha and crushed out his parental feelings.

Ishidomaro, however, was not satisfied, for he felt instinctively that the man before him was in reality his father, and once again he addressed the priest: "Good sir, on my left eye there is a mole, and my mother told me that on the left eye of my father there is a similar mark, by which I might at once recognise him. You have the very mark, and in my heart I know that you are my father." And having said these words the boy wept bitterly, longing for arms that never came to caress and soothe the unhappy little fellow.

Sayemon's feelings were again stirred; but with a great effort to conceal his emotion, he said: "The mark of which you speak is very common. I am certainly not your father, and you had better dry your eyes and seek him elsewhere." With these words the priest left the boy in order to attend an evening service. Sayemon continued to live in the temple. He had found peace in serving the Lord Buddha, and he cared not what became of his wife and child.

The Foundation of the Temple of Yakushi Niurai

IN THE DAYS OF OLD there was a priest called Jikaku, who at the age of forty years, it being the autumn of the tenth year of the period called Tencho (AD 833), was suffering from disease of the eyes, which had attacked him three years before. In order to be healed from this disease he carved a figure of Yakushi Niurai, to which he used to offer up his prayers. Five years later he went to China, taking with him the figure as his guardian saint, and at a place called Kairetsu it protected him from robbers and wild beasts and from other calamities. There he passed his time in studying the sacred laws both hidden and revealed, and after nine years set sail to return to Japan. When he was on the high seas a storm arose, and a great fish attacked and tried to swamp the ship, so that the rudder and mast were broken, and the nearest shore being that of a land inhabited by devils, to retreat or to advance was equally dangerous. Then the holy man prayed to the patron saint whose image he carried, and as he prayed, behold the true Yakushi Niurai appeared in the centre of the ship, and said to him:

"Verily, thou hast travelled far that the sacred laws might be revealed for the salvation of many men; now, therefore, take my image, which thou carriest in thy bosom, and cast it into the sea, that the wind may abate, and that thou mayest be delivered from this land of devils."

The commands of the saints must be obeyed, so with tears in his eyes, the priest threw into the sea the sacred image which he loved. Then did the wind abate, and the waves were stilled, and the ship went on her course as though she were being drawn by unseen hands until she reached a safe haven. In the tenth month of the same year the priest again set sail, trusting to the power of his patron saint, and reached the harbour of Tsukushi without mishap. For three years he prayed that the image which he had cast away might be restored to him, until at last one night he was warned in a dream that on the sea-shore at Matsura Yakushi Niurai would appear to him. In consequence of this dream he went to the province of Hizen, and landed on the sea-shore at Hirato, where, in the midst of a blaze of light, the image which he had carved appeared to him twice, riding on the back of a cuttlefish. Thus was the image restored to the world by a miracle. In commemoration of his recovery from the disease of the eyes and of his preservation from the dangers of the sea, that these things might be known to all posterity, the priest established the worship of Tako Yakushi Niurai ('Yakushi Niurai of the Cuttlefish') and came to Meguro, where he built the Temple of Fudo Sama, another Buddhist divinity. At this time there was an epidemic of small-pox in the village, so that men fell down and died in the street, and the holy man prayed to Fudo Sama that the plague might be stayed. Then the god appeared to him, and said:

"The saint Yakushi Niurai of the Cuttlefish, whose image thou carriest, desires to have his place in this village, and he will heal this plague. Thou shalt, therefore, raise a temple to him here that not only this small-pox, but other diseases for future generations, may be cured by his power."

Hearing this, the priest shed tears of gratitude, and having chosen a piece of fine wood, carved a large figure of his patron saint of the cuttlefish, and placed the smaller image inside of the larger, and laid it up in this temple, to which people still flock that they may be healed of their diseases.

Such is the story of the miracle, translated from a small ill-printed pamphlet sold by the priests of the temple, all the decorations of which, even to a bronze lantern in the middle of the yard, are in the form of a cuttlefish, the sacred emblem of the place.

Fox & Animal Legends

Introduction

MANY OF THE FOLLOWING STORIES are the tales a Japanese parent narrates to their child, for animal stories make a universal appeal to the child-mind. They are generally regarded as fairy stories, but they contain so much legendary material that it is necessary to include them in a book of this kind, for they tend to illustrate our subject in a lighter vein, where the miraculous is mingled with the humorous. Legends regarding the fox come first in this section, on account of the importance of the subject, but it must be borne in mind that the supernatural characteristics of this animal apply also to the badger and cat, for in Japanese legend all three animals have been associated with an incalculable amount of mischief.

Inari or other fox beings not infrequently reward human beings for any act of kindness to a fox. Only a part of his reward, however, is real; at least one tempting coin is bound to turn very quickly into grass! The little good done by Inari – and we have tried to do him justice – is altogether weighed down by his countless evil actions, often of an extremely cruel nature. The subject of the fox in Japan was aptly described by Lafcadio Hearn as 'ghostly zoology'.

As we have learnt earlier, many other animals feature in Japanese legend and folklore, whether as representations of spirits and deities, to act as vehicles for didactic messages, or even in origin tales (see 'The Jelly-fish and the Monkey'). So in this section you will encounter, in addition to the fox, hare, badger and cat, everything from a boar to a butterfly.

The Death-Stone

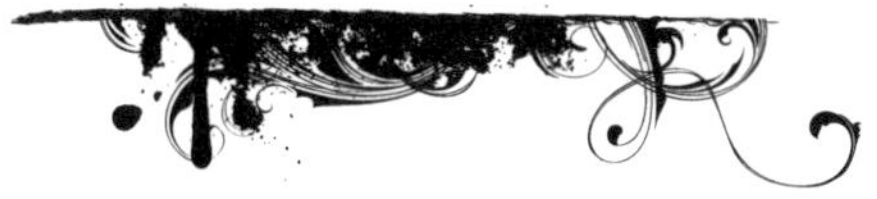

"The Death-Stone stands on Nasu's moor
Through winter snows and summer heat;
The moss grows grey upon its sides,
But the foul demon haunts it yet.

"Chill blows the blast: the owl's sad choir
Hoots hoarsely through the moaning pines;
Among the low chrysanthemums
The skulking fox, the jackal whines,
As o'er the moor the autumn light declines."

THE BUDDHIST PRIEST GENNO, after much weary travel, came to the moor of Nasu, and was about to rest under the shadow of a great stone, when a spirit suddenly appeared, and said: "Rest not under this stone. This is the Death-Stone. Men, birds, and beasts have perished by merely touching it!"

These mysterious and warning remarks naturally awakened Genno's curiosity, and he begged that the spirit would favour him with the story of the Death-Stone.

Thus the spirit began: "Long ago there was a fair girl living at the Japanese Court. She was so charming that she was called the Jewel Maiden. Her wisdom equalled her beauty, for she understood Buddhist lore and the Confucian classics, science, and the poetry of China."

"One night," went on the spirit, "the Mikado gave a great feast in the Summer Palace, and there he assembled the wit, wisdom, and beauty of the land. It was a brilliant gathering; but while the company ate and drank, accompanied by the strains of sweet music, darkness crept over the great apartment. Black clouds raced across the sky, and there was not a star to be seen. While the guests sat rigid with fear a mysterious wind arose. It howled through the Summer Palace and blew out all the lanterns. The complete darkness produced a state of panic, and during the uproar someone cried out, 'A light! A light!'"

"And lo! from out the Jewel Maiden's frame
There's seen to dart a weirdly lustrous flame!
It grows, it spreads, it fills th' imperial halls;
The painted screens, the costly panell'd walls,
Erst the pale viewless damask of the night
Sparkling stand forth as in the moon's full light."

"From that very hour the Mikado sickened," continued the spirit. "He grew so ill that the Court Magician was sent for, and this worthy soul speedily ascertained the cause of his Majesty's decline. He stated, with much warmth of language, that the Jewel Maiden was a harlot and a fiend, 'who, with insidious art, the State to ravage, captivates thy heart!'

"The Magician's words turned the Mikado's heart against the Jewel Maiden. When this sorceress was spurned she resumed her original shape, that of a fox, and ran away to this very stone on Nasu moor."

The priest looked at the spirit critically. "Who are you?" he said at length.

"I am the demon that once dwelt in the breast of the Jewel Maiden! Now I inhabit the Death-Stone for evermore!"

The good Genno was much horrified by this dreadful confession, but, remembering his duty as a priest, he said: "Though you have sunk low in wickedness, you shall rise to virtue again. Take this priestly robe and begging-bowl, and reveal to me your fox form."

Then this wicked spirit cried pitifully:

"In the garish light of day
I hide myself away,
Like pale Asama's fires:
With the night I'll come again,
Confess my guilt with pain
And new-born pure desires."

With these words the spirit suddenly vanished.

Genno did not relinquish his good intentions. He strove more ardently than ever for this erring soul's salvation. In order that she might attain Nirvana, he offered flowers, burnt incense, and recited the sacred Scriptures in front of the stone.

When Genno had performed these religious duties, he said: "Spirit of the Death-Stone, I conjure thee! what was it in a former world that did cause thee to assume in this so foul a shape?"

Suddenly the Death-Stone was rent and the spirit once more appeared, crying:

"In stones there are spirits,
In the waters is a voice heard:
The winds sweep across the firmament!"

Genno saw a lurid glare about him and, in the shining light, a fox that suddenly turned into a beautiful maiden.

Thus spoke the spirit of the Death-Stone: "I am she who first, in Ind, was the demon to whom Prince Hazoku paid homage.... In Great Cathay I took the form of Hoji, consort of the Emperor Iuwao; and at the Court of the Rising Sun I became the Flawless Jewel Maiden, concubine to the Emperor Toba."

The spirit confessed to Genno that in the form of the Jewel Maiden she had desired to bring destruction to the Imperial line. "Already," said the spirit, "I was making my plans, already I was gloating over the thought of the Mikado's death, and had it not been for the power of the Court Magician I should have succeeded in my scheme. As I have told you, I was driven from the Court. I was pursued by dogs and arrows, and finally sank exhausted into the Death-Stone. From time to time I haunted the moor. Now the Lord Buddha has had compassion upon me, and he has sent his priest to point out the way of true religion and to bring peace."

The legend concludes with the following pious utterances poured forth by the now contrite spirit:

"'I swear, O man of God! I swear,' she cries,
'To thee whose blessing wafts me to the skies,
I swear a solemn oath, that shall endure
Firm as the Death-Stone standing on the moor,
That from this hour I'm virtue's child alone!'
Thus spake the ghoul, and vanished 'neath the Stone."

How a Man Was Bewitched and Had His Head Shaved by the Foxes

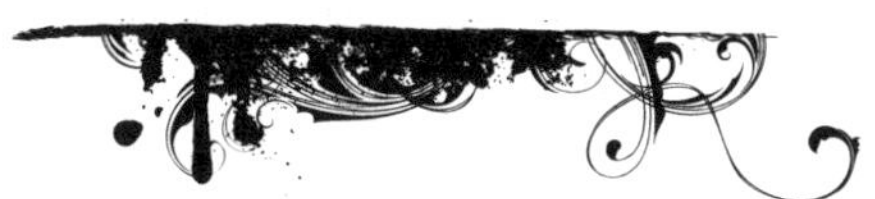

IN THE VILLAGE OF IWAHARA, in the province of Shinshiu, there dwelt a family which had acquired considerable wealth in the wine trade. On some auspicious occasion it happened that a number of guests were gathered together at their house, feasting on wine and fish; and as the wine-cup went round, the conversation turned upon foxes. Among the guests was a certain carpenter, Tokutaro by name, a man about thirty years of age, of a stubborn and obstinate turn, who said:

"Well, sirs, you've been talking for some time of men being bewitched by foxes; surely you must be under their influence yourselves, to say such things. How on earth can foxes have such power over men? At any rate, men must be great fools to be so deluded. Let's have no more of this nonsense."

Upon this a man who was sitting by him answered:

"Tokutaro little knows what goes on in the world, or he would not speak so. How many myriads of men are there who have been bewitched by foxes? Why, there have been at least twenty or thirty men tricked by the brutes on the Maki Moor alone. It's hard to disprove facts that have happened before our eyes."

"You're no better than a pack of born idiots," said Tokutaro. "I will engage to go out to the Maki Moor this very night and prove it. There is not a fox in all Japan that can make a fool of Tokutaro."

Thus he spoke in his pride; but the others were all angry with him for boasting, and said:

"If you return without anything having happened, we will pay for five measures of wine and a thousand copper cash worth of fish; and if you are bewitched, you shall do as much for us."

Tokutaro took the bet, and at nightfall set forth for the Maki Moor by himself. As he neared the moor, he saw before him a small bamboo grove, into which a fox ran; and it instantly occurred to him that the foxes of the moor would try to bewitch him. As he was yet looking, he suddenly saw the daughter of the headman of the village of Upper Horikane, who was married to the headman of the village of Maki.

"Pray, where are you going to, Master Tokutaro?" said she.

"I am going to the village hard by."

"Then, as you will have to pass my native place, if you will allow me, I will accompany you so far."

Tokutaro thought this very odd, and made up his mind that it was a fox trying to make a fool of him; he accordingly determined to turn the tables on the fox, and answered – "It is a long time since I have had the pleasure of seeing you; and as it seems that your house is on my road, I shall be glad to escort you so far."

With this he walked behind her, thinking he should certainly see the end of a fox's tail peeping out; but, look as he might, there was nothing to be seen. At last they came to the village of Upper Horikane; and when they reached the cottage of the girl's father, the family all came out, surprised to see her.

"Oh dear! oh dear! here is our daughter come: I hope there is nothing the matter."

And so they went on, for some time, asking a string of questions.

In the meanwhile, Tokutaro went round to the kitchen door, at the back of the house, and, beckoning out the master of the house, said:

"The girl who has come with me is not really your daughter. As I was going to the Maki Moor, when I arrived at the bamboo grove, a fox jumped up in front of me, and when it had dashed into the grove it immediately took the shape of your daughter, and offered to accompany me to the village; so I pretended to be taken in by the brute, and came with it so far."

On hearing this, the master of the house put his head on one side, and mused a while; then, calling his wife, he repeated the story to her, in a whisper.

But she flew into a great rage with Tokutaro, and said:

"This is a pretty way of insulting people's daughters. The girl is our daughter, and there's no mistake about it. How dare you invent such lies?"

"Well," said Tokutaro, "you are quite right to say so; but still there is no doubt that this is a case of witchcraft."

Seeing how obstinately he held to his opinion, the old folks were sorely perplexed, and said: "What do you think of doing?"

"Pray leave the matter to me: I'll soon strip the false skin off, and show the beast to you in its true colours. Do you two go into the store-closet, and wait there."

With this he went into the kitchen, and, seizing the girl by the back of the neck, forced her down by the hearth.

"Oh! Master Tokutaro, what means this brutal violence? Mother! father! help!"

So the girl cried and screamed; but Tokutaro only laughed, and said:

"So you thought to bewitch me, did you? From the moment you jumped into the wood, I was on the look-out for you to play me some trick. I'll soon make you show what you really are;" and as he said this, he twisted her two hands behind her back, and trod upon her, and tortured her; but she only wept, and cried:

"Oh! it hurts, it hurts!"

"If this is not enough to make you show your true form, I'll roast you to death;" and he piled firewood on the hearth, and, tucking up her dress, scorched her severely.

"Oh! oh! this is more than I can bear;" and with this she expired.

The two old people then came running in from the rear of the house, and, pushing aside Tokutaro, folded their daughter in their arms, and put their hands to her mouth to feel whether she still breathed; but life was extinct, and not the sign of a fox's tail was to be seen about her. Then they seized Tokutaro by the collar, and cried:

"On pretence that our true daughter was a fox, you have roasted her to death. Murderer! Here, you there, bring ropes and cords, and secure this Tokutaro!"

So the servants obeyed, and several of them seized Tokutaro and bound him to a pillar. Then the master of the house, turning to Tokutaro, said:

"You have murdered our daughter before our very eyes. I shall report the matter to the lord of the manor, and you will assuredly pay for this with your head. Be prepared for the worst."

And as he said this, glaring fiercely at Tokutaro, they carried the corpse of his daughter into the store-closet. As they were sending to make the matter known in the village of Maki, and taking other measures, who should come up but the priest of the temple called Anrakuji, in the village of Iwahara, with an acolyte and a servant, who called out in a loud voice from the front door:

"Is all well with the honourable master of this house? I have been to say prayers today in a neighbouring village, and on my way back I could not pass the door without at least inquiring after your welfare. If you are at home, I would fain pay my respects to you."

As he spoke thus in a loud voice, he was heard from the back of the house; and the master got up and went out, and, after the usual compliments on meeting had been exchanged, said:

"I ought to have the honour of inviting you to step inside this evening; but really we are all in the greatest trouble, and I must beg you to excuse my impoliteness."

"Indeed! Pray, what may be the matter?" replied the priest. And when the master of the house had told the whole story, from beginning to end, he was thunderstruck, and said:

"Truly, this must be a terrible distress to you." Then the priest looked on one side, and saw Tokutaro bound, and exclaimed, "Is not that Tokutaro that I see there?"

"Oh, your reverence," replied Tokutaro, piteously, "it was this, that, and the other: and I took it into my head that the young lady was a fox, and so I killed her. But I pray your reverence to intercede for me, and save my life;" and as he spoke, the tears started from his eyes.

"To be sure," said the priest, "you may well bewail yourself; however, if I save your life, will you consent to become my disciple, and enter the priesthood?"

"Only save my life, and I'll become your disciple with all my heart."

When the priest heard this, he called out the parents, and said to them:

"It would seem that, though I am but a foolish old priest, my coming here today has been unusually well timed. I have a request to make of you. Your putting Tokutaro to death won't bring your daughter to life again. I have heard his story, and there certainly was no malice prepense on his part to kill your daughter. What he did, he did thinking to do a service to your family; and it would surely be better to hush the matter up. He wishes, moreover, to give himself over to me, and to become my disciple."

"It is as you say," replied the father and mother, speaking together. "Revenge will not recall our daughter. Please dispel our grief, by shaving his head and making a priest of him on the spot."

"I'll shave him at once, before your eyes," answered the priest, who immediately caused the cords which bound Tokutaro to be untied, and, putting on his priest's scarf, made him join his hands together in a posture of prayer. Then the reverend man stood up behind him, razor in hand, and, intoning a hymn, gave two or three strokes of the razor, which he then handed to his acolyte, who made a clean shave of Tokutaro's hair. When the latter had finished his obeisance to the priest, and the ceremony was over, there was a loud burst of laughter; and at the same moment the day broke, and Tokutaro found himself alone, in the middle of a large moor. At first, in his surprise, he thought that it was all a dream, and was much annoyed at having been tricked by the foxes. He then passed his hand over his head, and found that he was shaved quite bald. There was nothing for it but to get up, wrap a handkerchief round his head, and go back to the place where his friends were assembled.

"Hallo, Tokutaro! so you've come back. Well, how about the foxes?"

"Really, gentlemen," replied he, bowing, "I am quite ashamed to appear before you."

Then he told them the whole story, and, when he had finished, pulled off the kerchief, and showed his bald pate.

"What a capital joke!" shouted his listeners, and amid roars of laughter, claimed the bet of fish, and wine. It was duly paid; but Tokutaro never allowed his hair to grow again, and renounced the world, and became a priest under the name of Sainen.

The Grateful Foxes

ONE FINE SPRING DAY, two friends went out to a moor to gather fern, attended by a boy with a bottle of wine and a box of provisions. As they were straying about, they saw at the foot of a hill a fox that had brought out its cub to play; and whilst they looked on, struck by the strangeness of the sight, three children came up from a neighbouring village with baskets in their hands, on the same errand as themselves. As soon as the children saw the foxes, they picked up a bamboo stick and took the creatures stealthily in the rear; and when the old foxes took to flight, they surrounded them and beat them with the stick, so that they ran away as fast as their legs could carry them; but two of the boys held down the cub, and, seizing it by the scruff of the neck, went off in high glee.

The two friends were looking on all the while, and one of them, raising his voice, shouted out, "Hallo! you boys! what are you doing with that fox?"

The eldest of the boys replied, "We're going to take him home and sell him to a young man in our village. He'll buy him, and then he'll boil him in a pot and eat him."

"Well," replied the other, after considering the matter attentively, "I suppose it's all the same to you whom you sell him to. You'd better let me have him."

"Oh, but the young man from our village promised us a good round sum if we could find a fox, and got us to come out to the hills and catch one; and so we can't sell him to you at any price."

"Well, I suppose it cannot be helped, then; but how much would the young man give you for the cub?"

"Oh, he'll give us three hundred cash at least."

"Then I'll give you half a bu; and so you'll gain five hundred cash by the transaction."

"Oh, we'll sell him for that, sir. How shall we hand him over to you?"

"Just tie him up here," said the other; and so he made fast the cub round the neck with the string of the napkin in which the luncheon-box was wrapped, and gave half a bu to the three boys, who ran away delighted.

The man's friend, upon this, said to him, "Well, certainly you have got queer tastes. What on earth are you going to keep the fox for?"

"How very unkind of you to speak of my tastes like that. If we had not interfered just now, the fox's cub would have lost its life. If we had not seen the affair, there would have been no help for it. How could I stand by and see life taken? It was but a little I spent –only half a bu – to save the cub, but had it cost a fortune I should not have grudged it. I thought you were intimate enough with me to know my heart; but today you have accused me of being eccentric, and I see how mistaken I have been in you. However, our friendship shall cease from this day forth."

And when he had said this with a great deal of firmness, the other, retiring backwards and bowing with his hands on his knees, replied:

"Indeed, indeed, I am filled with admiration at the goodness of your heart. When I hear you speak thus, I feel more than ever how great is the love I bear you. I thought that you might wish to use the cub as a sort of decoy to lead the old ones to you, that you might pray them to bring prosperity and virtue to your house. When I called you eccentric just now, I was but trying your heart, because I had some suspicions of you; and now I am truly ashamed of myself."

And as he spoke, still bowing, the other replied, "Really! was that indeed your thought? Then I pray you to forgive me for my violent language."

When the two friends had thus become reconciled, they examined the cub, and saw that it had a slight wound in its foot, and could not walk; and while they were thinking what they should do, they spied out the herb called 'Doctor's Nakase', which was just sprouting; so they rolled up a little of it in their fingers and applied it to the part. Then they pulled out some boiled rice from their luncheon-box and offered it to the cub, but it showed no sign of wanting to eat; so they stroked it gently on the back, and petted it; and as the pain of the wound seemed to have subsided, they were admiring the properties of the herb, when, opposite to them, they saw the old foxes sitting watching them by the side of some stacks of rice straw.

"Look there! the old foxes have come back, out of fear for their cub's safety. Come, we will set it free!" And with these words they untied the string round the cub's neck, and turned its head towards the spot where the old foxes sat; and as the wounded foot was no longer painful, with one bound it dashed to its parents' side and licked them all over for joy, while they seemed to bow their thanks, looking towards the two friends. So, with peace in their hearts, the latter went off to another place, and, choosing a pretty spot, produced the wine bottle and ate their noon-day meal; and after a pleasant day, they returned to their homes, and became firmer friends than ever.

Now the man who had rescued the fox's cub was a tradesman in good circumstances: he had three or four agents and two maid-servants, besides men-servants; and altogether he lived in a liberal manner. He was married, and this union had brought him one son, who had reached his tenth year, but had been attacked by a strange disease which defied all the physician's skill and drugs. At last a famous physician prescribed the liver taken from a live fox, which, as he said, would certainly effect a cure. If that were not forthcoming, the most expensive medicine in the world would not restore the boy to health. When the parents heard this, they were at their wits' end. However, they told the state of the case to a man who lived on the mountains. "Even though our child should die for it," they said, "we will not ourselves deprive other creatures of their lives; but you, who live among the hills, are sure to hear when your neighbours go out fox-hunting. We don't care what price we might have to pay for a fox's liver; pray, buy one for us at any expense." So they pressed him to exert himself on their behalf; and he, having promised faithfully to execute the commission, went his way.

In the night of the following day there came a messenger, who announced himself as coming from the person who had undertaken to procure the fox's liver; so the master of the house went out to see him.

"I have come from Mr So-and-so. Last night the fox's liver that you required fell into his hands; so he sent me to bring it to you." With these words the messenger produced a small jar, adding, "In a few days he will let you know the price."

When he had delivered his message, the master of the house was greatly pleased, and said, "Indeed, I am deeply grateful for this kindness, which will save my son's life."

Then the good wife came out, and received the jar with every mark of politeness.

"We must make a present to the messenger."

"Indeed, sir, I've already been paid for my trouble."

"Well, at any rate, you must stop the night here."

"Thank you, sir: I've a relation in the next village whom I have not seen for a long while, and I will pass the night with him;" and so he took his leave, and went away.

The parents lost no time in sending to let the physician know that they had procured the fox's liver. The next day the doctor came and compounded a medicine for the patient, which at once produced a good effect, and there was no little joy in the household. As luck would have it, three days after this the man whom they had commissioned to buy the fox's liver came to the house; so the goodwife hurried out to meet him and welcome him.

"How quickly you fulfilled our wishes, and how kind of you to send at once! The doctor prepared the medicine, and now our boy can get up and walk about the room; and it's all owing to your goodness."

"Wait a bit!" cried the guest, who did not know what to make of the joy of the two parents. "The commission with which you entrusted me about the fox's liver turned out to be a matter of impossibility, so I came today to make my excuses; and now I really can't understand what you are so grateful to me for."

"We are thanking you, sir," replied the master of the house, bowing with his hands on the ground, "for the fox's liver which we asked you to procure for us."

"I really am perfectly unaware of having sent you a fox's liver: there must be some mistake here. Pray inquire carefully into the matter."

"Well, this is very strange. Four nights ago, a man of some five or six and thirty years of age came with a verbal message from you, to the effect that you had sent him with a fox's liver, which you had just procured, and said that he would come and tell us the price another day. When we asked him to spend the night here, he answered that he would lodge with a relation in the next village, and went away."

The visitor was more and more lost in amazement, and; leaning his head on one side in deep thought, confessed that he could make nothing of it. As for the husband and wife, they felt quite out of countenance at having thanked a man so warmly for favours of which he denied all knowledge; and so the visitor took his leave, and went home.

That night there appeared at the pillow of the master of the house a woman of about one or two and thirty years of age, who said, "I am the fox that lives at such-and-such a mountain. Last spring, when I was taking out my cub to play, it was carried off by some boys, and only saved by your goodness. The desire to requite this kindness pierced me to the quick. At last, when calamity attacked your house, I thought that I might be of use to you. Your son's illness could not be cured without a liver taken from a live fox, so to repay your kindness I killed my cub and took out its liver; then its sire, disguising himself as a messenger, brought it to your house."

And as she spoke, the fox shed tears; and the master of the house, wishing to thank her, moved in bed, upon which his wife awoke and asked him what was the matter; but he too, to her great astonishment, was biting the pillow and weeping bitterly.

"Why are you weeping thus?" asked she.

At last he sat up in bed, and said, "Last spring, when I was out on a pleasure excursion, I was the means of saving the life of a fox's cub, as I told you at the time. The other day I told Mr So-and-so that, although my son were to die before my eyes, I would not be the means of killing a fox on purpose; but asked him, in case he heard of any hunter killing a fox, to buy it for me. How the foxes came to hear of this I don't know; but the foxes to whom I had shown kindness killed their own cub and took out the liver; and the old dog-fox, disguising himself as a messenger from the person to whom we had confided the commission, came here with it. His mate has just been at my pillow-side and told me all about it; hence it was that, in spite of myself, I was moved to tears."

When she heard this, the goodwife likewise was blinded by her tears, and for a while they lay lost in thought; but at last, coming to themselves, they lighted the lamp on the shelf on which the family idol stood, and spent the night in reciting prayers and praises, and the next day they published the matter to the household and to their relations and friends. Now, although there are instances of men killing their own children to requite a favour, there is no other example of foxes having done such a thing; so the story became the talk of the whole country.

Now, the boy who had recovered through the efficacy of this medicine selected the prettiest spot on the premises to erect a shrine to Inari Sama, the Fox God, and offered sacrifice to the two old foxes, for whom he purchased the highest rank at the court of the Mikado.

Inari Answers a Woman's Prayer

INARI is often extremely benevolent. One legend informs us that a woman who had been married many years and had not been blessed with a child prayed at Inari's shrine. At the conclusion of her supplication the stone foxes wagged their tails, and snow began to fall. She regarded these phenomena as favourable omens.

When the woman reached her home a *yeta* (beggar) accosted her, and begged for something to eat. The woman good-naturedly gave this unfortunate wayfarer some red bean rice, the only food she had in the house, and presented it to him in a dish.

The next day her husband discovered this dish lying in front of the shrine where she had prayed. The beggar was none other than Inari himself, and the woman's generosity was rewarded in due season by the birth of a child.

The Meanness of Raiko

RAIKO WAS A WEALTHY MAN living in a certain village. In spite of his enormous wealth, which he carried in his *obi* (girdle), he was extremely mean. As he grew older his meanness increased till at last he contemplated dismissing his faithful servants who had served him so well.

One day Raiko became very ill, so ill that he almost wasted away, on account of a terrible fever. On the tenth night of his illness a poorly dressed *bozu* (priest) appeared by his pillow, inquired how he fared, and added that he had expected the *oni* to carry him off long ago.

These home truths, none too delicately expressed, made Raiko very angry, and he indignantly demanded that the priest should take his departure. But the *bozu*, instead of departing, told him that there was only one remedy for his illness. The remedy was that Raiko should loosen his *obi* and distribute his money to the poor.

Raiko became still more angry at what he considered the gross impertinence of the priest. He snatched a dagger from his robe and tried to kill the kindly *bozu*. The priest, without the least fear, informed Raiko that he had heard of his mean intention to dismiss his worthy servants, and had nightly come to the old man to drain his life-blood. "Now," said the priest, "my object is attained!" and with these words he blew out the light.

The now thoroughly frightened Raiko felt a ghostly creature advance towards him. The old man struck out blindly with his dagger, and made such a commotion that his loyal servants ran, into the room with lanterns, and the light revealed the horrible claw of a monster lying by the side of the old man's mat.

Carefully following the little spots of blood, Raiko's servants came to a miniature mountain at the extreme end of the garden, and in the mountain was a large hole, from whence protruded the upper part of an enormous spider. This creature begged the servants to try to persuade their master not to attack the Gods, and in future to refrain from meanness.

When Raiko heard these words from his servants he repented, and gave large sums of money to the poor. Inari had assumed the shape of a spider and priest in order to teach the once mean old man a lesson.

The Foxes' Wedding

ONCE UPON A TIME THERE was a young white fox, whose name was Fukuyemon. When he had reached the fitting age, he shaved off his forelock and began to think of taking to himself a beautiful bride. The old fox, his father, resolved to give up his inheritance to his son, and retired into private life; so the young fox, in gratitude for this, laboured hard and earnestly to increase his patrimony. Now it happened that in a famous old family of foxes there was a beautiful young lady-fox, with such lovely fur that the fame of her jewel-like charms was spread far and wide. The young white fox, who had heard of this, was bent on making her his wife, and a meeting was arranged between them. There was not a fault to be found on either side; so the preliminaries were settled, and the wedding presents sent from the bridegroom to the bride's house, with congratulatory speeches from the messenger, which were duly acknowledged by the person deputed to receive the gifts; the bearers, of course, received the customary fee in copper cash.

When the ceremonies had been concluded, an auspicious day was chosen for the bride to go to her husband's house, and she was carried off in solemn procession during a shower of rain, the sun shining all the while. After the ceremonies of drinking wine had been gone through, the bride changed her dress, and the wedding was concluded, without let or hindrance, amid singing and dancing and merry-making.

The bride and bridegroom lived lovingly together, and a litter of little foxes were born to them, to the great joy of the old grandsire, who treated the little cubs as tenderly as if they had been butterflies or flowers. "They're the very image of their old grandfather," said he, as proud as possible. "As for medicine, bless them, they're so healthy that they'll never need a copper coin's worth!"

As soon as they were old enough, they were carried off to the temple of Inari Sama, the patron saint of foxes, and the old grand-parents prayed that they might be delivered from dogs and all the other ills to which fox flesh is heir.

In this way the white fox by degrees waxed old and prosperous, and his children, year by year, became more and more numerous around him; so that, happy in his family and his business, every recurring spring brought him fresh cause for joy.

The White Hare of Inaba

IN ANCIENT DAYS there were eighty-one brothers, who were Princes in Japan. With the exception of one brother they were quarrelsome fellows, and spent their time in showing all manner of petty jealousy, one toward the other. Each wanted to reign over the whole kingdom, and, in addition, each had the misfortune to wish to marry the Princess of Yakami, in Inaba. Although these eighty Princes were at variance in most things, they were at one in persistently hating the brother who was gentle and peaceful in all his ways.

At length, after many angry words, the eighty brothers decided to go to Inaba in order to visit the Princess of Yakami, each brother fully resolved that he and he alone should be the successful suitor. The kind and gentle brother accompanied them, not, indeed, as a wooer of the fair Princess, but as a servant who carried a large and heavy bag upon his back.

At last the eighty Princes, who had left their much-wronged brother far behind, arrived at Cape Keta. They were about to continue their journey when they saw a white hare lying on the ground looking very miserable and entirely divested of fur.

The eighty Princes, who were much amused by the sorry plight of the hare, said: "If you want your fur to grow again, bathe in the sea, and, when you have done so, run to the summit of a high mountain and allow the wind to blow upon you." With these words the eighty heartless Princes proceeded on their way.

The hare at once went down to the sea, delighted at the prospect of regaining his handsome white fur. Having bathed, he ran up to the top of a mountain and lay down upon it; but he quickly perceived that the cold wind blowing on a skin recently immersed in salt water was beginning to crack and split. In addition to the humiliation of having no fur he now suffered considerable physical pain, and he realised that the eighty Princes had shamefully deceived him.

While the hare was lying in pain upon the mountain the kind and gentle brother approached, slowly and laboriously, owing to the heavy bag he carried. When he saw the weeping hare he inquired how it was that the poor animal had met with such a misfortune.

"Please stop a moment," said the hare, "and I will tell you how it all happened. I wanted to cross from the Island of Oki to Cape Keta, so I said to the crocodiles: 'I should very much like to know how many crocodiles there are in the sea, and how many hares on land. Allow me first of all to count you.' And having said these words the crocodiles formed themselves into a long line, stretching from the Island of Oki to Cape Keta. I ran across their horny bodies, counting each as I passed. When I reached the last crocodile, I said: 'O foolish crocodiles, it doesn't matter to me how many there are of you in the sea, or how many hares on land! I only wanted you for a bridge in order that I might reach my destination.' Alas! my miserable boast cost me dear, for the last crocodile raised his head and snapped off all my fur!"

"Well," said the gentle brother, "I must say you were in the wrong and deserved to suffer for your folly. Is that the end of your story?"

"No," continued the hare. "I had no sooner suffered this indignity than the eighty Princes came by, and lyingly told me that I might be cured by salt water and wind. Alas! not knowing that they deceived me, I carried out their instructions, with the result that my body is cracked and extremely sore."

"Bathe in fresh water, my poor friend," said the good brother, "and when you have done so scatter the pollen of sedges upon the ground and roll yourself in it. This will indeed heal your sores and cause your fur to grow again."

The hare walked slowly to the river, bathed himself, and then rolled about in sedge pollen. He had no sooner done so than his skin healed and he was covered once more with a thick coat of fur.

The grateful hare ran back to his benefactor. "Those eighty wicked and cruel brothers of yours," said he, "shall never win the Princess of Inaba. It is you who shall marry her and reign over the country."

The hare's prophecy came true, for the eighty Princes failed in their mission, while the brother who was good and kind to the white hare married the fair Princess and became King of the country.

The Crackling Mountain

AN OLD MAN AND HIS WIFE kept a white hare. One day a badger came and ate the food provided for the pet. The mischievous animal was about to scamper away when the old man, seeing what had taken place, tied the badger to a tree, and then went to a neighbouring mountain to cut wood.

When the old man had gone on his journey the badger began to weep and to beg that the old woman would untie the rope. She had no sooner done so than the badger proclaimed vengeance and ran away.

When the good white hare heard what had taken place he set out to warn his master; but during his absence the badger returned, killed the old woman, assumed her form, and converted her corpse into broth.

"I have made such excellent broth," said the badger, when the old man returned from the mountain. "You must be hungry and tired: pray sit down and make a good meal!"

The old man, not suspecting treachery of any kind, consumed the broth and pronounced it excellent.

"Excellent?" sneered the badger. "You have eaten your wife! Her bones lie over there in that corner," and with these words he disappeared.

While the old man was overcome with sorrow, and while he wept and bewailed his fate, the hare returned, grasped the situation, and scampered off to the mountain fully resolved to avenge the death of his poor old mistress.

When the hare reached the mountain he saw the badger carrying a bundle of sticks on his back. Softly the hare crept up, and, unobserved, set light to the sticks, which began to crackle immediately.

"This is a strange noise," said the badger. "What is it?"

"The Crackling Mountain," replied the hare.

The fire began to burn the badger, so he sprang into a river and extinguished the flames; but on getting out again he found that his back was severely burnt, and the pain he suffered was increased by a cayenne poultice which the delighted hare provided for that purpose.

When the badger was well again he chanced to see the hare standing by a boat he had made.

"Where are you going in that vessel?" inquired the badger.

"To the moon," replied the hare. "Perhaps you would like to come with me?"

"Not in your boat!" said the badger. "I know too well your tricks on the Crackling Mountain. But I will build a boat of clay for myself, and we will journey to the moon."

Down the river went the wooden boat of the hare and the clay boat of the badger. Presently the badger's vessel began to come to pieces. The hare laughed derisively, and killed his enemy with his oar. Later on, when the loyal animal returned to the old man, he justly received much praise and loving care from his grateful master.

The Fox and the Badger

THERE IS A CERTAIN mountainous district in Shikoku in which a skillful hunter had trapped or shot so many foxes and badgers that only a few were left. These were an old grey badger and a female fox with one cub. Though hard pressed by hunger, neither dared to touch a loose piece of food, lest a trap might be hidden under it. Indeed they scarcely stirred out of their holes except at night, lest the hunter's arrow should strike them. At last the two animals held a council together to decide what to do, whether to emigrate or to attempt to outwit their enemy. They thought a long while, when finally the badger having hit upon a good plan, cried out:

"I have it. Do you transform yourself into a man. I'll pretend to be dead. Then you can bind me up and sell me in the town. With the money paid you can buy some food. Then I'll get loose and come back. The next week I'll sell you and you can escape."

"Ha! ha! ha! *yoroshiu*, *yoroshiu*," (good, good,) cried both together. "It's a capital plan," said Mrs Fox.

So the Fox changed herself into a human form, and the badger, pretending to be dead, was tied up with straw ropes.

Slinging him over her shoulder, the fox went to town, sold the badger, and buying a lot of *tofu* (bean-cheese) and one or two chickens, made a feast. By this time the badger had got loose, for the man to whom he was sold, thinking him dead, had not watched him carefully. So scampering away to the mountains he met the fox, who congratulated him, while both feasted merrily.

The next week the badger took human form, and going to town sold the fox, who made believe to be dead. But the badger being an old skin-flint, and very greedy, wanted all the money and food for himself. So he whispered in the man's ear to watch the fox well as she was only feigning to be dead. So the man taking up a club gave the fox a blow on the head, which finished her. The badger, buying a good dinner, ate it all himself, and licked his chops, never even thinking of the fox's cub.

The cub after waiting a long time for its mother to come back, suspected foul play, and resolved on revenge. So going to the badger he challenged him to a trial of skill in the art of transformation. The badger accepted right off, for he despised the cub and wished to be rid of him.

"Well what do you want to do first? said Sir Badger."

"I propose that you go and stand on the Big Bridge leading to the city," said the cub, "and wait for my appearance. I shall come in splendid garments, and with many followers in my train. If you recognize me, you win, and I lose. If you fail, I win."

So the badger went and waited behind a tree. Soon a daimyo riding in a palanquin, with a splendid retinue of courtiers appeared, coming up the road. Thinking this was the fox-cub changed into a nobleman, although wondering at the skill of the young fox, the badger went up to the palanquin and told the person inside that he was recognized and had lost the game.

"What!" said the daimyo's followers, who were real men, and surrounding the badger, they beat him to death.

The fox-cub, who was looking on from a hill near by, laughed in derision, and glad that treachery was punished, scampered away.

Kadzutoyo and the Badger

ON ONE OCCASION Kadzutoyo and his retainer went fishing. They had had excellent sport, and were about to return home, when a violent shower came on, and they were forced to take shelter under a willow-tree. After waiting for some time the rain showed no sign of abating, and as it was already growing dark they decided to continue their journey in spite of the inclement weather. They had not proceeded far when they perceived a young girl weeping bitterly. Kadzutoyo regarded her with suspicion, but his retainer was charmed by the maiden's great beauty, and inquired who she was and why she lingered on such a stormy night.

"Alas! good sir," said the maiden, still weeping, "my tale is a sad one. I have long endured the taunts and cruelties of my wicked stepmother, who hates me. Tonight she spat upon me and beat me. I could bear the bitter humiliation no longer, and I was on the way to my aunt, who lives in yonder village, there to receive peace and shelter, when I was stricken down with a strange malady, and compelled to remain here until the pain subsided."

These words much affected the kind-hearted retainer, and he fell desperately in love with this fair maiden; but Kadzutoyo, after carefully considering the matter, drew his sword and cut off her head.

"Oh! my lord," said the retainer, "what awful deed is this? How can you kill a harmless girl? Believe me, you will have to pay for your folly."

"You do not understand," replied Kadzutoyo, "but all I ask is that you keep silence in the matter."

When they reached home Kadzutoyo soon fell asleep; but his retainer, after brooding over the murder of the fair maiden, went to his lord's parents and told them the whole pitiful story.

Kadzutoyo's father was stricken with anger when he heard the dreadful tale. He at once went to his son's room, roused him, and said: "Oh, miserable murderer! How could you slay an innocent girl without the least provocation? You have shamed the honourable name of *samurai*, a name that stands for true chivalry and for the defence of the weak and helpless. You have brought dishonour upon our house, and it is my duty to take your life." Having said these words, he drew his sword.

"Sir," replied Kadzutoyo, without flinching at the shining weapon, "you, like my retainer, do not understand. It has been given me to solve certain mysteries, and with that knowledge I assure you that I have not been guilty of so foul a crime as you suppose, but have been loyal to the fair calling of a *samurai*. The girl I cut down with my sword was no mortal. Be pleased to go tomorrow with your retainers to the spot where this scene occurred. If you find the corpse of a girl you will have no need to take my life, for I will disembowel myself."

Early next day, when the sun had scarce risen in the sky, Kadzutoyo's father, together with his retainers, set out upon the journey. When they reached the place where the tragedy had taken place the father saw lying by the roadside, not the corpse of a fair maiden as he had feared, but the body of a great headless badger.

When the father reached home again he questioned his son: "How is it," said he, "that what appeared to be a girl to your retainer seemed to you to be a badger?"

"Sir," replied Kadzutoyo, "the creature I saw last night appeared to me as a girl; but her beauty was strange, and not like the beauty of earthly women. Moreover, although it was raining hard, I observed that the garments of this being did not get wet, and having noticed this weird occurrence, I knew at once that the woman was none other than some wicked goblin. The creature took the form of a lovely maiden with the idea of bewitching us with her many charms, in the hope that she might get our fish."

The old Prince was filled with admiration for his son's cleverness. Having discovered so much foresight and prudence, he resolved to abdicate, and proclaim Kadzutoyo Prince of Tosa in his stead.

The Miraculous Tea-kettle

ONE DAY a priest of the Morinji temple put his old tea-kettle on the fire in order that he might make himself a cup of tea. No sooner had the kettle touched the fire than it suddenly changed into the head, tail, and legs of a badger. The novices of the temple were called in to see the extraordinary sight. While they gazed in utter astonishment, the badger, with the body of a kettle, rushed nimbly about the room, and finally flew into the air. Round and round the room went the merry badger, and the priests, after many efforts, succeeded in capturing the animal and thrusting it into a box.

Shortly after this event had taken place a tinker called at the temple, and the priest thought it would be an excellent idea if he could induce the good man to buy his extraordinary tea-kettle. He therefore took the kettle out of its box, for it had now resumed its ordinary form, and commenced to bargain, with the result that the unsuspecting tinker purchased the kettle, and took it away with him, assured that he had done a good day's work in buying such a useful article at so reasonable a price.

That night the tinker was awakened by hearing a curious sound close to his pillow. He looked out from behind his quilts and saw that the kettle he had purchased was not a kettle at all, but a very lively and clever badger.

When the tinker told his friends about his remarkable companion, they said: "You are a fortunate fellow, and we advise you to take this badger on show, for it is clever enough to dance and walk on the tight-rope. With song and music you certainly have in this very strange creature a series of novel entertainments which will attract considerable notice, and bring you far more money than you would earn by all the tinkering in the world."

The tinker accordingly acted upon this excellent advice, and the fame of his performing badger spread far and wide. Princes and princesses came to see the show, and from royal patronage and the delight of the common people he amassed a great fortune. When the tinker had made his money he restored the kettle to the Morinji temple, where it was worshipped as a precious treasure.

The Badger's Money

IT IS A COMMON SAYING among men, that to forget favours received is the part of a bird or a beast: an ungrateful man will be ill spoken of by all the world. And yet even birds and beasts will show gratitude; so that a man who does not requite a favour is worse even than dumb brutes. Is not this a disgrace?

Once upon a time, in a hut at a place called Namekata, in Hitachi, there lived an old priest famous neither for learning nor wisdom, but bent only on passing his days in prayer and meditation. He had not even a child to wait upon him, but prepared his food with his own hands. Night and morning he recited the prayer "Namu Amida Butsu," intent upon that alone. Although the fame of his virtue did not reach far, yet his neighbours respected and revered him, and often brought him food and raiment; and when his roof or his walls fell out of repair, they would mend them for him; so for the things of this world he took no thought.

One very cold night, when he little thought anyone was outside, he heard a voice calling "Your reverence! your reverence!" So he rose and went out to see who it was, and there he beheld an old badger standing. Any ordinary man would have been greatly alarmed at the apparition; but the priest, being such as he has been described above, showed no sign of fear, but asked the creature its business. Upon this the badger respectfully bent its knees, and said:

"Hitherto, sir, my lair has been in the mountains, and of snow or frost I have taken no heed; but now I am growing old, and this severe cold is more than I can bear. I pray you to let me enter and warm myself at the fire of your cottage, that I may live through this bitter night."

When the priest heard what a helpless state the beast was reduced to, he was filled with pity, and said:

"That's a very slight matter: make haste and come in and warm yourself."

The badger, delighted with so good a reception, went into the hut, and squatting down by the fire began to warm itself; and the priest, with renewed fervour, recited his prayers and struck his bell before the image of Buddha, looking straight before him. After two hours the badger took its leave, with profuse expressions of thanks, and went out; and from that time forth it came every night to the hut. As the badger would collect and bring with it dried branches and dead leaves from the hills for firewood, the priest at last became very friendly with it, and got used to its company; so that if ever, as the night wore on, the badger did not arrive, he used to miss it, and wonder why it did not come. When the winter was over, and the spring-time came at the end of the second month, the Badger gave up its visits, and was no more seen; but, on the return of the winter, the beast resumed its old habit of coming to the hut. When this practice had gone on for ten years, one day the badger said to the priest, "Through your reverence's kindness for all these years, I have been able to pass the winter nights in comfort. Your favours are such, that during all my life, and even after my death, I must remember them. What can I do to requite them? If there is anything that you wish for, pray tell me."

The priest, smiling at this speech, answered, "Being such as I am, I have no desire and no wishes. Glad as I am to hear your kind intentions, there is nothing that I can ask you to do for me. You need feel no anxiety on my account. As long as I live, when the winter comes, you shall be welcome here." The badger, on hearing this, could not conceal its admiration of the depth of the old man's benevolence; but having so much to be grateful for, it felt hurt at not being able to requite it. As this subject was often renewed between them, the priest at last, touched by the goodness of the badger's heart, said, "Since I have shaven my head, renounced the world, and forsaken the pleasures of this life, I have no desire to gratify, yet I own I should like to possess three riyos in gold. Food and raiment I receive by the favour of the villagers, so I take no heed for those things. Were I to die tomorrow, and attain my wish of being born again into the next world, the same kind folk have promised to meet and bury my body. Thus, although I have no other reason to wish for money, still if I had three riyos I would offer them up at some holy shrine, that masses and prayers might be said for me, whereby I might enter into salvation. Yet I would not get this money by violent or unlawful means; I only think of what might be if I had it. So you see, since you have expressed such kind feelings towards me, I have told you what is on my mind." When the priest had done speaking, the badger leant its head on one side with a puzzled and anxious look, so much so that the old man was sorry he had expressed a wish which seemed to give the beast trouble, and tried to retract what he had said. "Posthumous honours, after all, are the wish of ordinary men. I, who am a priest, ought not to entertain such thoughts, or to want money; so pray pay no attention to what I have said;" and the badger, feigning assent to what the priest had impressed upon it, returned to the hills as usual.

From that time forth the badger came no more to the hut. The priest thought this very strange, but imagined either that the badger stayed away because it did not like to come without the money, or that it had been killed in an attempt to steal it; and he blamed himself for having added to his sins for no purpose, repenting when it was too late: persuaded, however, that the badger must have been killed, he passed his time in putting up prayers upon prayers for it.

After three years had gone by, one night the old man heard a voice near his door calling out, "Your reverence! your reverence!"

As the voice was like that of the badger, he jumped up as soon as he heard it, and ran out to open the door; and there, sure enough, was the badger. The priest, in great delight, cried out, "And so you are safe and sound, after all! Why have you been so long without coming here? I have been expecting you anxiously this long while."

So the badger came into the hut, and said, "If the money which you required had been for unlawful purposes, I could easily have procured as much as ever you might have wanted; but when I heard that it was to be offered to a temple for masses for your soul, I thought that, if I were to steal the hidden treasure of some other man, you could not apply to a sacred purpose money which had been obtained at the expense of his sorrow. So I went to the island of Sado,and gathering the sand and earth which had been cast away as worthless by the miners, fused it afresh in the fire; and at this work I spent months and days." As the badger finished speaking, the priest looked at the money which it had produced, and sure enough he saw that it was bright and new and clean; so he took the money, and received it respectfully, raising it to his head.

"And so you have had all this toil and labour on account of a foolish speech of mine? I have obtained my heart's desire, and am truly thankful."

As he was thanking the badger with great politeness and ceremony, the beast said, "In doing this I have but fulfilled my own wish; still I hope that you will tell this thing to no man."

"Indeed," replied the priest, "I cannot choose but tell this story. For if I keep this money in my poor hut, it will be stolen by thieves: I must either give it to someone to keep for me, or else at once offer it up at the temple. And when I do this, when people see a poor old priest with a sum of money quite unsuited to his station, they will think it very suspicious, and I shall have to tell the tale as it occurred; but as I shall say that the badger that gave me the money has ceased coming to my hut, you need not fear being waylaid, but can come, as of old, and shelter yourself from the cold." To this the badger nodded assent; and as long as the old priest lived, it came and spent the winter nights with him.

The Vampire Cat

THE PRINCE OF HIZEN, a distinguished member of the Nabeshima family, lingered in the garden with O Toyo, the favourite among his ladies. When the sun set they retired to the palace, but failed to notice that they were being followed by a large cat.

O Toyo went to her room and fell asleep. At midnight she awoke and gazed about her, as if suddenly aware of some dreadful presence in the apartment. At length she saw, crouching close beside her, a gigantic cat, and before she could cry out for assistance the animal sprang upon her and strangled her. The animal then made a hole under the verandah, buried the corpse, and assumed the form of the beautiful O Toyo.

The Prince, who knew nothing of what had happened, continued to love the false O Toyo, unaware that in reality he was caressing a foul beast. He noticed, little by little, that his strength failed, and it was not long before he became dangerously ill. Physicians were summoned, but they could do nothing to restore the royal patient. It was observed that he suffered most during the night, and was troubled by horrible dreams. This being so his councillors arranged that a hundred retainers should sit with their lord and keep watch while he slept.

The watch went into the sick-room, but just before ten o'clock it was overcome by a mysterious drowsiness. When all the men were asleep the false O Toyo crept into the apartment and disturbed the Prince until sunrise. Night after night the retainers came to guard their master, but always they fell asleep at the same hour, and even three loyal councillors had a similar experience.

During this time the Prince grew worse, and at length a priest named Ruiten was appointed to pray on his behalf. One night, while he was engaged in his supplications, he heard a strange noise proceeding from the garden. On looking out of the window he saw a young soldier washing himself. When he had finished his ablutions he stood before an image of Buddha, and prayed most ardently for the recovery of the Prince.

Ruiten, delighted to find such zeal and loyalty, invited the young man to enter his house, and when he had donc so inquired his name.

"I am Ito Soda," said the young man, "and serve in the infantry of Nabeshima. I have heard of my lord's sickness and long to have the honour of nursing him; but being of low rank it is not meet that I should come into his presence. I have, nevertheless, prayed to the Buddha that my lord's life may be spared. I believe that the Prince of Hizen is bewitched, and if I might remain with him I would do my utmost to find and crush the evil power that is the cause of his illness."

Ruiten was so favourably impressed with these words that he went the next day to consult with one of the councillors, and after much discussion it was arranged that Ito Soda should keep watch with the hundred retainers.

When Ito Soda entered the royal apartment he saw that his master slept in the middle of the room, and he also observed the hundred retainers sitting in the chamber quietly chatting together in the hope that they would be able to keep off approaching drowsiness. By ten o'clock all the retainers, in spite of their efforts, had fallen asleep. Ito Soda tried to keep his eyes open, but a heaviness was gradually overcoming him, and he realised that if he wished to keep awake he must resort to extreme measures. When he had carefully spread oil-paper over the mats he stuck his dirk into his thigh. The sharp pain he experienced warded off sleep for a time, but eventually he felt his eyes closing once more. Resolved to outwit the spell which had proved too much for the retainers, he twisted the knife in his thigh, and thus increased the pain and kept his loyal watch, while blood continually dripped upon the oil-paper.

While Ito Soda watched he saw the sliding doors drawn open and a beautiful woman creep softly into the apartment. With a smile she noticed the sleeping retainers, and was about to approach the Prince when she observed Ito Soda. After she had spoken curtly to him she approached the Prince and inquired how he fared, but the Prince was too ill to make a reply. Ito Soda watched every movement, and believed she tried to bewitch the Prince, but she was always frustrated in her evil purpose by the dauntless eyes of Ito Soda, and at last she was compelled to retire.

In the morning the retainers awoke, and were filled with shame when they learnt how Ito Soda had kept his vigil. The councillors loudly praised the young soldier for his loyalty and enterprise, and he was commanded to keep watch again that night. He did so, and once more the false O Toyo entered the sick-room, and, as on the previous night, she was compelled to retreat without being able to cast her spell over the Prince.

It was discovered that immediately the faithful Soda had kept guard the Prince was able to obtain peaceful slumber, and, moreover, that he began to get better, for the false O Toyo, having been frustrated on two occasions, now kept away altogether, and the guard was not troubled with mysterious drowsiness. Soda, impressed by these strange circumstances, went to one of the councillors and informed him that the so-called O Toyo was a goblin of some kind.

That night Soda planned to go to the creature's room and try to kill her, arranging that in case she should escape there should be eight retainers outside waiting to capture her and despatch her immediately.

At the appointed hour Soda went to the creature's apartment, pretending that he bore a message from the Prince.

"What is your message?" inquired the woman.

"Kindly read this letter," replied Soda, and with these words he drew his dirk and tried to kill her.

The false O Toyo seized a halberd and endeavoured to strike her adversary. Blow followed blow, but at last perceiving that flight would serve her better than battle she threw away her weapon, and in a moment the lovely maiden turned into a cat and sprang on to the roof. The eight men waiting outside in case of emergency shot at the animal, but the creature succeeded in eluding them.

The cat made all speed for the mountains, and caused trouble among the people who lived in the vicinity, but was finally killed during a hunt ordered by the Prince Hizen. The Prince became well again, and Ito Soda received the honour and reward he so richly deserved.

Shippeitaro and the Phantom Cats

A CERTAIN KNIGHT took shelter in a lonely and dilapidated mountain temple. Towards midnight he was awakened by hearing a strange noise. Gazing about him, he saw a number of cats dancing and yelling and shrieking, and over and over again he heard these words: "*Tell it not to Shippeitaro*!"

At midnight the cats suddenly disappeared, stillness reigned in the ruined temple, and our warrior was able to resume his slumber.

The next morning the young knight left the haunted building, and came to one or two small dwellings near a village. As he passed one of these houses he heard great wailing and lamentation, and inquired the cause of the trouble.

"Alas!" said those who thronged about the knight, "well may you ask why we are so sorely troubled. This very night the mountain spirit will take away our fairest maiden in a great cage to the ruined temple where you have spent the night, and in the morning she will be devoured by the wicked spirit of the mountain. Every year we lose a girl in this way, and there is none to help us."

The knight, greatly moved by these pitiful words, and anxious to be of service, said: "Who or what is Shippeitaro? The evil spirits in the ruined temple used the name several times."

"Shippeitaro," said one of the people, "is a brave and very fine dog, and belongs to the head man of our Prince." The knight hastened off, was successful in securing Shippeitaro for one night, and took the dog back with him to the house of the weeping parents. Already the cage was prepared for the damsel, and into this cage he put Shippeitaro, and, with several young men to assist him, they reached the haunted temple. But the young men would not remain on the mountain, for they were full of fear, and, having performed their task, they took their departure, so that the knight and the dog were left alone.

At midnight the phantom cats again appeared, this time surrounding a tomcat of immense size and of great fierceness. When the monster cat saw the cage he sprang round it with screams of delight, accompanied by his companions.

The warrior, choosing a suitable opportunity, opened the cage, and Shippeitaro sprang out and held the great cat in his teeth. In another moment his master drew forth his sword and slew the wicked creature. The other cats were too amazed at what they had seen to make good their escape, and the valiant Shippeitaro soon made short work of them. Thus the village was no longer troubled with ravages of the mountain spirit, and the knight, in true courtly fashion, gave all the praise to the brave Shippeitaro.

The Story of the Faithful Cat

SOME YEARS AGO, in the summertime, a man went to pay a visit at a certain house at Osaka, and, in the course of conversation, said:

"I have eaten some very extraordinary cakes today," and on being asked what he meant, he told the following story:

"I received the cakes from the relatives of a family who were celebrating the hundredth anniversary of the death of a cat that had belonged to their ancestors. When I asked the history of the affair, I was told that, in former days, a young girl of the family, when she was about sixteen years old, used always to be followed about by a tom-cat, who was reared in the house, so much so that the two were never separated for an instant. When her father perceived this, he was very angry, thinking that the tom-cat, forgetting the kindness with which he had been treated for years in the house, had fallen in love with his daughter, and intended to cast a spell upon her; so he determined that he must kill the beast. As he was planning this in secret, the cat overheard him, and that night went to his pillow, and, assuming a human voice, said to him:

"'You suspect me of being in love with your daughter; and although you might well be justified in so thinking, your suspicions are groundless. The fact is this: There is a very large old rat who has been living for many years in your granary. Now it is this old rat who is in love with my young mistress, and this is why I dare not leave her side for a moment, for fear the old rat should carry her off. Therefore I pray you to dispel your suspicions. But as I, by myself, am no match for the rat, there is a famous cat, named Buchi, at the house of Mr So-and-so, at Ajikawa: if you will borrow that cat, we will soon make an end of the old rat.'

"When the father awoke from his dream, he thought it so wonderful, that he told the household of it; and the following day he got up very early and went off to Ajikawa, to inquire for the house which the cat had indicated, and had no difficulty in finding it; so he called upon the master of the house, and told him what his own cat had said, and how he wished to borrow the cat Buchi for a little while.

"'That's a very easy matter to settle,' said the other: 'pray take him with you at once;' and accordingly the father went home with the cat Buchi in charge. That night he put the two cats into the granary; and after a little while, a frightful clatter was heard, and then all was still again; so the people of the house opened the door, and crowded out to see what had happened; and there they beheld the two cats and the rat all locked together, and panting for breath; so they cut the throat of the rat, which was as big as either of the cats: then they attended to the two cats; but, although they gave them ginseng and other restoratives, they both got weaker and weaker, until at last they died. So the rat was thrown into the river; but the two cats were buried with all honours in a neighbouring temple."

The Old Man Who Made the Trees Blossom

ONE DAY, while an old man and his wife were in the garden, their dog suddenly became very excited as he lowered his head and sniffed the ground in one particular place. The old people, believing that their pet had detected something good to eat, brought a spade and commenced to dig, and to their amazement they dug up a great number of gold and silver pieces and a variety of precious treasures as well. With this newly acquired wealth the old couple lost no time in distributing alms among the poor.

When the people next door heard about their neighbours' good fortune they borrowed the dog, and spread before him all manner of delicacies in the hope that the animal would do them a good turn too. But the dog, who had been on previous occasions ill-treated by his hosts, refused to eat, and at length the angry couple dragged him into the garden. Immediately the dog began to sniff, and exactly where he sniffed the greedy couple began to dig; but they dug up no treasure, and all they could find was very objectionable refuse. The old couple, angry and disappointed, killed the dog and buried him under a pine-tree.

The good old man eventually learnt what had befallen his faithful dog, and, full of sorrow, he went to the place where his pet was buried, and arranged food and flowers on the grave, weeping as he did so.

That night the spirit of the dog came to his master, and said: "Cut down the tree where I am buried, and from the wood fashion a mortar, and think of me whenever you use it."

The old man carried out these instructions, and he found that when he ground the grains of rice in the pine mortar every grain turned into a precious treasure.

The wicked old couple, having borrowed the dog, had no compunction in borrowing the mortar too, but with these wicked people the rice immediately turned into filth, so that in their anger they broke and burnt the precious vessel.

Once again the spirit of the dog appeared before his master, and informed him what had taken place, adding: "If you will sprinkle the ashes of the mortar over withered trees they will immediately become full of blossom," and having uttered these words the spirit departed.

The kind-hearted old man secured the ashes, and, placing them in a basket, journeyed from village to village and from town to town, and over withered trees he threw the ashes, and, as the dog had promised, they suddenly came into flower. A prince heard of these wonders, and commanded the old man to appear before him, requesting that he would give an exhibition of his miraculous power. The old man did so, and joyfully departed with the many royal gifts bestowed upon him.

The old man's neighbours, hearing of these miracles, collected together the remaining ashes of the wonderful mortar, and the wicked fellow went about the country claiming to be able to revive withered or dead trees. Like the original worker of wonders, the greedy old man appeared in the palace, and was commanded to restore a withered tree. The old man climbed up into a tree and scattered the ashes, but the tree still remained withered, and the ashes almost blinded and suffocated the Prince. Upon this the old impostor was almost beaten to death, and he went away in a very miserable state indeed.

The kind old man and his wife, after rebuking their neighbours for their wickedness, allowed them to share in their wealth, and the once mean, cruel, and crafty couple led good and virtuous lives.

The Jelly-fish and the Monkey

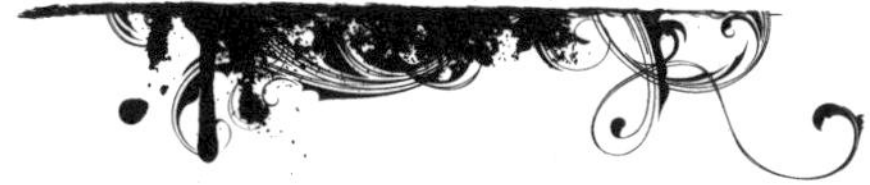

RIN-JIN, THE KING OF THE SEA, took to wife a young and beautiful Dragon Princess. They had not been married long when the fair Queen fell ill, and all the advice and attention of the great physicians availed nothing.

"Oh," sobbed the Queen, "there is only one thing that will cure me of my illness!"

"What is that?" inquired Rin-Jin.

"If I eat the liver of a live monkey I shall immediately recover. Pray get me a monkey's liver, for I know that nothing else will save my life."

So Rin-Jin called a jelly-fish to his side, and said: "I want you to swim to the land and return with a live monkey on your back, for I wish to use his liver that our Queen may be restored to health again. You are the only creature who can perform this task, for you alone have legs and are able to walk about on shore. In order to induce the monkey to come you must tell him of the wonders of the deep and of the rare beauties of my great palace, with its floor of pearl and its walls of coral."

The jelly-fish, delighted to think that the health and happiness of his mistress depended upon the success of his enterprise, lost no time in swimming to an island. He had no sooner stepped on shore than he observed a fine-looking monkey playing about in the branches of a pine-tree.

"Hello!" said the jelly-fish, "I don't think much of this island. What a dull and miserable life you must lead here! I come from the Kingdom of the Sea, where Rin-Jin reigns in a palace of great size and beauty. It may be that you would like to see a new country where there is plenty of fruit and where the weather is always fine. If so, get on my back, and I shall have much pleasure in taking you to the Kingdom of the Sea."

"I shall be delighted to accept your invitation," said the monkey, as he got down from the tree and comfortably seated himself on the thick shell of the jelly-fish.

"By the way," said the jelly-fish, when he had accomplished about half of the return journey, "I suppose you have brought your liver with you, haven't you?"

"What a personal question!" replied the monkey. "Why do you ask?"

"Our Sea Queen is dangerously ill," said the foolish jelly-fish, "and only the liver of a live monkey will save her life. When we reach the palace a doctor will make use of your liver and my mistress will be restored to health again."

"Dear me!" exclaimed the monkey, "I wish you had mentioned this matter to me before we left the island."

"If I had done so," replied the jelly-fish, "you would most certainly have refused my invitation."

"Believe me, you are quite mistaken, my dear jelly-fish. I have several livers hanging up on a pine-tree, and I would gladly have spared one in order to save the life of your Queen. If you will bring me back to the island again I will get it. It was most unfortunate that I should have forgotten to bring a liver with me."

So the credulous jelly-fish turned round and swam back to the island. Directly the jelly-fish reached the shore the monkey sprang from his back and danced about on the branches of a tree.

"*Liver*" said the monkey, chuckling, "did you say *liver*? You silly old jelly-fish, you'll certainly never get mine!"

The jelly-fish at length reached the palace, and told Rin-Jin his dismal tale. The Sea King fell into a great passion. "Beat him to a jelly!" he cried to those about him. "Beat this stupid fellow till he hasn't a bone left in his body!"

So the jelly-fish lost his shell from that unfortunate hour, and all the jelly-fishes that were born in the sea after his death were also without shells, and have remained nothing but jelly to this day.

The Sagacious Monkey and the Boar

LONG, LONG AGO, there lived in the province of Shinshin in Japan, a traveling monkey-man, who earned his living by taking round a monkey and showing off the animal's tricks.

One evening the man came home in a very bad temper and told his wife to send for the butcher the next morning.

The wife was very bewildered and asked her husband:

"Why do you wish me to send for the butcher?"

"It's no use taking that monkey round any longer, he's too old and forgets his tricks. I beat him with my stick all I know how, but he won't dance properly. I must now sell him to the butcher and make what money out of him I can. There is nothing else to be done."

The woman felt very sorry for the poor little animal, and pleaded for her husband to spare the monkey, but her pleading was all in vain, the man was determined to sell him to the butcher.

Now the monkey was in the next room and overheard every word of the conversation. He soon understood that he was to be killed, and he said to himself:

"Barbarous, indeed, is my master! Here I have served him faithfully for years, and instead of allowing me to end my days comfortably and in peace, he is going to let me be cut up by the butcher, and my poor body is to be roasted and stewed and eaten? Woe is me! What am I to do. Ah! a bright thought has struck me! There is, I know, a wild bear living in the forest near by. I have often heard tell of his wisdom. Perhaps if I go to him and tell him the strait I am in he will give me his counsel. I will go and try."

There was no time to lose. The monkey slipped out of the house and ran as quickly as he could to the forest to find the boar. The boar was at home, and the monkey began his tale of woe at once.

"Good Mr Boar, I have heard of your excellent wisdom. I am in great trouble, you alone can help me. I have grown old in the service of my master, and because I cannot dance properly now he intends to sell me to the butcher. What do you advise me to do? I know how clever you are!"

The boar was pleased at the flattery and determined to help the monkey. He thought for a little while and then said:

"Hasn't your master a baby?"

"Oh, yes," said the monkey, "he has one infant son."

"Doesn't it lie by the door in the morning when your mistress begins the work of the day? Well, I will come round early and when I see my opportunity I will seize the child and run off with it."

"What then?" said the monkey.

"Why the mother will be in a tremendous scare, and before your master and mistress know what to do, you must run after me and rescue the child and take it home safely to its parents, and you will see that when the butcher comes they won't have the heart to sell you."

The monkey thanked the boar many times and then went home. He did not sleep much that night, as you may imagine, for thinking of the morrow. His life depended on whether the boar's plan succeeded or not. He was the first up, waiting anxiously for what was to happen. It seemed to him a very long time before his master's wife began to move about and open the shutters to let in the light of day. Then all happened as the boar had planned. The mother placed her child near the porch as usual while she tidied up the house and got her breakfast ready.

The child was crooning happily in the morning sunlight, dabbing on the mats at the play of light and shadow. Suddenly there was a noise in the porch and a loud cry from the child. The mother ran out from the kitchen to the spot, only just in time to see the boar disappearing through the gate with her child in its clutch. She flung out her hands with a loud cry of despair and rushed into the inner room where her husband was still sleeping soundly.

He sat up slowly and rubbed his eyes, and crossly demanded what his wife was making all that noise about. By the time that the man was alive to what had happened, and they both got outside the gate, the boar had got well away, but they saw the monkey running after the thief as hard as his legs would carry him.

Both the man and wife were moved to admiration at the plucky conduct of the sagacious monkey, and their gratitude knew no bounds when the faithful monkey brought the child safely back to their arms.

"There!" said the wife. "This is the animal you want to kill – if the monkey hadn't been here we should have lost our child forever."

"You are right, wife, for once," said the man as he carried the child into the house. "You may send the butcher back when he comes, and now give us all a good breakfast and the monkey too."

When the butcher arrived he was sent away with an order for some boar's meat for the evening dinner, and the monkey was petted and lived the rest of his days in peace, nor did his master ever strike him again.

The Battle of the Ape and the Crab

ONCE UPON A TIME there was a crab who lived in a marsh in a certain part of the country. It fell out one day that, the crab having picked up a rice cake, an ape, who had got a nasty hard persimmon-seed, came up, and begged the crab to make an exchange with him. The crab, who was a simple-minded creature, agreed to this proposal; and they each went their way, the ape chuckling to himself at the good bargain which he had made.

When the crab got home, he planted the persimmon-seed in his garden, and, as time slipped by, it sprouted, and by degrees grew to be a big tree. The crab watched the growth of his tree with great delight; but when the fruit ripened, and he was going to pluck it, the ape came in, and offered to gather it for him. The crab consenting, the ape climbed up into the tree, and began eating all the ripe fruit himself, while he only threw down the sour persimmons to the crab, inviting him, at the same time, to eat heartily. The crab, however, was not pleased at this arrangement, and thought that it was his turn to play a trick upon the ape; so he called out to him to come down head foremost. The ape did as he was bid; and as he crawled down, head foremost, the ripe fruit all came tumbling out of his pockets, and the crab, having picked up the persimmons, ran off and hid himself in a hole. The ape, seeing this, lay in ambush, and as soon as the crab crept out of his hiding-place gave him a sound drubbing, and went home. Just at this time a friendly egg and a bee, who were the apprentices of a certain rice-mortar, happened to pass that way, and, seeing the crab's piteous condition, tied up his wounds, and, having escorted him home, began to lay plans to be revenged upon the cruel ape.

Having agreed upon a scheme, they all went to the ape's house, in his absence; and each one having undertaken to play a certain part, they waited in secret for their enemy to come home. The ape, little dreaming of the mischief that was brewing, returned home, and, having a fancy to drink a cup of tea, began lighting the fire in the hearth, when, all of a sudden, the egg, which was hidden in the ashes, burst with. the heat, and bespattered the frightened ape's face, so that he fled, howling with pain, and crying, "Oh! what an unlucky beast I am!" Maddened with the heat of the burst egg, he tried to go to the back of the house, when the bee darted out of a cupboard, and a piece of seaweed, who had joined the party, coming up at the same time, the ape was surrounded by enemies. In despair, he seized the clothes-rack, and fought valiantly for awhile; but he was no match for so many, and was obliged to run away, with the others in hot pursuit after him. Just as he was making his escape by a back door, however, the piece of seaweed tripped him up, and the rice-mortar, closing with him from behind, made an end of him.

So the crab, having punished his enemy, went home in triumph, and lived ever after on terms of brotherly love with the seaweed and the mortar. Was there ever such a fine piece of fun!

The Travels of Two Frogs

LONG, LONG AGO, in the good old days before the hairy-faced and pale-cheeked men from over the Sea of Great Peace (Pacific Ocean) came to Japan; before the black coal-smoke and snorting engine scared the white heron from the rice-fields; before black crows and fighting sparrows, which fear not man, perched on telegraph wires, or ever a railway was thought of, there lived two frogs – one in a well in Kyoto, the other in a lotus-pond in Osaka.

Now it is a common proverb in the Land of the Gods (Japan) that "the frog in the well knows not the great ocean," and the Kyoto frog had so often heard this scornful sneer from the maids who came to draw out water, with their long bamboo-handled buckets that he resolved to travel abroad and see the world, and especially the *tai kai* (the great ocean).

"I'll see for myself," said Mr Frog, as he packed his wallet and wiped his spectacles, "what this great ocean is that they talk about. I'll wager it isn't half as deep or wide as well, where I can see the stars even at daylight."

Now the truth was, a recent earthquake had greatly reduced the depth of the well and the water was getting very shallow. Mr Frog informed his family of his intentions. Mrs Frog wept a great deal; but, drying her eyes with her paper handkerchief, she declared she would count the hours on her fingers till he came back, and at every morning and evening meal would set out his table with food on it, just as if he were home. She tied up a little lacquered box full ofboiled rice and snails for his journey, wrapped it around with a silk napkin, and, putting his extra clothes in a bundle, swung it on his back. Tying it over his neck, he seized his staff and was ready to go.

"*Sayonara*" ("Good-bye") cried he, as, with a tear in his eye, he walked away.

"*Sayonara. Oshidzukani*" ("Good-bye. Walk slowly"), croaked Mrs Frog and the whole family of young frogs in a chorus.

Two of the froggies were still babies, that is, they were yet polywogs, with a half inch of tail still on them; and, of course, were carried about by being strapped on the back of their older brothers.

Mr Frog being now on land, out of his well, noticed that the other animals did not leap, but walked on their legs. And, not wishing to be eccentric, he likewise began briskly walking upright on his hind legs or waddling on all fours.

Now it happened that about the same time the Osaka father frog had become restless and dissatisfied with life on the edges of his lotus-ditch. He had made up his mind to "cast the lion's cub into the valley."

"Why! that *is* tall talk for a frog, I must say," exclaims the reader. "What did he mean?"

I must tell you that the Osaka frog was a philosopher. Right at the edge of his lotus-pond was a monastery, full of Buddhist monks, who every day studied their sacred rolls and droned over the books of Confucius, to learn them by heart. Our frog had heard them so often that he could (in frog language, of course) repeat many of their wise sentences and intone responses to their evening prayers put up by the great idol Amida. Indeed, our frog had so often listened to their debates on texts from the classics that he had himself become a sage and a philosopher. Yet, as the proverb says, "the sage is not happy."

Why not? In spite of a soft mud-bank, plenty of green scum, stagnant water, and shady lotus leaves, a fat wife and a numerous family; in short, everything to make a frog happy, his forehead, or rather gullet, was wrinkled with care from long pondering of knotty problems, such as the following:

The monks often come down to the edge of the pond to look at the pink and white lotus. One summer day, as a little frog, hardly out of his tadpole state, with a small fragment of tail still left, sat basking on a huge round leaf, one monk said to the other:

"Of what does that remind you?"

"The babies of frogs will become but frogs," said one shaven pate, laughing.

"What think you?"

"The white lotus flower springs out of the black mud," said the other, solemnly, as both walked away.

The old frog, sitting near by, overheard them and began to philosophize: "Humph! The babies of frogs will become but frogs, hey? If mud becomes lotus, why shouldn't a frog become a man? Why not? If my pet son should travel abroad and see the world – go to Kyoto, for instance – why shouldn't he be as wise as those shining-headed men, I wonder? I shall try it, anyhow. I'll send my son on a journey to Kyoto. I'll 'cast the lion's cub into the valley' (send the pet son abroad in the world, to see and study) at once. I'll deny myself for the sake of my offspring."

Flump! splash! sounded the water, as a pair of webby feet disappeared. The "lion's cub" was soon ready, after much paternal advice, and much counsel to beware of being gobbled up by long-legged storks, and trod on by impolite men, and struck at by bad boys. "*Kio ni no inaka*" ('Even in the capital there are boors') said Father Frog.

Now it so happened that the old frog from Kyoto and the "lion's cub" from Osaka started each from his home at the same time. Nothing of importance occurred to either of them until, as luck would have it, they met on a hill near Hashimoto, which is half way between the two cities. Both were footsore, and websore, and very tired, especially about the hips, on account of the unfroglike manner of walking, instead of hopping, as they had been used to.

"*Ohio gozarimasu*" ('Good-morning') said the "lion's cub" to the old frog, as he fell on all fours and bowed his head to the ground three times, squinting up over his left eye, to see if the other frog was paying equal deference in return.

"*He, konnichi wa*" ('Yes, good-day') replied the Kyoto frog.

"*O tenki*" ('It is rather fine weather today') said the "cub."

"*IIe, yoi tenki gozence*" ('Yes, it is very fine') replied the old fellow.

"I am Gamataro, from Osaka, the oldest son of Hiki Dono, Sensui no Kami" (Lord Bullfrog, Prince of the Lotus-Ditch).

"Your Lordship must be weary with your journey. I am Kayeru San of Idomidzu (Sir Frog of the Well) in Kyoto. I started out to see the 'great ocean' from Osaka; but, I declare, my hips are so dreadfully tired that I believe that I'll give up my plan and content myself with a look from this hill."

The truth must be owned that the old frog was not only on his hind legs, but also on his last legs, when he stood up to look at Osaka; while the "cub" was tired enough to believe anything. The old fellow, wiping his face, spoke up:

"Suppose we save ourselves the trouble of the journey. This hill is half way between the two cities, and while I see Osaka and the sea you can get a good look of the Kio" (Capital, or Kyoto).

"Happy thought!" said the Osaka frog.

Then both reared themselves upon their hind-legs, and stretching upon their toes, body to body, and neck to neck, propped each other up, rolled their goggles and looked steadily, as they supposed, on the places which they each wished to see. Now everyone knows that a frog has eyes mounted in that part of his head which is front when he is down and back when he stands up. They are set like a compass on gimbals.

Long and steadily they gazed, until, at last, their toes being tired, they fell down on all fours.

"I declare!" said the old *yaze* (daddy) "Osaka looks just like Kyoto; and as for 'the great ocean' those stupid maids talked about, I don't see any at all, unless they mean that strip of river that looks for all the world like the Yodo. I don't believe there is any 'great ocean'!"

"As for my part," said the 'cub', "I am satisfied that it's all folly to go further; for Kyoto is as like Osaka as one grain of rice is like another." Then he said to himself: "Old Totsu San (my father) is a fool, with all his philosophy."

Thereupon both congratulated themselves upon the happy labor-saving expedient by which they had spared themselves a long journey, much leg-weariness, and some danger. They departed, after exchanging many compliments; and, dropping again into a frog's hop, they leaped back in half the time – the one to his well and the other to his pond. There each told the story of both cities looking exactly alike; thus demonstrating the folly of those foolish folks called men. As for the old gentleman in the lotus-pond, he was so glad to get the "cub" back again that he never again tried to reason out the problems of philosophy. And to this day the frog in the well knows not and believes not in the "great ocean." Still do the babies of frogs become but frogs. Still is it vain to teach the reptiles philosophy; for all such labor is "like pouring water in a frog's face." Still out of the black mud springs the glorious white lotus in celestial purity, unfolding its stainless petals to the smiling heavens, the emblem of life and resurrection.

Jiraiya, or The Magic Frog

OGATA was the name of a castle-lord who lived in the Island of the Nine Provinces, (Kiushiu). He had but one son, an infant, whom the people in admiration nicknamed Jiraiya (Young Thunder.) During one of the civil wars, this castle was taken, and Ogata was slain; but by the aid of a faithful retainer, who hid Jiraiya in his bosom, the boy escaped and fled northward to Echigo. There he lived until he grew up to manhood.

At that time Echigo was infested with robbers. One day the faithful retainer of Jiraiya being attacked, made resistance, and was slain by the robbers. Jiraiya now left alone in the world went out from Echigo and led a wandering life in several provinces.

All this time he was consumed with the desire to revive the name of his father, and restore the fortunes of his family. Being exceedingly brave, and an expert swordsman, he became chief of a band of robbers and plundered many wealthy merchants, and in a short time he was rich in men, arms and booty. He was accustomed to disguise himself, and go in person into the houses and presence of men of wealth, and thus learn all about their gates and guards, where they slept, and in what rooms their treasures were stored, so that success was easy.

Hearing of an old man who lived in Shinano, he started to rob him, and for this purpose put on the disguise of a pilgrim. Shinano is a very high table-land, full of mountains, and the snow lies deep in winter. A great snow storm coming on, Jiraiya took refuge in a humble house by the way. Entering, he found a very beautiful woman, who treated him with great kindness. This, however, did not change the robber's nature. At midnight, when all was still, he unsheathed his sword, and going noiselessly to her room, he found the lady absorbed in reading.

Lifting his sword, he was about to strike at her neck, when, in a flash, her body changed into that of a very old man, who seized the heavy steel blade and broke it in pieces as though it were a stick. Then he tossed the bits of steel away, and thus spoke to Jiraiya, who stood amazed but fearless:

"I am a man named Senso Dojin, and I have lived in these mountains many hundred years, though my true body is that of a huge frog. I can easily put you to death but I have another purpose. So I shall pardon you and teach you magic instead."

Then the youth bowed his head to the floor, poured out his thanks to the old man and begged to be received as his pupil.

Remaining with the old man of the mountain for several weeks, Jiraiya learned all the arts of the mountain spirits; how to cause a storm of wind and rain, to make a deluge, and to control the elements at will.

He also learned how to govern the frogs, and at his bidding they assumed gigantic size, so that on their backs he could stand up and cross rivers and carry enormous loads.

When the old man had finished instructing him he said "Henceforth cease from robbing, or in any way injuring the poor. Take from the wicked rich, and those who acquire money dishonestly, but help the needy and the suffering." Thus speaking, the old man turned into a huge frog and hopped away.

What this old mountain spirit bade him do, was just what Jiraiya wished to accomplish. He set out on his journey with a light heart. "I can now make the storm and the waters obey me, and all the frogs are at my command; but alas! the magic of the frog cannot control that of the serpent. I shall beware of his poison."

From that time forth the oppressed poor people rejoiced many a time as the avaricious merchants and extortionate money lenders lost their treasures. For when a poor farmer, whose crops failed, could not pay his rent or loan on the date promised, these hard-hearted money lenders would turn him out of his house, seize his beds and mats and rice-tub, and even the shrine and images on the god-shelf, to sell them at auction for a trifle, to their minions, who resold them at a high price for the money-lender, who thus got a double benefit. Whenever a miser was robbed, the people said, "The young thunder has struck," and then they were glad, knowing that it was Jiraiya, (Young Thunder.) In this manner his name soon grew to be the poor people's watchword in those troublous times.

Yet Jiraiya was always ready to help the innocent and honest, even if they were rich. One day a merchant named Fukutaro was sentenced to death, though he was really not guilty. Jiraiya hearing of it, went to the magistrate and said that he himself was the very man who committed the robbery. So the man's life was saved, and Jiraiya was hanged on a large oak tree. But during the night, his dead body changed into a bull-frog which hopped away out of sight, and off into the mountains of Shinano.

At this time, there was living in this province, a young and beautiful maiden named Tsunade. Her character was very lovely. She was always obedient to her parents and kind to her friends. Her daily task was to go to the mountains and cut brushwood for fuel. One day while thus busy singing at the task, she met a very old man, with a long white beard sweeping his breast, who said to her:

"Do not fear me. I have lived in this mountain many hundred years, but my real body is that of a snail. I will teach you the powers of magic, so that you can walk on the sea, or cross a river however swift and deep, as though it were dry land."

Gladly the maiden took daily lessons of the old man, and soon was able to walk on the waters as on the mountain paths. One day the old man said, "I shall now leave you and resume my former shape. Use your power to destroy wicked robbers. Help those who defend the poor. I advise you to marry the celebrated man Jiraiya, and thus you will unite your powers."

Thus saying, the old man shrivelled up into a snail and crawled away.

"I am glad," said the maiden to herself, "for the magic of the snail can overcome that of the serpent. When Jiraiya, who has the magic of the frog, shall marry me, we can then destroy the son of the serpent, the robber named Dragon-coil (Orochimaru)."

By good fortune, Jiraiya met the maiden Tsunade, and being charmed with her beauty, and knowing her power of magic, sent a messenger with presents to her parents, asking them to give him their daughter to wife. The parents agreed, and so the young and loving couple were married.

Hitherto when Jiraiya wished to cross a river he changed himself into a frog and swam across; or, he summoned a bull-frog before him, which increased in size until as large as an elephant. Then standing erect on his warty back, even though the wind blew his garments wildly, Jiraiya reached the opposite shore in safety. But now, with his wife's powers, the two, without any delay, walked over as though the surface was a hard floor.

Soon after their marriage, war broke out in Japan between the two famous clans of Tsukikage and Inukage. To help them fight their battles, and capture the castles of their enemies, the Tsukikage family besought the aid of Jiraiya, who agreed to serve them and carried their banner in his back. Their enemies, the Inukage, then secured the services of Dragon-coil.

This Orochimaru, or Dragon-coil, was a very wicked robber whose father was a man, and whose mother was a serpent that lived in the bottom of Lake Takura. He was perfectly skilled in the magic of the serpent, and by spurting venom on his enemies, could destroy the strongest warriors.

Collecting thousands of followers, he made great ravages in all parts of Japan, robbing and murdering good and bad, rich and poor alike. Loving war and destruction he joined his forces with the Inukage family.

Now that the magic of the frog and snail was joined to the one army, and the magic of the serpent aided the other, the conflicts were bloody and terrible, and many men were slain on both sides.

On one occasion, after a hard fought battle, Jiraiya fled and took refuge in a monastery, with a few trusty vassals, to rest a short time. In this retreat a lovely princess named Tagoto was dwelling. She had fled from Orochimaru, who wished her for his bride. She hated to marry the offspring of a serpent, and hoped to escape him. She lived in fear of him continually. Orochimaru hearing at one time that both Jiraiya and the princess were at this place, changed himself into a serpent, and distilling a large mouthful of poisonous venom, crawled up to the ceiling in the room where Jiraiya and his wife were sleeping, and reaching a spot directly over them, poured the poisonous venom on the heads of his rivals. The fumes of the prison so stupefied Jiraiya's followers, and even the monks, that Orochimaru, instantly changing himself to a man, profited by the opportunity to seize the princess Tagoto, and make off with her.

Gradually the faithful retainers awoke from their stupor to find their master and his beloved wife delirious, and near the point of death, and the princess gone.

"What can we do to restore our dear master to life?" This was the question each one asked of the others, as with sorrowful faces and weeping eyes they gazed at the pallid forms of their unconscious master and his consort. They called in the venerable abbot of the monastery to see if he could suggest what could be done.

"Alas!" said the aged priest, "there is no medicine in Japan to cure your lord's disease, but in India there is an elixir which is a sure antidote. If we could get that, the master would recover."

"Alas! alas!" and a chorus of groans showed that all hope had fled, for the mountain in India, where the elixir was made, lay five thousand miles from Japan.

Just then a youth named Rikimatsu, one of the pages of Jiraiya, arose to speak. He was but fourteen years old, and served Jiraiya out of gratitude, for he had rescued his father from many dangers and saved his life. He begged permission to say a word to the abbot, who, seeing the lad's eager face, motioned to him with his fan to speak.

"How long can our lord live," asked the youth.

"He will be dead in thirty hours," answered the abbot, with a sigh.

"I'll go and procure the medicine, and if our master is still living when I come back, he will get well."

Now Rikimatsu had learned magic and sorcery from the Tengus, or long-nosed elves of the mountains, and could fly high in the air with incredible swiftness. Speaking a few words of incantation, he put on the wings of a Tengu, mounted a white cloud and rode on the east wind to India, bought the elixir of the mountain spirits, and returned to Japan in one day and a night.

On the first touch of the elixir on the sick man's face he drew a deep breath, perspiration glistened on his forehead, and in a few moments more he sat up.

Jiraiya and his wife both got well, and the war broke out again. In a great battle Dragon-coil was killed and the princess rescued. For his prowess and aid Jiraiya was made daimyo of Idzu.

Being now weary of war and the hardships of active life, Jiraiya was glad to settle down to tranquil life in the castle and rear his family in peace. He spent the remainder of his days in reading the books of the sages, in composing verses, in admiring the flowers, the moon and the landscape, and occasionally going out hawking or fishing. There, amid his children and children's children, he finished his days in peace.

Why There is Hatred of the Cock

THE GOD OF MIONOSEKI (a town now part of the city of Matsue) detests cocks and hens and everything pertaining to these birds, and the inhabitants respect his very marked dislike. On one occasion a certain steamer, shortly after making for the open sea, encountered a severe storm, and it was thought that the God of Mionoseki, who is the God of Mariners, must have been seriously offended. At length the captain discovered that one of his passengers was smoking a pipe adorned with the figure of a crowing cock. The pipe was immediately thrown into the sea, and the storm abated.

We are able to gather the reason for the hatred of the cock from the following legend. In the *Kojiki* we are informed that the son of the Deity of Kitsuki spent many an hour at Mionoseki in catching birds and fish. At that time the cock was his trusted friend, and it was the duty of this bird to crow lustily when it was time for the God to return from his sport. On one occasion, however, the cock forgot to crow, and in consequence, in the God's hurry to go back in his boat he lost his oars, and was compelled to propel the vessel with his hands, which were severely bitten by fishes.

How Yoritomo was Saved by Two Doves

YORITOMO, having been defeated in a battle against Oba Kage-chika, was forced to retreat with six of his followers. They ran with all speed through a forest, and, finding a large hollow tree, crept inside for shelter.

In the meantime Oba Kage-chika said to his cousin, Oba Kagetoki: "Go and search for Yoritomo, for I have good reason to believe that he lies hidden in this forest. I will so arrange my men that the flight of our enemy will be impossible."

Oba Kagetoki departed, none too pleased with the mission, for he had once been on friendly terms with Yoritomo. When he reached the hollow tree and saw through a hole in the trunk that his old friend lay concealed within, he took pity on him, and returned to his cousin, saying: "I believe that Yoritomo, our enemy, is not in this wood."

When Oba Kage-chika heard these words he cried fiercely: "You lie! How could Yoritomo make his escape so soon and with my men standing on guard about the forest? Lead the way, and I and some of my men will follow you. No cunning this time, cousin, or you shall severely suffer for it."

In due time the party reached the hollow tree, and Kage-chika was about to enter it, when his cousin cried: "Stay! What folly is this? Cannot you see that there is a spider's web spun across the opening? How could anyone enter this tree without breaking it? Let us spend our time more profitably elsewhere."

Kage-chika, however, was still suspicious concerning his cousin, and he thrust his bow into the hollow trunk. It almost touched the crouching Yoritomo, when two white doves suddenly flew out of the cavity.

"Alas!" exclaimed Kage-chika, "you are right, our enemy cannot lie concealed here, for doves and a cobweb would not admit of such a thing."

By the timely aid of two doves and a spider's web the great hero Yoritomo made good his escape, and when, in later years, he became Shogun he caused shrines to be erected to Hachiman, the God of War, in recognition of his deliverance, for the doves of Japan are recognised as the messengers of war, and not of peace, as is the case in our own country.

The Tongue-cut Sparrow

A CROSS OLD WOMAN was at her wash-tub when her neighbour's pet sparrow ate up all the starch, mistaking it for ordinary food. The old woman was so angry at what had happened that she cut out the sparrow's tongue, and the unfortunate bird flew away to a mountain.

When the old couple to whom the sparrow belonged heard what had taken place they left their home and journeyed a great distance until they had the good fortune to find their pet again.

The sparrow was no less delighted to meet his master and mistress, and begged them to enter his house. When they had done so they were feasted with an abundance of fish and *sake*, were waited upon by the sparrow's wife, children, and grandchildren, and, not content with these deeds of hospitality, the feathered host danced a jig called the Sparrow's Dance.

When it was time for the old couple to return home the sparrow brought forth two wicker baskets, saying: "One is heavy, and the other is light. Which would you rather have?"

"Oh, the light one," replied the old couple, "for we are aged and the journey is a long one."

When the old people reached their home they opened the basket, and to their delight and amazement discovered gold and silver, jewels and silk. As fast as they took the precious things out an inexhaustible supply came to their place, so that the wonderful basket of treasure could not be emptied, and the happy old couple grew rich and prosperous.

It was not long before the old woman who had cut out the sparrow's tongue heard about the good fortune of her neighbours, and she hastened to inquire where this wonderful sparrow was to be seen.

Having gained the information, she had no difficulty in finding the sparrow. When the bird saw her he asked which of two baskets she would prefer to take away with her, the heavy or light one? The cruel and greedy old woman chose the heavy one, believing that this basket would contain more treasure than the light one; but when, after much labour, she reached home and opened it, devils sprang upon her and tore her to pieces.

A Noble Sacrifice

THERE WAS ONCE A MAN who was extremely fond of shooting birds. He had two daughters, good Buddhists, and each in turn pointed out the folly of their father's cruel sport, and begged him not to destroy life wantonly. However, the man was obstinate and would not listen to his daughters' entreaties. One day a neighbour asked him to shoot two storks, and he promised to do so. When the women heard what their father was about to do, they said: "Let us dress in pure white garments and go down upon the shore tonight, for it is a place much frequented by storks. If our father should kill either of us in mistake for the birds, it will teach him a lesson, and he will surely repent his evil ways, which are contrary to the gentle teaching of the Lord Buddha."

That night the man went to the shore, and the cloudy sky made it difficult for him to discover any storks. At last, however, he saw two white objects in the distance. He fired; the bodies fell immediately, and he ran to where they lay, only to discover that he had shot both his noble, self-sacrificing daughters. Stricken with sorrow, the man erected a funeral pyre and burnt the bodies of his poor children. Having done these things, he shaved his head, went into the woods, and became a hermit.

Tama's Return

KAZARIYA KYUBEI, a merchant, had a maid-servant called Tama. Tama worked well and cheerfully, but she was negligent in regard to her dress. One day, when she had been five years in Kyubei's house, her master said to her: "Tama, how is it that, unlike most girls, you seem to have no desire to look your best? When you go out you wear your working dress. Surely you should put on a pretty robe on such occasions."

"Good master," said Tama, "you do well to rebuke me, for you do not know why, during all these years, I have worn old clothes and have made no attempt to wear pretty ones. When my father and mother died I was but a child, and as I had no brothers or sisters it rested upon me to have Buddhist services performed on behalf of my parents. In order that this might come to pass I have saved the money you have given me, and spent as little upon myself as possible. Now my parents' mortuary tablets are placed in the Jorakuji temple, and, having given my money to the priests, the sacred rites have now been performed. I have fulfilled my wish, and, begging for your forgiveness, I will in future dress more becomingly."

Before Tama died she asked her mistress to keep the remaining money she had saved. Shortly after her death a large fly entered Kyubei's house. Now at that time of the year, the Period of the Greatest Cold, it was unusual for flies to appear, and the master of the house was considerably puzzled. He carefully put the insect outside the house; but it flew back immediately, and every time it was ejected it came back again. "This fly," said Kyubei's wife, "may be Tama." Kyubei cut a small piece out of the insect's wings, and this time carried it some distance from his abode. But the next day it returned once more, and this time the master painted the fly's wings and body with rouge, and took it even further away from his dwelling. Two days later the fly returned, and the nick in its wings and the rouge with which it was covered left no doubt in the minds of Kyubei and his wife that this persistent insect was indeed Tama.

"I believe," said Kyubei's wife, "that Tama has returned to us because she wants us to do something for her. I have the money she asked me to keep. Let us give it to the priests in order that they may pray for her soul." When these words had been spoken the fly fell dead upon the floor.

Kyubei and his wife placed the fly in a box, and with the girl's money they went to the priests. A *sutra* was recited over the body of the insect, and it was duly buried in the temple grounds.

A Strange Dream

A YOUNG MAN OF MATSUE was returning home from a wedding-party when he saw, just in front of his house, a firefly. He paused a moment, surprised to see such an insect on a cold winter's night with snow on the ground. While he stood and meditated the firefly flew toward him, and the young man struck at it with his stick, but the insect flew away and entered the garden adjoining his own.

The next day he called at his neighbour's house, and was about to relate the experience of the previous night when the eldest daughter of the family entered the room, and exclaimed: "I had no idea you were here, and yet a moment ago you were in my mind. Last night I dreamt that I became a firefly. It was all very real and very beautiful, and while I was darting hither and thither I saw you, and flew toward you, intending to tell you that I had learnt to fly, but you thrust me aside with your stick, and the incident still frightens me."

The young man, having heard these words from the lips of his betrothed, held his peace.

The Vengeance of Kanshiro

IN THE VILLAGE OF FUNAKAMI there lived a devout old farmer called Kanshiro. Every year the old man made various pilgrimages to certain shrines, where he prayed and asked the blessings of the deities. At last, however, he became so infirm that he realised that his earthly days were numbered, and that he would probably only have strength to pay one more visit to the great shrines at Ise. When the people of the village heard this noble resolution they generously gave him a sum of money in order that the respected old farmer might present it to the sacred shrines.

Kanshiro set off upon his pilgrimage carrying the money in a bag, which he hung round his neck. The weather was extremely hot, and the heat and fatigue of the journey made the old man so ill that he was forced to remain for a few days in the village of Myojo. He went to a small inn and asked Jimpachi, the innkeeper, to take care of his money, explaining that it was an offering to the Gods at Ise. Jimpachi took the money, and assured the old man that he would take great care of it, and, moreover, that he himself would attend upon him.

On the sixth day the old man, though still far from well, paid his bill, took the bag from the innkeeper, and proceeded on his journey. As Kanshiro observed many pilgrims in the vicinity he did not look into the bag, but carefully concealed it in the sack containing spare raiment and food.

When Kanshiro at length rested under a pine-tree he took out the bag and looked inside. Alas! the money had been stolen, and stones of the same weight inserted in its place. The old man hastily returned to the innkeeper and begged him to restore the money. Jimpachi grew extremely angry, and gave him a severe beating.

The poor old man crawled away from the village, and three days later, with indomitable courage, he succeeded in reaching the sacred shrines at Ise. He sold his property in order to refund the money his good neighbours had given him, and with what remained he continued his pilgrimage, till at last he was forced to beg for food.

Three years later Kanshiro went to the village of Myoto, and found that the innkeeper who had treated him so badly was now comparatively well off, and lived in a large house. The old man went to him, and said: "You have stolen sacred money from me, and I have sold my little property in order that I might refund it to those who had given it to me. Ever since that time I have been a beggar, but be assured vengeance shall fall upon you!"

Jimpachi cursed the old man and told him that he had not stolen his money. During the heated dispute a watchman seized Kanshiro, dragged him away from the house, and told him that he would be arrested if he dared to return. At the end of the village the old man died, and a kindly priest took his body to a temple, respectfully burnt it, and offered up many holy prayers for his good and loyal soul.

Immediately after Kanshiro's death Jimpachi grew afraid of what he had done, and became so ill that he was forced to take to his bed. When he had lost all power of movement a great company of fireflies flew out of the farmer's tomb and surrounded Jimpachi's mosquito-curtain, and tried to break it down. Many of the villagers came to Jimpachi's assistance and killed a number of fireflies, but the stream of shining insects that flew from Kanshiro's tomb never lessened. Hundreds were killed, but thousands came to take their place. The room was ablaze with firefly light, and the mosquito-curtain sank beneath their ever-increasing weight. At this remarkable sight some of the villagers murmured: "Jimpachi stole the old man's money after all. This is the vengeance of Kanshiro."

Even while they spoke the curtain broke and the fireflies rushed into the eyes, ears, mouth, and nose of the terrified Jimpachi. For twenty days he screamed aloud for mercy; but no mercy came. Thicker and thicker grew the stream of flashing, angry insects, till at last they killed the wicked Jimpachi, when from that hour they completely disappeared.

The Firefly's Lovers

ON THE SOUTHERN AND SUNNY SIDE of the castle moats of the Fukui castle, in Echizen, the water had long ago become shallow so that lotus lilies grew luxuriantly. Deep in the heart of one of the great flowers whose petals were as pink as the lining of a sea-shell, lived the King of the Fireflies, Hi-o, whose only daughter was the lovely princess Hotaru-hime. While still a child the hime (princess) was carefully kept at home within the pink petals of the lily, never going even to the edges except to see her father fly off on his journey. Dutifully she waited until of age, when the fire glowed in her own body, and shone, beautifully illuminating the lotus, until its light at night was like a lamp within a globe of coral.

Every night her light grew brighter and brighter, until at last it was as mellow as gold. Then her father said:

"My daughter is now of age, she may fly abroad with me sometimes, and when the proper suitor comes she may marry whom she will."

So Hotaru-hime flew forth in and out among the lotus lilies of the moat, then into rich rice fields, and at last far off to the indigo meadows.

Whenever she went a crowd of suitors followed her, for she had the singular power of attracting all the night-flying insects to herself. But she cared for none of their attentions, and though she spoke politely to them all she gave encouragement to none. Yet some of the sheeny-winged gallants called her a coquette.

One night she said to her mother, the queen:

"I have met many admirers, but I don't wish a husband from any of them. Tonight I shall stay at home, and if any of them love me truly they will come and pay me court here. Then I shall lay an impossible duty on them. If they are wise they will not try to perform it; and if they love their lives more than they love me, I do not want any of them. Whoever succeeds may have me for his bride."

"As you will my child," said the queen mother, who arrayed her daughter in her most resplendent robes, and set her on her throne in the heart of the lotus.

Then she gave orders to her body-guard to keep all suitors at a respectful distance lest some stupid gallant, a horn-bug or a cockchafer dazzled by the light should approach too near and hurt the princess or shake her throne.

No sooner had twilight faded away, than forth came the golden beetle, who stood on a stamen and making obeisance, said:

"I am Lord Green-Gold, I offer my house, my fortune and my love to Princess Hotaru."

"Go and bring me fire and I will be your bride" said Hotaru-hime.

With a bow of the head the beetle opened his wings and departed with a stately whirr.

Next came a shining bug with wings and body as black as lamp-smoke, who solemnly professed his passion.

"Bring me fire and you may have me for your wife."

Off flew the bug with a buzz.

Pretty soon came the scarlet dragonfly, expecting so to dazzle the princess by his gorgeous colors that she would accept him at once.

"I decline your offer" said the princess, "but if you bring me a flash of fire, I'll become your bride."

Swift was the flight of the dragonfly on his errand, and in came the Beetle with a tremendous buzz, and ardently plead his suit.

"I'll say 'yes' if you bring me fire" said the glittering princess.

Suitor after suitor appeared to woo the daughter of the King of the Fireflies until every petal was dotted with them. One after another in a long troop they appeared. Each in his own way, proudly, humbly, boldly, mildly, with flattery, with boasting, even with tears, each proffered his love, told his rank or expatiated on his fortune or vowed his constancy, sang his tune or played his music. To everyone of her lovers the princess in modest voice returned the same answer:

"Bring me fire and I'll be your bride."

So without telling his rivals, each one thinking he had the secret alone sped away after fire.

But none ever came back to wed the princess. Alas for the poor suitors! The beetle whizzed off to a house near by through the paper windows of which light glimmered. So full was he of his passion that thinking nothing of wood or iron, he dashed his head against a nail, and fell dead on the ground.

The black bug flew into a room where a poor student was reading. His lamp was only a dish of earthenware full of rape seed oil with a wick made of pith. Knowing nothing of oil the love-lorn bug crawled into the dish to reach the flame and in a few seconds was drowned in the oil.

"Nan jaro?" (What's that?) said a thrifty housewife, sitting with needle in hand, as her lamp flared up for a moment, smoking the chimney, and then cracking it; while picking out the scorched bits she found a roasted dragonfly, whose scarlet wings were all burned off.

Mad with love the brilliant hawk-moth, afraid of the flame yet determined to win the fire for the princess, hovered round and round the candle flame, coming nearer and nearer each time. "Now or never, the princess or death," he buzzed, as he darted forward to snatch a flash of flame, but singeing his wings, he fell helplessly down, and died in agony.

"What a fool he was, to be sure," said the ugly clothes moth, coming on the spot, "I'll get the fire. I'll crawl up *inside* the candle." So he climbed up the hollow paper wick, and was nearly to the top, and inside the hollow blue part of the flame, when the man, snuffing the wick, crushed him to death.

Sad indeed was the fate of the lovers of Hi-o's daughter. Some hovered around the beacons on the headland, some fluttered about the great wax candles which stood eight feet high in their brass sockets in Buddhist temples; some burned their noses at the top of incense sticks, or were nearly choked by the smoke; some danced all night around the lanterns in the shrines; some sought the sepulchral lamps in the graveyard; one visited the cremation furnace; another the kitchen, where a feast was going on; another chased the sparks that flew out of the chimney; but none brought fire to the princess, or won the lover's prize. Many lost their feelers, had their shining bodies scorched or their wings singed, but most of them alas! lay dead, black and cold next morning.

As the priests trimmed the lamps in the shrines, and the servant maids the lanterns, each said alike:

"The Princess Hotaru must have had many lovers last night."

Alas! alas! poor suitors. Some tried to snatch a streak of green fire from the cat's eyes, and were snapped up for their pains. One attempted to get a mouthful of bird's breath, but was swallowed alive. A carrion beetle (the ugly lover) crawled off to the sea shore, and found some fish scales that emitted light. The stag-beetle climbed a mountain, and in a rotten tree stump found some bits of glowing wood like fire, but the distance was so great that long before they reached the castle moat it was daylight, and the fire had gone out; so they threw their fish scales and old wood away.

The next day was one of great mourning and there were so many funerals going on, that Hi-maro the Prince of the Fireflies on the north side of the castle moat inquired of his servants the cause. Then he learned for the first time of the glittering princess. Upon this the prince who had just succeeded his father upon the throne fell in love with the princess and resolved to marry her. He sent his chamberlain to ask of her father his daughter in marriage according to true etiquette. The father agreed to the prince's proposal, with the condition that the Prince should obey her behest in one thing, which was to come in person bringing her fire.

Then the Prince at the head of his glittering battalions came in person and filled the lotus palace with a flood of golden light. But Hotaru-hime was so beautiful that her charms paled not their fire even in the blaze of the Prince's glory. The visit ended in wooing, and the wooing in wedding. On the night appointed, in a palanquin made of the white lotus-petals, amid the blazing torches of the prince's battalions of warriors,

Hotaru-hime was borne to the prince's palace and there, prince and princess were joined in the wedlock.

Many generations have passed since Hi-maro and Hotaru-hime were married, and still it is the whim of all Firefly princesses that their base-born lovers must bring fire as their love-offering or lose their prize. Else would the glittering fair ones be wearied unto death by the importunity of their lovers. Great indeed is the loss, for in this quest of fire many thousand insects, attracted by the firefly, are burned to death in the vain hope of winning the fire that shall gain the cruel but beautiful one that fascinates them. It is for this cause that each night insects hover around the lamp flame, and every morning a crowd of victims drowned in the oil, or scorched in the flame, must be cleaned from the lamp. This is the reason why young ladies catch and imprison the fireflies to watch the war of insect-love, in the hope that they may have human lovers who will dare as much, through fire and flood, as they.

The White Butterfly

AN OLD MAN NAMED TAKAHAMA lived in a little house behind the cemetery of the temple of Sozanji. He was extremely amiable and generally liked by his neighbours, though most of them considered him to be a little mad. His madness, it would appear, entirely rested upon the fact that he had never married or evinced desire for intimate companionship with women.

One summer day he became very ill, so ill, in fact, that he sent for his sister-in-law and her son. They both came and did all they could to bring comfort during his last hours. While they watched Takahama fell asleep; but he had no sooner done so than a large white butterfly flew into the room, and rested on the old man's pillow. The young man tried to drive it away with a fan; but it came back three times, as if loth to leave the sufferer.

At last Takahama's nephew chased it out into the garden, through the gate, and into the cemetery beyond, where it lingered over a woman's tomb, and then mysteriously disappeared. On examining the tomb the young man found the name "Akiko" written upon it, together with a description narrating how Akiko died when she was eighteen. Though the tomb was covered with moss and must have been erected fifty years previously, the boy saw that it was surrounded with flowers, and that the little water-tank had been recently filled.

When the young man returned to the house he found that Takahama had passed away, and he returned to his mother and told her what he had seen in the cemetery.

"Akiko?" murmured his mother. "When your uncle was young he was betrothed to Akiko. She died of consumption shortly before her wedding-day. When Akiko left this world your uncle resolved never to marry and to live ever near her grave. For all these years he has remained faithful to his vow, and kept in his heart all the sweet memories of his one and only love. Every day Takahama went to the cemetery, whether the air was fragrant with summer breeze or thick with falling, snow. Every day he went to her grave and prayed for her happiness, swept the tomb and set flowers there. When Takahama was dying, and he could no longer perform his loving task, Akiko came for him. That white butterfly was her sweet and loving soul."

Just before Takahama passed away into the Land of the Yellow Spring he may have murmured words like those of Yone Noguchi:

"Where the flowers sleep,
Thank God! I shall sleep tonight.
Oh, come, butterfly!"

Flowers & Trees

Introduction

ONE OF THE MOST STRIKING, and certainly one of the most pleasing, characteristics of the Japanese is their intense love of flowers and trees. Merry parties set out to see the azaleas bloom, or the splendour of the pink-white cherry-blossom, or the scarlet glory of the maple-trees. The love of flowers is only a small part of the Japanese love of Nature. The great Japanese designer of gardens, Kobori-Enshū, said that an ideal garden should be like "the sweet solitude of a landscape clouded by moonlight, with a half-gloom between the trees."

The pine-tree is the emblem of good fortune and longevity, symbolising the comradeship of love, the peaceful and mutual devotion of old married people in Japan. The chrysanthemum is Japan's national flower and is certainly a fitting symbolism for the Imperial standard. Once, like the English rose, it figured as a badge in the War of the Chrysanthemums, a protracted civil war that divided the nation into two hostile factions. Now the chrysanthemum stands for a united Empire. The supreme floral glory of Japan takes place in April with the coming of the cherry and plum blossom, which are regarded with the most favour. The poet Motoori wrote: "If one should ask you concerning the heart of a true Japanese, point to the wild cherry flower glowing in the sun".

Lady White and Lady Yellow

LONG AGO there grew in a meadow a white and a yellow chrysanthemum side by side. One day an old gardener chanced to come across them, and took a great fancy to Lady Yellow. He told her that if she would come along with him he would make her far more attractive, that he would give her delicate food and fine clothes to wear.

Lady Yellow was so charmed with what the old man said that she forgot all about her white sister and consented to be lifted up, carried in the arms of the old gardener, and to be placed in his garden.

When Lady Yellow and her master had departed Lady White wept bitterly. Her own simple beauty had been despised; but, what was far worse, she was forced to remain in the meadow alone, without the converse of her sister, to whom she had been devoted.

Day by day Lady Yellow grew more fair, in her master's garden. No one would have recognised the common flower of the field now; but though her petals were long and curled and her leaves so clean and well cared for, she sometimes thought of Lady White alone in the field, and wondered how she managed to make the long and lonely hours pass by.

One day a village chief came to the old man's garden in quest of a perfect chrysanthemum that he might take to his lord for a crest design. He informed the old man that he did not want a fine chrysanthemum with many long petals. What he wanted was a simple white chrysanthemum with sixteen petals. The old man took the village chief to see Lady Yellow; but this flower did not please him, and, thanking the gardener, he took his departure.

On his way home he happened to enter a field, where he saw Lady White weeping. She told him the sad story of her loneliness, and when she had finished her tale of woe the village chief informed her that he had seen Lady Yellow and did not consider her half as beautiful as her own white self. At these cheering words Lady White dried her eyes, and she nearly jumped off her little feet when this kind man told her that he wanted her for his lord's crest!

In another moment the happy Lady White was being carried in a palanquin. When she reached the *Daimyō's* palace all warmly praised her remarkable perfection of form. Great artists came from far and near, sat about her, and sketched the flower with wonderful skill. She soon needed no mirror, for ere long she saw her pretty white face on all the *Daimyō's* most precious belongings. She saw it on his armour and lacquer boxes, on his quilts and cushions and robes. When she looked upward she could see her face in great carved panels. She was painted floating down a stream, and in all manner of quaint and beautiful ways. Everyone acknowledged that the white chrysanthemum, with her sixteen petals, made the most wonderful crest in all Japan.

While Lady White's happy face lived for ever designed upon the *Daimyō's* possessions, Lady Yellow met with a sad fate. She had bloomed for herself alone and drunk in the visitors' praise as eagerly as she did the dew upon her finely curled petals. One day, however, she felt a stiffness in her limbs and a cessation of the exuberance of life. Her once proud head fell forward, and when the old man found her he lifted her up and threw her upon a rubbish heap.

Chrysanthemum-Old-Man

KIKUO ('CHRYSANTHEMUM-OLD-MAN') was the faithful retainer of Tsugaru. One day his lord's force was overthrown, and the castle and fine estates were taken away by the enemy; but fortunately Tsugaru and Kikuo were able to escape to the mountains.

Kikuo, knowing his master's love of flowers, especially that of the chrysanthemum, resolved to cultivate this flower to the best of his ability, and in so doing to lessen a little of his master's remorse and humiliation in exile.

His efforts pleased Tsugaru, but unfortunately that lord soon fell sick and died, and the faithful Kikuo wept over his master's grave. Then once more he returned to his work, and planted chrysanthemums about his master's tomb till he had made a border thirty yards broad, so that red, white, pink, yellow, and bronze blossoms scented the air, to the wonder of all who chanced to come that way.

When Kikuo was about eighty-two he caught cold and was confined to his humble dwelling, where he suffered considerable pain.

One autumn night, when he knew those beloved flowers dedicated to his master were at their best, he saw in the verandah a number of young children. As he gazed upon them he realised that they were not the children of this world.

Two of these little ones drew near to Kikuo, and said: "We are the spirits of your chrysanthemums, and have come to tell you how sorry we are to find you ill. You have guarded and loved us with such care. There was a man in China, Hozo by name, who lived eight hundred years by drinking the dew from chrysanthemum blossoms. Gladly would we lengthen out your days, but, alas! the Gods ordain otherwise. Within thirty days you will die."

The old man expressed the wish that he might die in peace, and the regret that he must needs leave behind him all his chrysanthemums.

"Listen," said one of the ghostly children: "we have all loved you, Kikuo, for what you have done for us. When you die we shall die too." As soon as these words were spoken a puff of wind blew against the dwelling, and the spirits departed.

Kikuo grew worse instead of better, and on the thirtieth day he passed away. When visitors came to see the chrysanthemums he had planted, all had vanished. The villagers buried the old man near his master, and, thinking to please Kikuo, they planted chrysanthemums near his grave; but all died immediately they were put into the ground. Only grasses grow over the tombs now. The child-souls of the chrysanthemums chatter and sing and play with the spirit of Kikuo.

The Violet Well

SHINGE AND HER WAITING-MAIDS were picnicking in the Valley of Shimizutani, that lies between the mountains of Yoshino and Tsubosaka. Shinge, full of the joy of spring, ran towards the Violet Well, where she discovered great clumps of purple, sweet-scented violets. She was about to pick the fragrant blossoms when a great snake darted forth, and she immediately fainted.

When the maidens found her they saw that her lips were purple, as purple as the violets that surrounded her, and when they saw the snake, still lurking in the vicinity, they feared that their mistress would die. Matsu, however, had sufficient presence of mind to throw her basket of flowers at the snake, which at once crawled away.

Just at that moment a handsome youth appeared, and, explaining to the maidens that he was a doctor, he gave Matsu some medicine, in order that she might give it to her mistress.

While Matsu forced the powder into Shinge's mouth the doctor took up a stick, disappeared for a few moments, and then returned with the dead snake in his hands.

By this time Shinge had regained consciousness, and asked the name of the physician to whom she was indebted for saving her life. But he politely bowed, evaded her question, and then took his departure. Only Matsu knew that the name of her mistress's rescuer was Yoshisawa.

When Shinge had been taken to her home she grew worse instead of better. All the cleverest doctors came to her bedside, but could do nothing to restore her to health.

Matsu knew that her mistress was gradually fading away for love of the handsome man who had saved her life, and she therefore talked the matter over with her master, Zembei. Matsu told him the story, and said that although Yoshisawa was of a low birth, belonging to the Outcasts, the lowest caste in Japan, who live by killing and skinning animals, yet nevertheless he was extremely courteous and had the manner and bearing of a *samurai*. "Nothing," said Matsu, "will restore your daughter to health unless she marries this handsome physician."

Both Zembei and his wife were dismayed at these words, for Zembei was a great *daimyō*, and could not for one moment tolerate the idea of his daughter marrying one of the Outcast class. However, he agreed to make inquiries concerning Yoshisawa, and Matsu returned to her mistress with something like good news. When Matsu had told Shinge what her father was doing on her behalf she rallied considerably, and was able to take food.

When Shinge was nearly well again Zembei called her to him and said that he had made careful inquiries concerning Yoshisawa, and could on no account agree to her marrying him.

Shinge wept bitterly, and brooded long over her sorrow with a weary heart. The next morning she was not to be found in the house or in the garden. Search was made in every direction; even Yoshisawa himself sought her everywhere; but those who sought her found her not. She had mysteriously disappeared, burdened with a sorrow that now made her father realise the effect of his harsh decree.

After three days she was found lying at the bottom of the Violet Well, and shortly after Yoshisawa, overcome with grief, sought a similar end to his troubles. It is said that on stormy nights the ghost of Shinge is to be seen floating over the well, while near by comes the sound of the weeping of Yoshisawa.

The Ghost of the Lotus Lily

A CERTAIN DISEASE broke out in Kyoto from which many thousands of people died. It spread to Idzumi, where the Lord of Koriyama lived, and Koriyama, his wife and child, were stricken down with the malady.

One day Tada Samon, a high official in Koriyama's castle, received a visit from a *yamabushi*, or mountain recluse. This man was full of concern for the illness of the Lord Koriyama, and, addressing Samon, he said: "All this trouble has come about through the entrance of evil spirits in the castle. They have come because the moats about the abode are dry and contain no lotus. If these moats were at once planted with this sacred flower the evil spirits would depart, and your lord, his wife and child, grow well again."

Samon was much impressed by these wise words, and permission was given for this recluse to plant lotus about the castle. When he had accomplished his task he mysteriously disappeared.

Within a week the Lord Koriyama, his wife and son, were able to get up and resume their respective duties, for by this time the walls had been repaired, the moats filled with pure water, which reflected the nodding heads of countless lotus.

Many years later, and after the Lord Koriyama had died, a young *samurai* chanced to pass by the castle moats. He was gazing admiringly at these flowers when he suddenly saw two extremely handsome boys playing on the edge of the water. He was about to lead them to a safer place when they sprang into the air and, falling, disappeared beneath the water.

The astonished *samurai*, believing that he had seen a couple of *kappas*, or river goblins, made a hasty retreat to the castle, and there reported his strange adventure. When he had told his story the moats were dragged and cleaned, but nothing could be found of the supposed *kappas*.

A little later on another *samurai*, Murata Ippai, saw near the same lotus a number of beautiful little boys. He drew his sword and cut them down, breathing in as he did so the heavy perfume of this sacred flower with every stroke of his weapon. When Ippai looked about him to see how many of these strange beings he had killed, there arose before him a cloud of many colours, a cloud that fell upon his face with a fine spray.

As it was too dark to ascertain fully the extent and nature of his onslaught, Ippai remained all night by the spot. When he awoke in the morning he found to his disgust that he had only struck off the heads of a number of lotus. Knowing that this beneficent flower had saved the life of the Lord Koriyama, and now protected that of his son, Ippai was filled with shame and remorse. Saying a prayer by the water's edge, he committed *hara-kiri*.

The Spirit of the Peony

IT HAD BEEN ARRANGED that the Princess Aya should marry the second son of Lord Ako. The arrangements, according to Japanese custom, had been made entirely without the consent or approval of the actual parties concerned.

One night Princess Aya walked through the great garden of her home, accompanied by her waiting-maids. The moon shone brightly upon her favourite peony bed near a pond, and covered the sweet-scented blooms in a silver sheen. Here she lingered, and was stooping to breathe the fragrance of these flowers when her foot slipped, and she would have fallen had not a handsome young man, clad in a robe of embroidered peonies, rescued her just in time. He vanished as quickly and mysteriously as he had come, before, indeed, she had time to thank him.

It so happened that shortly after this event the Princess Aya became very ill, and in consequence the day for her marriage had to be postponed. All the medical aid available was useless to restore the feverish maiden to health again.

The Princess Aya's father asked his favourite daughter's maid, Sadayo, if she could throw any light upon this lamentable affair.

Sadayo, although hitherto bound to secrecy, felt that the time had come when it was wise, indeed essential, to communicate all she knew in the matter. She told her master that the Princess Aya was deeply in love with the young *samurai* wearing the robes embroidered with peonies, adding that if he could not be found she feared that her young mistress would die.

That night, while a celebrated player was performing upon the *biwa* in the hope of entertaining the sick Princess, there once more appeared behind the peonies the same young man in the same silk robe.

The next night, too, while Yae and Yakumo were playing on the flute and *koto*, the young man appeared again.

The Princess Aya's father now resolved to get at the root of the matter, and for this purpose he bade Maki Hiogo dress in black and lie concealed in the peony bed on the following night.

When the next night came Maki Hiogo lay hidden among the peonies, while Yae and Yakumo made sweet music. Not long after the music had sounded the mysterious young *samurai* again appeared. Maki Hiogo rose from his hiding-place with his arms tightly bound round this strange visitor. A cloud seemed to emanate from his captive. It made him dizzy, and he fell to the ground still tightly holding the handsome *samurai*.

Just as a number of guards came hurrying to the spot Maki Hiogo regained consciousness. He looked down expecting to see his captive. But all that he held in his arms was a large peony!

By this time Princess Aya and her father joined the astonished group, and the Lord Naizen-no-jo at once grasped the situation. "I see now," said he, "that the spirit of the peony flower had a moment ago, and on former occasions, taken the form of a young and handsome *samurai*. My daughter, you must take this flower and treat it with all kindness."

The Princess Aya needed to be told no more. She returned to the house, placed the peony in a vase, and stood it by her bedside. Day by day she got better, while the flower flourished exceedingly.

When the Princess Aya was quite well the Lord of Ako arrived at the castle, bringing with him his second son, whom she was to marry. In due time the wedding took place, but at that hour the beautiful peony suddenly died.

The Miraculous Chestnut

THE PRINCESS HINAKO-NAI-SHINNO begged that chestnuts should be brought to her; but she took but one, bit it, and threw it away.

It took root, and upon all the chestnuts that it eventually bore there were the marks of the Princess's small teeth. In honouring her death the chestnut had expressed its devotion in this strange way.

The Silent Pine

THE EMPEROR GO-TOBA, who strongly objected to the croaking of frogs, was on one occasion disturbed by a wind-blown pine-tree.

When his Majesty loudly commanded it to be still, the pine-tree never for a moment moved again. So greatly impressed was this obedient tree that the fiercest wind failed to stir its branches, or even its myriad pine-needles.

Willow Wife

IN A CERTAIN JAPANESE VILLAGE there grew a great willow-tree. For many generations the people loved it. In the summer it was a resting-place, a place where the villagers might meet after the work and heat of the day were over, and there talk till the moonlight streamed through the branches. In winter it was like a great half-opened umbrella covered with sparkling snow.

Heitaro, a young farmer, lived quite near this tree, and he, more than any of his companions, had entered into a deep communion with the imposing willow. It was almost the first object he saw upon waking, and upon his return from work in the fields he looked out eagerly for its familiar form. Sometimes he would burn a joss-stick beneath its branches and kneel down and pray.

One day an old man of the village came to Heitaro and explained to him that the villagers were anxious to build a bridge over the river, and that they particularly wanted the great willow-tree for timber.

"For timber?" said Heitaro, hiding his face in his hands. "My dear willow-tree for a bridge, one to bear the incessant patter of feet? Never, never, old man!"

When Heitaro had somewhat recovered himself, he offered to give the old man some of his own trees, if he and the villagers would accept them for timber and spare the ancient willow.

The old man readily accepted this offer, and the willow-tree continued to stand in the village as it had stood for so many years.

One night while Heitaro sat under the great willow he suddenly saw a beautiful woman standing close beside him, looking at him shyly, as if wanting to speak.

"Honourable lady," said he, "I will go home. I see you wait for someone. Heitaro is not without kindness towards those who love."

"He will not come now," said the woman, smiling.

"Can he have grown cold? Oh, how terrible when a mock love comes and leaves ashes and a grave behind!"

"He has not grown cold, dear lord."

"And yet he does not come! What strange mystery is this?"

"He has come! His heart has been always here, here under this willow-tree." And with a radiant smile the woman disappeared.

Night after night they met under the old willow-tree. The woman's shyness had entirely disappeared, and it seemed that she could not hear too much from Heitaro's lips in praise of the willow under which they sat.

One night he said to her: "Little one, will you be my wife – you who seem to come from the very tree itself?"

"Yes," said the woman. "Call me Higo ('Willow') and ask no questions, for love of me. I have no father or mother, and some day you will understand."

Heitaro and Higo were married, and in due time they were blessed with a child, whom they called Chiyodo. Simple was their dwelling, but those it contained were the happiest people in all Japan.

While this happy couple went about their respective duties great news came to the village. The villagers were full of it, and it was not long before it reached Heitaro's ears. The ex-Emperor Toba wished to build a temple to Kwannon in Kyoto, and those in authority sent far and wide for timber. The villagers said that they must contribute towards building the sacred edifice by presenting their great willow-tree. All Heitaro's argument and persuasion and promise of other trees were ineffectual, for neither he nor anyone else could give as large and handsome a tree as the great willow.

Heitaro went home and told his wife. "Oh, wife," said he, "they are about to cut down our dear willow-tree! Before I married you I could not have borne it. Having you, little one, perhaps I shall get over it some day."

That night Heitaro was aroused by hearing a piercing cry. "Heitaro," said his wife, "it grows dark! The room is full of whispers. Are you there, Heitaro? Hark! They are cutting down the willow-tree. Look how its shadow trembles in the moonlight. I am the soul of the willow-tree! The villagers are killing me. Oh, how they cut and tear me to pieces! Dear Heitaro, the pain, the pain! Put your hands here, and here. Surely the blows cannot fall now?"

"My Willow Wife! My Willow Wife!" sobbed Heitaro.

"Husband," said Higo, very faintly, pressing her wet, agonised face close to his, "I am going now. Such a love as ours cannot be cut down, however fierce the blows. I shall wait for you and Chiyodo – – My hair is falling through the sky! My body is breaking!"

There was a loud crash outside. The great willow-tree lay green and dishevelled upon the ground. Heitaro looked round for her he loved more than anything else in the world. Willow Wife had gone!

The Tree of the One-eyed Priest

IN ANCIENT DAYS there stood on the summit of Oki-yama a temple dedicated to Fudo, a god surrounded by fire, with sword in one hand and rope in the other. For twenty years Yenoki had performed his office, and one of his duties was to guard Fudo, who sat in a shrine, only accessible to the high-priest himself. During the whole of this period Yenoki had rendered faithful service and resisted the temptation to take a peep at this extremely ugly god. One morning, finding that the door of the shrine was not quite closed, his curiosity overcame him and he peeped within. No sooner had he done so than he became stone-blind in one eye and suffered the humiliation of being turned into a *tengu*.

He lived for a year after these deplorable happenings, and then died. His spirit passed into a great cryptomeria-tree standing on the east side of the mountain, and from that day Yenoki's spirit was invoked by sailors who were harassed by storms on the Chinese Sea. If a light blazed from the tree in answer to their prayers, it was a sure sign that the storm would abate.

At the foot of Oki-yama there was a village, where, sad to relate, the young people were very lax in their morals. During the Festival of the Dead they performed a dance known as the Bon Odori. These dances were very wild affairs indeed, and were accompanied by flirtations of a violent and wicked nature. The dances became more unrestrained as years went by, and the village got a bad name for immoral practices among the young people.

After a particularly wild celebration of the Bon a young maiden named Kimi set out to find her lover, Kurosuke. Instead of finding him she saw an extremely good-looking youth, who smiled upon her and continually beckoned. Kimi forgot all about Kurosuke; indeed, from that moment she hated him and eagerly followed the enticing youth. Nine fair but wicked maidens disappeared from the village in a similar way, and always it was the same youth who lured them astray in this mysterious manner.

The elders of the village consulted together, and came to the conclusion that the spirit of Yenoki was angry with the excesses connected with the Bon festival, and had assumed the form of a handsome youth for the purpose of administering severe admonition. The Lord of Kishiwada accordingly summoned Sonobe to his presence, and bade him journey to the great cryptomeria-tree on Oki-yama.

When Sonobe reached his destination he thus addressed the ancient tree: "Oh, home of Yenoki's spirit, I upbraid you for carrying away our daughters. If this continues I shall cut down the tree, so that you will be compelled to seek lodging elsewhere."

Sonobe had no sooner spoken than rain began to fall, and he heard the rumblings of a mighty earthquake. Then from out of the tree Yenoki's spirit suddenly appeared. He explained that many of the young people of Sonobe's village had offended against the Gods by their misconduct, and that he had, as conjectured, assumed the form of a handsome youth in order to take away the principal offenders. "You will find them," added the spirit of Yenoki, "bound to trees on the second summit of this mountain. Go, release them, and allow them to return to the village. They have not only repented of their follies, but will now persuade others to live nobler and purer lives." And with these words Yenoki disappeared into his tree.

Sonobe set off to the second summit and released the maidens. They returned to their homes, good and dutiful daughters, and from that day to this the Gods have been well satisfied with the general behaviour of the village that nestles at the foot of Oki-yama.

The Burning of Three Dwarf Trees

IN THE REIGN OF the Emperor Go-Fukakusa there lived a celebrated Regent, Saimyoji Tokiyori. When thirty years of age this Regent retired to a monastery for several years, and not infrequently his peace of mind was sadly disturbed by stories of peasants who suffered at the hands of tyrannical officials. Now Tokiyori loved above everything the welfare of his people, and after giving the matter careful consideration he determined to disguise himself, travel from place to place, and discover in an intimate way the heart of the poorer people, and later on to do all in his power to suppress malpractice on the part of various officials.

Tokiyori accordingly set out upon his excellent mission, and finally came to Sano, in the province of Kozuki. Now it was the time of winter, and a heavy snowstorm caused the royal wanderer to lose his way. After wearily tramping about for several hours in the hope of finding shelter, he was about to make the best of the matter by sleeping under a tree when, to his joy, he noticed a small thatched cottage nestling under a hill at no great distance. To this cottage he went, and explained to the woman who greeted him that he had lost his way and would be much indebted to her if she would afford him shelter for the night. The good woman explained that as her husband was away from home, it would be disloyal as his wife to give shelter to a stranger. Tokiyori not only took this reply in good part, but he greatly rejoiced, in spite of a night in the snow, to find such a virtuous woman. But he had not gone far from the cottage when he heard a man calling to him. Tokiyori stood still, and presently he saw someone beckoning him. The man explained that he was the husband of the woman the ex-Regent had just left, and cordially invited one whom he took to be a wandering priest to return with him and accept such humble hospitality as was available.

When Tokiyori was sitting in the little cottage simple fare was spread before him, and as he had eaten nothing since the morning he did full justice to the meal. But the fact that millet and not rice was provided clearly conveyed to the observant Tokiyori that here was poverty indeed, but with it all a generosity that went straight to his heart. Nor was this all, for, the meal finished, they gathered round the fire that was fast dying out for want of fuel.

The good man of the house turned to the fuel-box. Alas! it was empty. Without a moment's hesitation he went out into the garden, heavily covered with snow, and brought back with him three pots of dwarf trees, pine, plum, and cherry. Now in Japan dwarf trees are held in high esteem; much time and care is bestowed upon them, and their age and unique beauty have made them dear to the people of Nippon. In spite of Tokiyori's remonstrance his host broke up these little trees, and thus made a cheerful blaze.

It was this incident, scarcely to be fully appreciated by a Westerner, that caused Tokiyori to question his host, whose very possession of these valuable trees strongly suggested that this generous man was not a farmer by birth, but had taken to this calling by force of circumstance. The ex-Regent's conjecture proved to be correct, and his host, with some reluctance, finally explained that he was a *samurai* by the name of Sano Genzalmon Tsuneyo. He had been forced to take up farming owing to the dishonesty of one of his relatives.

Tokiyori readily recalled the name of this *samurai* before him, and suggested that he should make an appeal for redress. Sano explained that as the good and just Regent had died (so he thought), and as his successor was very young, he considered it was worse than useless to present a petition. But, nevertheless, he went on to explain to his interested listener that should there come a call to arms he would be the first to make an appearance at Kamakura. It was this thought of some day being of use to his country that had sweetened the days of his poverty.

The conversation, so rapidly suggested in this story, was in reality a lengthy one, and by the time it was concluded already a new day had begun. And when the storm-doors had been opened it was to reveal sunlight streaming over a world of snow. Before taking his departure Tokiyori warmly thanked his host and hostess for their hospitality. When this kindly visitor had gone Sano suddenly remembered that he had forgotten to inquire the name of his guest.

Now it happened that in the following spring a call to arms was instituted by the Government at Kamakura. No sooner had Sano heard the joyful news than he set out to obey the summons. His armour was shabby in the extreme, his halberd covered with rust, and his horse was in a very poor condition. He presented a sorry figure among the resplendent knights he found in Kamakura. Many of these knights made uncomplimentary remarks concerning him, but Sano bore this insolence without a word. While he stood, a forlorn figure, among the sparkling ranks of *samurai* about him, a herald approached riding on a magnificent horse, and carrying a banner bearing the house-crest of the Regent. With a loud, clear voice he bade the knight wearing the shabbiest armour to appear before his master. Sano obeyed the summons with a heavy heart. He thought that the Regent was about to rebuke him for appearing in such a gaily decked company clad in such miserable accoutrements.

This humble knight was surprised by the cordial welcome he received, and still more surprised when a servant pushed aside the screens of an adjoining room and revealed the Regent Saimyoji Tokiyori, who was none other than the priest who had taken shelter in his little home. Nor had Tokiyori forgotten the burning of the dwarf pine, plum, and cherry-trees. Out of that sacrifice, readily given without a thought of gain, came the thirty villages of which Sano had been robbed. This was only Sano's due, and in addition the grateful Tokiyori had the happy idea of presenting this faithful knight with the village of Matsu-idu, Umeda, and Sakurai, *matsu*, *ume*, and *sakura* being the Japanese names for pine, plum, and cherry.

The Pine-tree Lovers

IN ANCIENT DAYS there lived at Takasago a fisherman, his wife, and little daughter Matsue. There was nothing that Matsue loved to do more than to sit under the great pine-tree. She was particularly fond of the pine-needles that never seemed tired of falling to the ground. With these she fashioned a beautiful dress and sash, saying: "I will not wear these pine-clothes until my wedding-day."

One day, while Matsue was sitting under the pine-tree, she sang the following song:

"No man so callous but he heaves a sigh
When o'er his head the withered cherry flowers
Come fluttering down. Who knows? the Spring's soft showers
May be but tears shed by the sorrowing sky."

While she thus sang Teoyo stood on the steep shore of Sumiyoshi watching the flight of a heron. Up, up it went into the blue sky, and Teoyo saw it fly over the village where the fisherfolk and their daughter lived.

Now Teoyo was a youth who dearly loved adventure, and he thought it would be very delightful to swim across the sea and discover the land over which the heron had flown. So one morning he dived into the sea and swam so hard and so long that the poor fellow found the waves spinning and dancing, and saw the great sky bend down and try to touch him. Then he lay unconscious on the water; but the waves were kind to him after all, for they pressed him on and on till he was washed up at the very place where Matsue sat under the pine-tree.

Matsue carefully dragged Teoyo underneath the sheltering branches, and then set him down upon a couch of pine-needles, where he soon regained consciousness, and warmly thanked Matsue for her kindness.

Teoyo did not go back to his own country, for after a few happy months had gone by he married Matsue, and on her wedding morn she wore her dress and sash of pine-needles.

When Matsue's parents died her loss only seemed to make her love Teoyo the more. The older they grew the more they loved each other. Every night, when the moon shone, they went hand in hand to the pine-tree, and with their little rakes they made a couch for the morrow.

One night the great silver face of the moon peered through the branches of the pine-tree and looked in vain for the old lovers sitting together on a couch of pine-needles. Their little rakes lay side by side, and still the moon waited for the slow and stumbling steps of the Pine-Tree Lovers. But that night they did not come. They had gone home to an everlasting resting-place on the River of Souls. They had loved so well and so splendidly, in old age as well as in youth, that the Gods allowed their souls to come back again and wander round the pine-tree that had listened to their love for so many years. When the moon is full they whisper and laugh and sing and draw the pine-needles together, while the sea sings softly upon the shore.

Legends of Mount Fuji

Introduction

MOUNT FUJI, OR FUJI-YAMA ('The Never-dying Mountain'), seems to be typically Japanese. Its great snow-capped cone resembles a huge inverted fan, the fine streaks down its sides giving the appearance of fan-ribs. A native has thus fittingly described it: "Fuji dominates life by its silent beauty: sorrow is hushed, longing quieted, peace seems to flow down from that changeless home of peace, the peak of the white lotus." The reference here to a white lotus is as appropriate as that of the wide-stretched fan, for it refers to the sacred flower of the Lord Buddha. Indeed, Mount Fuji has been a place of pilgrimage for hundreds of years, and Lafcadio Hearn described its peak as "the Supreme Altar of the Sun".

The very name Fuji has been argued to derive from 'Huchi', or 'Fuchi', the Ainu Goddess of Fire or the Hearth, and the mountain itself has its own deities. Sengen, the Goddess of Fuji, is also known as Ko-no-hana-saku-ya-hime ('Radiant-blooming-as-the-flowers-of-the-trees'), and on the summit is her shrine. In ancient days it is said that this Goddess hovered in a luminous cloud above the crater, tended by invisible servants, who were prepared to throw down any pilgrims who were not pure of heart. Another deity of this mountain is O-ana-mochi ('Possessor of the Great Hole', or 'Crater').

It is not surprising to find that legend has grown round this venerable and venerated mountain. Like so many mountains in Japan, and, indeed, in other Eastern countries, it was associated with the Elixir of Life. The Japanese poet's words, "We being round thee forget to die," though written in recent years, seem to reflect the old idea. We have already seen, in the legend of 'The Bamboo Cutter and the Moon Maiden', that Tsuki was commanded by the Lady Kaguya to ascend Fuji and there burn the Elixir of Life, together with a certain scroll. As we shall see, the desire to wrest from Mount Fuji the secret of perpetual life never seems to have met with success.

As well as dealing with the subject of everlasting life, the tale 'The Rip van Winkle of Old Japan' also gives an account of that legendary coming of Fuji in a single night.

Fuji, the Abode of the Elixir of Life

THE FAME OF FUJI, so an old legend informs us, reached the ears of an Emperor of China. When he was told that this mountain had come into being in a single night he conjectured that Mount Fuji must needs yield the Elixir of Life itself. He accordingly collected about him a number of handsome youths and maidens and set sail for the Land of the Rising Sun. The junks rushed before the roaring wind like a shower of gold petals; but eventually the storm abated, and the Emperor and his people saw the white splendour of Fuji rise up before them.

When the junks had run in upon the shore the Emperor formed his company in procession, and, walking very slowly, led the way up the mountain. Hour after hour the procession climbed, the gold-robed Emperor ever walking in advance, until the sound of the sea was lost, and the thousand feet trod softly on the snow where there was peace and life eternal. Nearing the journey's end, the old Emperor ran forward joyously, for he wanted to be the first to drink of the Elixir of Life. And he was the first to taste of that Life that never grows old; but when the company found him they saw their Emperor lying on his back with a smile upon his face. He had indeed found Life Eternal, but it was through the way of Death.

Sentaro's Visit to the Land of Perpetual Youth

SENTARO ON ONE OCCASION prayed at this shrine, and was presented with a small paper crane, which expanded to a vast size directly it had reached his hands. On the back of this great crane flew Sentaro to the Land of Perpetual Youth, where, to his amazement, the people ate poisons and longed in vain to die!

Sentaro soon grew weary of this land, returned to his own country, and resolved to be content with the ordinary span of years allotted to mankind – as well he may have been, considering that he had already spent three hundred years in the country where there was no death and no birth.

The Goddess of Fuji

YOSOJI'S MOTHER, in common with many in the village where she lived, was stricken down with smallpox. Yosoji consulted the magician Kamo Yamakiko in the matter, for his mother grew so ill that every hour he expected her to be taken from him in death. Kamo Yamakiko told Yosoji to go to a small stream that flowed from the south-west side of Mount Fuji. "Near the source of this stream," said the magician, "is a shrine to the God of Long Breath. Go fetch this water, and give it to your mother, for this alone will cure her."

Yosoji, full of hope, eagerly set forth upon his journey, and when he had arrived at a spot where three paths crossed each other he was in difficulty as to the right one to take. Just as he was debating the matter a lovely girl, clad in white, stepped out from the forest, and bade him follow her to the place where the precious stream flowed near the shrine of the God of Long Breath.

When they reached the stream Yosoji was told to drink himself, as well as to fill the gourd with the sparkling water for his mother. When he had done these things the beautiful girl accompanied him to the place where he had originally seen her, and said: "Meet me again at this place in three days' time, for you will require a further supply of this water."

After five visits to this sacred shrine Yosoji rejoiced to find that his mother was quite well again, and not only his mother, but many of the villagers who had also been privileged to drink the water. Yosoji's bravery was loudly extolled, and presents were sent to the magician for his timely advice; but Yosoji, who was an honest lad, knew in his heart that all praise was really due to the beautiful girl who had been his guide. He desired to thank her more fully than he had hitherto done, and for this purpose he once more set out for the stream.

When Yosoji reached the shrine of the God of Long Breath he found that the stream had dried up. With much surprise and not a little sorrow he knelt down and prayed that she who had been so good to his mother would appear before him in order that he might thank her as she so richly deserved. When Yosoji arose he saw the maiden standing before him.

Yosoji expressed his gratitude in warm and elegant language, and begged to be told the name of her who had been his guide and restored his mother to health and strength again. But the maiden, smiling sweetly upon him, would not tell her name. Still smiling, she swung a branch of camellia in the air, so that it seemed that the fair blossom beckoned to some invisible spirit far away. In answer to the floral summons a cloud came down from Mount Fuji; it enveloped the lovely maiden, and carried her to the sacred mountain from which she had come. Yosoji knew now that his guide was none other than the Goddess of Fuji. He knelt with rapture upon his face as he watched the departing figure. As he gazed upon her he knew in his heart that with his thanks love had mingled too. While he yet knelt the Goddess of Fuji threw down the branch of camellia, a remembrance, perhaps a token, of her love for him.

The Rip van Winkle of Old Japan

MANY YEARS AGO there lived on the then barren plain of Suruga a woodman by the name of Visu. He was a giant in stature, and lived in a hut with his wife and children. One night, just as Visu was about to fall asleep, he heard a most extraordinary sound coming from under the earth, a sound louder and more terrible than thunder. Visu, thinking that he and his family were about to be destroyed by an earthquake, hastily snatched up the younger children and rushed to the door of the hut, where he saw a most wonderful sight. Instead of the once desolate plain he perceived a great mountain from whose head sprang tongues of flame and dense clouds of smoke! So glorious was the sight of this mountain that had run under the earth for two hundred miles and then suddenly sprung forth on the plain of Suruga that Visu, his wife and family, sat down on the ground as if under a spell. When the sun rose the next morning Visu saw that the mountain had put on robes of opal. It seemed so impressive to him that he called it Fuji-yama ('The Never-dying Mountain'), and so it is called to this day. Such perfect beauty suggested to the woodman the eternal, an idea which no doubt gave rise to the Elixir of Life so frequently associated with this mountain.

Day after day Visu sat and gazed upon Fuji, and was just conjecturing how nice it would be for so imposing a mountain to be able to see her loveliness, when a great lake suddenly stretched before him, shaped like a lute, and so called Biwa.

The Adventures of Visu

One day Visu received a visit from an old priest, who said to him: "Honourable woodman, I am afraid you never pray." Visu replied: "If you had a wife and a large family to keep you would never have time to pray." This remark made the priest angry, and the old man gave the woodcutter a vivid description of the horror of being reborn as a toad, or a mouse, or an insect for millions of years. Such lurid details were not to Visu's liking, and he accordingly promised the priest that in future he would pray. "Work and pray," said the priest as he took his departure.

Unfortunately Visu did nothing but pray. He prayed all day long and refused to do any work, so that his rice crops withered and his wife and family starved. Visu's wife, who had hitherto never said a harsh or bitter word to her husband, now became extremely angry, and, pointing to the poor thin bodies of her children, she exclaimed: "Rise, Visu, take up your axe and do something more helpful to us all than the mere mumbling of prayers!"

Visu was so utterly amazed at what his wife had said that it was some time before he could think of a fitting reply. When he did so his words came hot and strong to the ears of his poor, much-wronged wife.

"Woman," said he, "the Gods come first. You are an impertinent creature to speak to me so, and I will have nothing more to do with you!" Visu snatched up his axe and, without looking round to say farewell, he left the hut, strode out of the wood, and climbed up Fuji-yama, where a mist hid him from sight.

When Visu had seated himself upon the mountain he heard a soft rustling sound, and immediately afterward saw a fox dart into a thicket. Now Visu deemed it extremely lucky to see a fox, and, forgetting his prayers, he sprang up, and ran hither and thither in the hope of again finding this sharp-nosed little creature. He was about to give up the chase when, coming to an open space in a wood, he saw two ladies sitting down by a brook playing *go*. The woodman was so completely fascinated that he could do nothing but sit down and watch them. There was no sound except the soft click of pieces on the board and the song of the running brook. The ladies took no notice of Visu, for they seemed to be playing a strange game that had no end, a game that entirely absorbed their attention. Visu could not keep his eyes off these fair women. He watched their long black hair and the little quick hands that shot out now and again from their big silk sleeves in order to move the pieces. After he had been sitting there for three hundred years, though to him it was but a summer's afternoon, he saw that one of the players had made a false move. "*Wrongs* most lovely lady!" he exclaimed excitedly. In a moment these women turned into foxes and ran away.

When Visu attempted to pursue them he found to his horror that his limbs were terribly stiff, that his hair was very long, and that his beard touched the ground. He discovered, moreover, that the handle of his axe, though made of the hardest wood, had crumbled away into a little heap of dust.

Visu's Return

After many painful efforts Visu was able to stand on his feet and proceed very slowly toward his little home. When he reached the spot he was surprised to see no hut, and, perceiving a very old woman, he said: "Good lady, I am amazed to find that my little home has disappeared. I went away this afternoon, and now in the evening it has vanished!"

The old woman, who believed that a madman was addressing her, inquired his name. When she was told, she exclaimed: "Bah! you must indeed be mad! Visu lived three hundred years ago! He went away one day, and he never came back again."

"*Three hundred years*!" murmured Visu. "It cannot be possible. Where are my dear wife and children?"

"Buried!" hissed the old woman, "and, if what you say is true, your children's children too. The Gods have prolonged your miserable life in punishment for having neglected your wife and little children."

Big tears ran down Visu's withered cheeks as he said in a husky voice: "I have lost my manhood. I have prayed when my dear ones starved and needed the labour of my once strong hands. Old woman, remember my last words: *if you pray, work too*!"

We do not know how long the poor but repentant Visu lived after he returned from his strange adventures. His white spirit is still said to haunt Fuji-yama when the moon shines brightly.

Bells, Mirrors, Fans & Tea

Introduction

THE BELL OF ENKAKUJI, which features in the first short tales, is the largest bell in the city of Kamakura and is designated a National Treasure. When rung, a great note quivers forth, "deep as thunder, rich as the bass of a mighty organ." The sheer physical presence of these great bells affirms their *spiritual* heft.

The great legendary idea underlying Japanese mirrors is that the mirror, through constant reflection of its owner's face, draws to itself the very soul of its possessor. Long before the Japanese mirror was a familiar object in the house it had a very deep religious significance in connection with Shintoism. The Divine Mirror into which the Sun Goddess gazed is said to repose at Ise. Other mirrors are to be found in Shinto shrines. The mirror is said to "typify the human heart, which, when perfectly placid and clear, reflects the very image of the deity." In the *Kojiki* we are told that Izanagi presented his children with a polished silver disc, and bade them kneel before it every morning and evening and examine their reflections. He told them to think of heavenly things, to stifle passion and all evil thought, so that the disc should reveal a pure and lovely soul.

The Japanese fan is not merely a dainty feminine trifle to be used in conjunction with a smile or with eyes peeping behind some exquisite floral design. It has a fascinating history quite outside the gentle art of coquetry – it has been used, for instance, by ancient warriors on the battlefield as a means of giving emphasis to their commands. And yet, the fan appeals to us most in its more tender aspect. The fan that has a love-poem upon it and a love-story behind it is the fan that will always be the most precious to those who still keep a place for romance in their hearts. Hence we include here the legend entitled 'The Love of Asagao'.

Tea-drinking in Japan has been influenced most particularly by the Zen sect of Buddhism. The priests of this order drank tea from a single bowl before the image of Bodhidharma (Daruma). This Zen observance, strictly of a religious nature, finally developed into the Japanese tea ceremony. And so it is unsurprising that there are tales concerning legendary tea masters and even the origin of the plant itself.

Tales of the Bell of Enkakuji

The Return of Ono-no-Kimi

WHEN ONO-NO-KIMI DIED he went before the Judgment Seat of Emma-O, the Judge of Souls, and was told by that dread deity that he had quitted earthly life too soon, and that he must at once return.

Ono-no-Kimi pleaded that he could not retrace his steps, as he did not know the way. Then Emma-O said: "By listening to the bell of Enkakuji you will be able to find your way into the world again." And Ono-no-Kimi went forth from the Judgment Seat, and, with the sound of the bell for guidance, once more found himself in his old home.

The Giant Priest

ON ONE OCCASION it is said that a priest of giant stature was seen in the country, and no one knew his name or whence he had come. With unceasing zest he travelled up and down the land, from village to village, from town to town, exhorting the people to pray before the bell of Enkakuji.

It was eventually discovered that this giant priest was none other than a personification of the holy bell itself. This extraordinary news had its effect, for numerous people now flocked to the bell of Enkakuji, prayed, and returned with many a wish fulfilled.

Faith Rewarded

ON ANOTHER OCCASION this sacred bell is said to have sounded a deep note of its own accord. Those who were incredulous and laughed at the miracle met with calamity, and those who believed in the miraculous power of the sacred bell were rewarded with much prosperity.

A Woman and the Bell of Miidera

IN THE ANCIENT MONASTERY OF MIIDERA there was a great bronze bell. It rang out every morning and evening, a clear, rich note, and its surface shone like sparkling dew. The priests would not allow any woman to strike it, because they thought that such an action would pollute and dull the metal, as well as bring calamity upon them.

When a certain pretty woman who lived in Kyoto heard this she grew extremely inquisitive, and at last, unable to restrain her curiosity, she said: "I will go and see this wonderful bell of

Miidera. I will make it sound forth a soft note, and in its shining surface, bigger and brighter than a thousand mirrors, I will paint and powder, my face and dress my hair."

At length this vain and irreverent woman reached the belfry in which the great bell was suspended at a time when all were absorbed in their sacred duties. She looked into the gleaming bell and saw her pretty eyes, flushed cheeks, and laughing dimples. Presently she stretched forth her little fingers, lightly touched the shining metal, and prayed that she might have as great and splendid a mirror for her own. When the bell felt this woman's fingers, the bronze that she touched shrank, leaving a little hollow, and losing at the same time all its exquisite polish.

Benkei and the Bell

WHEN BENKEI, the faithful retainer of Yoshitsune, was a monk he very much desired to steal the bell of Miidera, and bring it to his own monastery. He accordingly visited Miidera, and, at an opportune moment, unhooked the great bell. Benkei's first thought was to roll it down the hill, and thus save himself the trouble of carrying such a huge piece of metal; but, thinking that the monks would hear the noise, he was forced to set about carrying it down the steep incline. He accordingly pulled out the crossbeam from the belfry, suspended the bell at one end, and – humorous touch – his paper lantern at the other, and in this manner he carried his mighty burden for nearly seven miles.

When Benkei reached his temple he at once demanded food. He managed to get through a concoction which filled an iron soup-pot five feet in diameter, and when he had finished he gave permission for a few priests to strike the stolen bell of Miidera. The bell was struck, but in its dying murmur it seemed to cry: "I want to go back to Miidera! I want to go back to Miidera!"

When the priests heard this they were amazed. The abbot, however, thought that if the bell were sprinkled with holy water it would become reconciled to its new abode; but in spite of holy water the bell still sobbed forth its plaintive and provoking cry. No one was more displeased by the sound than Benkei himself. It seemed that the bell mocked him and that arduous journey of his.

At last, exasperated beyond endurance, he rushed to the rope, strained it till the beam was far from the great piece of metal, then let it go, hoping that the force of the swift-rushing beam would crack such a peevish and ill-bred bell. The whirling wood reached the bell with a terrific crash; but it did not break. Through the air rang again: "I want to go back to Miidera!" and whether the bell was struck harshly or softly it always spoke the same words.

At last Benkei, now in a towering rage, shouldered the bell and beam, and, coming to the top of a mountain, he set down his burden, and, with a mighty kick, sent it rolling into the valley beneath. Some time later the Miidera priests found their precious bell, and joyfully hung it in its accustomed place, and from that time it failed to speak, and only rang like other temple bells.

A Bell and the Power of Karma

NEAR THE BANKS OF THE HIDAKA there once stood a far-famed tea-house nestling amid lovely scenery beside a hill called the Dragon's Claw. The fairest girl in this tea-house was Kiyo, for she was like "the fragrance of white lilies, when the wind, sweeping down the mountain heights, comes perfume-laden to the traveller."

Across the river stood a Buddhist temple where the abbot and a number of priests lived a simple and devout life. In the belfry of this temple reposed a great bell, six inches thick and weighing several tons. It was one of the monastery rules that none of the priests should eat fish or meat or drink *sake*, and they were especially forbidden to stop at tea-houses, lest they should lose their spirituality and fall into the sinful ways of the flesh.

One of the priests, however, on returning from a certain shrine, happened to see the pretty Kiyo, flitting hither and thither in the tea-garden, like a large, bright-winged butterfly. He stood and watched her for a moment, sorely tempted to enter the garden and speak to this beautiful creature, but, remembering his priestly calling, he crossed the river and entered his temple. That night, however, he could not sleep. The fever of a violent love had come upon him. He fingered his rosary and repeated passages from the Buddhist Scriptures, but these things brought him no peace of mind. Through all his pious thoughts there ever shone the winsome face of Kiyo, and it seemed to him that she was calling from that fair garden across the river.

His burning love grew so intense that it was not long before he stifled his religious feelings, broke one of the temple rules, and entered the forbidden tea-house. Here he entirely forgot his religion, or found a new one in contemplating the beautiful Kiyo, who brought him refreshment. Night after night he crept across the river and fell under the spell of this woman. She returned his love with equal passion, so that for the moment it appeared to this erring priest that he had found in a woman's charms something far sweeter than the possibility of attaining Nirvana.

After the priest had seen Kiyo on many nights conscience began to stir within him and to do battle with his unholy love. The power of Karma and the teaching of the Lord Buddha struggled within his breast. It was a fierce conflict, but in the end passion was vanquished, though, as we shall learn, not its awful consequences. The priest, having stamped out his carnal love, deemed it wise to deal with Kiyo as circumspectly as possible, lest his sudden change should make her angry.

When Kiyo saw the priest after his victory over the flesh she observed the far-away look in his eyes and the ascetic calm that now rested upon his face. She redoubled her feminine wiles, determined either to make the priest love her again, or, failing that, to put him to a cruel death by sorcery.

All Kiyo's blandishments failed to awaken love within the priest's heart, and, thinking only of vengeance, she set out, arrayed in a white robe, and went to a certain mountain where there was a Fudo shrine. Fudo sat, surrounded by fire, a sword in one hand and a small coil of rope in the other. Here Kiyo prayed with fearful vehemence that this hideous-looking God would show her how to kill the priest who had once loved her.

From Fudo she went to the shrine of Kompira, who has the knowledge of magic and is able to teach sorcery. Here she begged that she might have the power to turn herself at will into a dragon-serpent. After many visits a long-nosed sprite (probably a *tengu*), who waited upon Kompira, taught Kiyo all the mysteries of magic and sorcery. He taught this once sweet girl how to change herself into the awful creature she desired to be for the purpose of a cruel vengeance.

Still the priest visited Kiyo; but no longer was he the lover. By many exhortations he tried to stay the passion of this maiden he once loved; but these priestly discourses only made Kiyo more determined to win the victory in the end. She wept, she pleaded, she wound her fair arms about him; but none of her allurements had the slightest effect, except to drive away the priest for the last time.

Just as the priest was about to take his departure he was horrified to see Kiyo's eyes suddenly turn into those of a serpent. With a shriek of fear he ran out of the tea-garden, swam across the river, and hid himself inside the great temple bell.

Kiyo raised her magic wand, murmured a certain incantation, and in a moment the sweet face and form of this lovely maiden became transformed into that of a dragon-serpent, hissing and spirting fire. With eyes as large and luminous as moons she crawled over the garden, swam across the river, and entered the belfry. Her weight broke down the supporting columns, and the bell, with the priest inside, fell with a deafening crash to the ground.

Kiyo embraced the bell with a terrible lust for vengeance. Her coils held the metal as in a vice; tighter and tighter she hugged the bell, till the metal became red-hot. All in vain was the prayer of the captive priest; all in vain, too, were the earnest entreaties of his fellow brethren, who implored that Buddha would destroy the demon. Hotter and hotter grew the bell, and it rang with the piteous shrieks of the priest within. Presently his voice was stilled, and the bell melted and ran down into a pool of molten metal. The great power of Karma had destroyed it, and with it the priest and the dragon-serpent that was once the beautiful Kiyo.

Hidari Jingoro the Sculptor

THE FAMOUS SCULPTOR HIDARI JINGORO on one occasion happened to fall in love with a very attractive woman whom he met in the street on his return to his studio. He was so fascinated by her rare beauty that as soon as he had reached his destination he commenced to carve a statue of her.

Between the chiselled robes he placed a mirror, the mirror which the lovely woman had dropped, and which her eager lover had at once picked up. Because this mirror had reflected a thousand thousand times that fair face, it had taken to its shining surface the very body and soul of its owner, and because of these strange things the statue came to life, to the extreme happiness of sculptor and maid.

The Soul of a Mirror

THE SHRINE OF OGAWACHI-MYOJIN fell into decay, and the Shinto priest in charge, Matsumura, journeyed to Kyoto in the hope of successfully appealing to the Shogun for a grant for the restoration of the temple.

Matsumura and his family resided in a house in Kyoto, said to be extremely unlucky, and many tenants had thrown themselves into the well on the north-east side of the dwelling. But Matsumura took no notice of these tales, and was not the least afraid of evil spirits.

During the summer of that year there was a great drought in Kyoto. Though the river-beds dried up and many wells failed for want of rain, the well in Matsumura's garden was full to overflowing. The distress elsewhere, owing to want of water, forced many poor people to beg for it, and for all their drawing the water in this particular well did not diminish.

One day, however, a dead body was found lying in the well, that of a servant who had come to fetch water. In his case suicide was out of the question, and it seemed impossible that he should have accidentally fallen in. When Matsumura heard of the fatality he went to inspect the well. To his surprise the water stirred with a strange rocking movement. When the motion lessened he saw reflected in the clear water the form of a fair young woman. She was touching her lips with *beni*. At length she smiled upon him. It was a strange smile that made Matsumura feel dizzy, a smile that blotted out everything else save the beautiful woman's face. He felt an almost irresistible desire to fling himself into the water in order that he might reach and hold this enchanting woman. He struggled against this strange feeling, however, and was able after a while to enter the house, where he gave orders that a fence should be built round the well, and that from thenceforth no one, on any pretext whatever, should draw water there.

Shortly afterwards the drought came to an end. For three days and nights there was a continuous downpour of rain, and the city shook with an earthquake. On the third night of the storm there was a loud knocking at Matsumura's door. The priest himself inquired who his visitor might be. He half opened the door, and saw once more the woman he had seen in the well. He refused her admission, and asked why she had been guilty of taking the lives of so many harmless and innocent people.

Thus the woman made answer: "Alas! good priest, I have never desired to lure human beings to their death. It is the Poison Dragon, who lived in that well, who forced me against my will to entice people to death. But now the Gods have compelled the Poison Dragon to live elsewhere, so that tonight I was able to leave my place of captivity. Now there is but little water in the well, and if you will search there you will find my body. Take care of it for me, and I shall not fail to reward your goodness." With these words she vanished as suddenly as she had appeared.

Next day well-cleaners searched the well, and discovered some ancient hair ornaments and an old metal mirror.

Matsumura, being a wise man, took the mirror and cleaned it, believing that it might reveal a solution to the mystery.

Upon the back of the mirror he discovered several characters. Many of the ideographs were too blurred to be legible, but he managed to make out "third month, the third day." In ancient time the third month used to be called *Yayoi*, or Month of Increase, and remembering that the woman had called herself Yayoi, Matsumura realised that he had probably received a visit from the Soul of the Mirror.

Matsumura took every care of the mirror. He ordered it to be resilvered and polished, and when this had been done he laid it in a box specially made for it, and mirror and box were placed in a particular room in the house.

One day, when Matsumura was sitting in the apartment where the mirror reposed, he once more saw Yayoi standing before him, looking more beautiful than ever, and the refulgence of her beauty was like summer moonlight. After she had saluted Matsumura she explained that she was indeed the Soul of the Mirror, and narrated how she had fallen into the possession of Lady Kamo, of the Imperial Court, and how she had become an heirloom of the Fujiwara House, until during the period of Hogen, when the Taira and Minamoto clans were engaged in conflict, she was thrown into a well, and there forgotten. Having narrated these things, and all the horrors she had gone through under the tyranny of the Poison Dragon, Yayoi begged that Matsumura would present the mirror to the Shogun, the Lord Yoshimasa, who was a descendant of her former possessors, promising the priest considerable good fortune if he did so. Before Yayoi departed she advised Matsumura to leave his home immediately, as it was about to be washed away by a great storm.

On the following day Matsumura left the house, and, as Yayoi had prophesied, almost immediately afterwards his late dwelling was swept away.

At length Matsumura was able to present, the mirror to the Shogun Yoshimasa, together with a written account of its strange history. The Shogun was so pleased with the gift that he not only gave Matsumura many personal presents, but he also presented the priest with a considerable sum of money for the rebuilding of his temple.

A Mirror and a Bell

WHEN THE PRIESTS OF MUGENYAMA required a large bell for their temple they asked the women in the vicinity to contribute their old bronze mirrors for the purpose of providing the necessary metal.

Hundreds of mirrors were given for this purpose, and all were offered gladly, except the mirror presented by a certain farmer's wife. As soon as she had given her mirror to the priests she began to regret having parted with it. She remembered how old it was, how it had reflected her mother's laughter and tears, and even her great-grandmother's. Whenever this farmer's wife went to the temple she saw her coveted mirror lying in a great heap behind a railing. She recognised it by the design on the back known as the *Shō-Chiku-Bai*, or the three emblems of the Pine, Bamboo, and Plum-flower. She yearned to stretch forth her arm between the railings and to snatch back her beloved mirror. Her soul was in the shining surface, and it mingled with the souls of those who had gazed into it before she was born.

When the Mugenyama bell was in course of construction the bell-founders discovered that one mirror would not melt. The workers said that it refused to melt because the owner had afterwards regretted the gift, which had made the metal hard, as hard as the woman's selfish heart.

Soon everyone knew the identity of the giver of the mirror that would not melt, and, angry and ashamed, the farmer's wife drowned herself, first having written the following: "When I am dead you will be able to melt my mirror, and so cast the bell. My soul will come to him who breaks that bell by ringing it, and I will give him great wealth."

When the woman died her old mirror melted immediately, and the bell was cast and was suspended in its customary place. Many people having heard of the message written by the deceased farmer's wife, a great multitude came to the temple, and one by one rang the bell with the utmost violence in the hope of breaking it and winning great wealth. Day after day the ringing continued, till at last the noise became so unbearable that the priests rolled the bell into a swamp, where it lay hidden from sight.

The Mirror of Matsuyama

IN ANCIENT DAYS there lived in a remote part of Japan a man and his wife, and they were blessed with a little girl, who was the pet and idol of her parents. On one occasion the man was called away on business in distant Kyoto. Before he went he told his daughter that if she were good and dutiful to her mother he would bring her back a present she would prize very highly. Then the good man took his departure, mother and daughter watching him go.

At last he returned to his home, and after his wife and child had taken off his large hat and sandals he sat down upon the white mats and opened a bamboo basket, watching the eager gaze of his little child. He took out a wonderful doll and a lacquer box of cakes and put them into her outstretched hands. Once more he dived into his basket, and presented his wife with a metal mirror. Its convex surface shone brightly, while upon its back there was a design of pine-trees and storks.

The good man's wife had never seen a mirror before, and on gazing into it she was under the impression that another woman looked out upon her as she gazed with growing wonder. Her husband explained the mystery and bade her take great care of the mirror.

Not long after this happy home-coming and distribution of presents the woman became very ill. Just before she died she called to her little daughter, and said: "Dear child, when I am dead take every care of your father. You will miss me when I have left you. But take this mirror, and when you feel most lonely look into it and you will always see me." Having said these words she passed away.

In due time the man married again, and his wife was not at all kind to her stepdaughter. But the little one, remembering her mother's last words, would retire to a corner and eagerly look into the mirror, where it seemed to her that she saw her dear mother's face, not drawn in pain as she had seen it on her death-bed, but young and beautiful.

One day this child's stepmother chanced to see her crouching in a corner over an object she could not quite see, murmuring to herself. This ignorant woman, who detested the child and believed that her stepdaughter detested her in return, fancied that this little one was performing some strange magical art – perhaps making an image and sticking pins into it. Full of these notions, the stepmother went to her husband and told him that his wicked child was doing her best to kill her by witchcraft.

When the master of the house had listened to this extraordinary recital he went straight to his daughter's room. He took her by surprise, and immediately the girl saw him she slipped the mirror into her sleeve. For the first time her doting father grew angry, and he feared that there was, after all, truth in what his wife had told him, and he repeated her tale forthwith.

When his daughter had heard this unjust accusation she was amazed at her father's words, and she told him that she loved him far too well ever to attempt or wish to kill his wife, who she knew was dear to him.

"What have you hidden in your sleeve?" said her father, only hair convinced and still much puzzled.

"The mirror you gave my mother, and which she on her death-bed gave to me. Every time I look into its shining surface I see the face of my dear mother, young and beautiful. When my heart aches – and oh! it has ached so much lately – I take out the mirror, and mother's face, with sweet, kind smile, brings me peace, and helps me to bear hard words and cross looks."

Then the man understood and loved his child the more for her filial piety. Even the girl's stepmother, when she knew what had really taken place, was ashamed and asked forgiveness. And this child, who believed she had seen her mother's face in the mirror, forgave, and trouble for ever departed from the home.

The Love of Asagao

KOMAGAWA MIYAGI, a retainer of one of the *daimyōs*, came to a suburb of Kyoto. As it happened to be a warm summer evening he hired a boat, and, forgetting all his worries, he watched many bright-robed little ladies catching fireflies. In the air and on the grass these bright insects shone, so that the laughing ladies had many opportunities of catching these living jewels and placing them for a moment in their hair, upon poised finger, or against a silk flower on a *kimono*.

While Komagawa watched this pretty scene he saw that one of the ladies was in difficulty with her boat. Komagawa at once came to her assistance, and there and then fell desperately in love with her. They lingered together in a cool recess on the river, and no longer troubled about fireflies, for both were eager to express their love.

In order to pledge their vows these two lovers, according to an ancient custom, exchanged fans. On Miyuki's fan there was a painting of a convolvulus. Komagawa wrote a poem about this lovely flower upon his own fan before presenting it to the woman he loved. So it was that their fans and their vows were exchanged, and the convolvulus, in picture and in verse, became the pledge of their troth.

Eventually the lovers separated, to meet again a few days later at Akasha, where it chanced that their ships touched each other. When they had exchanged many a fair and loving word they returned to their respective homes.

When Miyuki reached her home, radiant with thoughts of her true love, she discovered that her parents had already arranged a marriage for her with someone the poor little woman had never seen.

Miyuki heard this piece of news with an aching heart. She knew that children must obey their parents, and when she was lying down on her *futon* she did her utmost to comply with her parents' wish. But the struggle proved useless, for the form of her lover kept on coming back to her, and the river and the gleaming fireflies. So she arose, crept out of the house, and walked towards a certain town, hoping to find Komagawa, only to discover on her arrival that he had departed, no one knew whither.

This bitter disappointment much affected Miyuki, and she wept for many days. Her salt tears flowed so persistently that she soon became quite blind, as helpless a creature as "a bird without feathers or a fish without fins."

Miyuki, after she had given way to grief for some time, discovered that if she did not wish to starve she must do something to earn a living. She made up her mind to make use of her excellent voice and to sing in streets or in tea-houses. Her voice, combined with her beautiful and pathetic face, won instant recognition. People wept over her plaintive singing without knowing why. She loved to sing the little poem about the convolvulus Komagawa had written on his fan, so the people who heard her called her Asagao ('Convolvulus').

The blind maiden was led from place to place by her friend Asaka ('Slight Fragrance'), till someone killed her, and Asagao was left alone to tap out her dark journeys without a loving hand to guide her. There was only one thought that consoled Asagao, and that was that she might, in her wanderings, eventually meet her lover.

When a few years had passed by it chanced that Komagawa, accompanied by Iwashiro Takita, was sent on business by his *Daimyō*. While on their journey they happened to enter a certain tea-house. Iwashiro Takita was sullen and morose, and sat in gloomy silence, not deigning to notice his surroundings. Komagawa, on the other hand, looked about him, and saw on a screen the very poem he had written about the convolvulus, the poem he had so lovingly inscribed for Asagao. While pondering the matter in his mind the master of the tea-house entered the apartment. Komagawa questioned him concerning this little love-poem, and the master of the tea-house told the following story:

"It is a very sad story," said he. "The poem was sung by a poor blind lady. She ran away from her home because she could not marry the man her parents had chosen for her. She was unable to consent to the union because she already had a lover, and this lover she sought up and down the country, ever singing this little poem about the convolvulus, in the hope that some day she might have the good fortune to meet him. Honourable sir, at this very moment she is in my tea-garden!"

Komagawa could scarcely conceal his joy when he requested that the master of the tea-house would bring in the blind woman.

In another moment Asagao stood before him. He saw in her delicate face an added beauty, the beauty of a hope, of a love kept bright and clear through the long, sorrowful years of waiting.

Asagao touched the *samisen*. Very gently she sang:

"Down fell the shower of silver rain and wet the poor Convolvulus,
The sweet dew on the leaves and flowers being taken away by the jealous sun."

Komagawa listened intently, longing to speak, longing to reveal his love, yet keeping silent because his ill-bred companion still remained in the room. He watched her dark eyes fixed upon him, but they were without expression, for they could not see. Still the *samisen* tinkled, and still the voice sounded sweet and low and unspeakably pathetic in the apartment. With an aching heart and without a word of love he dismissed her with the usual fee. She walked out of the room as if conscious of a new, acute sorrow. There was something in her patron's voice that was extremely tender, something that moved her deeply, and it made her heart ache and yearn without knowing why.

The next day Komagawa gave the master of the tea-house a fan, saying: "Give this fan and money to Asagao. She will understand." With these words Komagawa and his companion proceeded on their journey.

When Asagao had received the fan she felt it eagerly with her small white fingers. "Who has given me this fan and money?" she inquired. "Oh, tell me what the fan is like. Has it a drawing of a convolvulus?"

The master of the tea-house looked at her gently, "He to whom you sang last night gave you this fan," said he. "There is a drawing of a convolvulus upon it."

Asagao gave a cry of joy. "Last night," she said softly, "I was with my lover again! And now, and now...."

At this very moment a servant from Asagao's old home arrived, asserting that he had been sent by her parents to bring her back again. But Asagao, true to her old love, determined to fight down all opposition.

Now it happened that the master of this tea-house had once been employed by Asagao's father. He had committed a great wrong in that capacity, a wrong worthy of death; but Asagao's father had taken pity upon him. He had dismissed him with money, which had enabled the wrongdoer to set up in business for himself. During this crisis the master of the tea-house thought oven the kindness that had been shown him, and resolved to commit *seppuku* in order that his old master's child might receive her sight again by means of this brave man's liver.

So the master of the tea-house killed himself, and Asagao received her sight. That very night, though there was a fierce tempest raging, she set out in search of her lover, accompanied by a faithful little band of servants. All night the maiden journeyed over rough and rugged roads. She scarcely noticed the heavy rain or her bleeding feet. She was urged on by a joyous love, by the fond hope of finding her lover again.

As she climbed a mountain, now bathed in sunlight, she fancied she heard a voice calling her name. She looked about her and discovered Komagawa. Peace came to her then. All the weariness of long search and almost endless waiting were over for ever, and in a little while the lovers were married. The convolvulus, or morning glory, is a flower that only blooms for a few hours; but Asagao's love had the beauty of the convolvulus combined with the strength and long life of the pine. In their happy union they had remained true to the pledge of love upon their fans, and out of blindness and much suffering Asagao could hold up her fair head to the dew and sunshine of her lover's sheltering arms.

The Passing of Rikiu

RIKIU WAS ONE OF THE GREATEST OF TEA-MASTERS, and for long he remained the friend of Taiko-Hideyoshi; but the age in which he lived was full of treachery. There were many who were jealous of Rikiu, many who sought his death. When a coldness sprang up between Hideyoshi and Rikiu, the enemies of the great tea-master made use of this breach of friendship by spreading the report that Rikiu intended to add poison to a cup of tea and present it to his distinguished patron. Hideyoshi soon heard of the rumour, and without troubling to examine the matter he condemned Rikiu to die by his own hand.

On the last day of the famous tea-master's life he invited many of his disciples to join with him in his final tea ceremony. As they walked up the garden path it seemed that ghosts whispered in the rustling leaves. When the disciples entered the tea-room they saw a *kakemono* hanging in the *tokonoma*, and when they raised their sorrowful eyes they saw that the writing described the passing of all earthly things. There was poetry in the singing of the tea-kettle, but it was a sad song like the plaintive cry of an insect. Rikiu came into the tea-room calm and dignified, and, according to custom, he allowed the chief guest to admire the various articles associated with the tea ceremony. When all the guests had gazed upon them, noting their beauty with a heavy heart, Rikiu presented each disciple with a souvenir. He took his own cup in his hand, and said: "Never again shall this cup, polluted by the lips of misfortune, be used by man." Having spoken these words, he broke the cup as a sign that the tea ceremony was over, and the guests bade a sad farewell and departed. Only one remained to witness, not the drinking of another cup of tea, but the passing of Rikiu. The great master took off his outer garment, and revealed the pure white robe of Death. Still calm and dignified, he looked upon his dagger, and then recited the following verse with unfaltering voice:

"Welcome to thee,
O sword of eternity!
Through Buddha
And through Daruma alike
Thou hast cleft thy way."

He who loved to quote the old poem, "To those who long only for flowers fain would I show the full-blown spring which abides in the toiling buds of snow-covered hills," has crowned the Japanese tea ceremony with an immortal flower.

The Legend of the Tea-plant

DARUMA WAS AN INDIAN SAGE, whose image, as we have already seen, was associated with the ritualistic drinking of tea by the Zen sect in Japan. He is said to have been the son of a Hindu king, and received instruction from Panyatara. When he had completed his studies he retired to Lo Yang, where he remained seated in meditation for nine years.

During this period the sage was tempted after the manner of St. Anthony. He wrestled with these temptations by continually reciting sacred scriptures; but the frequent repetition of the word 'jewel' lost its spiritual significance, and became associated with the precious stone worn in the ear of a certain lovely woman. Even the word 'lotus', so sacred to all true Buddhists, ceased to be the symbol of the Lord Buddha and suggested to Daruma the opening of a girl's fair mouth. His temptations increased, and he was transported to an Indian city, where he found himself among a vast crowd of worshippers. He saw strange deities with horrible symbols upon their foreheads, and Rajahs and Princes riding upon elephants, surrounded by a great company of dancing-girls. The great crowd of people surged forward, and Daruma with them, till they came to a temple with innumerable pinnacles, a temple covered with a multitude of foul forms, and it seemed to Daruma that he met and kissed the woman who had changed the meaning of jewel and lotus. Then suddenly the vision departed, and Daruma awoke to find himself sitting under the Chinese sky.

The sage, who had fallen asleep during his meditation, was truly penitent for the neglect of his devotions, and, taking a knife from his girdle, he cut off his eyelids and cast them upon the ground, saying: "O Thou Perfectly Awakened!" The eyelids were transformed into the tea-plant, from which was made a beverage that would repel slumber and allow good Buddhist priests to their vigils.

THE END

Biographies

James S. de Benneville

James Seguin de Benneville was a nineteenth-century author whose writings concerning Japan include *The Fruit of the Tree* ('travel notes on thoughts and things Japanese, experienced during a four years' sojourn in the country'), *Tales of the Wars of the Gempei* ('being the story of the lives and adventures of Iyo-no-Kami Minamoto Kurō Yoshitsune and Saitō Musashi-Bō Benkei the Warrior Monk), *Tales of the Samurai* ('being the story of the lives, the adventures, and the misadventures of the Hangwan-dai Kojirō Sukéshigé and Ternte-hime, his wife) and his *Tales of the Tokugawa* – in two volumes (1917 and 1921) and 'retold from the Japanese originals': *The Yotsuya Kwaidan; Or O'Iwa Inari* and *Bakémono Yashiki (The Haunted House)*, the latter including the *Bancho Sarayashiki*.

Dr Alan Cummings

Foreword

Alan Cummings is Associate Head of the Department of East Asian Languages and Cultures at SOAS. He teaches Japanese and courses on Japanese literature, drama and culture. He has published a collection of haiku from the 1600s to the present day, called *Haiku: Love*, and has contributed to many other books.

F. Hadland Davis

Frederick Hadland Davis was a writer and a historian – author of *The Land of the Yellow Spring and Other Japanese Stories* (1910) and *The Persian Mystics* (1908 and 1920). His books describe these cultures to the western world and tell stories of ghosts, creation, mystical creatures and more. He is best known for his book *Myths and Legends of Japan* (1912).

William Elliot Griffis

Born in Philadelphia, William Elliot Griffis (1843–1928) went on to serve as a corporal during the American Civil War. He studied at Rutgers University after the war and graduated in 1869. He tutored Latin and English to a samurai from Fukui and then travelled around Europe for a year prior to studying at what is now known as the New Brunswick Theological Seminary. In 1870, Griffis went to Japan and became Superintendent of Education in the province of Echizen because of his organisation of schools there. During the 1870s, Griffis and his sister taught at many different institutes and he wrote for many newspapers and magazines. In 1872 he prepared the *New Japan Series of Reading and Spelling Books* and left Japan in 1874, having made many connections and friendships with Japan's future leaders. On returning to the United States he worked in several churches on the east coast but retired in 1903 to write. With the help of his extensive knowledge of Japanese and European culture, he produced a number of books, such as *Japanese Fairy World* (1880), *The Fire-fly's Lovers and Other Fairy Tales of Old Japan* (1908), *Japanese Fairy Tales* (1922), *Korean Fairy Tales* (1922), *Belgian Fairy Tales* (1919) and many more.

Lafcadio Hearn

After being abandoned by both of his parents, Lafcadio Hearn (1850–1904) was sent from Greece to Ireland and later to the United States where he became a newspaper reporter in Cincinnati and later New Orleans where he contributed translations of French authors to the

Times Democrat. His wandering life led him eventually to Japan where he spent the rest of his life finding inspiration from the country and, especially, its legends and ghost stories. Hearn published many books in his lifetime, informative on aspects of Japanese custom, culture and religion and which influenced future folklorists and writers whose writings feature in this collection – standout examples of Hearn's output include *Glimpses of Unfamiliar Japan* (1894), *Kokoro: Hints and Echoes of Japanese Inner Life* (1896), *Japanese Fairy Tales* (1898, and sequels), *Shadowings* (1900), *Kottō: Being Japanese Curios, with Sundry Cobwebs* (1902) and *Kwaidan: Stories and Studies of Strange Things* (1903). In 1891 Hearn married and had four children but later died of heart failure in Tokyo in 1904.

Stephen Hodge
First half of Introduction to Japanese Mythology
A linguist in Japanese and an author with a specialist knowledge of Japanese culture, oriental religions and theology, Stephen Hodge (b. 1947) graduated from the School of Oriental and African Studies, did MA research in Japan and taught at the University of London.

A.B. Mitford, Lord Redesdale
Algernon Bertram Freeman-Mitford, 1st Baron Redesdale (1837–1916), was a writer, collector and British diplomat. He was educated at Eton and at Oxford University, and later went to Japan as second secretary of the British Legation. His stay in Japan and his meeting Ernest Satow inspired the writing of *Tales of Old Japan* (1871). The book allowed several Japanese classics to be exposed to the Western world.

Yei Theodora Ozaki
The translations of Japanese stories and fairy tales by Yei Theodora Ozaki (1871–1932) were, by her own admission, fairly liberal ('I have followed my fancy in adding such touches of local colour or description as they seemed to need or as pleased me'), and yet proved popular. They include *Japanese Fairy Tales* (1908), 'translated from the modern version written by Sadanami Sanjin', and *Warriors of Old Japan, and Other Stories* (1909).

Text Sources

The core body of tales in this book have been selected from F. Hadland Davis's *Myths and Legends of Japan* (George G. Harrap & Company, London, 1912). To these have been added a number from *Tales of Old Japan* by A.B. Mitford, Lord Redesdale (Macmillan and Co., London, 1910 edition), some from *Japanese Fairy World* by William Elliot Griffis (Trübner & Co., Ludgate Hill, London, 1887), and a few from *Japanese Fairy Tales*, compiled by Yei Theodora Ozaki (Tokyo, 1908). The two long ghost stories, *The Yotsuya Kwaidan or O'Iwa Inari* and The *Bancho Sarayashiki or The Lady of The Plates*, are from James S. Benneville's *Tales of the Tokugawa* – volumes I (J.B. Lippincott Company, Philadelphia, 1917) and II, Part II only, (Yokohama, 1921) respectively.

GOTHIC FANTASY